André Brink

AN ACT OF TERROR

André Brink was born in South Africa in 1935. He is the author of eight novels, including *A Dry White Season*, *A Chain of Voices*, and *States of Emergency*. He has won the most important South African literary prize, the CNA Award, three times, and his novels have twice been shortlisted for the Booker Prize, in 1976 and 1978. In 1980 he received the Martin Luther King Prize, and in France the Prix Médicis Étranger. In 1982 he was made a Chevalier of the Légion d'Honneur and in 1987 was named Officier de l'Ordre des Arts et des Lettres. He is Professor of English at the University of Cape Town.

INTERNATIONAL

ALSO BY ANDRÉ BRINK

A Chain of Voices
Looking on Darkness
The Ambassador
States of Emergency
Mapmakers
A Land Apart (with J. M. Coetzee)
The Wall of the Plague
An Instant in the Wind
Rumours of Rain
A Dry White Season

AN ACT OF TERROR

AN
ACT
OF
TERROR

André Brink

Vintage International
Vintage Books
A Division of Random House, Inc.
New York

FIRST VINTAGE INTERNATIONAL EDITION, JANUARY 1993

Copyright © 1991 by André Brink

Library of Congress Cataloging-in-Publication Data
Brink, André Philippus, 1935–
An act of terror / André Brink. — 1st Vintage International ed.
p.   cm.
ISBN 0-679-74429-0 (pbk.)
I. Title.
PR9369.3.B7A65   1993
823 — dc20   92-56373
CIP

Manufactured in the United States of America
10 9 8 7 6 5 4 3 2 1

For Herta

Contents

AN ACT OF TERROR

NOTE

Thomas Landman's reconstruction of the thirteen generations of his family chronicle forms a supplement at the end of the novel. This supplement should be regarded as a floating presence in the text, to be read where and when the reader chooses – whether at the beginning, as a background and preparation; or at the end, as reflection; or at any suitable pause in the narrative; or even piecemeal, as certain figures, or places, or events from that history surface in the story.

Readers may also find it useful to refer to the Glossary of words, phrases and acronyms at the end of the book.

The crayfish get used to it.

West Coast fisherman

We all want to discover what we're alive for,
there's no doubt about that: it's one of the main
sources of all the violence in the world.

Robert Musil

I did not participate in the rebellion of the West.
Yet I carry the burden of the questions they
raised. As I and you emerge into the universe,
it is no longer silent. I and you are forced to
confront the ugly question of murder. Is it
still possible to begin with innocence? Damn
William Blake!

Noel Chabani Manganyi

Chapter 1

1

Observing the two of them stroll hand in hand through the Cape that late summer's day – Kirstenbosch, the Gardens, up the Mountain, across the burning sand of Camp's Bay, through the alleys of the Malay Quarter and downhill again, across the Parade (past the Castle), to the bare grassy slope where only a few desolate churches and mosques remained as witnesses to the long-vanished boisterous life of District Six – no one could have imagined, not even in an outrageous fantasy, that next day they would take part in a bomb attack. Two ordinary young lovers, so ordinary in fact that an hour later, even if one had noticed them to start with, it might be difficult to recall what they had looked like. The man tall, angular, his skin suffused with an underlying darker hue, more than a tan; carrying as always his camera round his neck; black longish hair; in his appearance a boyishness which made him look younger than his twenty-eight years. What must strike the observer would be the intensity of his almost-black eyes; and then his hands, the kind of hands that would elicit from older women over their teacups the observation that he must be a pianist, and from farmers the comment that it was obvious he hadn't done a day's honest hard work in his life. She: slight, especially in the faded boiler-suit several sizes too big for her, the bands held in place over her white T-shirt with safety-pins, her mousy hair unevenly cropped (a do-it-yourself job executed soon after, early last December, the group had moved into the sprawling old farmhouse near Paarl; the short hair being more practical for the wig she was wearing there), the sharp, challenging features of her severely freckled face without any make-up; and two unexpectedly large, startlingly green eyes.

What singled them out was, simply, the awareness of, the resignation to, their own death; for that was something they had come to terms with from the very first day they had embarked on the planning of the attack. It might happen at any moment. Perhaps tomorrow at fifteen minutes to eleven in front of the Castle, when the bomb exploded. Or twenty minutes later, on the way to the safe house in Observatory. Maybe at half-past twelve at the airport; or a year from now, in the Central Prison in Pretoria, one morning at six. It *need* not happen like that: if all went according to plan – and everything had been arranged to the last detail, together with Justin, and David, and Rashid (and, before that unfortunate event in February, Christine) – it wouldn't. But it remained a possibility; and without being alert to it, and living with it every day, they could never have sauntered through the city like that, on such a morning.

Strolling along the leafy lane in the Gardens – mottled with shadows, cooing with pigeons, rippling with quicksilver squirrels – his whole life seemed to converge in this moment, as if in walking there like that, holding in his hand that of the girl Nina, innumerable other promenades from the past were being gathered into this one. Those gnarled oaks were at the same time the flame-trees and msasas of Harare, dark toonas in Luanda, horse-chestnuts in London, birches in Moscow. Not one of them excluded the others, not one was complete without the rest.

'I can't stand goodbyes,' he said suddenly.

She glanced up at him (he was so much taller), pressing his hand: he could feel the delicate bones under the skin. 'This isn't goodbye, Thomas. We'll often be together like this again.'

'But here? In Cape Town?'

'Of course.' Was there something just a bit too emphatic in her voice? But he didn't look at her. 'We're only going away for a while.' More urgently: 'You're not having any doubts, are you?'

'No, I'm not. I know we've done all we could.'

'It's only the waiting that gets me,' she said. 'I wish we could have wrapped it all up today –'

'By this time tomorrow –'

'What time is it now?'

'Ten past eleven.'

'–'

'Nina.' He stopped, clasping her by the arms for a moment and looking her in the eyes. The front of her boiler-suit was sagging from the inadequate hold of the two safety-pins. 'Let's not talk about it now,' he said. 'Remember what Justin said: today we're free to

2

do whatever we like, except think about tomorrow.' Followed by a small strained laugh: 'It's like the infallible recipe for making gold, remember? – keep stirring for an hour, with a wooden spoon, a cup of sand in a bucket of water, without once thinking the word "gold".'

'Perhaps,' she said, pursuing her own train of thought, 'perhaps one day, when we look back, our lives will be divided into two neat halves: Before-the-Bomb, and After. You know, like BC and AD.'

'"Between the idea and the reality, between the motion and the act –"?'

'Look, we've made up our minds. We know what we're doing, and why. All that remains is to go ahead and actually do it. I wish it was tomorrow.'

'And I wish we had more time!' he said. 'You know what I would have loved to do? I was lying awake last night, thinking about it: I'd like to take a long trip through the country before I leave, go to all the places I've ever been, look up all the people I've ever known.'

'To say goodbye?'

'No. Just to make sure I'll never forget.'

'You won't.' She sighed. 'It's hard to believe it'll really happen tomorrow, isn't it? After all these months. All the preparations, the scares, the hard work, the planning. Now, at last – Somehow it doesn't feel real, as if I'll suddenly wake up – and all I'm scared of, Thomas, is that you may not be beside me when I open my eyes.'

'I'll be there. After all, this – thing – what's going to happen tomorrow – it's come with us all the way, hasn't it? You spoke about it the very first day we met, remember?'

'You think I'll ever forget?'

'It was only a joke then.'

'For me it's never been a joke, Thomas.'

On a bench near them a small boy sat beside an absent-minded smoking mother, his legs folded under him, his eager little face puckered with concentration as with a small pointed finger he drew an invisible picture, wrote an inscrutable message, in the air.

2

-- It's the wind I remember first of that day in Crossroads, the wind, even before the noise and the movement comes back: the phalanxes

3

of yellow Casspirs (the 'Mello-Yellos'), the brown Buffels, the troop-carriers, like prehistoric animals rumbling and lumbering in the gloomy winter day below fast-drifting tattered clouds; the jeering of the people, the hail of stones and bottles and other desperate projectiles; the plumes of teargas; the first houses bursting into flames; the vigilantes with their distinguishing white cloths tied to their arms, storming in, flanked by police; then the shooting ('My God, they're using real bullets today!'). The wind cutting like a blade through one's anorak and layers of clothing (and what about those people in the dunes, scarecrows with sticks for arms and legs, bare-bottomed snot-nosed kids among the shacks and shanties and haphazard shelters of black plastic sheets and corrugated iron and cardboard insufficiently protected by windblown Port Jackson willows?) and driving the sand of the Cape Flats into one's eyes and right through one's body. Yesterday was bad enough, with its pelting rain, but at least nothing could burn in the wet. In this wind there is nothing to prevent the police and the army and their *witdoeke* collaborators from setting fire to the squatters' huts and smoking them out of their wretched 'illegal' settlements in Crossroads and KTC.

There's a weariness in my bones even as I get up that morning; standing at the kitchen window in my small flat in Vredehoek, nursing a bright green mug of scalding black coffee between my hands to wake me from the dead, I have little stomach for the day ahead. It's as if the pallid predawn is desperately scraping its corroded lungs to cough up a slimy sun above the horizon, a gob of mucus streaked with blood.

Apathetic, I wait for the others to turn up: we've decided that it would be safer for us, journalists and photographers, to work in groups. In the combi, unlike other mornings, no one tries to make jokes or cheer us up. Most of the roads have already been cordoned off, but Johnny Oliphant from the *Weekly Mail*, who knows the whole network of bush roads through the Cape Flats, leads us right into Crossroads – only to find that the people who have been helping us the past few days are today morose and resentful. 'You better fuck off here. We got shit coming. They said they going to raze this camp to the ground. It's *witdoeke* all over the place. And the cops want the press out, they got it up to here with all the bad publicity.'

But we refuse to budge. Taking photographs even while we run and duck and hide and scamper among the burning huts. There's a unique excitement in this kind of danger. Possibly because one can

4

never really accept – not even when you've been shot at before (that day, with Ntsiki, in Guguletu; those many other days and nights) – that your life is being threatened. The very danger seems to give meaning to what you're doing; trying to do. Each photograph, each minute on TV, every paragraph in the paper, is a small triumph. There may be those in our group for whom it is no more than a job to be done. But I know that some of us, exhausted as we may be, our bodies aching and sticky with sweat, plastered with dust, carved up by the edge of the wind, persist in believing, fiercely, irrationally, that what we're doing *must* be done. How else would the world find out what is happening? And it is imperative it should know about these children clubbed with the butts of guns, these women savaged by dogs let loose, these men driven into their burning shacks to be charred among their meagre possessions.

But at a given moment even the most intrepid among us cannot go on. Behind us, in front of the first row of burning shanties, a row of *witdoeke* are lined up, armed with *kieries*, with pangas, with automatic rifles (I have photographs of the police distributing these guns, and their brand of napalm, among them). And from ahead the blue rows of riot police are approaching, a front line of men with sjamboks and dogs, followed by those with teargas and guns. Our first reaction is to stand our ground, convinced they are merely out to intimidate us: it must be obvious to them that we are from the press. But after the first sudden salvo – strange how almost detachedly one registers it, as if it is happening very far away; like a star streaking through the sky light-years after it has burnt out – we scatter in all directions. At a time like this one does not think of heroism. One's life becomes very small and tight and immediate. Some of us, in twos or threes, drag with us those wounded in the first round of firing. Others simply scuttle away among the shacks and scraggly bushes, discarding in their flight notebooks, bags, even cameras.

I have already reached the combi parked behind the third row of shanties – the engine revving urgently, frantic arms reaching out from the sliding door, voices shouting: 'Come on, Thomas! Jump! Hurry up, dammit!' – when against the general din in the background I hear new, separate screams, defined as sharply as a red blob on a grey photograph. Glancing back (the lugubrious grey tower of Portland Cement in the background) I see a clutch of policemen grappling with someone. You, Nina. It is immediately clear what has been happening: in full pursuit of a small half-naked boy (his

5

only clothing a man's tattered jacket reaching down to his rickety shanks), they all set upon him when he stumbled and fell – some with sjamboks, others with their heavy boots. You must have been close by, for by the time I discover what is going on you're already in the fray, fighting off the cops like a wildcat. In the turmoil, thank God, the child manages to scamper to his feet and run off, crying, smeared with blood and grime: upon which the men all turn on you. My first impression is that you must be a child, you look so slight and frail among those burly bodies. You're still wearing your hair long, it's only much later that you will hack it off: gathered in a ponytail, it thrashes this way and that as you try furiously to break away from the constable who's grabbed you by the arm. I see him raise his other hand, the obscene pink sjambok high above his blunt head, see the blow strike you in the face, leaving a bloody weal on your right cheek. For a moment you are clearly dazed from shock. Then I hear you scream, not in pain but in rage.

'Let me go! Fuck off!'

Then you jerk your knee up between his legs with a violence I would not have thought such a frail female figure capable of. Without waiting another instant I start sprinting towards you – behind me I can hear the combi's engine revved more urgently than before, voices calling out in desperation – convinced they're going to kill you. Over the shoulder of the blue constable, as he crouches, I see his companions approaching with the dogs. We reach you almost simultaneously. For a while we tug and pull and jerk you to and fro by the arms, like dogs fighting over an empty bag; then, suddenly, you tear yourself away from us all.

'Let me go! Goddammit!'

'Come with me, they'll kill you.'

We've both had it, I know that for sure. The dogs are going crazy. Then there's an angry shout from behind. Perhaps an officer? (But why should he wish to intervene? I've seen them, an hour ago, tearing into the crowd with as much abandon as their men.) There is a brief hesitation among men and dogs. I grab you by the arm and start running, while you curse and shout abuse at me as if it is all my fault.

'You want to get us both killed?' My breath breaks from my throat in burning gasps.

'Just leave me alone, I didn't ask you any favour.'

Behind us the dogs are starting up again.

By the time we reach the third row of shacks, the combi is gone.

For a moment all the noise around us seems to drain away like water from a bath. Only the wind remains, the thin sound of the wind among the Port Jacksons and the shanties and the broken shacks. Sand in my eyes. Smoke billowing up on all sides. Sporadic flames.

You're crying. With fury, not fear or pain.

Helpless, cornered, I look around. Over your shoulder I can see the police reforming their ranks, then approaching resolutely in a solid blue tide, all their forces mustered against the miserable two of us. Grabbing both your hands I try to restrain your flailing and struggling. In the process I feel the strap of my camera snap. Desperate, I make a grab for it, but I need all my strength to hold on to you. At least my tog bag is still intact.

At that moment someone clutches my by the elbow from behind: 'Come with me.'

'My camera —!'

But there is no time to retrieve it. It's a man from the township. A thin man in a torn red poloneck jersey and a much-mended brown jacket, his feet below his stick like legs grotesquely shod in two huge mud-caked boots.

I have no idea of how we reach his home. Not much of a home either: a mere wooden framework covered with corrugated iron and waterlogged ribbed cardboard; inside, a coughing woman with a speckled *doek* round her head, and five or six children huddled on a rickety single bed, under which a brooding hen sits clucking angrily; the whole interior smothered in blue smoke from a large drum in which a pile of wet leaves and pieces of green wood lies smouldering desperately. Yet that is where we crouch throughout the interminable windblown day (you cowering in such a rage, and so feverish from pain, that you stubbornly refuse to say a word); they even share a meagre meal with us: thin bitter coffee, a chunk of mouldy bread, a handful of potatoes.

In the early evening, the man — the only name he's given is Samuel — cautiously slips out, returning soon afterwards with the laconic announcement that someone's waiting to take us home. Even though I realise it's no use, I insist on first returning to where he found us and scour the place for my camera, and he meekly allows it. Of course it has disappeared. The fires in the burning shacks have been doused, but a bank of smoke still lies heavily over the scorched earth. Outside the squatters' camp, where glaring floodlights have been turned on long before dark, a cordon of military vehicles and armed men has been drawn, like a besieging army. But, for the time being, the violence has ended. It is eerily quiet. There is only, unremittingly, the wind.

A man hobbling on a lame leg, curiously good-humoured but silent – grinning at us as if there's something unspeakably funny about the situation – leads us to a battered green Escort, the left front door so hopelessly corroded that the handle has fallen off, so that it has to be secured with wire from the inside once the passengers have been piled in; and one rear wing badly smashed in, causing the wheel to spin against it with a nerve-racking scraping sound.

On the way back you still remain stubbornly silent, except for asking the driver his name ('Bennie,' he replies, shaking with repressed laughter, as if this is the biggest joke of all). For the first few kilometres, through windblown bushes, we drive on recklessly without headlights – Bennie must have cat's eyes – but once we've left the townships and reached Lansdowne Road we make easier progress, even though only one of the lights is working. Even before we reach De Waal Drive the poor old Escort has shuddered to a standstill twice; both times Bennie, unperturbed, and without dropping his grin for a moment, gets out, dives in under the bonnet to apply some arcane ministrations to the protesting engine, then comes back to drive on in a cloud of smoke. I suggest we drop you off first, but it turns out you live much further, in Green Point, and you remark tartly that it will suit you fine if I get out: as if you have still not forgiven me (for what?). But two blocks from my flat building, high up on the foot of the mountain in Vredehoek, the car breaks down again; and this time it looks more serious.

'She won't make it up this hill,' says Bennie, the first words he has spoken of his own accord, and looking mightily pleased with himself.

'We can walk from here,' I say. Looking at you: 'I can take you home. I have a motorbike.'

'–'

I give Bennie a hand to get the engine going, sending him downhill with a final shove after a futile last attempt to press some money on him; and suddenly, for the first time in this long day, we are alone. Even the wind has died down. It is bitterly cold. The moon is not yet out. The sky is clear, spattered with huge winter stars.

'Come.'

We must go up to my flat first to collect the keys. When I return

8

from the bedroom, you are still standing in the middle of the small lounge; and, perhaps because of the unflattering light, I'm shocked to see you like that – your face smeared with dirt and dried blood, swollen and bruised, deathly pale, your hair a mess.

'You look bloody awful.' It suddenly occurs to me that I do not even know your name. 'By the way, who *are* you?'

'Does it matter?'

'Listen.' With all the sympathy I feel for you I'm damned annoyed too. 'I don't know why you're so angry with me. I'm not asking you to be grateful or anything. As far as I'm concerned you can go to hell. But do you realise what would have happened if I hadn't dragged you out of there? Those people were ready to commit murder. Or did you *want* to act the martyr?'

'I'm not acting, damn you. Not ever. You understand?' After the brief outburst you unexpectedly close your eyes. I do not realise immediately what is happening, staring at you bemused as you sway on your legs for a moment like a drunk. Through pale lips you mutter: 'Nina Jordaan.' Emphatically, as if it is important for me to grasp each separate syllable. And then I see you slump.

It surprises me to feel how light you are when I pick you up and lay you down on the sofa. I hurry to the kitchen for a glass of water, but when I come back you are already sitting up again.

'I'm sorry, I didn't mean to –'

'I'm going to run you a hot bath. Make you something to eat.'

'I've been a bloody fool, haven't I?' A bitter, apologetic smile. 'But we've been working right through the last two nights on affidavits and things, and I suppose I didn't have much to eat either. There was so much to –'

'Which newspaper are you with?'

'I'm not a journalist. I work for the legal aid clinic at UCT. We were monitoring the situation with the Black Sash. The others scooted when things warmed up.'

'You just stay on this sofa for a while.'

As I reach the door on my way to the bathroom opposite the narrow passage, you say behind me, 'I hope you will forgive me. I suppose you did save my life.'

'My good deed for the day.'

I have to clean up the bathroom before I can run a bath. It's only a few weeks ago that, back from Europe, I moved into the flat and the bathroom is still used as a makeshift darkroom until I have time to equip one. Thanks to the influence of my friend Sean I can make my final prints at the *Cape Times*; but the bathroom is useful for developing and making proof prints. Visitors keep on complaining about the smell of the chemicals, the rows of negatives dangling from washing pegs on a line above the bath, the ghostly glow of the red safety light, the enlarger poised on a square table which takes up all the space between the bath and the opposite wall, the rows of brown bottles on a makeshift shelf, the developing dishes on the floor. But for me it's the holy of holies, my sanctuary, wonderfully secluded and secure, the one place where I can close the door behind me, not to exclude the world but to draw it in with me, my most intimate space. I've often wondered whether one can get high on the smell of developer and fixer. If so, I'm incurably hooked. Even normal time is suspended here: I never take my watch into this room with me; there is only the phosphorescent glimmering of the timer in the dark (the whizzing of the mechanism measuring the seconds continuing afterwards to regulate my dreams). No matter how old I grow, I shall never get bored by, or take for granted, the constantly renewed miracle of white paper breaking into the stains and blotches of new life. ('Bloody Jungian shadows,' Sean once mocked me. 'Your unconscious must be really fucked up.') Not a simple registering of whatever I have previously caught in the sensitive silver bromide, but a completely new world coming into being right here, now, before my eyes. Mine, devised by myself; and for which I take responsibility.

I clear up the place, clean it, cursorily sweep the floor (by which time you have already turned up in the doorway – with a cup of hot chocolate you've made in the kitchen – to find out what is keeping me so long), then rinse the tub and run the water. Afterwards, while you're lolling in the bath, I prepare salad and schnitzels in the kitchen; when you emerge at last, your hair damp and curly, you're wrapped in the dressing-gown, much too big for you, which you've discovered behind the door. Your teeth are chattering lightly; you crawl almost right into the heater. Only after you have greedily devoured everything on your plate do you look up at me through dun-coloured strands of hair – the shock of your green eyes – and ask with unexpected restraint, 'Did you see what happened there today?'

'I'm a photographer. It's my job to see.'

'Those people they drove into the burning shacks. That child they –' Your voice breaks. You take too large a gulp from the glass of red wine clutched tightly in both hands: I notice how short your nails are, chewed to the quick. 'Do you think they'll get away with lies and cheating again?' Evidently not expecting an answer, you get up from where you've been huddling in front of the little convex heater and go to the large front window. Staring out over the scene I know so well, the spectacle of the city, down to where the farthest row of lights is reflected on the oily surface of the sea in the harbour. Do you notice it at all? Without turning your head, after a long silence, you ask, as if talking to yourself, 'You think our honourable state president will be sleeping well tonight?'

'Oh undoubtedly. The forces of law and order have triumphed again, haven't they?'

'There must be a special little corner in hell reserved for him.'

'It's not one man alone who keeps the system going, Nina. He's only a small, miserable cog in the whole machine.'

'But he could stop it. If he really wanted to, he could stop it.'

'_'

You swing round so suddenly that it startles me. 'You agree?'

'Sure.'

'Then he _is_ responsible. He is to blame.'

'He and many others.'

'So you don't deny he is evil?'

'He represents it.'

'But do you really feel strongly about it?'

'There are few things I feel more strongly about.' (I wish I could tell you about these past months in Europe; Africa. About Sipho.)

'Then why don't you go and kill the bastard?'

I honestly cannot believe that you are serious. So I say, 'Right, why not? Let's go.'

Your voice as cold as the night outside: 'I happen to be serious.'

'Now wait. One can't just start killing people left, right and centre just because you think they're evil.'

'How else can you destroy evil?'

'Nina, it's murder you're talking about.'

'Murder? _They_ are the murderers. Didn't you see it with your own eyes? _He's_ a murderer. To wipe out someone like that isn't murder. It's a favour to humanity.'

It is my first, unsettling, glimpse of the fire inside you.

Only much later do I discover how calm and methodical you normally are, how suspicious about the emotional desperation that drives individuals to believe they must change the world. How lucid your appraisal of the situation. How resolute and dedicated once you've set your mind on something.

But on this evening we do not discuss it any further. After a while you come back from the window, past me. Saying casually, 'I'm going to get dressed. Can you take me home now?'

'Of course.' Why this sudden reluctance to see you go, this real sense of impending loss? But I try not to show anything of my feelings, and ask instead, 'Wouldn't you like another glass of wine before you go?'

Without expecting you to say yes. But you do. With a slight flickering in your lower lip. And after the glass, which you empty in a few gulps, you pour another and – more relaxed, it seems – seat yourself on a corner of my unwieldy second-hand sofa to drink more quietly. Of the next chunk of conversation, unremarkable and even, I have no clear recollection. Except, in the middle of it, your sudden impatient question: 'Thomas Landman: who *are* you?'

'Freelance photographer, I've already told you.'

'I wasn't asking about your job. I want to know *who* you are.'

I'm standing, at that moment, in front of the window, the side window, peering into the night. On this side, where the city lights are not so obtrusive, one has a clear view of the night sky: that black blackness peculiar to winter, the stars enormous and icy in their geometric patterns. It was these stars that guided the first Portuguese explorers round this Cape: Dias, Vasco da Gama, d'Almeida, followed by Dutch, Huguenots, Germans, English; Malay and Angolan slaves herded into ships smelling of phenol and death. And by that time the people of Africa, too, had been ordering their lives according to the coming and going of Evening Star and Morning Star, the Pleiades, the Southern Cross. From the beginning of time, this unstoppable, reassuring, slow careening of the Zodiac, always in the same sequence, first Aries, then Taurus, then Gemini, then Cancer; and Leo, Virgo, Libra, Scorpio, Capricorn, Aquarius, Pisces. And then once more, Aries, Taurus, Gemini, Cancer –

'I was born under Cancer,' I say suddenly, lightly, returning to her question. 'If that means anything to you.' (Thinking: I should be ashamed of myself.)

'Crabs and crayfish. Scavengers. Or are you one of those who argue that they keep the sea clean?' Are you mocking me, or are you really trying to grasp at clues?

'We're supposed to be moon people,' I say, eager to drop the seriousness. 'You know? Melancholy and vulnerable. And inclined to hoard up stuff, as my poor mother will testify. Besotted with the past. Always, poor creatures, in search of security. I read somewhere that Noah must have been a Cancerian.'

'I don't have much experience of Cancerians.'

'What are you?'

'I was born under the sign of neon,' you say tartly.

Outside, undiminished: the vast night, the slow spiral of the Zodiac turning past, calm, remote, inured to Crossroads and Cape Town, as it is to Maseru, Lusaka, Dakar, Accra, Washington, Moscow, Prague, Berlin, everywhere I've been and not been, the places I should like to have been to, might have. Through what accidents of birth and genes is one relegated to one's corner of the earth, what responsibility does one assume for it? – and how outrageous to ascribe it to the stars. As Capricorn sinks away, Orion rears up in the east with bow and dagger; as Scorpio descends, the Pleiades rise. And these are the familiar ones, the known and named, the visible. Behind them: what unfathomable nocturnal abysses reeling back, with yet more constellations and milky ways and zodiacs, invisible exploding stars that make our earthly catastrophes – earthquakes, volcanic eruptions, typhoons, floods – dwindle to insignificance. Supernovae, black holes: the invisible presences known only through their influence on nearby bodies: no light shining from them or through them: stars subsided into themselves, sucking in energy and emitting nothing: drawn into that vortex, you suddenly find yourself in another dimension, a different time and space.

And here we are. You and I. With everything we have lived through today. We are exhausted. We are terribly small. Terribly insignificant.

I turn towards you and see your eyes on me, unwavering, disarming.

'Stay with me tonight,' I say.

A simple nod, no word, in reply.

Remember? – in this lies our beginning.

Very early the following morning, it is still dark, barely five o'clock, there is a thunderous knocking on my door, repeated impatiently as I grope for something to put on. There can only be one explanation for it, I know only too well. My first thought is how to keep you out of it. And afterwards: where to hide the camera bag and the film rolls

13

from yesterday. (Losing the camera was bad enough.) But there is no time. They seem intent on breaking down the front door. I stumble towards it, with an urgent gesture in your direction, for God's sake, to stay where you are.

On the threshold, when at last I draw back the latch, the middle-aged man. Behind him a commotion of others, a whole scrum. Colonel Bester: only much later in the day do I discover his name, but I shall not forget it. Checkered sports jacket drawn tight across the barrel of his torso, the heavy shoulders. A smell of stale tobacco. A man who inspires earthy confidence; one might be tempted to call him 'Uncle'.

'You Thomas Landman?'

'_'

'You a photographer?'

'_'

'This your camera?' Holding it out to me.

'Oh, thanks.'

With a heavy, contented expression on his face he pulls it back. The broad, sallow face, brooding eyebrows, grooves beside the mouth. I'm fascinated by his large hands. He asks, 'Were you in Crossroads yesterday?'

'So what if I was?'

'Will you please come with us? We're from the Special Branch.'

I know you must be listening. I know you're standing, naked, in the passage. But thank God they know nothing about you. Yet. –

3

Nina and Thomas emerged at the upper end of the lane, past the twittering aviaries with parakeets and canaries, sad grey red-beaked birds, nervous pheasants, great tortoises embedded like rocks in the conscience of a continent, a timeless angry stare in the bright eyes at the tips of outstretched necks. They walked past the statue of a gesturing Rhodes (*Your hinterland lies there*: that forgotten imperial dream of a British Africa from Cape to Cairo). Here they could turn left, past the state president's office building, back into the city. (Perhaps there was time for a cup of tea with the great man? – 'We've just come to make sure you will be at the parade in the Castle tomorrow morning. We have an appointment with you, remember, at a quarter to eleven. It's all arranged. At this very moment Rashid must be checking the bomb for the last time.') But neither of them glanced in that direction, as if the building existed only in their more lurid fantasies.

Past the round pond and the bright flower beds where convicts under the supervision of a fat armed guard were digging in manure; on the far side of the rose garden two young constables were chatting up a painted blonde girl in a yellow miniskirt. From Queen Victoria Street a thin 'coloured' man was laboriously coming up the broad steps on all fours, a blaring transistor radio clutched possessively to his chest. Finally reaching the top level he staggered to his feet and approached unsteadily, singing passionately out of tune with his music: 'Bye-bye love – Bye-bye happiness – Hello loneliness – I think I'm going to die' – interrupted, every time he stumbled and fell, by a bout of earsplitting cursing that exposed his toothless gums, his eyes closed tightly as he hurled his imprecations into the resplendent day: 'So fuck you! I say fuck you! Fuck the whole blarry lot of you!' Until one of the young constables ambled towards him from the rose garden (conscious, no doubt, of the fake blonde watching him through thickly blackened eyes) and grabbed him by the shoulder:

'Hey? What's this racket? You're causing a public nuisance.'

'Lemme go! Blarry cunt! Lemme go!'

In the struggle that inevitably followed he dropped his radio.

'Now jes' look at it! I say fuck you, man. Blarry Boer!'

'Come on.' The constable made a grab for his arm, managing to tear the whole ragged sleeve from the shirt. The drunken man sat down heavily and refused to move, shouting abuse all the while.

And now the second constable also approached. As if it had all been previously arranged, they began to drag the invader along the gravel path, back to the stairs that lead down to the street. At the top of the stairs they stood balancing him for a moment between them, then let go. For a yard or two his legs thrashed through the air like a man trying to walk on water, then he missed the top step and tumbled down like a bundle of rags. Laughing, the two constables turned back. One of them stopped where the still loudly blaring radio had fallen, picked it up and carried it to where the drunken man was lying sobbing in the gutter, and dropped it on him. The music stopped abruptly. The sunny morning resumed its course as if nothing had happened.

Thomas had been aware, from the beginning, of Nina's hand

15

clutching his more and more tightly, her fingers cutting into his palm. Knowing her he did his best to restrain her.

'Let's get out of this place,' she whispered.

'The museum?'

'Anywhere.' As they drew level with blondie and her escorts, Nina hissed, 'Well done! You're real heroes, aren't you?'

Uncomprehending, they stared after her.

Thomas pulled her hand. Whatever happened, they should not attract attention today.

In one of the halls of the museum the San family stood and squatted, as always, in their glass cases, pursuing their every-day activities of hunting and preparing food and mixing poison and drinking curdled milk from calabashes or ostrich eggs and sharpening arrows. The first time he'd come here with his parents on one of his father's indefatigable 'educational excursions', Thomas had been so startled by their lifelike appearance that he'd whispered, 'How do the Bushmen manage to sit so still?' Whereupon his brother Frans had calmly answered, 'They're not alive, man. They're stuffed, like all the other animals in this place.' It was only years later that he'd discovered they were plaster casts. But the exhibition continued to disturb him. Those little people simply looked too naked, too exposed, to the 'civilised' eyes staring at them as at monkeys in a zoo. Africa's oldest inhabitants? Perhaps. Now reduced to an anthropological curiosity.

They wandered past the animals. Elephants, lions, jackals, wilde-beest. A petrified Africa: Atlas Mountains and moonscapes, Saharas and Kalaharis, savannah, Ngorongoro craters, extinct volcanoes, the cone of Kilimanjaro (would it still harbour the skeleton of a leopard?), ilala palms and acacias and baobabs, bleeding sunsets, tropical rainforests, mopani thickets, outcrops of chalk or tiger's eye, sandstone and granite and scale, aloes, erosion ditches like deep red scars, ridges, the cairns of the Khoin's ancient hunter-god Heitsi-Eibib, dried beds of brown rivers, koppies, jonas rock, flint, bluestone, fossils and parched white bones, thistles and tumble-weeds, arid lands and landscapes, sisal trees, desolate coasts, the cries of fishing eagles, of gulls, of small patridges and *kiewiets* and hadedas: God, an entire continent summarised, here, in a few popular emblems. And borne with one, wherever one went, forever, part of your fibres and your dreams; a profound presence, intimate lightning; shadows of the sun.

'Perhaps, one day, they'll make room for a stuffed Afrikaner too,' said Nina in his ear. 'Our wretched species is already an anachronism. But who do you think will be chosen to represent us? Who is "typical" enough?'

'Brigadier Bester?' he proposed. (The colonel had moved swiftly through the ranks. Services rendered.)

'I'm not sure. His tan is suspicious.'

'Like mine?' he grimaced.

'What about our state president?' she suggested.

'Not after tomorrow. They won't ever get all the pieces together again.'

'Can you think of anyone else?'

'One of us perhaps?'

'We don't count any more.'

(– *'What I do, I do* because *I'm an Afrikaner. In the name of my Afrikanerhood. I've got to try and redeem something before it's too late.'* Do you remember? –)

They wandered on. Fossils. Reptiles. Reconstructions of prehistoric animals. The curiously delicate skeleton of a smaller dinosaur from the Orange Free State: 200 million years old according to the notice that accompanied it. As they watched, something moved among the vertebrae of the *Massospondylus*.

'Look,' said Nina, chuckling, 'a cockroach! The cheek of it. Aren't they supposed to be even older than the dinosaurs? And they're still with us. Long after human life has been destroyed the cockroaches may inherit the earth.'

'Tomorrow there'll be one cockroach less in the world.'

'We may die with him.'

He pressed a finger to her mouth. 'You promised, remember? Not to talk about it again.'

'You're getting me wrong, Thomas. I'm not afraid of dying.'

'Neither should you *want* to die,' he said. 'We've had enough martyrs as it is.'

'No need to tell *me* that.' She gestured angrily. 'It's too stuffy in here. Too dead. Let's go.'

'Where to?'

'Since we're tourists today, why not up the mountain with the cableway? To see what the Promised Land looks like from above.'

Back in the sun, outside, the light was momentarily blinding. What he saw first, was a wave of purple flowers – *vygies?* – in the distance: the purple of purple bougainvillea. It shook him. He grabbed her hand. Because all of a sudden he was back in that other day – that beautiful, devastating day – with Sipho and Noni in Lusaka.

Today, nothing was simply here and now. Each moment carried in it the scars and signs of other observations, experiences, thoughts. Was this, he wondered, a variation of the old belief that your life unfolds before your eyes before you die?

4

How do you set about eliminating the state president? If you ignore for the moment the philosophical, the moral, even the political questions involved – assuming that these would have been sorted out first, in urgent explorations and soul-searchings that might take days or weeks or months – what remains is the logistics. That is, once the decision has been taken, and after the possibility has been weighed up against innumerable others; after it has been submitted to the Organisation, which in its turn has taken it through all conceivable further stages of evaluation before coming back, at long last, with the directive: right, go ahead. After all the personal and collective objections and misgivings have been dealt with and a core group selected – no more than five or six, for security reasons – who may be relied on in all respects, in all circumstances. When it comes to the planning, the scheme, as such: what then?

It is ironical, even curiously reassuring, to know from the outset that it need not even succeed in practical terms. Success is, of course, always, preferable; and everything has to be done to ensure that it succeeds: but should something unforeseen go wrong, the impact of an *attempt* is in itself powerful and disconcerting enough to ensure devastating disruptions of the political situation. The mere knowledge, in the consciousness of the head of state and all his subjects, that an assault *was* planned, that the unthinkable has become manifest within the framework of the possible, that he has been very nearly blown up, that in future he can never again, wherever he may find himself, feel wholly secure, and that his entourage must come to terms with the fact that it may happen again, that his regime has been demonstrated to be vulnerable, can act like a destructive virus on the entire dispensation. For this is the heart of a totalitarian regime: that the despot forgets about, ignores, his own mortality. And the simple confrontation with this most basic of truths – the fact that he is mortal – signals the beginning of the dictator's end.

The president and his men (they are all men) might still cope with hate, it is given in the very nature of the situation: in the course of time the hate of the oppressed masses even becomes a necessary pretext for the means applied to keep the regime in power. But an assault, the mere attempt at an assault, implies a transition from an attitude or a sentiment to a political reality, from untouchability to vulnerability. And even if, at least temporarily, this should lead to greater oppression, the natural psychological reaction, still, the principle of defeat, the germ of death, has been introduced into the fabric of the regime. There are dictators who survive whole series of assaults, who even pretend to flourish on them: but historically their eventual decline and destruction can invariably be traced to that first attempt, that first discovery of the body's frontiers in time.

Hence 'success' – or what in the circumstances can be defined as 'success' – is guaranteed in advance. Even so, the aim remains to succeed in real and concrete, rather than virtual, terms. Which means that the ultimate of professional action is required: in a struggle which has been going on for so many years, it is often inevitable that the initiative for assaults be delegated to small groups in the field, even to trusted individuals who can act under difficult circumstances with a minimum of help or equipment: in such cases, what is important is the simple statistical *fact* of the action. In most cases victims, even actual explosions, are not mandatory: it is the very discovery of a *planned* attack, a bomb *planted*, that enhances the general climate of unease. But the present project is too daring, there is too much at stake, to rely on anything less than professionalism. It cannot be entrusted to amateurs. At the very outset this determines the selection of members of the core group. There can be no weak link. Which means patient, painstaking deliberation, experimenting, training. Only after that has been concluded to the full satisfaction of the controllers can the planning proceed: and here, too, the most accurate calculations, the most elaborate precautions, are necessary. It may take weeks; months. (It was for this purpose that the group initially rented the old Cape-Dutch farmstead outside Paarl: out of the way, remote, ideal for unobtrusive comings and goings, even for test runs and experiments.)

The first task – after extensive reconnaissance, and consultation

19

with all possible informants; but without raising suspicion or even curiosity – is to compile a list of possible procedures.

The official domain of the state president would be an obvious target: to strike at the cockroach in its own habitat: the residence, Westbrooke; the office building, Tuynhuys. A car bomb or limpet mine at the main entrance, for example. The problem of constant surveillance might be overcome through precise timing, but ideally an assault of this kind would demand a kamikaze strategy. And that is unwise. The Organisation is not eager unnecessarily to sacrifice the lives of its members; there have been enough victims as it is. If automatic weapons or hand grenades were used, the scene might be transferred to the Houses of Parliament. Maximum spectacular impact guaranteed; but the strict round-the-clock security measures create, once more, too great a risk. Also, the president seldom appears outside the buildings.

So other strategies must be explored. A big Party gathering in Parow or Bellville or elsewhere in the Peninsula? The Goodwood Agricultural Show, to be opened this year by His Majesty in person? (Two comrades in police uniform arriving minutes before the opening with written instructions to remove the lectern, pronounced 'unsafe', and install a new one with a bomb built into it. Even more audaciously – Rashid loves this – the bomb can be concealed inside the microphone set up by a person with an SABC clearance pass.) Another possibility: any of the countless parades of army or police attended by the great man who is besotted with uniforms. Or a rugby match at Newlands, to strike at the very soul of the *volk*?

What is selected at last, based on information from inside the army (the Organisation is represented everywhere, in almost every training camp or regiment), is a medal parade in the grounds of the Castle. The symbolic importance of the venue – the first white fortress at the southernmost tip of the continent, its impregnability, its arrogance – is decisive. In addition, it is situated more conveniently than the well protected Tuynhuys or the official residence: right on the Parade with its crowds, its traffic, its accessibility.

This is, in broad outline, the likely scenario:

At exactly fifteen minutes to eleven on that Friday morning the state president and his escort are expected at the gateway to the Castle on the eastern side of the Parade. The advantage of bureaucratic precision in timing is that it also makes it possible for the opposition to plan accurately, down to the last second. At, say, twenty minutes to eleven a person unlikely to attract much attention, a little old lady for instance, arrives in an unobtrusive car of mature age, bearing the registration plates of some small *dorp* in the deep interior: there will be roadblocks, of course, but having no experience of such things, she blithely drives on with all the death-defying confidence an inhabitant of Garies or Darling or Godknowswhere can muster. At the last moment, briefly unnerved by the confusion she has caused, the noise, the traffic cops, she brakes jerkily, and the little car stalls right opposite the Castle gate. With a brief motion, unnoticed by anyone outside, she presses a button hidden under the instrument panel, which effectively disconnects the battery. Now no one can drive the car away. More important, it sets in motion the timing mechanism of the bomb, allowing five (or, again depending on the circumstances, ten) minutes before it explodes inside the carefully sealed boot. (Remote control will naturally have been considered first, manipulated from a car parked well beforehand at a safe distance, let's say near the City Hall. But such a car may arouse suspicion; may be towed or ordered away by the traffic police; moreover, after careful reconnaissance, it is evident that visibility would be a problem.)

Our lady of the car gets out, opens the bonnet of her recalcitrant vehicle, starts tugging at the wiring. Guards, traffic cops and others descend on her, some to reprimand and fulminate, others to offer help. The atmosphere is tense, everybody is nervous, anxious, hurried. Only the old tortoise from Garies remains unperturbed. One finds her sort all over the world: in the middle of an earthquake they will shake the dust from their prim clothes and make a cup of tea among the debris.

In all this confusion a traffic cop in uniform arrives on his motorcycle. He starts yelling at the old lady. Quietly annoyed, she approaches, presumably to admonish him, perhaps even to belt him with her handbag (the cheek of today's young people: how dare they speak to an elderly person like that?). In the general panic and consternation she jumps on the pillion seat of his cycle and they charge off. The other bystanders, flabbergasted, remain behind beside the stalled car. A minute later, on the appointed second, the state president's cavalcade arrives.

The rest of the enterprise has been planned with equal finesse: safe escape, after all, is as important as the assault itself. It is the test of professionalism. It determines the ultimate efficacy of the Organisation. Briefly: the constable drops his passenger in Adderley Street, opposite an entrance to the underground shopping centre in the Golden Acre. In a ladies' toilet, a startling metamorphosis. The wig comes off, the demure dress, the shoes and stockings are removed – under the clothes she is already wearing a T-shirt and shorts which will make her look about seventeen. From the sensible handbag she takes flipflops for her feet, dark glasses, chewing gum, a Walkman with earphones. The redundant costume is bundled into a Garlicks shopping bag also taken from the handbag. Within minutes the skinny teenager, her body swaying to the rhythm of her inaudible music, moves up an escalator and emerges in St George's Street.

In the meantime the traffic cop has gone to Long Street where he stops beside a parked car and gets off the cycle. He appears to discuss with the driver behind the steering wheel the state of his tyres, a broken rear light. The man leans over to open the passenger door. The cop gets in. Seconds later they are on their way. Perhaps they drive via St George's Street to meet Miss Walkman; alternatively, one of the other cars on standby may already have picked her up. For every stage of the scenario there are two or three alternatives; one must plan for all contingencies.

Twenty minutes later they arrive at the address in Observatory where the group moved in two months ago, in February (after the unexpected mishap in Paarl). By this time, his helmet, glasses and moustache removed, and divested of his uniform, the erstwhile traffic constable is no longer recognisable. While the two of them undergo yet another change of appearance, their previous costumes are dispatched from the house to places in Athlone and Manenburg, from where, bit by bit, they will be dispensed with, along old trusted routes, with the help of people who themselves have no inkling of the clothing's origins (the Organisation runs a network of specialised concerns and individuals all over the country: from panel beaters and spray-painters to photographers, suppliers of documents, pawnbrokers and junk dealers, you name it; and it is in their common interest that each will contribute his or her bit without knowing or ever enquiring about the others); and so in due course the clothes, if for some reason they cannot be disposed of by burning, will find their way to rubbish bins or second-hand shops throughout the Peninsula, or as far afield as Port Elizabeth or Johannesburg; an item like the uniform may end up deep in the sea, dropped from a fishing trawler.

Less than an hour after the explosion two passengers, in separate cars, will arrive at different departure halls at the airport

22

— a bookish young lady with square glasses and dark fringe; a nonchalant tousle-haired young bloke, presumably a student, in jeans and yellow T-shirt — to check in for their respective flights: he on the direct flight to Johannesburg (SA 322), she to Port Elizabeth (SA 608). On her arrival in Port Elizabeth she will be met by a girlfriend in a souped-up Volkswagen; forty minutes later (this is cutting it fine indeed!) a man in a new Opel will drop a short-haired girl in a frivolous Foschini dress in front of the departures building, in time for flight SA 412 to Johannesburg. In the meantime, the long-haired student, upon his arrival at Jan Smuts airport, has gone to the Holiday Inn where he is transformed into an eager young executive with short dark hair, glasses, briefcase and leather suitcase. In his hotel room he negotiates one of the last critical tests of the day when with a lightly perspiring hand he dials the well-memorised number to make sure that everything is still on track, that he has the go-ahead for the final manoeuvre. An acquaintance arrives to drive him to the international departure lounge. (The next morning the same acquaintance, having spent the night in the reserved room, will check out of the Holiday Inn, pay the bill, hand over the keys.) And just in time for flight BA 054 to London he moves through passport control and customs. As he goes down the escalator to the departure hall he may notice stunned passengers thronging around special late-afternoon editions of newspapers. The entire front page of the *Star* is bordered in black, while huge letters filling up all the available space within the frame proclaim:

PRESIDENT KILLED IN BLAST

Perhaps he notices, at a distance, the sprightly young girl in the queue waiting to board flight LH 571 to Frankfurt which leaves twenty minutes before his own; but neither gives any sign of knowing the other.

It is conceivable that, months or years later, they return to the country. In the meantime the other members of their cell will have regrouped, moved to other operational areas, pursuing in their professional, determined way the preparation and execution of other assaults. For it can never end. The pressure must never be relaxed. To remain effective, sporadic failures must be followed up as rapidly as possible with success; and success with ever more spectacular enterprises.

They left the blue Mini they'd removed from Sean's garage during his absence abroad, in the shade of pine-trees in the parking lot at the lower cableway station. As it was a weekday, there were few tourists around and the cable car going up the Mountain was empty. They stood, he behind her, at the end window watching the landscape ebb away below them: the city and the Lion's Head, the harbour, the smoking townships of the Cape Flats, the blue-flame mountains of the Hottentot's Holland range. Everything became smaller, more crisply defined, receding not only in space but in time.

'It's like flying,' Nina said, whispering to exclude the pale youth with the acne-scarred face manning the door. 'Just think away the car and the cable. All my most special dreams are about flying. Every time you cross a ridge a new valley opens up below you. It's scary, a hollow feeling in your stomach, but terribly exciting at the same time – like when I was small and my father pushed me on a swing. It's a very physical sensation, almost sexual. One night I woke up with an orgasm from a dream like that.' Without any bridge in her thinking she added, 'Can we make love on the mountain? I feel sexy.'

Thomas glanced at the young conductor, but he was leaning over the railing, obviously not paying any attention to them. 'Why do you always want to make love in the most impossible places?' he asked against her cheek.

'Otherwise it gets boring. I'll get the creeps if I have to lead a bourgeois life like my parents'.'

'Not much chance of that, for you.'

Another of her disconcerting switches: 'Do you think, if they caught us tomorrow, they'd get my father to try us?'

'Of course not. You of all people should know that.'

'Yes, I know. Still, it's a pity. It would have been poetic justice. Then, at last, I would have known how his mind really works. What justice means to him. "Judge sentences own daughter to death." Nice ring to it, don't you think?'

'No. For one thing, they're not going to catch us.'

'I know.' She leaned out over the window ledge to stare more intensely at the Cape below them, then pressed her mouth against his ear again: 'You remember how my father pulled out the last time the minister tried to plant him in a "terror" trial? – said he was concerned about his family. Suppose the comrades of the accused came to blow up the house or something. You know' – her green eyes burned in his – 'I wish I could find a reason to respect him, even it was only as a jurist.'

'Is that really important?'

She didn't answer directly. 'Sometimes,' she said, 'sometimes I wish I could have grown up in an ordinary home, in Bellville or somewhere, with veneer furniture, and classicord wall-to-wall, and vibracrete around the Sundance pool in the back garden, and a caravan on the pavement in front of the house, and men coming round on Sundays for barbecue, discussing the Province flyhalf or fuel injection, while the women in the kitchen gossip about miscarriages and foolproof recipes: and to have felt proud of my father.'

– Proud? That Saturday in the back garden. From the kitchen, I was mixing Oros at the wash-up, I heard the outburst of noise outside and rushed to the door to look. Father had caught the gardener, Solomon, picking an orange, and was shouting blue murder as if he was God Almighty who'd just surprised Adam and Eve at the Tree of Knowledge. 'Put back that orange immediately!' Honest to God, that was what he said. And the poor gardener, a kind-hearted abject soul who did his work for next to nothing simply so that he could be with his wife Sabien, the 'domestic' in our kitchen, he was just standing there, bewildered, staring at Father and at the orange in his hand, not knowing what to do. Then Sabien came round the corner of the servant's room to see what the noise was about. That must have been the worst of all for the man, to be humiliated in front of his wife. He tried to explain: It was only an orange, Baas, the whole tree was full of them. Father got beside himself. 'Don't you talk back at me! You bloody good-for-nothing parasite on my property – you think you can gobble up every damn thing in sight?' It went on and on. I never even thought he knew such words. Unexpectedly, worked up into a frenzy, Father made a grab for the orange, wrenched it from the man's hand and threw it at him. Hitting him on the shoulder. Quite ridiculous. But for Solomon it was the last straw. He bent down, and suddenly he had a half-brick in his hand. I stood petrified in the doorway. Sabien too, at the corner. Solomon came a step nearer, the brick raised above his hand. There was murder in his eyes. I could see their whites, shot with red. And all of a sudden Father started pleading. Stepping gingerly back as he whined, 'Now come on, Solomon, it's not so bad, hey. You can pick all the oranges you want, okay?' Solomon came another step closer. 'I'll give you a raise, Solomon. You hear? You've always been a good worker. Now just put down that brick. I'm not angry with you. I'll give you new overalls too. Just listen to me, please.'

Suddenly Solomon had had enough. He dropped the brick on the ground and turned on his heel, stalked past Sabien to the servant's room and closed the door behind him.

The same door was kicked down from its hinges by the police later that afternoon when they came to fetch him. I watched wide-eyed as they hurled him into the back of the van like a bag of potatoes. And before dark Sabien, too, had left, having packed all her things into a large cardboard box – everything she and her husband possessed in a box – and gone off without even asking for her pay. On that day I knew I'd lost my father. I could never again respect a person like that. –

'Neither your father nor mine has much reason to be proud of us,' Thomas said wryly. 'And after tomorrow, if they ever find out –'

'Can you imagine the newspapers? *What could have possessed two talented young Afrikaners from good homes to betray everything that is dear to their people?*'

'They'll find reasons enough. They've got to, their salvation depends on it. Proving that we're aberrations, that something's gone wrong with us: that we've been trying to fill a psychological void, to compensate for guilt or fear or whatever, that having made a fuck-up of ordinary relations we were forced to turn to other possibilities. Two paranoid, twisted pariahs incapable of love, turning to the enemy to hide their own shortcomings.' He reflected for a moment. When he spoke again, his voice was more restrained: 'Do you think someone among them, anyone, even if it's only one, will ever stop to consider that an ordinary decent Afrikaner can be driven to a point where he's *got* to do a thing like this, just because he cannot take it any longer?'

'Does it matter whether they understand it or not?' she asked. 'What matters is that *we* know we've thought it through and there's nothing else we can do.'

'Still, it would have made it easier to know there was *someone* outside who understood.'

'We've always known it wouldn't be easy, Thomas.'

'I know. It's just – all of a sudden one feels – I don't even know *what* I feel – it's just so damn lonely.'

26

Impulsively she pressed her face against his chest. He held her head, feeling in his hands the soft uneven hair, the stubble on her neck, the hardness of her shoulders. He felt her body against his, the pressure of her ribcage and her hips. And below them the world receded: that must be how astronauts saw it. To drift away like that, surrounded by nothing, by space, and nothing to refer to, to depend on, but oneself, this small fierce urge to survive, this irrational angry faith that you're doing what you must do, that you must do what you're doing. Tomorrow, he thought, tomorrow night they would be even lonelier than now, each on a plane winging towards a different destination, surrounded by night, not even a hand to touch, someone's breathing in one's ear, the caress of a cheek. All things considered they were still better off now. And he felt almost ashamed. Because how could he think of this as loneliness? They were still together, he and she, containing in them everything they'd ever been, the whole long road they'd travelled together from that first windswept day in Crossroads, that first night in his high flat: but even from much further back, infinitely further, beyond generations and ages in this tragic land. What was the meaning of 'beginning'? Where were the roots of what was to happen at fifteen minutes to eleven tomorrow morning? Were they already there, obscure, in the arrival of the very first Landman, the first Jordaan, at this Cape of Storms?

Or is this, he wondered in anguish, the most terrifying loneliness of all? – this solitary confrontation with one's own history, with everything that has made you what you are, brought you to where you happen to be? Knowing that the present is pervaded by yesterday and the day before; and that today is coloured in advance by tomorrow's solitude? Cain's loneliness in the land of Nod –?

He kept his eyes pressed tightly closed until the car – that frail little surrogate of a space vessel – arrived, scraping and swaying, at the top station and the apathetic young conductor opened the door to let out his two passengers.

Hand in hand they walked up the uneven path to the top. It was cool up there. A touch of wind. As if, so high up, one were closer to an autumn the world below did not yet suspect; exposed to a greater emptiness. Rock-rabbits reluctantly darted off a few paces along the grey lichen-stained rocks. Below, to the south, lay the vertebrae of the Peninsula, an angry Adamastor, a vast prehistoric skeleton thrust against the ink-blue ocean:

further on, invisible beyond their provisional horizon, Antarctica would sprawl below its ice-caps, the largest continent of all, inhospitable, inhuman, starkly beautiful. Their eyes returned to the more familiar: the crescent of False Bay on one side, Table Bay on the other. The almost imperceptible motion of white wavelines breaking. Here and there the hulls of wrecked ships: how many lives had been sacrificed through the centuries before Europeans had caught a hold on this stern continent and learned to adapt to it? – How impudent of us, to set out sowing and planting and building in this place, and then to start lording it over others, pretending it belongs to us, against all sense and reason.

Yet at the same time, how can we not cling to it, now that we're here? Once one has taken root in Africa, it is impossible to acclimatise elsewhere. Remember Sipho and Noni and all the others withering in exile, like thorn-trees or baobabs transplanted in a cold climate. –

Earlier, when they'd still had the time, the luxury, to indulge in such pastimes, they'd discussed the persistent attempts of Europe, through the ages, to insert itself into the interstices of the continent, lured by Prester John, or the fabulous riches of Monomotapa (*Hic sunt leones* on ancient maps), or prompted simply by the practical need to find a resting-place on the long journey to the East: they'd discussed the rape and desolation and destruction of the continent – starting in this place, in this angry blue sea – and how it had never really succeeded. Africa was still Africa, no longer romantic or virginal, but a wild subconscious in the mind of the world. Sometimes, on fifteenth- and sixteenth-century maps (he, especially, found them irresistible), they'd traced with their fingers the progress of Portuguese caravels, millimetre by millimetre down the curving coast and round the Cape of Storms. Once he'd brought her a book which had haunted him since his student days, *The Lusiads*, in a charmingly old-fashioned prose translation (the last time it had been taken out, according to the library stamp, had been twenty-one years before); and amused, yet curiously touched as well, they'd read the prophecy ascribed by Camoens in the fifth Canto to the giant Adamastor, who in the Portuguese version had been turned into the great rocky outcrop of the Cape Peninsula as punishment for rebelling against Zeus. In this Canto the petrified giant warns future generations of Europeans never to hope for survival in this place: Adamastor himself, the land itself, would see to that, a dark fate embedded in mountain and rock:

'Listen to me now and learn what perils have been laid up against such excess of presumption, what penalties await you over the vast expanse of ocean and on the land that you will eventually subdue in battle ... Here, unless I am deceived, I count on avenging myself to the full on him who discovered me —'

Nina, of course, had been cynical; but she, too, had been moved by the apocalyptic vision of one explorer after the other succumbing to the land, culminating in the emblematic couple, man and woman, burnt into this etching plate, Africa:

'Another will come, too, one noble, liberal, greatly esteemed, and in love, and with him the beauteous lady whose affections he will have had the rare good fortune to win. A sorry plight is theirs, and black the fate that brings them into my realms: for, incensed against them, it will allow them to survive cruel shipwreck only to vent on them sufferings still more grievous.

'They shall see their children, the fruit of so much love, die of hunger; rough, grasping Caffres shall strip the gracious lady of her garments after a long and painful trek across the hot sands, leaving her crystal limbs exposed to all the rigours of the elements. And their fellow-survivors from so much misery shall see still more: they shall see the two hapless lovers fall victims of the hot, implacable bush, where their tears, for the grief that is in them, will melt the very stones, until after a last close embrace their souls will take leave of their bodies even more wretched than they were comely.'

But once she couldn't help saying, 'Only a European could have thought up such a vision. We know better, don't we?' Persisting, with more emphasis, when he did not answer immediately, 'Don't you agree, Thomas? One can only think of Adamastor as fate if you treat him as your enemy. But if you show him respect instead, and surrender yourself to his mercy? I'd much rather think of us as the children of Adamastor, Thomas, not his victims.'

'I think it's up to him to decide whether he wants to accept us or not.'

'Touché,' she said, laughing.

Today, he thought, today they'd reached an extremity: a moral cape as ultimate as this horn with which Africa gaffs into the southern seas. And tomorrow would decide whether, and how, they would be accepted. Whether they would be judged worthy.

Mechanically, more from habit than from any conscious decision, he took a few photographs of Adamastor, blue on blue.

'What are you going to do with them?' asked Nina.

'Mementoes to refresh our memory. It may be years before we come back here.'

'But we will.'

There was, suddenly, so much to be said, no matter how many times they had discussed it between themselves, and with the others, during the past months. A last chance of reaching ultimate certainty? Making a gesture with his head towards the distant city, without looking at her, he said, 'We could have been down there like all the others today, doing our shopping or lying on a beach. So what makes us different from them? How did we get here? Do you think we've gone crazy?'

'Suppose it's the world that's crazy, not us,' she said, 'then everything becomes its own opposite, not so? Then being ordinary, being normal, would mean we're mad.'

'So we don't really seem to have a choice, after all.'

'We're here precisely because we *have* a choice.'

'I know.' A strained smile. 'I'm just playing devil's advocate. To make doubly sure. There is so much at stake.'

She walked a few yards away from him, jumped on a flat rock poised precariously on the edge of the precipice, stained a rusty red, and dull green, and yellow with lichen, to get an uninterrupted view. Without looking round, she said, 'Shall I tell you what really scares me? It's the thought that even when all this is behind us it will still not be the end of injustice and horror and everything.'

'Of course it won't be the end,' he said with sudden urgency. 'As long as there are people living – my God, you know it as well as I do! – the world will be a mess. That's just about all we can be sure of. Life will never be good or sensible or beautiful. But that doesn't mean it can't be *better* than it is. It can always be better. And as long as there's that possibility, it's worth while to keep on risking everything, doing what we're doing.'

'I know you're right,' she said quietly. 'But then we must be truly mad. Risking everything for a mere possibility.'

He came to her, put an arm round her from behind, his hand under the flap of her boiler-suit on her breast, a gesture not of possession, not even of protection, merely of affirmation. 'You're not having misgivings, are you?' he asked gently. 'I don't believe it. It's been you, you more than anyone else, who's helped me to believe in our cause.'

'Don't worry,' she said, 'one day we'll come back to celebrate. You and I, and with Justin and Rashid and David. And everybody else.'

'Can you imagine it? All the fugitives, all the exiles, streaming back from all over the world. And all the jails opening their doors to let out their prisoners. And from the island over there –' Together they stood, staring in awe across the narrow stretch of azure dividing the mainland and Robben Island which, from up there, appeared disconcertingly small and flat, a dun-coloured stain on the sea. So close to the beach. But light-years away for those looking from out there. In Thomas's ears was the memory of Henry's voice speaking about the years he'd spent there; and Sipho's; the voices of countless others through the years, in dingy rooms blue with smoke in Soweto or Alexandra or New Brighton or Langa, basement flats in London, a room with a high ornate ceiling in Prague, a hostel room on the outskirts of Moscow, a kitchen in a derelict blue building in Lusaka, all of them variations of the same experience, all the voices identical – a single irrepressible sound, a timeless shofar resounding over the tumbling walls of Jericho, like the collective scream one might imagine erupting from the ochre slave-house on the isle of Gorée off the coast of Senegal, ringing out across the ocean, the cry of the slaves shipped from there through three centuries and more: Gorée where his own ancestral mother Catharijn had come from – On that resplendent future day all the history and prehistory of Africa would converge, beams of light bent inward through a burning-glass to a single searing point where it erupts in fire.

How unreal that vision appeared at this moment, a mirage, a hallucination above the placid smoky facts of the Cape as it lay below them: and yet it was thinkable, not as a miracle, but as the final outcome of innumerable small, ordinary actions, sacrifices and deprivations along the road. And tomorrow would be, for them, the eye of the needle.

'Come.'

In the restaurant they ordered tea. There were dried proteas in an arrangement against the stone wall: even that seemed emblematic. Afterwards they began to amble across the uneven top of the mountain, away from the clusters of sightseers in the vicinity of the restaurant.

Nina pointed at the city and its many tentacles groping up the foot of the mountain, the series of coastal towns stretching round the curve of False Bay. 'That's what fascinated me in Australia when I was there,' she said – in her matric year she'd gone down under as a Rotary exchange student, a gesture to her father's expectations of her (except it turned out differently from what he'd hoped!) – 'how almost desperately their cities cling to the coastline, all round the continent: and then that vast empty interior. As if people were afraid of venturing too far, preferring instead to stay as close as possible to the sea that had washed them up there. Perhaps it's an old colonial urge, only much more pronounced there than elsewhere. But here it's different. Remember this morning, in Kirstenbosch? – Commander van Riebeeck's hedge of wild almonds still growing there, three hundred years after he'd planted it, the first pathetic attempt to keep Africa out of the small European settlement. But somehow it never worked. Not here. Here the people, even the Europeans, started moving away from the sea as soon as they could, into the interior.'

'I'm sure Freud would have had something to say about it,' said Thomas. 'The Afrikaner turning his back on the mother sea and heading for the barren male hinterland. Or is that something in our favour after all, something we picked up from the Africans themselves?' He chuckled at a memory. 'The craziest sign of it I've ever seen was a navy unit in the middle of the desert, at Oshakati, in Namibia, when I did my military service. The dreary little bar they had there, the Makalani, had a parachute for a roof, and inside the walls were covered in murals of technicolour seascapes and palm trees.' (But was that more crazy, he wondered, than his own ancestor Fransoois Lodewickus, who'd trekked into the desert on a ship, an ark? Or his great-great-grandfather Petrus who'd seduced a woman with palm trees on his bedroom wall?)

'You see?' she said. 'You cannot deny something inside yourself and not expect to be punished. You of all people ought to know that: you're a Cancerian. Somewhere in your most secret self the sea must be hiding away, you can't betray it.'

They had crossed the spine of the mountain; there was no one else in sight. They were above Africa Face, the almost perpendicular cliffs plummeting from their feet to very far below where the wind left footprints on the goose-flesh of the sea. A single gull swept past them, wings motionless, riding the invisible currents to which it abandoned itself unquestioningly. From time to time it uttered its raucous call, a forlorn grey squawk lost in time. Nina sat down on a large boulder, leaning back on her arms, her face raised to the sun. After a few minutes she got up impatiently, undid the safety-pins that held her straps, stepped out of the faded denim boiler-suit and kicked off her panties, then pulled the thin shirt over her head. She resumed her earlier posture; under the cool caress of the wind her nipples tautened. The gull came sweeping by again.

'What if someone comes?' he asked.

'No one will come this far. Come and sit by me.'

He looked round, then squatted beside her on the rough boulder, prying with a fingernail a small crust of lichen from the surface; then moved his hand to caress, almost absently, her shoulders and breasts. How strange, he thought, to be so remote from the world, as if they'd dropped out of time. She lay back on the scarred rock, her knees drawn up.

'We've got to soak up the sun,' she said. 'It's our last chance for God knows how long. Day after tomorrow we'll be dumped in winter. Have you seen the papers? Snowstorms all over Europe just when they thought spring had settled in. No wonder our ancestors fled down here.'

Once again the soundless gull sailing past, then the single desolate cry.

'I want to take a picture of you,' he said suddenly, and stood back, began to move this way and that, squatting, climbing on rocks, to find the best angle. Then opened the lens as wide as it could go, selected a shutter speed of 1/1000, and focused on her body – freckly and pale and slight on the mottled boulder, the background a blue blur – and pressed the button. Stretched his back for a moment, and positioned himself to take another – how startlingly all relationships in space changed at every step to the left or right, backward or forward – reducing her to a speck in the landscape. Then stopped to consider what it would appear like from higher up, that boulder over there, looking down on her from above, heraldic, spreadeagled on the rock –

'Come back to me,' she called, her eyes still closed.

Zipping his camera bag shut he returned to her and sat down beside her. She reached for his hand, and placed it between her breasts, where he could feel under his open palm the light throbbing of her heart.

'Whatever may happen after this,' she said quietly, her eyes now wide open, staring intensely into the blue as if she could discern invisible constellations in that glaring light, 'whether it's tomorrow, or the day after, or whenever: if ever we are tempted to have misgivings about what's happened, then try to remember, Thomas, try to remember it *was* worth while. All of it. Promise?'

He moved the tips of his fingers down over her belly between the sharp points of her hips. His palm braced on the small promontory between her thighs (underneath the softness the solidity of bone) he moved his middle finger along the ridge of her sex.

But at that moment he heard voices on the wind; and looking up, he saw a group of tourists approaching among the rocks in the distance, ten or twelve of them, foreigners by their looks, elderly men and women with cloth hats and sunglasses, loud shirts, bermudas or floppy trousers, their oustretched necks straining against the weight of cameras and binoculars.

'Oh no.' Thomas bent over quickly to pick up her clothes.

'What's the matter?' she asked, annoyed.

He motioned. 'People. Coming this way.'

'Let them.'

As she made no attempt to put on her shirt, he angrily placed himself between her and them.

The group drew closer, chattering loudly. They were only a few yards away when some of the women became aware of them. 'Oh my goodness –' 'Oh no, for heaven's sake –' 'Come *on*, Harry –'

Nina got up, stretching her arms with the luxurious delight of a cat, then placed her hands on her hips and scowled at the bewildered strangers as if they were the ones who had to explain their presence. There were a few more exclamations before the women took charge of their menfolk (one or two had begun to grope furtively for their cameras) and marched them off, some of them clearly fractious, others myopic and meek.

Thomas pressed the bundle of clothes against her body. 'Better put them on, Nina.'

Resentful, she began to fold out the short sleeves of her T-shirt. 'What's it matter? Not one of them will ever see us again.'

'But they may remember us, dammit. And no one must remember us.'

Still smouldering with chagrin, standing defiantly, legs astride, on the tallest boulder, she pulled the shirt over her cropped head, stepped into the boiler-suit (stuffing her panties into a pocket to assert her independence), and fastened the safety-pins; then stood looking in the direction where the last of the tourists were scurrying off among the grey boulders; one portly man glancing back for a final peep, stepping on a loose stone, and scuttling out of sight on all fours. Nina sat down on the rock.

'You do understand that, don't you?' He was standing lower than she, looking up at her, blinded for a moment by the sun behind her.

'Of course, my love.' In a furious gesture she pressed her head against her knees. 'It's just – such a pity. We have so little time left.'

Following a different route – to avoid the sightseers; and to stretch this hour as long as possible – they returned to the upper cable station. There were still other appointments with the city to be kept.

6

The sand beyond the narrow lawn under the palm trees was warm under their feet (his more sensitive than hers: she went barefoot whenever she could). They'd left their shoes in the car, after they had eaten the hamburgers and greasy chips he'd bought at the café – a guilty meal, as only a few yards away a wretched old beggarwoman was rifling a rubbish bin in search of scraps. The sudden question: Tomorrow, after the bomb – or the day after – or a month from now – or after the revolution – would anything have changed in the life of this miserable creature? Or would she still be coming back here for the rejects of the rich? And if it were so, what would it all have availed, all their sacrifices and suffering, the anguish, the sleepless nights, calculations, danger, violence? What an unsettling day this was turning into, behind the even surface of its flow, with all these questions coming back, questions they'd explored and thought they'd settled long ago, like poisonous bubbles released by weeds submerged deep in the mud below?

Nina ran to the sea ahead of him, after pressing most of her food into the hands of the old beggarwoman. She thrashed into the shallow water, laughing at the sogginess that crept, a dark stain, up her trouser legs; knee-deep, she turned to wait for him. Behind him the houses of Camp's Bay reached up the tall slope, through tumbling gardens; far above stood the Twelve Apostles. Thomas bent over to roll up the legs of his jeans above his calves.

'Cold?' he asked, unnecessarily.

'Fearsome.'

Like ice crystals the cold shot up through his very bones as he waded in. He hesitated, approached a few more steps, then gave it up and turned back and ran out, gasping, to the beach, where he squatted down to rub his aching ankles.

After a few minutes he looked up and saw her still standing, legs astride, fiercely resolute, in the cold water, her denim boiler-suit soaked to the thighs. Her teeth were chattering, but she made no attempt to come out.

'Are you bloody mad?' he called. 'You'll freeze to death in there.'

Small waves were breaking against her. She tried to laugh, but managed only a grimace.

'Nina, what are you trying to prove?'

'That I'm better than you.'

Only after he'd finally persuaded her to come back to the hot sand, where she dug her legs in to warm them up, did she continue: 'I tried to imagine it was the SB torturing me; I wanted to see how long I could stand it.'

A crazy whim? No, it was much more. A kind of passion. He knew that well enough. There was nothing whimsical about it, no mere impulse of rebellion, emotional recalcitrance. That was what he'd had to convince the Organisation of when he'd first proposed that she be part of their core group: they had no interest in, no place for, hotheads, people with axes to grind, romantic rebels. He'd first discussed it at length with Justin. Then enquiries were made, exploring every corner of her life through a magnifying glass. After the enquiry a different picture emerged. That bohemian year in Stellenbosch? A question mark in the margin, but judged in context it no longer appeared so outrageous. Then the impressive record at UCT: academic achievements running parallel with hard, dedicated work in different organisations: the SRC, ECC, Black Sash, the UDF, NUSAS (on the national executive in her final year). The ability to work on a project with others, through days and nights, for weeks, months – organising, collecting data and interpreting them, distributing food and clothing among refugees of squatter settlements bulldozed by the police, conducting interviews in the embattled townships, taking affidavits from victims of unjust dismissal from domestic or factory employment, of persecution or exploitation, following up information, negotiating with police officers about the particulars of detainees and their conditions of detention, liaising with the families of prisoners. Hardly sleeping for a week sometimes, going almost without food: such things she would readily give up if the well-being or freedom of others were at stake. Protests, demonstrations? Oh all the time. But that had never been as important to her as working in the legal aid clinic, or in an advice office, or among the people in the townships. Okay, so gestures sometimes had value, could not always be discounted; but her concern had been to get something *done*. ('It's no damn use kicking up a fuss about injustice: we've got to change it. And in order to do that we need to find out how it works, how it's structured, what makes it tick.') Where the passion came in was in her impatience with everything that was inessential or evasive, that wasted time, that postponed results. In this respect, the Organisation had found, she could do with more restraint. But she had the dedication, and the talent, and the ability, no doubt about that; she also had the experience of working with others, of adapting to changing circumstances, of obeying orders. Even then she still had to be tested, those first few months at Paarl – to make sure that she did not only have initiative, but that she could also accept discipline; that she could show, not only creativity, but obedience as well; that she was prepared to handle inspiration, but also hard and boring work. He, too, had been subjected to the same tests. And Christine. Unlike Justin, and David, and Rashid, who had been tested long before, and had worked together on other projects. And that was how they'd got here: he and she, today, on this unexpected holiday, on the hot sand beside the icy indigo sea.

Nina rolled over on her stomach, her sandy feet raised high, staring up at the chain of mountains. 'Which one of those peaks do you think is Judas?'

'Why on earth do you ask a thing like that?'

'They're the Twelve Apostles, so one of them must be Judas.'

'I don't think anybody has ever thought of naming them separately. It's a collective name. I'm not even sure there are twelve of them.'

For a while she lay staring at the jagged peaks, as if trying to count them, losing track, starting again.

'I'd love to climb Judas if only I knew which one it was,' she said, pensive. 'Don't you agree the poor man had a raw deal?'

'No one can forgive a traitor.'

'Not even his kind? Think of what he must have been expecting of Jesus: to throw off the Roman yoke, to end the oppression, to set the Jews free in their own land. But at the crucial moment he chickened out, saying it was some unworldly pie-in-the-sky kingdom he'd been talking about. And whining on and on about turning the other cheek, and the meek inheriting the earth: all that sweet, hopeless stuff you and I used to believe in too. The way I see it, and I know it's not all that original but at least it makes sense, Judas calculated that if he could force the guy's hand, manipulate him into a position where he'd have to choose between being thrown into prison and *doing* something, he would – at long last! – go for some action. Instead of which all his expectations were dashed.'

'Jesus was his friend. He relied on Judas.'

'And not the other way round? You must remember, all we have is the official version. Who has ever tried to see it from Judas's perspective? If you ask me, he was concerned with much more than personal sentiment. It was a matter of his whole nation, his whole society, everybody oppressed by the Romans.'

'Your turn to play at devil's advocate?'

'You said nobody could forgive a traitor?'

'Sure. Anything wrong with that?'

'You'll have to define "traitor" very carefully first, Thomas,' she said calmly. 'What do you think people are going to call this thing we're doing? To them we're all a bunch of Judases. And in our case, too, only the official version will be sent into the world.'

'No. We know that what we're doing is the right thing. The necessary, inevitable thing. It's the only moral choice.'

'I'm sure that is exactly how Judas argued. Or do you think it only depends on which side wins in the end? Morality can't be as provisional as that.'

He looked up at the nearest of the Apostles. 'My lord,' he said, 'the advocate for the defence is drawing conclusions not warranted by the facts.'

'My lord,' she retorted, 'my learned friend is twisting the facts to suit his own misguided argument.'

The peak, which might have been any of the Apostles, gazed imperturbably into the distance, as implacable as Adamastor himself.

– To think that I've brought up a Judas in my own home,' said my father. 'And that it should have been you.'

For heaven's sake, I thought, don't start again. I know it by heart.

That all your life you've wanted a daughter (the ultimate wish of the male chauvinist? – to have a female made by himself, to fulfil his every wish, and with whom, barring incest, he can do what he wants); added to this, the disappointment that not one of your four sons showed any interest in law. Not one to follow in your footsteps. (Perhaps, my poor father, you never left any visible footprints to follow?) And then, at long last, I. Not that I was by 'nature' interested in law. But it was a base to negotiate from. Because you were adamant I should go to Stellenbosch, your alma mater, the cradle of Afrikaner intelligentsia. I was just as adamant: I wanted to go to UCT. For once you thought you could have it your way. But after I'd made a total balls-up of my first year at Stellenbosch (the disgrace! the brilliant Nina Jordaan, exchange student in Australia, top pupil at Bloemhof Girls' High, one of the top twenty in the province, finalist in the English Olympiad, you name it) and you discovered that I'd joined the 'alternative' scene, booze, dagga, sex, opposition politics, failing all my subjects at the end of the year, you relented, and I promised to pull myself together. I even undertook to swot law, provided I could go to UCT, otherwise you could stuff it.

And then, at the end of my fourth year, this confrontation. I remember every word of it:

'Nina, I'm talking to you.'

'You're not leaving me much space to say anything.'

'Not even that you're sorry?'

'I'm not sorry.' Adding deliberately (what is it in you, between us, that always provokes me? to renew, every time, my shame at how weak you are? because it is the one thing I don't *want* to know?): 'I'm sorry I'm not sorry, Father.'

'Do you realise what you've done?'

'I did almost nothing. I was one of a whole crowd.'

'A crowd of *demonstrators*.'

'No one asked the police to attack the campus. We weren't disturbing anybody. It was they who acted like savages. You haven't once asked me to tell you my side of the story. What about *audi alterem partem* and all that? And you're supposed to be a judge.'

'I know only too well what happened. I've spoken to Colonel Bester personally.'

'Did he tell you how they went for the women first? How they deliberately aimed at our faces and boobs with their sjamboks?

How they set their dogs on bystanders who'd only gathered to see what was going on? Did he tell you that the VC had arranged with them that we'd disperse at three o'clock? And that they'd charged at exactly five to three when most of the students had already begun to move away?'

'Colonel Bester had no reason to lie to me, Nina. I've known him for years.'

'You think *I* have reason to lie? I'm your daughter, Father. Or is it because you made me yourself that you don't trust me?'

The familiar pained expression on your face. That tone of long-suffering. 'Nina, you must admit that you're inclined to react emotionally.'

'Always a weakness in a jurist.'

'I know you can't really help it, you're a girl. But at least you should be prepared to admit your own weaknesses.'

'You should have left me in the cells. Then the press wouldn't have come to me.'

'All I expected of you was some sense of responsibility. This deplorable incident may affect your whole future. Nina, I want a daughter I can be proud of. You may be admitted to the Bar next year!'

Don't you realise, I wanted to ask you, how desperately I want to be proud of *you*? Not because you're a judge, but because you're just. Not because you're respectable, but because you are respected? I know why you feel threatened, I wanted to tell you. It's because they made you a judge after you'd done the Party's dirty work in that big case against the English press. You're not concerned with right and wrong. All that matters to you is quid pro quo. Your friends. Your contacts. And the power they give you access to. And for that, I swear before God, I cannot forgive you.

Was what had happened really so terrible? Decisive, yes – but 'terrible'? It started with the mass meeting that was broken up by the police: we'd been demonstrating against the killing of children in Athlone the day before. A protest march was planned for the following day. But a handful of us in the SRC managed to persuade them not to be too provocative, not to play into the hands of the authorities: a march like that was exactly what the Boere had been waiting for. Moreover, it might alienate the moderates on campus. So we urged them to accept the VC's proposal to gather on the Jameson steps and not to leave the campus, a peaceful demonstration, in academic dress, with posters; for an hour, in silent and dignified protest – that above all – we would make known our grievances without provoking anyone. But then it turned out differently. And after they'd had enough of beating us up, they dragged off everybody they could lay their hands on. That's how I also ended up in detention.

Until deep in the night they worked on 'processing' us. During all that time no one was allowed to sit; we were not given anything to eat or drink. (My friend Patsy had a hard time: she'd been ill for several days and we were scared she might faint; when a constable finally responded to our pleas for water and handed her a bottle of liquid, it turned out to be petrol.) The university had appointed a team of lawyers to speed up matters, but this time the police refused to accept admissions of guilt. We had been threatening state security, we were informed. So we were handed over to the SB. Twenty-four hours after we'd been arrested Father learned that I was among the detainees. An hour later I was called out: I could go, charges against me had been dropped.

'I'm not going unless the others can go free too,' I told the officer who came to fetch me.

'Cheeky, hey?' he said. 'In that case you can bloody well stay here.' And I was pushed back into the overcrowded cell, and the door was locked again.

A few hours later four scowling men arrived to escort us back to the ordinary police. An uncle with a broad chest covered in medals told us in tortured English that, this time, we were allowed to go, 'but let this be a warning to you, hey?' An obsequious young registrar from my father's chambers was waiting to take me home in his car. Mother was, naturally, laid up behind closed doors with a migraine. Father, stern and strained, told me laconically that, 'All I ask of you is not to let anybody find out you were in that bunch.' Then I was sent back to my residence on the campus. (The poor, patient, young registrar never uttered a word.) From there I telephoned the *Argus* to ask whether they were interested in an interview.

Father, I swear: I didn't do it on purpose. No matter how often we had quarrelled in the past, it had always remained between the two of us. I'd never opposed you in public or done anything to embarrass you. But don't you understand? – Whatever might have happened to me or to others in the past, whatever I had *seen* happen, I'd always persuaded myself that sooner or later, somehow or other, justice would triumph. I forced myself to believe that *you* were

41

on the side of justice. That's what I *wanted* to believe. I need to have something to believe in, Father. Something, someone. But that afternoon the world I used to believe in was finally shattered. And the last few shreds you destroyed with your own hands: when you used your influence to set me free – not because you believed in my innocence or because you thought an injustice had been done, but because you wanted to protect your own reputation, the Jordaan name. Would I have reached that point anyway, sooner or later? Maybe. I'd been heading in that direction for a long time. But the drastic way in which it happened made the destruction more complete, irrevocable. Perhaps one needs to experience a thing like that oneself, physically, before you can truly acknowledge it. Still, I wish there could have been another way. I didn't want *this* to happen between us. If only I could convince you of it. Don't you know, Father, can't you see, how desperately I wanted to love you? –

7

On the way from Camp's Bay they passed a block below the house she rented in Green Point, a narrow tall Victorian building with bay windows, white walls and peeling green woodwork covered by mauve wisteria. They remembered it with some nostalgia: although it had hardly been cosy, or even comfortably furnished, it was still 'her place', filled with memories of working through days or nights, sorting through her notes and reports, or his photographs; endless conversations; dreams about the future; emptying large mugs of coffee; shared showers after playing squash; making love, often, interminably, passionately.

A memory of space rather than of homeliness. Tall Victorian moulded ceilings, bare walls, pine floors with no sign of a carpet. In one bedroom a collection of mattresses, sleeping bags and bedding was piled up; guests staying over (and there used to be a never-ending variety of them: colleagues who'd come over to work on a project, friends who'd dropped in, people from the townships in hiding from the police, strangers sent there by acquaintances of acquaintances) were expected to help themselves to whatever they needed. Provided they cleared up afterwards: she was very strict about that.

An impression of temporariness, provisionality, an in-transit existence which might be suspended at any moment. Yet the impression was deceptive, for by the time Thomas first came there she'd been living in the house for over two years, since the completion of her legal studies; and it was the first place she'd ever felt at home in. Officially she was still the tenant and the rent was paid monthly by stop order; but the social worker friend who'd shared it with her, Gerda, was now in charge. Six months earlier Nina had announced that she was going to move in with a lover in Johannesburg and might come round to pick up her things at a later, unspecified, stage. And from time to time she did pitch up with a suitcase or a box to select some clothes or books, stopping a while to chat (but without divulging where she was living now or what she was doing; and of course no one knew about the old farmstead at Paarl), then went off again. For two months now she hadn't been back at all, although she'd telephoned once or twice, pretending she was speaking from Johannesburg, to keep in touch. Nobody who knew her would think twice about it.

And now, the Mini left behind in Shortmarket Street, where at this very moment it was being ticketed for an expired meter, they were wandering through the Malay Quarter. Behind a black gate in a white wall enclosing a small backyard – barely big enough for the fig-tree spreading from it, with a swing suspended from a horizontal branch, and a small pigtailed girl squealing shrilly as she swung to and fro – a dog barked. 'Sharrap!' shouted the child; her pigtails, which one could see as she swung up above the wall, ended in two bright ribbons, red as geraniums.

'We must have one like that some time.'

'This place is in too much of a mess to think about children.' But she relented: 'Later perhaps. When it's peaceful again.'

'What about a dog?'

'You know I can't stand animals. They're too cringing, too dependent.'

They came round a corner. A block away a funeral procession was moving downhill – veiled women, grave men wearing kofias – towards a waiting hearse. A slight shiver moved through the day. Autumn wasn't far away. Already dark shadows were moving down the slope below them. There was an air of mortality among the whitewashed houses.

'Christine –' Nina began, then checked herself, guilty.

'What makes you think of her?' he asked, reproachful, knowing the answer; then continuing much too fast, 'I'm sure she's out of danger by now.'

'She didn't deserve what happened. It was all so unnecessary. She should have been with us tomorrow.'

'She'll get another chance, I'm sure.'

'Even if she gets well, they won't let her off so easily.'

'They can't prove anything. Sooner or later they'll *have* to let her go.'

It had all come upon them entirely without warning. The day at Paarl when they had to clear out so hurriedly, loading all they could into the cars. (Except the guns. There was no time to run up and down the ladder to the loft. And they couldn't risk being stopped on the road with the load. They could only hope that no one would think of searching the loft before they had time to come back in the night and clean up.) And then there was Christine to worry about. She'd gone in to town as usual that morning, to her work with the Performing Arts Board (her access to the workshops and the theatre wardrobe proved invaluable); she wasn't expected home before dark – with some of the wigs, make-up, clothes she had been working on. Below the small postbox beside the dusty track that led to the main road, they'd placed the newspaper, weighted down by two bricks. That was the sign. The moment she saw it, she would turn round and drive away as fast as she could.

How were they to know about the kids coming home from school and removing the newspaper? At least, that was what they deduced afterwards, trying to reconstruct what could have gone wrong: for the police had kept quiet about the whole thing, not a word in the newspapers. Until this very day not a soul outside – not even her family in Upington – knew that for the last six weeks Christine had been in intensive care in Tygerberg Hospital with a bullet in the brain, under armed guard. It was only Judy, the nurse working for the Organisation, who managed from time to time to smuggle out a message about her condition. That mishap had nearly caused them to abort the whole plan. Justin, especially, wanted to postpone it, at least until they were sure of how much the SB knew. That they would by now have found the arms in the loft was to be expected: how ironical, as the stuff hadn't even been theirs, they'd merely hidden it while it was 'hot', until Justin received the go-ahead to pass it on to Mabusa's group in Langa. But even that discovery did not necessarily have to be fatal, for there was no evidence to tie the six of them – five, now – to the cache. No one knew their real identities. What did concern them was the new explosive, the Semtex, hidden under a chair in the lounge. Everything would depend on that.

But there had been no news at all, not the slightest indication that the Semtex had been found. (True, the presence of an armed guard at Christine's bedside was alarming; but that might have been a simple precaution, no more.) And after a few weeks of waiting and reflecting and considering, and urgent contacts with Lusaka, Justin relaxed. Fortunately there was the other safe house in Observatory intended as the base for the next attack; for the time being they could move in there. It was important not to let a chance like this slip by. Everything was ready. Rashid had subjected the Semtex to countless experiments in distant places, even in the Karoo, and at night – this remarkable new plastic explosive from Czechoslovakia, colourless, odourless, which they had collected in Europe: infallible, undetectable even by X-rays or any other conventional method. In a thin flat layer between the lid and the lining of a suitcase. No, they simply *had* to go through with it. And tomorrow –

The coffin was loaded into the hearse, and slowly the procession began to move down the narrow cobbled street.

So many funerals: in an endless procession they moved through Thomas's memories. In times when no ordinary gatherings, meetings, demonstrations were allowed, funerals had become the only occasions for the community to meet, to give vent to all their pent-up passions: more than rituals to bury their dead, the funerals offered the opportunity to protest against oppression, to muster forces, to celebrate a coming freedom. Crowds, processions, flags; songs, slogans, *Viva! Viva! Viva!* Police cordons, vans, trucks, Casspirs. Clouds of teargas. Wild stampedes. People offering Vaseline or lemon juice or bicarb to treat inflamed eyes. Soweto. Cradock. New Brighton. Langa. Guguletu. And then *that* day: the row of coffins in Lusaka, the wreaths and flowers, the black-and-green-and-gold flags, the bougainvillea, the great elegiac wave of *Nkosi sikelel' iAfrika*. Followed by the reverberating thunder gathered from the depths of seas, from eternal mountain ranges, across the desolate plains of Africa, Africa: 'Amandla! Ngawethu!'

'Let's go,' said Nina beside him. Her hand was moist with perspiration; perhaps she, too, had heard the sound.

Downhill, back to Shortmarket Street. Finding the ticket on

45

the front windscreen, Thomas was annoyed for a moment, then shrugged. He would settle it with Sean later.

They spent some time among the market stalls – clothing, cheap homemade jewellery, old bottles, shoes – their concentration disturbed by loud music. A group of (presumably) Zulu dancers were kicking up clouds of dust, without much enthusiasm – it was hot, it was getting late – on a small stage. A handful of foreign tourists evidently found it amusing, urging on the dancers, taking photographs. Was it a symptom of civilisation itself growing old, wondered Thomas, this ethnic, ethnic über alles? On the terrace of the hotel semi-clothed people sat drooping over beer and cold drinks. From the streets came a waft of old, sweaty air.

Mechanically, they moved on again, down through the busy city centre to the Parade. Tomorrow this area, now invaded by cars, would be cordoned off for the state president's visit. In these modern surroundings the low squat walls of the Castle appeared unimpressive. Yet it had been a formidable fortress in its time. After van Riebeeck's wild-almond hedge and the first earth wall surrounding a temporary little fortress, this solid structure must have inspired awe of some kind. The first rebels against the first despot, thought Thomas, had been imprisoned there, in chains in the Dark Hole. Adam Tas, Henning Husing. And Carel Guillaume Landman, his own ancestor. It had been in that same struggle, against governor Willem Adriaen van der Stel, that a drunken young man, Bibault, had resisted arrest by the soldiers of the district commander, the *landdrost*, with such futile bravado: 'I won't go. I am an Afrikaner, and even if the *landdrost* beats me to death or throws me in prison, I won't shut up.'

I am an Afrikaner.

What a tricky, precarious, unmanageable word. Anachronism and swearword to the world. But was it really unavoidable? Could it not be chiselled and hammered into other meanings? Afrikaner: native of Africa. Was it really all illusion and pretext?

Would tomorrow, perhaps, change something about the way in which it would be defined in future? There had been others before him, hadn't there? – Bram Fischer, Jan Hendrik Hofmeyr, Beyers Naudé. Not many, but some. And they hadn't fallen ready-made from heaven: in every generation of the long past they had been there. They were not mere exceptions, deviants. Were his own expectations unrealistic? – that one day, when the history of this country was written down at last, including the events of this late

April day, among the names of those present, his own would also feature? I am an Afrikaner.

(– 'Violence? Come on. It's simply the easiest way out. And the most foolish.' Was it really I who'd said that, during one of our endless arguments, at a time when such questions were still, to me, 'academic'?

And Sipho, of course: 'The Organisation didn't choose violence for ethical or humanistic reasons, but because after fifty years of peaceful protest we had no other option left. And because it was effective.' –)

From the bare hill of shame that used to be District Six (the wind had come up again, it was no longer warm, a cloud was beginning to obscure the head of Table Mountain), from below a deserted green mosque, they watched a procession moving along De Waal Drive towards the city. Police vehicles, army trucks, moving in unearthly silence – perhaps because of the wind? – and slowly, a deliberate slowness that demanded to be seen, like a film shown in slow motion, time suspended or irrelevant. On their way, undoubtedly, from the black townships on the Flats, Langa or Guguletu, or further away, Crossroads, Mitchell's Plain, Khayelitsha, where some evil job had once again been done in the name of law and order. (Unless, having learned about the planned attack, they were reinforcements brought in for tomorrow?)

For twenty years this whole area had been lying fallow, scarred and exposed; the tumultuous streets and buildings of the Cape's most colourful, most human quarter now a mere image in memory or conscience, the people driven out to the sandy plains: and still the disfiguring wound lay visible, uncured, incurable, like earth on which the devil had left his imprint, causing everything to wither and die, forever barren. All that was left was, here and there, a desolate church or mosque. Stooping to look closely, one might still find, overgrown by coarse grass and scrub, the almost obscene bits and pieces of a vanished world: shards of porcelain, broken bottles, the carcass of an old stove or fridge, the faded blue plastic of a baby pot, the broken arm of a doll.

Aimless, they wandered about, archaeologists without a map. What had prompted them to come here, today of all days? There was nothing here. Only the wind.

The desolation of the hillside – a trough to let the wind through; at night, who knows, a breach for ghosts from a guilty past – seemed

47

to make them more aware of the surrounding city, spreading relentlessly up the mountain and across the plains, a cancerous growth. Sometimes, thought Thomas, one might be tempted to believe that humanity itself had become a disease on earth, infecting and laying waste wherever it went, deserving to be destroyed in turn, like its predecessors who'd also tried to conquer the earth, the dinosaurs. Until, again, only the cockroaches remained. Was that why it was necessary, from time to time, for someone – a small handful of individuals alerted to the danger – to eradicate the disease, eliminate the cockroaches? Even if it demanded one's own life. And even if it were, in many respects, unnatural, against the grain. To demonstrate that the entire species was not abhorrent. That humanity *could* be different.

The wind seemed to be blowing gulls from the clear sky. They came swooping past like balls of crumpled paper, seemingly helpless, ready to be dashed to the ground. But it was deceptive: at a given moment one of them, apparently effortless, would dive up again, through all the treacherous currents, to where, high above the wind, it would sail and career on motionless wings, gazing brightly at whatever was moving down below, a God's-eye view, peering right through the wind currents of history: perhaps, on this obscene bare hill, they still saw the suburb that had sprawled here long ago.

'I wonder where Justin's family used to live?' said Nina.

'I'm not sure. All I know is that it was close to a church. Remember, his father was an elder and he had a bad leg, so he couldn't walk far.'

Justin, the oldest of them all, just over forty, leader of the group. A man of experience. Small in stature, almost puny, with that thin wisp of a beard. The soft voice, the delicate hands, the sad but mocking eyes. 'We've always lived there. Three generations before me. My great-grandpa was a bricklayer, he built the house with his own hands. We've always been practical people. My grandpa was a fisherman. My dad a carpenter. I can still remember the sharp smell of the shavings in the small shed in the backyard where he used to work. I was the first one in the family to get an education. My dad was very upset about it in the beginning, but my mother backed me.'

'How come?'

'Well, she was kind of middle-class, higher up than him. Her people were Muslims. She only came over to my father's church after they got married. Quite an upheaval in her family. Anyway, she had her matric, my dad only standard five, and she put her foot down. That's how I went to Hewatt College, and once the education bug bit me, I just kept on, through correspondence mostly. Many days, I tell you, it was hell. When we were driven out of District Six, I'll never forget it to the day I die, my father told me to write to the people, the council, the minister, the whole lot of them. 'Otherwise what's the use of all your eddycation if you can't even tell them to let us keep our own house?' But in the end we had to get out, even though he hung on till the very day the bulldozers came. If I hadn't dragged him out, I swear he'd have stayed right in there to be trampled into the ground with his house and all. The house his grandpa had built. But anyway, we had to go, I helped them move into a little house in Bishop Lavis. There was *nothing*, I tell you. Just that little brick building and the bare yard. Not even a tree, not a shrub. What was worst for him was that he could no longer go to his church. That's what killed him. Just six months in that place, then he died.'

'I'd have started throwing bombs long ago if I were you,' Nina had said, indignant, when she'd first heard the story. It was on one of the early occasions just after the group had moved into the farmhouse outside Paarl, when the Organisation had finally approved of her and of the project: they'd all been there, Justin, and Thomas and Nina, and Rashid, and David, and of course Christine; a hot summer's night in December, frogs and crickets outside, insects on the gauze in front of the open windows, moths circling the lamp.

In his quiet way Justin looked right through her 'You don't throw bombs in anger, Nina. You do it because you've thought it right through and decided on the best strategy. You don't throw bombs with your heart or your guts, you do it with your head.'

'I know. You convinced me of that long ago. All I meant was that you've had a hell of a lot more reason than any of us. Yet even so, it took you a long time before you turned to bombs.'

He shrugged his narrow shoulders. 'I suppose I'm just a peaceful kind of person by nature. I've seen too many people breaking their heads against a brick wall. And if you have a family, it's worse. You got to think about *them*. On your own you can face any kind of danger. But what do you do if your kids are small? And I had two. Until 'seventy-six. That's when things changed for me.'

He was suddenly reluctant to continue. It was only much later that they heard the rest: about the pupils who'd gone on strike in his school, like everywhere else in the Peninsula that year; the police who'd picked up every child they'd found in the streets ('Look, it's straightforward,' the officer had explained when Justin had gone to the station to enquire, 'if they're not in school then they must be criminals'); the group playing on the street corner in front of Justin's house when the Casspir drew up: they'd scattered in all directions; the police had jumped out and followed them, shooting haphazardly as they ran. Justin's son had received a bullet in the lung, so he was thrown into the Casspir and driven through the townships as they continued on their rounds; only late that evening, weary and satisfied with a good day's work, had they dropped him off at a hospital, by which time he was already dead. He'd lost his first milk tooth that morning. It was still in his shoe under his bed, waiting for the mouse, when the message came from the hospital. 'That night,' said Justin, 'I realised it no longer made sense to keep turning the other cheek to people who fight like that. I had to start fighting back. I did it because I'm a Christian. To help break down the forces of evil in this world. It's the only way.'

The bomb at Caledon Square, some years ago, had been his first action. Then the one at D.F. Malan airport. Another outside Pollsmoor prison, a year ago. By that time Rashid and David had already joined his group. But all of those had been mere trial runs. Demonstration attacks, aimed at intimidation. This time it was serious.

The long debate, the meticulous exploration preceding the actual planning, after Thomas had returned from his brief intensive training in Angola and was first contacted by Justin. Exploring it between the two of them, motivating his proposal and discussing its feasibility; then submitting it to the Organisation. Couriers; messengers; all of it time-consuming but necessary. For this was no exercise in daring, no adventure; it was not even a matter of eliminating a dangerous or hated individual. What concerned them was efficacy, the unemotional, disinterested evaluation of results and consequences. Strategy. To demonstrate the vulnerability of the system, true; but it went farther than that. Farther even than Rashid's arguments inspired by Fanon: the polarisation of the colonial consciousness, the need for the damned of the earth to rid themselves of the coloniser; the need for cathartic violence and retribution. It was, rather, a matter (Justin's argument) of using as a starting-point the situation of the whites in the country, the class of owners, of rulers, ensconced in their prosperous and secure existence – BMWs, barbecues, hunting trips, opera, five-star hotels, mink-and-manure – and consequently supporting the system that offered them their material benefits; the need to shock them out of this syndrome of the 'good life' and to open their eyes, if not to its injustice, at least to its precariousness. To achieve this, any soft target would serve, any disruption of their suburban smugness, any extension of the armed struggle, an attempt against any public figure, but nothing could be as dramatic as an attempt on the life of the one person who symbolises the entire system. Attack the state president – not because he is authoritarian or evil, but because he is the *president* – and a seismic shock-wave must move through the whole of society, destabilise the whole system.

But what about other consequences? A swing to the right among whites? revulsion even among blacks? condemnation by allies abroad? retaliation across a broad front, on countless organisations, movements, activists, even innocent individuals? All these pros and cons had to be weighed, then weighed again, discussed, reviewed. More couriers abroad, and back. Only then the moment of final approval. On condition that Justin be in charge; he had already proved his mettle, he was experienced, reliable, thorough. With David Blumer as his right hand. And then, Rashid: young and angry, but a masterly technician. And Thomas Landman: this would be his baptism of fire, after he'd already been approved by none other than Sipho Mdana and made an impression during his training. It was Justin himself who recommended Christine: ironically enough David had initially been the one to object, arguing that she was too inexperienced; but Justin could vouch for her reliability, her integrity, above all her practical value – and then, after the first few weeks in Paarl, it was David who'd become so attached to her. Last of all, after intensive enquiries and research, Nina was approved.

That was when, early in December, like a medieval conclave of devotees, they'd detached themselves from the world, the Garden of Earthly Delights, and withdrawn to the old Cape-Dutch homestead Thomas had discovered a few kilometres from Paarl.

Now, five months later, they were here. And tomorrow was D-day. For all of them, as members of a group, of an organisation. But for him there was a private reckoning involved as well.

Thomas looked at his watch. He took Nina by the arm. It was time for them to go back. David would be coming over in the evening. There was still much to clear up, round off, prepare.

— Bougainvillea, the colour of that day. Purple cascades, interspersed with scarlet and sudden outrageous orange. The msasas in flower. Large shady flamboyants with long pods like donkey penises; some already split open, their black and red seeds scattered on the sandy ground. There are days one associates with smells, with particular sounds. But of this day in Lusaka it is the colour that will be burnt into my mind forever. Long before daybreak, oppressed by the heat, I disentangle myself from the mosquito net in my hotel room and stagger to the lukewarm shower, then stumble off into the day. The greenish shimmering of the sky as the stars begin to fade. Then it changes into opal, a mother-of-pearl sheen, a hint of mauve running into a darker red below. Like the round sweets of my childhood we called, disgracefully, 'nigger-balls', all different layers of colour one could suck off and then hold up against the light for inspection. (The day Frans and I took turns, until from sheer perversity he swallowed the whole sweet before it had even turned purple.) The stark black silhouettes of acacias on the outskirts of the city. And then the sun, like a scream in the sky. Flies beginning to buzz, people unwrapping their wares under the mota trees and on the long wooden trestle-tables of Kamwala Market. The hum of Singer sewing machines. A barber arranging boxes under his thatched shelter and sorting his scissors and combs and old-fashioned leather strops. An old woman popping small round tomatoes one by one into her mouth from which they emerge a glistening red, ready to be stacked in a pyramid. Piles of shrivelled mopani worms or termites. Dried fish. Mangoes. Bunches of bananas, virulent yellows, strident greens. Small pawpaws like barely nubile breasts. Everything bursting with emphatic life. The anachronistic skyline of the city in the distance, to the west; the post-office tower, the tall ziggurat of the ZNBS; as if one is existing simultaneously in two dimensions, a Western and an African. Two dimensions of time. A lethargic desire stirring in the blood. Sweat in one's armpits, a prickling of dust in eyes and nostrils. Even heat acquires its own colour in this place, a greyish-brown precipitation in the brain. Africa. Nowhere else, nothing else, is quite like this, timeless, without beginning or end, Africa.

The kind of day on which, from the moment you get up, you know that something is going to happen, something important, something special. Perhaps a bride has that presentiment on the morning of her wedding day, or a pregnant woman who rises one morning knowing, serenely, confidently, that her time has come. Will one have this knowledge, too, on the day of one's death, a knowledge that has nothing to do with consciousness? This day in Lusaka looks different from others. As if the colour of bougainvillea has started to run on a sheet of porous paper, staining everything. From my earliest days Mum has taught me to keep my purple crayons separate from the rest: it gives off, she said, it makes stains nothing can ever get out. Once, opening furtively a packet of Condy's crystals in the bathroom, which Mum had expressly forbidden me ever to do, I accidentally dropped it in the bath: to me that was the worst sin I'd ever committed, simply because it was so frightfully visible. Whenever I heard about the single unforgivable sin against the Holy Ghost I associated it with that colour. To me it's always been the original colour from which all others sprang. God himself must be purple.

On my return from the market, Sipho is already waiting for me. I must go to the airport with him to meet Noni.

'I'm sure you want to be alone with her,' I protest. 'You haven't seen her in three months.'

'Noni'd love to see you again. And you can give me a hand with Govan in the car.'

'Govan isn't a baby any more. He's four.'

Also, he's the most independent child I've ever met. As well as one of the most beautiful.

'Come on,' Sipho insists. And that's that. It's through this firmness, this obstinacy at times, that he's reached a key position in the Organisation at an age when most others are still learning the ropes. Not a very big man, but strongly built, like a good rugby centre. What impresses one is his presence more than his appearance (even though no one can ignore or forget those two piercing black eyes): a presence which causes people to fall silent when he enters a room. He is always abundantly *there*. Yet it is a serene presence – no doubt the pipe contributes to the impression, always that pipe glued to his mouth, a true calabash pipe from the Little Karoo – but the serenity of a cat: one is aware of a readiness to react to whatever is happening around him: nothing can catch him unawares. (Nothing?) There is something in his voice that contributes to the presence. Not a very strong voice, he's no great orator in the accepted sense; but it has a timbre that inspires confidence, as if it has been produced, not by his throat, but by his whole body. And, to me, his body says 'Africa'.

I'm prejudiced, of course; he is the best friend I've ever had. Still, when I'm with him I have a sense of knowing Africa, the way one senses it in an aloe, a flintstone rock, a camel-thorn, a tall anthill. Yet the imagery seems ill-chosen, for when one first meets Sipho, it is his 'Western' look that strikes the observer. The result, no doubt, of the years he studied at the LSE, and Oxford, later Harvard. Always dressed – even on this morning when we drive the fifteen kilometres to the airport, by rights a holiday for him – as if he's on his way to an important conference. (Which is usually true.) Quite misplaced in the heat of Africa, really. Yet he always seems relaxed, at ease, never crumpled or sweaty like the rest of us.

And then Noni. I recognise her immediately as she comes down from the plane, even though it's a year since I last saw her. Tall and beautiful in a flowing West African robe that reaches down to her feet, her hair an intricate affair of tiny plaits. When she walks one is reminded of a ship, a tall yacht, its spinnaker billowing in the wind. Even when there is no movement of air, as on this stifling, blazing day – now and then the shrill call of an unfamiliar bird in the bush, just to confirm the heat – she reminds one of wind. I keep to the background as she sweeps up little Govan and presses him against her in the great throng of bodies (most have come to the airport simply for the adventure of it), dancing a few steps. Then, still clutching Govan in one arm, she embraces Sipho. There's something heraldic about the three of them: man, woman, child, a seamless statue hewn from gleaming dark wood, like the one in the foyer of the hotel, something archaic, archetypal, timeless, beautiful.

Then she notices me. 'Thomas!' And finds room for me in her large embrace, with Govan and Sipho. 'What a lovely surprise!'

'I was supposed to fly out the day before yesterday, but I couldn't bear to miss you. Now I'm leaving in the morning.'

'But you *must* stay for the conference.'

'I'd love to, but I can't. I must be in London tomorrow night.'

'Then we must make the most of today. I've got so much to tell you.'

'How'd it go?'

She has just been on a fellowship to Princeton. How I envy her students: I've heard Noni lecture before – her subject is the sociology of literature; Third World literature – and I know few others who can compare with her.

'I suppose it was okay,' she replies to my question. 'But you know, the Americans are strange people. Madly enthusiastic about any noble cause that's geographically far enough away not to make demands on them. But tell me, what's the news from home?'

Somehow we manage to force our way through the milling, jostling crowd – her luggage, thanks to Sipho's prior arrangements, is swept through customs without delay – and drive off in Sipho's battered Austin. On the way back, while we are all talking more or less at the same time, Govan sits pressed against his mother, straight as a meerkat, not letting go of her hand for a moment. Only his enormous eyes betray his joy.

'Don't you find it terrible to be separated from him so often?' I ask her later, when the child has gone to play for a while (although he comes back every few minutes to make sure she's still there).

'Of course. It's unbearable. But Sipho and I have to travel so much, we just have to take turns.' Her eyes darken briefly, which I would not even have noticed if I hadn't known her so well. 'But in the long run it's better for him this way, you know. He must learn to be independent, to get on without us. One never knows what may happen – and then he must be able to fend for himself.'

'But Noni, he's only four.'

'I know. But in our kind of life –'

Against my better reason I persist: 'You're barely thirty.'

'In this job not many of us grow old, Thomas. You know, I've sometimes thought the only survivors are the ones who are in jail.'

A confusing day, impossible to sort out afterwards. A flood of impressions: people, conversations, small precious moments of sudden discovery, explosions of laughter, glasses of beer on which the foam slowly subsides, then a new wave of people. They're converging from everywhere for the big conference planned to start tomorrow: from Harare and Maputo and Luanda and Nairobi and Dar-es-Salaam, from Accra and Dakar and Abidjan, from London, from Washington, from Melbourne, from Amsterdam and Stockholm, Oslo and Paris, from Prague and Berlin and Moscow. Old friends, some of whom haven't seen each other for years. Colleagues. Rivals. Men and women, black and white and Asian, Jews and Muslims, old and middle-aged and young. All of them exchanging memories, discussing projects, comparing scenarios, telling jokes. The one discovery that never ceases to catch me by surprise, like so many times over the last few years, is how all these people, no matter how far they've been scattered across the globe, are still tuned in to the same geographic reality. 'And where do *you* come from?' one asks a stranger you've met a minute ago. 'Oh I was born in the Western Transvaal,' he tells you. 'Schweizer-Reneke.' Or: Kimberley. Boksburg. Cape Town. P.E. Uitenhage. Nigel. Durban. Kroonstad. Or the village off the Cape West Coast where Sipho and I come from. Here we are: three thousand kilometres away, yet we all belong *there*. It doesn't matter that they're posted in Paris or Addis Ababa or Leningrad, when we talk about 'home' it is the same place we have in mind. Through all that has happened, through danger and loneliness and misery and failure and success and betrayal and love, that home is still there, awaiting us.

It is especially moving when in the late afternoon a whole contingent of youngsters arrive – not one of them over twenty-five, some of them barely sixteen – who have all fled South Africa during the last year, to Mozambique, Tanzania, Zimbabwe, Zambia, Angola: one after the other, as they discover that I was in Johannesburg only a month or two ago, they rush up to me, and embrace me, give me the threefold Africa greeting, and explode into questions: 'So how *are* things at home? D'you know so-and-so? Is such-and-such still in Pollsmoor? Or in Central? The Fort? On the Island?' Like long-lost relatives we talk about the beloved land, laughing, crying, laughing again. (Because on a day like this everything, suddenly, seems funny: events which at other times would have made you gasp for breath in shock or anger, now sound so funny that you collapse with laughter until your belly aches.)

Throughout the whole long day I meet only one who is openly dejected. I never come to hear his name. He's not a delegate either, he's just turned up, one of Africa's pieces of driftwood, not so much old as the worse for wear, shot with alcohol, offering to whomever he encounters the tale of his daughter, killed a month ago, he says, in Boksburg: no one knows if it's true, but that's what he says, and every now and then he bursts into tears, cursing through his sobs the South African government and the whole system and everything white. In the end it is Sipho who, pipe in mouth, puts one arm round his shoulders and starts comforting him in that soothing voice, 'Now come on, man, come on, pull yourself together. So she's dead. So nothing can hurt her any more, right? So she's better off than most of us. And tomorrow we're all going home together, you too, and we'll put flowers on her grave. Okay? Who's going with us?'

A whole chorus responds.

Then Sipho shouts, 'Amandla!'

And we all, the whole lounge, past the latticework of the wooden partitions, through the open doors to the paved terrace under the toona-trees, in one voice we all respond: 'Ngawethu!'

Later, freedom songs erupt, beginning with a low, throbbing, provocative pulse of sound, songs without end, each one more compelling than the others – and some of the people, Noni among them, jump up and start dancing, because that music makes it impossible to stay in one place. It amazes me to see the total change that comes over a woman like her the moment her body tunes in to the music: a beautiful sophisticated woman, professor of literature, citizen of the world, with an aura of untouchability (those high cheekbones, the slight slant of the eyes, like those of a mask, the full mouth, the delicate skin, a woodcut from Bamako), transformed in an instant into a sensual earth-mother, swaying and dancing like something sprouting from the earth and moving in invisible currents of air, an elemental motion as ancient as the earth. And proceeding from there, as the songs become louder, more extravagant in their satire and provocation and affirmation, there is yet another metamorphosis into, perhaps, a shebeen queen, loud, vulgar, voluptuous, throwing her body this way and that in total abandon. In this dance all conversation stops. Whatever has been rational or premeditated or calculated before, is decanted into a new dimension of pure emotion, irrational faith: tomorrow, tomorrow we're going home, tomorrow we're back in the land that is ours, the land to which we belong like leaves and fruit and flowers to a tree, tomorrow the gates will open, and Nkosi sikelel' iAfrika: Maluphakamis' uphondo lwayo, Yiva imithandazo yethu, Nkosi sikelela, Thina lusapho lwayo – And, below that exuberant surface, a sadness as deep as the sea, for Africa is indeed an ancient continent, and patience and suffering are its nature.

Not for a moment am I made to feel an impostor. I'm simply there, Sipho's friend, one of them, absorbed into their midst.

Some time during the long afternoon, while clusters of people gather in the hotel lounge where the air-conditioning has packed up, or on the broad terrace where the heat lies dozing, in lobbies and corridors and pale green rooms with tatty bedspreads and threadbare patches in the carpets, I notice – as I make my way to the terrace with an armload of tepid beer (the ice has run out) – Noni sitting under an acacia on the grass, chatting to her child: I see him wave his little arms, hear his peal of laughter, see her picking him up in her arms and raising him above her head and pressing him against her and kissing his bare belly.

It is dark already – that sudden African dusk that descends like a huge bat the moment after the sun has burnt itself out on the horizon – by the time I'm gathered up again, with Sipho and Noni and a sleepy but bravely resisting Govan, in the battered Austin and driven back to their apartment in a building with peeling blue paint, its balconies strung with lines of multicoloured washing, on the other side of Kamwala market. As we pull up there is another sudden view, in the glare of the headlights just before Sipho turns them off, of a massive wave of bougainvillea.

'You sure you don't want to go back to the others?' I ask. 'I can baby-sit for you –'

'We'll be seeing more than enough of them tomorrow, and you're leaving. Tonight we want to be with you.'

Noni makes food in the kitchen while Sipho and I settle in the small lounge, Govan nestled in my lap, where he drifts slowly into sleep. I know, even as I look at them, that I shall always remember the paintings and lithos on the walls, mostly by artists from the Third World, and Beethoven's Third on the tape-deck. Later Sipho goes to lay the table and open more beer. Throughout the meal the talk keeps flowing, easy, relaxed, unpremeditated.

Once, perhaps a bit maudlin from the beer and the heat, I ask, 'Sipho, are you really sure I can be useful to the Organisation?'

'You still got doubts?' He laughs quietly.

'When all is said and done I'm still white.'

'Haven't you seen today's crowd? All colours of the rainbow. All that matters is whether *you* really mean it seriously.'

'I'm only a photographer.'

'We need all kinds of people, Thomas. And we have more use for a good photographer than for a bad soldier.'

'Even if the photographer is an Afrikaner?'

'And why not?' from Noni. 'Don't you belong to Africa?' With a sly smile: 'Have you forgotten then? – a century ago you Boers sometimes joined ranks with our people to drive out the English: then *they* were the foreign oppressor. We've come a long way together. We've all got Africa in our blood.'

'God knows –' I shake my head. 'Can you tell me how a thing like this is possible? That sitting here with you tonight I'm feeling more at home than in my own parents' house?'

'In this terrorist hole?' Sipho bursts out laughing. 'Next time you

58

come back, bring a couple of your friends with you. Otherwise they'll never believe you.'

'That's the worst: I cannot even tell them that I've been here. Tomorrow in London I must leave Cedric the British passport you organised for me and go back to Johburg with my little blue job.'

'It's only temporary. One of these days —'

Like Jews, I think, wherever they meet in the world: 'Next year in Jerusalem.' How far across the face of the earth has our own sad diaspora scattered us? But one day we'll all be back. It's a promise. One day the centripetal forces will become stronger than the centrifugal ones that have disseminated us.

Close to ten o'clock I get up to leave. They won't hear of it: I must stay the night. There are so many more questions they still want to ask, so much to tell —

But I am adamant. 'Noni's been away for months, you have a lot to catch up with. And tomorrow you'll be tied up by the conference.'

'You think I want to be alone with this guy?' asks Noni, laughing, bending down his head in her arm to kiss him.

Govan is fast asleep now, spreadeagled in a chair. I lean over to kiss him on the forehead.

'Sleep well, Noni.'

'Hamba kahle, Thomas.'

In spite of my protests Sipho insists on driving me back to the hotel, a different route from the one we've come by, past the Kalingalinga hospital. Outside, the night is vast and peaceful. Insects in the dark, from time to time a night bird inserting its call in immeasurable space. Overhead, as I get out, the stars. Orion moving over. The Pleiades. The Southern Cross. Familiar, reassuring, the stars of home. Everything is well. All will be well.

'Night, Thomas.'

'Night, Sipho.'

First the triple handshake, then the embrace, our bodies pressed close together. (How sad, it occurs to me, how Anglo-Saxon, that we whites have abandoned this naturalness of bodily contact, this affirmation of brotherhood.)

Deep in the night I hear the rumbling noise in the distance, but in the confusion of sleep I take it to be thunder. Only the next morning, when I enter the lobby on my way to the airport and find the place crowded with excited people, do I realise that something else must have happened. A sobbing woman tells me the story: a contingent of the South African army, eager, no doubt, to profit from the great gathering of delegates for the conference, has launched a mortar raid on 'terrorist bases' in the city. At that stage no one knows the extent of the damage yet, but there must have been casualties.

There's something inside that makes you realise immediately when an event concerns *you*. Forgetting all about my flight to London I rush about looking for someone who can take me to Sipho's apartment. (They have no telephone at home.) It turns out to be near-impossible. But even when at last, frantic, I manage to persuade one of the delegates, a stocky, bespectacled man from Nairobi, to drive me, it turns out to be futile. We are not allowed anywhere near the blue building. Everything has been cordoned off by the police. After what seems like hours someone suggests that we go to the state mortuary, but there, too, we are turned away. Then, through obscure, roundabout channels, there is a signal. We should go to the morgue in Chachacha Street, opposite the central market. (What an unlikely place, this unprepossessing face-brick building across the street from the open square where long lines of patient people stand queuing for overcrowded buses, exposed to the aggressive black-market strategies of the mashangu boys.) There, at seven minutes past twelve, I learn the news. There have been eighteen injured, six dead. A sweating man in a blue shirt, with a broad lurid tie, reads out the names. Among them: Sipho, and Noni, and Govan Mdana. The others I don't recognise. A Zambian typist, a teenage boy, a German tourist, we learn afterwards.

A good photographer, Sipho said, means more to us than a bad soldier. But in that blazing noon outside the morgue, near the *Freedom Ladies Hair Salon* and the *Good Job Good Time Tailors*, I make up my mind. I shall train; I shall learn. I'll be patient, and work with dedication, and assimilate whatever is necessary to become a good soldier. –

9

They'd hardly entered the humble little house in Observatory that had been their base for the previous six weeks or so – the only sign of extravagance a pot of blood-red geraniums on the front stoep, which Thomas had brought her three weeks ago for her birthday – when there was a loud knock on the front door. Startled, they looked at each other in the skimpy little kitchen. It was much too early for David; Justin and Rashid weren't due before the next morning

60

('During this last week there must be as few comings and goings as possible, we don't want the neighbours to become suspicious') – and who else knew that they were there? Even Sean's Mini was parked several blocks away.

'Don't make a sound,' Thomas whispered. 'Perhaps they'll go away.'

Another reverberating rattling on the door. It could only be the SB. Perhaps Christine had regained consciousness and said something? But surely she wouldn't!

'We'll have to open,' he said, 'before the neighbours start wondering.'

Nina drew a deep breath and prepared to go.

'If it's them –' he began.

She nodded impatiently. She knew what to do.

The knock was repeated, this time quite deafening.

On the stoep, as she opened, were a young man in a brown suit and a mousy woman with her hair in a tight bun, each with a black briefcase; the man had a bible in his hand.

'Peace!' the man greeted her, beaming. 'We've come to ask you a very important question.'

Nina gaped at them, for a moment too flustered to respond.

'Have you found the Lord?' asked the woman.

Immediately she was furious; at the same time she felt so relieved she could burst out laughing.

'No, I haven't,' she snapped. 'But I'll keep on looking.'

For a moment they seemed nonplussed. Then the man began to slide past her across the threshold.

'What do you think you're doing?' asked Nina, blocking his way.

'Lady.' His eyes measured the space between her and the doorpost. 'This is serious. It concerns the salvation of your immortal soul.'

'You can leave that to me.' She started closing the door, but he stopped it with his foot.

'Don't you realise,' asked his wife, 'one cannot postpone a thing like this? What if something happens to you tonight?'

'It won't,' said Nina. 'Tomorrow perhaps, but definitely not tonight.'

'Can't we just read a few verses with you and say a prayer?' the man offered.

'Why don't you come back tomorrow evening?' Nina said in a rush of good will. 'Same time. Then we can pray right through the night.'

61

'Our message is much too urgent to wait,' the wispy woman said brightly.

'Fuck off!' said Nina, lifting her foot and bringing the heel down hard on the man's toes.

With a yelp of pain he danced out of the way.

'Even if your sins were as scarlet,' said the mouse, retreating gingerly down the steps, 'they shall be white as snow.'

Thomas, who must have been listening round the corner, appeared behind Nina. 'What's going on?'

The man hesitated at the front gate, careful not to step on his lame foot. 'What about you, sir?' he asked hopefully, but staying safely out of reach. 'Are you prepared to invest five minutes in your soul? It's a matter of life or death, of heaven or hell.'

'We've already opted for hell,' Nina informed him.

The two visitors exchanged stricken glances, and the man made a last half-hearted gesture in their direction, but whether of benediction or damnation was hard to tell. Then they disappeared into the street towards the house next door, the man limping.

They were about to close the door when something moved at the front gate. For a moment they froze, then discovered a small boy staggering on spindly legs under the weight of a large basket.

'Merrim!' he shouted anxiously when it seemed they were going to close the door on him. 'Maste'! How 'bout a little crayfish or two?'

'Where'd you get them?' Thomas asked suspiciously. 'Do you have a licence to catch them?'

'Don't need no licence, Maste'. Got 'em from my fader.' Adding urgently as he saw his chances slipping away, 'Jesus, Maste', you got to take a few, else my fader will kill me tonight.'

'I'm sure they're all dead already,' said Thomas, hesitating.

'No, look fo' yourself. Live en' kicking.' He put the basket down at their feet and removed the wet hessian bag covering it. Inside a number of crayfish were indeed slithering and crawling about, most of them looking decidedly smaller than the permitted minimum size.

'Nina?'

'Tell him to say yes, Merrim. Is good for de sex-life too, is crayfish. If de Maste eat dis lot he'll keep de merrim busy till daybreak.'

'How much?' asked Nina, struggling to suppress a giggle.

'Jus' make it five rand a piece, 'cause it's late.'

'You have money?' she asked Thomas.

62

'I'll get some.' He returned with the money and a plastic basin.

'De Lo'd will bless de Maste'.'

'I'm not your master,' said Thomas angrily.

The boy looked warily at him, decided against a retort, and disappeared into the night as soundlessly as he'd arrived.

'What are we going to do with this lot?' asked Thomas after the door had been closed again.

'I'll cook them. There's enough for David too. Let's make a proper feast of it.' A brief pause. 'People condemned to death usually have the right to choose what they want for their last meal, don't they?'

'You're being morbid. Anyway, they're served chicken.'

'I didn't mean it, Thomas. Honest.' She kissed him briefly, holding the dish with the dark, angular shapes of the crayfish between them. 'Give me a hand?'

He followed her. But when the salt water came to the boil and she thrust in the crayfish and they started clawing frantically up the sides of the big aluminium pot, uttering almost inaudible screeching sounds, he hurriedly turned away.

'What's the matter?' she asked.

'Sorry, but I can't stand it. It makes me sick. It's too human.'

She calmly dislodged the crayfish claws from the edge of the pot and put on the lid to force them down. Was it his imagination, when he looked back from the middle door, or was she trembling lightly? Very straight and taut, she kept her back to him.

'You shouldn't let yourself be put off by a little thing like this, Thomas,' she said, but quietly, as if she were talking to herself. 'Tomorrow it's a man we'll be killing, not a crayfish.'

'I don't want you to say such things.' Quickly, he returned to her and grabbed her shoulders. 'Nina, do you hear me?'

'I do.' Almost angrily she detached herself from his grip, and turned round to face him squarely, her dark green eyes filled with night shadows. 'But I've *got* to say it. Don't you understand? We've got to be prepared. It's no use talking all the time about the cause, the cause, my soul, about the reasons for doing it, the system he represents, the monster he is. When that bomb explodes tomorrow it will be a human being that's blown to pieces. Perhaps several of them. Not an idea, or a concept, or a system, an abstraction, but people. People just like the two of us. If we want to be sure, absolutely sure, that we can go through with it, then we must accept in advance that it's *people* we're going to kill. We must be prepared for every drop of brains and blood and shit. And take responsibility for it. Otherwise we're kidding ourselves.'

He nodded slowly. So many other voices were clamouring in his ears with hers: the instructors and commissars in Luanda – Sipho – Justin – Behind her the sounds on the stove had died down.

'If you can't face those crayfish,' Nina persisted, 'how the hell are you going to get through the rest of your life with tomorrow's screams in your ears?'

'I can face it,' he said softly.

'It's murder, Thomas,' she went on very calmly. 'Okay, so we know why we're doing it, why we think it's absolutely necessary, unavoidable. We've discussed this a thousand times. But after you've peeled away everything else, you're left with the stone inside. And that stone is murder. And maybe – God knows – maybe committing murder is just as lonely an experience as dying. I mean, if you do it our way: not in anger or passion or in a flush of inspiration, but calculating, clear-headed, cool. Knowing exactly what is at stake.' She continued to stare fixedly at him. But after a while her head dropped and she pressed her forehead against him. 'Hold me, Thomas,' she whispered. 'Don't let go. You must hold me very tight all night.'

'Are you frightened?'

She shook her head angrily. 'No. No, of course I'm not afraid. It's just – what you said on the mountain today, remember? – it's so bloody lonely.'

'We're not alone.' He pressed her against him. 'We're in it together. And if you think about it, there are thousands, there are millions with us tonight, tomorrow.' He paused for a moment. 'It helps to remember that.'

She moved her head against his chest, but he couldn't make out whether it meant yes or no.

After a while he let go of her, and went to the drawer in which they kept their few bits and pieces of cutlery, and pulled it open, and began to set the table. The activity calmed his agitation.

'If you want to have mayonnaise with the crayfish, we can leave it to cool off for a while. We can start clearing up in the meantime, before David arrives.'

There were only a few of their possessions in the place. When they'd arrived here, after the panicky flight from Paarl, it had already been furnished with the basics: a few pieces of impersonal furniture, bedding, cutlery and crockery and cooking utensils, acquired at auctions or in junk shops to ensure strict anonymity in case of a raid. The few personal possessions they had brought with them must be cleared out tonight. Clothes, including what they'd been wearing today. The few books, especially his notebooks. The last bits and pieces of his photographic equipment. An assortment of letters and photographs that had come with him, like burrs or fleas he couldn't shed. Even now he felt reluctant about parting with them. Secret sins.

She stripped off her boiler-suit and T-shirt, emerging from them smaller than she had been. All her other clothes were stuffed into an OK bag. In the cupboard remained only the shorts and shirt in which she would be leaving in the morning, and returning later. And the sober outfit into which she would then change to go the airport.

'My going-away,' she said from the open cupboard.

Leafing through his notebooks, he didn't look up.

'You must get rid of that stuff,' she warned. 'It's incriminating.'

'It's not. There's no name in it. And the notes are so cryptic, no one beside myself could make head or tail out of them. David can stow them away for me. And one day I'll come back for them. Once all this is behind us and part of history.' Behind the lightness of his words lay a darker weight. Taking leave like this of notes, papers, photographs, meant leaving behind a part of himself. Snatches of his family history, thirteen generations of Landmans – dreamers and losers, prophets, savages and lechers, traitors, crooks, builders, trekkers, warriors, labourers – without whose company he was going to feel unprotected, vulnerable. Almost compulsively, through the years, he'd been working on compiling this chronicle; even when he'd had to leave out names to avoid identification in case the books fell in strange hands, he'd felt bolstered by their presence, reassured, at peace with himself. He would have to come to terms with a new kind of nakedness.

Nina knelt in a corner to sift through a pile of magazines and newspapers for anything personal that might have strayed among them. He went on with his own work. From the pages of a faded green notebook fell a photograph. He picked it up. Not very sharp, one corner yellowed where it hadn't been fixed properly, but he recognised it immediately: it had been taken with his very first camera, given to him for his thirteenth birthday, that June. He'd been taking photographs of every imaginable subject that came his way. And this had been a special occasion: their arrival at their new home, in the village in the Little Karoo. (In the Eastern Transvaal they'd only lasted a year. Too lush, too fertile for their liking; they had literally felt threatened by such natural extravagance after the more barren regions, the whiter sun that had shaped them before. Also, his father had run into problems with the Transvaal school syllabuses. In fact, it had been a rash venture from the start, but his father had got it into his head that this was a way of coming to know the country; his real reason, Thomas had suspected, was to retrace some of the steps of their ancestors, driven by an atavistic romanticism. But now they had come back to the Cape Province.)

Five epic days' driving in the old 1959 Chev – his father had never kept a car for less than fifteen years; and on their way through the Orange Free State the dilapidated old thing had broken down twice – brought them to the Little Karoo. He took the photograph a minute after they'd stopped in front of the house his father had rashly bought on his own when he'd come down for the interview three months earlier. In the background of the faded picture loomed the drab, unimaginative house from the Thirties, with its pitched roof and tall chimneys, a dark verandah propped up by sturdy pillars in front, bluegums, an iron postbox on the front gate, two cypresses. At the gate, in the dusty street, the triumphant Chev, and four of the five exhausted, disgruntled travellers lined up in front of it.

His father, the vice-principal, in jacket and tie (he'd driven in his shirt-sleeves, but had insisted on making himself 'decent' for the photograph): the fixed, annoyed frown between the eyes, the thinning hair combed back severely, short back and sides, shoulders drooping, unhappy grey moustache below the nose, chin raised defiantly in a gesture of assumed authority, left hand in a Napoleon pose, holding together the lapels – an unexpectedly rough hand, a farmer's hand, suggesting a youth of hardship.

His mother small and narrow, but with generous maternal breasts, light reflecting from her glasses so that one could not make out the eyes. Her hair, prematurely grey, obviously 'done' before the journey but now somewhat undone, sitting on her head like a hen brooding with wings outstretched. The kind of looks that prompt the thought: what an attractive girl she must have been –

Maria. How old would she have been then? Seven years older than he; twentyish. Presumably her last year at university. Not pretty in any conventional sense, but attractive in a strong, assertive, even defiant way: as yet untamed by life.

Frans. His father's child. Hair cut very short, the hint of a thin moustache. His attitude suggested that he would have felt at ease with either a gun or a bible in his hand. A touch of arrogance: the look of a born-again soul who knows he has right on his side.

Thomas tore up the photograph and added the shreds to the heap of papers to be burned. Hardly incriminating; but nothing should be left behind which might in any way be traced back to them later. Mopping up a phase, a period, a stretch of life. Something of themselves that would cease to exist. (Justin: 'They took away my childhood, my whole history.') This was the final stage of the stripping and clearing up that had begun months ago when they'd first started working on the project. He giving up his flat in Vredehoek, she moving out of her house in Green Point, to resume temporary existences elsewhere, a life without traces. Not just the shedding of an old skin, like a reptile, but a reinvention of the self; divesting oneself of all one had been. At the same time it was a deceptive lightness. One can never, really, start from scratch again, the slate can never be wholly cleared: one drags along one's history, one's own and that of one's people, a snail's trail through time, often invisible, but never absent.

'Finished,' said Nina, returning the last magazine to her pile. A collection of objects she'd retrieved – a writing pad, a few pages with handwritten notes or sketches, even a small initialled handkerchief that had somehow survived from her previous life – was added to the pile destined for the fire. 'David's late. I think we'd better eat first.'

Their food supply was running low, but she managed to scrape the last bit of mayonnaise from a jar to accompany the crayfish; and there were a few lemons in a basket on the small fridge; half a loaf of brown bread in the bin.

They ate in silence, with the solemnity of a last supper.

'I wish we could all have spent the night together,' said Thomas. 'David. Christine. Rashid. Justin. Especially Justin. He has a way of putting one at ease. And all those little jokes of his.'

She looked at him, questioning him with her eyes.

'I'm just missing them. We've been together for so long.'

'They'll be there tomorrow.'

'That's different.' After a while she rose. 'I'm going to do the dishes. Why don't you start your bonfire?'

In the small barbecue behind the house he stacked a fire and began systematically to burn everything they had set aside. With a long fire-iron he poked around in the flames until everything had been reduced to ashes. As he was dousing the coals with a watering can, Nina came out to announce that their guest had arrived. She had put on a longish man's jacket, a garment they'd inherited with the house; it reached down to her knees.

When Thomas came in, David was already seated at the kitchen table, methodically dismembering the two small crayfish they had kept for him. Pale, except for two fever spots on his almost transparent cheeks, on his nose a pair of thick-rimmed spectacles through which his black eyes peered in a shy, fishy stare, he sat under the bare bulb suspended from the ceiling, a piece of bright red crayfish shell stuck to the sparse crescent of beard which hung on his jaws like mould. He had a monkish look, ascetic, older than his forty-odd years, his hair greying and thin.

'So you chaps are finishing in style, I see.' He sucked his long white forefingers.

'It used to be food for the poor,' Thomas reminded him, amused at the thought.

'So the Afrikaners have travelled the same route,' said Nina. 'Rejected to start with, now in the pound seats.'

'Perhaps there's hope for you yet,' said David, with mocking eyes.

'I protest,' said Nina. 'I'm not an Afrikaner.'

'So I'm not a Jew,' said David. *'Eppur si muove.'*

'Did you see Justin?' she changed the subject, irritable.

'Everything's fine. Saw Rashid too. He's so wrapped up with his toy, it's like Christmas. Checking it all again tonight, including the car. Then he'll weld the boot shut. He's keeping the number plates until tomorrow morning. Sweet little car, everybody'll think it's really Aunt Sannie from the farm come in to town for her shopping.'

'Are my clothes okay? Remember, the wig was too tight when I tried it on last.'

'It's been stretched.' For a moment he showed anxiety, dejection. 'We really needed Christine for this.'

'It's tough on you,' she said warmly. 'You made such a good couple.'

'"Made"?' David flared up; then sighed and gave a wan smile. 'It's all right, I don't mean it. It's just – well, yes, it *is* bloody hard. For years and years you stick to the resolve never to lose your heart to someone again, to give everything to the struggle: then a girl like her comes along: and just as suddenly she's gone again.'

Strange: in a way all the members of their little group knew each other better than family: yet there were landscapes in each of them the others had never seen. What did she know about Justin's life at home, his wife, his remaining child, his teaching? Or about Rashid, who could be so scathing about 'bloody intellectuals', nurturing behind his half-closed eyes something like contempt for the whites in the group: why did he never talk about other people in his life – father or mother, brothers and sisters, lovers, friends? And David: after Christine's mishap he'd sometimes come to her, Nina, when the others weren't around: him she knew better; she knew he'd been married for a while, not long; that he'd had a daughter; that at some stage his wife had left with the child; knew that his parents had survived Auschwitz and that in some mysterious way they had drifted from Germany to South Africa. But apart from this handful of 'facts'? What did she know about his life, about the man, David Blumer, hidden behind his thick lenses? Well, at least she had Thomas. Yes, Thomas. And yet: even he – Even today she'd discovered things in him she hadn't known of before: moments of doubt, impulsiveness, resistance, acceptance. A country of which she knew the coastline, but not the dark interior.

'I'll come to pick you up at eight in the morning,' said David. The moment of melancholy had passed; he was again the businesslike man she had come to know.

'So early?'

'It's better to play it safe. Don't want to take chances with the traffic.' He looked at Thomas. 'And at half-past you'll be driving to Sean's house, right? Lock up the Mini in the garage.'

'And Justin will meet me there?'

'He'll be there at nine, with the bike. By which time you must be dressed and ready. The outfit will be waiting in Sean's cupboard. Justin will check through everything with you. After that I'll come round in the Avis car to collect him and leave him, with the car, in Loop Street. From there I walk down to the Stalplein parkade where the other car will be waiting, so that I can pick you up if anything goes wrong with the main plan. And Rashid will be monitoring the scene from the Nico side in case you have to change course in that direction. The moment it's done, we all charge back here. Until then you're on your own.'

Sudden fingers of fear whispering on his skin, a cold caress: his scalp, down his spine, his scrotum.

'So that's that,' David added, as if to provoke an answer. He snapped off another crayfish leg, but put it down without trying to pick out the sliver of succulent white meat inside.

'I can't believe we've come so far,' said Nina. 'All one's life, without realising it, one keeps getting closer to this point. Yet it seems so far away, so preposterous. And then, suddenly, on an ordinary evening like this, around an ordinary kitchen table, you know you're there. The moment has come.'

'You can still change your mind.' said David. His black eyes bore into her.

She pulled together the lapels of her unwieldy jacket. 'You think I'll chicken out?'

'I just wanted to remind you. Sometimes it helps to realise you *have* a choice.'

'I made my choice a long time ago,' she replied. Then, without warning, kneeling on her chair and leaning forward, her elbows on the table, she said, 'It's *you* I sometimes wonder about, David.' She silenced him before he could speak. 'What I mean is: Thomas, and I, and Rashid, and Justin – all our families have been living here for generations. We have nowhere else to go to. We have no choice but to make this country a place one can live in. But you – don't get me wrong! I know how dedicated you are – but if it really came to the push, you *could* go somewhere else, couldn't you?'

'You mean Israel?' He stared at her through his thick glasses: that must be how he looks at his patients, she thought, examining the symptoms of some strange disease – 'Yes, you may be right,' he said with disarming candour. 'Even though I'm damned depressed about what's happening on the West Bank. But I don't *want* to leave. Can you understand that? My parents had to flee from Germany to come here. Why should I have to leave again? Somewhere in this world there must be a place for me. I listen to my parents comparing this country to the Third Reich they knew, discovering new similarities every day. For years now they've been predicting every step that's happened. But that is precisely what I must help prevent, before it is too late. It cannot be allowed to happen again. Not ever. At some point one's got to break out of one's own history.' He got up suddenly, as if the conversation was becoming too intimate. The crude light reflected on his glasses. 'Got to go. In a year or two there will be time for leisurely chats. Not tonight.'

They accompanied him to the front door, where Nina handed him the shopping bags filled with the things they'd salvaged.

'Make sure it's looked after,' said Thomas. 'It's two whole lives you're carting off there.'

Nina pulled a face. 'Actually it's a relief to be rid of the stuff. You get claustrophobic with too many things cluttering up your life.'

They did not turn on the front light when David left. In democratic darkness they looked after him. The street was deserted. A single sheet of newsprint rustled in the wind, caught in a hedge; a Coke can rolled downhill with an empty clatter.

When at last they lay together on the broad mattress in the corner of the bare room, they seemed curiously shy of each other, even more shy than that distant first night in his flat in Vredehoek, after the violence in Crossroads. They couldn't sleep. There was nothing left to talk about. In the end it was she who silently took his hand and placed it between her legs.

'Do you want to?' He felt, strangely, almost frightened.

Her answer caught him by surprise: 'Make me a child, Thomas. Thomas, I want your child.'

'But you've always   this very afternoon –'

'I want your child! Thomas, I want to take *something* of you with me.'

The wind was still outside, a gusty obtrusive presence now that the light was out. Through the window they could not see the night sky, but the stars must have been there regardless, the southern late-summer sky, the Milky Way, and Orion high above, the blackest black of the Coal Sack, old burnt-out stars, layer upon layer, one dimension after the other, world without end: but in here there were only the two of them in the pale glow of the night seeping into their darkness, body against body, man and woman, sad and desperate, here, terrifyingly here – and on the periphery of their consciousness, huge as a sun, as an exploding star, the knowledge of death and violence to which they had given themselves in trust, a future as inescapable as the past.

Provisionally, they, here. But tomorrow – God, what then?

Chapter 2

In that instant: the bomb exploding. The realisation scorching through them like a flame: *It has happened*. The force of the explosion was like a great hand grabbing them and flinging them through space, into the future. There was the knowledge that even if they could turn round now and rush back, against the momentum of their own speed, to where they'd come from, nothing would be the same any more. It had exploded right inside them, and turning back was impossible; because everything that had previously existed had now been relegated to another dimension: and the only point of contact, fragile and febrile, was this instant.

Yet there was no elation, no exuberance in the experience. A long slow love relationship had unfolded meticulously to debouch in this: and the eagerly expected, necessary orgasm had simply not happened.

They had been thwarted after all.

Even for the improbable they'd been prepared, with David stationed close enough, just round the corner in Plein Street, so that, should the bomb explode too early, before they could get away, he could rush to the Castle and, as a doctor, offer help; with Justin in Loop Street and Rashid in front of the Nico Malan theatre, ready to pick them up regardless of the direction they fled in; with radio contact to keep in touch with everything.

The single stupid variable they had not foreseen was the irascible traffic officer in the white patrol car who'd tried to book Nina for a smoking exhaust even before she'd turned right out of Strand Street towards the Parade. And who had lost his temper when she'd refused to pull up, and swerved in front of her to force her to a standstill half a block away from their target, the Castle. Should she be held up, they had arranged that she would get out immediately and start arguing with whoever had stopped her: and then Thomas in his traffic cop's uniform would intervene and drive the car to the appointed spot himself, while she would follow on his cycle. But when the white traffic car cut in so sharply in front of her she was forced to brake very hard, and that caused the engine to stall; and she couldn't get it going again. The carburettor had flooded, and to prevent anything else from going wrong, before the officer appeared beside her window, she'd pressed the button below the instrument panel; the man was standing so close to her, swearing and gesticulating, that she could not open the door to get out.

Thomas pulled up beside them to ask, calmly and professionally, 'You need help?'

'It's this bloody old lady who —' The officer frowned. 'And who the hell are *you*?'

'Germishuys,' Thomas said smartly. 'From the Wineberg station. Shall I try to start the car for her? She's blocking the traffic.'

'Can't you see I'm handling it? What are you doing here if you're from Wineberg?'

'They sent four of us down to help at the ceremony in the Castle.'

Nina tried again to get out, but the officer stood pressed so tightly against the shoddy little car that she couldn't move. And she was conscious of the time ticking away, and the need to warn Thomas that the mechanism had been activated.

'I'm sorry, Mister,' she said in a wavering voice that was more than play-acting, 'but I'm sure there's something wrong, there's a ticking noise in the engine. Can you please help me —?'

'No ticking noise in front can give off smoke at the back like this,' the officer said sharply. 'Why didn't you stop when I first signalled?'

'I'm a woman on my own, Mister. I can't just stop for any man trying to force me off the road.'

'Let me have a look,' Thomas said. And to Nina, 'Madam, can you help me open the bonnet?'

The officer lost his temper. 'I told you I will handle this. You stay out of it. Why don't you go and do your job over there?' He glanced at his space-age watch. 'The state president will be here any moment now.'

My God, thought Thomas, *something ticking in the engine!* They had only five minutes, from the moment she'd switched it on. And weren't those the sirens of the cavalcade approaching in the distance?

He looked round anxiously. There was one way out. Without explanation, propping up his idling motorcycle, he ran towards the white traffic car whose driver's door was still ajar.

'What do you think you're doing?' shouted the officer.

Yes, those were the sirens. How much time did they have left? A matter of seconds.

The officer came after him. At last Nina could get out. In the brief scuffle that developed among the three of them she took a swipe at the man's head with her handbag. Dazed, he staggered back. She and Thomas jumped on the motorcycle and thundered off. But within moments the fuming officer in the traffic car had started off in pursuit, siren screaming and blue lights flashing.

And then the blast, such a short distance behind them that its impact caught the bike like a sudden gust of wind, a squall that sent them swaying dangerously left and right, momentarily out of control. But then they were round the corner, up Plein Street, past David's idling car.

The traffic car was still hard on their heels, block after block.

In front of them, at the corner of Roeland Street, a pantechnicon was pulling up at a red traffic light. Thomas swerved right, preparing to cross against the light; but accelerating rapidly, the white car drew up abreast of him to cut them off. 'He's going to squash you!' Nina shouted in his ear.

'Hold on! We're turning back.'

At full speed he raced towards the back of the stationary truck, then stood up on the brakes, threw his weight to the side and spun the bike round. But the front wheel caught the kerb. They fell. Thomas was on his feet instantly. The traffic officer was already emerging from his car. Thomas let fly with a kick that caught the man's head in the door; then he swung round to help Nina. The bike's handlebar had slammed her hand against the edge of the kerb and it was bleeding profusely, but for the moment she wasn't even aware of it. What concerned her was that in the fall her wig and prim little hat had shot off her head. It was lying a good ten yards away against a parking meter, like the carcass of a grey cat after a hit-and-run accident. Reacting instinctively, still on all fours, she scuttled after it. The traffic officer, clutching his head, was hard on her heels.

'Nina!' Thomas shouted. 'Leave it! Come here!'

He was back on the bike, revving furiously, driving straight at the man who just managed to jump clear. Thomas grabbed Nina by the arm. 'Come on!' She obeyed, half-dazed. Charging back in the direction they'd come from, then sharply left up the narrow single lane of Barrack Street, against the traffic (thank God there were only a few cars, not one of them in a hurry), in a zigzag motion across Church Square and up Buro Street, along the side of the Groote Kerk and right again into Adderley. There was no sign of the traffic car behind them.

Now they could slow down to avoid attracting any more attention. Near Garlicks, opposite an escalator going down into the Golden Acre, he braked briefly to let her off. A funny sight with her chopped-off hair and old woman's clothing, she ducked into the crowd; a few passers-by looked after her in wonder, some sniggering.

The rest went strictly according to plan. Up in Loop Street Justin was waiting. Thomas got in beside him.

Justin briefly touched his shoulder. 'Everything okay?'

'Not sure yet.' Now that the worst seemed to be behind them he had to struggle to contain a reaction of hysteria. 'Nina lost her wig.' As Justin turned the key, Thomas quickly began to get rid of his outfit: crash helmet, sunglasses, moustache, uniform jacket. 'Have you heard anything? Did we get him? A bloody cop stopped her before she could −'

'That bomb was powerful enough. With a bit of luck −'

'That's not how it was supposed to be.'

'There's always something you cannot foresee. Don't worry. I'm sure you did very well. Now relax, Thomas.'

In St George's Street, at one of the top exits from the Acre, Nina stood waiting, her right hand thrust into the Garlicks bag with the old woman's clothes. It was to hide the blood, they discovered as she got in.

She began to cry as she closed the back door and they pulled off. 'Oh my God, it was a fuck-up.'

'It's your imagination,' said Justin. 'You did it, my girl.' As fast as possible he sped on his way to Wale Street, then into Long, round the bend at the Synod Hall, along Orange; within minutes they were on De Waal Drive. 'Can you make out anything down there?'

No. But every siren in the city was screaming. Police, ambulances, fire brigade. From Kloof Nek all the way down to the harbour.

'It's all my fault,' Nina sobbed. 'I panicked and pushed the button. And then I went and lost the wig.'

'Let's see your hand,' asked Thomas, leaning over to reach the back seat.

It was still bleeding heavily. He tried to wipe it off with a handkerchief, making an effort not to panic.

'What are we going to do if she –?'

'She's okay,' said Justin, his voice quiet, reassuring, 'Nothing to worry about.' He picked up the microphone of his civic band radio and called David's code name. 'Doc?' He spoke very calmly. 'It's the old man. I think you'd better come out to the clinic, you got a patient.' He replaced the microphone, weaving skilfully through the traffic, giving Nina a reassuring glance and a thumbs-up sign in the rear-view mirror. 'Keep cool, my girl. We'll be home in a minute, then David can take a look at you.'

At Groote Schuur they turned down towards the Main Road, and two blocks further left again into a narrow lane compressed between rows of unsuspecting suburban cottages. A block from their house Justin stopped.

'Can you make it from here?' he asked Nina. 'Come on, now, stop crying. Keep your hand in the bag, we don't want anyone to see.'

With an effort she swallowed her tears, blew her nose, got out of the car, and set out resolutely. Justin drove a few blocks further to park in the street above the house. From there he and Thomas sauntered down with an air of nonchalance, chatting away, taking their time. Rashid opened to their knock.

He seemed anxious, as if he'd been pacing impatiently up and down the passage for some time: boyishly lean, dark, long black forelock over his eyes, looking even younger than his twenty-two years.

'What happened to Nina?' he asked, fuming. 'She came past me like a madwoman.'

'Hurt her hand,' Thomas said curtly. 'Where is she now?'

'In the bathroom.'

Thomas ran down the passage.

'But we've done it, haven't we?' Rashid asked urgently. 'Better than any Guy Fawkes I've seen. Right, Justin? It worked, didn't it? The bastard was blown to pieces?'

'Your Semtex certainly did the job,' Justin said briefly. 'The rest we'll still have to find out. Let's hope for the best.' He also hurried past. Rashid followed more slowly.

Behind the closed door they heard water running. Thomas knocked, his head pressed against the door. It took a while. Then they heard the toilet flushing. Nina's voice called something, and he went in. She was leaning over the bath, a small ruffled sea-bird with a wounded wing.

'I can't stop it,' she said. But her voice was calmer now than before. She had wrapped a towel round her bleeding hand.

'There's a drop of brandy in the sideboard,' said Thomas. 'I'll get it.'

He was pouring it when David arrived; he must have driven like a maniac.

As if he knew instinctively where to find her, he went down the passage, past Rashid, into the bathroom; gave Nina a professional pat on the shoulder, unwrapped her hand, opened his bag.

'Nice work, my girl.'

'It was a fuck-up,' she said again, now without emotion. 'I just know it. And it's all been my fault.'

'Don't be silly.' He was examining the hand, swiftly, expertly. Blood dripped through his fingers to the floor.

'You seen anything?' asked Justin.

'No, it was chaos. I was still waiting to hear from you.'

'Did we get him?' asked Thomas.

'Well, *something*'s happened. All hell was loose.' David was still working quickly and smoothly to disinfect the wound.

'How does it look?' enquired Justin.

'Not very good, I'm afraid.' He pushed Nina down on the rim of the bath and began to daub the wound with mercurochrome. 'Badly bruised. There may be a fracture. And the cut is nasty. I'm going to put in a few stitches.' He looked at Nina. 'You want an anaesthetic or can you take it?'

'Of course I can take it. There's no time for fancy stuff anyway.'

'Right, here goes.'

She clenched her teeth hard as he stuck the needle into the living flesh of her palm and pulled through the thread, tied it up, snipped it off. A second time. A third. Her face was very pale, and there were drops of perspiration on her forehead and her upper lip. Holding her tightly round the shoulders, Thomas coaxed her into swallowing a few mouthfuls of brandy.

David took crêpe from his bag. 'Now we're going to bandage it up as tightly as we can,' he said. 'When you change your outfit in P.E., you can take off the bandage and put on gloves. We'll send them a message. It's all under control. I'm going to give you an anti-tetanus injection too, just to play it safe. And I'll give you some tablets to kill the pain on the night flight. But I want you to see a doctor in Frankfurt or London tomorrow to check up, right?'

'If you'd given me the job like I asked you from the beginning, this wouldn't have happened,' Rashid suddenly said from the door. 'I *told* you. You can't leave a thing like this to a pair of novices.'

Justin moved in very swiftly. 'In this organisation we're all equal and everybody gets a chance. The bomb did go off. And for all we know it was a success.'

'But look at her. We can't take chances like this.' Viciously: 'We could have been bloody heroes.'

'We have no place for heroes, Rashid,' Justin reprimanded him sharply. 'We're plain ordinary folk doing a job. And that job's still far from done.'

For a moment Rashid's eyes continued to flare. Then he nodded. 'Sorry, chaps. I suppose I also got a fright when she came in bleeding like that. I know we're all in it together. I just don't want anybody to get hurt unnecessarily, we need you all.' He came to her. 'So, no hard feelings?' He touched her shoulder with his hand.

Knowing how wary he usually was of any kind of physical contact, she nodded, giving him a brief tense smile.

'Here, have some more of this,' said David, handing her the brandy glass she'd given back to Thomas. 'We don't have time to waste. We must get you to the airport.'

'I think you'd better take her yourself, David,' suggested Justin. 'She may need attention on the way.'

'Right. But what will we do to get the news then?' It had been arranged that he would either remain in town or return there as soon as possible, to offer his assistance as a doctor, so that he could report back first-hand.

'We can always find out later. It's more important to make sure that Nina is all right.' He looked at Thomas who was still hovering in the background, anxious, eager to help. 'Pull yourself together, man. Get dressed and put on your wig. I'll take you to the airport.'

'All right.' He shook his head. 'You know, I still can't believe it.' He looked embarrassed as he started unbuttoning his shirt. 'I suppose it's all in a day's work for you, you've been through it before –'

'One never gets used to it, Thomas,' Justin said very quietly, suppressed emotion lighting up his dark eyes. 'Every time it's the first time.' A brief silence. Then he added, almost reluctantly,

'And every time something gets lost along the way.' He became matter-of-fact again: 'Right, guys, move your backsides.'

'If only one could be sure –' Nina checked her thoughts and got up. 'I'm so very sorry, Justin. I've let the Organisation down.'

'What the hell makes you think we've messed it up?' he demanded. 'We all did our jobs. And now it's time for the next step. Okay? It's never what you've done that's important: what matters is what you doing next. Just remember that. Rashid, where's their clothes?'

Thomas and Nina were left alone in the bathroom. She changed into her demure secretary's outfit and put on the wig with the fringe, while Thomas hurriedly tucked his hair in under the unkempt brown wig they'd chosen for him.

'If Christine had still been with us, that damned wig would not have fallen off,' she said in another flush of anger. 'Now they all saw me. You should have seen the looks I got in the Golden Acre.' Mechanically she took a comb from the shelf in front of the mirror and pulled it through his hair. 'I wish we could have driven to the airport together. I'm scared, Thomas.'

'You mustn't!' He took her by the arms. 'You hear me? Nina, from the very beginning you were the one who kept us going. Even when Justin wanted to abort it after they'd caught Christine. And now we've pulled it off. And it was worth it. Yesterday it was you who said it, now I want you to remember this: *it was worth it.* Nina, do you hear me?'

She looked him in the eyes, for a long time, then nodded. 'I'm sorry, Thomas. I didn't mean to crack up like that. I'm okay now. Come, will you zip me up behind? I'm afraid this hand isn't very useful right now.'

'It'll be all right soon.'

'I know.'

He helped her, then pulled on his own casual clothes. A weird feeling, all of a sudden, as if he were – temporarily? – taking leave of himself. With her sound left hand Nina straightened his hair for the last time. 'You look like a total stranger,' she said. 'Rather sexy too.'

The clothes they'd taken off he carried in a small bundle to give to Rashid, who had already bundled the traffic cop's uniform in a rucksack.

Nina suddenly turned to Thomas. 'Aren't you hungry? You didn't have any breakfast either.'

'You can have a bite at the airport,' said Justin. 'Or on the plane. We can't waste any more time now. David, you go first. I'll give you ten minutes.'

'By this time tomorrow I'll already have joined you in London from Frankfurt.' She looked at Justin. 'You sure it's all been double-checked?'

'Of course. Here's your ticket to P.E. For the next couple of hours you'll be Anna Esterhuysen. There you will become Elaine Munroe, with new luggage and everything. Suzy will meet you with your passport and the new tickets. Make sure you check your suitcase right through to Frankfurt, you won't have much time at Jan Smuts. You'll have to run straight from Arrivals to International Departures. In Frankfurt our chaps will meet you and help you through to London.' She knew it all by heart, but it was reassuring to hear it repeated. He took her lightly by the elbow and kissed her. 'You were great, my girl,' he said, emotional for a moment. 'We'll be missing you, hey?'

'As long as it hasn't all been in vain.'

'How many times have I told you? It's better to light a candle than to curse the dark. Not so? And your little candle will be burning for a hell of a long time yet, I promise you that.'

He opened the door. Violent daylight broke into the interior. David went out, checked the street, then turned to take Thomas's hand in his for a moment, and went down the steps to the trellis gate.

For a moment Justin considerately stepped back.

And then they were alone on the porch. He, she. Later he would think, or remember: It's only in moments like these that one is truly alive, that you are what you are, where you are: moments like when the bomb exploded, or when we stood on that porch in the aggressive light; moments in which all times converge like rays of light in a lens, when you exist in a kind of total awareness: when you know where you are, fully present in your knowing. An almost unbearable intensity. Which is why these moments are so rare.

He might have wished to say this to her. But how could it be pronounced? At least he might have wanted to put his arms around her and hold her. But almost brusquely she said, in a tone that suited her secretary-bird looks, 'Thomas, I'm not going to say goodbye. It's only until tomorrow, for God's sake. You know I hate goodbyes, they're too soppy.'

Before he could answer, one hand still raised anxiously as if to detain her, she briefly waved a kiss at him with her white bandaged hand, and hurried down the steps to David who was holding open the gate.

2

The even drone of the plane created a different kind of suspension. Yesterday it had been the suspended existence preceding the action, now it was the petrifying moment of not knowing, isolated in that tube which excluded all contact with the surrounding space and within which the flow of time between departure and arrival had been arrested. Until he *knew* what had happened, how the attack had ended, it had not yet occurred, its existence remained only virtual, not real. The president might be dead, a nation plunged into disarray, shedding crocodile tears; violence might have broken out in black townships throughout the country; reprisals on a massive scale might be in progress; the land down below might be going up in flames: but as long as he did not know about it, hurtling in splendid isolation through space at dizzy speed, kilometres above the earth, tens of degrees below zero, he was not yet involved, it had not happened yet. Like a body stored in ice for a future era when scientists would (hopefully) know how to resuscitate it, a real and conscious existence was excluded. Only when he stepped out again at Jan Smuts to learn about the news in the airport building, whatever that news might be, would life resume.

Perhaps that was why he reacted so eagerly, rather than with diffidence or mere amusement, to the young woman next to him. For it was a way of keeping him occupied, of restraining the thoughts milling in his head, suspending memory or expectation, even of temporarily displacing his anxiety about Nina. Normally he would hardly have noticed the girl – not unattractive, but plain, with straight shining black hair (a hundred strokes, at least, a night?) forming a fringe on her forehead and swinging down in a pony-tail behind; a small sharp nose with an unexpected refractious tilt at the end, and a wide mouth, a generous no-nonsense mouth, a Carly Simon mouth (his mother would disapprove, 'Girls with big mouths –' leaving the rest, most decently, unsaid), radical eyes: a blue-stocking, one might conclude, wearing no visible make-up, a long Indian cotton dress no longer much in fashion except in communes here and there, with handmade brown thong sandals she quickly kicked off her narrow feet (he noticed the two strands of bright beads round one ankle) – but from the moment she entered the plane he couldn't but notice her. The flight steward was already preparing to close the door when she came stumbling up the steps, breathless, red in the face, lugging a bulky denim bag (she'd been too late to check it in, she later explained, unasked, and the ground staff was not prepared to let her through unless she took the bag on board with her); when she tried to force the unwieldy bag into the luggage bin above his head, a clasp broke and a rain of objects came showering over him: folded or rolled-up shirts, socks, a pair of white shoes, pantyhose, three minuscule brightly coloured panties, a white bra, a hefty black book which, if it had hit his head, would have knocked him out cold, a toothbrush and a terribly out-of-shape tube of toothpaste, even a small pink box which spilled tampons like a pod bursting open and distributing its seeds.

A small wave of giggling rippled down the aisle while he helped her to collect her possessions and stuff them back into the blue canvas bag. (The lethal book, he discovered, was the *I Ching*.) Was she blushing or was it the exertion it took to carry the bag on board that had stained her cheeks such a deep crimson?

'It's because I couldn't pack before the last minute.' She moved past him to the window; the seat between them was open. 'Thanks a bundle. Hell, I never thought I'd make it. I suppose it's my punishment for sneaking off this weekend.' There was something compulsive about her talking; the torrent of words flooded him, whirling and eddying unabated for the rest of the flight, as if the mishap with the bag was being continued in a different key. Her voice was hoarse, like sandpaper rasping through her throat, an unusual quality that drew attention not only to what she was saying but to the voice itself. 'Until the very last moment I was sure old Siebert was going to send somebody after me to stop me. He's the principal. A real shit. My dad would get a fit if he knew. How does one explain that kind of thing to a *dominee*?' That was when she kicked off her sandals. Looking sideways at him with a touch of guilt: 'Sorry, I suppose you don't want to be talked to. Why do people on planes always feel threatened when a stranger starts talking to them?' A brief hesitation. 'Would you like me to shut up?'

'Oh no, do go on.'

Without waiting for an answer she continued, 'You see, for a whole week now I couldn't say a word about it to anyone, and I was beginning to think I'm going to burst if someone doesn't stop to listen. Bloody unfair, if you ask me, I mean, I've got to be at their disposal like twenty-four hours a day if they want to talk to *me*, but the moment I've got something to tell *them* —'

'Who's forcing you to listen to them? Who are "they" anyway?'

'Oh.' For the first time she seemed to realise that he had no idea of what she was talking about. 'I'm a school psychologist, you see. At an industrial school, of all places. You know what that is?'

'Not very well.'

'Don't worry, I didn't know either. Otherwise I'd never have landed there. It's, well, not quite like a reformatory, but almost. The children who end up in there are usually sent by the court. Petty theft, prostitution, that kind of thing. But others are simply girls who somehow landed in trouble. They're not criminals, just ordinary kids. Difficult, but ordinary. All they need is a bit of love. But that's not how Siebert's crowd see it. Oh no, to them it's a question of discipline. Authority. Decency. Jesus, have you ever thought what's all done in the name of decency? Basically there's only one solution: the kids must be broken in. Like horses or dogs. With the cane. Or with solitary. Just one misstep – never mind how ridiculous it is, and let me tell you, there's *thousands* of rules – and the girl is locked up in a cell for a week. Not even a bath. She sits there naked, they don't even allow her clothing, there's no mirror, nothing. A toilet and a basin, and that's it. And you know what's the worst? – some of those girls break the rules deliberately so they can be sent to solitary. That's how bad it is outside. I tell you, I can't take it any more. I started there in January this year, all starry-eyed, like anybody just starting a new job. But before the first week was out I was in trouble with Siebert. Do you know that Siebert once called me in because I chewed gum? A pernicious influence on our children, Miss Lombard. A bad example. It fosters liberalism. You see why I said I couldn't take it any more? If you think I'm off my rocker, that's exactly what I am. No human being can survive in that place.'

'Why don't you leave if it's really so bad?'

'And admit that I've been a failure? Maybe I am. But it doesn't make it any easier to accept. The worst is: I keep thinking about the kids. Okay, so I know there's almost nothing I can do for them, I'm hemmed in on all sides. Still, I can offer them *something*, even if it's only because I'm not much older than them. And because I haven't sold out yet. It's like they trust me. And what's to become of them if I leave?'

'Is it really so bad?'

'It's worse. I ask you: who are the really sick ones? The real criminals?' She dug a tissue from the front of her dress and blew her nose. A wry smile caused her nose to pucker. 'I hope you're not a psychiatrist too, or I'll be certified myself.'

'No, I'm harmless. A student.'

'You look too old for that.'

For a moment he was startled, but he tried to cover up. 'Postgrad. I'm working on a Ph.D.'

'And what are you going to do in Johburg?'

'I live there,' he answered without blinking an eye. 'I've just been down to Cape Town for a while to sort things out with my prof.'

'Sounds like a good life.' He couldn't make out whether she was mocking him. 'All around you the world's going to blazes while you carry on swotting. What's your subject?'

'Philosophy.'

'Naturally. Your folks must be stinking rich. Or are you the bright type that's loaded with grants and scholarships?'

'No, I'm working like hell to pay my way.'

'What kind of work?'

Inquisitive bastard, he thought, not without amusement. 'I clean the chamber-pots in a whorehouse in Hillbrow,' he said.

She burst out laughing so loudly that the flight attendant behind the trolley in the aisle two rows before them spilled tea on the shoulder of the man she was serving; several of the passengers turned their heads.

With a generous fluttering of her wide colourful dress the girl scooped her feet in under her on the seat to sit crosslegged. She pressed her dark head against the window – her breath made a small cloud of fog on the inside pane – and gazed out with great concentration. Thomas leaned forward to look past her. Far below the desolate brown land rolled past, with the shadow patches of drifting clouds, geometric patterns of hills and plains, the ancient water marks of an inland sea. Now and then the double stain of a town: houses on large square plots set in a grid of broad streets; and to one side, apart, the identical matchboxes or the conglomeration of shacks and shanties where the blacks lived. How clear and exposed the anatomy of apartheid, he thought, like the skeleton of an animal picked clean by vultures. Visible even

84

from ten thousand metres up: we here, you there. And underneath it all, disfigured by the patterns of towns and villages which from up here looked as temporary and coincidental as a skin disease, measles on the brown skin of the earth, stretched the ancient carcass of Africa, scarred by the depredations of sun and wind, snow, occasional floods, but untouched in its essence, untouchable, eternal.

'So what do *you* do to keep sane?' she asked.

He shrugged. The conversation was approaching more precarious territory; he had to avoid questions, postpone answers, remain uninvolved.

'Or have you given up already?' she pressed him. Adding almost immediately, 'Who am I to talk? Perhaps this is the worst of growing up the way we do.' (He was amused by the 'we', but said nothing.) 'I mean, from the very beginning one is forced to think of ways of breaking out, even if it's only to shock them. Then, one day, you discover that the worst you can think of is farting in church. In a manner of speaking. Even in high school I used to wonder what there was I could do that would really shake them to their foundations, just to prove that I was *I*, not one of them? Falling pregnant? Kicking the principal in the balls? What else, besides? Does anyone have the guts for anything more than that? Surely there should be something truly terrible one could do. Like burning down the school. Or necklacing Siebert. Or blowing up the state president. Something like that.'

He felt the blood drain from his face.

'Why are you looking so terribly serious all of a sudden?' she asked.

'I suppose it's because I've been asking myself those very questions for so long.'

'And?'

'It's very confidential. Promise you won't tell a soul?'

'Okay. Is it really so important?'

'It is. You see, I'm organising a countrywide strike of whores. That's the real reason why I went to the Cape.'

She giggled. 'You think that will solve our problems?'

'Absolutely. Can you imagine what will become of the three houses of parliament, or the Cabinet, the whole tutti, if the whores shut up shop?'

She looked at him with sudden intensity. 'Is that all you can do?' she asked. 'Make jokes?'

'I'm not joking. It's serious. Considering that we're all whores living off the system.'

Her eyes − unusual eyes: but what was it about them that intrigued him so? − narrowed. 'Perhaps you're deeper than I thought after all.'

'I told you I'm a philosopher.'

She shook her head; her hair swayed. 'And what do you think *I* should do?'

'I can't answer that for you. As I see it, the only solution for anybody is to make the thing you *want* to do coincide with what you've *got* to do, with what your bit of history demands of you.'

She gazed at him with her narrowed eyes, in silence.

'What would you recommend yourself?' he asked, realising it was necessary to remain on the attack. 'What, provided it's not impossible?'

'One should *start* with the impossible,' she said sharply. 'What will become of us if there's nothing impossible left to try?' Her eyes were a truly remarkable colour, he decided: not blue, more a dark smoky grey, like some semi-precious stone. 'Don't you see?' she went on. 'That's why the school is driving me crazy. People like Siebert can't handle anything irrational. Everything's got to be shrunken to a size they can manipulate. And then it becomes tyranny. A power game. Have you ever thought what tyranny *means*? What power comes down to if you try to analyse it? It's very simple, really. It's the power to kill. That's the ultimate meaning of power. The power to kill. Through your armies, your police, your gallows, sure: but it can operate in a million other ways too: through an education system, a church, through people like Siebert. To break a child's spirit is also a way of killing. And what are we doing to stop it? What *can* one do? When it comes down to it, we're all scared of dying.'

'But if you don't try to stop it −?'

'Exactly. That's what bugs me. Here I am, I'm twenty-five years old: it feels as if the whole world is drifting past and there's nothing I can do to stop it. It's like a car, I've got four pistons, or whatever you call those things, but I'm running on only one.'

'I honestly don't get the impression that *you're* running on only one,' he said, smiling.

'What do you know about me?' she asked aggressively. 'You think because I've been spilling all my beans over you −' She looked at him, then turned away and once again pressed her forehead against

86

the window. After a while, more composed, she said, 'My nerves are shot. You see, my very best friend is getting married in Pretoria tomorrow. I *must* be there with her tonight. I asked Siebert to give me the day off. He hardly even listened, simply said no, it was impossible, against the fucking rules. So I just stayed away. I suppose he'll give me hell on Monday.' She shrugged. 'Anyway, that's next week's worries. First I'm going to live it up this weekend. Where in Johburg do you live?'

'I'm sharing a flat in Hillbrow.'

'With a girl?'

'Yes,' he said, smoothly.

'Hm. Perhaps you two can show me the city if I come up again one day'.

'And you?' he asked: it was safer to keep her talking. 'Where in the Cape do you live?'

'Do you know the Cape?'

'Not well. I go there very seldom.'

'Fransie and I used to share a cottage in Claremont,' she said. 'Fransie's the one who's getting married tomorrow. Now I have the place to myself. Look, if you ever come down again, you can stay with me if you like. Provided you aren't fussy. I can show you the whole Cape. You got something to write with? I'll give you the address.'

'Just tell me, I'll remember.'

'I see,' she said accusingly. 'So you don't really mean it.'

'I do. Cross my heart. But I don't have a pen on me.'

She stretched out her arm and pushed the overhead button to call the flight attendant, and with an air of condescension requested pen and paper from the woman she'd ruffled earlier. Then wrote down the particulars for him (using no capitals, he noticed): *lisa lombard*, followed by a telephone number and an address. She folded the sheet, tore it down the middle, and gave him the inscribed half.

He studied it as if to memorise the particulars.

'What about you?'

'What about me?'

'Your address. Or don't you give it to strange women?'

'Not usually. The madam in my brothel is very strict about that. But I'll make an exception in your case.' He wrote down the name on his flight ticket: *Anton Swanepoel*, and thought up, with a touch of perversity, an address, *President Flats*, in Pretoria Street, and underlined it. 'We don't have a phone yet, we haven't been there long.'

He was thinking: What a pity. He'd have liked to meet her again; Nina should take to her too. But now it was over, he would never see her again, trains in the night. For an hour and fifty minutes they'd been sitting beside each other, and now it was over. For ever. In a few hours he would be on his way to London. On Monday when she – what was her name again? he checked the large italic script on the piece of paper, *lisa lombard* – on Monday, when she was back in Cape Town to see her Mr Siebert, he would be ten thousand kilometres away.

'Please fasten your seat-belts,' the flight attendant announced, followed by the rest of her jingle, in two languages, both botched.

The young woman beside him bent over to put on her sandals. The thin bright lines of the beads on the tanned skin of her narrow ankle. Lovely slim feet, he thought; likeable toes.

The plane touched down. Thomas stood up to retrieve her blue bag from the luggage bin.

'Now please be careful,' he said in a paternal tone of voice.

She put out her tongue at him.

(His mother, once more: 'Decent girls *never* do that.')

On their way to the bus, where they were separated in the throng of hurried passengers, she called: 'See you in the Cape, Anton. Sometime.'

'It's a date.'

In the airport building extraordinary safety measures were being applied. A whole contingent of police surrounded the luggage conveyance system, searching every suitcase, checking every ticket. It took almost half an hour before he could go to the bookshop to buy a newspaper.

CAPE TOWN BLAST KILLS FOUR, said the front page. And below it: NARROW ESCAPE FOR PRESIDENT.

Now it has happened, he thought. Only now, now that we have failed, has it happened.

3

– My hand has begun to bleed again. I've been to the toilet twice, but I cannot get it to stop. One doesn't want to attract attention. Fortunately there's no one sitting next to me. So I'm trying to keep my hand, under cover of the newspaper, hidden inside the air-sickness bag. I'll put the glove on again when we reach Jan Smuts.

I should have liked to have this hour, without interruption or distraction, to collect my thoughts. On the night flight to Frankfurt, I suppose, there will be more than enough time. But it's *now* I need the time. To write you a letter in my mind. A kind of stock-taking, perhaps. Unsentimental, but not disinterested.

Dearest Thomas: but what next —?

As far as P.E. it went smoothly. I must have been in a kind of stupor still, I wasn't really aware of what was going on around me. Not even of my hand. A vacuum. In P.E. the woman called Peggy met me and took me to a flat in Summerstrand. There I changed. Still in a haze. The man, Stanley, took me back to the airport in a different car. By that time I'd already heard the news. They told me in the flat. The president's car, warned no doubt by the security people in the Castle, had swung round at the corner of Darling Street and raced away. But four other people were killed in the blast. Two army conscripts. A young white woman. A baby. God knows how many others wounded, some critical.

All the preparations. So many months. Now this.

All right, we've always known there might be, had to be, other casualties. Crossfire in a civil war. One weighs gain and loss. Four lives are entered against our names today. Not abstractions, not statistics, Thomas. We spoke about it last night. *People.* People like you and me. Flesh and bone and blood. An amazing amount of blood. Look at my hand in this air-sickness bag. Soaked with blood. Mine. But that is only the visible part. Invisibly, it is stained with the blood of those four people. A child among them. Not for a moment can I deny the horror of it. But Thomas, I've also seen the bodies of children shot in Crossroads, in Langa, in Guguletu, in Athlone. I know I had to be involved in what happened. Even though we failed in our first objective. There is more at stake than this. Killing: so that the killing might stop. That is why. How did Mandela put it, so many years ago? — 'It is an ideal I hope to live for and to achieve. But if needs be, it is an ideal for which I am prepared to die.' This is what sustains me. This knowledge inside myself. That I am not sending, in cold blood, others — 'innocents', that charged word — to their deaths, but that I am prepared, if I must, to give up my own life.

Actually I am relieved, you know, Thomas — please forgive me for this — that I could be alone, without you, on this journey. One needs to be alone sometimes. I needed it. I am prepared, now, for whatever may come. And I regret nothing.

It is time to fasten my seat-belt. Not easy, with this hand. But I think it isn't bleeding quite so much now.

I may yet see you, if only at a distance, in one of the departure halls, before we leave.

Hamba kahle, Thomas.

Amandla ngawethu, Thomas. –

4

Time, which had been suspended, began to flow again. Although he had to remain in the Holiday Inn for the time being – minute after devastating minute dragging past interminably – it was different from the plane. The man who had met him at the airport (he'd nearly missed the cardboard notice bearing his new name on it, *Anton Swanepoel*) was a silent, serious young Indian with long smooth hair swept glossily off his forehead. With what seemed like unnecessary cloak-and-dagger extravagance, he'd first driven for some distance in the direction of Pretoria, then had turned off the freeway to make a long loop back to the Holiday Inn.

'Do you know anything more than the paper said?' Thomas asked along the way.

'All hell is loose.'

'Will Nina and I be able to get out tonight?'

'We'll play it by ear. You got the number you must phone at six?'

'Yes, I memorised it.'

'Remember to say as little as possible.'

'Of course.' He tried to suppress his anxiety. 'But what about Nina? I still have time to change, but she'll have to run straight from one plane to the next.'

'She has a good chance. Remember, according to the SAA records she's a new passenger who only boarded in P.E.'

They stopped in the parking lot of the hotel. From the inside pocket of his immaculate suit the man drew a small sheet of paper. 'Here's another number, in case the shit hits the fan.' The number was written in two rows, like an addition sum. 'You start on the second line, okay? Right to left, skipping every second figure. On the top line, you skip the first, then read from left to right.'

'I know.'

The man handed him a long white envelope. 'Passport, traveller's cheques, air ticket to London. From the time you set foot in the airport again, you will be Dennis Johnstone. Here in the hotel you are Peter Ward. Here's your key and the card to the room. Somebody else did the checking in for you this morning. There is a suitcase with clothes and stuff in the room. Inside is a carrier bag for the clothes you are wearing at the moment and anything else you want to leave behind. Remember to give all of that, with the key, to the man who picks you up at half-past six.'

Then he was alone.

Like an automaton he went through the routine he'd practised so many times. Browsed through the shops on the ground floor, feigning interest in the African curios in ivory and wood, semi-precious stones and T-shirts with wild-life prints; bought something; then, having made sure he wasn't followed, he went up to the third floor. Secured the door of his room with the metal chain, opened the suitcase waiting on the luggage stand, chose a suit for the journey, ran a bath. Among the bottles and tubes on the dressing table was brown hair-dye.

It was seventeen minutes past five.

He turned on the radio, then quickly set to work, trimming his hair considerably shorter and washing it in the dye. The end result was a dull dirty brown. Not very appetising, but more comfortable than the wig.

It was the main item on the news at half-past five.

The death toll in this morning's bomb explosion in Cape Town has risen to five after an elderly Coloured man succumbed to his injuries in Groote Schuur hospital. The names of the dead have not yet been released. Twenty-three persons were discharged after treatment; eighteen are still in hospital, seven of them in a critical condition. The chief of police has announced that a bomb of Russian origin has been found in the wreck of the car used in the attack. It is of a kind often before used in explosions in the Peninsula, and the police are following several clues. Important information on the two suspects who fled from the scene of the crime on a motorcycle immediately before the explosion has been supplied by Mr Daniel van Eck, the traffic officer who risked his own life pursuing them. The criminals allegedly fired several shots from a Makaroff pistol at Mr van Eck before they managed to escape. In the chase one of the two, a short-haired woman, lost her wig, which is at present being examined by the police. Roadblocks have been set up on all main roads in the Peninsula, and passengers at stations in Cape Town and at D.F. Malan airport are being screened to prevent the terrorists from escaping. The full co-operation of the public has been requested. In the meantime the Minister of Justice –

He turned off the radio and returned to the bathroom. In less than half an hour now he had to telephone the contact number – a public booth somewhere, no doubt – for the final go-ahead. Fifteen minutes later Nina's flight SA 412 from Port Elizabeth should land. *She has a good chance*, the man had said.

At exactly six o'clock he picked up the telephone and dialled the number he'd memorised. His hands were moist. It rang and rang in his ear.

'Come on, Jesus!'

At last the unknown voice.

'Peter Ward,' Thomas said.

'Your lift to Pretoria has been cancelled,' the voice said in his ear. 'We've had a breakdown. Sorry.'

'Listen –' said Thomas.

'Pass on the message,' the voice interrupted. 'If you can get through.'

A click. The receiver had been replaced.

A numbness spread through his body. He sat staring at the empty receiver in his hand. Dropped it back after a long time. Picked it up again, and dialled, once more, mechanically, the number.

It rang and rang, but no one answered.

It was not the cancellation that upset him most, but the command that followed it. *Pass on the message*. It meant they couldn't contact Nina themselves. *If you can get through*. If it was at all possible; if he thought he could risk it; if it wouldn't endanger his own life.

Did that matter?

Leaving everything behind – the expensive suitcase packed with strange clothes, the briefcase with financial reports, the toilet bag in the bathroom, even the wallet with his passport and ticket – he hurried out, down to the lobby. The courtesy bus was ready to leave, but he was stopped by the driver.

'It's only for guests checking out, sir.'

He pressed a twenty-rand note into the man's hand. Saw him hesitate, then smile. Behind him the combi's sliding door was slammed shut.

At the entrance to the domestic departures hall he got out, went through to the arrivals hall – it was difficult to keep from running – and went to the enquiries desk. Flight 412 had landed on time, twenty minutes earlier. It was now twenty-five to seven.

There were police in blue uniforms everywhere, with dogs and automatic weapons.

A whole squad of them blocked the upper entrance to the international departures counters. A woman directly in front of Thomas was stopped.

'Only passengers with tickets are admitted, madam,' said the officer in charge.

Thomas moved deftly out of the throng. With a crowd of other people who had come to see off friends and relatives, he went round the departures area to the glass walls on the far side through which one could watch passengers coming through customs control on their way to the duty-free shops and the escalator running down to baggage control and departure lounges.

In there, too, the police were everywhere.

He knew it was hopeless. He couldn't possibly stop her. And to try to attract her attention might be disastrous. For both of them.

But he had to keep cool. Nobody knew that she was Nina Jordaan, nobody knew that she came from Cape Town. She could not be connected in any way with the secretary bird, Miss Anna Esterhuysen, who'd left D.F. Malan airport earlier today on flight SA 608 to Port Elizabeth, because there a brand-new Ms Elaine Munroe had boarded the plane for her connecting flight to Frankfurt, the ticket for which had been purchased in P.E. more than a month ago. Once she had passed through passport control the last obstacle would be cleared. Tomorrow morning she would be in Frankfurt. He would go underground for a while – that was what the message had implied – and in due course he would join her in London. It was, at most, an irritation, nothing serious.

Then why couldn't he stop perspiring?

She should be through by now. She must be safe.

But he remained at the glass partition, among the many members of a large family swarming around him with packets of crisps and chewing-gum and tins of Coke and Fanta, evidently waiting for someone whose appearance was imminent.

Absently he kept an eye on the airport clock. From 19h13 it had flipped over to 19h14, then 19h15, 19h16, now 19h17. Strange, it struck him, how this clock, at first sight so accurate – the infallibility of electronics – ignored the seconds. Each time, in

93

the precise moment when it flipped over, it was absolutely correct. But from there, while time moved on, for a full minute, it stood motionless on a figure no longer relevant. Quantum leaps. But everything in between was suppressed, all the gathering tension and energy, all the forces that made the next jump possible. 'Official time.' For but a single second out of every sixty the clock was on time: for the following fifty-nine, roughly ninety-eight per cent of the time, it was slow. And yet everything was running smoothly, as if it made no difference; planes arrived and took off, millions of people came and went, firmly believing that they knew where they were, in what time-frame they existed: but it was all false, a mere illusion of reliability.

He should go. Undoubtedly she had already passed through customs and gone down to the departure gates, free.

But something held him there, while the untimely clock went its deceitful way to 19h18, 19h19.

With a feeling of hopelessness he looked round. Through the tall glass wall overlooking the tarmac, he could see the high noses of waiting planes, staring at him through slanting suspicious eyes. Alitalia. UTA. TAP. KLM. SAA. Lufthansa. British Airways. Beyond those glass walls lay the whole of the free world.

He turned back again.

It was 19h21.

And then she appeared.

He had to suppress the impulse to wave, call out her name. (Or should he try, 'Elaine!'?)

It unrolled before his eyes like a film. An old-fashioned movie without sound, for the thick glass excluded it.

He saw her stop for a moment to rearrange her ticket and papers and passport in her left hand. Saw the dark red bloodstain breaking through the white glove. Even imagined that he could see her tremble. Then she stooped to pick up the small overnight bag she'd put down. Began walking on towards the escalator.

Where had they appeared from so suddenly? There were now two men in checkered jackets and grey flannels behind her. They appeared to be talking to her. She turned her head briefly, gripped her bag more resolutely, began to walk faster. They came up beside her. Now they had taken hold of her arms. One of them was making a gesture. Was he calling someone? Four or five men in uniform were approaching from the side. They were hemming her in, making it impossible for her to move. It was difficult to see what was happening. The

94

family beside Thomas broke into wild shouting and waving. A fat woman in a red tracksuit, who had emerged from customs a moment after Nina, waved back. They did not even seem to notice the commotion.

Thomas did not move. The glass felt cold against his forehead. But it was difficult to see through the fog caused by his breath on the pane.

Perhaps they were only double-checking her passport and her ticket. Then everything would be fine. No one could possibly tell those documents from real ones. Zeke was a master, even better than Cedric in London. In a few seconds (unmarked by the clock), a minute at most, she would be allowed to proceed.

There was a sudden churning motion in the group surrounding her. She came bursting through them. A policeman grabbed at her, but she beat him off with her overnight bag and broke into a run, though it was clear she had no idea where to go. Straight ahead she ran, like a hunted animal, in the direction of the shops and the restaurant.

He saw two of the policemen take aim with their automatic rifles. (Why in God's name didn't they run after her? She could not possibly get away.) This time the sound was audible enough, and only too familiar. A brief salvo, tacatacatac. Centimetres from his face the whole glass wall splintered into pieces. All around him people were screaming, some falling down on the floor, others stampeding towards the distant exit. A child choked on his crisps. A Coke tin rolled. Then it was very quiet.

His mouth formed a word, but he, too, uttered no sound: 'Nina.'

Through the glass, as if through the wall of an aquarium, isolated, remote, improbable, he saw her shudder briefly where she'd fallen. Now it was no longer just her hand that bled.

Chapter 3

He was lying on his back, his arms under his head, on the single bed
with the tall white posts and brass-coloured plastic knobs, copied
from some antique model. The ceiling white, the walls pale green;
there were flokatis on the beige wall-to-wall carpet on the floor;
above the bed was a framed tapestry of Gainsborough's *Blue Boy*
stitched by Belinda's mother; on the opposite wall, a watercolour
seascape and a butcher's calendar with a colour photograph of a
little girl with a large shaggy dog; on either side of the old-fashioned
washing stand with its small floral tiles, were two wall-texts:
Kipling's *If*, and, in Afrikaans, the words of an erstwhile prime
minister, *Believe in God, believe in your people, believe in yourself.*
The Kipling used to hang in Frans's bedroom when they'd been kids,
a present from their mother on his fourteenth or fifteenth birthday
(in spite of the father's protests about the English); it had now
been relegated to the guest-room. Beside the bed, in a small shelf
stacked with old copies of *Reader's Digest*, a number of women's
and family magazines, Afrikaans translations of Konsalik, a bible,
an *Illustrated Great Trek*, books on guns, on the Angolan war, the
Boer War; rather unexpectedly, probably picked up by Belinda at
a sale, Linda Goodman's *Sun Signs*; also a Morris West, two thin
collections of daily prayers, Roberts's *Birds of South Africa*, a tourist
guide to Boston where Frans had spent two years at MIT, a German
grammar book from the time Frans had done research at the Max
Planck Institute in Munich.

– How can one feel such a stranger in one's own brother's home? I
can remember only one other occasion when I was so displaced. We
were on our annual visit to Ouma Muller in the Eastern Cape, and
on that particular afternoon Dad had taken me with him to some

people, strangers, on a farm, somewhere. While the grownups are discussing business in the sitting-room I am left to my own devices in the 'ram camp', a closed-in room on the porch occupied by the sons of the family, now presumably away at university. The day is dark with pouring rain. Nosing about desultorily in search of something to do, I come upon a *Penthouse*, worn and torn, with tell-tale stains on all the pages with naked girls. From the tall tales of Frans and his friends I've learned all about 'such things' since an early age, but eager inspections of my own equipment have shown up disheartening shortcomings compared to the claims of the bigger boys. This afternoon, too, the eager erection in my shorts (and oh, the anguish at the thought that Dad may find me in that condition!) remains fruitless. Still, looking at those photographs, for the first time in my life, with all the force of revelation, I suddenly know what the others have been talking about. The discovery leaves me breathless. Still shaky, I steal to the door to make sure the grownups are still busy, and then, in my first experience of real sin, tear the provocative pages from the magazine, shove them under my shirt (I am wearing a thick sweater over it), and hide away the *Penthouse* again. The afterglow of my discovery is still throbbing in my body as I sit on the bed, one eager hand in my pocket, staring through the large window at the lightning that stands in the sky like flaming trees.

Then Dad comes to call me and stiff-legged I follow him through the (fortunately) half-dark house, scurry across the backyard in the rain, and jump into the car beside him. We have to drive very slowly, as the dirt road is like a flood coming down: all one can see in the headlights is churning red water. And then we reach the river, no more than a *spruit* really, but in this downpour the low-water bridge is covered by such a churning mass of water that the low white wall at the edge is barely visible. Dad drives resolutely down the slope, hesitates for a moment at the edge of the angry water – big branches come careering over the bridge – and announces that if it is God's will we will get through. Not daring to say it out loud, I think 'If God knows what I've got hidden under this shirt, and I'm sure He does, this is the end.'

But we survive. It is a nightmare driving through that flood – once we actually graze the side wall – but through God's unfathomable mercy or Dad's resolution (or quite simply his mulishness) we make it. However, the plugs must have got wet in the process for we have barely reached the top of the opposite bank when the car stutters and stops in its tracks. We stumble out. Almost instantaneously we are drenched to the skin.

We can still count ourselves lucky. Afterwards we learn that a pick-up that tried to cross the stream later that night has been washed away by the current: the vehicle will be found a few days later several kilometres downstream, but the farmer and his wife who were inside it are never seen again.

I follow Dad at a trot. Where to? I have no idea. Neither, as far as I can make out, does Dad. Only the two of us in this night of black water above us, below us, all around us; and in that torrent Dad's torch is a fart against thunder. Were it not for the terrifying, never-ending lightning we might well get lost for good. At long last, somewhere in the distance through the streaming rain, miraculously, there is a dull glow of light. And, as we trudge closer, a small square building with a verandah, a farm store with a few rooms added at the back where the shopkeeper lives. Never again will I see a Joko advertisement without remembering this night. In one of the back rooms there is light, a dull orange glare caused, as I discover when the owner opens to Pa's urgent knocking, by an ordinary lantern. The storm has blown out the electricity. Stooped, tanned, with the large rough hands of a labourer, the stranger stands in the orange doorway, his hollow cheeks unshaven, eyes bleary and circled with red, a heavy smell of brandy on his breath. Dumbly he stares at us.

An equally decrepit woman wearing a dirty flowery apron over her dress appears in an inside door, her hair gathered in a straggly bun behind her narrow beaked head. 'Who is it, Lewies?'

'People.'

'Well, aren't you going to ask them in? They must be soaked. I told you someone would turn up.'

Dripping wet, we go inside and stop on the worn linoleum where dark puddles soon form around our feet. In the dull light of the lantern on the cluttered dining table in one corner one can see the lugubrious shapes of furniture here and there: the room is evidently part dining-room, part lounge; but in the far corner there are a stove and a sink as well; two oval frames surround the stark faces of ancestors staring ferociously into the gloom.

From another room comes, suddenly, a sound: not quite human, more like the moan of some animal.

'I'll go,' says the woman and she goes out, moving so silently on her slippered feet that one cannot be sure she has been there at all.

The man makes a helpless gesture in the direction his wife has gone in, mumbling with sunken toothless gums, 'It's my mother-in-law. She's all rotten with cancer. My *bakkie* broke down, so we were hoping somebody would come to give us a hand.'

'My car stopped down there at the stream,' Dad explains.

'You don't happen to be a doctor?'

'No, I'm a teacher.'

'Oh well, that's no use then. When the Lord does decide to send someone it's always the wrong kind. You can count on that.' The blasphemous remark sounds strangely resigned in that man's mouth.

'Perhaps we can first try to start up my car again. Then we can go and look for help.'

The woman appears in the doorway again. 'Can the man help us, Lewies? Ma is very bad now.'

The rest of the night will remain a dark smudge on my memory, with only a few moments standing out in sharp relief. Dad going out into the night with the man, leaving me behind, pressed against the wall, numb with terror, too scared to sit down. The woman moving soundlessly between the bedroom and the living-room like a thin dark ghost. The sounds from next door, like the lowing of a cow, but muted, as if they come from very far away. The smell in that dusky interior, a smell I will associate with death for ever after. The ancestral faces of the people in the oval frames. The searing knowledge of the sinful pictures pressed against my body under my clothes like the fox concealed by the Spartan boy.

At some stage Dad and the man come back, streaming with dark rain, their errand futile.

'Won't you come and have a look at her anyway, Mister?' the woman asks dully.

'But Madam, I –'

'Even if you will only read something to her.'

In a small dark huddle the grownups move past the light of the lantern towards the inside door, the men still dripping with water. From the threshold the woman looks back at me: 'You can come too, my boy. It's always a good thing.'

(Good for what? For whom? I have still not found an answer.)

I am too scared to move, but I cannot refuse. I am intimidated by those evil eyes staring at me from the photographs so accusingly, *knowingly*. And in spite of everything I have to admit to morbid curiosity as well. *Rotten with cancer*. What does that look like?

There isn't much to see. Beside the huge canopied bed in the room next door a short candle stands burning in a saucer, flickering in an invisible draught (from the hereafter?), making it difficult to distinguish between sight and imagination. Something resembling a human frame lies lost among the crumpled sheets and pillows: a small skull with a few wisps of hair stuck to it, a large bony yellow nose like the beak of an exotic bird, sunken red eyes; and two large gnarled talons clutching the edge of the blanket. Covering everything else like a visible sheet is the sour, unearthly smell of death. My stomach is scorched by the still-damp pages of my sin. Monstrous shadows on the walls. Dad's low droning voice – the only reassuring thing about this night – interrupted regularly by the inhuman lowing sound from the frail skeleton below the canopy.

After the prayer, as we begin to move away, there is a different sound from the bed. The old creature is trying to speak. Her daughter leans over her, pressing her ear against the oral slit in the skull, holding in her hand the talons clawing at the sheets.

'Yes, Ma. All right, Ma.'

On her soundless feet the woman comes shuffling towards me and places a hand on my shoulder. I pull away in fear, wishing I could make myself invisible, but the hand holds me very tightly. 'Son, my mother has something to tell you.'

Now it is coming, I know. This old creature, already in the clutches of death, whose eyes have located me in the dark, staring at me from the shadows of whatever lies beyond: she *knows*; she has seen everything; she is going to tell. I arch my back. I know that at any moment something inside me may give way and I shall run into the night screaming. But they hem me in. Escape is impossible.

'Come on, Thomas.' Dad's deep strange voice. 'You heard what the auntie said.'

How on earth do I reach that canopied bed? All I shall remember to the end of my life is the sour smell from that cavernous hairy mouth. She whispers so softly I have to press my head right against her to hear.

'Sonny.' A confused mumbling. Her clammy death's breath inside my ear. Then I can make it out: 'Sonny – the – Kaffirs – are – coming.'

Then, somehow, we are back in the front room where the lantern is still glowing grimly in the gloom. And at last I scrape together the courage to whisper, 'Dad, I – I got to go and pee, Dad.'

It is sheer terror going out into that stormy night. Even worse is the fear that Dad may offer to go with me. For what I have to do I can only do alone. It is a duty I have to perform, both exorcism and sacrifice, to persuade God to withdraw death from this wretched little house and remove me from the reach of evil. There is no other way: I *have* to do it; and without delay.

Clutching Dad's torch I creep into the night, crossing the evil howling space that must be the backyard, into the dingy outdoor toilet. There I take the crumpled damp photographs from under my shirt, flatten them with infinite care – risking one last breathless, urgent, terrified look at their blatant sexuality now unreal and defused in that uncertain light – and drop them, one by one, into the pit. Spiders flicker soundlessly along the walls.

Stumbling through the rain I hurry back; there are demons grabbing at my heels as I run, crashing back into the house with something like a sob breaking from my chest.

Some time afterwards – but whether it is minutes or hours later I cannot tell – Dad and I follow our morose host through the house to the store in front where, in the light of a candle steadied in its own wax on a dark counter, we take turns with a pocket knife to scrape pilchards in tomato sauce from an open can, while the man stands slumped at the end of the counter pouring brandy from a flat halfjack into a tin mug and gulping it down.

Later the man brings a mattress stuffed with mealie leaves which he throws down in a corner, and a kaross of jackal-skins to cover us, a foul-smelling thing that has clearly not been cured properly.

It must be from pure exhaustion that I eventually fall asleep behind Dad's back on that scratchy, rustling mattress under the smelly kaross; but it is a sleep disturbed by a mixture of nightmares and dreams of lust.

In the early dawn, it is still dark, we are awakened by the stranger, now clad in an old-fashioned striped flannel shift which barely covers his hairy legs down to the knees – he looks like a baboon spider, I think, not sure whether I am awake or still entangled in dreams – still (or again) carrying the candle, which shows up his eye-sockets like those of a skull. 'Mister,' he announces in a tone of awe, 'the old lady has gone out.' Adding as an afterthought, 'It pleased the Lord.' On the counter the open pilchard-can still stands. And the whole house is pervaded with the smell of death nothing can ward off any longer.

And it is the same feeling of having drifted loose from all my moorings, out of touch with all that used to be familiar, which haunts me tonight – an early traveller with nothing to guide him but a map that says, *Here be monsters* – in this suburb of Hatfield, in Pretoria, in my brother's house. –

When at last he emerged from the airport building with the rest of the crowd, herded out, like sheep, by the police, Thomas avoided the Holiday Inn bus and got into the one from Southern Sun, shook his head absently when the driver enquired about his luggage and, ten minutes later, dialled from one of the public telephones in the hotel the emergency number the young Indian man had given him.

'Peter Ward,' he said quickly, covering the mouthpiece with his hand. (Wondering anxiously for a moment whether he should have said 'Dennis Johnstone'.)

A momentary silence. Then an unfamiliar male voice replied, 'Where were you? Someone went to look for you, but he phoned in to say he couldn't find you.'

'I had to go out. Something's happened.'

'Where are you now?'

'In the flat.' Strange how it all came back, took over, all the codes memorised before, untouched by the last half-hour.

'Stay right there. Give us forty-five minutes, an hour. Patrick will come to pick you up. Wait at the poolside.'

A brilliant, translucent turquoise, the rectangle of water lay in the embrace of the mock-Spanish building. Colourful sunshades bloomed on the lawn like large tropical flowers; in their shade people sat drinking or talking while children splashed and cavorted. Perspiring black waiters, immaculate and exotic like penguins, moved to and fro performing balancing feats with their trays (tinkling ice-cubes in tall glasses, minute paper parasols), stepping deftly over sprawling half-naked bodies: men with hairy chests, men with unbuttoned white shirts and golden chains, men with bulging stomachs, plump mother figures, blonde or dark straight-haired nymphs in tangas, with long tanned legs, perfect navels, breasts almost bare, smooth buttocks flickering with muscles, oiled satin skin. For all of them it was the end of another perfect day, perfumed with coconut oil, in the luxurious caress of the late sun on emerald grass among palms: an ad for the perfect life, come and relax in Africa. Thomas was the only one to sit hunched up, contracted as if in cramp, at his table under a yellow and blue shade, turning his glass of orange juice round and round. This wasn't possible: the simple terrifying discovery of life going on as if nothing at all had happened. It ought not be possible. A mere kilometre, perhaps two, from here – Yet he'd been there; he was here now. Unbelieving, absent, petrified, he stared at his glass.

It was a shortish middle-aged man, bald, with an unbuttoned lemon-yellow long-sleeved shirt (the initials of Yves Saint-Laurent on the pocket), who finally came through the french doors and hovered at the edge of the lawn, looking left and right, his dark glasses pushed up on his forehead. He might have been anybody, but when Thomas approached him casually and asked, 'Patrick?', he reacted immediately. They returned to the white table under the shade to have a drink – he could choke with the tension, but he realised the show of nonchalance had to be maintained – before Patrick escorted him to a small white Mazda in the parking lot.

He unlocked it, leaned over to open the door for Thomas from the inside, and asked briefly as they drove off, 'What happened?'

'They shot Nina.' Even when he heard himself say it he could not believe it.

'Shit.' The tanned face grew a shade paler. 'You sure?'

'It happened right in front of me.' He stared straight in front of him. 'I was sent to warn her, but I was too late.'

'Vic went to look for you at the Inn.'

'–'

'You sure they didn't notice you?'

'I made absolutely sure.'

Patrick took off his dark glasses and, steering slowly with his elbows, wiped the lenses with a handkerchief. Then his perspiring forehead. Slowly and meticulously, as if he was trying to arrange his thoughts. His eyes looked younger than they had appeared through the glasses, worried. Then, once again, 'Shit.'

'What do we do now?'

'We'll have to get you to a safe place first.'

Thomas said impulsively, 'I have some good friends in Soweto. I suppose you know them? – Jakes, and Zeke.'

'Don't be daft. You'll stick out like a dog's balls. You want to land them all in trouble? No, you better come with me. I'll think of something.'

That was when it occurred to him: 'I have a brother in Pretoria. Nobody will look for me there. He works at Armscor, of all places.'

'I don't believe it.' Patrick looked sharply at him, then laughed, shaking his head. 'That's obscene. Will he let you in?'

'We've been at odds all our lives. But we're family.'

'You Boers.' He shook his head again.

'Can you think of a safer place? No one will ever suspect that I've been involved.'

'Suppose your brother isn't home, or something goes wrong?'

'Then I can phone again. I have the number.'

'No. Don't use the same number. Here.' He took a small green notebook and a golden ball-point pen from his shirt pocket and, slowing down, scribbled a number, once more on two lines. Then he hesitated again. 'I'm not sure you should be on your own right now, you know.'

'Please, Patrick.'

'All right then. But phone the moment you need anything. From a public booth.'

'Of course.' He hesitated. 'My things are still in the Inn.'

'We can stop there. I'll fetch them for you. You stay in the car. I'm sure no one suspects you, but we don't want to take any chances.'

'How do you think they picked up Nina's tracks?' he asked through his teeth.

'Anybody's guess.'

'She changed her disguise in P.E.'

'Must have been her wounded hand. And I hear she lost her wig in the Cape when you rode off?'

'Yes. Wouldn't have happened if Christine had been with us. Perhaps it was a sign. We should have known not to go through with it after that.'

'Now stop that!' Patrick said sharply. 'What's happened has happened. We're looking at the future now.'

'Easy for you.'

'What do you know about me?' Patrick stared through the windscreen, waiting for a traffic light to change, then took the turn into the loop that leads to the Holiday Inn. The sun was down. On the horizon lay a dark smudge of smoke. A plane taking off drew a steep graph against the blackening sky. On its way somewhere, far away, free.

'Sorry, Patrick.'

'Forget it.'

They stopped in front of the hotel from where, two hours earlier, he'd set out for the airport in the courtesy bus to warn Nina.

'Here's a newspaper,' said Patrick. 'Keep it in front of your face. Give me your room key.'

In less than ten minutes they were on their way.

'I'll get off in Sandton,' said Patrick. 'You can keep the car, it's rented from Avis.' He straightened his legs to reach into his trouser pocket. 'Here's some bucks. Don't outstay your welcome. This weekend at the most.'

On his way to Pretoria – once again, as on the airport clock, time gave a hiccup; when Patrick had been deposited in Sandton they'd agreed to meet the following morning at ten at the Kruger statue on Church Square – he wondered whether it might not be wiser to telephone his brother first. But it was too late now. And if Frans was not at home, he would simply check into a hotel. Perhaps he should do that in any case? He could not really face people tonight, he felt the need to hide, to curl up somewhere out of sight and allow this unbearable pain to heal, to try and understand something about it. (At the moment all he could do, over and over, was obtusely to think her name – Nina, Nina, Nina – but it was like the title of a poem whose words one has forgotten.) On the other hand the idea of family offered a kind of consolation; it might ease the agony. Even if it had to be Frans.

– Nothing has ever bridged the six years that separate us. In your eyes I've always been the irksome little brother tagging after you and your friends, a spoilt brat, an afterthought in a family that had been perfectly balanced while you and Maria were the only siblings, a whining little pest. And to me you've been the difficult, ambiguous older brother: hero and model, but at the same time bully and petty tyrant, whose achievements at school – in application, zeal, neatness, obedience, in rugby or cadets, in impossible subjects like maths and science – were held up to me by parents and teachers alike as examples of 'what can be done'. You and Maria were close, in spite of the gulf of gender, because at least there is only a year's difference between you; and at school she was as bright as you were. Whereas I – ('Oh, Mrs Landman' – I heard with my own ears my class teacher say this to Mum – 'it's not that the boy isn't gifted, his IQ is among the highest in his class, but he can be so contrary.') Faced with a project I liked – history, geography, art – I easily obtained top marks in the class. But in tests or exams there was always trouble. Even in my finals I would write a paper only until, in my calculation, I had enough marks to pass – then I'd up and leave. ('Why waste my time and the examiner's? I know I can do the work. So what am I supposed to prove? What's in a symbol?') You were head boy in your time, Maria head girl. Everybody expected me to follow in your footsteps. But I didn't. ('It isn't easy to say it to your face, Mrs Landman, but one really cannot rely on Thomas. He can be so recalcitrant. The other day he stood with his hands in his pockets while we sang the anthem.') You came down on me, Frans, like a mountain of shit. (By that time you had already blazed your trail through university to a high-profile job at the CSIR.) 'Thomas, do you realise how you've let Dad and Mum down? They were *expecting* you to become head boy. I honestly don't know what's going to become of you yet. There's such an irresponsible streak in you.' I was more amused than surprised. 'What makes it such a big deal to be head boy, Frans? All the prefects are a pain in the backside.' You: 'What do you think will happen if we all adopt such an attitude?' I: 'Who are "we all"?' You were getting impatient: 'We Afrikaners, of course. How do you think we managed, a handful of us against a great mass of English and blacks, to get to the top? There was only one way: by being the best. In everything. We can't afford to let up. If we give them half a chance they'll step right over us.' I yawned. 'Ag don't be such a bore, man. There's more to life than that.' You, in your condescending tone: 'You can be so flippant.' I hurled a magazine at you, laughing: 'Don't put up such a holy face, Frans. That girl on the beach the other day, was it the future of Afrikanerdom the two of you discussed in the evenings when you drove into the dunes in Dad's car? One night she even lost her bra under the seat.' You were furious: 'Thomas, you're talking absolute nonsense!' I rolled over on my back, laughing: 'Instead of preaching to me you should thank your stars it was I who found it. Can you imagine what Dad would have said?' And so on. All these years. –

It was Frans himself who opened the front door of the house in a lane where street lights shone a dark green through dense jacaranda foliage. He was shorter than Thomas, more sturdily built, tanned, in a light green safari suit. For a moment, nonplussed, incredulous, he stared at his visitor.

'Frans? Don't you know me any more?'

'Good heavens, Thomas.' Then he paused, evidently in two minds about the visit. Perhaps to win time, he asked guardedly, 'What brings you back to civilisation?'

'I've been in Johburg these last two weeks and the weekend suddenly came free –'

'You could have phoned.'

'Look, if it's inconvenient, I can always –' Now he regretted having come at all. It would have been much better to go to earth in an anonymous hotel room. (Nina, Nina –!)

'What have you done to your hair?' Frans asked, disapproving. 'For a moment I didn't recognise you. And the suit and tie? I don't know you like this.' A pause. 'You haven't turned queer, have you?'

'No.' He grinned, embarrassed. 'I just thought it was time to do something about my image.'

In the inside door of the tall entrance hall behind Frans his wife appeared, Belinda, carrying a baby on her hip and trailing behind her two small boys with crew cuts, the younger proudly baring gap-toothed gums. 'Frans? Who is it?'

'Guess.' Frans stood aside. 'The prodigal son. Without a word of warning.'

'My goodness, Thomas.' Belinda appeared tired, worn down, her long hair unbrushed, without make-up; but in an arch way, recognising him, she began to bloom. 'Well, why don't you come in, for goodness sake.'

The hall was impressive, almost overwhelming (the moment he entered he remembered: how could he ever have forgotten?): a full two storeys high, all four walls covered in hunting trophies, the mounted heads of kudu, buffalo, nyala, oryx, eland, warthogs, wildebeest, a black rhino, the entire long neck of a giraffe; and on the slate floor – smoothly polished flagstones of different colours – were two leopard skins and a lion skin, the great male maned head stuffed with awesome kitsch realism, mouth gaping, yellow eyes flaring. The inside door, cut out in a tall arch, was flanked by two great elephant tusks which repeated the curve of the opening. And, in the corner, an elephant trunk mounted as a standing lamp.

Frans, with a rush of boyish excitement: 'You remember these? Look, here's a few I'm sure you haven't seen before. And next week I'm getting another lion. Shot it in Botswana last year.'

Whereupon the two boys (six and eight? five and seven?) took over in eager syncopated rhythms: 'Uncle Thomas, have you seen this one –?' 'You know what this is?' 'Uncle, uncle, my dad says, next year –' 'Uncle Thomas, can I show you –?'

Belinda's cat's eyes were smouldering as she purred, 'Are you staying over, Thomas? It's been *such* a long time –'

The baby on her hip broke wind and vomited milk on the front of her dress.

'You won't know this one either,' said Frans, indicating the baby.

'Maria junior. We're fruitful and multiplying. As long as Belinda's figure is up to it.' (But already her figure was broadening, loosening up, becoming stout around the hips.)

'Ag, Frans,' she protested, blushing, but without taking her eyes off Thomas, as if to coax approval from him.

'In that case you can have a dozen,' he said gallantly, shamelessly. 'She still doesn't look a day older than twenty.'

'Uncle Thomas, uncle, uncle –!' The boys were pulling him by the arms.

'Come on, Belinda,' Frans said sternly, 'get the kids out of the way. Sophie can look after them. And ask Agnes to make us something for supper.'

'I think Sophie and them have gone to bed already, Frans. They had a long day between them.'

'Then wake them up. They're getting spoilt in this house.'

Sophie, he learned after Belinda had dragged out the two protesting boys and the hiccuping baby, was a real gem. Thomas probably hadn't heard yet, but Frans had bought himself a small farm in the Bushveld near Warmbaths – 'very primitive, pure Africa, just a couple of rondavels and a *lapa*' – and the old foreman's extended family had grown so alarmingly that something had to be done about putting the people to better use. Consequently young Sophie and her elder brother Filemon had been brought from the farm with their mother Agnes to run this place, the older woman as 'house girl', Sophie as nanny, Filemon as gardener.

'The good old indenture system?' Thomas couldn't help asking. (Watch out, he checked himself immediately: no matter what happened, this time he had to play it cool.)

For a moment Frans stared hard at him, his eyes narrowed; then – fortunately – decided to treat it as a joke. 'Still the pale pink liberal?' he said forgivingly, clearly conscious of putting a younger brother down. 'What do you people understand about these things anyway? I tell you, on the farm they breed like flies, there isn't enough food for them all. Whereas here –' He rubbed his hands with satisfaction. 'You can ask them yourself. They're practically part of the family. They have everything they need; wherever we go, Sophie goes with – last month she even flew to Durban with us, stayed in our hotel, her own room, room service, the works – and Filemon looks after the house. We don't even need a dog, he's so trustworthy. You see, that's what's so good about it: they're still the salt of the earth, not spoilt or anything. But look' – he went through the arch, followed by Thomas, to the bar, devised from a wine vat, skilfully cut up and varnished in the corner of the sitting-room – 'what about a drink?'

'You have red wine?'

'You Capeys.' He poured himself a brandy, added water, then ducked behind the counter to look for wine.

Thomas inspected the room: squat furniture with mahogany back-rests and legs, a zebra skin among the carpets, a large hi-fi against the far wall, an art book with colour reproductions (from the library, he discovered when he opened it) on the glass-top coffee table; on the walls a few prints (Vermeer's girl with the blue headscarf, a landscape by Erich Mayer) and three original oils – a Gordon Vorster veld scene with springbok and wildebeest; a nude of a coloured girl by Father Claerhout in the Free State; and a portrait, bought in Europe, of a beggar child with huge Spanish eyes brimming with tears – besides a few of Belinda's own watercolours, most of them seascapes on the brink of abstraction. For the rest, on the floor and in the large open spaces on the modular shelves surrounding the TV and video recorder, there were ornaments, predominantly 'ethnic': woodcuts, soapstone sculptures, bottles filled with layers of coloured sand or covered in Ndebele beads, unbaked pots sprouting tall plumed grasses.

'Here you are. Bottoms up!' Frans sat down opposite him on the sofa, took a large mouthful, pulled a contented face. 'Well, well, well. So what brings you here? You say you're in Johburg for a while?'

'A few weeks, yes. A project for *National Geographic*.'

'Slinging mud at the country again?'

'It's a record of our mineral wealth. I'm doing the shots on the gold mines.'

'And for that you'll be talking, no doubt, to all the poor exploited blacks from Lesotho and Mozambique and Zimbabwe who stream in here because they can't get decent jobs in their own countries?'

'No, Frans,' he said patiently, and continued to improvise: 'It deals with the gold itself, the processes of excavating it and refining it and smelting it and so on.'

'How come you're suddenly so meek and mild?' Frans studied him over the rim of his brandy glass. 'Or have you finally got some sense into your head?'

'I suppose we all grow older.'

'Hm.' Frans emptied his glass and got up to fill it again. 'I still don't know what got into you that time you held the exhibition overseas. A bloody disgrace. I mean, how can a man stab his own people in the back like that?'

'Let's not start on that again. You remember all the unpleasantness it caused at home. In front of Mum and Dad, and on Christmas day too.'

'So whose fault was it? You were bloody irresponsible, Thomas. No matter how much they paid you for it.'

'You know very well it wasn't for money.'

'I'm sure that's what Judas also said.'

(The sudden shock of memory: yesterday, was it only yesterday, Nina, on Camps Bay's blond sand, below the Twelve Apostles.)

'Did you watch the news at eight?' he asked abruptly.

'Yes. Why?' Frans sat down again, leaning far back.

He tried to phrase it very casually. 'Just before I left Johburg someone told me they'd heard of a – he wasn't quite sure – an explosion or a shootout at the airport or somewhere. Did they say anything about it?'

'Not as far as I can remember. Almost the whole news was about this morning's explosion in Cape Town. Horrible.' He took another large mouthful. 'But this time, I tell you, those terrorists went too far. The cheek of it. They nearly got the president. Right in front of the Castle. Can you beat it?'

'What do you know about "those terrorists", Frans?' he asked, annoyed. (– Careful, now, for God's sake. –)

Frans settled more comfortably against the cushions. 'I damn well know enough,' he said, stung. 'At least I'm sure I know more than *you* with all your nice little stories from the townships. The moment that lot see a photographer or a journalist on the horizon they come running. And the bloody world press is only too eager to shout it from the rooftops.' He took another big gulp, choking slightly.

'A camera doesn't lie, Frans.'

'Says who? I tell you there's *nothing* that beats a camera when it comes to lying. You ought to know. You shoot what's happening in one square metre and ignore all the kilometres around you. Or don't you call that lying?'

'You prefer to pretend, like the government, that nothing at all is happening?' (– Thomas, you're *asking* for trouble. Stop it. –)

'Look' – Frans sat up on the very edge of the sofa, leaning forward as far as possible, his knees almost touching the floor – 'nobody's saying everything that happens is right. But the government is busy cleaning up the place. It's already a hell of a lot better than a year ago. Thanks to the state of emergency. And even if they overdo it now and then – hell, man, don't you know the stress and the provocation the security forces are working under?'

'You think their opponents are not working under stress and provocation?'

'Thomas.' Frans stood up. 'Look, I won't tolerate –' He restrained himself, but not without effort; sat down again. 'Don't tell me you're now going to condone what this morning's bunch of terrorists did?'

Thomas pulled up his shoulders and busied himself with his wine. Deep in the dark red liquid shuddered the reflection of the light.

'Come on,' Frans insisted. 'Come clean. I want to know exactly where you stand. I have a right to know. I'm your brother.'

'All I'm trying to say, is that we shouldn't be too quick to judge. Even the ones responsible for what happened this morning: don't you think they're just people like you and me?'

'The hell they are!' His brother stood up once more, made a wide detour through the room to compose himself, then topped up his glass which wasn't quite empty yet. He leaned on his elbows on the bar counter. 'Creatures like that aren't human, man. I refuse to accept that. Those five people who got killed – two national servicemen, a young woman, a baby, an old man – all of them innocent – blown to pieces – they said the remains had to be gathered in plastic bags – and all the others who got wounded, who lost arms or legs or eyes or God knows what, confined to wheelchairs for the rest of their lives – *they* were people. While the animals who blew them up – how can you talk about human beings? You're fucked in your head, man. But I'll tell you one thing: they're going to hunt those terrorists down. And once they've caught them, oh Jesus – I tell you, the death penalty is not enough for them. They should be killed slowly, the way they did in the Middle Ages.'

'And you call that civilised, Frans?' He had difficulty controlling his voice. His eyes were burning.

'Who talked about civilised? Those – those things you called human beings – you call *them* civilised?'

'Isn't all this simply a sign of how far things have gone, Frans? Of how close to the abyss we have all come? I mean, the very fact that people can be driven to something like that –'

'Who's driving who? What about everything that's been changed over the last few years, all the reforms we've had, everything that's in the process of changing? And all one gets for it is bloody ingratitude. Why? Sometimes I ask myself whether it's really so far-fetched to think that there are fundamental differences between the races. I mean as far as intelligence is concerned, mental capacity, call it what you will. There must be something organic, something genetic. But even if it was only a difference in culture, they still have about five hundred years to catch up – and that's a generous reckoning.'

'I thought you were a scientist, Frans!'

'At least I'm trying to be realistic. Hell, man, I'm not a racist or anything. I'm just trying to be an ordinary decent Christian. But there are *facts* to be considered, facts you tend to overlook in your nice humane arguments. And those facts tell me that blacks are quite simply not able to handle the things they're shouting for. That's why they react like savages when they get frustrated.'

'Apart from anything else you're saying, you're just taking for granted that this morning's – the people who threw the bomb – that they must be black?' he asked through clenched jaws.

'What else? My God, man, surely you don't think *whites* can do a thing like that?'

'Whites have done it before.'

'Foreigners, perhaps. Irishmen. Jews. Arabs – but they're not really white either, are they?'

'You're talking against your own better reason, Frans.'

'And you're talking shit.'

Frans emerged from behind the counter, without his glass, white in the face, his fists clenched. How many times in the past had it come to this between them? But at that moment Belinda came down the stairs.

'Ag no man, Frans!' she called. 'Don't tell me the two of you are at it again?'

She had changed into a pale blue summer skirt and a white blouse, the two top buttons undone; white sandals. Her dyed blonde hair was hanging loose on her shoulders; she'd evidently taken special trouble with her make-up, particularly the eyeshadow, and she was preceded by an invisible cloud of Anneline Kriel's perfume.

'Hell!' said Frans. 'If you looked like this every evening we'd have had a dozen children by now.'

The blush returned to her cheeks, glowing through the slightly overdone make-up. 'Aren't you going to offer me a drink?' With unnerving ease she raised her voice to shout in the direction of the kitchen, 'Agnes!' Turning back to Frans, she asked, once again in a musical modulation, 'Cane and cream soda, please. I'm feeling reckless tonight.' Followed by a new earsplitting yell to the kitchen.

But nothing materialised from there, and Belinda had to excuse herself for a while. She returned unruffled. 'Food's almost ready.' She took her glass and smiled at Thomas. 'Do you know why she didn't answer when I called? She has a thing about the name, can you imagine? After she chose it herself.'

'What do you mean?' he asked, holding his glass to Frans for a refill.

'She used to be Mary, you see. But when we had the baby and christened her Maria it was a bit confusing, so we asked Mary to choose another name. That's how she became Agnes.' She raised her sea-sick green glass. 'Cheers. And welcome, Thomas.' She crossed one leg over the other, offering him a generous glimpse of long tanned thighs and hail-white panties. 'Well, did you come up north to take all kinds of sexy photos of naked girls?'

'I suppose you're sorry he didn't ask you?' Frans asked, a sting in his voice, a hint of venom which had nothing to do with the earlier tiff.

'I'm afraid he's waited too long,' said Belinda, pouting her full mouth, her eyes turned eagerly to Thomas. 'I've lost my figure.'

'I think you're beautiful,' he said with the chivalry expected of him. 'Just say when.'

'Now don't go over the top, please.' Frans clearly did not approve of the new turn in the conversation. 'You're a mother of three children. In any case, Thomas is doing a thing on the mines.'

'Tough luck,' said Belinda. She cast Thomas an almost yearning look. 'Your work never stays the same for two days running, does it now? And travelling all the time.' She nodded towards Frans. 'Frans too, of course, with his hunting trips every year. But he never takes me with him. I wish you'd speak to him, Thomas.'

'You can't take a busload of children with you,' Frans said curtly. 'Perhaps when they're a bit bigger.'

'And when are *you* going to settle down?' she asked Thomas. 'You must be nearing thirty?'

'I'll be twenty-nine in June.'

'And still no wedding plans? You must have a girl in every city.'
And, when he gave no answer: 'Well?'

'No,' he said quietly. 'There's no one at the moment.'

'Come on, I don't believe you.'

Briefly, he closed his eyes, aware of how tight his scalp had
become, then looked at her again. 'No, it's true.'

'You don't have a girl at all?'

He shook his head, and with a show of fierce concentration tilted
the wine glass to his mouth.

'You men, really. You can be so secretive. I've begun to wonder
whether I shouldn't also take a *skelm* on the sly.' She winked at
Frans. The drink, which she'd emptied surprisingly fast, had brought
the blush back to her cheeks.

'I really don't think it's very funny,' said Frans. 'Shouldn't you go
and check up on Mary-what's-her-name-Agnes?'

She gave him an offended look, swung back her leg – another
sweeping gesture offering Thomas a privileged view – and floated
towards the kitchen.

Frans sighed, disgruntled. 'You must forgive her. Ever since the
baby she's changed a lot. Stroppy. And she doesn't look after herself
the way she used to. You know, tonight's the first night in I don't
know how long that she's put on some make-up. Between the two of
us, brother to brother: every single night she finds a new excuse. If I
didn't pull rank sometimes – and I mean, she isn't even thirty-five
yet. This isn't much of a life for a man.'

'Not for her either, I should imagine,' remarked Thomas.

Frans got up so quickly that he spilled the remains of his drink
on the floor. 'Why are you all ganging up against me?'

'Come on, Frans, it's not so bad.'

Hurt, suspicious, Frans glared at him for a moment, then went
to the bar to pour another drink. A thickset black woman with
permanent lines of weariness carved into her face appeared in the
doorway. 'Baas, the madam says the food is ready.'

'Thank you, Agnes.' He picked up the bottle of red wine he'd
opened for Thomas.

'And the children? Has Sophie put them to sleep?'

'I think so, baas.'

'Then you two can go to bed now, all right? You needn't wait up.
The madam will clear up when we've finished.'

'Thank you, baas.' She nodded to both of them in turn. 'Good
night, baas. Good night, baas.'

'Good night, Agnes.'

'Good night, Mary,' said Thomas.

She gave him a surprised look, glanced anxiously at Frans, and hurried out.

At the table Frans poured the wine, only a half-glass for Belinda.

'You can fill it up,' she demanded.

He hesitated, reluctant, sceptical, but she held out her glass and looked him straight in the eyes. There was a small muscle flickering in his cheek as he poured her glass steadily to the rim, so that she could not avoid spilling a few drops as she moved her hand. No one made any remark about it.

'Shall I say grace?' Frans took Belinda's hand on the table. For an instant she hesitated, then put out hers and placed it on Thomas's. 'For what we are about to receive, may the Lord make us truly thankful. Not because we deserve it, but through thy infinite mercy. Amen.'

'That used to be Dad's prayer,' said Thomas.

Frans looked at him as if he was expecting an explanation, then held out his plate for Belinda to dish out the food.

The macaroni and cheese was savoury, but not one of them ate much. Frans, it transpired, had had some biltong earlier; Belinda was tired, and slightly tipsy. And in the sudden pause brought on by the meal Thomas felt so overcome by all the events of the past day that he had no appetite. The food seemed to curdle in his mouth; it was purely out of a sense of obligation that he emptied his plate. Was it only this morning that they'd left the cottage in Observatory to prepare for what was, then, still ahead of them? And then, this afternoon, that scene through the window. The soundless mime in which he could not intervene, as if it were a film already predetermined, the end fixed, the sudden explosion of sound, the Coke tin rolling past his feet, Nina falling down, trying to crawl on hands and knees, then toppling over, and the slow pool of blood growing larger as he stared.

Belinda, in a warm, suggestive tone: 'What are you thinking about so deeply, Thomas?'

'I'm sorry. I've had a busy day.'

'Who hasn't?' She tensed up suddenly. 'Was that little Maria crying?'

They all pricked up their ears, but there was no sound.

'You're imagining things,' said Frans.

'How old is the little one?' asked Thomas.

'Ten months. She was born last June, when Frans was in Botswana.'

'I'll never hear the end of that,' said Frans. 'But what could I do? It was the chance of a lifetime. And the baby was three weeks early, you must admit.'

'Was that when you shot the last lion?' asked Thomas.

'Ja. I must tell you about it sometime.' He used his fork to dislodge a sliver of tomato between his front teeth. Then chortled with unexpected glee. 'You must come with me one day, I'll show you what Africa really looks like. Did you know I've even been to Uganda? Next year I hope to organise a trip to Zaïre. I still need an okapi head on my wall. Now that's something you don't see every day. Want to go back to Angola too. Even while the war was at its worst one could still go hunting there. Some of my pals in the army organised it. Went along to shoot elephants for Savimbi's boys. Hell, I tell you, there were days it looked like Samson and the Philistines. Carcasses all round. And the tusks! No man, I promise you, you chaps go farting all over Europe and America and heaven knows where, and then you talk about Africa. But has one of you ever set foot across the Limpopo?'

'I've been in a few places,' Thomas said cautiously.

'Like Malawi, I suppose? Or Zimbabwe?'

'There too.'

'Things looking bad in Zimbabwe, hey? You should have seen it when it was still Rhodesia. You can't imagine a place going down the drain so fast. I remember one of the saddest things I ever saw in my life, it was last year we passed through there on our way to Botswana. There was a farm, not far from Wankie – it's got a different name nowadays, but I can't remember it – the people had obviously left in a hell of a hurry. Whole sheds full of oranges. And the orchards covered in the stuff, all fallen on the ground and rotting. Green with mould. And that smell: I swear I'll never forget it. The overripe smell of a world that's been destroyed, a civilisation that's disappeared. For me, that is the smell of Africa. After the white man has left and everything he's built up is falling apart.'

'There's something I read somewhere,' said Thomas quietly. '"We fear Africa, because if we leave it alone it works."'

'*Read*, yes,' Frans snorted. 'I'm talking about reality. About what I've seen with my own two eyes. Not like you liberals who get it all from books.'

'Ag Frans,' said Belinda, 'how can he help it? Not everybody has the chances you have.'

'Well, then he shouldn't pretend he knows all about it.' His voice had a curiously satisfied ring.

'Coffee?' she asked with a small sigh. Without waiting, she stacked the plates to carry them to the kitchen.

'Let me help you,' said Thomas, pushing back his chair.

'Sit down!' Frans ordered.

Belinda brushed a strand of hair from her cheek. The heavy heat had caused her make-up to run. Her face looked greasy now, the eyeshadow had smudged. Above the lamp some moths were turning, round and round.

After some time, Frans asked, 'Smoke?' and got up to retrieve his packet of Winstons from the sideboard.

'No, thanks.'

'Virtuous.' Frans lit his cigarette, allowing the match to burn for a while, watching it intently, before he blew it out. The sharp smell of sulphur remained with them. 'Do you *have* any sins?'

'I want to make sure I'll go to hell one day, so I'm only interested in big ones. The little ones aren't worth the trouble.'

'Don't come to *me* when your number comes up.'

Belinda returned with the coffee. Soon afterwards Frans pushed back his chair and got up.

'Come, there's something I still want to show you.' He went to a closed door next to the one they'd come through, and opened it, turned on a light. There was a flight of stairs running down.

'Can I come with?' asked Belinda.

'Leave this to the boys,' he snapped. Then, relenting, he winked. 'Why don't you wait for me in bed?'

'Where are we going?' asked Thomas. 'Don't tell me you've added a cellar.'

'Better than a cellar.' At the bottom of the stairs Frans took a key from his pocket and unlocked a heavy metal door, then stood aside to let Thomas pass. 'So, what do you say?'

It was a smallish room, a strongroom, with a large collection of guns and rifles resting on hooks in the walls, all of them very obviously new. Even a layman like Thomas could tell that they were of the very best; presumably the most expensive too, each butt so shiny and smooth one could mirror oneself in it; with the latest in telescopic lenses and other accessories and trimmings.

Almost with reverence, Frans lifted one from its hooks and

handed it to Thomas. 'Hold it. Feel it. Look through the visor.'
His eyes were shining with cold fire. 'Isn't she a beauty? Cost you
fifteen thousand in the trade, that's to say if you can get one. I
tell you, no elephant has a chance against it. And this one –' So
it went on.

'But this is a fortune in arms, Frans,' he said at last, his voice
guarded.

'You telling me. I get them through my job, of course.'

'You can run a revolution all on your own.'

'I can bloody well *prevent* a revolution on my own.' His eyes
gleamed with enthusiasm; he was like a child on Christmas
morning.

'Come, let's go,' said Thomas. 'It's stuffy in here.'

'Stuffy, my arse. I've had special air-conditioning installed in here,
man. Night and day.' Reluctantly he stowed away his guns again and
locked up after them; Thomas was already waiting on the stairs.

'Can I give you a hand with your luggage?' Frans asked when they
arrived upstairs again.

'I'll be all right.'

'Oh come on.'

As Thomas pulled his suitcase from the boot – the smart
expensive leather suitcase that had awaited him in his hotel room
– he went cold with shock: the handle still bore the name tag in its
leather frame: *Dennis Johnstone*. He tried to shield it from Frans,
but his brother pushed him aside.

'Here, I'll take it.' Then frowned, and looked askance at Thomas.
'What's this? Picked up the wrong case? Who's Dennis Johnstone?'

'I borrowed it for the weekend,' he said quickly. 'Dennis is
working on the photo project with me. He does the text.'

(How many different people had he been in the course of this
single day? Thomas Landman. A traffic cop. Anton Swanepoel.
Peter Ward. Dennis Johnstone. And how many others were still to
come? Would he ever find his way back through so many different
selves?)

He was perspiring when they reached the bedroom prepared for
him; there were fresh white towels draped over the bedpost. A faint
scent of Belinda's pink perfume still stained the air.

'Got everything you need?'

'Yes, thanks. 'Night, Frans.'

At last, thank God, he was alone.

He had a bath. Crept in under the sheets. But it was too hot to sleep. There was too much to think about. Too much had happened. A lifetime in one day.

Nina. Nina. Nina.

He only became aware of his surroundings again when a sound from the neighbouring room was insinuated into his consciousness. He propped himself up on an elbow to listen. Was someone crying? It wasn't the baby. Belinda? It could only be she. A strange rhythmic moaning sound. As if it was forced out of her. Only after a while did he realise what was going on. He didn't want to hear it. He would have covered his head with the pillow but it was too hot.

The night pressed down heavily on the world.

After some time the house fell silent again. Was she still sobbing quietly? He wanted, and did not want, to hear. But no sound came through the walls: and yet he suspected that it was there.

He was too exhausted to sleep.

Exasperated, he began to page through books and magazines from the shelf beside the bed, but it couldn't hold his attention. Almost with an urge wilfully to inflict pain on himself he opened the *Sun Signs*. Without having meant to – although subconsciously, he realised afterwards, it must have been inevitable – he turned to the Aries chapter. Nina's sign. (On that distant first night she'd said so emphatically, 'I was born under the sign of Neon.') *The Aries Woman*. Cynical, he began to read, discovering after a while that it was indeed hurting. The quote from Carroll:

'But aren't you going to run and help her?' Alice asked . . . 'No use, no use!' said the King. 'She runs so fearfully quick you might as well try to catch a Bandersnatch!'

Now he wanted to put it down, but he couldn't.

This woman is capable of deep passion and mystical idealism, woven together in strange patterns . . . There's something clean and fresh about the utter simplicity of her emotions, but even so, they often get her into waters way over her head –

He turned the pages quickly, trying to force himself to close the book – it was subversive reading – but a last statement broke through his defence: *Don't forget that she bruises easily, in spite of her bright, brave smile.*

Disturbed, he thrust the book back on the shelf. Tried to think of something, anything, else. But now it was haunting him.

But aren't you going to run and help her? No use, no use!
Her bright, brave smile.

He sat up again to listen whether there were still sounds, however muffled, coming from next door, but the house was very silent.

He turned off the light. Heavily the hot night pressed down on him. Once again he followed the tracks of the day's events: whence this feeling that something was eluding him, something he *had* to discover, a key, a clue, something without which he would never be at peace with himself again?

It kept tugging at the loose ends of his thoughts, just beyond the fringe of consciousness. Weary, dejected, he retraced once again his movements through the day, a detective searching for clues. From the whole welter of memories came the instant of their fall on the motorcycle. He saw the wig fly from Nina's head. Saw her crawling on all fours to retrieve it, her hand streaming with blood. Saw the officer coming after her. Heard his own voice shouting in his ears: 'Nina!'

And suddenly he knew that this was why it had all gone wrong. This was how they had managed to trace her, to lie in wait for her at Jan Smuts. They'd known who she was. In spite of all the disguises, all the elaborate precautions. They had heard her name. And it was he who had given it to them.

2

Justin: 'It's never what you've done that's important: what matters is what you doing next.'

3

It was on the front page of the newspaper the next morning. Thomas lay sprawled in a deckchair under a red parasol, reading, beside the pool. Frans had left early, for even if it was Saturday he had work, he'd explained, to catch up with. Belinda was somewhere inside, busy with the baby. The two boys were cavorting in the water with an assortment of small cloned friends.

A female terrorist was shot dead by police last night in the international departure lounge at Jan Smuts airport. According to a police spokesman a hand grenade was found on her, and if it had not been for the efficient intervention by the security forces acting in self-defence, a large-scale massacre might have resulted in the hall crammed with passengers, or even inside a plane on an international flight. The Minister of Justice has expressed his appreciation to the officers whose alertness had prevented a catastrophe. Five people were taken to the General Hospital afterwards and treated for cuts and bruises, but there were no serious injuries. Neither the identity of the terrorist nor any further information has so far been divulged by the authorities.

According to our information Brigadier Kat Bester of the Special Branch in the Cape Peninsula flew to Johannesburg late last night to confer with his northern colleagues. The possibility of a link between the shooting of the terrorist at Jan Smuts and yesterday morning's horrifying bomb explosion in Cape Town, in which the State President had miraculously escaped death, has not been excluded.

In the meantime the death toll in the Cape explosion rose overnight to six, when the twelve-year old Renier de Wit succumbed to his injuries in Tygerberg Hospital. The other casualties –

He wanted to put down the paper, but was mesmerised by it.

In an interview, the Commissioner of Police confirmed that important clues had been discovered and that a breakthrough in the investigation was expected soon, possibly this weekend. Although there are indications that the leader of the terrorist group, undoubtedly acting under instructions from abroad, may already have skipped the country, presumably to Swaziland, the police net around the remaining killers is tightening rapidly. The State President, who is kept informed of the latest developments on an ongoing basis, has personally instructed –

– When we were small, do you remember, Frans, we often played the immemorial game in which all the children are lined up, and the one at the beginning of the line whispers in his neighbour's ear a sentence he has thought up, and the message is then transmitted from one end of the line to the other. The child at the far end has to repeat out loud what he has heard. And then we all fell about screaming with laughter at the mangled way in which the original message had reached its destination. 'Two birds in a tree' might be transformed into something like 'Who heard the scream?' I'm beginning to think that newspapers operate on the same principle. And not just newspapers. Perhaps it is true of all our attempts to chronicle our history or our time. My own reconstruction of all the generations of Landmans that have produced me. How can one ever get to what 'really' happened? (And this anguish is compounded by another: suppose the beginning was as incomprehensible, made as little sense, as the end? suppose there *was* nothing to begin with? what substance can we claim?)

Is this not also the basis of public life? The very organisation of society, of government, makes it possible – inevitable – that all decisions are taken at a remove, that all information is filtered through innumerable membranes. No one is ever directly involved any more. No one need feel guilty or responsible. In earlier times people had to wage their wars through physical combat; the hunter had to gore his prey, or cut its throat, with his own hand. Today we live in a time of increasing distance, space, between the actor and his actions. Even your achievements as a hunter, Frans: your rifles and telescopic sights and God knows what else: it is no longer a simple, direct relationship between yourself and some animal. An entire science has interposed itself between you. Everything has become abstract, disembodied. What used to be immediate and original loses its meaning in distance and indeterminacy. If I whisper 'Two birds in a tree' in someone's ear, I need not take responsibility if it emerges at the other side as 'Who heard the scream?' That is the way we expect it to be. We *bank* on disembodiment and abstraction. The very finger that presses the red button in an ultimate war has been absolved of responsibility in advance, as all it does is execute some anonymous decision or instruction, unleashing a war that takes place at a distance. The victims are real enough; but the chain of events resulting in their destruction stops at a distance. Which makes ever-increasing violence possible, even, ironically, indispensable, as a kind of scream *against* abstraction and distancing. No one is *present* any more. No message is ever fresh, or immediate, or innocent.

I wonder whether you will ever understand, Frans, if you were to find out what I have done? That *this* was the reason for it, the explanation for my involvement? I had to be present, I had to be *there*. (And then even that went awry: we were already out of reach when the explosion came: we were *not* there, not on the spot. Something, I fear, will remain forever incomplete.) –

– He never played rugby. Not that I want to blame that for everything, of course! But it should have been a warning to us. And once one has become aware of a thing like that, there's a whole lot of other signs too. If only we'd noticed them in time. But one always tends to find excuses for one's family. I mean, he *is* my brother. All right, so we never got on well, the age difference between us was too big. But he was my brother.

Even the weekend he turned up so unexpectedly on our doorstep, I never suspected a thing. Although I realise now that something was evidently very wrong. It's easy, with hindsight, to be wise. But when you're confronted with it out of the blue like that, you're blind. Of course there was much about him that irritated me no end. The way Belinda sucked up to him, which he actually encouraged by suggesting in a roundabout way that she pose in the nude for him. I mean, honestly. And the way he tried to condone the bomb attack, finding all sorts of excuses for the terrorists, that kind of thing. Even so, I didn't suspect him. Also, I didn't feel like quarrelling with him. I was actually glad that he'd decided to come and look us up. He'd hardly ever done that before. Now, of course, it's obvious why he came. Shamelessly using us. But at that stage I was prepared to believe that family ties still mattered to him. It's something I've always regarded as important.

To think how we went out of our way to make him feel at home. Even arranged a barbecue for Sunday. He wasn't familiar with our Transvaal *pap* and I wanted to offer him a special treat. With a couple of good friends I'd specially invited over so that he could meet the kind of people he no longer seemed to associate with. I wanted him to rediscover what genuine, generous people there really are among us Afrikaners. He'd strayed from the fold so long ago. Always ready to lash out against his own people, but what did he really know about them? Ever since he got mixed up with journalists and agitators he began to forget where his true roots were.

It was only too obvious on the Sunday, when he deliberately provoked arguments with all my friends. I was irked by his intolerance. That was not how Mum and Dad had brought us up. But I'm afraid it was already too late by then, he'd long passed the point of no return. I still tried my best, of course, to act as peacemaker between him and the other guests, but it wasn't easy. Later he withdrew completely. As he'd done on the Saturday, too, come to think of it, when I had to go to work and Belinda offered to take him in to town. It was seldom enough he came to Pretoria, and it was quite a sacrifice for her to leave the house and the children and everything just like that to show him around: but then, what did he do? Announced haughtily that he wanted to go by himself.

And when he came home, late for lunch and everything, what did he bring with him? The *Weekly Mail*. Which is not a newspaper I like to see in my house. But once again, for the sake of peace and quiet in the family, I didn't say a word. Just had the rag disposed of quietly after he'd finished reading it. The children are still small, but I didn't want one of them to look at that kind of filth.

The only occasion during the whole weekend when he did show enthusiasm for anything, and that was only too obvious, was when I showed him my collection of guns. Once again I must confess that at the time I saw nothing untoward in it, since I obviously had no suspicion of the blood already on his hands. Only now do I realise the unnatural, unhealthy eagerness in his reaction. He couldn't get enough of handling the guns. In fact, on the Sunday, can you imagine the temerity?, on the Sunday, I say, he could hardly wait to see the guns again. Thinking that he was truly interested, and that we'd finally found a base for future understanding, I unsuspectingly accompanied him back to the strongroom. Not even when he started taking photographs of my collection did I smell a rat. In retrospect, of course, his motives became only too transparent, but on that relaxed morning I let him have his way, and even encouraged him, only too relieved for once to see him interested in something that was important to me. Thank God he never succeeded in achieving his diabolic ends with those photographs. I never breathed a word about this to Mum and Dad either, they've been going through deep enough waters as it is since the news broke.

Looking back today, I cannot but blame myself for not having sensed something amiss in his attitude. But how could I have imagined in my wildest dreams what was going on? He'd always pretended to be such a pacifist. It just shows how one can misjudge even those closest to oneself. I have already mentioned that he never played rugby at school. Even in those days we regarded him as something of a sissy. Only once, when he was about nine or ten, we finally managed to coax him into coming with us on a hunt. The poor kid was so desperate about doing things with us older boys. And from our point of view, he couldn't be allowed to remain a sissy all his life. One weekend we stayed on the farm of a friend, Hendrik. His father, Oom Kerneels, was a difficult man who wouldn't think twice of laying into you with his sjambok if you happened to wound an animal. And he never allowed the boys to go hunting on their own when there was no grownup present. Except for that Saturday, when for some reason he relented. What happened then still gives me nightmares. We were deep in the veld when we saw something moving in a thicket below us. Immediately we went down on all fours to stalk it. Me, my friend Hendrik, and Thomas. In such circumstances one waits until you're close enough, and below the wind. You've got to have a clear view of your target before you shoot. But Thomas, I presume, wanted to impress us, or perhaps he simply couldn't contain his excitement. Whatever the reason, while Hendrik and I were still crawling along through the scrub, we heard Thomas's gun go off right next to us, aiming haphazardly at the invisible animal in the bushes. At first we thought it really was something, for we could see a big black thing falling in its tracks. But when we went closer we saw it was one of the farmer's prize cows.

Afterwards, Hendrik and I tried all we could to explain. I mean, Thomas was a mere child, but the old man brushed us aside and with a mean-looking hippo-hide whip gave Thomas the thrashing of his life. And when we got home, Dad, having been told on the telephone of what had happened, took off his belt and gave it to him again. I honestly thought they were going to flog my little brother to death. I ran to my bedroom and pulled the pillow over my head to shut out the sound. On the other hand, I suppose it really was the only way he could learn his lesson. Except I'm not so sure any more. Thomas never went hunting again. But look at what has become of him. Perhaps it was all driven inside, the way old people used to talk about catching a cold when you have measles. It's the only explanation.

That incident undoubtedly increased the distance between us, as for some reason or other Thomas appeared to blame *me* for what had happened. But I doubt whether we could ever have become close anyway, however much it pains me to admit it. A matter, not just of the age difference, but of temperament.

I have always had the impression that Maria understood him better than I did. But she was even older, which meant that she and I had more in common. On the whole, we have always been a tightly knit family.

How often I yearn back for what I can only describe as the innocence of those times. A happy youth, which prepared me for being a good father to my own children.

Hopefully it will not be long now before we have our fourth. I wouldn't mind having half a dozen. I find it one of the most lamentable phenomena in our country that the birth-rate among whites is declining so alarmingly, while the blacks continue to multiply like vermin. We Afrikaners have traditionally brought up large families. But urbanisation is changing all that. Which wise leader was it who said that we have been able to overcome all temptations except that of prosperity? We have always been at our best in times of suffering. That drove us back to the family as a bastion for society as a whole. If only we could return to the time-honoured practice of rearing large families, I know we should be able to face the future with greater confidence. Surely they cannot just be allowed to carry on breeding like that. It would serve their own interests to be, in a manner of speaking, hamstrung.

Here we are today, almost alone against the world, and against the overwhelming black masses in our own country. Isolation has made it increasingly difficult for us to keep up with the world, but it has also strengthened us. Armscor is a case in point. A shining example, in fact. Today, thanks to international sanctions, we have become self-reliant in terms of arms. We even export to other countries, including African states. I am proud to have a share in this success. Only two months ago I went on that highly confidential mission to Tel Aviv. What would Thomas have said if he'd known of our collaboration with Israel on nuclear arms?! (The Israelis, in turn, don't know that we also supply arms, developed through their technology, to Arab states.) But of course he would have been blinded by the surface facts only. If only he'd had some understanding of the true need of our people, he would never have sided with our enemies. All the arguments we had during that weekend –

Perhaps I should spell it out in no uncertain terms. I am not a racist. I am fundamentally a moderate and well-balanced person. I do not wish anyone to suffer injustice. But then others must also respect *my* right of survival. And that of my people. For no matter how humane or liberal one may be, the interests of one's own people must always come first. It has always been like that.

The most humble animal obeys the instinct to protect its own. The territorial imperative. It is a matter of survival, nothing less. And so no one can expect of me to watch passively while we are ploughed under in the land *we* tamed and civilised. What would have become of the blacks without us? Where would they have been today? This continent is a disgrace to humanity. Give everybody a chance, that's fine by me. But only when he's proved that he is capable of handling responsibility.

This is something Dad has taught me from a very early age. Look at our history, he would say. But it is not a matter of repeating parrot-like what he told me. I know exactly what I'm talking about. I know what death looks like from close by. If Thomas had seen something of it before he got involved with those terrorists, he would have thought twice. I was in Angola myself, in seventy-five. Called up for three months' border service. A difficult time, in my work. Others asked for deferrals, pleading this and that, and got it. It would have been easy for me to argue that I was involved in essential work, that my services could not be dispensed with, that I was serving the army in my own way already; but did I do it? No. I believed I had a duty to fulfil. I was on that long trek up to the outskirts of Luanda, when we tried to make sure the right people took over after independence. Not a soul at home even knew we'd crossed the border. There was all kinds of flak afterwards. But I knew what I was doing there. It was a struggle for civilisation, for Christianity, for values. *That* was what we were defending up there in Angola, before the bloody Americans chickened out and left us with all the chestnuts in the fire.

I don't hate kaffirs. But I have seen with my own eyes what happens when savages take over. Look at Mozambique today. Zimbabwe. Angola. All of them prosperous colonies in their day. And today? Can anyone in his right mind expect me to allow that to happen in South Africa too? Never. That's what I told Thomas when he spoke so glibly about 'negotiating' and 'sharing' and 'mutual respect'.

I wish there had been time over the weekend to drive out to my farm at Warmbaths. I should have liked him to see it. That in itself might have helped. To call a small tract of Africa your own. To possess it. Your own trees. Your own rocks. Your own herds of buck and zebra and giraffe. It does something to a man. It tunes you in to the heartbeat of Africa. It reveals to you what it means to belong *here*, and not to want to belong anywhere else in the world.

There he would have met the blacks who work for me, who depend on me. People who would have died like flies if I hadn't helped them. What has Thomas ever understood of such relationships? Has he ever seen the gratitude in the eyes of a man who knows that he owes his food, his clothes, everything he has and is, to you? The irony is, of course, that so many of those people don't properly appreciate it themselves. Take a boy like Filemon whom I brought from the farm to work here in my garden. I have noticed in recent times that he is no longer the humble, grateful boy he used to be. Started calling me 'sir', instead of 'baas'. One of these days, if he goes on like this, I shall have to let him go. And what will become of him then?

I am trying my utmost, Lord knows, to remain loyal towards a man who through an accident of birth became my brother. Just as I tried that weekend, with such sincerity and so much good will. I guess I should have realised something was amiss when I saw that strange name *Dennis Johnstone* on his suitcase. For all I know there may have been bombs inside. And I carried it to his room myself! If I think of what might have happened – But that is not even necessary. I only have to consider what actually happened. This blot on our family name. An honest and honourable name like Landman. In the long run I may even be forced to resign my job at Armscor. From their point of view it might jeopardise security to keep on their payroll the brother of a terrorist. How can I ever look my friends and acquaintances and superiors in the eye again? I doubt that I can ever lift my head in this country again. I can only entrust myself to the infinite understanding of the Lord. Revenge is His, not mine. And He, I know, will see to it that Thomas will be wailing and gnashing his teeth in the lake that burneth with fire and brimstone, for ever and ever, amen. –

5

On Sunday morning, Thomas stayed in bed late, reluctant, after another bad night, to face the day and other people. He had planned to go to bed early the night before – it had been a turbulent day, especially after he'd come back from his appointment in the city – but it had turned out otherwise. He had spent the evening with the children: he'd been invited to the State Theatre with Frans and Belinda, but he'd used as a pretext the need to update his notes for the *National Geographic* photographs. As soon as their parents had left, the boys descended on Thomas with breathless accounts of their day's exploits; and after an hour or two of energetic games and tussles on the sitting-room floor, they prevailed on him to tell them stories. The baby had been put to bed hours before, but the tired Sophie had been instructed to stay awake and keep an eye on the boys, and she bravely sat up even after Thomas had tried to persuade her that he would take over. ('I can see you're tired, Sophie. Why don't you go to bed? I'll look after them.' 'No baas, the madman he will be angry.' 'Please don't call me "baas".' 'Yes, baas.' Once again he was struck by the young girl's beautiful eyes.)

It was very late before the lively twosome, at last too exhausted to listen to more stories, dropped off and Thomas went to the kitchen to boil a kettle and make some instant coffee. He took Sophie a cup too; she was still sitting on the floor in the lounge. At first she didn't know how to handle it; after a while she carried the cup back to the kitchen where she poured the coffee into one of the enamel mugs set aside for the servants, and returned to her post. He went up to his room, but once again found it impossible to sleep, while his headache, the result of the afternoon's family quarrel, ruled out reading. All he could do was turn off the light and lie on his back in the dark, until long after he'd heard Frans and Belinda return.

He relived their quarrel. He'd been delayed on his way back from the city where he'd met Patrick at the Kruger monument on Church Square – a brief, earnest discussion below the bronze rifle, green with age, of an early Boer freedom fighter below the hulking mass of the dour old president – and arriving home late for lunch, which must have annoyed Belinda, he'd dropped a *Weekly Mail* on the table before pulling out his chair.

'What's that?' asked Frans, an edge of warning in his voice.

'I bought a newspaper.'

'That's no newspaper. It's subversive communist filth.'

'Ag please, Frans,' from Belinda.

'You stay out of this. I won't allow me or my family to be contaminated by a thing like that.' Frans, more and more upset, suddenly jumped up and made a grab for the paper; Thomas tried to prevent it. There was a tussle. With large round eyes the children stared at them. Belinda was standing with a soup ladle in her hand, making helpless gestures in the empty air.

And now, on Sunday morning, for the first time, he took up the crumpled newspaper again and began to page through it, desultorily, grasping at any pretext to postpone for as long as possible his immersion into the new day. Outside, he felt, the moment he left his room, Nina would return with the full force of what had happened. He couldn't face the predictable sensationalism of the Sunday papers (a colour photograph, all blood and broken limbs, spread across the front page of *Rapport*? respectable liberal outrage, redolent of colonial toryism, in the editorial of the *Sunday Times*?). The conversations. The whole terrifying world in which she had happened. At least here, in the unfamiliar guest-room, he could withdraw, even from himself.

But before he was halfway through his crumpled *Weekly Mail*, when the house had just fallen silent after Belinda had left to drive the boys to church or Sunday school, the first commotion of the day broke over him: an explosion of voices like a sudden squall, Belinda, the boys, Frans, all yelling at the same time. He tried to ignore it, but his last peace of mind had been destroyed. After spending a long time in the bath, and shaving, and getting dressed, he finally left his room to face the day, more resigned than fortified.

What had happened, Frans and Belinda reported in syncopation, was that their younger son had disgraced them all on the way to church by jumping from the car at a stop sign and running off. The child had refused point-blank to get back into the car unless she promised never to force him to go to church again. As by that time it was already too late for the service, she'd returned home, where she had vented her frustration on Frans, telling him straight out that she refused to take the boys to church again unless their father went with them; while *he* argued that it was his good right to spend his only free day reading his papers at leisure at home. But first, he announced, the child had to be given the thrashing he deserved, whereupon Belinda intervened, saying he had no right to punish the child if he himself remained at home.

Thomas was spared the embarrassment of being forced to choose sides by the outbreak of the second domestic crisis of the day – this time caused by a snake in the kitchen discovered by Sophie, her mother, and the boys. So great was the pandemonium that Frans was convinced someone must have been bitten; but as, amid all the sound and fury, the snake was preparing quietly to slither out of sight, the anxious inquisition had to be suspended temporarily while Frans went to get a gun from his strongroom and Filemon and family scattered into the yard in search of picks, spades, forks and other weapons, leaving Belinda (the screaming baby pressed to her sagging bosom), to control the boys and keep a peeled eye on the reptile. It was useless for Thomas to try and find out from them whether the snake was really poisonous after all; in the confusion no one was paying any attention to him.

Between them, Frans with his pistol – thank God he hadn't brought the elephant gun – and Filemon with a pick-handle shot and bludgeoned the snake to death, biblically crushing its head: a rather disappointing little thong of a reptile, and whether it had in fact been a poisonous adder or a harmless house snake was now impossible to tell. At least they could show enough destruction for their efforts.

After a while Frans picked up the snake by the tail, measured it with his eyes, and handed it to Filemon for burial in the garden.

'Real bastard, wasn't it?' he remarked, rubbing his hands, an unnerving glint in his eyes. 'Who was expecting this on a peaceful Sunday morning?'

'It just shows,' Thomas said, with an irony that went unnoticed, 'one can never relax one's guard. This *is* Africa.'

'Not in my house it isn't,' Frans said, indignant.

From there it wasn't far to the next crisis: the boys diving into the pool in spite of a ban on Sunday swimming. This time not even Belinda tried to avert the deserved punishment. And this third commotion had barely subsided when the guests started arriving in their BMWs (only one turned up in his wife's battered Volkswagen) and preparations were made for the barbecue.

Thomas would have liked to withdraw from it, but he couldn't so openly offend his brother, not while relations in the household were already under so much strain. There were four or five couples, most of them with children; and it soon transpired that this was a long-established custom on Sundays, each week at a different home, whether for a straight Boer *braai*, or a Chinese barbecue, or the dubious delights of *potjiekos*, a hotchpotch in an iron pot. Husbands named Dolf or Daan or Marius or Quintus; wives whose names sounded like washing powder or insect repellent; men wearing Rolex watches (occasionally two on one wrist, one showing South African time, the other the hour in New York or Tokyo), in shorts or long white slacks, in Lacoste or Pierre Cardin shirts; women drinking Perrier or brandy-and-Coke, and flashing chunky ethnic jewellery round necks or arms. Among them (Thomas found it impossible afterwards to match names and occupations) were, as far as he could make out, an economist, a top broadcasting official, a lawyer, the MD of an advertising firm, someone from the Council for Scientific and Industrial Research.

For the general peace of mind (this, too, appeared to be an accepted custom) the domestic ban on Sunday swimming was suspended and the Landman children were allowed to join their friends, in a steady pool of sound, in the water forbidden them an hour earlier. Occasionally, more from habit than with much conviction, one of the fathers would roar a dire threat or warning in their direction, but without any noticeable effect on the volume. In any case, the grownups were much too involved in doing their own thing: the men gathered in a circle around the slasto barbecue, clutching cans of beer or crystal glasses of whisky, some sporting cloth hats against the sun; the women, initially, indoors, making salads or putting babies to sleep or accompanying Belinda on esoteric conducted tours into the hidden recesses of bedrooms or bathrooms, before they emerged to drape themselves, like Dali watches, over deckchairs at the far end of the pool among the cycads. Metamorphosed into skimpy floral sunsuits or bright bikinis, in a slither of imported suntan lotions, they were locked in urgent discussion of liposuctions, weigh-less, goodwill drives among domestic servants, progressive women's organisations, the scholastic achievements of their offspring, and various endeavours in ballet, elocution, drama, athletics, the maintenance of gardens stocked exclusively with rare indigenous trees and shrubs, Portuguese farmers from smallholdings on the outskirts of the city who could be relied upon to supply special products at special moments, private dressmakers and new boutiques, an exhibition at the Art Gallery, the increase in servants' wages, a sensational rape in Lynnwood, the latest inside information about who'd been hired or fired by the SABC, travels to Taiwan and Thailand, Chile, Mauritius or Nepal, breast-feeding, who-was-sleeping-with-whom in the Cabinet, AIDS in Africa, microwave recipes, courses in pottery, French, and target shooting.

Eager to find a reason not to be drawn into either of the two groups, Thomas went inside to fetch his camera and (amid the eager protests of the ladies) started wandering about taking photographs. But from time to time he had no choice but to join the men again. How many times had he heard those conversations? Perhaps, he thought, this was the worst of all: a country choking in its own clichés, a country no longer able to express its realities in anything but slogans.

The new rugby season. The latest about the state president. But have you heard this one? Keep your voices down, the girls are listening. And Ilandré is as suspicious as hell nowadays, all to do with that new little secretary I hired, I must have told you guys about her, gave it to her last Wednesday, Ilandré thought I was at golf, but Jesus, can she do it? – she's got a way of churning that arse of hers, sort of round-and-sideways, round-and-sideways, makes you see stars in bright daylight. Which reminds me: you heard the one about van der Merwe who got married to the whore? Followed by a flood of other stories, until the conversation moved, predictably, from sex to business. The latest on the Stock Exchange. Properties. Invest in uranium. In platinum. In gold. And in case you decide it's time to get your money out of the country: provided you're prepared to do your bit, you can get help from right inside the Cabinet. *Now*'s the time to bring in the profits. As well as to make provision for future knocks, in case the explosion hits us. Matter of using your head. Your contacts. Your influence. At the end of the day it's the guy with bucks in his back pocket who survives. If you play this thing right, no bomb needs to scare you.

– Shall I throw another bomb into your midst? Tell you about my meeting with Patrick at the Kruger statue yesterday morning? Tell you which organisation *he* represents? Give you inside information about *our* discussion? It all seems to belong to another country, another as yet undiscovered planet. –

The conversation wended its inexorable way from business to politics.

'Had that American with us yesterday.' (Who was talking? The economist, most likely; or perhaps the SABC man: after a while they all became interchangeable.) 'All righteous indignation about the way we're oppressing our blacks. So I asked him, Haven't you ever travelled in this world? Can't you open your eyes? No matter where you go, I told him, there's Catholics blowing up Protestants, or Protestants blowing up Catholics, Jews oppressing Arabs or Arabs killing Jews, Muslims and Hindus trying to exterminate one another, Australians treating Aborigines like animals, or Norwegians lording it over Lapps, Canadians over Red Indians, Sikhs setting fire to others if they're not set on fire themselves, indigenous peoples hunted like game from helicopters, women sold as slaves, you name it. So why single us out? It's because we're too honest to lie about it. I told him. The simplest and cheapest solution for all our problems in this country is just to start lying like the rest of the world.'

– Patrick had received confirmation from the Cape. 'Justin and David and Rashid are safe, no need to worry about them. And as far as we know Christine is still in a coma. So she hasn't said a word. And she won't either, even if she regained consciousness. Which means there is no reason they'll ever find out. Just play it cool. The only cause for alarm is this news about Brigadier Bester, who's flown up to Johburg now. He's a bastard. If ever *he* picks up the trail –' I know that, I know only too well: I've met the man. And if Nina hadn't intervened that time, through her father, when they came to pick me up early that morning, I don't know what would have happened. I have no wish to cross his path again. –

Frans: 'You should have told him to take a trip through Africa. Our blacks live in luxury compared to the rest of the continent. They say, in Tanzania –'

Whereupon Thomas interposed, 'Would you like to change places?'

For a moment the hands holding the cans and glasses stiffened; the eyes were turned to him.

'What do you mean?' asked Frans.

'Just what I said. No matter in how much luxury "our" blacks are supposed to live, would you care to change places with any one of them?'

'Have you seen some of those houses in Soweto?' asked Frans, challenging him. 'Bloody palaces, man.'

'What's the use of living in a palace if you cannot even choose where you want to build it? Or if you go out your front door and cannot vote?'

'I'd much rather have a decent house and no vote than to have the vote and beg for food and clothing.'

'Easy for you: you've got it all.'

'But there was a time when we Afrikaners did *not* have it all. The difference between us and them is that instead of grovelling and lamenting to the world how unjustly life was treating us, we set to work and fought our way to the top. Right?'

– 'The best news as far as you are concerned,' Patrick had said, 'is that the Organisation wants you back in the Cape. Nobody has the faintest suspicion that you were involved. But even *if* they knew, the very last place they'll be expecting to find you now is Cape

Town. So that's where you're going to go to earth. Keep the Avis car, we'll extend the lease, and in Cape Town Rashid can give it an overhaul. Just to be safe.' –

'And we didn't use violence either, on our way up,' said the advertising man (or it might have been the lawyer). 'Remember, when Paul Kruger tried to use strong-arm tactics against Britain, he broke his balls. It was only after the Boers gave up the violence game that they started getting somewhere. That's what these blacks can learn from us.'

'There is a difference,' Thomas reminded him. 'No matter how miserable our situation was, we always had the vote. Peaceful means were an *option*. What chances does a black person have?'

'You in favour of violence?' The lawyer (presumably).

– Patrick: 'But you've got to pull yourself together, Thomas. You can't go on thinking about Nina. No matter how hard it is: it's happened, it's over. You hear me? It's over. The struggle goes on, and we need you. All of you, not just part. Especially if Bester is on the job. If he's about, it takes one little slip and you've had it. It's now a battle of wits. And of guts. This is much harder than exploding a bomb. It's what separates the men from the boys. Are you with me?' –

'You can afford to reject violence,' said Thomas, 'because you are the right colour. You're on the right side of the fence. All the power of the state is at your disposal.'

'And you?'

'I'm just trying to imagine how a person might argue who did *not* have all of this going for him. Someone who's got to survive in a system that never stops keeping him "in his place" with whatever force is required.'

'Violence has no place in the mind of any rational being!'

'For you, violence is a philosophical concept,' said Thomas. 'Or a moral one. If you were black, you might discover that it is the only way to stay alive.'

'It's only because they still have so much to learn,' said Frans. 'But, hell, man, we have thousands of years of civilisation behind us.'

'You think it's "civilised" for the government to send Casspirs into a crowd of children or to bulldoze a whole township?'

'If you ask me, the government has shown incredible restraint so far,' said the CSIR man, or perhaps the economist, 'It hasn't even *begun* to flex its muscles yet.'

'And after all, how else do you deal with a bunch of savages? Someone at the Urban Foundation told me the other day how they'd built new houses for these people, decent houses, kitchens and bathrooms, everything. And what happened? They hoard up their coal in the baths and do their cooking on a primus in the back yard. These the people you want to give the vote to?'

Then it became time for anecdotes. The man from the SABC, unless it was the lawyer: 'If you don't believe this, ask Lindalene: her mother, who lives up in Tzaneen, hired a new kitchen boy some time ago, okay? On the very first Sunday they expected the dominee or the school principal for dinner, and she asked the cook whether he knew how to roast a suckling pig. Sure, he said, sure. And did he know how to dish it up, with parsley over the ears and an apple in the mouth? Sure, madam, sure. Right, so when it was time for dinner, this is the gospel truth, hey, you can ask Lindalene, this blockhead brought in the pig on a tray, with two sprigs of parsley draped over his own ears and an apple in his mouth.'

Someone else: 'Reminds me –'

'No, wait, wait, listen to this one first –'

At last, after the roar of laughter had subsided, Frans turned to Thomas and asked, 'Well? What do you have to say now? Still in favour of general franchise?'

'I don't think they are in this country for comic relief,' he said, repressing his anger. 'They're here because it happens to be their land. And *if* they decide one day to allow us to stay on, it'll be – what is that prayer you say at table? – not because we deserve it but from their infinite mercy, amen.'

'Ag, fuck you!' shouted Frans, so loudly that the women at the far side of the pool were startled into silence and even the children for a moment interrupted their screaming and splashing.

'It's thanks to *our* infinite mercy that they're here at all,' said one of the others. 'In the States and in Australia the settlers were sensible enough to eradicate the lot of them: but just because we chose to be decent and Christian, we're treated like lepers.'

In the midst of the argument Thomas said, 'It's strange not to see any vultures circling over us today. Surely they can smell the decaying carcass?'

'Thomas, if you think I'm going to let you insult my friends in my own backyard –'

Briefly, the argument threatened to become ugly. Then one of the guests, who had just torn open a new can, laughed airily:

'Don't worry, Frans. When things really get bad we'll ask your brother here to negotiate with the vultures.'

'Thomas?' Frans jeered. 'Not a hope in hell. The moment things go sour he turns and runs. Always been like that.'

'Well, I'd rather be safe than dead myself,' answered his friend. (The economist, most likely.) '*I* certainly don't intend struggling on in a country razed to the ground. The politicians have fucked up the place to start with, so let them find the solutions. As long as they leave me out of it I'm happy.'

'What makes you think they'll leave you out?'

'Because if they don't I'll up and get out before they can touch me. I've already bought myself a place in Perth.'

'Bloody disgraceful,' said Frans. 'No one will ever see *me* selling out. I'm here to stay.'

'It's all right for you,' teased one of his guests. 'You have the weapons.'

– Patrick: 'I guarantee you, Thomas, the moment the dust has settled we'll smuggle you across the border. You just be patient. What they're going to do now is to round up people in droves. It's already started. That'll keep them busy for a while. You just lie low. We'll get you out of here.' –

At last the discussion had brought Frans where he'd wanted to be all along. 'Have I shown you the baby I got this week?' he asked, beaming. 'Cost me a whole case of whisky for the guy at Customs to bring it in, but thank God I have this contact. Come, I'll show you.'

Excited, the men trooped after him; Thomas was the only one to turn away, squatting on his haunches beside the pool to take a few shots of the children.

But Frans came back from inside, calling, 'Thomas, where are you? You too good for us again? Come on, man.'

'I've already seen it.'

'Not everything.'

Grudgingly he followed. More from petulance than out of interest he even took a few photographs of the eager men handling the guns in the strongroom. Even here, he noticed, not without glee, there were cockroaches scuttling along the walls. Preparing to take over.

– 'Only two things, all right? Put Nina out of your mind. And watch out for the brigadier. The rest we can handle.' –

Frans was clearly disapproving when he saw Thomas at work with his camera. 'You could have asked me first,' he said pointedly. 'What are you going to do with those photos?'

He shrugged, and pulled a face. 'I think I'll send them straight to the enemy.'

General laughter. 'Go on, go on, do it,' said one of the men. 'That'll scare the shit out of them.'

'They're shit-scared as it is,' said one of the others, who had brought along his whisky. 'Biggest lot of cowards you've ever seen. It's obvious from their whole way of fighting. When it's women and children they can blow up, they're bloody heroes. But don't think they'll ever take on anyone their size. Just look at what happened day before yesterday in Cape Town.'

A chuckle from someone: 'Ja, if only they'd aimed better. Then we would all have applauded.'

'It's not something to joke about,' Frans said severely. 'Nobody can stand the turd, all right. But people got killed. Totally innocent people.'

'Who can still plead innocent in this country?' asked Thomas.

'Hell, boys, it's Sunday, we've come over to get away from it all,' one of the guests complained. 'So why are we all so gloomy? Dammit, Frans, we're thirsty.'

'Now you're talking,' said Frans, waxing enthusiastic again. 'Let's go back to the fire. I've soaked those chops in a marinade like no one here has ever tasted before.'

Chapter 4

— People get used to everything. That is what we in the Special Branch bank on. Can work out good or bad. Just a matter of knowing how to use it.

Can be bloody annoying when in the course of an ordinary *braai* or a bunch of men having a beer, you discover how little they care about what's going on. Can't be bothered. Take the first couple of times there were bombs exploding. The first landmines on dirt roads in northern Transvaal. Hell of a rumpus. But then they got used to it. Don't even think twice about it, nowadays, putting up tall security fences all round their farms on the border. Or seeing their kids off to school in army trucks. Or women carrying their guns with them when they take their husbands coffee in the fields. That kind of thing. Big scare when something happens. But give them a month and they're used to it. Keep telling them: you must watch out. You getting too casual. That's what the communists are waiting for. Their eyes peeled, watching us day and night, prowling like predators. Waiting to grab our country. You all think it's just talk. It's *mos* become fashionable to be liberal. You think a leopard can change its spots? Got to be prepared, every minute. So *you* can sleep safely in your beds. Keep on telling them that. But they shrug it off. That's how this thing in the Cape caught them unawares. People are no longer on the alert. That's the bad side of getting used to things.

The good side is this: gives one a hold on them. Matter of time. You start something new, and everybody's shouting blue murder. But you just wait it out. A week, a month, then it becomes quiet again. They get used to it. Look at the State of Emergency. Even inside the Cabinet there were some who protested. What do those shits know about it anyway? We're the ones in the know. The security forces. We take the decisions. Anyway, so they moaned. Not to speak about the newspapers. The English press, my God. Screaming to high heaven. Even the Afrikaans press, in the beginning. But you just wait. Gradually they calm down again. Get used to it. Then we can get on with our job the way we know.

You can bring it all down to that. Suppose someone is brought in for interrogation. In the beginning he's on the defence, right? Can't get through to him, no way. Bloody stone wall. Matter of method. If you know the ropes, he'll break down in the end. But first you got to wait until he gets used to it. Begins to relax, thinks he knows what's going on, can't be surprised any more. Drops his guard. No matter how little. You just got to read the signs right. Like a fish getting used to the bait. Then you tug at the line.

Way I see it, it works particularly well with women. Would have been the same with this one. Nina Jordaan. The one they bagged at Jan Smuts. Never got a chance to lay my own hands on her. Bloody pity. If only they hadn't been so trigger happy. It's one thing to shoot your prey if there's no other way. Or if it no longer matters. Or if it's got to be silenced. But not while it's still useful to you. Even fish you don't just pull out. You first play with it, test it, get to know it, get the feel of it. Otherwise where's the joy?

If only they hadn't got to her first. Would have been a hell of a lot further in this case today. The whole lot rounded up, no doubt about that. It's not arrogance. Just a matter of knowing my job. Would have given anything to bring this one in. Goes back a long way, really. Been waiting for her, you might say. One gets to know one's people. Saw it coming. Perhaps not this particular thing, because then she'd been brought in long ago. But something along the lines. Know her type only too damn well. Only, in those early days there was never enough reason. And there was her father too, of course. The judge. Intervened much too soon. Pity. Because it was clear as daylight the cookie had guts. Like them that way. A game must never be too easy. Give me a fish that knows how to fight back, any day. One that gives you a run for your money. You must put in a day's work to bring it in. Makes you feel it's worth while.

Recognised her immediately. The moment they opened the drawer in the mortuary. Nina Jordaan. Strange feeling you get when things turn out exactly the way you expected. Got a hunch the moment the traffic cop in Cape Town mentioned the name the lightie had called out when she fell. If only the cop hadn't been such a prick. Could have had both of them right there. But we'll get them, don't worry. Promised the president. More than that: promised myself. Before God. Because if it works this time the road is open. Head of

Security: sounds good. Commissioner of Police: sounds even better. Road's clear. That is what matters. Always been those who said Kat Bester couldn't make it. Pa. Wish he was alive today, even he would have had to swallow his words. Admit Kat Bester isn't so hopeless after all. For once he would have seen his son was worthy of him. Had to wait fifty-seven years for this. Now's the chance.

Hard man he was. Hard on the lot of us. Ma, Sis Nakkie, Johanna, Bettie, Sissy, me. Worst on me though. Only son. Example to the rest. The one bearing his name. Pa's own child. Who turned out a disappointment, never could do what was expected of him. Like my books. He said he wasn't bloody well raising a sissy. Wanted to make a man of me. Only way he knew was the strap. Nights he burst into my room at two or three or four o'clock, drunk as a lord, dragged me from the bed, started thrashing away. For the pure hell of it. His way of doing. Don't think a single day went by without the strap. Except for the time he spent in the concentration camp. In the war. For the rest it was hell all the way.

But somehow one learns to take it. There was nothing one could do against him. Strong as an ox. Savage as anything. Anyway, there *was* no way to please him. But one gets wiser. Tried to anyway. Decided to show him. Learned to restrain myself when he beat me. Took it like a man. Clenched my teeth until the world was reeling. Learned to count the blows, way to concentrate the mind. It helps. Anything: anything to keep from crying. So he could *see* his son could take it, his son was tough. A real man. Even began to look forward to the beatings in a way, occasion to show him what his son was made of. But it never made any difference to him at all. If only he could have been alive today. For once he would have been proud of his son.

For that is what it was. Always been. Not ashamed to admit it: Pa was my hero. All the way. All he ever wanted to do was to make a man out of me. A kid a man could be proud of. That's what he was to me. My hero.

During the war Pa was in the OB. In the beginning we didn't know about it. Of course not. It was a secret. Life or death. But then they blew up the railway bridge five miles out of town. Story only came out afterwards. Pa'd known exactly what time the train was coming past. Crammed with men in red tabs on their way to Cape Town to be shipped up north, to fight for Jan Smuts. But that night the train was five minutes late. Had it been on time, that whole trainload of joiners would have been blown sky-high, bridge and all. As it happened it was only the bridge. A week later they came to take Pa away. Someone in his own group must have betrayed him. Can you imagine? A Boer betraying his fellow Boers. Nothing more despicable than that under the sun.

So Pa had to go to the camp. Great men in there with him. But for us who stayed behind it was grim. Thank heavens it was already February 1945, not far to go to the end of the war, and then they let him go. But of course he was a marked man, couldn't get a job again. Least not before forty-eight when the people's heroes were reinstated. So for three years we suffered. Shitting bricks. But no one complained. My pa was a bloody hero. Destined from the beginning to be one.

Had to give up school to help bring in some money. Worked in a butchery first. Then joined the Force. Ma crying her heart out. Always wanted her son to study. But gave her my solemn word. Hush-hush, of course. And did it too. Through correspondence. Worked day and night, and got my matric. Later passed the Force exams. One by one. Rank of Brigadier today. Even Pa would have had reason to be proud.

Pity he couldn't live to see much of it. His health was broken in the camp. Never the same man afterwards. Only the bottle could cheer him up. Would have given anything to have him here today. He should have seen what has become of his son. Close to the president. Calls me Bester. Not Brigadier. Nothing formal. Bester. And this thing that's happened in Cape Town is going to be my break.

Gave him my personal assurance. 'Leave it to me, Mr President. Will take this on my own shoulders. Already working on a few clues. They won't get away.'

Back at Caledon Square the message was waiting. Passenger with a heavily bandaged right hand observed on flight SA 608 to P.E. There they lost track of her. But then another woman joined the plane at P.E., proceeding to Johannesburg. Also a bandaged right hand. Never expected them to move so fast. But when it happened we went into gear. Nothing more satisfying than a chase. Requested Pretoria to stop her. Never said to shoot her.

This Nina Jordaan. Father's a judge, but one has respect for a man like him. Some judges make life difficult for us. Don't realise that in a time of war there are no rules. Question of survival. Them or us. You can't argue fine points of law with a terrorist. But old Jordaan understands the circumstances we're working under. Knows when to look the other way. All one has to do is whisper a word in his ear. When there are detainees to be visited, affidavits to be signed. Always consults me first. Get on well together. Only those few times we got stuck, every time his daughter was involved.

That time they had the protest march. Bunch of students like that make me see red. The men made a proper job of cleaning up. Should have seen them scurrying for cover when we moved in. Shat themselves. And then they're the ones who talk of the armed struggle. Beat the piss out of them that day. But then old Jordaan's daughter happened to be among them. Didn't get much time to talk to her myself. But got the impression the doll had guts. Didn't break down like some of the others. But then her father phoned, so what could one do? One hand washing the other.

Another occasion too. But then it concerned that other lightie. The photographer. Thomas Landman. Picked him up in Crossroads. Had a whole thick file on him already. The photos he'd sent overseas to the newspapers. Stabbing his own people in the back. Good family too. Had a long chat with the boy myself. Stubborn as anything. Had to call in Swanepoel and his gang to soften him up a bit. He needed a little work-over. Question of getting your hand in before it's too late. But then we had to let him go too, before Swanie could get warmed up properly. Just started feeling him up, checking him out, then old Jordaan phoned. Only found out much later from Swanie that it was the girl who'd poked her nose into it. Asked her father to intervene.

Thick as thieves, those two were at the time. Birds of a feather.

Must look into it, back in Cape Town. Dig up all her contacts. Hell of a job. Know from experience. Like undoing a crows' nest in your fishing tackle. All kinds of things coming to light. But one needs time for it. Now they're all pushing me. Haven't even had time to tidy up that Mabusa thing. Now it's the bomb. Just when it was all beginning to look so good. Because the Mabusa story was a bloody fun fair. Kicked open the whole terrorist nest in Langa. Enough arms to blow up the centre of town. Took three weeks hard work to make Mabusa talk. One of the toughest we ever had. Not that he really broke into song yet, but he was on the brink. Could feel that in my balls. Good job, young Swanie at his best.

At that very point the minister came round. Party going through a bad patch and a by-election coming up. Something solid needed to distract the public. Told him all we needed was just another day or two, Mabusa had reached breaking-point. But then instead of waiting, can you beat it?, the minister went on TV that night to announce that the terror trial was starting in a week's time, Cape Supreme Court, and they had a state witness from the bosom of the enemy. Who else but Mabusa? Long spiel about all the 'information' we got straight from the horse's mouth. Dissent in the ranks of the enemy, people peeling away, the leadership breaking up, dissidents caught and tortured in camps in Angola.

Mabusa hauled from jail and paraded before the press. All the foreign correspondents called up. No questions allowed, of course. Sub judice. But here the nation and the world could see with their own eyes. And after the press conference Mabusa was brought back to me. Now they expected me to deliver the goods. To save the minister's arse. And that was the moment Mabusa chose to play his trump. Can you believe it? One would expect a bastard like that to be grateful for the chance we gave him. State witness instead of accused. Indemnity. All he needed to say in court was what the others had done. But then he turned tail and said no, he'd decided against it. Wasn't going to spill anything after all. Didn't care if we killed him, he said.

That was real shit. Because the minister was now waiting for results, and the press sat watching our every move.

So what could we do? That's where one needs an artistic touch. Got that from fishing. You must know exactly at what moment to relax your grip and give the fish some line. So we released Mabusa. Made sure the press knew about it. But what they didn't know was that Swanie was following him home with a small group of hand-picked men. Couldn't take chances, could we? And that night they zapped him. Inside his house. Big stories in the papers about factions among the terrorists taking revenge on Mabusa for defecting. The minister pleased like hell. If he was a dog he'd have wagged his tail.

Very happy with young Swanie. Noticed him the first day he joined the Branch. Handsome chap, blonde, lean but tough, knows his job. Orphan, grew up poor. Gave him one look and knew immediately he was one to keep my own eye on. Infallible programme for that kind of thing. Take him in your confidence. Give him a couple of special jobs. Get him a promotion or two. Then pull him into an operation like this Mabusa business, and you've got him for life. Fierce, devoted, burning with ambition. And up to his ears in shit. Can't move his arse. Because after a shooting job like that you've got him by the balls. From that moment on you can use him for anything, because he can't refuse. Nicest thing of all is he thinks it's his own choice. No two ways about it, Swanie is my man. My right hand. Like a son, in a way. And he regards me as a father. So it works out well, both ways.

Only problem was that the case was still not tied up. The terror trial was postponed, of course, as we'd lost our 'witness'. Bought some time anyway. And the Party won the by-election. But then we had to start from scratch on Mabusa's comrades. And these bastards seem to get tougher all the time. So our hands are tied. And now this new bomb as well.

One needs fifty hours a day. Hardly sleep a wink at night. And if there are a couple of hours it's not really what you would call rest. Nightmares. Never bothered by insomnia before. Only these last months. Flesh and blood cannot stand it indefinitely. Not that people show any understanding. Just keep pressing for results, results, on the double all the time. Easy for them to push us. Easy for him to shit on us. But at the end of the day we're only human.

When was my last proper holiday? Must be three years. Hard on Anna. But just let me get this case behind me. Then it's up and away. Overhaul the caravan, borrow a ski boat, prepare my tackle, load Anna and Hendrina into the car, and off we go. For at least a month.

Meeting at HQ last night. Wachthuis. Decided not to tell old Jordaan just yet. He'll blow his top. And he's friendly with the Pres. too. But that wasn't the only reason. More important is not to let *anyone* know who she was. That way we keep the initiative. Got to act quickly now. Round up every individual Nina Jordaan had been in contact with over the last few years. My hunch is they're all in hiding somewhere in Cape Town. Seems logical they would have tried to smuggle her out, she was the only one identified at the scene of the blast. Her helper, that cop, was too heavily disguised. So he and the others must still be there. Banking on it that we'll be looking elsewhere. First sign they give, we zap them. Can't wait for that moment. This is *my* case. The one case that will open up the road all the way to the top. For Pa's sake. Main thing is to play the cards very close to one's chest. And be patient. Let the press rant and rave. Patience. Give them time to relax. Drop their guard. Grow tame. Then they grow careless and slip up. People get used to everything. –

Chapter 5

A kilometre out of Vereeniging, on the first leg of his long journey back to the Cape, Thomas stopped to pick up the hitchhiker. A youngish man, in his early thirties, Thomas guessed, very tall, lanky, in a shirt that must have been a flaming red once, now past its first furious bloom, and pale yellow trousers, takkies without socks. His head shaved very bald, showing his skull like a gleaming black egg with a face carved into it. What probably decided Thomas was the battered old cardboard box he had with him, tied up with a leather belt, a piece of baggage so unexpected, so pathetic beside the desperate flair of his outfit, that one could not resist it. The man looked surprised, almost taken aback, when he stopped, remaining cautiously at the edge of the road until Thomas turned down his window.

'Well, want a lift?'

'Thanks. Please. I –' He still looked hesitant about where to get in, front or back, waiting for Thomas to lean over and open the passenger door before he made his move. Then he reacted eagerly enough, seating himself with an air of satisfaction, the battered box poised high on his pointed kneecaps.

'Why don't you put it in the back? It'll be much more comfortable.'

'Thank you, sir.' He put the box on the back seat, and shifted into a comfortable position, his legs so long that his articulated knees came almost up to his ears.

Thomas pulled off again.

'What's your name?'

Another quick, cautious glance, as if he wasn't sure what Thomas expected of him. Then, in a neutral voice, 'It's Raymond, sir.'

'I'm –' A brief hesitation. What name should he give this time?

He could say anything. Neither of them would ever see the other again. Between them, a name was not a point of reference, merely a coincidence. Still, one had to be careful. Avoid risks. But that meant that one couldn't offer anything of oneself, or expect anything in return. With a name one placed oneself at stake. He said, 'Thomas.'

A smile broke the taut surface of the man's oval face. (Why? Because Thomas, white, had volunteered a Christian name, not a surname, not a 'Mr'?) Against the unusual blackness of his features – West African rather than austral – his gums showed up like a smear of blood. He held out his hand. Thomas had to change his grip on the steering wheel to take it, reaching with his right hand under his left arm. Raymond greeted him with gusto, the triple Africa handshake, smiling unwaveringly.

'Yes, Thomas!' he said. 'So how's it, man?'

'Where are you going to?'

Raymond grinned with a hint of embarrassment. The moment of spontaneity was over. They were, once again, white and black. 'It's a long story.'

'We've got time.'

He needed the company, the conversation. He was beginning to feel claustrophobic within himself. For the first while after he'd driven away from Frans's house – Belinda at the front gate, the baby on her hip, the gardener in blue overalls moving about out of focus among the flowering shrubs in the background – it had been a relief to be on his own again. But it was depressing too, demanding. There were so many arcane memories the weekend had stirred up in him, things he'd thought he had forgotten, not even relevant: and yet he found they bothered him, perturbed him. He was thinking about how lonely he'd grown up: and yet he'd had what most people would regard as a 'happy' childhood, ordinary, unremarkable years. If he and Frans had had their differences, surely those had never been serious enough to cause this chasm between them? Their temperaments were different, but their origins had been the same. Where, then, had the gulf begun to gape? Perhaps, he thought as he drove on, the fault lay in the very 'ordinary', the very unsuspecting 'happy' aspect of that youth, its appearance of normality. Because, in retrospect, what could conceivably have been 'normal' about it? All the images returning to him as he tried to recall it now, were concerned with his family, his few friends, a world inhabited exclusively by whites. As if the others simply had not existed. The labourers in their garden or their kitchen. His mother used to get along well with them, her servants would stay with her for years, she would care for them and dispense medicine to them when they were ill, and present them with old clothes for their families, and sometimes even give them a cake or a whole batch of rusks that hadn't come out as well as usual: yet today he had to strain himself to wonder: who were they? Who *were* they? On the stoep in front of the Checkers supermarket, in the Greek café, in the shade of the trees on the sidewalks, they thronged and sprawled; at night, sometimes, one could hear them singing in the 'location': but always at a distance, far away, remote. On the other side of the wooden partition in the post office; outside the side window of the takeaways, never inside; the separate door at the butchery. Who *were* they? Only if he made a special effort could he introduce them into his memories of childhood: and yet they must always have been there, indispensable, ubiquitous. The accoutrements and trappings of a 'normal' youth.

– I was born in the year of Sharpeville. Does that mark one for life? Perhaps it is insinuated into one with one's mother's milk, like a vitamin or a germ in one's blood; and then it runs its course. –

Unexpectedly, a single more sharply defined incident did detach itself from the vague mass of his memories. An afternoon (it must have been a week or two before Christmas, because the next day they were leaving on the annual trek to his grandfather's farm near Kuruman), when he accompanied his mother's 'kitchen maid' – but who *was* she? what was her name? after all these years he still only knew her as 'Aia', which was the form of address one had used for all elderly black women – to her house. She had a lot to carry that afternoon, his mother had just distributed all the Christmas provisions – 'useful' things, overalls and headscarves and sugar and samp and coffee and flour, a packet of liquorice allsorts for the children, and mince and shanks and jelly and a rare bottle of Oros to mix cool drinks over the festive days – and he'd offered to help her carry. It really was a pretext to accompany her into the 'location', that mysterious forbidden world of black people where no white ever set foot, where terrible things happened at night, where *tsotsis* jumped from dark places to slit your throat, a place of smoke and loud voices, of bare-bottomed children, women in *kopdoeke*, men sitting on the ground with cartons of beer, of streets crisscrossed with erosion ditches and stagnant pools of dirty water, open spaces littered with the carcasses of rusty cars, of chickens scratching in the streets, mangy dogs, an alien planet. The woman had protested at first, said his mother would be angry, but for once he could not be dissuaded (presumably his mother was having tea with friends, his father in the garage busy with his woodwork, Frans and Maria at play somewhere, the house deserted). He could remember how children in the 'location' had stopped to stare at him when he and the woman came past – she balancing a large box on her head, her arms loaded with parcels, he staggering under the weight of two plastic shopping bags – and how he'd hollowed his back as he walked past, cold with fear; but then the woman had called out something to the children, and they'd responded, their faces breaking into smiles. She'd turned round – the grace of that movement, balancing the box on her head – and said to him, 'They're greeting you, *Kleinbaas*.' He uttered a hesitant hello, and suddenly they waved and laughed in reply, and a whole procession began to follow them.

The woman took him into her house – the rickety door remained open, children swarmed in the bright light on the doorstep but did not enter – and poured him some of her precious Oros in a tin mug. He sat down at the table covered with a floral plastic cloth, and greedily gulped down the orange drink, stopping only to catch his breath and ask for ice, but she explained patiently that there wasn't electricity in the 'location', and gas was too expensive. With the memory of a photographer he recalled the newsprint cut into patterns on the shelves of the old kitchen dresser; a transistor radio on the table, its antenna pulled out to its full length; an old-fashioned Singer sewing-machine on an apple box against the wall; pictures from magazines, and a butcher's calendar; a coal-stove with a few battered aluminium pots on it, which he seemed to recollect having seen in his mother's kitchen before; the concrete floor. There were only two rooms in the little house; the kitchen-cum-front-room where they were sitting, and a bedroom next door, where he could make out two beds pushed together, and some rolled blankets against the far wall. Everything was pervaded with the smell of woodsmoke. There was no ceiling, and it was blazing hot. Through small holes in the corrugated iron roof sharp thin nails of light stabbed into the dark interior.

When he'd finished his Oros, without stopping to think, he asked for more. Did she hesitate before she opened the bottle again and carefully poured out another tot of the bright liquid? Then discovered that there was no more water in the bucket near the door, and asked him to wait while she went to get some. He sat watching her from the table – but later he got up and went to the door, from where the crowd of children had by then disappeared – as she walked past the patched houses and shacks, in the shocking white wash of summer light, towards the public tap that had no handle, streaming night and day, with poultry and children and even a black pig messing about in the mud: he suddenly felt his heart contract; and when she came back, the blue pail balanced on her head, said abruptly that if she didn't mind he'd rather not have any more, he was no longer thirsty. And then he went home.

No wonder he stopped for the hitchhiker standing beside the road. This, it occurred to him, was what that talkative young woman on the flight to Johannesburg – what was her name again? Lisa something, Lombard – must have felt like when she'd cornered him on the plane and forced him, willy-nilly, to listen to whatever she had to say: because she could not contain it any more. Now it was his turn. Except that he could never be as frank as she had been. Perhaps that wasn't even important. It didn't matter *what* he said: he just needed another person to be close, to listen to him, to save him from being alone with himself.

But after the surprising enthusiasm in the man's reaction when Thomas had said his name, there was that noticeable withdrawal in Raymond when he asked, 'Where you going to?' (Did he, also, have something to hide? A game to play? Was nobody in the country capable of conducting a simple conversation any more?)

'It's a long story.'

'We've got time.'

'How far you going?'

It was his turn to hesitate. 'Bloemfontein.'

'You live there?'

'God, no.'

Raymond grinned. 'Good for you.'

'No, I live in Johannesburg,' said Thomas. (Already we are being separated by lies, he thought. What guarantee do I have that *you* will be telling the truth?) 'And you?' he tried again, not to labour the point, merely to keep the conversation going.

'P.E.'

'I've spent a lot of time there,' said Thomas. 'Just after the State of Emergency was first declared. It was a bad time.'

'The P.E. you know won't be the same as mine,' said Raymond (if it was his name). It was a statement, not a rebuke or a reproach.

'I'm talking about the townships. New Brighton. Zwide. Soweto.
Without turning his head he was aware of his passenger looking at
him sharply. He motioned towards the back seat where his camera
sat. 'I'm a photographer.'

'Newspaper?'

'American papers.' He gave it time to sink in. Then asked, 'So
where in P.E. do you live?'

'New Brighton.' The voice was still guarded.

'I remember a couple of times I was there I thought it was tickets
with me,' said Thomas, as casually as he could. Staring ahead as if
intrigued by the straight road and the colourless plains dotted with
thorn-trees. 'If I spent the night with friends we would listen to the
Boere driving past. You can tell a Casspir from a mile off. And then
the sounds of marching as the troops moved in. Left-right, left-right.
One night I spent under a bed, house in D Street, with two small
children on top of me.'

Something he said, some secret password he was not even
conscious of himself, must have penetrated Raymond's defences.
He appeared less sceptical than before.

'Yes, I'm on my way home,' said Raymond, with a hint of the
enthusiasm that had illuminated his first greeting. 'Times are bad,
man. People started fighting on the mines, you know, Xhosas and
Zulus, those Inkatha people, now they close the place down and
send us all home. I'm a boiler-maker, you see, they trained me, I
been there seven years now. But now nobody knows what's going
to happen. I must sell my cattle, I think, it's too bad. They grazing
on the farm where my father works, Alexandria district. That farmer
is a good man. But you see, the cattle is my guarantee, for my family.
I don't know what will become of us if we don't have them any more.
And the prices are bad in this drought. But what else can I do?' He
suddenly beamed. 'I got twins at home, you know. Just a year old.
That's the good part of going back. Sipho and Siphiwo.'

'Two gifts?' asked Thomas, referring to the meaning of the Xhosa
names.

Raymond laughed with pleasure. 'You know what those names
mean?'

'One of the best friends I ever had was called Sipho.'

'Had?'

'Yes. He died.'

'Tsk, tsk.' He shook his head. 'Everybody dying these days.' He
leaned his tall body up against the backrest and felt under the seat

to adjust it; but even after he had moved it back as far as it could go there was barely enough space for his long legs. 'I tell you, Thomas, I can't wait to see Sipho and Siphiwo again. And my wife. But you know what, I'm also scared to go back. I don't know how to bring up children in this place. Life is too bad, man. You got sons?'

'No, I'm not married.'

'I don't know if that is good or bad.'

'I had a girlfriend, but she also died.'

'Hau, it's tough.'

Raymond put a hand on Thomas's knee and pressed it for a moment, as if it were the most natural gesture in the world.

'Last time I was back home,' said Raymond, 'was when the twins were born last year. It was a too-bad time for the township, jeez. The Boere had big sports with us. You know, they wait until it is night, then they come in with the Casspirs into the streets. And then they start shooting, at nothing, left and right. So then the people come out to see what is going on. And then they pick you up, because you broke the curfew. That is if you lucky, because other times they just keep on shooting. For the hell of it, you know. When I was there we were working in the yard. The place belongs to my wife's mother, so we put up shacks to rent to people, it's a way of making some extra money when times are bad. Now we are working there in the yard, me and my *buti*, my brother, we are putting up a scaffolding, then there's this big noise in the street. It's a Land-Rover with two cops, young lighties, man, not more than eighteen or so I think. They chasing some black kids down the street, falling about laughing because the kids are so shit-scared of being hit and trampled, it's zigzag all the way, I tell you. One of the kids, I heard afterwards, get so scared, and the hell in too, of course, he bends over and picks up a stone. Jeez, that was asking for it, hey? I mean, that's terrorism and treason, the works. The two Boere come jumping from the Land-Rover and now they chasing the boys with their guns. So this is when the kids come running into our yard, right into the house, cops after them. Me and my brother, I tell you Thomas, hell, we get such a fright we think this is the end. My *buti* just drop everything, stop working on the spot, he run after them into the house to find out what's going on, I mean he don't want them to break down the whole place. The moment he come in at the back door one of the cops begin to shout, "That's him! That's him!" And they move in on him with their rifle butts. Drag him out to the Land-Rover, it's kicking and beating him all the way.

"Hey!" I shout at them. "Hey, what you doing? He's my brother, he didn't do you nothing." One of them look at me over his shoulder, he says, "You shut up, kaffir, or you also come with us." Now I tell you, Thomas, I'm ashamed to say this to you, but I just stopped right there and looked away. It was because of my children, man. How could I try to stop them, even if it was my *buti*? They took him away. We never seen him again from that day. That was last year, in January. And when we go to Louis le Grange Square, or we go to St Alban's prison, they tell us they know nothing of such a man, he is not in their books. That's all. So now he's gone, disappeared, just like that. And I am ashamed, ashamed, ashamed. But what could I do?' He shook his head again. 'Now I'm going home again. Perhaps there will be some news this time.'

'Why do you work so far from home?' asked Thomas.

'What else can I do? It's a good job, I tell you. And there's nothing in Ibhayi. When the motor-car companies started moving out there's *mos* no more jobs. The people are too poor. I got to send home something for my children. But sure, this is not a life for a man. No, it's not a life, honest to God.'

'At least you have something.'

'Sure. But it's touch and go all the time. Now the mine people send me back.'

'You said you'd been working on the mine for seven years?'

'Yes, seven years. Good job, I tell you, but it's difficult too. Last year, you know, when I went home, it wasn't just because of the twins. The mine *sent* me. You see, the government suddenly decided I was a citizen of Ciskei. Don't make no difference that I was born in Alexandria, like my father, like his father. No, all of a sudden we're Ciskeians. And if I don't get the right papers the mine can't keep me. That's the law. So I go to get my Ciskei papers. But you see how dicey it is now? They can turn round any day and say, "Look, you not South African, go back to Ciskei, you migrant labour now." They can throw us out of our house and everything. Anytime. Soon as I have trouble with the law, or if they get fed up for some reason, or if the government tells them to. So that's another reason why I had to shut up about my *buti* that time. Because now I am on their books, they watching me. A man got to know his step, I tell you.'

Against his better judgement Thomas said, 'Well, they promised the other day they wouldn't throw out the homeland people.'

'What's a Boer's promise worth?' asked Raymond. 'All they been doing, right along the line, is telling lies. You know, there was a time my people used to say there's one thing about a Boer: he'll fuck you around and treat you like dirt, but he'll never lie to you. You always know where you stand with him. But now it's different. Today, if you say "Boer", you mean "liar". Don't tell me you don't know it.'

'I know only too well,' said Thomas. He turned his head to look Raymond in the eyes. 'Because I'm a Boer myself, you see.'

'Come again.'

'Genuine. And you know what's the worst? I am ashamed for having to feel ashamed.'

'Don't worry.' Raymond burst out laughing, shifting his spindly legs. 'You'll survive.' He gave Thomas a brotherly pat on the shoulder. '*We*'ll survive, what you say?'

'Let's drink on it.' They had reached the outskirts of Frankfort. Thomas swerved right at the first turn-off from where he could see the signboard of a hotel, and stopped at the Off Sales. 'What'll it be? Beer?'

'Spot on.'

He went in through the open door – inside it smelled of stale beer and wine – and bought two cans of Castle, which he took back to the car. He handed Raymond one through the open window. 'Here. Cheers.'

'Cheers.'

They filled up at a garage; then they were on their way again, across the monotonous plains covered in bleached summer grass. (Through these open spaces, Thomas thought, his great-great-grandfather must have travelled with the intrepid wanderers of the Great Trek, Petrus, the Seer: first as a child, after Blood River and the British annexation of Natal, on his way to the Transvaal and the sweet illusion of Jerusalem; and in the last days of his life in the opposite direction, in search of an apocalyptic commando. And here he was, today, on his way – where? No end to the journeys of the Landman family.) Raymond turned down his window, threw out his beer can, shifted his legs, resumed the conversation – about his children, his young wife, his father on the farm, his job on the mine, his time in the veld, years ago, when he underwent circumcision and the rites of passage to manhood, New Brighton, whatever came to mind. And while Thomas listened, reacting mechanically from time to time, asking a question, offering a comment, his thoughts wandered off on their own.

– Is there a line, tentative and often obscure, from the distant

154

December day in the 'location' when I first entered that Other World (the shock both of its strangeness and its familiarity, its ordinariness), to that month of June, in midwinter, just before my sixteenth birthday, when the shock-waves of the children's revolt in Soweto were registered throughout the country?

The first that struck me – not the news as such, the discovery that the children were rebelling against the Afrikaans language in their schools: but the breakthrough into a layer of my mind where it *mattered*, where it touched a nerve and remained smouldering like a red-hot coal – was that photograph. The now famous photograph by Sam Nzima of the pupil carrying the body of Hector Peterson in a street of Soweto. There are photographs that break through a level of consciousness as a Mirage shatters the sound barrier.

How many other photographs have marked turning-points in my life like that one? Every time another barrier broken. Moments in which one is changed irredeemably, breaking through to other spaces inside oneself. The small boy with the black cap in the ghetto of Warsaw. The naked girl, burning with napalm, running on the open stretch of road among the paddies in Vietnam. A shot of a lion catching a wildebeest, in an old *National Geographic* (the fury in the lion's amber eye; the realisation of death in the wild bulging eyes of the wildebeest). Some of Peter Magubane's early photographs from the townships. Another by Robert Capa: refugees in the Spanish Civil War, on their way from Barcelona to the frontier, most of them women and children, staggering under their bundles and boxes. More often than not one doesn't even remember the name of the photographer: they become archetypal images burnt into the conscience of the world. Such a one is that photograph of Hector Peterson, the first victim of Soweto on that 16th June 1976, which introduced a whole new era in South African history, an era marked by a long frieze of its own images, landmarks for memory: Biko's body, the faces of his murderers; the dumb face of the Cabinet minister whose immortality rests on that single phrase, 'It leaves me cold'; children throwing stones; youthful policemen hurling teargas canisters or brandishing sjamboks; the bodies of people shot in the back in Langa outside Uitenhage; Alan Boesak and Desmond Tutu leading a protest march to Pollsmoor prison; a maimed body in a still smouldering tyre, contorted like a piece of driftwood on the beach; the beaming Aryan faces of the new Hitler Jugend gazing over the edge of a Buffel or a Casspir; a young white soldier posing with his rifle, one foot on the body of a 'terrorist' he has bagged, like a hunting trophy. Even some of my own photographs may have found their way into this gallery. But it was that winter's day, it was that photograph of a young man marching on, unstoppable, sobbing, with the body of a child in his arms, which first brought home to me the discovery that my land was no longer the land I once thought I knew. It was that photograph which made me realise what I wanted to do, what I had to be one day: all at once I knew what 'photography' meant; knew that what had been no more than a hobby before, had now, through looking at that one image, moved into the passionate centre of my life's interest.

I wanted, there and then, to put it to the test. Money I'd been saving for something else – I no longer even remember what for – I spent on rolls of film and on darkroom equipment. Our chemist telephoned the order through to Cape Town. Previously I had developed my own films, but the chemist had done the printing; from now on I wanted to do it all myself. That week or two before the equipment arrived must have been the most impatient wait of my life. (I didn't know, then, not yet, about the waiting that precedes a bomb.) In the meantime I built up a collection of negatives.

In my enthusiasm, of course, I overestimated the possibilities of our village in the Little Karoo. The tension in the country had reached even our remote region: a cordon of police and army vehicles was drawn around the 'location'; even a school was burnt down. But I had no access to anything that might cause people to sit up. The police – even the commanding officer, my own Oom Boet, Mum's brother, the local sergeant – would not allow me into the township at all. (The whole roll of film devoted to the burning school, taken at a kilometre's distance, showed only a few blobs of light on a back background.)

Photographically speaking, it was an unpropitious debut. But it didn't put me off. At least I learned to keep my eyes open. And it was only years later, when I dug up those beginner's negatives again from the biscuit tin in which I'd kept them, that I discovered how, on some of them, quite unawares, I had captured something of those turbulent days. A photograph of women from the 'location' approaching at sunset to bring food to the policemen on patrol, because they thought the men might be cold and hungry. A row of soldiers looking on while children play with ingenious wire carts. My Oom Boet's face from a few yards away (in those days I possessed neither telephoto nor close-up lenses): the crow's feet of laughter etched a startling white on his tanned face, the eyes drawn to slits from lack of sleep, the weary lines on his cheeks, small crusts of dried spittle in the corners of his mouth. I can still hear him say, one evening at supper, 'Ag, you know, sometimes I do feel sorry for those people. It's not an easy life. And to be guarded day and night like this –' Dad: 'It's for their own sake, Boet.' My uncle only sighed. 'Even so. Would *you* have liked to be watched over like that?' The broad white line across the top half of his forehead, where the cap kept out the sun; the bristles of hair in his nostrils and ears which used to fascinate me as a child. 'And where is it all leading to? It's bad enough as it is. Sometimes I honestly think we've made a mess of this country.'

There was another conversation I had with him, in the days following the burning of the school. It was just after his men first ventured into the township to look for the arsonists; and some of the constables were so badly wounded by stones that they had to be taken to hospital. As a result, reinforcements were brought in from elsewhere. Oom Boet shook his blunt head. 'Now our men will move in there tomorrow to take revenge for what happened today. I can't stop them. It's only human. And we're acting under orders. But you see, Thomas, then the blacks will have to take revenge again. And so it goes on, over and over, like a dog chasing its own tail. Will there ever be an end to it? Violence never solves anything. Not for anybody.'

'But sometimes people get desperate, Oom Boet.'

'Of course they do. But as I see it, once you start using violence to change the world to your liking, you're stuck with violence to keep it going. And then there's no way out again.'

I have no illusions about Oom Boet. His vision was alarmingly narrow. In the final analysis he sincerely believed in law and order. But behind everything that constituted his day's work he'd seen something of the terrifying complexity of it all.

I, too, was beginning to learn. Something had begun, and even if I myself did not know yet what it was, I was already on the long road that has brought me here today. –

In Kroonstad Thomas bought hamburgers and chips and Cokes at a roadhouse; and a little distance away they stopped under some dusty trees at a picnic spot to eat the lukewarm food. It wasn't far to Bloemfontein now. He could easily drive right past to Port Elizabeth and drop Raymond. What did it matter whether he arrived in Cape Town tomorrow, or in three days, or even next week? But something in him held on to the idea of stopping over in Bloemfontein first, to see Maria. A conscious effort to attach himself again, to places, people, now that he'd lost Nina? Perhaps a test to find out whether the very possibility of attachment still existed, was still conceivable, after what had happened last Friday? Or simply a postponement of the inevitable arrival in the Cape, where he yearned to be yet also dreaded to be again? The reason was not important. He *had* to stay over, and that was that.

At the first exit towards the city he swerved off the road. 'Here we'll have to say goodbye, Raymond.'

'There's an end to everything,' Raymond said gaily as he opened his door. 'Thanks for the chat.'

'Hope it goes well.' He also tried to be lighthearted. 'Just grin and bear it. Viva the struggle.'

'Fuck the struggle,' Raymond said calmly. 'I just want to be left alone, man. You understand what I mean? They must leave my wife and kids alone so we can live in peace. All I'm asking.' He stretched out a long thin arm and gave Thomas the triple handshake. 'See you, Thomas, God bless.'

2

He did not go directly to Maria's house after all. There was a possibility that she might have gone somewhere with the children, and he didn't relish the idea of being received by her senior lecturer husband Tertius; relations between them had always been, if not strained, at least guarded. Whatever differences there had been between them had never surfaced openly – mainly for Maria's sake they had maintained a very polite front – but neither could ever approve of what the other (in his view) represented; they were like two dogs sniffing at each other without really risking to come close. But what was there to do on an empty afternoon in Bloemfontein?

That was how he landed in the zoo. On a bench in a shady spot opposite the lion enclosure he installed himself as comfortably as he could, with a carton of orange juice he'd bought at the café. He just sat, trying not even to think. And in a way it was an escape, for the first time since the previous Thursday, in the Gardens, on the mountain, on the beach. Only four days ago. It was hard to grasp. Thursday did not seem to belong to the 'past' as much as to a different space, another kind of existence. This, he thought with a rueful smile, might have been how Adam felt, stopping for a moment in the shade to wipe his brow, trying to remember what it had been like in the Garden before the picking of that fruit. How stripped and bare the hoary old Tree of Knowledge seemed from here. Only the aftertaste still lingered; would always be there, acrid, acrid on the tongue.

But in a way he was also the opposite of Adam. Adam had been driven out from where he'd believed he belonged. For him, Thomas, it was different. If he had to resume, now, the argument spanning so many years, with so many people, about the Afrikaner's 'schizophrenia', living with one foot in Europe and the other in Africa, about the yearning to arrive and the stubborn refusal to yield to it, then he was not so much driven out as driven inside. That impact of the explosion on Friday, that moment of violence, marked in a strange way the acknowledgement of his final arrival in Africa. (But can one say, 'I love you' with a bomb?) And if it had really been an arrival, how did this journey come about then, a journey provisionally without a destination, and with no end in sight? Surely one can be an exile only abroad, in some foreign land? Or is another kind of exile conceivable, inside the place you love?

It was quiet in the zoo on a Monday afternoon, out of season. Here and there a few mothers with small children. Groups of black or 'coloured' pupils in school uniform. Gardeners poking about desultorily in flower beds or snipping at hedges. And he. Even the animals were lethargic. Golden brown, the lions lay sprawling on flat boulders or under straggly trees, only one female gnawing at a piece of raw meat, more black than red; and small clouds of flies and bluebottles rose up every time she tugged at it. Poor, half-tamed Africa. Ersatz. Yet there was something in zoos that held an atavistic attraction for him, ever since he'd been a child, when a visit like this, on the rare occasions they ever saw a big town, had been an extraordinary holiday treat.

The morning in the Amsterdam zoo, in Artis: his friends could not get over their amusement at 'an African from Africa' insisting on going to look at animals in Holland of all places. Their comments, good-humoured as they were, ranged from 'misplaced romanticism' to 'lunacy'. And then it turned into a quite unexpected adventure in front of the monkey house. More specifically, the large cage housing the orang-utans, consisting of tall glass walls which, theoretically at least, permitted of no escape; and an open top. But the designers of the cage had not reckoned with the initiative of one young male who, on that bright spring morning, got it into his head to escape: evidently one who refused to abide by what was 'expected' of a primate.

There were few visitors that morning, and apart from Thomas only five or six others were watching the young orang-utan as he patiently tried, over and over again, to wriggle himself up the smooth glass walls in one of the far corners, progressing a yard or two further at every attempt, followed by a thudding fall back to the ground, and a new beginning. Sisyphus was an amateur by comparison. And unlike Sisyphus, this orang-utan finally, however impossible it had seemed, did reach the top ledge of the tall glass wall where he perched to survey the scene. With their heads thrown back, like people watching an eclipse of the sun or moon, Thomas and the other spectators stood staring at the orang-utan as he balanced himself on the high ridge. Inside the cage, too, the other orang-utans had also abandoned their usual pursuits: the largest, oldest male in the family took up position at the very top of the dry tree in the middle of the cage (what a depressing paradigm of the Tree in the Garden!), to keep watch from as close by as possible; the others huddled below, not missing a single movement.

A moment of choice had arrived. The young adventurer rose on his hind legs on his ledge, one hand shielding his eyes to explore the horizon like a sailor waiting to shout 'Land ahoy!', then looked down into the cage again: one step this way, one step back, then another towards freedom, and back again. Ahead of him was the row of rooftops on the monkey house leading up to a tall parapet; behind it were the trees and the skyline of Amsterdam – distance, space, freedom – while on this side stood the cage in which he had obviously been born, where he had grown up, and where all the members of his family were spending their lives in contented and pampered imprisonment.

By that time, through some secret system of communication, the news had spread throughout Artis. Perhaps that was the most remarkable event about the whole morning, the one thing Thomas would remember most intensely: how all the birds and animals in the adjacent enclosures began to react to this young orang-utan's attempt to escape. Geese and ducks and other water-birds, even tall graceful swans, watched with necks outstretched as the escapee proceeded inch by inch along the rooftops; they were flapping their wings as if to urge him on, cackling and cawing and hissing and squawking with excitement; smaller monkeys clung to the wire-mesh of their cages while they screeched and squeaked as if possessed; strange hairy antelopes from remote tundra regions, gazelles from the savannah of Africa or South America were bleating or barking, their necks poked through the railings of their pens; even the lions and tigers began to roar. The whole zoo had taken notice. A wave of eagerness swept through the place like a vast wind flattening the grass on a prairie. As if – preposterous thought – this thing that was taking place before their eyes was not simply a young orang-utan's attempt to escape, but an adventure, a feat undertaken on behalf of all the creatures in that zoo. They were all aware of it: they were watching: they shared every hesitant step along the hazardous way: suddenly their own existence, their own possibilities of survival, in that translucent morning, were at stake.

Inside him Thomas could feel his guts contract. His whole body was pleading: Please, please, do it, please succeed, don't turn back, go, go! While at the same time he realised how impossible and dangerous and unwise it was: for what was to become of a young orang-utan let loose in the streets of Amsterdam? But the logic of consequences had been suspended: the only thing that mattered was that the ape should succeed in its outrageous enterprise.

Step by step the orang-utan shuffled away. First, from the ridge of his cage to the edge of the roof; then up along the slope of the roof to a section of wall, following a gutter to the main roof above, and further towards the triangular parapet. It felt like hours. Every few minutes the ape hesitated, stopped to stare this way and that, to retrace a few steps, lowering his head to ponder what was happening, what still lay ahead. Once he came back all the way to the top ridge of his cage as if his courage had finally deserted him. There he sat for God knows how long, his eyes covered by his hands. Everything in the zoo below him grew very quiet. (Only inside Thomas a voice was shouting, so loudly that he thought the ape could not but hear: 'Go! Go! Don't come back! Go!') The orang-utan rose on his hind legs again as if he were the first of all creatures to do so. Looked around. Once more the zoo erupted in squawks, hoots, calls, cries, roars, grunts, barks, every sound a living creature was capable of. And once again he followed that long, lonesome road up the roof to the parapet, no more than a small hairy silhouette against the sky. This time, surely, he was gone. He was free.

But evidently it was not his first attempt. The keepers must have been alerted to that streak in him. While a couple of them stood watching, amused, from below, another climbed a ladder to the roof, from the back of the building: and when at last the orang-utan reared up on his high rooftop, the keeper appeared from behind a chimney, waving his arms.

Below, all sound ceased. The ape began to scream and gesticulate at the man, standing his ground for a minute or two, then lost confidence and began to retreat step by step. On the top rim of his cage he stopped. It was a last resolute stand. In a tragic grimace he bared his teeth. The keeper made another shooing movement. Very, very slowly, inch by inch, the escapee began to shuffle down the inside glass wall of his cage once more. A second keeper appeared inside the sleeping quarters, trying to lure him through a hatch with a banana. At first the young male reacted with rage, grabbing a stick and hitting out in all directions until it splintered on the ground. But he could not resist the banana. Five minutes later he was back in the sleeping quarters, the hatch slammed shut. He would, most likely, have to spend the rest of the day in that dark inner cubicle: not so much as punishment as to make him forget what he had attempted, what had so nearly happened. For his own good. That above all. For his own good.

An event which had nearly been transformed into a miracle had gone awry. The animals in the zoo returned to their normal business. The spectators disappeared among the cages. But Thomas remained in front of the orang-utan cage. Would something, he wondered, some small glimmer of light, the hint of a memory, continue to smoulder in the mind of that audacious and now tamed young animal, the knowledge – not even knowledge, merely a dim suspicion – that the ends of his cage were not the limits of his world, that somewhere beyond it loomed another world, something vast and great, something hazardous perhaps, something which had no end at all, and which he had almost reached? And if he were indeed to remember, would it make him happy with an awareness of which none of his peers had the slightest inkling? Or would it haunt and plague him, a wound in his mind, chafing, smarting, aching, never to be healed?

Still seated on his bench in the Bloemfontein zoo, Thomas closed his eyes for a moment; then got up. The lions were still sprawling in their enclosure, like golden skins with mounted heads. Over the bare earth beyond the deep moat that separated the predators and their world from that of their human spectators, the late afternoon sun came pouring, sticky and slow like Golden Syrup, sweetness from strength. It was time to go. Maria should be home by now.

'Boetie! What a surprise.' Followed, inevitably, by the question, 'What have you done to your hair?'

'Tried to regain my lost youth,' he smiled. 'Unfortunately it didn't work.'

'Lost youth? You're not even thirty yet. Leave that kind of desperation to me.'

'You're looking good.' He studied her. 'Tired. But good.'

'I'm putting on weight.'

'Not another baby, I hope? You have so many already.'

'Oh come on. Only four. It's still respectable.' She pulled a face, and on her nose appeared small, funny wrinkles he remembered from their childhood. 'Who are you to talk anyway? You're still a bachelor. Unless –?'

'No, I still tread warily. Mum and Dad have enough grandchildren for now.'

'Shame on you, Boetie.' She called out into the house. Some of the children ran out to carry his luggage. Two rowdy white Labradors made it difficult.

'So where's Tertius?' he asked cautiously.

'In Pretoria. He's on some steering committee or other organising the Great Trek thing. No end to their meetings. Patriotism rampant.'

He could barely conceal his relief. But he kept his pose. 'I thought you also became a patriot when you married him?'

Without answering, she went inside ahead of him, to a bedroom in the passage, scattering children from their course. 'Tommie, will you move in with Vicky while Uncle Thomas is here? He'll be sleeping in your room.' With a stern stare she nipped all protest in the bud. 'Come on, you're named after him and all. It's not so bad, is it?' To Thomas, 'How long will you be staying?'

'Just for the night. I'm on my way through.'

'That's all Bloemfontein is good for, it seems to me. A halfway station for people passing through.'

'That's not how I meant it.'

'I know. But I wish you'd give the place a chance, sometime. It's not so bad if you live here.'

'Who're you trying to convince?'

She didn't answer. In a few decisive motions she stripped the

163

bedclothes from the single bed and carried them to another room, followed by the children; then returned with an armful of fresh sheets and towels, and prepared to make the bed.

'Let me help you.'

'You sit down over there,' she said. 'What do you know about housework anyway?'

'I'm used to doing it all myself,' he reminded her. And suddenly stopped, stunned by the violence with which pain suddenly invaded him: Nina, Nina, dear God –

'Something happened?' Maria asked calmly. Her grey eyes scrutinised him. He wanted to deny it, avoid it, but had to clench his teeth to restrain the emotion.

She came from the bed to put her arms around him. He thought: She's become exactly like Mum, conditioned by the need to comfort children and heal wounds. But mine cannot be kissed better. And yet it helped to lose himself for a moment in her embrace. But only for a moment: then he detached himself from her, and she was wise enough to let him go.

'Would you like to talk about it?'

'I don't think I can.'

'Come,' she said, as if she'd taken an important decision. 'Come and sit in the kitchen while I make us something to eat. I'll try to think of something special for you.'

Exactly like their mother: no matter what happened, how great the upheaval, there was nothing she could not redeem with a good meal.

But the kitchen was full of children, and he wandered off through the house on his own. Past the open door of Tertius's study: the backs of the books on the shelves perfectly straight, the pens on the desk meticulously in line, every pile of documents fastidiously squared. Children's rooms where chaos prevailed; on the walls large softboards covered with their drawings and cuttings. A sitting-room with heavy practical furniture that showed the ravages of children and dogs: stains on the carpet, an ink mark on a cushion, a cover frayed at the seam, scratches on the woodwork.

'Oh here you are,' Maria said behind him. Her youngest, two years old, Katrien, was perched like a small monkey on her hip, studying him with solemn eyes, a red bow bobbing cheekily on a wisp of a pigtail.

'She looks exactly like you when you were small,' he said.

'You didn't know me when I was small.'

'There were snapshots.'

'I wish you'd make me a nice one of her. You *are* her godfather, you know. Or have you forgotten?'

'How can I forget?' But he had, as a matter of fact. He put out his arms towards the baby. She sized him up for another moment, then suddenly, unreservedly, flung her body at him. He caught her, laughing, threw her up in the air, pressed his face against her fat belly until she shrieked with laughter.

'Why don't you take some now?' asked Maria. 'She's on her way to her bath.'

'I didn't bring my flash. But first thing tomorrow morning, before I leave. I'd love to.'

'How come you're on the road without your equipment? That's very unlike you.'

For a moment he was caught unprepared. Then, hastily — too hastily? — tried to cover up: 'A friend of mine took it through to Port Elizabeth. I'm meeting him there tomorrow.'

'Oh.' Unconvinced, disappointed, she held out her arms to her daughter, but the child clung to Thomas, laughing. 'She's crazy about men,' said Maria. Was she deliberately trying to sound lighthearted? 'We're in for a lot of trouble with this one.'

Later, after the baby had been bathed and put to bed, Thomas joined Maria in the kitchen where the boys were having their supper, as voracious as silkworms on a mulberry leaf. They had their own meal in the midst of all that eager grazing. And then, at last, the house grew quiet. She made tea; he carried the tray to the sitting-room. The Labradors had already settled cosily on the shaggy brown carpet, licking and groaning, yawning, dozing off.

'The children are a handful,' said Thomas, shifting into a comfortable position on the sofa.

'I'm not complaining.'

'Is this all you want from life?'

They were interrupted by the news on television. A Who's Who of the power establishment, all of them equally pompous. Long sentences bristling with interpolations and non sequiturs and sub-clauses, diving in at one end of a muddy lake in search of a verb and re-emerging at the other without it. A welter of clichés, pronounced so many times that even the speakers had begun to believe them. This, for them, was, per definition, the 'truth'.

Thomas did not pay attention to what the state president on the screen was intoning in his lay-preacher's voice: he was staring at

165

the face itself, his own face cold, as if perspiration had evaporated from it. He was thinking: If this man had been dead tonight, the way we'd planned, if everything had gone well and he had been killed, would the evil in this country have been eradicated with him? (That was what Nina had asked, long ago, wasn't it? Wasn't it?) Would it have made a *difference*? Or was it already too late for anything to make a difference? On the other hand, even if the man had been no more than an instrument of evil, wasn't it better to start somewhere instead of allowing it all to hurtle towards disaster? Evil is not an abstraction, not in our post-metaphysical world: it exists only inasmuch as it is embodied in *people*, in individuals or their institutions, in someone like that talking, arrogant face on the screen.

At last the interview was over. Even the newscaster seemed relieved. But the reprieve did not last long. Another image from Madame Tussaud's replaced the first. A minister of defence – of law and order – of justice – of something: they were interchangeable, it made no difference to the clichés or to the undulations of ungrammatical language.

Maria got up to refill their cups.

Next, the commissioner of police. And now the sound was breaking through to him: '– give the assurance that my men are working round the clock following up clues in connection with last Friday's bomb explosion in Cape Town. Already more than eight hundred people have been arrested in various parts of the country in police raids over the weekend. Among them –' Names, names: leaders of organisations and movements, students, members of COSATU, of the UDF. Many of them he had met over the years. But not one of the names shook him as deeply as the one suddenly scorching through the others: Henry Bungane.

Henry. On how many journeys had they been together, criss-crossing through the vast land, from one city to another, one township to the next, he with his cameras, Henry with his UDF briefcase. Ever since that first meeting in Guguletu, when Henry had been released from Robben Island. The crowd that had surrounded him that day. Ntsiki's laughing face. At last the silence that descended on them, the interior of the small house in the white light of the gas lamp, Henry's gravelly voice, the child sleeping on his lap. It had been like the beginning of a new world. And today? Perhaps he shouldn't be unduly worried. How many times had Henry been detained since then? They would release him again.

In a week, a few months, one day. But it was different this time: this time it was because of something *he* had done, he, Thomas. Because they were looking for *him*, even if they themselves were still unaware of it. And, with Henry, there were others, hundreds of others, 'in various parts of the country'. Detained. Probably tortured. And how many more to come? For this could only be the beginning; it could get worse. While here *he* was —

The commissioner had finished his statement. Back to the newscaster. Words, words. Still circling the explosion, like a swarm of flies. A sickening parade of the injured in Tygerberg hospital, sobbing relatives, a playback of material that must have been repeated daily since the previous week.

Thomas got up and turned off the screen, aware of Maria's quizzical, reproaching look.

'If you don't mind?' he said. 'They just keep on repeating the same thing.'

'But it was awful, wasn't it?' she asked. 'The screams of those children. And the little baby. All I could think was, God knows what I would have done if it was my child — I didn't sleep a wink that night. Kept on going into the children's rooms. They were sleeping so peacefully. One is so utterly helpless. A thing like that might happen anywhere, anytime.' She was so upset that she had to get up. Cup in hand, she wandered aimlessly through the room, stopping at last beside the blank TV. 'It's just violence everywhere, every day. As if there is no more room for reason in the world. And it affects every one of us. The most ordinary people, who just want to be left in peace.' She turned her anxious eyes to him. 'Thomas, how can anyone in his right mind do such a thing?'

'Don't you think,' he said, his voice restrained, strained, 'people can be driven to a point where there is no other option left, nothing except violence, if they really want to change the world?'

'But what about reason?' she repeated. 'Violence is so utterly unreasonable.'

'Suppose it isn't a case of blindly threatening the lives of others, but of consciously choosing to risk one's own life too?'

'You sound like a voice from the distant past,' she said. 'I've almost forgotten about it, you know. Philosophy, at varsity. Was it Camus?' She sounded almost irritable. 'But this isn't philosophy, Thomas. It's real bombs we're talking about. Real people being blown up.'

'I'm just trying to imagine the reasoning behind it —'

'You really think philosophical or moral considerations play a part in the actions of a terrorist?'

'Aren't you being too simplistic? I can easily imagine that people like that – *particularly* people like that – might struggle for weeks or months or even years with problems of that kind.'

'You've always been a romantic.'

'That's no answer, Maria.'

'Forgive me, Boetie.' She sat down beside him. 'My nerves are frayed. It's as if everything has gone out of control in my life. One doesn't know from day to day what may happen. Everything that used to be so infallible, so much taken for granted, suddenly appears hollow. Our lives used to be so relaxed and easy. But nowadays –' She made a helpless gesture. 'You must have noticed when you arrived. We've raised the garden walls. Security gates. Alarm systems. Dogs. It's like living in a prison. And even with all that one doesn't feel safe. When Tertius is away I hardly sleep at night – and you know for yourself I never used to be a nervous person.'

'Surely, here in the Free State life couldn't have changed much?'

'It may seem like that on the surface. I mean, we read in the papers about blacks going on strike elsewhere in the country, even domestics staying away, things like that; we don't have much of that around here, not yet. But it's not like it used to be before. If I talk with my *ousie* and she tells me how they're being intimidated and threatened – all the agitators – they are in danger of their lives.'

'You really swallow that story about agitators from outside?'

'What do you know about what's going on here?' She sighed. 'Don't let us argue about that now. We see each other so seldom and heaven knows, life is hard enough. But I tell you, even here in the Free State things are not the way they used to be. Even when it looks calm on the surface I feel uneasy. Because if it *is* calm, it's only because the old relations of *baas* and servant are so ingrained. And that's awful too. Sometimes I feel the urge to talk to my *ousie*, you know, just ordinary woman-talk. But I cannot get through to her. She says Yes, Madam. If I persist, she tells me something about her children or her parents, but it's all on the surface. What happens to her when she closes the back door behind her in the afternoon and goes home? I don't know. I don't know anything about her. Yet we spend eight or nine hours in each other's company every day of our lives. It makes me feel guilty. And I don't *want* to feel guilty. Because, dammit, it isn't my fault!' She put her hand on his knee. 'Or is it?'

He placed his hand on hers. 'Now that sounds more like the old rebellious Maria I used to know.'

'One grows older, Thomas. Rebellion is for the young ones who have nothing to lose.'

'I don't believe it!' he said, indignant. 'Not of you, Maria.'

'We'll talk again, five or ten years from now,' she said calmly.

'Indeed, I hope so.'

(He thought of Nina: her rebelliousness and anger and passion. That was more like the Maria of old. And it couldn't just be a matter of growing older, shouldering more responsibilities, building a family. Nina would never have compromised or given up! But Nina was never allowed to grow older.)

'You seen Frans recently?' asked Maria.

'I spent the weekend with them.' He grimaced. 'He nearly threw me out.'

'Oh, you two. Cheese and chalk. Always been.'

'Do you remember –' And so began the inevitable return. Until they were stranded together, as so often in the past, on the small island of their childhood. So far away. So secure, that above all. Secure? No, hardly. The enchantment of distance, he thought, could not take away the lucidity of insight. Even in those days their island had been obscured by clouds; and there were rifts running through the meadows.

'I cannot understand how Frans and I managed to grow up in one home,' he confessed.

'It was Mum,' she said without hesitation. 'If it hadn't been for her – She could keep anything together. She never blamed anybody for being what he was.'

'That didn't stop her from taking the strap to our backsides.'

'That was different. What we did wrong, was one thing. What we *were* was something else. And Mum respected that. Right?'

– Can I respect Frans for what *he* is? He is my brother. We share the same blood. But what does that really amount to? A man like Sipho: I find it much easier, much more natural, to think of him as my brother. Does blood really bring a special responsibility with it? Perhaps it's different for parents and children. But brother and brother? In Maria I recognise something of myself; I love her. But I'm not sure about Frans. Or is one obliged to take responsibility for one's shadow too?

An insignificant memory, perhaps. (But what is 'insignificant'? Who has the right to judge?) That Saturday afternoon on Oom

Kerneels's farm. I didn't want to go, I never liked hunting. But Frans and Hendrik used all kinds of threats and promises to force me. I knew why: to prevent my telling anybody that they'd gone hunting on their own after Oom Kerneels had expressly forbidden them to. And also to do their dirty work should they bag something. Skinning the buck, taking out the insides, carrying the carcass home. Ostensibly from generosity, to 'teach me the ropes'. And then there was the thing moving in the thicket and Frans firing blindly – I was still shouting at him to wait until we could see what it was – and the cow slumping to the ground. One of Oom Kerneels's stud animals. I just turned tail and ran, but they caught up with me and dragged me back. And then the begging and pleading and arguing. If I confessed to the deed I would be forgiven, I was too young to know better, the grownups would understand and forgive. Whereas if it came out that it had been one of them, Oom Kerneels would kill them. I didn't want to, I was scared to death. Then Frans began to make promises. All the things he'd give me, everything I'd be permitted to do in future. I can't even remember the particulars. But in the end – under pressure of dire threats and physical force – I was persuaded. My heart weighed like a stone in my chest. And well it might, for never in my life have I been given a beating like that. While Frans kept a straight face about the whole thing; and afterwards forgot all about his promises. –

From one of the bedrooms came a small moaning sound. Maria was on her feet immediately.

'Katrien,' she said. 'She wakes up so often. She's always scared. I don't know where she gets it from.'

She stood listening, her body taut. It was quiet again. Outside a small owl screeched.

3

– So this is what you tried to tell me with that visit. No, I don't blame you for not confiding in me then. How could you? Even if you had, I would not have understood. Not the way I understand it now. But is it inevitable for understanding always to come too late? Perhaps this is the wrong question. Understanding can never come too late: too late, perhaps, for practical intervention; too late to help this one or that: but always, exactly, at the right moment for oneself. Because it can only come when one is ready for it.

Thomas, Thomas, Thomas. My boetie. I never slept at all last night. I did not *want* to. I wanted to, had to, stay up, the way one watches with someone ill or dead. *In extremis.* A kind of atonement, perhaps, not for you but for myself. And if there is regret in it, then it is for not being ready in time for this understanding, for not being able to do more while I could. Regret for the loss. Because loss there has been; devastating.

It sounded unreal on the TV news, a piece of cheap sensation about a stranger who by pure coincidence was also called Thomas Landman. Some Thomas Landman who, a few weeks ago, that Friday at the end of April, had in an attempt to blow up the state president taken the lives of six people and maimed and wounded I don't know how many others. It was not the Thomas I know. That was my first thought: that they didn't, couldn't possibly, know *you*. But afterwards, in the course of this long night, I thought: no, this isn't the way to think about it. I must not try to keep my Thomas separate from theirs. They are one and the same. And only if I can succeed in reconciling them can there be any hope of discovering any kind of sense in it all. Can there be any hope of understanding you. The Thomas I knew – the baby who once lay in my arms, with the flicker of a heartbeat in his soft fontanelle, gazing up at me with his grave black eyes, so wise and peaceful, and with whom I played as with a doll while Mum was ill (I was only eight myself); the little boy who sobbed out his heart in my lap because Frans had killed a grasshopper in the garden, tearing off legs and wings one by one; the thin-legged lad who could spend hours listening to Oupa's stories and who, when he was only thirteen, devoted months of hard labour to translating Great-grandfather's Boer War journal from High Dutch into Afrikaans (asking Mum for the meaning of every other word and driving her up the wall), and whose tears stained the black ink in the journal pages where he read about the women and children in the concentration camps; the youngster dancing about with joy, clutching the newspaper that had printed his first photograph; the young man who, on the morning he left my home for the last time, cavorted in the swimming-pool, Katrien screaming with glee as he pressed her small blonde bare body to the light brown of his own, the 'tan' I'd always envied him: it was the innocence of his body that morning, its smooth, unblemished narrowness, that gave me a lump in the throat – that Thomas was the same person who had detonated a bomb and blown people into bloody little bits. Bookworm, dreamer, photographer, collector of anything he could lay his hands on, his head filled with wild and wonderful schemes, loner lost in thought with a solemn line between the eyes (on your forehead the sign of Cancer: my darling crustacean, so vulnerable in your carapace), playful prankster, music lover, handyman in the house, my brother, Thomas, you: murderer and terrorist.

The moment after we'd heard the news Tertius began to rant and stamp about like a madman. He was absolutely white, trembling as if he was in fever. He smashed his fist on the table, strutting and fretting like a ham actor in a bad play. 'This is the end! How can I ever look my colleagues in the face again, Maria? There's no hope of my ever becoming a professor now. All I've been working for, for years –'

I suddenly became so angry I could not contain myself. I heard his voice again, the way it sounded years ago, after he'd resigned from his teaching job to work fulltime on his thesis; we were subsisting on my salary, but then I fell pregnant, and when I told him he stared at me in gawking incomprehension: 'But Maria, how could you be so irresponsible? What about my studies.' I was too flabbergasted at the time to answer, but afterwards it was too late, it didn't matter any more; but this time I refused to be silent.

'Is that all that matters to you, Tertius?' I asked. '*Your* professorship, the things *you*'ve been working for?'

'Are you saying it's not important to you any more?'

I felt singularly calm. 'As a matter of fact, it isn't.' I got up. 'I'm going to phone Mum. They'll be needing help.'

'I'm talking to you, Maria. Are you listening at all?'

I telephoned in the passage. Mum could not speak to me, she was crying too much, just stood there sobbing into the mouthpiece until Dad took it from her. I had a sensation of moving about in a dream, looking down on what was happening from a great distance, observing my own gestures and motions, listening to my voice. For the moment feeling was excluded, unimaginable.

'I'll go down to them as soon as it can be arranged,' I told Tertius when I came back into the dining-room. 'I'll take Katrien with me.'

'What about the boys? Can you imagine, when they arrive at school tomorrow –' He rose again from the chair into which he had slumped.

'It will be difficult, but they'll just have to learn to live with it. Like the rest of us. I'll still be here for a day or two to help them. After that –'

'You don't expect me to look after them?'

'Why not, Tertius? They're your children too. And right now Mum and Dad need me more.'

172

'Sure. Blood is thicker than water.'

'Tertius.' I could feel my body beginning to tremble. Leaning forward on my two straight arms on the table I stared at him. 'Exactly what is that supposed to mean?'

'Well, it's your family, isn't it?'

'You mean, "Thank God I'm not like the rest of those poor sinners"?'

'That's not what I said.'

'It wasn't necessary to spell it out.'

I could see his nostrils flaring and contracting. Like a rabbit's. It was as if I was looking at him for the first time in my life. And this, I thought, was the man for whose sake I'd given up everything – my dreams of independence, a job of my own, travelling, writing, fulfilment – so that he might achieve what he'd been destined for.

Two weeks ago little Leendert came home from school, breathless with excitement because their second grade class had been taken on a trip in a Casspir. The first step to 'manhood'. Is it for this I brought my sons into the world? To be drawn into the carnage, killing and being killed, the perpetual celebration of death?

Tertius continued to rage. 'Doesn't the man have any brains? Is it necessary, after thousands of years of civilisation, to act like an ape or a troglodyte? This is not the jungle any more!' I didn't even try to react. What does our own – 'civilised' – history amount to other than a catalogue of violence? Through what else, if not violence, does our Christian country maintain its law and order?

This shocking thing you did: was that *your* way of trying to put an end to it? Using violence to stop violence? But if it is so, what have you achieved, my Thomas? Was it not, in the final analysis, a *man*'s response? Or was that the measure of your despair? Perhaps the biggest shock of all, this night, has been the discovery of how little I really know about you. My own brother. And about myself.

I remember so well the very first time I learned to regard and love you, not simply as my little brother, but as a person: the first time I was forced to think about who you are, what you are. We were still living in the village off the West Coast then, and you couldn't have been older than six or seven. One evening I heard you go out the back door, with the torch. Usually you came back very quickly, for you were dead scared of the dark. But this evening you stayed away a very long time. And then came running back to call me from my room. 'Maria! Maria, come, look, there's an angel in the outhouse.' You'd found it, you explained, near the backdoor, while you were peeing: a small creature lighting up the night. You'd followed it this way and that through the back yard, into the outhouse. A firefly, I guessed. But you were adamant. It *was* an angel. Keeping a straight face, I went outside with you to have a look, but the deep well below the round hole in the outhouse was pitch-dark. No sign of angels. And after a long search we went home again.

At supper the following evening you asked, 'What kind of food do angels eat?'

Frans choked on a mouthful of bread and peanut butter, and began to tease you unmercifully, until I kicked him under the table. Dad glared his disapproval. It was Mum who said in her quiet way, as if it was the most natural thing in the world, 'Sugar water. Angels drink nothing but sugar water.'

That, I thought, was that. But an hour later I heard you go out again, as usual, for your evening pee; and once again you stayed out very long. And because I knew how scared you were of the dark, I went out to look for you. And found you. Sitting hunched up on the wooden seat in the outhouse, the torch beside you, staring into the hole. The light made a huge black shadow on the corrugated-iron wall. I remember every detail of the scene. The open door with the uneven heart-shape sawn into it (Dad's brave but unconvincing handiwork). The long nail holding squares of newsprint. The cardboard box with old copies of magazines. The smell of Jeyes' Fluid. And you crouching there, staring into the malodorous darkness, a saucer of sugar water in your hand.

When the angels failed to appear you left the saucer on the edge of the seat and returned home with me, your sticky little hand warm in mine.

The following evening you did it again. And many evenings after that. Nothing could bruise your faith. There *had been* an angel with shining wings. It would come back.

You were never afraid of the dark again, either.

How often through the years have I envied you that faith. Yet what have you achieved?

I have no wish to speculate, as in my more audacious, blinder youth I did, on the good or evil of humanity. Perhaps I've left my years of philosophy at university too far behind: being a housewife keeps one, literally, close to the ground. And that is why I am dubious, suspicious, even cynical. What about the ordinary little person – that's what I'd like to ask of you, Thomas – what about the ordinary little person, like me, who simply struggles to stay alive; who does not want to see big bullies determine her life for her; who only wants the humble freedom to take her own small decisions? Is that asking too much?

And I *must* find out. Because I, too, have momentous decisions to take in my life, decisions I can no longer postpone. What am I to *do* with everything you have exposed to my view in this long-closed room of my life? Once one has opened a door like this, it is useless to try and pull it shut again as if it hasn't happened. In a few months I shall be thirty-seven. It isn't young any more. But it isn't old either. I *can* still do something: think – decide – act.

Even if I abhor what you have done, there is something in me that shamelessly envies you: not for what you have done, but for having done something. Because I know now that I, too, have a right to live, to take my life in my own hands, here and now. That is what you have made me see. I've been wrong, all these years, to persist in thinking of myself as the victim of exploitation or oppression by others. I wasn't just, poor creature, a pitiful sacrificing spouse who'd given up her life to be used by others. I was, I am, an accomplice. It was too easy trying to persuade myself my life was hard. That is simply not enough. It can never be enough only to see, or to state, the truth. That can only be a beginning. It is only doing something about it that really matters. I think I am ready for it now. –

4

It struck him like a sjambok in the face when he saw the roadblock, a kilometre after the airport, on the road to Thaba Nchu. He had been lost in his thoughts; by the time he noticed the obstruction it was too late to brake and turn back and race away. Lights flickering. A convoy of military vehicles beside the road. Scores of soldiers with automatic rifles. Police in riot uniform.

This was the jackpot. And it was his own fault. Patrick had ordered him to return to Cape Town. That was what the Organisation had decided. It was one of the first things one was taught: you obey orders; you never act impulsively. There are enough situations in which the initiative is left to you. But when you've been given a specific instruction, you obey it to the letter. That is what you are there for. He had failed them; betrayed them: this was the first, and the worst, he thought of. Not the danger to himself, but the knowledge that he had let them down. He deserved whatever was going to happen now.

Madness. That was what it was, last night, when he couldn't sleep: this decision not to continue today to Cape Town but to turn off to Thaba Nchu, to Ladybrand, from there to the Lesotho border. If he could make it to Maseru, he would be free. A plane to Gaborone or Harare, from there to London, and this whole episode would be behind him. (Except for this horror burnt into him like the brand mark of a slave, the memory of Nina, Nina.) But Patrick had warned him. The security forces were *expecting* everybody involved in the attack to attempt leaving the country as soon as possible. And it wasn't a crisis, a sudden panic, that had prompted his change of plans. It was a calm, considered decision in the middle of the night. He'd had time to think. In the dark it had all seemed so feasible. As if, in a way, he owed it to Nina to put this matter behind him once and for all, as if his safe escape would somehow compensate for what had happened to her. Only now – too late – he realised the idiocy of the decision. Madness.

Why hadn't he considered the possibility of roadblocks? It was the first, the most elementary of eventualities. It wasn't being caught as such that dismayed him, he'd always been prepared for that. But failing the expectations, the requirements of the Organisation, that was different. Because he'd been too certain of success from the beginning. Even when that horrendous, still incredible scene had taken place in front of his eyes in the airport building, he hadn't really considered that he, too, might be apprehended. It had been a postponement, that was all. And last night, when once again he couldn't sleep, that was the way he'd thought about it.

Last night: he'd stood, exhausted but wide awake, in front of his open window breathing in the clean night air. Insects peacefully chirping in the grass. The night sky above, familiar and reassuring, shedding a milky light over the shrubs in the garden. A night one could smell: grass, dark soil, subterranean water. Now and then a whirring of wings or the screeching of the owl. And then, an apocryphal sound, so low one hardly heard it with one's ears, it was insinuated into the bones and the subconscious, the roaring of the lions in the zoo. An ancient tragic Africa that refused to come to rest. A sound, he thought, his ancestor, the Seer, Petrus, would have heard when he'd camped here as a child, with the Enslins and the Greylings, before they set out for Jerusalem. In those days one could withdraw into a laager and be safe against the predators: today the enemy was inside the laager; the laager itself had become the enemy. Great-great-grandfather Petrus, he thought, tonight I'm on the run from my own people.

Maria had said, 'Thomas, why don't you stay longer? What's driving you? Only one more day, it can't make so much difference to you?' It would have made all the difference in the world if he'd stayed. Or if he'd turned off, as he should, to the N1. Then he wouldn't have come up against this roadblock. Fifty yards ahead of him a soldier, presumably the C.O., walked to the middle of the road, his automatic rifle casually cradled in one arm. Perhaps he could still brake very hard, make a U-turn, race away at full speed. Or step on the accelerator and drive straight at the man in the road, ducking low behind the wheel. But of course either choice would be fatal. Better to maintain a last bit of dignity. All right, arrest me. I know this is it. It's all over. Here I am, a lion in your den of Daniels.

'Good morning, sir,' the officer greeted him with a friendly, apologetic smile. A smell of perspiration wafted into the car as he leaned through the window to peer inside. 'Just a routine check. Do you mind opening the boot for us?'

He felt like bursting out laughing, uttering a war-cry, performing a wild dance in the road. But with as much restraint as he could muster he walked round the car, unlocked the boot, opened the hood, and stood back.

Without much interest the soldier poked at the suitcase. (Thomas had removed the name-tag the previous day, a block from Frans's house, and disposed of it in a waste-paper bin.) Then asked, 'Any firearms?'

'I'm not a terrorist,' said Thomas.

'I didn't mean that, sir.' A hint of warning in the voice. 'And it's not a joke.'

'Sorry.'

For a moment their eyes met.

'May I go now?'

'Of course.'

As he turned the starter the officer suddenly said, 'Just a moment!'

Thomas felt his heart contract. 'What's the matter?' His throat was dry.

'That box on the seat next to you?'

Relieved and furious at the same time, he felt like answering, It's a bomb. But he said demurely, 'Have a look,' and handed it to the officer, through the window. The man opened the lid, glanced at the food Maria had packed for him: sandwiches, two hard-boiled eggs, a chicken drumstick, tomatoes, two late-summer figs. 'I hope it's not against the emergency regulations?' Thomas asked.

Annoyed, without a word, the officer thrust the box back into his hands and motioned him to drive on. Thomas kept an eye on him in the rear-view mirror until the roadblock disappeared in the distance behind him. He was expecting to feel relieved; instead, he was nauseous. There was perspiration on his forehead. For several kilometres he drove on mechanically, until he felt he couldn't go any further. Opposite a turn-off to the black township of Botshabelo he steered off the road and sat there motionless, waiting for the turbulence in his chest to subside.

Opposite him, close to the road, was a group of imposing houses that would not have been out of place in any white suburb; which was why they had been placed in full view of the main road. To the right, a series of blue postmodernist constructions were going up. Further along the side road, half hidden behind a low hill, there was an intimation of a sprawling township, small box-houses and shacks, growing more miserable and dilapidated the further one moved away from the road as if, ashamed, they were trying to hide their naked ugliness behind the hill. He remembered an earlier visit to the place, with Henry, on UDF business. There had been a secretary from the Canadian Embassy with them. Part of an enquiry to determine what assistance the Canadian government could offer. Here in Botshabelo, like everywhere they had been, Henry had invited the inhabitants to a discussion. Explained to them that the Canadian government was eager to sponsor a community project, some kind of self-help scheme, something the whole township would benefit from: the people were free to choose what they wanted most. The leaders seemed overwhelmed by the offer, and asked for time to discuss it with the people. A report-back meeting was arranged for the afternoon. When they came back, the people humbly announced their decision: what they needed most, they said, was a mortuary.

He felt an urge to follow the side-road to the township. There, among people so abject that even the thought of revolution was a luxury, he would be more at home than in the affluent white suburbs of Pretoria or Bloemfontein. Total strangers would stare at him from a safe distance at first; then approach him to take their photographs, and invite him home, and share their scraps of food with him, offer

him a place to sleep. How often had it not happened to him before –
in Guguletu or Langa outside Cape Town; in New Brighton or Zwide
at Port Elizabeth; Duncanville at East London, Mamelodi at Pretoria.
Ubuntu. That was what Sipho had called it. That untranslatable
word missing from Afrikaans and English dictionaries. (Perhaps
his ancestors had known an equivalent, lost in the deep interior,
out of sight even of a neighbour's smoke? – the savage Diederik,
the obsessive builder Jan-Jonas, or Benjamin, the frontier farmer
with the ready hands? Yes, they might have known the meaning.
But where, along the road, had they lost it, where had they taken
the wrong turning, how could you lose a thing like that once you'd
known it?) *Ubuntu*: sharing, generosity, hospitality, humanity. All
of that, and more. Oh much more. It was *ubuntu* that prompted
you to invite a stranger to spend the night, even when you possessed
nothing. That made you shelter, at the risk of your own life, on a
windblown day in Crossroads, two white strangers on the run from
the police. That made you invite a friend to share with you, some
distant purple day in Lusaka, the homecoming of your wife.

But he did not turn off. Not for fear that Botshabelo might
have changed; but because Patrick had warned him: Don't! Stay
away from all the black townships on your way. There are spies
everywhere, and you'll be as visible as a dominee in a whorehouse.
Keep out. He'd done one impulsive thing today. It could have cost
him his life. Back to Cape Town. The Organisation knew what was
going on. He had to keep cool, obey the instructions.

The sound of faint thunder in the distance. High above – his
eyes grew tearful from staring into the light – the speck of a plane
streaked past, from south to north. The route he had travelled
last Friday. There had been that talkative girl beside him, who'd
showered him with the contents of her bag. Lisa. He could do
with her company right now; that gravelly voice; it would have
held his own thoughts in check. She'd talked too much, but it had
been from dismay, anxiety, rage. (*What was there I could do that
would really shake them to their foundations, just to prove that
I was I, not one of them! There should be something truly terrible
one could do. Like burning down the school. Or necklacing Siebert.
Or blowing up the state president. Something like that.*) He smiled
ruefully. By now her little cavale would be over: she'd attended her
friend's wedding, flown back to Cape Town, survived a talking-to
by her principal, demurely resumed her work. She wouldn't really
jeopardise her security. There were so many safe rebels around. But

it was neither here nor there. She belonged to yesterday. The world before the Flood.

He felt calmer now. He started the car again, checked the rear-view mirror, turned back into the road. Over the next few kilometres there were several more small dirt tracks turning off to Botshabelo. On the edge of visibility, in the distance, one could distinguish the smear of sad dwellings continuing, it seemed, forever: a subconscious to the white city he'd left behind; rejected, naked, crude.

Just before he reached the junction at Ladybrand – his last chance to turn off to Lesotho, less than twenty kilometres away, if he still wished to; but he no longer considered it – there was a news bulletin on the radio. He put out his hand to turn it off and silence that smug voice; he didn't need any more reminders. But this time there was something new, which touched him like a shudder of wind moving across water. *A spokesman in the office of the state president has announced that the joint funeral of the victims in last Friday's bomb tragedy in Cape Town will be held this Friday afternoon at three o'clock in the Groote Kerk. The relatives of –* At the memorial service – *It is expected that –* He thought: Now he *had* to go back. Clear and unambiguous it stood before him. He had to be there. Provided the Organisation gave permission, of course; he would have to find out first. It was not the kind of decision he could take on his own. But he had to try. It was unavoidable. Even if he had trouble explaining it to himself. The criminal returning to the scene of the crime? No, it wasn't so easy. It had to do with the need to round off what had begun, to follow through, all the way to the very end, wherever that might be, the assumption of an illogical responsibility.

In a strange way it calmed the restlessness in himself: a focus for his thoughts, something to do, something to aim for.

That was, undoubtedly, what Nina would have done if she had been on this road today, heading back, through wide plains of late summer grass turning to pale yellow. Only half conscious of his surroundings – Wepener, Zastron, Aliwal North – he gave his thoughts free rein, not *wanting* to restrain them any more.

– That early dawn in my flat in Vredehoek when Colonel Bester arrives with his stormtroopers to arrest me, my first thought is: you. You, Nina, listening in the passage, naked. They must not find you there. Yesterday in Crossroads I had a glimpse of your way of doing things. If they find you here today you will undoubtedly fight back. And then God knows what will happen. For a moment I even wish I had taken you home to your own place last night, as you first asked me to. But if I think about last night I know I would not want to change that.

My front door is full of men. And behind me, in the short dark passage, you. In the bedroom, on the floor, my camera bag; all the films I took in Crossroads. I cannot afford to lose them all. I've always been so fastidious, after that first raid while I was abroad, about keeping films, negatives, 'exhibits' in other places, not in my flat. A whole network of contacts all over town. But this once – and it is such a vital occasion – I have neglected to do so. And now they're here.

I try to stall for time. Ask if they have a warrant. Try to argue. Try to keep very calm, even though my heart is pounding and I know I am short of breath. My very nonchalance makes the colonel furious. 'Take him in!' he finally orders two of his men. 'The rest of us will work through this place. Keep him quiet until we come back. We have a lot to talk about.'

It is their custom to detain one on the spot while they search one's possessions. Not that they are much concerned with the letter of the law; but usually, I should imagine, it adds a certain sadistic glee to the situation if they can wreck a place in the presence of the victim. Not this time. And that is what upsets me so. Now I don't even know what they've found in my absence. Or what they've done to you. I can only suspect the worst. That week in detention is the longest in my life. I cannot understand why they keep on asking about the Crossroads films. The bag was left standing in the middle of the bedroom floor; during the night, when you went to the bathroom, you stumbled over it, and cursed, and I came to help you, and we burst out laughing, and continued our lovemaking on the floor. So I know the bag was there. What could have become of it?

Towards the end of the week things are beginning to look bad. Bester's patience, I can see, is wearing thin. It's obvious he won't be satisfied with threats and insinuations for much longer. I believe the colour of my skin (even if, as is the case of so many Afrikaners, there is the faintest hint of a deeper tint in it, inherited from my worthy forebears) will protect me up to a point, but then no more. If they so decide, I need never step out of this place again. Not alive. I may be a very small pawn, not comparable to the true martyrs, but there is always the risk. Nowadays even the insignificant ones are in danger: in the State of Emergency no rule and no law restrains the SB any more.

That is exactly what Colonel Bester tells me.

And then I am released. Just like that. Taken from my cell one morning, bundled into a car, driven to Caledon Square, 'booked out', into another car, and dropped at the front entrance to my flat building.

I remember very clearly what Bester has told me in his office, his face a centimetre from my face: 'You can go. This time, my friend, you can thank your lucky stars. But we'll be seeing each other again. Will you remember that? We two will be seeing each other again. It's a date. And I never miss a date.'

But for the moment I am too overwhelmed by everything to be concerned about that appointment.

When I look up, you are sitting on the bottom step in the cold foyer, waiting. Huddled in an anorak much too big for you.

'So it was *you*!' I say. 'How did you manage it?'

You get up, your head barely reaching my shoulder; I've forgotten how small you are. 'I was hoping you wouldn't ask me that. I'm not exactly proud of myself.' Then, furious, 'And don't ever, ever expect a thing like this from me again. Because I won't.'

'I don't know what you're talking about, Nina. I *wasn't* expecting anything from you. Will you please tell me what is going on? How did you know to wait here for me?'

'Can we go somewhere? Outside. I feel cornered in here. And your place will be bugged by now.'

Up the mountain. It is the first time we go there together.

'Now will you tell me?'

'It was my father who arranged your release.' You look down at your hands.

'Your father?'

'I told you about him. He's a judge.'

'I know, but – You didn't *ask* him, did you?'

'What else could I do, Thomas?' In a rage, you tug at my sleeve. 'I thought I'd go mad with worry, all this week. I'd sworn long ago I'd never ask him another favour in my life. If it had been anyone else I – And he was so bloody awful about it too. But, damn it, Thomas, I couldn't just let you stay there!'

I am so confused that it is only much later it occurs to me to ask, 'But what happened to *you* after they took me away? And my photographs – my films?'

You seem very casual about it all. 'I could hear from the passage what was going on. They were talking so loudly. So I took the bag and slipped out the back way, down the fire escape. It was only when I reached the bottom that I realised I wasn't wearing a stitch.'

(That explains their insistent questions: 'Who were you with that night? Who was the woman? Don't lie to us, we know there was someone with you!')

'But how did you —?'

'One of the garages downstairs was open. I slipped in there and closed the door. I don't know what I would have done if somebody had come in. There was a lot of junk lying about. Paint tins, brushes, building material. And that black plastic stuff, what d'you call it?, damp course. I made a kind of tunic out of it. Not exactly stylish. People must have thought I was a *bergie* or something when I crept out. It must have been noon already, I'd been too shit-scared to go out earlier. And when I reached the top of Long Street there was a yellow police van behind me. Kept cruising after me for God knows how long. Must have thought I was a whore on my way to the harbour. I was expecting them to stop at any moment and throw me into the back.'

'You had to walk all the way to Green Point?'

'What else? Never knew it was so far from Vredehoek. And barefoot too. Jesus, I thought I was going to freeze. But I got there. And your films are safe.'

'My God, Nina —'

You are breathless, I too, when I let you go at last. Wind in your unkempt hair. Your green eyes defiant.

'The worst is,' you say — are you mocking? are you serious? — 'I have an idea this is only the beginning. Because we can't possibly leave each other after this, we both know too much.' —

5

— 'Viva the struggle!' was what he said, hey. And I said, 'Fuck the struggle, man. I just want to be left in peace.' That's what I said. Because after everything that happened, I mean, the trouble on the mines, and those Ciskei papers, and my brother they took away to Louis le Grange Square, I mean, no ways. And I was pissed off too. What did he mean, saying, 'Viva the struggle'? I mean, what did he know about it? It's easy for him to talk, he's white. But what's he know? All right, he was a nice chap, we had a good chat on the way, it's not every white man that can speak to you in your language, and what he told me about his experiences in the Emergency, I mean, that sounded all pretty genuine. I could see he meant it all right. But I wasn't going to let any white man just come and say 'Viva the struggle' to me, right? Whose struggle is it anyway?

But so okay, he dropped me outside Bloemfontein and that was, I thought, that was the last I was to see of him. Stood there for twelve hours before I got another lift, the Free State is hell to hitch a hike in if you're black. But I knew sometime someone would stop, and they did, it was a combi from Queenstown, full-full-full of people, but they found place for me. And in Queenstown they knew someone else who was going to Ibhayi, so from there I got to New Brighton, no problem. And there was Ntomzana and the twins, just fine, it was good to be back.

Never thought of the man again. There was such a lot of things to do anyway, trying to find out about a job and everything. Days and days walking the streets, from factory to factory, just useless. Then in the white suburbs, all those smart houses, hey, from one house to the other, and all those bloody dogs at your heels, all the time. Sorry, Madam, I'm looking for a job. Anything. Handyman, painting, gardening, anything. At home the twins are growing up, they don't even know their father any more. Now I must come home day after day with empty hands, no job, nothing. It's not a good life for a father of sons.

But then suddenly, okay, here's Vuyisile. My brother. Can you believe it? They let him go from Louis le Grange Square. He looks bad, he's *deurmekaar* in his head. But he's free. After nearly two years, that's a hell of a long time, man. So we have a big party, I mean, really big, everybody comes to welcome him. Only, I don't recognise my brother no more. When our friends speak to him of jail, he just shakes his head, no, he's not going to talk about it. It was too bad. Now you must know, he was always the hot-headed one. Ready to fight anyone. Not a troublemaker, but a man with a spark in his guts. Only that spark is gone now. I talk to Vuyisile, I talk, I talk, but he just shakes his head. Then one day he says, 'Buti,' he says, 'I'm going to take a job with the police. There's no way.'

He's broken, man, broken. He can't get no job, nowhere. His spark is gone. So now he wants a job with the police. They will pay him, he says. Good pay. They will give him a new house. They will send his children to school. He will have a good life. But to me, hell man, I mean, it's the worst thing I have heard in my life. I mean, I was never a man for trouble. I don't like what I see around me, it's too bad, but I just want to live my life in peace with Ntomzana and the kids, right? The young comrades in the

184

townships, they talk about Free Mandela, about Azania, about lots of things. All I say is, leave me out of it. I say, suppose they free all the prisoners, suppose they bring back the exiles, suppose they call this place Azania, suppose we can all stand in the streets and shout Amandla! Ngawethu! Then what? Is that going to feed my children? Is that going to solve my problems? No, just leave me out of it, is what I always said. But this thing about my brother, about Vuyisile, that was too bad.

It broke my heart to see that man put on a police uniform and come home with his baton and his gun in the evening. It's like he is a stranger now, he's not the brother I grew up with, I went to the bush with, we were *amakweta* together, that's not the one I know. I try to talk to him, we talk, we talk, we talk, but it's no use, and in the end he just gets angry. He tells me what do I know about jail? Who am I to tell him what to do and what not to do? And there I am without a job too, and we must sell two more cattle, there are not many left, and what is going to happen to my wife and my kids? Must I also go into the police? So help me God, no. I can't do a thing like that. I mean, it's not like I'm against them or anything. Just keep me out of it to live my life. Except I say what is this thing I call my life? Please, Madam, I'm looking for a job. Anything, Madam.

That is when I see the man's face in the newspaper at the fish and chips shop. Jesus, it gives me such a shock. Too bad, man. If I read the newspaper every day I would have seen it long ago, but now it is the first time. Thomas Landman, it says, and it tells the whole thing about a bomb in Cape Town, everything. This is the terrorist the police are looking for.

Thomas. That was what he said his name was. Thomas. And this one is Thomas Landman.

Suddenly I remember everything, man. I mean, what he told me about visiting his friends in the townships, and how he listened to the Casspirs coming past in the streets, and the Boere marching in the night, and his best friend that was called Sipho, and who died. And his girlfriend, too, who died. I remember that, and later I see in the newspaper this girl was killed at Jan Smuts airport. So now I know. He was telling the truth all the time.

I tell you, it was like what they talk about, the ones they take to Louis le Grange Square: when they tie the wires on to you and they give you shock treatment. This was the kind of shock I got. What I have in my mind is this: Here I am, look at me, I am black. And all I can say is leave me out of it, I want to live in peace with my wife and children. But what kind of peace have I got? And now my own brother has joined the police. My own *buti* is walking about with a gun strapped to his belt. It is now his turn to kill people, to kill for the Boere. Now he is one of them, because he suffered too much, he could not take it. Okay, and here is this white man, this Thomas, I mean, he's got everything, he is white. 'I'm also a Boer,' is what he said. Now he is running away. If they catch him, they going to kill him, sure as God. And all the same, he did it. He didn't care that they may kill him. What did he do it for? Not for himself. How can he? He already got everything, he is white. So he did it for other people, he did it for people like me. Who say: Leave me out of it.

This is a very wrong thing, it is too bad.

I tell you, I did not sleep, I did not eat, I did not do nothing. For days and days. Just thinking about this thing.

But now I have peace in my mind. I know what I am going to do.

It is this young man, this Thomas, this one who gave me the lift, who made me see it. If he can do a thing like this, who am I to say I want to stay out of it? If I try to stay out, what happens? It just gets worse, that is what happens. Look at my own brother. A traitor. So there is something for me to do. I have already packed my things. I shall be going to Botswana. From there I shall go to Lusaka. I shall present myself to them and tell them: Here I am. My name was Raymond, now I am Kholisile, the name my father gave me. The name I want people to know me by, the name I shall be proud of one day. It is not for the sake of this young man, Thomas Landman, that I do it: but it is he who made me do it. The reason I do it is for myself. It is for my wife, it is for my children. So that one day, when people ask them who their father was, they can say: He was a freedom fighter. And they will be proud of me. And in a way I know I am also doing it for my brother. To ask pardon for him. For what he has done. Because he does not know it himself.

Perhaps one day I shall meet Thomas Landman again, over there. Look, I shall say to him, look, I have come. It is good to see you here. But you must know, Thomas, it is not to meet you that I have come. It is to meet myself.

And perhaps, one day, one day, perhaps, we shall both go home together. Brother and brother. For that is what we are. —

186

He had meant to work his way back, progressively, to the N1, from Aliwal North over Burgersdorp, and past the Verwoerd Dam to Colesberg; or via Steynsburg and Middelburg. But at Middelburg, in the late afternoon, it occurred to him that he could easily drive on to Graaff-Reinet from there, and via Aberdeen and Willowmore to the Little Karoo, and look up his parents; there he could rest and recover, prepare himself for the last half-day's drive to Cape Town. It was barely a detour. And it made sense, on a level deeper than logic.

7

– I still cannot believe it. There must be a mistake. I've thought so from the beginning. Not *our* child. Not Thomas. To see the papers referring to him as a 'terrorist'. How is such a thing possible? Over and over. Dear God in heaven, how is it possible? Where have we gone wrong? Because it must have been our fault. All the time one believes one is bringing up a child in the fear of the Lord, then this. Reveal to me my sin, Lord. It's all I'm asking. He would never have done it on his own. Not my son. I know him. I suckled him on my breast. Such a greedy little animal. I brought him into the world. For nine months I carried him deep inside my own body. I had endless conversations with him that no one will ever know about. Just the two of us. Months in which the shadow of death was over me. Three times the doctor told Christiaan he'd better prepare himself, I wasn't going to make it. What brought me back, every time, what kept me alive, was the child inside me. I wanted him. I would have him. That is what I told him, over and over again. It was our secret. Neither of us could face the world without the other.

The poor child was exhausted when he arrived here that afternoon. It was the Wednesday afternoon, I remember exactly, because I was just getting ready to go to the WAA. With the jar of canned peaches for the competition. Very nearly hadn't made it either. Because early that morning, just when I'd filled up the jar to the brim, ready to screw on the lid, it slipped from my hands. I was ready to cry, I tell you, because I'd selected all the best halves. And as Bettie and I were crawling about on the floor on hands and knees, trying to save what could still be salvaged in a soup plate, one of the blue and white ones Ma had given me as a wedding present, I had this terrible thought. Like a sudden gust of winter wind blowing into the kitchen. What I thought was how many things had started breaking around the house lately.

First the jug in the room, the heirloom from Ma's family, the Mullers. As I was filling it up with water in the bathroom to pour into the vase in which I'd arranged the roses, it's such a good year for roses, I struck the lip against the tap. A whole big chip out of it.

And that same night, which means it was the Tuesday, there was the crash in the passage. Burglars, I thought. Crept there, with Christiaan, torch in hand, my heart in my throat. And then what should we see but that the Landmans' old family mirror had fallen from its nail on the wall. On top of the earthenware pot we'd brought from the Transvaal all those years ago. The pot in smithereens. The mirror, which had survived so many generations, even after it had first cracked, was also damaged. One corner, bottom left, quite splintered off. That heavy hand-carved old thing. Christiaan promised he'd mend it, but I prefer him to keep his hands off it. I know he means well, but no piece of wood is safe in his vicinity.

Thirteen generations of Landmans, if one includes Thomas and the other children, have looked into that mirror. It travelled into the interior in oxwagons. It survived Bloukrans, where the Zulus murdered the *trekboers*. Even the angel Gabriel, if one can repeat the Landmans' claim without committing blasphemy, appeared in it. And all of that it survived, except for the crack that was supposed to have split it when God Himself, can you imagine, looked in it. Now this. The wire at the back had rusted right through. We'd never noticed before. But who ever thinks of taking down a heavy thing like that to check the wire? It's easy to be wise afterwards.

Christiaan was pale with shock. I didn't feel too well either. But I wanted to soothe him, bolster his confidence. 'It's just an earthly possession,' I told him.

Which, I suppose, was the wrong word.

'Earthly possession, Helena?' His voice was shaky. 'Here I stand with my whole family in my two hands and you.' Christiaan never finishes his sentences.

'Let me make us some bush-tea,' I offered. 'Then we can go back to bed.'

'How can you think of going to bed again? You'll never.'

As I stood in the kitchen with the teapot in my hands, the old Limoges pot my ancestors had brought with them when the

Huguenots first fled from France – the Landmans aren't the only ones with a family history, even though Christiaan would like to think so – I was suddenly shaken by a bout of uncontrollable trembling. As if I was looking right through the old teapot. Right through the kitchen. The walls. Everything. As if there was nothing solid and secure around me any more. Everything transparent. And terribly, terribly vulnerable. This old teapot would also break, I thought. Another chunk of our history gone. A chunk from myself. Piece by piece we are being broken up. Nothing lasts. These very walls will cave in and crumble to dust. This house.

I've always had this thing about the house. Could never reconcile myself to it. Because I'd been denied a say in buying it. Christiaan had come here ahead of the rest of us, decided it was a good buy, and when he brought the family down in the car it was already registered in his name, and all we could do was move in. He kept promising, 'It's only temporary, Helena, I promise you I'll. As soon as there's something better on the market we can.'

We're still living here, temporarily. Sixteen years, come July. And I'm still not feeling at home. I know we'll die here one day. I have resigned myself to it. Even if I still don't think of it as mine. Temporary. We live by the grace of God. Perhaps it's wishful thinking anyway, being tied to a place or a time. Yet it's in our nature. One can't really be a person without this urge. And children need it. The security. There are two things, I've always thought, a parent should give his children. And I'm not sure, today, that I've been able to provide either. One is roots. The other, wings.

The tea water must have been boiling for minutes before I became aware of it again. And Christiaan was fast asleep when I took the tray to the bedroom. Snoring to high heaven. And I was the one who couldn't sleep.

So it wasn't a Wednesday that started very propitiously for me. And when at last I had the second jar of canned peaches ready, not as good as the first, the strange white car pulled up beside the house and there was Thomas.

Quite flaked he was when he arrived. Hadn't slept a wink, he told me. He'd pulled off the road somewhere between Middelburg and Graaff-Reinet and tried to sleep, but of course it didn't work. He should have booked in at a hotel, I told him. No, he said, it was unnecessary expense and he couldn't sleep in a strange bed anyway. Children always know better. And what was he up to, I asked him, on the road like that? Some kind of project. I just hope, I said, it wasn't another thing on the protests and stuff. You know, your Dad and I still have a hard time because of that exhibition you had last time. Even some of our best friends keep on harping on it. And Dad has had an inspector from the Department. Very friendly man he was, I invited him to lunch, but he made sure we knew it was an embarrassment to the Department. If you ask me, that's where Dad got his first setback from. This latest news was just the final nail, in a manner of speaking, in his coffin, bless him. It's not that I blame the boy, heaven forbid, not a word of reproach will ever cross these lips. But he had to realise he wasn't making things easy for us. All our lives we've never bothered other people or caused them to raise their eyebrows, and that's how it should be.

Now just listen to them. Even at night, sometimes, in the wee hours, the telephone will start ringing. Mostly they don't even say who they are. Just ranting and raving. As if *we* are to blame. Gossips. Troublemakers. Cowards without a name. I wipe my backside on them. But it's hard on Christiaan. Every time he wants to know who it was that phoned. How can I possibly tell him? He won't survive another shock like that. Worst is, every time he thinks it's Thomas. Waiting and waiting for news. And it never comes. I cannot even tell him what it is I fear. Alone I must bear it, for it will be the death of him. But God is always there to support one in the hour of need. He knows the reason and the end of it all. His ways are higher than our ways, and His thoughts than our thoughts.

Strange how concerned Thomas was about the broken mirror in the passage. The very next morning he went to town to buy new picture wire and threaded it through the hooks at the back of that ostentatious old frame and hung it up again. Even as a child he would always straighten the pictures, couldn't bear them hanging askew. Many times I found him there in the passage in front of the old mirror, peering into the mottled glass, as if he was trying to stare right through it. What he said when I asked him about it. 'One can't see it with the naked eye, Mum. But I'm sure they're still somewhere in this glass. They're soaked into it. And if only one knew how to look, they would still be there, looking back at you.' Made one feel quite funny. So many dead and departed in one's home.

On a sudden inspiration, more to hide my embarrassment than anything else, I said, 'I think you should take the mirror for you when we're no longer there.'

To my surprise he reacted very seriously. 'You really mean it,

190

Mum?' And before I could answer, a sudden hesitation, 'But it's supposed to go to Frans, he's the eldest.'

I remembered how Christiaan and them wrote their names on the back of each piece of furniture in their father's house long before the old man died. There was something disrespectful about it, the way I saw it. Like robbing a corpse. And I knew Frans would insist on having what by rights should go to him. That child. But perhaps for that very reason I answered, 'I'll discuss it with your father. Some time, when he's in the right mood.'

Now I still haven't done it. And there Christiaan lies outstretched in his bed, half paralysed. The blow was simply too much for him. When those policemen turned up. Actually it goes back to the night before, when we first heard the news on TV. In the beginning I was much more shocked than he. When Maria phoned just after the news I was the one who couldn't get a word out. Selfish of me. If I'd paid more attention to Christiaan then, I might have prevented what happened the next day.

Five security policemen, driven all the way from Port Elizabeth in their big beige car just to see us. No, let me be precise. They came to question us. (Even that was nothing compared to what happened later. The swine. God forgive me, but that's the only word I have for them. But I'd rather not talk about that now. My nerves are still too raw.) When had we last seen Thomas? Had we noticed anything strange in his behaviour? Had he by any chance asked us to keep anything for him?

I acted dumb. Didn't even offer them coffee. Must have been the first time in my life I did that to visitors. I told them Thomas hadn't been home for over a year. The child was kept so busy all the time. In fact, we know nothing about his doings at all. I glanced sideways at Christiaan once, thinking: Now you just try to put in a word. To deny what I'm saying. Then you'll have me to reckon with like never before in all our years together. Because I was fighting for my child's life. But Christiaan said nothing. I don't think he even heard our conversation. Just sat there staring into space. Too shocked, too angry to move, it looked.

They grew more difficult. Would I show them Thomas's room? And if that wasn't enough, they dug up all his possessions he'd been storing there for years and years. All those boxes of magazines, photographs, letters, files, school-books, university books, lecture notes. Always been like that, Thomas. Never threw anything away. I told the men: Over my dead body. Those are my son's things. But they just shrugged. Sorry, Mrs Landman, but this is serious. Other people's lives may depend on it. But it's all *old* stuff, I told them. Look, it comes from his school days, his student days. Doesn't matter, Mrs Landman. We'll give you a receipt for everything. A receipt in exchange for my child. Because it was as if it was *him* they were carrying out of here in those boxes. Taking from me something that had been my very own. For almost twenty-nine years. A child who'd nearly cost my life when he was born. For months I hovered in the shadows of death. Maria was the one who had to mother him. That is why he's always been as precious as my own life to me. Now they were taking him away. But I did not cry. I wouldn't humiliate myself before people like that.

While they were packing up, I went back to Christiaan in the sitting-room. I needed his help. He's a man, he has more authority. But he was still sitting rigidly in his chair, hadn't moved since we'd gone out. Staring into whatever was ahead of him, as if he was looking into the valley of death. Christiaan, I said, Christiaan, for heaven's sake, come and *do* something. These people want to take all Thomas's things away. If you don't stop them I may be tempted to do something I won't take responsibility for. Christiaan! But he just *sat* there. The man can be such a bloody mule. Forgive me for saying these words, but that was what I thought in my rage. I've always been quick-tempered, God has had His hands full with me most of my life. But I calm down again. It's a matter of working myself up, and exploding, and then it's over. Not like Christiaan or Frans who can mope and sulk for days. Once he didn't speak to me for four weeks. That was, so help me God, why I thought it was just one of his moods again.

Helpless, I went back to the room. I didn't want to leave them alone with Thomas's things. You can't trust those people with anything. Sorry, but it's true. I discussed it with Boet afterwards. Boet, I said, I need your help. You've *got* to help me. You're my brother, and you're a sergeant in the police. Your word must count for something.

But he just sighed and threw up his arms. Nobody's word counts for anything with the security police, he said. Not even the minister can stop them. I didn't want to believe him, but that's what he told me and he's been in the police for longer than I can remember. Will be retiring soon. Sixty-five, and he started at eighteen. Told me to be patient. Things might sort themselves out.

God doesn't sleep, Boet, I told him. That was all I could say. God doesn't sleep. That's what I told them too, those five men, the five who filled their big beige car with their big bodies when they left at last, the five who came from Thomas's bedroom carrying the boxes loaded with his possessions, taken from under his bed, from his drawers, from his wardrobe. God doesn't sleep. And only then I began to cry, when they'd left. Because then I couldn't hold back any more.

Christiaan, I couldn't believe my eyes, was still sitting in his chair. Paying no attention to anything I said. You're heartless, I cried out. More loudly than I'd ever spoken to him before. And then ran to Thomas's room and fell down on his bed and just cried and cried. Later I went over to Boet's, as I've said. He gave me a stiff neat brandy to calm me down. It's not something I easily take, except for medicine. And then with buchu. But this time I needed medicine. And it was only when I came home again in the early dusk, more composed at last, and found Christiaan still sitting in his chair, unmoving, in the half-dark, that I realised there was something very wrong. Something in the way he sat. And for the first time I discovered that this was no sulk; he'd had a stroke.

When I touched his shoulder he fell against the backrest of the chair, and his mouth remained open. He was drooling. I had such a fright I even forgot about the telephone. Ran all the way to Dr Cronjé's house. And I'm not a spring chicken any more. Christiaan and I will both be sixty-one this year. Dr Cronjé gave one look and called the ambulance. Took Christiaan through to Oudtshoorn, where I don't know how many doctors went over him. It was two weeks before he could manage to move the fingers of his left hand again. By that time, fortunately, Maria had come to help me out. He's better now, and back at home, but there's almost nothing he can do for himself. Lies there with his eyes wide open, day and night, staring, and no one can tell what he sees.

The second time they came there were nine of them, in two cars. Once again I refused to offer them coffee. I didn't even invite them to sit, but they did it unbidden. People like that have no manners. And started questioning me again, on and on, no end to it. I gave no more answers than I had the first time. When they left I said, I hope you're satisfied now. Or are you going to continue until I've also had a stroke? Is that what you're aiming for? I'm sorry, Mrs Landman, one of the men said. The leader, I think. Some corporal or general or something, I don't know one rank from another. Terribly polite. I'm sorry, Mrs Landman, it is most unfortunate that you should react like this. But you must realise, we cannot take chances with terrorists. I'm not so sure who the real terrorists are, I said. You've almost succeeded in driving my husband to his grave, and how far you're going to hunt my son I don't know. I can't take much more either. So why don't you just continue like this? You're doing a good job.

A guard in front of my mouth. That was what Ma told me ever since I was a child. And then Christiaan. But I've never learned. And now I think it is too late.

And then, yet another time, the big boss came straight from Cape Town. Brigadier Bester. In charge of The Case. A big man, on the dark side, very friendly. But I don't trust their friendliness. And what he did here I'd rather not talk about. I must leave it to God to forgive, if He can. It's asking too much of *me*. Sorry.

That I should be saying such things. I who used to impress it on my children always to be generous, forgiving. Including the last time the whole family gathered here for Christmas. Two years ago. It was good to have them all together. All the grandchildren too. But then there was the terrible fight. It started with such a small thing. On the sacred day of Christmas, at table, the festive meal spread out before us. The children began by teasing me for filling up their plates like that. When they were small I used to keep them at table after school until their plates were clean. Even if it took them until after sunset. Always put down my foot. Now they started telling me about the things they'd done to get around it, to fool me. I couldn't believe my ears. Even the exemplary Maria told me how she'd fed the meat and potatoes to the dog under the table. And Frans had stuffed his spinach and cabbage into his trouser pockets. Thomas was the only one who didn't join in, because he'd been the latecomer, I'd never been so strict with him.

Which provoked Frans into saying, 'Yes, you've always been the favourite. Never got hidings like Maria and me. Brought you up for the gallows, they did.'

Thomas, still amicably, as it seemed to me, 'Except for the times you deliberately landed me in trouble.'

Frans, indignant, 'Like when? You're talking nonsense, man.'

Christiaan, always the teacher, 'Now, now, children. You're talking about years ago. Please show some respect for the birthday of the Lord.'

But Frans went on. 'Yes, Dad, but Thomas shouldn't think he can get away with all kinds of unfair accusations.'

Thomas: 'What about the time you shot Oom Hannes's cow and then blamed me for it?'

We all remembered the occasion very clearly, because it had been the worst hiding ever administered in our home. If I hadn't stopped Christiaan he would have killed the boy. But can you believe it, this Christmas was the first time we'd ever heard Thomas's side of the story.

I thought Frans was going to have a fit from anger. Jumped up from the table, threw his chair to the floor, lunged at Thomas. Quite funny, I thought afterwards, they in their Christmas hats and all. But it really wasn't funny then. All the shouting and scuffling. And Frans repeating over and over that Thomas had deserved what happened. And then Thomas also lost his temper. 'Look here,' he said to Frans, 'I've forgiven you long ago for putting the blame on me. But that you should still go on lying about it today, twenty years later, that I won't forgive you.'

It got completely out of hand. The little ones crying. The in-laws joining in. That was just the time when all the newspapers were going on about Thomas's photographs. And Frans brought up that too, accusing Thomas of bringing shame on his family and being in cahoots with the enemy. And Thomas retorting that there were people among the enemy more honourable than his own brother. And if he had to be ashamed then he'd prefer to be ashamed of his brother. Frans threatening to beat him up good and proper, and Christiaan pulling and tugging at them to separate them, otherwise there would have been blue murder. Their father still standing between them, panting and shoving, Frans shouted at Thomas, using words that made me blush, that he should take his bloody things and clear out, he didn't belong with respectable people any more.

'What do you know about respectability?' said Thomas. 'You hypocrite!'

And then Frans started off again about traitors and communists and backstabbers and heaven knows what else.

In the end it was Thomas who left. Scooped up his belongings in the room – the notebooks in which he'd been working on the Landman story, and his cameras, and bits and pieces of clothing, leaving behind more than he took with him – and drove away. Everybody in the house was miserable. Maria cleared the table without saying a word. All the half-eaten Christmas food remained on the plates, no one was in the mood for eating any more. I kept on pleading with Frans to phone his brother and make peace again. He was the eldest, he ought to know better, set an example. But he just said if anyone had to apologise it was Thomas, not he. And the next morning he left with Belinda and the children, even though they'd planned to stay until after New Year's Day. The most wretched Christmas of my life. That stubborn refusal to forgive. And now here I'm doing the same thing today.

All these years I've been the peacemaker in the family. Not because of the Bible or the Lord, but simply because I don't like people arguing or fighting around me. But how does one keep the peace between two brothers like that?

To think how reluctant I was about bringing up the subject again, those two days Thomas spent with us, the business about him and Frans. About the need for brothers to live together in love and peace. And when at last I found the courage to broach it, he just smiled and said, 'I've just spent the weekend with them, Mum.' It made me so happy. Can you believe it, it was the first time they'd spoken since that Christmas Day. He didn't say much about the visit, but the mere fact that he'd gone was enough. And when he left here, early the Friday morning, he said he was going back north. Will you look up Frans again? I asked. He was reluctant at first. But in the end he took my two hands in his and kissed them. All right, Mum, he said, I promise. As soon as I'm back in Pretoria I'll look him up. And stay with them? And stay with them.

I remember thinking: Look how it all gets sorted out when one grows older. I've been worrying quite unnecessarily. God has His own way of solving problems. Just leave it to Him. Don't try to take it in your own hands.

He was tired, those few days. Slept a lot. Lay on his bed reading. Always been like that. But somehow I felt concerned about him. He didn't seem as forthcoming as he used to be. Or was it my imagination? It's so easy to put a different look on things afterwards.

'No, there's nothing wrong with me,' he said when at last I asked him straight. It was the evening I went to sit with him as I'd done when he was small. The second evening. The last. Held his hand in the dark. Soothing him, comforting him. 'I've had a tough time, that's all.'

'You're working too hard.' I wondered whether I dared risk it: it was the one thing that used to make him angry, if we went on about it. Especially his father. But I felt I had to. 'It'll be so much easier if you got another job, Thomas. Teaching. Anything. Photography isn't the sort of work one does for a living. There's no future in it.'

'There's nothing else I want to do, Mum.'

'But Thomas.' I weighed my words carefully. 'You'll be twenty-nine soon. Next year you'll be thirty. Sooner or later you'll have to think about getting married. About starting a family. And what security can you offer them?'

He pressed my hand. A small laugh in the dark. 'You're just counting grandchildren again.'

'No, I'm thinking of *you*, Thomas. You always shy away from it.'

'I suppose I'll get married if the time is ripe.'

'What about the Nina you brought home that time? I know she was a bit too sharp with her tongue to your father's liking. But she seemed a nice girl.'

He clutched my hand so tightly it made me start. I wished I could see his face. For a long time he didn't speak.

'Thomas?' Perhaps I shouldn't have gone on like that. I never know when to stop. 'Why didn't you bring her with you this time?'

That was when I discovered he was crying. Without a sound. But his body was shaking. Oh my God, I thought, helpless, bewildered. Oh my God. Oh my God. What have I done? What do I do now?

'Thomas? Boetie, what's the matter? Is something wrong? What has happened between you and Nina?'

After a long time, his voice in the dark. Dull. 'I can't talk about it now, Mum.'

'Did she drop you?'

I could feel him shaking his head vigorously.

'You dropped her?'

'Mum, please.'

'You've always discussed things with me, Thomas. Don't you remember? Ever since you were very small.'

'I know. And I promise I'll do it again. When I'm ready.'

'I can see you still love her. Promise me you'll try again.'

I couldn't hear his answer. It sounded like a strained laugh.

'Don't give up so easily, Thomas.'

'I haven't given up, Mum.'

'All right then.' I leaned over and kissed him on the forehead. And then left him behind in the dark.

And yet it did him a world of good to be here. I could see that from his pottering in the garden. He'd always enjoyed planting and sowing. In this same barren backyard, when he was fourteen, he'd started gardening on a scale such as we'd never seen. As if he was running a whole vegetable farm. Carrots and beetroot and pumpkins and beans and mealies, you name it. Not for the money he could make. There was something else that drove him. Perhaps the way everybody, Frans especially, had told him it was impossible to get a proper vegetable garden growing here. The earth is too barren, too hard. There's no water. Nothing. But he paid no attention. With one of his friends he drove out to a farm on a donkey cart to collect manure. In the blazing sun. And dug and raked until his hands were all blisters. I had to scrounge for all my ointments and oils. He dug furrows from the tap to the vegetable beds. But he was forced to give it up, because it was uphill. And the soil was too hard anyway. So he had to water everything from buckets and watering cans, staggering under their weight on his thin long legs. It was still all right while the plants were small. But when they grew bigger it was hopeless. It was one of the worst summers we've ever had in this place. Looked like a landscape on the moon. Bare stones and parched earth. On the farms the farmers had to slaughter their sheep. Many of them sold out and moved away. And it was the end of Thomas's garden too. He kept on manfully for a while. Carrying those heavy pails until long after sunset. But he couldn't keep it up. And one summer night I went to sit with him, like this night, and held his hand and let him cry. Which was something he hardly ever did. I used to be amazed at how tough he could be. But that garden had broken his heart. Not because he'd failed. Because when I tried to comfort him by telling him he could try again the next year, he answered fiercely through his tears, 'It's the garden itself, Mum. All the little plants that died. I tried to help them through, but I couldn't.'

Now they call him a terrorist.

How easy it is for them to talk. They don't know him. If only I could have made them see him the way I knew him. Know him. But even if they'd let me, I wouldn't. He is mine. I shall protect him like a hen covering her last remaining chicken. That resolve in me was only hardened the day that Brigadier Bester came here. I suppose I shall have to tell it after all. May God give me strength. Not that there is all that much to tell. I went back to Oudtshoorn with friends of ours to visit Christiaan in hospital. They waited outside the hospital in the car while I went in to Christiaan's private room.

By that time he was out of intensive care. And there I found the two strange men outside his door. Didn't want to let me through. Look, I said, he's my husband. And I don't care who you are, but you try to stop me and we'll see what happens. And when I pushed past them I saw the man kneeling at Christiaan's high bed, next to the cabinet beside the bed, looking through his things. Christiaan lying there, helpless, uttering sounds. By that time his speech hadn't returned yet. It's better now. And making small desperate motions with his left hand. Mumbling with his thick, unwieldy tongue, 'The man – the man –' So upset it was a miracle he didn't have another stroke right there.

At that time I hadn't met the stranger yet. But I pulled him back by the shoulder with so much force that he sprawled backwards on the floor. Plucked Christiaan's things from his big paws. The little diary. The Bible. Cards and letters people had sent him to wish him well.

'Madam, do you know who I am?' the man asked, veins bulging on his forehead.

'You can be Beelzebub himself straight out of hell for all I care,' I answered. 'But what you're doing here will make a pig blush.'

Furious. 'I am Brigadier Bester, and I've come all the way from Cape Town to –'

'Then you can drive all the way back again. I have no time for your sort.'

He changed his tone. All milk and honey. 'Mrs Landman, look, I can understand that you must be upset.'

'You can stuff your understanding up your arsehole.' In all my grownup life such words have never crossed my lips.

I went to call the hospital superintendent. In his presence I told the brigadier that if any one of them ever set foot in that hospital again I would tell every newspaper in the country what he'd done. The brigadier tried to say something, but I paid no attention.

It was only the following day he turned up here at the house. I spoke to them on the front stoep. I refused to invite them in. I cannot even remember any more what was said. I didn't bother to listen.

Now Christiaan is back home again. What will become of him, what will become of us, I don't know. All I know is that life can never be the way it was before.

The nights are the worst. When I wake up and hold my ear to his face to hear whether he is still breathing. And afterwards I cannot fall asleep again. There is nothing to put a stop to one's thoughts. They wash over one like water. Suppose, I sometimes think, suppose Frans was right that Christmas Day when he raged about Thomas being a traitor and a sell-out and God knows what else? But no, not Thomas.

And the mirror in the passage remains blank too. Mottled and stained with too much history. There's nothing one's eyes can pry from it. If ever there was anything at all. –

8

Afterwards, in Cape Town, and again later, when his journey was no longer one of simple displacement but of flight, he would remember this visit to his parents as an almost desperate attempt to recapture everything that had been familiar and reassuring about his youth. And, on the surface at least, it seemed as if his surroundings were prepared to assist in making possible this return to the past. From the first moment he stopped outside the depressing square house with the red roof and the curved verandah behind the row of bluegums lining the broad street, and walked inside – the wire-mesh back door slamming sharply behind him; on either side of the back stoep the rooms added on as an unsuccessful afterthought: the bathroom and a narrow pantry left, and right his father's study; his mother in the kitchen, small and grey and plump, a jar of canned fruit in her hands, a red-checkered dishcloth on her shoulder – there was a feeling of the past flooding over him. (– When we were small, in the village off the west coast, diving for crayfish or abalone: the sudden breaking of a wave through a narrow breach in the rocks, the ice-cold water of the Atlantic taking our breath away. –) He surrendered himself to it without even a token resistance. He needed it.

Where else could she have been but, in that archetypal attitude, in her kitchen? Not because it was the place she had been relegated to by custom or her family, but because she had turned it into a power base. She actually seemed to derive a satisfaction beyond the reach of words from washing up and cleaning, baking and cooking, tidying, ordering her world – assisted, naturally, by a black charwoman, Bettie, who had become a trusted companion and accomplice – to her taste, and to her image.

His sudden appearance gave her a fright. It amused him.

'What's the matter?' he asked. 'You look as if you've seen a ghost.'
He greeted her companion and winked at her.

'It must be a ghost,' said his mother. 'Where do you come from?
What's happened?' In a daze, she thrust the jar of peaches into
Bettie's waiting hands and embraced him – standing on tiptoe to
reach his face – then stood back to look at him, but without letting
him go, her glasses hanging from one ear now; on her left cheek
the mole with the hard bristles; and repeated anxiously, 'What's
happened?'

'What makes you think something happened?' (With a fleeting
unnerving thought: Perhaps she knows, in her submarine way, as
she has always known everything.)

'Why else should you turn up so unexpectedly?'

'I had to come to this part of the world for a project, so I
thought –'

'Take your things through. We'll have to air the room. I'll make
us some coffee. Bettie?'

'You were on your way out?' he asked.

'No, of course not.'

'Then why this smart dress, and your hair all done up?'

'Oh come on.' She shooed him out with her dishcloth.

From the inside door of the kitchen the main passage led straight
to the front door, left open to let in the autumn sunshine. At the
end, looking out over the bright red front stoep below the curved
verandah, were the lounge and the dining-room, left and right; then,
again left and right, his parents' bedroom and Maria's. There the
main passage was intersected by another, which used to be dark and
depressing until his father had had side windows put in, one next to
Frans's bedroom door, the other next to his. Yellow afternoon sun
came pouring in through the window on his side, a long bright patch
that stretched all the way along the passage to where the broken
family mirror had been propped up. A dark rectangle on the wall
marked its usual place.

'Happened last night,' his mother said behind him. She had
followed him, anticipating his question. 'We had such a fright. It
sounded like a thunderclap right inside the house. It's the old wire
that's snapped.'

He carried his suitcase – the dark green suitcase packed with
strange clothes – into his bedroom next to the kitchen. Opened the
wardrobe still filled, reassuringly, with the much-worn old clothes
he had never had the heart to discard; chose a frayed and faded pair

of jeans to change into; then sat down on the edge of the bed – the
familiar old mattress gently gave way under his weight – to put on
his shoes again. His heels struck an object under the bed. Behind
the spread, as he leaned over to look, he discovered the cardboard
boxes crammed with the accumulated possessions of his past, still
waiting with an air of placid assurance.

Back in the kitchen he found his mother at the narrow window
above the zinc. The colourless, forbidding light – the back of
the house, facing due south, was always in shadow; she'd often
complained about the rheumatism it was bound to give her – fell
across her grey hair. Years ago it had been as shiny black as the
wing of a crow. Now it shocked him to see how old she had
become, how much smaller. It had happened so unobtrusively.
It was only now, after such a long absence, that he became
aware of it. She had not yet discovered his presence behind
her. She was looking out, across the dark porch, into the white
backyard where chickens were scratching and cackling. Not that
she was really looking: it was a vacant stare. Motionless, like
a painting. A Vermeer, perhaps. Except that Vermeer's women
were usually younger. He thought: all her life, or at least that
part of it he'd shared, she had been staring out like that. As
if there was something out there, another world, invisible yet
undeniable, where she would never set foot, of which she would
never be part; her space was here, inside. It was here she'd grown
so grey.

She turned round abruptly. She looked trapped. 'My goodness,
Thomas, for how long have you been standing here?'

On the kitchen dresser the jar of canned fruit still sat, the
peach halves gleaming a dark orange in the light that lovingly
fingered them.

They drank their coffee at the old scrubbed pine table in the
kitchen. All the grain lay bare and exposed in grim yet acquiescent
nakedness. Wide slits had opened up between the boards. A few
old-fashioned square nailheads protruded.

'I suppose I should have taken out the new coffee set you sent me
last Christmas,' she apologised. 'But it's too good for everyday use.'
He knew that if he opened the unwieldy cupboards his father had
made himself with such fierce determination and at the risk of life
and limb, he would find them stacked with boxes full of unused
things, each box marked with the name of the donor. ('One day
when I'm dead you can have it all back.') Dinner services. Electric

whisks and frying pans. A small microwave oven. All the utensils that might have made life easier for her.

'Where have you been?' she asked.

Early that morning he had visited New Bethesda, then stopped at Graaff-Reinet, taking photographs as he went, driven this time not by the usual curiosity of his profession, but by a compulsion to register whatever he could of the itinerary he and Nina had followed more than a year ago, before that fatal Christmas Day, when he had first brought her home to his parents; from there, on his motorcycle, they had explored far and wide the region of his youth and some of his more intrepid ancestors, she perched behind his back and clinging to his body like a small baboon. (If only she'd held on like that – not a lifetime ago, a mere five days – in Cape Town, in Plein Street.) As if the photographs, once developed, might – quite literally! – bring to light traces of that trip no longer visible to the naked eye, yet lurking tenacious and nude in the recesses of the mind. Because they *had* been here; together. But there was a wind, swirling dust through the streets and spinning the wheels of the windmills, and there was no sight of her narrow footprints.

The Owl House with its eerie birds on the stoep. He didn't want to go round the corner and down the street again in search of the old lady who kept the keys. This was a hollow in the subconscious he no longer wished to penetrate, not without Nina – the shimmering of finely ground coloured glass on walls and ceilings; red window-panes that transformed an outside view into a flight of fancy; memories of an ancient lonely woman who on a Friday afternoon had swallowed washing soda to end it all – and what was visible, across the tall hedge, of the camel garden at the back, had been enough: weird heads, outlandish jewel-eyes (where was the tortured woman on the rack, with her red nipples of splintered glass?), fabulous monsters, misshapen creatures from wishful dreams. What had once seemed magical to him – an Aladdin's cave, a Garden of Earthly Delights, Fugard's Road to Mecca – had now become, in Nina's absence, a nightmare, a vision of hell in which evil lurked within the shapes of fantasy. He regretted having come at all. And yet he knew he'd hardly had a choice.

Even the tranquillity of Graaff-Reinet on a weekday morning seemed deceptive this time. The town his ancestor Benjamin had once lived in; in some back street the small cottage might still be standing, where young Gideon had met the missionary van der Kemp and turned to religion. A one-horse Wild West hamlet in those frontier days, now a town of decent citizens. Yet one could imagine how, as in a fairy-tale, they might suddenly turn into birds of prey or a pack of wild dogs if they were to find out who this stranger really was who wandered so casually through their righteous streets. He no longer belonged among them. (Had he ever?) The very ordinariness of the scene – people doing their shopping, mothers pushing babies in prams, old men hosing patchy gardens, farmers coming in to town in their *bakkies*, labourers in the back, coloured children clustered in front of a store – was ominous. How was it possible that life could go on like this, that nothing had shifted, nothing had changed at all? Except himself, moving through those sane, salubrious streets like a virus through the veins of a body as yet unaware of its own infection. Almost in a panic, he'd returned to his car and driven on, and never stopped again, except once, in Willowmore, for petrol.

'Some more coffee?'

But then his father came in, stern in his charcoal school-suit (he'd been on library duty), his hair sparser than Thomas had remembered it, combed back in long dendrites over the thin round shell of his skull, his moustache like a long-used toothbrush on his upper lip. The pitch-black eyes – unexpectedly meek, but constantly on the lookout for someone who might doubt his authority – lit up brightly as he recognised his son; then focused resolutely on Thomas's left shoulder, an unsettling habit which invariably prompted one, after a minute or two, to bring a hand up to that shoulder and brush or flick at it, convinced that there must be something on it that shouldn't be there, a thread, a stain, perhaps a spider.

'So you've remembered us again?'

'Now come on, Christiaan,' said his wife. 'Aren't you glad he's come?'

'For how long are you staying?'

'I have to move on again tomorrow, Dad.'

It was she who protested, 'No, Boetie, I won't allow that. You look so tired, you need a good rest first. Look how thin you are.'

'What about yourself?'

'Don't change the subject. Promise me you'll stay longer.'

He made a quick calculation. Everything was determined by that sole fixed point in the future: the funeral service on Friday afternoon. It was only five hours to Cape Town from here. Even less. And it *was* tempting to stay. Provided he could set out early enough.

'All right, I promise.'

His father went to change into his working clothes, a pair of old white overalls like a mechanic's, rather too big for him; and Thomas accompanied him to his workshop in the garage – past the late-afternoon chickens in the yard: and, honest to God, he stepped in their excrement again, as always when he'd been a child, only this time at least he wasn't barefoot – to see what Christiaan Beyers Landman was working on at the moment. It turned out to be a cupboard, meant for the side passage, for his mother's things: her cooking books, her sewing, her odds and ends, her prize cups: but at the first glance Thomas could tell that it was too wide, it would never get through a door into the house. But he didn't have the heart to say anything. Who knows how many months' work, how many spoiled and broken boards, how many blisters and chips and gaping wounds on well-intentioned hands had gone into the making of that crooked thing. Just as well, he thought, his father would never be required to set up a bomb. He would blow himself up months before the attack. (But had *they* fared any better?)

If he closed his eyes – in his nose the pungent smell of wood, in his ears the rasping, uneven sounds of his father's shaving – he could imagine himself a child again, as if no time had passed at all.

The impression was even stronger after supper – a stew, bean salad, even vinegar pudding – when he fetched from the sideboard the family bible, perched squarely and sedately on top of the worn old brown State Bible (he thought: if he were to be awakened in the middle of the night and told to fetch the bible, he would be able to go straight towards it in the dark and, without a moment's hesitation, place his hand on it), and his father put on his reading glasses and opened the book on the page marked with a small yellow heart of silkworm silk, near the beginning. He cleared his throat and, before he began to read, looked at Thomas over the rim of his glasses:

'Two nights ago, your mother and I started at the beginning again.' He stretched out his hand across the table to take hers. 'It's twelve times we've worked through it now, from Genesis 1 to Revelations 22.'

Thomas surrendered himself to the even drone of his father's voice, the words so familiar that he could recite them soundlessly as the passage unfolded. And yet, he realised afterwards, this was the turning point of his visit.

> Now the serpent was more subtil than any beast of the field which the Lord God had made. And he said unto the woman, Yea, hath God said, Ye shall not eat of every tree of the garden?
> And the woman said unto the serpent, We may eat of the fruit of the trees of the garden:
> But of the fruit of the tree which is in the midst of the garden, God hath said, Ye shall not eat of it, neither shall ye touch it, lest ye die.

How serene was law and order. How unproblematic, if one could keep to it.

> And the eyes of them both were opened, and they knew that they were naked –

A brief, blinding memory of Nina on the mountain. Naked on her back on the boulder. He hovering over her, his hand on her sex. The emblematic man and woman in the wilderness. And then the spell had been broken by the bunch of tourists who'd invaded their little paradise. My God, he thought, he still had those photographs, on one of the films in his suitcase. It was *something*. He must develop it as soon as he was back in Cape Town.

> And the Lord God said, Behold, the man is become as one of us, to know good and evil: and now, lest he put forth his hand, and take also of the tree of life, and eat, and live forever:
> Therefore the Lord God sent him forth from the garden of Eden, to till the ground from whence he was taken.
> So he drove out the man; and he placed at the east of the garden of Eden Cherubims, and a flaming sword which turned every way, to keep the way of the tree of life.

This was how it had begun, he thought as he knelt beside his chair, his father's voice washing over his back in prayer. *This* was how. This religion is itself the foundation of an entire dispensation of power, a way of thinking. It is the beginning of fascism. The moment Adam and Eve acquire knowledge they are driven out. God does not wish them to distinguish between good and evil. *He* wants to make the decisions himself, keep them in the dark. And even before that, when the angels first rebelled, he cast them out of heaven too. Afrikaners merely followed his example.

206

All he knew about sin and evil, came from that book. In a manner of speaking it was through the bible that he'd lost his innocence. All those dire commandments and proscriptions and warnings to the children of Israel: about whoring and sodomy and onanism and idolatry and betrayal and revenge and murder and violence. Because a thing forbidden becomes a possibility suddenly introduced into the domain of the thinkable. (A sudden, disturbing memory of Henry: 'Has it ever occurred to you for how many centuries the bible – the New Testament – has been used by missionaries to persuade the oppressed to turn the other cheek, to bear the yoke with humility, to expect their reward not on earth but, safely after death, in heaven? To make sure they would be more manageable, collaborating in their own oppression? And we meekly swallowed it all, Thomas. We have to learn to read from scratch.')

'– not because we deserve it, but through Thy infinite amen.'

They rose and pushed back their chairs. He avoided his parents' eyes as if he were ashamed that they might see in his what he had just gleaned from the Word that had shaped them. While his father went to his easy chair in the sitting-room to read the paper, he and his mother cleared the table. Ignoring her protests, he helped her wash up. (Bettie had left, as usual, at sunset.) Before they had finished, Oom Boet's booming voice preceded him down the passage – the front door was still open – shouting to wake the dead. His mother's brother, the sergeant. He could have retired long ago, but he'd stayed on in the force. Ever since his wife had died, of cancer, three years before, he'd avoided his own home as much as he could. Whenever he wasn't on duty, working unnecessary long hours, one could find him in the hotel; otherwise he would be doing the rounds of his many friends, knowing he would be welcome wherever he went. It was a matter of pride, and he made sure no one was in any doubt about it, that he had no enemies in the world, white or black.

'Is there no coffee in this place for a thirsty man?'

He waved at Christiaan from the passage; he kissed his sister. Seeing Thomas made him stop in his tracks.

'Well, I'll be blowed,' he said. 'Hasn't the police picked you up yet?'

Thomas felt the blood drain from his face. 'What do you mean, Oom Boet?'

He received a staggering blow between the shoulders in reply. Then a huge hand gripped his like a vice; he could swear he heard the bones cracking. 'No, I'm just asking. You've been looking for trouble for so long now, haven't you?' His laugh reverberated through the house. 'Well, what are you standing there like a chicken with lice?' He lowered his body on the sofa. The wood creaked in protest. Light spilled on his bald head like milk. Below his nose his moustache spread like a winnowing broom.

'Well!' He crossed his heavy legs and cast a generous stare at Thomas. 'So you're still on the loose?'

'Why shouldn't I be?' asked Thomas, with a small strained grimace.

'We got word that the Special Branch people are spreading their raids all over the country. Last night. Cape Town, Johannesburg, Durban, everywhere.' For a moment he grew serious. 'It's still that bomb blast last Friday. Picking them up at random now. Obviously hoping they'll land on someone who can help them. The way we sometimes do when there's sheep stolen or something like that. It's not a way of doing I've ever liked. But you can imagine the president wants to see a couple of them swinging. Of course, if you ask me, the bastards have fled the country long ago. Thanks, Helena.' Taking the cup she offered him, and adding four heaped teaspoonfuls of sugar. 'Shit, it's an ugly story, man.'

'Are you referring to their raids, or to the bomb?' Thomas asked with a straight face.

'How can you have the one without the other?' His uncle pursed his lips to test the temperature of the coffee. 'Yes, it's an ugly story. Ugly. The world isn't what it used to be. Ever since 'sixty, when it first started.' He looked at Thomas. 'It came into the world with you.'

'I think it started when the Dutch first arrived, Oom Boet.'

'Oh, if you insist on going back, why not all the way to Adam? Then you know you've got the culprit.'

'It's not something to joke about,' Helena reprimanded him. 'Such a terrible, terrible thing. One of these days we'll have to start locking our doors at night like the city people. The Devil is on the rampage among us.'

'They've got to be caught and hanged,' said Christiaan with angry emphasis.

'We're all agreed on that.' Oom Boet emptied his cup; he had a throat of iron. 'But that by itself will solve nothing. That's only the fruit of the tree. We've got to get to the roots, and they are buried deep.'

'You've always been too soft for your kind of work,' said Christiaan.

'I'm only human, and contrary too.'

'No one respects a soft person,' Christiaan persisted. 'I don't say one must be cruel or unreasonable. But firm. Otherwise they don't know who's the boss. It was only yesterday when I.'

'Shh,' said Helena. 'It's time for the news.'

A ceremony as solemn as family prayers.

It was again the main item on the news. The raids. (Would Justin still be safe? David? Rashid?) Two of the injured still in a critical condition. Questions in parliament about the female terrorist shot by police in self-defence at Jan Smuts airport last Friday night as she was preparing to blow up an SAA plane. The minister of police: The public is requested to stay calm, no stone will be left unturned and extremely important clues are being followed up around the clock.

'Which means they've got sweet blow-all,' Oom Boet said quietly.

Like a large smug toad the female news reader stared into the sitting-room with bulging eyes. The report went on and on.

Arrangements for Friday's funeral service have been finalised. In the Groote Kerk, at three o'clock. The government will be represented by the Minister of Constitutional Development and Planning. Unfortunately, under strict medical orders, the state president will remain confined to his bed for several days.

'Hope they can keep up with changing the sheets,' said Oom Boet.

'You should be ashamed, Boet.'

'Well, the man did get a fright, didn't he?'

'He could have been killed.'

'But now it's other people,' said Christiaan. 'It's always the innocents who have to pay.'

'– by the moderator of the Dutch Reformed Church,' the toad completed her report with a defiant shake of the red buttons.

It was followed by a survey on prospects of a rugby tour. Maize production. A minister of something commenting on something. Three more government officials indicted on charges of corruption. Two people condemned to death. Another minister. The rand dropping to its lowest level in two years. Another minister. Financial reports. Sport. The weather.

'Well, time to go.' Oom Boet rose from the sofa. 'One gets sleepy of so much rubbish.' He bent over to kiss his sister. 'Still got to go to the station, I've got a chappie in the van.'

'Who is it?' asked Thomas.

'Don't know. Found him on the corner over there.' He motioned. 'He couldn't give me any good reason why he was loitering here in the white part of town, so I picked him up. I mean, he doesn't belong here.'

'One can't be too careful these days,' said Helena.

The three men went through the open front door. Outside, the night was soundless. Not a breath of air. Through the tattered branches of the bluegums one could see a white half-moon above the rooftop opposite the street. Somewhere a dog barked. Through the open sitting-room window of the neighbours' house a TV screen flickered, blue and white. In the air hung a timeless smell: dried grass, dust, acrid scrub, and something sweet, like evening flowers, like freesias; only it wasn't that. 'It's the stars,' his mother had told them when they were small. 'Some nights the stars hang down so low one can smell them.'

In silence, as the three of them stood in a row below the bluegums with their smell of bruised eucalyptus, they performed the immemorial ritual of male companionship and trust, their three separate jets glistening in the moonlight and forming a communal black stain on the pale parched lawn.

'Well,' said Oom Boet, with a deft bending of his knees and a thrust of his solid hips as he tucked away his member for future reference, 'I must be off.'

In the back of the van, as he pulled away, something moved. It was too dark to distinguish anything. All one could make out was a dark hand clutching the heavy wire-mesh. Like an orang-utan in a cage.

This was why I did it, thought Thomas; this was why I *had* to.

'Shall we go in?' asked his father.

'I think I'm going for a walk first.' He couldn't face, right now, the oppressive interior and the light.

In the distance the dog was still barking, monotonously and without much conviction. Crickets were chirping in the large irrigation plots beside the street. Behind a house a windmill screeched in a sudden irresponsible gust of wind. Then it was silent again. On the main road, far ahead, a car approached soundlessly, the beams of its headlights probing the dark like antennae, turned up the steep incline beyond the town, disappeared around a bend.

If he went up that slope now, he knew, the whole town would lie exposed at his feet in the elementary reassurance of its geometry, predictable, straight dotted lines of light drawn on a black map. Everything that here enclosed him like a net would be visible and comprehensible from up there. If only, he thought, there were another kind of mountain to whose summit one could climb, to look down on what was happening here, to acknowledge the pattern, to see where it began and especially where it was to end.

His parents were still in the sitting-room when he returned to the house. The curtains undrawn. The window wide open to let in the night air. In quick, brilliant curves and circles moths were flitting about in the light that came from inside. On the edge of the yellow rectangle on the dry lawn he stopped to stare at them, fascinated, as if he were looking into something strange and inexplicable. His father with the newspaper – he'd started on the advertisements; he'd paid for it, he wouldn't skip a thing – his mother with her knitting. How soothing, reassuring, ever since his childhood, her mumbled accompaniment to the flickering of her needles: knit one, purl one, slip one, plain, purl, knit two together. Even a bomb couldn't disturb the tenor of their lives. Innumerable times he'd seen them together like this. But never, as far as he could recall, exactly in *this* way: as if he were peering through a telescope from very far away, immeasurably far. Milky ways and galaxies whirling between them.

After a long time he entered through the open front door. Saw them looking up as he came past in the passage. He went to the bathroom; returned with a glass of water. In the dining-room, on the sideboard, in the dark, he picked up the Dutch State Bible. With the glass in one hand and the great leatherbound book in the other he stopped in the doorway. 'I'm off to bed. I'm tired.'

'Good night, Thomas. Is there anything you need?'

Crosslegged, the heavy book on his knees, he sat on his bed, no longer knowing why he'd felt the need to bring it with him. If it was security he was looking for, it wouldn't be in the printed text (behind the words on the paper he could hear, like distant thunder, the voice of his grandfather reading), but in the human imprints his family had made in it: the traces left by the guilty conscience of the stonemason Jan-Jonas, in marginal notes obscured by blots and exclamation marks; anonymous underlinings and cryptic comments in many handwritings, some barely literate, barely legible;

thumbprints and dog-ears; the leather binding discoloured by an ancestor's blood in the massacre of Bloukrans; wax droppings, crushed insects, indecipherable and questionable stains; the names and dates of all the Landman generations in gradations of black and dark blue ink on the flyleaf at the back, starting with flourishes and a supreme disregard for space, and becoming more and more cramped on the way down.

In the small space next to his own name there might yet have been room, if one wrote very carefully, for *Nina Jordaan*. But below that? There wasn't really any space left anyway. One of the early scribes had spilled ink on the bottom of the then blank page – a Rorschach blot with the smudged outline of a palm impressed on it – at a time when the page must have seemed as open and boundless as the land. As if it had been predestined this way. So far, and no further.

Halfway through his researches the book became too heavy. He put it down on the bed and stretched out more comfortably beside it. Slow waves of fatigue began to move over him. It became more and more difficult to decipher names and connect them with memories. When he woke up in the late morning, the heavy binding of the book had left a dent in his cheek. (Impulsively he brought his hand to his face and checked his fingers for a sign of that blood spilled so long ago, but there was nothing.) Someone must have come in to put out the light. On the bedside table stood a cup of coffee, but it was already cold.

He swung his feet from the bed, still confused, vaguely conscious of an uncomfortable erection he'd brought with him from some untraceable dream. Once again his heels brushed against one of the boxes under the bed. Without much conviction, his movements still dulled by sleep, perhaps with a touch of detached amusement, he sat down on the floor and pulled the box from under the bed, pried open the flaps, began to burrow in the books and papers. Notes. Old certificates and school reports. ('Nice work, but Thomas can do better.' 'Thomas is a good pupil, but he does not always pay enough attention.') A Sunday-school diploma covered in colourful seals, including the coveted gold one. All things bright and beautiful. Two prize books from the Christian Students Association. On Tuesday afternoons when they'd held their meetings in the church hall, he'd used to play the harmonium to accompany their desultory singing. His whole youth came flickering past. Covered in dust. Fish-moths scurrying across the pages.

It really was time he brought some order to this confusion from his past. With great concentration he began to make two piles: one to keep, the other to throw away. From his years at university, hoarded in the second and third boxes, came the inevitable notebooks, roneos, shreds of assignments and essays and test papers, parts of letters; as well as theatre programmes (one adorned with the signatures of all the cast members), the torn halves of cinema or concert tickets, rugby tickets, menus or invoices from restaurants, a small red-and-black notebook in which he'd listed 'themes for photographs', another with his monthly budgets. A torn glove. A single grey sock with a hole in the heel. Unexpectedly, a girl's panties – barely the size of an old Cape triangular postage stamp, off-white, the lace edge frayed, a minuscule red bow strategically placed – which he pressed impulsively to his nose, but the scent had long disappeared. (Whose had it been? Had she given it to him? Had he stolen it to keep as a sentimental memento? Or was it simply a lost trophy from a panty raid?)

One whole big box was crammed with the remains of his early photographic endeavours. A green album filled with strips of negatives, accompanied by a meticulous index on the front page. Two lens hoods. An assortment of filters in plastic containers. Unsorted photographs, proof prints, most of them discoloured from bad fixing, the corners bent and torn, some completely crumpled. His parents. Frans. Maria. Babies and offspring of acquaintances. School friends. University friends. Girlfriends in various stages of undress: here a mere shoulder coyly bared, there a shy breast, an 'artistic' torso, figure studies with heavily dramatised lighting, a few frontals in provocative poses more erotic than aesthetic.

Even now, he discovered from the signs of life throbbing in his penis (a sad, resigned salute to the past?), they did not leave him cold. He thought: One returns to a lost love like a criminal to the scene of his crime. For a while he sat with his eyes closed, abandoned to what no longer existed, to what no longer had any right of existence; then, almost ashamed, as the momentary excitement ebbed from his body, he returned to the photographs.

Of some negatives there were ten or twenty different prints: experiments with lighting, developers, texture screens, grain. On the backs of some of them he'd noted technical details; others bore only reference numbers. Many were unmarked, had lost all reason. The patient exploration of hours, days, months, an all-encompassing apprenticeship. Whole segments of his life had been summarised in them, yet now they could no longer be traced, he'd lost the key to their code; perhaps they were no longer relevant anyway.

Bulbs for his enlarger. A few red ones, yellow ones. Brown jars with chemicals long evaporated, leaving only hard dark crusts. A thermometer. A (presumably broken) time-switch. Empty styrofoam containers. A camera bag from which he shook loose negatives, a sheet of paper covered in cryptic data, a dead spider and a live cockroach.

What could he discard, what should he keep? In a kind of desperation he burrowed on, lost among clues leading nowhere, sesames that no longer opened magic doors, keys that could unlock nothing. But others too, that chased up memories like insects, faded black and white images on paper transformed in his mind, as he looked at them, into violent colour and movement, joys and agonies that plucked at his heart, irritations and longings – all, all of it relegated to the contents of boxes under a bed, at the bottom of a wardrobe, in the insides of drawers smelling of camphor or naphthalene.

A knock on his door. His mother came in with a large wooden tray and the emphatic smells of bush-tea, toast, bacon and eggs.

'But my goodness me, Thomas, what are you doing? It looks like Tutankhamun's grave.'

He stretched out his arms to take the tray (he couldn't get up: he'd slept naked; slightly embarrassed, he kept the box between his legs). 'I've finally begun to sort out this mess.'

She took the cup from the bedside table, and clicked her tongue. 'You haven't had your coffee.'

'I overslept hopelessly.' He stretched his arms. 'It's the first time in a week I've had a proper sleep.'

'Your conscience troubling you?'

'_'

'Now make sure the food doesn't get cold.' She went out.

After he'd finished his breakfast he stood up, staring down at the litter on the floor. Then squatted beside the nearest empty box and, methodically, began to repack everything; half an hour later he stowed all the boxes where he'd found them. In fact, there was more in them now than when he'd started unpacking. His mother's flippant remark about his conscience had disturbed him; and among the paraphernalia in the boxes he'd thrust, also, the rolls of film taken on his trip so far, including the one of Nina on the mountain. All the signs of his second life. Whatever he'd decided, rashly, the previous evening, he knew now that he couldn't keep them with him. And he couldn't destroy them either. There might yet be a day in the distant future when he could reclaim them openly. But for the time being they had to be hidden; and what better place was there, what safer, than this? He wrapped a towel round his waist and went to the bathroom.

Later that morning he visited the co-op store a couple of blocks away and returned with picture wire to restore the mirror to its appointed place. He dug a few flower beds in the garden, brought manure in a wheelbarrow from the compost heap at the bottom of the garden, repaired a plug for his mother, repainted the top of the wash-stand in the bathroom, then had his tea on an up-ended box in the back garden, watching the chickens. And felt his heart break inside him. Because whatever he looked at was crumbling to pieces in his mind. All objects became transparent; holes appeared in whatever had seemed so solid. And through the holes he stared into a blank space where children where being killed, funerals disrupted by teargas, students beaten with batons and sjamboks, anonymous detainees convulsed by electrodes attached to their feet, wrists, nipples, genitals, where bombs exploded and people died; a space in which, over and over again, Nina came crawling forward on hands and knees to collapse in a black pool of her own blood.

Lunch was late, because they had to wait for his father to return from school. The canned peaches from the jar filled the previous day were delicious. 'You could have won a prize with this, I'm sure,' he told his mother. She only smiled. After lunch she withdrew for her afternoon nap. His father, on his way to a staff meeting, or library duty, or sports training, something, hesitated for a while in obvious embarrassment before he said, almost apologetic, 'If you don't have anything better to do until I. I've been working quite steadily on the family tree lately, trying to. I thought perhaps you'd.'

'I'd love to look at it, Dad.'

'Only if you have time.'

'Of course I have.'

'You know where it is?'

'In the second drawer.'

He went to the study, the stuffy little box on the back stoep, filled with a few functional bookshelves, a grey filing cabinet, a hulking homemade cupboard whose doors could not close properly, a few uncomfortable armchairs, and a desk on which papers and school-books were arranged in precisely squared piles; two small ceramic jars sprouted bunches of red and blue pens, neatly separated. From a row of small, identical standing-frames the members of his family smiled or scowled fixedly. On the wall behind the desk was a large map of the country, flanked by group photographs from his father's student days at college, and a framed teaching certificate. On the floor, a zebra skin, a gift from Frans.

From the second drawer on the left Thomas took the box containing his father's family files. Two separate files for each generation in the family tree: one blue, in which, in a small, precise handwriting on ruled folio paper his father had made a clean copy of the information already sifted and weighed and finally accepted as fact; the other pink, containing loose sheets of rough notes, photocopies and other material still to pass his rigorous tests. Apart from those, at the bottom of the drawer, was the hefty ledger in which his great-grandfather had written, in High Dutch, his memoirs of the Boer War; and a retyped copy of the translation Thomas had made of it when he was only twelve or thirteen (with his father's stern corrections in red). Intrigued, he began to page through it. This, above all – this extension of the faded handwriting in the State Bible – was what he associated with his father.

He wished he'd brought his own manuscript of the family chronicle with him to compare. But perhaps it was just as well he hadn't. It could only have led to renewed disagreements. It was good, and necessary, that for once he and his father should spend some time without those interminable arguments.

Could there have been, as he sat there that afternoon, he would think afterwards – after the news had broken and his father had been brought down by the stroke – a subaquatic presentiment in himself of an end approaching, of death already looming over them like a falling shadow? Was that the apprehension that brought into being a new considerateness, more patience, a new compassion between the two of them? And if not the possibility of his father's death, then at least the certainty of Nina's; and the awareness of his own mortality he'd already borne inside him that morning in the Gardens, as sharp as nostalgia or the smell of freesias in the dark.

216

In a tidy cavalcade the procession of generations passed across the pages in front of him, file upon file, savage and chaotic life reduced to meticulous handwriting, like the tracks of small sea-birds on a dune, off into the wilderness.

Hendrick Willemszoon, with whom it had all started – stowed away, who knows, on a ship, emerging at night to feast on salted hams and barrels of arrack and precious fresh water; landing at the mouth of the Salt River; settling beyond the limits of the small colony with the young slave girl he'd saved from the stake (in possessive lust? or in a moment of reckless compassion?) – was missing from those rigorously ordered files. The title page of the State Bible – the book Hendrick Willemszoon had brought with him from Holland, with the 'wall mirror in ornamental wooden frame', and the silver bell, passed on from hand to hand in the long relay race of the generations – bore his name, presumably signed by a son or grandson as he himself had been illiterate; and there can be no doubt that he had founded the Landman family in Africa, the thirteen generations sprung from the loins of his slave-girl bride, to extend, for all time, the shadow of Gorée across the subcontinent. But here, in his father's 'definitive' history, he had not been canonised.

In his father's documentation the family history began with Fransoois Lodewickus who, assisted by his Huguenot wife Manon, had staked out the Landmans' first outspan on the Cape west coast, near Lambert's Bay. Where this late branch of the family had returned to. His own childhood had been spent there. A circle that had to be completed. Intrigued, Thomas turned the pages. The building of Fransoois Lodewickus's ark was duly recorded, but the magical end which his grandfather had intoned with such robust self-assurance was missing. There was only an acknowledgement (scientifically commendable) of a lack of information to record beyond all doubt the conclusion of the patriarch's life. The only surmise that merited mention was that in the absence of the rest of the family the ambitious boat-builder had been attacked and murdered by 'natives', who might then have proceeded to chop up the ark for firewood. This chronicle did not allow for miracles.

Then followed that worthy descendant of an ancient race of Dutch Protestants (remember the Eighty Years' War?), Carel Guillaume, who'd distinguished himself in the liberation struggle of colonists against the despotic governor Willem Adriaen van der Stel, leading to his incarceration in the Dark Hole of the Castle; after which he'd fled the petty politicking of the Cape to found, back on the West Coast, with his fifteen children, a race that would brook no despotism.

The savage Diederik merited only a brief, sober inscription as the man who'd shod his cattle and sheep in home-made shoes for the epic trek to the Little Karoo, which he'd tamed and cleared of 'Bushmen and other vermin', before he died ('following, as far as can be established, an unfortunate family quarrel') and was laid to rest by his only surviving son Jan-Jonas.

Jan-Jonas had become, in this chronicle, a famous builder whose stone walls had claimed the wilderness for civilisation. At long last he'd settled in what appeared to be the vicinity of New Bethesda, where he had married a woman, Fransina, legendary for her obesity, from a leading Swellendam family; sadly, a few years after the birth of their son Benjamin, she'd died tragically when part of the roof of their homestead had collapsed on her. As for the boy, he'd run away from home at an early age and never saw his father again. Fortunately, Benjamin was assisted by a loyal Hottentot servant, one Toas, who stayed with him like a second mother to the end of her days.

Benjamin was represented as a brave fighter in the ranks of the leaders in the Graaff-Reinet rebellion, Adriaan van Jaarsveld and the Prinsloo brothers and others, who'd protested against the increasing liberalism of a despicable Cape government: an early patriot and republican, inspired by the ideals of the French Revolution, prepared to fight to the death for what he believed in, ending his noble life, inevitably, in martyrdom in the struggle between civilisation and savagery on the Eastern frontier.

Benjamin's father-in-law, the wonderful old mythomaniac Yitshak Kirschbaum, barely featured in his father's narrative; even the comely Leah was relegated to a minor role, presumably because she was both Jewish and female. But it was evidently unfeasible to minimise the importance of Thomas (Tommie) Lourens, the girl who'd caught David Gideon Landman's fancy when he'd surprised her in the wood near his home. Even so, her story in that thin blue file was much less exciting than in Thomas's reconstruction. Toned down to sobriety, above all to propriety, the emphasis fell squarely on the woman she'd become after their marriage: a staunch pioneer and frontierswoman who'd ruled husband and children, serfs and neighbours, with an iron hand and had buried most of them in her lifetime. And beside her, less impressive but pious and worthy all the same, David Gideon himself, prominent among the Zuurveld farmers at the time British rule found its most obnoxious expression in the Black Circuit, the court set up to investigate Hottentot allegations (prompted by evil missionaries) about Boer atrocities; and provoking the tragic failure of the rebellion at Slagtersnek. From his youth this piquant episode had been recorded: how the half-mad philanthropist van der Kemp had tried to involve the young man in the unholy activities of the squalid mission station at Bethelsdorp, and how the staunch young Afrikaner, refusing to fall for the lure of the Antichrist, had broken away to pursue his own vocation.

Barely a page on Frans Jacobus. It surprised Thomas, because he had personally sent his father photocopies of the diary by the British settler Cunningham he had discovered in Grahamstown, on that motorcycle trip with Nina. No sign of it here. On the events after the death of Frans Jacobus's brother, when the broken young widow Hendrina had been taken in marriage by her brother-in-law, only this neutral comment: 'In the absence of further information on Frans Jacobus one may conclude that he and his wife joined the trek of Piet Retief early in 1837, and that both were killed in that terrible night of 16/17 February 1838 at Bloukrans, when Dingane's bloodthirsty impis so treacherously massacred the sleeping Trekkers.'

There was rather more on Petrus, born on the Great Trek, survivor of Bloukrans and Blood River. (His father had observed: 'It is fitting to cite here the winged words of the historian S. F. N. Gie: "The future of civilisation and a large part of South-Africa was in the balance at that juncture, and it is important to note that not only the fire-arms of the white man, but his spiritual superiority as well, proved decisive." Such were the circumstances in which the character of the young Petrus Landman was shaped.') There were fewer discrepancies here – the account traced the hero's life from Natal to the Orange Free State, and from there, in the company of the fanatical Enslin clan, to the Transvaal, on their fatal trek through a fever-ridden region in search of a Jerusalem that turned out a hallucination; and up to his final years as a clairvoyant – but the famous conversations with the angel Gabriel, and with God Almighty himself, were handled with commendable circumspection. Except for a single concession: 'How can an ordinary mortal judge the ways God chooses to reveal Himself to man? If He did it in His Scriptures, why not in the events of peoples and nations as well? Who are we to deny that He might have chosen this man as His servant to reveal His will to his people?' And the end was quite impressive: that final image of Petrus mounting a commando of thirty-three men to free Southern Africa from the British yoke, only 'to succumb to the angel of death' near Bloemfontein, on his way to Cape Town.

The account of the two lives following that of Petrus did not deviate much from Thomas's own version either. There were differences in emphasis and perspective – Gabriel's part in the Boer War appeared more heroic; his attempt, towards the end of his life, to import a German wife, was omitted altogether; and Grandpa Pieter Gerhardus Landman's role as soldier in the Rebellion of 1914, as striker on the gold mines in the Twenties, as campaigner in the great national movements of the Thirties and the subversive activities of the OB in the War, was massively inflated – but the broad outline, at least, had remained unchanged.

There was nothing in the definitive blue file on his father's own life; but the pink file was bursting at the seams with notes and corroborating documents. Thomas had just come to it when the door opened and his father came in. It was after four. He hadn't realised that time had passed so swiftly.

'I've just reached your own file,' he said.

'I see.' A discreet cough. 'I did not think it fitting that I myself should. But perhaps it is something you might like to.'

'If you will trust me with it.'

'Well, you know, Frans doesn't really have the time. And I know you've always been interested in. So if you.' He approached a few steps. He looked much older than the last time. His collar seemed to have become too wide for his scrawny neck. 'What do you think about the rest?' he asked eagerly.

'I'll need more time to study it,' he said, as delicately evasive as he could. 'I've been working hard on my own notes these last few months. Perhaps we can sit down together one day and compare.'

His father seemed both anxious and wary. 'Of course, I only wrote down what could be established beyond doubt. I don't think it's right to let one's private feelings intrude into a. It's only hard facts that count, isn't it? And as you know I.'

He decided to risk it: 'That Settler diary I sent you photocopies of – you don't seem to have used it at all?'

His father went to the filing cabinet, aimlessly pulled open a drawer, closed it again. 'I'm still thinking about it,' he said, uncommunicative. 'One cannot be too careful with that kind of. Remember, it's an Englishman who wrote those things about our. It's quite clear from the diary that he was rather fond of his bottle. That Cape Smoke they used to. One'll have to check with other sources first to see if.'

Thomas looked through the files again. 'While we're at it,' he said, now with more resolution; his father tensed. 'Here. About Diederik. And Jan-Jonas.'

'We've spoken about them so many times already,' his father said, closing up defensively.

'But what about that little notebook Diederik's granddaughter had written about her father and grandfather? I know it's not a pleasant story. Diederik drove his own son to his death. Among other things. And Jan-Jonas disowned his son by Toas when his white wife refused to accept the boy. But if one decides to write a history one has to face up to both good and bad. Don't you agree?'

'When it comes to such abominations, one has to be doubly careful, Thomas. Look, I don't want to say anything against your grandpa Pieter. He did a lot to get all the bits and pieces of our family history together. But he was a storyteller, not a. And the way I see it, if you cannot find evidence for something, it's better to remain silent. It's a matter of.'

'Don't you believe what Diederik's own grandchild wrote about him?'

'How can we be sure that stuff was written by his grandchild? There's no evidence.'

'If she'd written good things about him, would you have used her diary?'

'It's always better to speak well of someone rather than. That's what the Bible.'

'What about Jan-Jonas's own handwriting in the State Bible? In the margin next to the piece about Abraham driving out Hagar and Ishmael? Or about Ahola and Aholibah? All those passages?'

'Those are your own conclusions, Thomas. He never said anything openly.'

'_'

'We're just poor sinners, my son. It's only in the hereafter that we'll see face to face. Just a couple of days ago I. And it's wise to be humble in all matters, including one's own.'

'If we really want to be humble, Dad, wouldn't it be better to admit that our own ancestors were small and sinful people too? That they were capable, not only of doing good, but of the worst as well? Otherwise, how will we ever learn?'

'If there's something in it for us to learn, Thomas, whether it's about our ancestors or about the Afrikaner people, it is that God has cherished us in His hand. How do you think the Afrikaner has managed to survive against all the odds of history, all the? There's only one explanation. It's because God has been on our side. And how could He have been with us if we hadn't been right? The mere fact that we are here proves that we've been right. It's a.'

He could not restrain himself: 'But Dad, if that is your argument, it would mean that we lost the Boer War because God was on the side of the English.'

'Don't blaspheme, Thomas! Don't you know the bible then? Sometimes God chastises those He loves. *Because* He loves them.'

'Then it is equally possible that he chastised the Zulus at Blood River because He loved *them.*'

'Thomas, this is preposterous. Use your intelligence. How could He have loved them? They were heathens.'

He persisted. 'If we really use our intelligence, Dad, then ordinary common sense would tell us that all the Landmans couldn't possibly have been heroes, or even decent Godfearing people. What about our sinful nature?'

His father went to the narrow window. The spare light coming from it made the room look grey, as if winter had already invaded it. After a while Christiaan Beyers Landman turned round again. 'When you grow older, Thomas,' he said, 'I think you will agree with me. What some of the accounts have to say about people like Diederik or Jan-Jonas is. I don't even want to pronounce those words. The things that savage did. Jan-Jonas having a bastard child with a. Frans Jacobus selling guns to the enemies of his.' He paused. 'Thomas, don't you see? It's just not thinkable.'

'Dad.' He tried to restrain himself. 'How can we ever know who we are, who we really are, unless we accept that we're not somebody else? *Us*: everything we are, and nothing but what we are. Not so?'

His father stared at him for a while. Then he drew a deep slow breath. He squared his narrow shoulders and raised his head. 'Thomas, I want you to listen very carefully: there are things no Landman will ever do. There are depths no Landman can ever sink to.'

'And you really believe that, before God?'

Christiaan Beyers Landman remained silent for a long time. It was as if the grey light was slowly eroding his outline, diminishing him, unravelling him, subverting his substance. 'If I can no longer believe that, Thomas, what will become of me?'

Once again, that night, he could not sleep. After his mother had left him (that disconcerting conversation in which Nina had so unexpectedly returned to break down his last defences), he paged through a 'family' magazine for a while, hoping that the accumulation of sensation, sentimentality and smug moralising would induce sleep; but it had the opposite effect. And after some time he put out the light (afraid that the give-away line of light under his door might attract his mother) and remained lying on his back, his whole body tense, arms under his head. It felt as if he were stretched out on a very narrow, very sharp ridge. The slightest movement would cause pain, might endanger his life. A ridge between what had been and what still lay ahead.

In his imagination he could already see himself getting up in the morning, and putting on his clothes, and eating in the kitchen the copious breakfast his mother would no doubt force on him – standing, perhaps, to persuade her of his hurry; like an Israelite preparing for the trek through the desert (forty years, great God!); blood on the doorposts, and the whisper of the wings of the angel of death outside – and how they would say goodbye (and how the two of them would shrink in the rear-view mirror, their arms around one another, grown old together, arrived at a high even plateau beyond romanticism or disillusionment, slowly being bent down, back towards the earth, growing ever smaller and more frail, like his grandmother when she'd had cancer, his grandmother to whose grave, already dug, the whole family had undertaken their weekly pilgrimage in order to pay homage, in advance, to that impending death) and how he would follow the broad main road out of the town, up the steep incline, round the bend at the top, along the mountain pass winding among the kloofs and cliffs, jagged and grotesque like the entrails of the earth, dark red and orange, discoloured by lichen; and on and on, across arid plains and moonscapes, through the final mountain range towards more fertile valleys where the vineyards would already be turning to the reds of cabernet and hermitage, a journey upstream against the early trek of his ancestors, back, back to where it had all begun, back to where the blast of a bomb a week ago had redefined his whole existence, back to the place he could no longer avoid or circumvent, back to Cape Town.

Chapter 6

The whole of the Cape – 'the whole country', the afternoon newspapers proclaimed – came to a standstill on that first Friday afternoon in May. Every shop and office closed at noon, ordinary citizens drained off the streets, traffic ebbed to almost nothing, even the piercing voices of the newspaper vendors had temporarily fallen silent. A dismal grey day with intermittent showers. The mountain was practically invisible through the fog. Down the whole length of Adderley Street rows of soldiers in uniform, miserable as wet chickens, tried to stay in line. All the flags were at half-mast, soaked like washing on a Blue Monday. Only on the Parade in front of the Castle, and at the upper end of Adderley Street near the entrance to the Groote Kerk, crowds had gathered since mid-morning, controlled and intimidated by nervous police on horseback: and in the streets cordoned off on either side police vehicles and Buffels and Mello-Yellos stood parked in solid phalanxes, crammed with men in riot gear, automatic weapons bristling like porcupine quills.

For days the place had been rife with rumours: that an explosive device would be set up in the Groote Kerk (as a result of which, since the moment the service had first been announced on the Wednesday, the church had been transformed into a barracks), that the Castle was going to be blown up, that terrorists were planning a large-scale attack – linked, it had been whispered in far-right circles, to the appearance of Russian submarines in Table Bay and an attack on Robben Island. According to the Afrikaans papers the city had experienced such a state of siege only once before in living memory, and that had been after Sharpeville in 1960, when the mass march of black protesters had streamed into the city along De Waal Drive, heading for the Houses of Parliament. (And how dismally that had ended, when after announcing he would meet Philip Kgosana, the

225

leader of the march, if the protest were abandoned, the minister promptly had him thrown into prison.)

The morning papers appeared on the streets with their front pages framed in black, surrounding colour photographs of the six victims, accompanied by their biographies, in honour of the latest martyrs who had sacrificed their lives on the altar of innocence and civilised values, in their brave attempts to keep the nation's head above water (here the metaphors broke down) in the war against savagery and terror:

– Jonathan Owen, white, national serviceman (23), who had completed his theological studies at the University of Cape Town the year before: according to his mother, he had postponed his military service for as long as possible, having considered for some time to become a conscious objector – he had even thought of emigrating, 'but he loved his country too much' – but she and her husband, a retired attorney in Queenstown and a veteran of the Second World War, had finally persuaded him that he could make a more meaningful contribution to society once he'd put the two years of service behind him;

– Ahmed Padayachee, Indian, national serviceman and member of the navy orchestra (19), only son of a widowed mother in Cato Manor in Natal who had told the newspaper how proud he'd been of his uniform and how he'd planned to work himself up through the ranks 'to make our country a safer place for all who live in it';

– Gertruida Carstens, white (21), a newly married woman from Boksburg, spending her honeymoon in the Cape with her husband, a mechanic: 'They had only arrived the previous evening, and neither of them had seen the sea before';

– Renier de Wet, white (12), a boy from Bellville, who on the fatal morning had been brought to town by his teacher with the rest of his class, to attend the ceremony in the Castle as part of a course in Youth Preparedness;

– Cornelis Botha, coloured (73), a retired farm labourer from Tulbagh, who had come to Cape Town with two of his children and four grandchildren, on the back of a farmer's truck, to buy herbs for a stomach complaint on the Parade;

– Charlie Webster, white (7 months), who had come from Wineberg with his mother (who was still in a serious condition) and a friend to do shopping in the Golden Acre: 'The Websters have been childless for eight years,' said the friend who requested not to be named, 'and God alone knows how they will survive this tragedy.'

Thomas had bought the newspapers from a surly woman in a café in Montagu (she was reading a woman's magazine, and he practically had to pull the papers from under her elbows and ponderous breasts); but a brief glance at the front pages had so nauseated him that he'd put them away again. Was there really any point in trying to obtain permission to attend the funeral? Afterwards, when he'd discussed it with Rashid, his comrade had not minced his words:

'Thomas, you're off your rocker.'

'_'

'Is it to pay your last respects, or because you're suddenly suffering from a bleeding conscience?'

'It's something I just *have* to do, Rashid.'

'I'll have to check with Justin first. Why did you wait till the last minute?'

'You wanted me to discuss it on the phone?'

'Oh, all right then.' Grudgingly. 'But I can't see him clearing it.'

But Justin had consented after all, even if he was very hesitant; he probably knew Thomas better, or read him more thoroughly, than Rashid.

And here he was now. He'd made sure, well in advance, to find a seat in the church: right at the back, against the wall, from where he could see the baroque pulpit, if not the gleaming wooden lions that supported it. The front seats had been reserved in advance for Cabinet members from all three Houses of Parliament, administrators, officers of the security forces, the diplomatic corps, and relatives; in that order.

The most remote corners of the interior were flooded by television lights; the crews gathered left and right on the gallery – amazingly, even they had dressed, for the occasion, in suits and ties: orders from above, no doubt – behind cameras mounted to capture every secret sob and blowing of a nose to inform the mourning nation across the length and breadth of the land. (The Afrikaans daily: 'A nation plunged in sorrow, united in its anguish, unanimous in its resistance to the forces of darkness.') Thomas, camouflaged behind thick-rimmed glasses and a moustache, had to sink down low in his pew behind the rows of heads in front of him to stay out of range; with the uneasy feeling that nothing could remain hidden in that apocalyptic glare.

Only four coffins, all of them white, one the size of a shoe-box, were lodged on the trestles in front of the pulpit. 'Other arrangements', the newspapers reported, had been made by the families of the two remaining victims, and the state had respected their wishes. But Rashid had already told him what the *Weekly Mail* was to confirm the following week, of how nearly – and why – the entire impressive ceremony had been shipwrecked. Initially, not only a communal service but a communal burial as well, in Woltemade cemetery, had been planned, in order truly to grip the imagination of the nation. Consideration had even been given in high places to the temporary suspension of separate entrances at the cemetery in order to emphasise the shared nature of the sorrow. But, to begin with, the relatives of the young Indian soldier had refused to co-operate: the official reason given was that Islamic custom did not permit the body to remain unburied for so long; but a more informed guess was that no imam could be found to appear with the other men of God in the Groote Kerk. An even more serious problem had arisen when the Boksburg mechanic, Theuns Carstens, who had lost his wife, had refused 'to let her be buried with a bunch of hottentots'; and when pressure was applied, he'd threatened to take his story to the newspapers. As a result his wife's remains had been transported to Johannesburg by air, at the state's expense, to be buried in a separate ceremony attended by Boer guards in khaki uniform, with pseudo-swastikas on aggressive red and white flags surrounding the grave.

Even Jonathan Owen's parents, Rashid had learned, had been dead against the idea of a military funeral for their pacifist son, but after a visit by a delegation of top brass (apparently with the hint of an enquiry into the possibility of awarding the father a belated medal for services rendered at El Alamein) they had consented to attend, on the condition that the coffin would afterwards be sent to Queenstown for private burial.

Hence the final arrangement of a communal service followed by private, separate funerals.

Archbishop Tutu of the Anglican Church was – to the relief of the government (and, it should be said, the Owens) – on a visit abroad; consequently a less radical bishop could be co-opted to appear with the moderator of the Dutch Reformed Church, the chief chaplain of the armed forces, and a pastor of the Assembly of God (for the Webster family) at the interdenominational service.

– For all flesh is as grass, and all the glory of man as the flower of grass. The grass withereth, and the flower thereof falleth away: But the word of the Lord endureth for ever.

Thomas was aware, when the squad of officers in uniform entered and the doors were blocked behind them by a double row of constables with mounted rifles, of a sudden claustrophobia: he wanted to get out, get away, fight his way free through that solid blue wall. And also nausea. And yet he knew he had to go through with it. Behind all rational consideration, overriding Rashid's angry objections, he knew that this was what he had to do; this was where he had to be. In spite of his revulsion at the way in which the state had taken over everything – the soldiers lining the streets outside, the police at the doors, the officers in the front seats, the unfolding of the ceremony itself, the carefully chosen texts, the hypocrisy of the prayers – in spite of all that he had to be there, a ritual of purgation, in its own way harder to get through than all the preparations for the assault. And then there was the searing of a coal in live flesh, in the beginning, when they first came in; at the end, when they followed the coffins into the drizzle outside: the families. The Owens: a dignified little man, lean as a greyhound, resisting with military straightness the ravages of rheumatism; and his wife, large and limp, wearing a black veil over her hat; and their four older children, two of them with children of their own. Charlie Webster's young parents: a sturdy man with longish red hair, in a black suit borrowed for the occasion from a smaller relative, embarrassed by his wife who wept monotonously throughout the service, supported by an older sister who tried to keep her upright, obviously annoyed at her brother-in-law for not offering any assistance. The parents of the boy Renier de Wet, in their thirties: the woman, a lecturer at the Cape Technicon, vaguely blonde and attractive, kept busy by an infant on her lap; her husband, an insurance agent, wearing a white carnation in his buttonhole, a fixed expression of blunted amazement on his face. And then a dozen or more members of the Botha family from Tulbagh (an accurate count was difficult in that throng): a very thin, very straight, wholly toothless old woman in a black dress with white dots, on her head a white hat bedecked with purple flowers, on her lap a yellow shopping bag from which, with the disturbing rustle of crumpled plastic, she continually took peppermints to keep her grandchildren quiet; divers other elderly people, presumably brothers and sisters, uncomfortable in Sunday suits from which protruded peasant hands like gnarled vine stumps; an in-between generation, some marked with the lines and scars and passivity of farm labourers, others evidently more well-to-do, city people in a cloud of eau de cologne and Brylcreem; and children, ranging from babes in arms (one of whom had to be breast-fed during the service) to teenage.

– Say to them that are of a fearful heart. Be strong, fear not: behold, your God will come with vengeance, even God with a recompense; he will come and save you.

– It isn't you I wanted to hurt! For God's sake, believe me. If not today, for that is asking too much, then some day in the future. One day when we have all broken free from this whirlpool that has sucked us in and churns us round and round, madness, darkness, evil. It was to get us *out* of it that we have done it. To hasten its end. Can you understand that? If only I could take you with me, I would let you see the countless other funerals I've been to over the years. In Uitenhage, when twenty-eight people were buried together, nineteen of them – men, women, children, babies – shot in the back by police. There were a hundred thousand of us at that funeral. Or in Cradock, when they carried, in four coffins, the tortured and charred bodies of Goniwe and Calata and Mhlauli and Mkonto high above the heads on their hands through the crowds, and in tragic defiance the black and green and gold flags moved ahead of the throng like the columns of fire or smoke leading the children of Israel through the desert in search of a promised land. And all the others, the countless others of the countless nameless: men and women tortured and murdered, their bodies carted away like night-soil from police stations and dumped on deserted beaches or in rivers or among bushes or dunes behind rows of squatters' shacks; children beaten to death with the butts of guns, or with sjamboks, or batons, or blown to pieces by buckshot fired at point-blank range. The small bodies of babies who'd died of hunger or measles or cholera or typhoid. Come with me, and I'll show you the photographs, hundreds of them, taken over years and years, here in the Cape Peninsula, or in the townships of Port Elizabeth and Cradock and East London, in the Valley of a Thousand Hills in Natal, on white-frosted mornings on the Free State plains outside Thaba Nchu. Come back with me to a day that nothing can obliterate, a purple bougainvillea day in

Africa, white cumulus clouds in the bluest of skies, Lusaka's broken skyline behind dark masses of trees, a day that smells of mangoes, a day red with flamboyants, as of blood, a day when the hum of the sewing machines in the market-places grows quiet and the fires below the grids in the food-stalls are doused, and the scissors of the barbers stop snipping, and even the birds in the toona-trees fall silent: as a huge funeral procession moves through the city and everything is transformed into the black and green and gold of the flags over the single deep grave into which three coffins are lowered, father, mother and child, the archetypal family, as immemorial as that statue of fertility in the lobby of the hotel: that day when they were folded back into the soil of Africa, the cheerful big-eyed child Govan and his beautiful mother Noni and the man whose name means 'Gift', my friend, the best of friends, Sipho. Come with me, let me show you. Weep, weep today: it is your right to weep. My own eyes, as I am sitting here, are filled with tears, I cannot restrain them. I am weeping with you. But for God's sake: weep with me, too, cry the beloved country: weep with me over a land, a continent that has seen too much of exploitation and cruelty and violence and death; blood, blood, blood –

– Verily, verily, I say unto you, That ye shall weep and lament, but the world shall rejoice: and ye shall be sorrowful, but your sorrow shall be turned into joy. A woman when she is in travail hath sorrow, because her hour is come: but as soon as she is delivered of the child, she remembereth no more the anguish, for joy that a man is born into the world. And ye now therefore have sorrow: but I will see you again, and your heart shall rejoice, and your joy no man taketh from you.

A school choir sang, girls in white, *Our Father*, first in Afrikaans, then in English.

A few people were sobbing loudly.

In one of the front pews where the relatives were seated there was a sudden commotion. The young Webster woman had fainted and half slipped from the seat. Over-zealous police at the front door, ready for action, stormed to the pew to intervene, then hesitated, embarrassed, when they discovered what had happened, and prepared to return to their posts when they were stopped in their tracks by a loud whisper from one of the officers. They scrambled over people blocking their way, and at last marched towards the vestry on heavy boots, carrying the limp woman among them like

231

a rag doll. The sister followed, casting back a last accusing glance at the wretched husband who stared ahead, his face burning with shame. The vestry door closed behind them.

The moderator raised his head in the direction of the TV cameras and appeared satisfied.

An eloquent message from the state president was read by a member of the white Cabinet, followed by shorter speeches (the length of each determined rigorously in advance) by the chairmen of the House of Representatives and the House of Delegates. At the end of the final speech there was another disruption. One of the widow Botha's grandchildren had lost his peppermint, and as he emerged from under the pew where he'd collected it, there was the sound of a resounding slap – his grandmother stood no nonsense – which caused the child to start screaming blue murder. One of the other women in the group, presumably the mother, gathered the sobbing child to her bosom, trying to smother the sound. Through the commotion the old lady's voice cut like a razor through church and country:

'Johnny, if you don't sharrap jes' now, I'm not ever bringing you to a funeral again.'

The brief stir soon subsided before the great continuing sweep of familiar phrases.

– Behold, I shew you a mystery; We shall not all sleep, but we shall all be changed – in the twinkling of an eye, at the last trump: for the trumpet shall sound, and the dead shall be raised incorruptible – Death is swallowed up in victory. O death, where is thy sting? O grave, where is thy victory? The sting of death is sin; and the strength of sin is the law –

Then the trumpets of the navy band resounded at the front door, the police moved aside, navy officers in white raised the four coffins on their shoulders and marched solemnly into the grey day outside where, for a moment, even the rain had stopped.

Of the whole occasion there would afterwards remain only one moment transfixed in Thomas's mind, as if nothing else had mattered – not the last respects paid to the dead, not the offering of atonement, not the attempt to complete a circle, but only this – as if, as far as he was concerned, everything had happened so that this single instant of shock could be registered in his memory. In the throng of people pushing through the doors towards the vast crowd that had collected outside, for a brief moment – no more, a mere moment – the pushing and shoving brought him face to face with a big dark-complexioned man with grey hair cut short in a horse-shoe round his bald head; liver spots on the crown, and on the hairy back of the hand that removed an already half-smoked, somewhat crumpled cigarette from his pocket to light it up again. They were so close to one another that he caught the smell of old tobacco from the man's worn brown suit. Stale perspiration. Something physical. A man who looked like a farmer forced, against his will, into a suit. Below the heavy brows the round eyes, bulging slightly, stared in myopic innocence at the world; they were so pale as to seem colourless, the eyeballs yellowish, with a fine network of red veins. A brush moustache. The sharp, brief flare of the match illuminated each detail. Then he flicked out the flame – a swift, deft motion as if he were wringing the neck of a small bird – and threw the match away. His eyes stared straight at Thomas. Just for a moment; then he looked elsewhere. There was no sign of recognition in his expression. (Thank God, the glasses, the short hair, the moustache had done the trick. For now.) But Thomas, unable to move, felt his guts contract like a ball of stiff porridge coagulating inside his body. Mouse and snake, he thought. A hare caught in the deadly spotlight of its hunter. Total paralysis. Because he'd looked into those eyes before; and might again. Brigadier Kat Bester.

Four hearses, piled high with wreaths in which orange, blue and white predominated, took the coffins to their separate destinations: Jonathan Owen's remains (and with sickening clarity Thomas suddenly wondered: what *had* remained?) to the station for the journey to Queenstown; Renier de Wet's on the way to Bellville; old grandpa Cornelis Botha's to Tulbagh; Charlie Webster's shoe-box to Wineberg. There were buses waiting to take the funeral-goers to the different destinations; at the door to each police were already positioned to search all passengers.

Someone had once said, thought Thomas – no, not someone: Nina: Nina had said – that in some remote society in the world people believed that if you killed a person, he became part of you, and lived the rest of his life inside you. For ever.

He watched the funeral buses filling up with people. He considered getting into one of them – to counter the emptiness and the revolt, the resentment the service had kindled in him; to try and round off, perhaps, what had been left so agonisingly incomplete (*this* was not what he'd come for!) – but the risk was too great. And where, even if he could, should he go? A suburban cemetery in Bellville – a child's grave in Wineberg – a muddy farm graveyard outside Tulbagh?

But it was not only the risk. Perhaps risk had nothing to do with it. It was the discovery, which without the service he could never have made, that there are circles which *cannot* be completed. Not ever. (One coffin, especially, had been altogether missing today. It was as if she had not even existed. Her name had not yet been announced. Unless they really didn't know? But they must.) It was not enough to return to the city where it had all begun a week before. Because the ends didn't meet; it was not a circle. It was a spiral. Moving irredeemably onward, inward. And it was not a week ago that it had begun! But where then? With the first Landman, Hendrick Willemszoon, who had set foot on this shore? Or, even if one remained within a single lifespan, with that purple day in Lusaka? the day in Crossroads when he'd dragged Nina away from the policemen and their dogs? the exhibition he'd held in London?

How could one ever be sure that *this* was the point where all began?

2

– Perhaps in an Old Flat in Langa. Or in a 'zone' in that township, or in Nyanga. ('Langa', 'Nyanga': 'Sun', 'Moon': only a Boer government could seriously think up such names.)

I'm in my third year at university, still intending to proceed to the Teacher's Diploma the following year and follow in Dad's footsteps. Together with three or four others – in due course more will join – I volunteer to lend a hand with the running of a club in the township: under the pretext of 'recreation' – darts, a ping-pong table, the rudiments of pottery and drawing – some unofficial night-school education is smuggled in. Standard 5 to begin with, then Standard 6, eventually Standard 8. There must be an atavistic missionary zeal in me inspired, perhaps, by what Oupa and Pa have – wrongly, but with the best of intentions – told me about Fransoois Lodewickus Landman. Or maybe it is simple curiosity that drives me, to find out more about the dark side of the moon, in those places with the beautiful names and the terrifying reputations.

Without too many hassles we obtain permits which entitle each of us to devote two evenings per week (plus, occasionally, another few hours of a Saturday) to the basic teaching programme: mainly reading and writing; some Afrikaans and English, a smattering of history and geography, elementary mathematics. The lessons are given in the 'front room' of one of the eight or so New Flats buildings in Langa: four-storey structures looking ill at ease among the swarming hovels surrounding them, desperately trying to maintain some old-world 'status' against the ravages of poverty and decay. Red-brick from the late Forties, with proud crowns that ought to have disappeared with the Third Reich. Practically the only furniture in the 'front room' is two rows of dilapidated bare tables flanked by long benches. But the overwhelming impression is that of sound: innumerable radios on all the floors; the hissing of Cadac or primus stoves on which, in blackened aluminium pots, samp and beans are simmering; dark groups of people clustered round a table, vociferous in their eating, or drinking, or playing cards, mothers breast-feeding their babies. Because although the building, like all the other single quarters – 'zones' and 'flats' and 'special quarters' – has been constructed for migrant workers, a population of temporary unattached males, it houses more women and children than men; and some of the 'temporary' residents have been there for thirty years and more.

Not an easy task. Beyond the two tables we occupy for our lessons, the ordinary life of the building continues. People eating or chatting or listening to the radio; appearing from a dingy narrow passage or disappearing into the night; others huddled together, their dark faces illuminated sharply by a candle or a lamp, as on a Rembrandt painting. We cannot stay too late, because after a long working day most of our pupils – some of them old men in their seventies – are tired, their concentration flagging; and many of them must rise at four in the morning to catch intricate combinations of buses and trains and buses again to their distant working places. In any case the 'front room' must be evacuated in time for the young boys who bring down their bedding from the upstairs bedrooms to spread it on the floor down here: because every man with a precious claim to a bed of his own is in charge of relatives who have moved in over the years – some of the older ones have only a woman; others have accumulated a vast extended family of cousins and descendants and distant relatives and hangers-on.

In the beginning I feel diffident and awkward. It's only after I have come to know the old man from Mdantsane, Khaya Ntshenge, that the place relents and welcomes me. He is seventy-three, has spent thirty-two years in his flat. (Or rather, his cubicle, because a bed is all any inhabitant can precariously claim as his own.) Originally, when he first arrived in the Cape in search of work, he intended staying only for a year to earn money for the wife and five children he'd left behind. From year to year his stay has been extended. At first, he used to go home for a month every year; but for fifteen years now he hasn't been back at all. He met another woman and took her in with him, started a second family. She died six years ago and most of the children were taken in by her relatives. Since then he has been mostly alone, although some of his Cape children still drop in occasionally. For a while, when he was ill, a female cousin moved in under his bed to look after him. News from the Ciskei children has been coming at ever greater intervals. This is why he's decided to learn to write. So that he can send a letter to Mdantsane from time to time, to inform his children that he's still alive, even if he now has a cataract in one eye, and in winter he is crippled by gout in the left foot.

Before he acquires the skill himself – half a page covered in large, hesitant letters, which takes him an hour, the paper getting more and more wrinkled, and stained with candle-wax – I am charged with the duty of writing on his behalf. Those are confidential letters. He doesn't want to have them written in the 'front room' among all the other people, but high up on the third floor, on his own bed. His 'room' – a small space around his iron bed partitioned off from his neighbours' with a wooden frame he's made himself, draped with red and blue floral curtains – is pervaded by the smell of cough medicine. The little place is immaculate: the grey, white-striped blankets folded with military precision; the sheet and pillow-case a dazzling white; the bottom end has a red-checkered rug folded on it. The wall is covered with colour photographs cut from magazines, as precisely squared as the lines of a crossword puzzle. On a narrow shelf beside the bed sits his large alarm clock, flanked by a radio with shiny knobs, two or three blue enamel mugs, his primus stove, a packet of candles, medicine bottles. Under the bed he keeps a dark green tin trunk which is moved out for me to sit on when I write; for the whole duration of the ceremony he remains standing rigidly to attention, watching my every scrawl.

After the third letter I venture to ask him whether he will have

236

any objection if I bring along my camera to take photographs of his quarters.

The old man gazes suspiciously at me. 'What for?'

'It's so colourful.'

He looks around him in surprise, as if he has never seen it properly. (Perhaps he hasn't, with that cataract.) 'What is nice about him? It is my life. He is very little.'

'It will look good on a photo.'

'If other people see him, perhaps they will throw me out.'

'Why should they?'

'One never know.'

'If I take a photo of the room you can send it to your children, then they can see how you live here.'

That seems to touch something in him.

'We can make a portrait of you too,' I proposed.

All of a sudden he becomes enthusiastic. 'How long will it take?'

'Not long. I do everything myself.'

By this time I already have a regular income from my photography. Enough to pay my fees and lodging, which has allayed Dad's initial misgivings. I accept whatever comes my way. Photographs of residence balls, intervarsity, parties, panty raids, rag, the occasional wedding, the girlfriends and boyfriends of acquaintances. A portfolio in *Panorama* on grape harvesting in the Western Cape brought the first breakthrough. And when, soon afterwards, at the end of my second year, I won two awards – a competition in the *Cape Times*, a Kodak prize – and three of my photographs were accepted for a national salon in Johannesburg, a studio in town hired me part-time, and now allows me to use their darkroom over weekends.

It has stopped being a hobby long ago, although I have not yet tried to formulate exactly what it means to me. 'Art'? Yes, rather. There are photographs I take to earn money and learn my trade. But there are others with which I try to prove something – but what? – to myself. Many of them will, in retrospect, appear over-dramatic in their lighting or posing, over-textured, as I pass, inevitably, through a period of addiction to grain, manipulating development time, experimenting with chemicals, varying temperatures: but this is all part of a process of breaking away from the mere mechanical recording of what has been observed by the lens. I derive from it the deep satisfaction others get from painting or writing. And for the time being it is sufficient in itself. Or is there already, deep down, an uneasiness, an irritation, a dissatisfaction, however vague and unformulated still, with a notion of art as something essentially disconnected from the very world it relies on? This, I think, must lie at the root of what the old man in Langa has begun to drive home to me, a process that will result in my changing all my previous notions of photography.

Old Khaya Ntshenge awaits me in his Sunday suit when I arrive the following Thursday evening. This is how I shall always see him, as he poses in the colour photographs: stern and dignified, his gaunt body straighter than usual, big hands on his thighs, elbows pointed outward, eyes staring fixedly into the lens. Above him, the magazine pages behind the bedstead. Hangers on the walls, draped with his few shirts and single jacket. The sharp reflection of the flashlight on the enamel mugs. A much too rigid pose. And the artificial light makes it all look much too glamorous. So I persuade him to arrange a repeat session on the Saturday, in daylight. However meagre the light that filters into those dark cubicles.

His watery eyes spill over the high erosion banks of his cheek-bones when he looks at the first batch of photographs, held close to his face to make out what is on them. What can he really see of that ancient weatherbeaten face, furrowed and wrinkled like a relief map? Perhaps the brightness of the colours is enough for him.

'Now they will see me,' he says. 'Now it is all right if I die, they will see me.'

For an hour I sit with him while he laboriously pens a letter to his children in Mdantsane. The address on the envelope I print in my own hand before I take it to the post office. From that day there is something in his attitude towards me I can only describe as paternal. He derives particular pleasure from introducing me to the customs of his people – the circumcision of the boys, the choosing of a wife and the paying of *lobola*, family responsibilities, witch doctors and ancestral spirits, funeral rites – and to the oral traditions transmitted to him by his grandmother: especially about the tragic massacre of his people after the young girl Nunqawusa had told her uncle about the conversation she'd had with spirits at the waterhole – spirits who'd urged the amaXhosa to slaughter all their cattle and destroy all their grain in preparation for a Day of Judgement when the ancestors would rise from the dead to join forces with the living in driving the white people into the sea. Stories I've known from my school history books, or from the

238

chronicle of our family composed by my grandfather and my father, suddenly spring to life in a wholly different perspective. Literally everything is changed into its opposite: what used to be the eastern frontier to my ancestors becomes a western to Khaya Ntshenge; our Black Peril has been transformed into their White Peril; what to us has been a heathen mass-suicide of the Xhosa has changed, in his view, into a sly design of the British colonial authorities, in cahoots with the gullible Nunqawusa, to exterminate the black race. It's like a photograph, it strikes me in the darkroom one afternoon as I'm developing some black and white film taken in Langa: positive/negative. Such an obvious comparison, yet to me it has the shock of revelation. And it is this revelation, I believe, which makes the old man so special to me. Because it fuses his existence with an activity that is fast becoming the passion of my life – so much so, that occasionally I even neglect my current girlfriend, the effervescent Carla, so that I can have more time for photography.

More and more flows from it. Since Khaya Ntshenge has adopted me as a surrogate son – he has long been a father, a chief, to all the inhabitants of his hostel – the others also begin to accept me with a generosity that often humbles me. On every wall and partition in that cavernous building my photographs are stuck with Sellotape or drawing-pins; they are dispatched in letters far and wide across the country, to the most remote places the people have come from.

It is not confined to this one hostel either. It is Grandpa Khaya himself who insists, 'This place he give you the wrong idea, Thomas. This is the Old Flats, we living in luxury here. You must going see how the other people live, the people in the zones, yes, here in Langa, over there in Nyanga, and in Guguletu. You must be seeing for yourself.'

'But they won't let me in there, Grandpa Khaya.'

His voice rasps in dry laughter; his eyes are watery again. 'I shall speak to them.'

This is how, for the first time, I really immerse myself in the world of the shadow people. Because in a way the Old Flats have remained on the edge of this world, more or less settled, more or less 'decent'; but the New Flats, and the other council hostels, the single quarters, are a whole new world to me. I go on a photographic spree. (Within limits, of course: later, after my international breakthrough, I will work with photographers from *National Geographic* and other magazines, people who produce forty thousand colour slides for a single project: compared with them, I have always had a puritanical streak. All the more so at this time, when I have to think twice about every roll of film, even if I can now acquire it at cost from the studio I work for. But whereas previously I set out on a project like an old-time Boer hunter who, if he'd gone out with four bullets, expected to return with four carcasses, during these months in the black townships I'm hunting with a shotgun as it were.)

How clear, the images on these photographs. In the distant background: Table Mountain, Lion's Head, Devil's Peak, the timeless, incomparable blue range of Adamastor; or the two cool-towers on Settlers' Way, where traffic sweeps past without an inkling of this lost world, the subconscious of the Cape which only on rare occasions breaks out in nightmares on the surface. The New Flats, two storeys high, bare brick, or whitewashed half-heartedly without plastering it first, subsiding into ruins (from inside, one can see daylight through the cracks), doors or window-frames an unexpected bright red, or blue, or yellow; the long depressing rows of 'zones'. Hordes of children playing with their wire-cars in the sand that never stops sifting or blowing through the straggled Port Jacksons; or splashing in puddles where a dead rat is a special treat. Lorries parked like old-fashioned trading wagons in vacant lots among mounds of rubbish, their back flaps turned up to display their merchandise, tinned food and Omo and toilet rolls and soccer balls, you name it. Women sitting beside rickety tables, or straight-legged on the ground, some under parasols, with whatever can be bought or sold: small items like razor-blades and matches and candles and shoelaces; foodstuff like *pap* and intestines, or samp, *marog*, sheep's heads. (Surrounding the images is the sound: the never-ending ocean of children's voices, quarrels and squabbles, exuberant dialogues conducted across three or four blocks of intervening space, radios, barking dogs, cackling or crowing chickens, even the grunting of pigs here and there.)

And indoors: crumbling walls bravely, defiantly, painted blue or green. Multicoloured curtains or strident blankets in the dusk, bare light bulbs, long, lugubrious corridors, the ubiquitous primus stoves and radios. The indomitable urge in each bed-owner to make his little space his own, with a family snapshot, a potted plant, a handful of feathers in a broken pot, a small mat on the floor. Front rooms with concrete blocks on pedestals to serve as tables; others with the more human feel of wooden tables and benches. 'Kitchens' with lock-up cupboards or shelves lining the wall. Green bathrooms with open showers which also serve as urinals. Everywhere, the stench of blocked toilets, broken sewage pipes, old boiled cabbage leaves.

But what the photographs cannot show is what really matters. The people, the parties, the conversations, the eruptions of laughter, the ever-readiness to help, whether someone falls ill, or is sacked at his work, or receives news of a death at home, hundreds of kilometres away, or is mugged and robbed by *skollies* on the way from work, or returns home from the horses on Saturday, cleaned out. Each bed has family attached to it: sometimes there are seven, or eight, or nine people who must be accommodated at night, either under or beside the bed. But in a sense the entire 'zone' is a vast extended family. Nothing happens to anyone which does not affect them all. No matter how bad it is – and sometimes it is horrendous, especially after a police raid, when all the women and children are picked up and carted off – it can be borne because it is always shared. This is my first exposure to *ubuntu*. And I learn it from people who officially do not even exist, who are not supposed to be there, or who have, at most, a claim to only temporary residence.

The whole experience, to me, is coloured by the presence and the personality of Ntsiki Yaya. It is to his care the old man entrusts me when I first venture into the unknown. A distant relative, as far as I can make out; Grandpa Khaya refers to him as his 'son', but that can mean anything. The most casual, nonchalant person I've ever known in my life, the archetypal cool cat, always 'ready for something', and on the verge of exploding in laughter, even when things are going badly – in fact, most especially when they are going badly. ('So what, Thomas, that's life, man.') Thirtyish, I guess, but I suppose he can be anything between twenty and forty; with Afro hair and dark sunglasses in white frames, invariably bedecked with a zoot scarf flung over his shoulder, Isadora Duncan style, and two-tone takkies (which he insists on calling 'sneakers'); not particularly tall, sturdily built, but with a premature bulge in his stomach which makes him look permanently pregnant. Ntsiki is, officially at least, a hawker. He has his own combi, an old jalopy whose doors are held to their frames with blue-wire, and which is regularly impounded by the traffic police for being unroadworthy. In unfathomable ways he always succeeds in retrieving it: sometimes by having it repaired in some Nyanga backyard, but mostly, I believe, through the devious intervention of friends and 'contacts' at the pound. He doesn't always hawk the same wares. It depends on whatever pays better at any given moment: sometimes fish, sometimes vegetables, sometimes second-hand clothing, sometimes groceries – mostly, I fear, stolen goods. In summer he occasionally drives through the Boland and returns with a load of plums, peaches, grapes, watermelons. And at least once a month he goes off to Transkei, ostensibly to look up his 'people'. But when he comes back, one can count on a fair consignment of dagga in the combi, smuggled in some unimaginable manner through all the raids and roadblocks on the way. Until that last time, of course.

And it is Ntsiki who is responsible for introducing me to Henry. Henry Bungane, the man from Robben Island. But that comes later.

Ntsiki takes me wherever he goes. Right into Freedom Square in Nyanga, the quarter where, mostly, young men go to earth when they have problems with the law; and it is well known that even the police are too scared to venture into that place. Hard-boiled types, comrades, shaped by the violence of 1976. But even in their midst, with Ntsiki Yaya as my guide and bodyguard I am received with a generosity and a warmth, a naturalness, as if it is the most ordinary of visits. (Except that I'm not allowed to take photos here, Ntsiki has warned me in advance. There are too many faces whose mugshots adorn the notice-boards of police stations all over the Peninsula.)

Early in the following year, just after the university has reopened, Grandpa Khaya Ntshenge dies suddenly in his sleep one night. To me it is a blow as bad as that of my own grandfather's death, three years before. Another storyteller's voice has fallen silent. And in a way it is even worse than my grandfather's death, because he, at least, has left a written record of his stories. With Grandpa Khaya, it seems to me, a whole dimension of the country's memory has vanished. Snatches of it I have recorded over the past months; but there is so much more, so much no one will ever be able to retrieve again. And it is not this, alone, that shakes me, but the very loneliness of his death.

What will be remembered of him in the distant valley where he comes from, and which he hasn't seen for so many years? All the time he has been living in this no-man's-land behind the cooling towers – this temporary residence of thirty-five years' duration: what is left of it? A small pile, I've seen it myself after the neighbours have assembled it, of blankets, a curtain, two cardboard boxes of clothing and odds and ends. And somewhere in an official register his name will now be erased, and a new name will be entered beside the number of his bed. With a stroke of a civil service pen he will be written off. His whole life cancelled.

His is the first township funeral I have ever attended. Quite different from those of subsequent years, because the old man has never been involved in politics of any kind. All the people from his building are there, this Sunday morning, and a handful of relatives traced in the city; from the Ciskei, no one. Carla and I are the only whites. She resists, at first – 'Please, Thomas, I don't want to know about things that will depress me' – but in the end she agrees, more from curiosity, I think, than from any understanding of my grief. After the service and the short ceremony at the grave, we accompany the others back to the tall brick building where a funeral meal has been prepared. The baked sheep's head nearly causes Carla to throw up; it takes much pleading to coax her into tasting, diffidently, a charred, stone-hard mealie cob roasted on a fire (and afterwards it leads to one of our worst quarrels). I must confess that I, too, have trouble eating the fare offered us, but I don't want to offend our hosts. (One photograph shows Ntsiki in a triumphant pose, holding one whole blue-boiled eye from the sheep's head in his hand.) And in the end there is something profoundly satisfying in the event: the putting away of the old man, the communal meal and the drinking afterwards, a reconciliation of life and death.

On the way back from the township, Carla still sulking beside me, I decide that the time has come to do something with all my photographs of the past months. A kind of homage to an old man who has shifted my consciousness of the world. An exhibition on campus: *The World of Khaya Ntshenge*. The SRC has no objection. (No one dares to, I've taken photographs, at cut rates, of all of them, and all their girl- and boyfriends too.) But on the day of the exhibition, a mere hour or two before the opening, I am summoned by the rector.

'I'm sorry, Mr Landman, but this exhibition must come down. I cannot allow it on my campus. People will get the wrong impression.'

'But Professor –' Flabbergasted, I grope for words. 'I've worked on it for *months*. All I've tried to do is to show the way these people live –'

'I respect your talent, Mr Landman, but if you want my honest opinion, I don't think you're using it to the best advantage. Suppose the English press got hold of it, can you imagine –'

I can no longer listen to him. Stammering with excitement I start arguing back. But he rises behind his wide desk and says laconically, 'Mr Landman, I am not interested in discussing the matter. I have given you an instruction. You may go.'

Seething, I leave the office. All kinds of extravagant schemes of revenge rage through my mind; but in the end Carla persuades me not to do anything rash. By the evening there is no sign of the exhibition left.

The next morning I load a selection of the mounted photographs into a car borrowed from a friend (my own, only, means of transport is a 500 cc bike), and take them to the office of the Afrikaans Sunday paper *Rapport* in Cape Town, where an assistant editor offers encouraging comments and undertakes to forward the material by courier to their head office on Johannesburg.

When, six weeks and several telephone calls later, there has still not been any reaction from the paper, I borrow my friend's car again and return to Cape Town. They're still waiting for a decision from Johannesburg, the assistant editor informs me; but he knows they've been having serious space problems lately. Perhaps it will be wise to give up the idea. Well, may I have my photographs back? Without a moment's hesitation, and without batting an eyelid, he retrieves the parcel – still unopened since my first visit – from a grey filing cabinet in the corner and hands it to me.

I walk the few blocks to the offices of the *Sunday Times* where I deposit the photographs with a secretary.

A fortnight later, without bothering to contact or consult with me, they publish a selection on an inside double page: in black and white, badly reproduced, cropped at random, without any attempt at coherence. But at least they're published.

It is, of course, a Sunday.

On the Monday afternoon three strangers in flannels and sports jackets arrive at my digs. Major Somebody, and two lieutenants. Just an informal chat. I do have time, don't I? They know exactly when my next lecture begins. Small-talk to begin with. Do I play rugby? Do I at least take part in some student activities? What are my plans for next year? Nice chick I've got, real hot stuff, don't I agree?

At long last, the major: 'You interested in photography, I notice.'

'I have been for years. Why?' My throat feels dry.

'Just asking. Saw the spread in yesterday's *Sunday Times*. By the way, what made you choose an English newspaper?'

'I showed them to *Rapport* first.'

'I see. Yes, I suppose it's pretty obvious why they turned them down.'

'I don't know what you mean, Major. I thought people would be interested. It's a whole world most of them know nothing about.'

'Problem is, this kind of thing can so easily create the wrong impression.'

'Like what?'

'I mean, suppose the overseas press got hold of it. Gives them ammunition for all kinds of stories about oppression and heaven knows what else. That kind of thing, you know?'

'But it's the truth, Major!'

'Thomas.' He switches, significantly, to my first name; his tone now confidential, trustworthy, fatherly. 'You come from a good Afrikaner home. Your parents must have high expectations of you. And well they should, if I may say so. Look, I'm convinced you acted in good faith. You only wanted to use your undeniable talent. But you see, in these times we live in we can never be too careful. There are people everywhere just waiting to pounce and make use of anything they can hit us with. Now, you're still young. You're probably not even aware of all the dangers threatening us. But often, before you know where you are, the enemy starts using you for its own evil purposes.'

I am furious. At the same time – there's no need to deny it – I am scared too. Shit-scared.

After a while I manage to ask, 'Is this a warning, Major?'

'Sonny.' He gets up and puts his hand on my shoulder. 'Let's just call it a bit of friendly advice. We wouldn't like to see –'

The rest of the sentence, unuttered, still hangs in my room, like smoke, after they have left.

The next afternoon, on my way back from a lecture, I find my landlady waiting for me outside my room. An urgent message from the photographic studio that employs me. The manager wants to see me as soon as possible. Intrigued, I hurry in to town on my bike. But the manager is, reportedly, 'out', and has left a letter with the receptionist. They regret to inform me that as they are forced by circumstances beyond their control to cut down on their overheads they cannot afford to make use of my services any longer. A postscript: much to their regret they are obliged to terminate my access to their darkroom as well. –

As the church-goers and the curious bystanders began to disperse – all the way down Adderley Street, further and further in the grey cotton wool of the afternoon, resounded military commands which caused the lines of soldiers to break up and march away – the city's everyday life returned to the streets. On the squares in the neighbourhood the Casspirs and Buffels and police buses were started up and moved off. The hearses had disappeared. What had happened had happened. The Cape reverted to normal.

Thomas looked on his watch. Four o'clock. It was too early for his meeting with Rashid. Over the lunch-hour they'd agreed to meet again at six. To make himself even less inconspicuous, he had put on the grey plastic mac he'd bought that morning on the way to Cape Town – in Montagu, just before he'd picked up the troopie – but the rain, it seemed, had stopped. Light filtered through the drifting grey clouds. But the city was still drained of colour, like a badly developed photograph that lacked contrast, neither blacks nor whites sufficiently defined. He sauntered through the Gardens. It was too wet to sit down on a bench, but he did so nevertheless, protected by the plastic coat, opposite the birdcage where budgies and canaries twittered and a pheasant strutted up and down along the wire-mesh. A few puffy pigeons on the soaked lawn strewn with fallen leaves were watching him sideways. A single damp squirrel came flitting past his feet. How different from a week ago, with Nina, when everything was washed in sunlight.

No. He mustn't think of her again.

He was on the point of getting up when he was stopped by a sudden commotion as something came crashing through the branches of the nearest shrubs and swooped down on him: something like a huge dark bird thrashing about on the ground with a broken wing. One claw grabbed Thomas by the shoulder. Petrified with shock, he drew himself into a tight bundle. Then caught an overwhelming whiff of alcohol and glanced up. It was a sordid old man in rags and tatters – broken shoes without laces, frayed grey trousers with gaping rents and holes, a floppy khaki trenchcoat – who'd grabbed hold of him, peering at him through red eyes overshadowed by protruding brows, his hair and beard unkempt and covered in dried leaves and twigs and tufts of grass. Yellow spittle drooled from his toothless mouth. In his other talon he clutched a bottle in which a few fingers of mauve methylated spirits still splashed. A *bergie*.

'Are you –' The scarecrow pressed his face right against Thomas's; the fumes took his breath away. 'Are you Jeremy?'

His throat still taut with fright, Thomas stammered, 'Why do you want to know?'

"Cause I'm looking for Jeremy. I *got* to find Jeremy.'

Thomas got up, so relieved he was ready to laugh or cry. 'Mister,' he said, 'you're absolutely right. We should all be looking for Jeremy.'

The *bergie* gawked at him. Thomas was already some distance away when the old man called after him, 'I say!' Thomas stopped to look round. 'Will you tell me when you found him?'

'I promise,' Thomas said solemnly. He walked on, suddenly feeling extraordinarily carefree. At the gate the peanut vendors and newspaper boys, driven away by the rain (where to?), had resumed their posts. He took a rand from his pocket to buy an *Argus*. 'Keep the change,' he said. 'And if you happen to see Jeremy, please tell him there's someone waiting for him at the birdcage.'

The boy stared after him as if he'd lost his mind.

A stare different from the desolate gaze of his parents in the rear-view mirror when he'd left home in the early dusk, driving into the gloomy day. He'd waved one last time from the corner. They believed he was on his way back to Johannesburg. But when he reached the main road he turned left, down into the dip – on the hill opposite, the white mission church, the row of sisal plants, the Apostolic church with its cracked wall – and up again, towards the mountains, the crumbling cliffs blood-red in the rain. It did not seem like a pass through the mountains, but like driving into the very entrails of the earth, the rocks still glowing with primordial fire, the dull green lichen on it like ancient dried algae and flotsam from a prehistoric sea.

Now the open road stretched ahead. Something urged him on. He drove faster than usual. And yet there was trepidation in him too; he almost wished to encounter barriers and obstacles to cut him off, to postpone what he wanted both to see and not to see. When he reached Montagu he turned off towards the main street. The rain was coming down in a solid dark sheet. At the first shop in the main street he bought the plastic mac and a black umbrella; then went in search of a café for a cup of coffee. Which was where he bought the papers, casting his eyes guardedly across the front page with the biographies of the dead.

He could postpone it no longer. But he knew, as he swung back into the main road, that for the first time he was really scared now. Not the sudden fright at the roadblock on his way to Thaba Nchu, but a calm, deep presence. His hands felt moist on the steering wheel. In his armpits and in his groin cold specks of perspiration prickled his warm skin. He was almost relieved when, on the outskirts of the town, he saw the troopie hitchhiking beside the road. It was more than compassion that made him stop for the young man drenched to the skin, there was calculation in it too: the soldier's presence in the car was a useful camouflage, protection, an alibi.

'Jesus. Thanks, man. Fuck, but it's wet.' The boy squeezed his bulging kitbag into the front beside his feet, shaking himself like a dog.

'Put it on the back seat,' Thomas offered. 'There's room enough.'

'It's okay like this.' Rivulets of water ran down his limbs on to the seat and the floor. He shivered. His short-cropped hair was plastered tight to his skull. A callow child, Thomas discovered, with a feeling almost of pity. A shadow of peach-down on his upper lip. He'd probably not even started shaving yet. 'Hennie van Rensburg.' An uncomfortable shaking of hands in the cramped space.

Thomas mumbled a name, hoping the hitchhiker would let it pass. But he asked emphatically, 'What was that?'

'Tertius Wessels.' He hoped Maria wouldn't blame him one day for appropriating her husband's name like that; or would she be amused? It was time he thought up other names for moments like this. Names no one could trace back to him, no matter in what roundabout way, afterwards. 'You on your way to Cape Town?'

'Villiersdorp. My parents live there, like.' An unexpected teenage blush. 'And, you know, my girl.' He became talkative. 'We got, you know, a long pass, I mean, like a fortnight. Because I mean, when I get back to Oudtshoorn, it's off to the fucking border.'

'For how long?'

'Oh you know, three months, Jesus.'

The curses, the evasions and obfuscations, seemed ill-suited to the precise innocence of his face, the frankness of his blue eyes: as if language was a suit of armour he'd put on, and which didn't fit him properly.

'I don't want to be a wet blanket, but when I did my stint on the border some lighties spent up to eighteen months up there.'

'Shit.' The troopie gulped. Then decided to risk it: 'Is it –' He had to clear his throat first, his voice wavered. 'I mean, is it really as fucking tough as they say?'

Thomas shrugged, and braked; they were caught behind a pantechnicon. 'It all depends. When I was there – ten years ago, already – it was all quiet. I was involved in only one battle when someone got killed, and that was a fake.'

'How d'you mean, you know, like a fake? Was the fucking ouk killed or wasn't he?'

'Oh he was killed all right. It's the battle that was a fake.'

'I don't figure you.'

'Don't worry, Hennie. I still can't figure it out myself.'

It was a relief to tell it to the blond boy.

Like many times before, the government had been in a spot about some recent incursion into Angola, the 'destruction of Swapo bases'. In the US and Europe television films were shown of a massacre of Angolan civilians, an entire village wiped out by mistake; among the conscripts stories did the rounds about a whole company of South Africans who, returning from the massacre, were ambushed by Cubans and more or less annihilated. Morale was low. Rumours were rife. In Parliament the Opposition put questions which were evaded by the Minister of Defence with the skill of an oxwagon making a U-turn in mud. 'Security reasons.' (He did emphasise, unasked, that morale in the forces was 'one hundred per cent. I am proud of my men.') Something had to be done to salvage a miserable situation; and in pillow talk between Foreign Affairs and Defence the idea was hatched to call television to their aid. A 'documentary' had to be compiled post haste to reveal the courage and heroism of the South African forces and the rout of Swapo.

The TV team arrived in the Caprivi soon after Thomas's company had been transferred there from Ondangua. Everything had to be done at breakneck speed in order to get the film to Johannesburg within a day: the public had to be deluded into believing that it had been shot during the raid of the previous week. The problem was that in the dense bush the men could not spread out as far as they would have on an actual manoeuvre: everything had to be adapted to the range of the cameras.

'That's how it came that one lightie was accidentally shot by someone behind him, not fifty yards from where I was crawling in the dust. One of his own pals. Actually, when I think back now, it's a miracle that only one got killed. The whole thing was a disaster.'

'And the, you know, the film, I mean, was that like screened?'

'Of course it was screened. And back home it was announced that the lightie had been killed the previous week, during the attack on the Swapo base. The reason, they said, they hadn't announced it before was that they couldn't trace the troopie's parents.'

'And nobody spilled the beans?'

'We were all put under oath. You can imagine. Even so, once we were home, some of the chaps began to drop hints. Nobody dared to go on record, of course. The shit nearly hit the fan when the troopie's father revealed that his son had written them a letter two days after the date he was supposed to have been killed. But the army just mumbled something about the wrong date, and that was that.'

'Jesus.' There was light perspiration on the boy's forehead, and on the disarming down of his upper lip. 'And otherwise?'

'Otherwise I suppose it was okay.'

– Otherwise: throwing darts in the dust, playing soccer in the dust, writing letters at the big table in the tent in the dust, swimming in a hole lined with plastic and surrounded by sandbags, going out on recce, riding convoys to Oshakati or Ondangua or Grootfontein (sometimes with loads of ivory from the countless elephants slaughtered by Savimbi to pay South Africa for its precious support), looking for landmines, shooting target at the 'enemy' across the Molopo, scouring each other's bodies for ticks, drinking lukewarm beer and Coke and rum and cane, talking about sex, killing flies or mosquitoes or gnats or countless other crawling or flying insects, digging shit trenches, masturbating over girlie magazines – sometimes a contraband *Playboy* – in the shower, or in the back of a Buffel, or in the bushes, or in bed, or in the latrines, trying to read, attending church services or prayer meetings or the rare concert (invariably by some sweet pale-pink singer who needed publicity for a new record, or tried to regain a lost reputation in the Heart of Africa, in the Bush, surrounded by hundreds of perspiring randy bodies, hundreds of agonising burning brains from which a cloud steamed up, like a bubble in a cartoon, inscribed hugely with the single word CUNT), or roasting meat and serving drinks to visiting VIPs. God, those VIPs.

It was among those visitors that I first saw, in the flesh – the too, too solid flesh – the man who later became president. If only I'd had, then, the slightest presentiment: how easy it would have been to arrange an accident with a grenade. At the *braavleis* fire. In the officers' mess. Even, spectacularly, in the latrine. How much could have been avoided by that timely act. Shit thou art and to shit thou wilt return. Even at that time – and I was only nineteen then – the encounter was a total disillusionment. Just to see a man like that, a Nebuchadnezzar of a man, His Excellency, for he was already in the Cabinet, getting pissed out of his mind, and stumbling about, the brass scurrying this way and that to amuse him, to be of service, to roar at his hoary jokes, keep his glass filled.

The next day, before the VIPs left again, His Excellency addressed us. All the customary shit: 'I know I am expecting a lot of you. Here in the wilds of Africa where you are fighting for the maintenance of our Christian values. But I know I can rely on you. I am proud of you. And it is my prayer that at the end of your term of service each and every one of you will return to the Republic safe and sound. But if God in His infinite wisdom should decide that some of you must give your lives for the cause to which we are all dedicated, then you must know in advance that your names will be inscribed indelibly on the scroll of honour of your people.' Something along those lines. But all I could think of as I stood at attention with the others, was, My God, what *are* we here for? Not to defend any 'values'. Not 'for the fatherland and its people'. But for individuals like you. Fat cats who, at most, are trying to get some political mileage out of us, we who are living and dying here, oh South Africa, dear land. *You* – look at you, still hung over from last night's boozing – *you* don't care a fuck about 'South Africa, dear land'. It's only your own arse you want to have licked. And you can't care less whether some of us die so that you can catch the shine for it.

'But at least you, I mean, Jesus, here you are, what the fuck, you're still sort of alive,' stammered the blond boy, as if to force, by fair means or foul, a positive response from Thomas.

'Sure, and you will be too. You know what they say' – why this viciousness in him? – 'War makes a man of a boy as a whorehouse makes a woman out of a girl.'

'Jesus, is it really so bad?'

'It depends, I suppose.'

'You spent all your fucking time like in the Caprivi?'

'After those first few weeks at Ondangua, yes. Two months at Omega, two at Katima Mulilo. Then another month back at Oshakati. For the rest I trod the dust at Voortrekkerhoogte.'

Omega, surrounded by camel-thorns and the dark foliage of tall bloodwood trees; a feeling of being abandoned in the wilderness.

251

(Major Henning, one night, when he was even more fazed than usual, 'Hell, boys, here in Omega cunt is so scarce a man has to fuck his own wife.') The woeful tattered remains of 'Bushmen': it turns one's stomach to look into the beautiful eyes of a people already extinct. For what has remained of their nomadic life? Only when a storm comes up, and they tear off their clothes and run about naked in the rain, something of an original spark seems to flare up again. But apart from that? Wizened old men with wrinkled faces entertaining, like trained monkeys, their paying visitors. Trackers who return from the bush and drink themselves into a stupor on whisky some of the men sell to them at five times the going price ('what do these gooks know about money anyway?'); women crocheting tea-cosies or doilies under the beaming eyes of a prim little mother from Pretoria; two church services on Sundays, prayer meetings on Wednesdays, as if an invisible remote moon still controls the religious tides in this place. And 'all-out night' once a month, concerts featuring accordion solos and 'sketches' and communal singing, because it's very important, says the commandant, 'to know who we are and to hold on to our values'.

Katima Mulilo, 'the place where the fire burns out': the deafening shrill of the cicadas in the mopanis, a heavy audible heat pressing down on the brute wilderness; parched and brown in drought, but at the slightest provocation, within a week of the first rains, an eruption of extravagant green luxuriance – the suddenness with which the seasons arrive – filling the river with dark swift water; the long low clubhouse at Wallela, serving both as church and as bar, with a plaque above the pulpit proclaiming *God is Love*, and another, directly above it, reading *Dry Inn*, with a machine-gun sling stacked with bullets draped over it. This was where I first became aware of the continent, this Africa: its expanse and its harshness, its sudden changes of mood; how it can press down, a hard lump of reality, on one's heart and guts, a presence one never escapes for the rest of one's life. This must have been what the land looked like, I think, when the first Landmans set foot in the south. And suddenly I understand more about them, and about the continent, and myself.

How many times, as I stand guard or loiter off-duty, I stare across the khaki-green water of the Zambezi or the Molopo to the far side, in me a longing so urgent it leaves me parched with thirst, to be *there*, to trek into Africa, see more of it, get deeper inside it. (And not for a moment do I suspect that it may become true one day!)

Oshakati: white grass, underbrush, bare patches, an occasional stark-green jackal-berry, sometimes thickets of camel-thorn, shallow dried-up lakes brimming with water in the rainy season, mottled long-horned cattle; the ragged plumes of makalani palms at the edge of the sandy stretch where we play handball in 42 degrees, and kick up dust, until it gets so bad we have to give up and retire to the coffee bar – *Ons Anker: Our Anchor* – where we while away the heavy time writing letters to real or imagined girls at home, playing chess or draughts, fray each other's nerves. Once, the handful of Swapo prisoners in the back of a closed truck that stays overnight before resuming the long trek to Grootfontein: parked, deliberately, in the full glare of the sun; some of them wounded, moaning, pleading for water, that interminable hoarse pleading for water, just a drop of water. We have stern instructions to keep away from the truck. ('They're fucking terrs, man, not human beings.') But in the predawn shift, when Henk Wepener and I stand guard, we cannot take their moaning any longer and offer them a few gulps from our mugs. And one of them – I cannot even see his face, it is too dark – thrusts something into my hand, a crumpled bit of paper I don't want to accept, yet cannot refuse. It is three, four days later before I dare to look at it – sick with a feeling of betrayal, of playing with fire – and discover a note, in Afrikaans, to a mother and father, an address near Okahandja. This, to me, is the turning-point of the war. Not what he has written, I do not even take it in properly, but the address. Here, I think, we've been fighting against terrorists from across the border: but among them is a man from Okahandja right in the middle of Namibia. And the others? Otavi, Rundu, Grootfontein? All the places near by. *Their land.* The discovery Frans Jacobus Landman made in the land of the Xhosas when his two brothers were killed beside him: why does one never learn? Why must each generation rediscover the same simple truths?

And why have I – all of us, I swear, every single troopie among us – why have we never realised it? Why has no one told us? It is their own land these 'enemies' are fighting for, are being killed for, are being shot or wounded or captured or tortured for. Three days, five days in a truck in the sun, without water. So what if they don't reach the destination alive? *Their land.*

In my mind the haunting words: *Nkosi sikelel' iAfrika* –

'Hey, listen, I mean, d'you mind if I ask you a kind of question?'

For a moment Thomas stared, uncomprehending, at the boy next to him; he'd forgotten about him. Then nodded. 'Sure.'

'I suppose you'll, you know, think I'm kind of megasoft in my head?' Hennie stared straight ahead through the monotonous hiss of the wipers. 'But tell me, I mean, were you ever, like scared?'

'You still asking? Of course I was.'

'I'm talking about, you know, sort of, *shit*-scared. You know, so fucking scared you can't fucking well sleep at night.'

Thomas nodded.

'I never wanted to go to the bloody army. Now I know what you're thinking, okay, so it's no big deal, shit, you think I'm a fucking sissy. That's what my dad thinks anyway. But I mean, Jesus, what fucking choice does a guy have?'

They were driving along the glistening wet road through Robertson. The air was heavy with the smell of young wine.

'Don't kid yourself,' Thomas said without looking at his passenger. 'Of course you have a choice.'

Hennie shook his head. 'Like what? Six fucking years in jail?'

'It's still a choice, isn't it? No matter what you choose: you've got to pay for it. Sometimes more, sometimes less. You can't expect to have a choice without a price tag.'

In a sudden surge of protest the boy asked, 'If you were, you know, suppose you were like in my place, suppose it's you who sort of had to go to the fucking border now, see what I mean, if you knew then what you know now, shit, if you could choose again today, what the fuck would you do?'

'I would regard six years in jail as a cheap alternative. Considering what it cost me in the end.'

'Still, you say you, I mean, you never saw bloody action?'

'I saw enough.' – A minister so pissed that he narrowly missed falling into the fire. A 'Bushman' arriving at the office to record the birth of his child in exchange for twelve beers. A crumpled ball of paper covered in almost illegible handwriting, an address in Okahandja. – 'I'd take the six years any time. Or clear out.'

'I don't bloody well want to, like, leave. I mean, where the hell will I, you know, kind of feel at home again?'

'There's always a chance of coming back. One day.' He stared ahead.

'If I go to jail now, hell, I mean, I'll be fucking twenty-four when I get out. You know how bloody old that is?'

Thomas suppressed a smile. 'I'm twenty-eight. I don't feel very old yet.'

'It's easy for you to bloody well talk.'

'Says who?'

He was silent for a long time. Only the wipers continued their unimaginative motion.

'And what d'you think, I mean, Jesus, what will my old man say?'

'Is it his choice, or yours?'

Hennie glanced quickly at him, then looked away. After a while he said, 'You don't know my old man.'

'_'

In the landscape around them Karoo and Boland overlapped. Orchards as yellow as turmeric. Patches of dark green Karoo scrub. Here and there a vineyard catching fire, smouldering red. On the right, prussian-blue mountains looming in the mist. A sheaf of white light falling through layers of cloud. On the outskirts of Worcester he slowed down. He looked at his watch. Not quite half-past nine. They'd made faster progress than he'd expected.

'I can take you through to Villiersdorp if you want to,' he offered. 'I have time.'

'Hell, it's fucking decent of you, man.'

'It's much of a muchness whether I go through Paarl or that way. Then you needn't stand in the rain again.' He grinned. 'That's one advantage of being in uniform: you seldom have to stand for long.'

'It's just because it's an easy way for people, you know, to work off like their fucking guilt-feelings. I mean, it makes them all feel nice and fucking safe at night. Because we're there to keep away the fucking Black Peril, right? Know what I mean?' He shifted his legs. 'Only, it's not as bloody easy as they think. I mean, there's some blokes —' He seemed reluctant to continue, as if he was unsure of what might come out; but after a while he did go on: 'You know, one of my school pals, he was a year before me, right, went to the bloody army like last year, see, up to the fucking border, and there he sort of got bushed, you know, and they brought him back. Few months in the fucking hospital and then, I mean, back to the camp, just after I got there. Okay? So one day he goes bloody AWOL, taking his fucking gun with him, you know. Anyway, then some bloody old couple picks him up, sort of, and Jesus, he just threw them out and took the fucking car and drove off, and then, I mean, shit, he just started shooting left and right at anything that fucking moved. Bloody miracle that only one of them died, like. But several others, I mean, in the fucking hospital, shit. Now they've, you know, put him away. And I tell you, man, he was the most ordinary fucking guy you can imagine. I mean, never even played rugby or that kind of thing. At school they used to, you know, tease him, said he was a fucking queer. Always, you know, drawing and things, that kind of stuff? Wanted to become, I mean, imagine, a fucking designer. Like fucking women's clothes and stuff, right? Just couldn't take it, know what I mean, just couldn't fucking well take it.' Suddenly his voice was breaking in urgency. 'So do you understand, Jesus, can you see why I'm, I mean, shit, I'm fucking scared, man. I mean, like if it could happen to him, hell –'

'What do *you* want to do one day?' Thomas interrupted, to steer the boy away from what had agitated him so. 'When you come back from the army?'

'Me? Drama. Always wanted to act, man. I mean, how can they expect me to bloody well go and, you know, shoot people?' He looked at Thomas. 'What do *you* job?'

'I?' Thomas thought quickly. 'Oh I'm freelancing for a couple of magazines. Articles, that kind of thing. Actually, I'm still working on a thesis.'

'That what you *wanted* to do?'

'I think so,' said Thomas, evasively.

'Your old man, I mean, like how's he take it?'

'That's a funny question.'

'Is it? Well, I can tell you, *my* old man –'

Thomas looked at him. 'Is he difficult?'

Hennie unexpectedly closed up. 'Ag, forget it, man.'

Thomas turned his head, but the boy was staring grimly ahead; he seemed to be clenching his teeth; perhaps he was close to tears. After a while he shifted his legs again, obviously cramped in the small space beside his bag.

'Why don't you put the thing on the back seat? You'll be much more comfortable.'

'Okay.' This time the boy obeyed. He first removed the newspaper and kept it on his lap, glancing without much interest at the front page. Thomas looked askance at him, then turned his head away, but still watching from a corner of his eye.

For a few minutes Hennie studied the front page, framed in black; the photographs, the large headings.

'Shit.' He folded it up angrily, slapping his hand on. 'You seen it?'

'Not really.' Thomas was aware of his hands perspiring on the wheel again.

'The bastards. I mean, Jesus.' A long pause. 'What a fuck-up. I mean, there we go to the bloody border to fight the bloody terrorists, and all the while they're, shit, I mean, they blow us up behind our backs. Right here among us.'

The last few kilometres they covered in silence, driving through billowing hills covered in vineyards. White streaks of mist lay in the valleys. As they entered Villiersdorp, there was once again the heady smell of young fermenting wine.

Hennie showed him the way. Two streets towards the mountain, then left. A modern house, but sporting a mock Cape-Dutch gable.

'Don't you want to come in, I mean, perhaps you'd like to, you know, what about a cup of tea or something?'

'No, I've got to move on.' He turned down his window and put out his hand. 'Good luck, Hennie. With whatever you decide to do.'

He thought, watching in his mirror the blond boy who remained standing, disconsolate, in the drizzle, It's not only the dead who enter your existence and become part of you: it's every single person who travels a part of the journey with you: each one rubs off on you, you on them. You are never on your own; there are always others. And nothing happens here and now only. Everything trails with it long fragments of the past. Or drags you into the future, long before you're there.

Rashid. He'd felt like embracing the slight young man when he made his appearance on the top deck of the parking garage. But naturally he hadn't: one never knew who might be watching. It was hard to keep his composure – in one swoop everything of the week before had swamped him again, becoming real in a way that hadn't been possible over the previous days: then it had been memory only, recollection; now it was, suddenly, here and now – but he merely nodded his head and unlocked the door of the small white car. (On the rear seat, the newspaper, now crumpled with reading and rereading during the hour he'd spent there waiting; and a wet patch where Hennie van Rensburg's kitbag had lain.)

Over the last stretch of road after he'd dropped the hitchhiker – through the black-green apple orchards and bluegum plantations of Grabouw; up the steep incline of the Hottentot's Holland range, heavy with the wet smell of heather, proteas, fynbos (he'd turned down the window to inhale); the sudden panorama from the summit, across the broad sweep of False Bay, the sea a matt leaden plate, here and there through the rain a fleck of tin; across the dreary expanse of the Cape Flats and past the cooling towers where, in a remote, earlier life, he'd so often turned off into the townships – he'd prepared himself for the meeting, steeling himself against the emotion he'd known would flood him. Even so, now that it was happening, he was still unprepared for the violence of the moment. After they'd got into the car, he leaned forward, his head pressed heavily against the wheel to restrain the urge to cry. His body shook.

'Rashid, Rashid, Rashid.'

'Come on.' Rashid's voice sounded reprimanding, almost severe; but when he put his hand on Thomas's shoulder, it was trembling. 'It's okay, man. You've made it. Never look back, right?'

Cool, mechanical, clinical, he'd headed straight for this parking garage when he'd reached the city, and stopped, like how many other times, in the busy weeks before the blast, on the top deck. Ducking under his new black umbrella, he'd made a detour through the city centre to make sure there was no one following him before he'd gone to a public telephone in Leeuwen Street where he'd dialled the familiar number: a taxi business in Salt River.

'Miss Gouws? It's Peter. Will you please tell Jimmy I'm waiting for him in the boarding house? Top floor. Tell him I'm in a hurry.'

Even so, it had taken almost an hour. By that time there was nothing left to read in the paper. But he repressed his impatience. He was back in the city, that was all that mattered. In a way it was a homecoming, a return to a safe harbour. Now there would be others to look after him. Rashid would come. Soon, today or tomorrow, he would see Justin and David again. All of them exactly as before. (No! – not all of them. Christine, for all he knew, was still in Tygerberg. And Nina, and Nina –)

What did he really know about Rashid? All attempts, in the past, at direct questioning had met with blunt rebuffs. ('What counts, is the struggle, not the people, okay? I'm nothing. You're nothing. So what is there to know?') But in the course of their working together Thomas had picked up a few snatches, mainly through Justin. He grew up in Chatsworth, in Natal. In those days he had a different name, Thomas never found out what it was. They were poor people. It took an effort to scrape together the money for his first year at university, Durban-Westville; but he was bright and some of his teachers had personally intervened to obtain bursaries. Physics and electronics were his passion. But halfway through his first year his father died and the family was in straits. The mere thought of having to give up his studies gave him nightmares. But what could he do? His mother was helpless, his two younger brothers and three sisters were all still at school. That was when the Special Branch man paid him a visit. Persuaded him to go for a drive, towards Kloof. Look, we can see you're a bright chap. But it seems you've got financial problems. Now, if you were prepared to help us –? Nothing much. We'll give you a list of names, people from your class, all you have to do is keep your eyes open and report back from time to time. In exchange, we'll pay your fees, as far as you want to go, including Ph.D. if you feel like it, even in America or Germany or wherever. Plus a salary. You and your family won't ever have worries again. Surely you'd like to help your mother, your brothers and sisters?

The names on the list included some of his close friends.

He was so confused – the man was so insistent – that he didn't know what to do or say. Scared out of his wits. 'But I don't know anything about politics,' he objected, 'and I'm not interested either. I just want to get on with my studies.' The man persisted, almost paternal in his understanding. He was in such a state that, for his mother's sake, he agreed. But two weeks later, when he had to deliver his first report-back, he burst into tears and pleaded with them to let him go, he couldn't go through with it. In the beginning they were understanding, prepared to give him time to think it over. Gradually the promises changed into threats. He gave up his studies and fled to Johannesburg where he went underground, changed his name, became an apprentice with an electronics firm.

In his heart he'd resolved to fight back. Previously he'd never been interested in politics at all; now he joined the UDF. Not for long. Then he left the country, clandestinely, without even letting his family know, for military training in Angola; in Cuba. Even Justin knew very little about his time abroad: unless he kept to himself what he knew. The young man had learned to put his interest in physics and electronics to the best use. After a year, possibly longer, he returned under yet another name, Rashid Amien, and found employment in the Cape, where the Organisation put him in touch with Justin.

Thomas quickly pulled himself together again.

'I'm sorry,' he said, embarrassed. 'It was just – suddenly seeing you again and everything. After what happened to Nina.' His voice got stuck; after a moment he managed to control it.

'It's okay. We're only too glad to see you back. They're looking for us at the airports and border posts, not here.'

'Has anything new happened? How much do you know?'

Rashid shook his head. 'They playing it close to the chest. No news at all. Not about Nina, not about nothing. They're stumped, that's for sure.'

'Justin?'

'Busy, as always. Still got an itch in his arse. Saw him yesterday.'

'David?'

He hesitated momentarily. 'David's – okay too, really.'

'What's the matter?'

'Oh, nothing. Just –' He shrugged. 'This business about Christine is eating him.'

'Why *now*? She's been unchanged for a long time. Or has something new happened?'.

'I suppose it's what happened to Nina that really shook him up. Now he can't get Christine out of his mind. And –' Another hesitation, 'Something fishy going on. We can't find out what it is, but something's not *lekker*.'

'Like what?'

'You know Judy? The nurse in the team that looks after her in Tygerberg?'

'Of course. What about her?'

'Well, she sent a message to Justin – it was Tuesday or Wednesday already – saying there's a lot of coming and going around her. Doctors, cops, all kinds of people. So Judy's worried.'

'Nothing she could put her finger on?'

'Not so far. But Justin's working on it.'

'Surely there's no way they can link Christine with us? As long as she remains in a coma –'

'That's the way I figure it too. But it's tough on David. You can imagine.'

'He'll bear up.'

'Sure. We'll all bear up. You're the one we're most worried about.' He turned down his window and looked out. 'Look, we shouldn't sit here talking too long. This place is too tight. Let's go somewhere else.'

'You want to drive?'

'No, stay where you are. There may be someone at the entrance that remembers you coming in. Can't be too careful.'

'Shall we go to Sea Point?'

'Why not? Nice weather for the sea.'

They went down the spiral tracks. This could have been the inside of hell: circle upon circle, all the decks identical, as if one continually passed the same point − only to discover it was not the same; until one lost all sense of direction or level, drawn into a slowly churning eddy, round and round, over and over, a senseless motion that took one ever more deeply into oneself. Occasionally they passed people on their way down: caretakers in uniform, pedestrians on their way to or from their cars. But no one paid any attention to them. At the cashier's cubicle, when they finally reached the ground floor, Thomas paid his ticket and turned into Bree Street.

They followed the high-level road across the rump of the Lion, along the higher slope of Green Point (below, somewhere, was Nina's house: he did not want to drive past it), turning down towards the sea only when they'd reached Sea Point. The parking lot below the President Hotel, overlooking the beach, was deserted. The rain came in dull, gusty showers, driven by the wind. On the surface of the restless grey sea it chased up white spray from the large swell; the waves broke right over the wall.

For some time they sat looking through the spray-splashed windscreen, across the ponderous breaking of the waves. Melancholy as he was, Thomas also found it deeply satisfying. Just to be there, back at the sea.

'Made any plans?' Rashid asked at last.

'I'm in your hands.'

'Well, we'll have to find out what Justin thinks. We can't just indulge every whim, you know.'

'That's not what I'm asking either. If he says no, I'll stay away.'

'What worries me is that you even *thought* of it.'

'What's the next step?' he asked Rashid, to steer the conversation back on course.

'Justin will discuss that with you. Meanwhile there's a few practical things to be done.'

'Like?'

'This car. It's got to be taken in for an overhaul as soon as possible. It's much too conspicuous with its Transvaal plates. As for you –' He studied Thomas critically. 'Whether you go to that funeral or not, you'll need a tune-up too.'

'No one suspects me.'

'I know, but we've got to play it safe.' He looked at his watch. 'What time's your game start?'

'Three.'

'Then we've got time. Let's go. But stop at the Pavilion first, I must make a call.' And when, ten minutes later, he came scurrying from the telephone booth through the drizzle and slid into his seat again, he said, 'It's okay. We can go to Observatory. Justin will be there too.'

'You still in the same place then?'

'No, it's another house, a few blocks on. A transit place we mostly use for messages and stuff like that. Right, move. I'll navigate.'

They drove past the old safe house on their way to the new one. It shook him. Without looking at Rashid, Thomas slowed down, almost brought the car to a standstill; turned down his window and looked out to see better: the cottage with the red front stoep and the intricate broekies lace under the verandah, the dark green door with its brass knocker, the pot of red geraniums on the sill. It seemed deserted. The curtains were drawn.

Inside there will still be the bathroom mirror, stained with damp, in which I watched David trying to sew up your bleeding hand; the mirror in which, that late last night, you gazed so intensely at your own reflection. And I came and stood behind you and put my hands on your shoulders. And you asked, 'Do you think it's possible, if we go to the bedroom now, that something of us will be left behind in this mirror, deep inside?'

'Left here,' said Rashid. 'And then the first right.' A hundred yards further on, 'You can stop here.'

He took his suitcase from the boot. They walked a block or two on foot, down a narrow lane to the left. At an ugly little house – a century old, it seemed, but disfigured by steel windows and a frosted-glass front door, curlicued burglar-proofing everywhere – Rashid opened the gate, glanced swiftly up and down the street, and motioned to Thomas to enter. There were people inside, from the kitchen one could hear voices and a clattering of crockery; but no one came to look. In a bedroom Rashid helped him choose a dark suit from the suitcase, a white shirt, a demure tie, black shoes. While Thomas was changing, Rashid ferreted in an iron trunk he'd dragged from under the sagging bed and emerged with a handful of hair-tufts in his hand, selected a black moustache and pasted it to Thomas's upper lip. For a moment, his head turned sideways, he inspected his handiwork. 'You got glasses?' he asked.

Thomas retrieved a jacket from his suitcase and took from the inside pocket the gold-rimmed glasses he'd worn in Johannesburg. 'Will these do?'

'One can see right through you,' said Rashid. 'Hang on.' From his trunk he took several pairs of spectacles and selected one with a heavy tortoise-shell frame. He poised it on Thomas's nose. 'Mm. Looks good. Dependable. *Poephol* from Bellville. Brings out your true self. Okay with you?'

'Anything to make you happy.' He motioned to the trunk. 'And if this place is raided?'

'No problem. As far as other people are concerned, it's two gay actors who live in this place. One a transvestite.' He sighed. 'We're still missing Christine. That girl was a genius with disguises.'

'She'll be all right yet.'

Rashid pulled a face. 'Irony is, at the moment it's better for all of us if she stays in a coma. But you try to tell that to David.'

Soon afterwards Justin arrived; entering from the back, so quietly that they hadn't even noticed. Immaculate, as always, in a grey suit, as befitted a teacher (even one who, like Justin at the moment, was on long leave); the wispy beard and thin moustache trimmed with care. An unobtrusive person: it was only by looking into his eyes that one discovered both his sadness and his quiet determination.

'Thomas! Welcome home.' It felt like greeting a father; closer to him than his own.

But Justin was in a hurry, and couldn't stay long.

'Rashid told me you had something to discuss.'

'Yes. The funeral this afternoon. I'd like to go.'

'Why?' Calm, amicable, but with a touch of warning.

'I think it's important.'

'For you? Or for the Organisation?'

'Probably more for me. But not because I'm selfish. We had a plan: in a way it worked, we sowed panic, but we missed the target, we hit others. We're not cold-blooded terrorists, Justin. I want to be there, on behalf of all of us. I think it's necessary.'

'But no one will know, no one *dare* know. So what difference will it make?'

'I'll know. We'll know.'

'Hopeless bloody romantic,' Rashid said curtly. 'I already told him. He can't expose us all to danger just because *he* can afford the luxury of a conscience.'

'You really think it's just a matter of a private conscience, Rashid? Anyway, I've already told you: how can it possibly put anyone at risk if no one has the slightest suspicion that I was involved? Even if I went there quite openly, not a soul will ask questions about Thomas Landman and his camera. It'll be the most obvious place in the world for a photographer to be.'

'It shouldn't even occur to anyone that Thomas Landman is in town,' said Rashid.

'With this disguise no one *will* know.'

'You still taking a chance.'

'You wait here, Thomas,' said Justin laconically. 'I want to have a word with Rashid.'

From the room next door, through the door they'd closed behind them, Thomas could hear from time to time the sound of their voices, especially Rashid's, when he raised it. Strangely resigned, he waited. If they really decided against it, he knew he would have to accept it.

But when they came back after a few minutes, Justin announced briefly, 'Okay, you can go. I can see it'll be better for you. And so, in a way, it will be better for us too.' He put his hand on Thomas's shoulder, and pressed it. 'But watch out, hey? We can't afford to lose you too.'

'Thanks, Justin.'

Rashid said nothing. But he did not appear resentful any more.

Justin looked at his watch. 'Got to go.'

'Will I be staying on in this place?' asked Thomas.

'No,' said Justin. 'We're still working on it. If you can find something to do after the funeral, Rashid will pick you up in town later. About six?'

'Where?'

'Wherever it suits you,' said Rashid.

'In front of the Sun in Strand Street?'

'Right.'

Justin pressed Thomas's hand. Without another word he went out. From the kitchen they heard his voice; another male voice answered. The back door was closed. After a while Rashid made a gesture with his head and they left through the front door. This time Rashid drove. They stopped at a Kentucky Fry where, without consulting with him, Rashid went in and emerged with two red and white cartons and two Cokes. Some distance away, in front of a furniture shop off Main Road, they stopped to eat. Well before two Rashid dropped him near the Synod Hall: the streets in the centre had already been cordoned off for the funeral.

As Thomas got out, Rashid took him by the arm. 'Don't let it get you,' he said. There was an unexpected warmth in his voice. 'I know it's been tough on you, but you've been first-class so far. You'll be first-class all the way. Right?'

'Right,' he said, a tightness in his jaws.

During the time he'd been in the Gardens the last signs of the funeral had been cleared away. In front of the Groote Kerk, and further down in the street, thin lines of people were queuing at their bus stops. He thought: Yes, there's enough time; why not? That morning, when he'd driven to Sea Point with Rashid, he'd found it impossible to take the Beach Road; but something had changed. Through the conversation with Rashid and Justin, the glimpse of the cottage in Observatory with, on the sill, the red geraniums he'd given Nina on her birthday, through the funeral service, he'd been prepared to face it now.

He joined a bus queue. The wait was short. Presumably most office workers had used the funeral service as an excuse to take off the afternoon, and even in the rush hour traffic was much easier than normal.

Behind the *Argus* he had bought, he hid from the people around him; but he wasn't reading. Nervously, his body tense, he watched their progress through the large side window. It did not take long. At a stop in Green Point he descended, stopped for a moment to button up his plastic mac and turn up the collar; and although it was no longer raining he opened the umbrella and held it in front of him like a shield. Two blocks on, then left into a steep alley leading towards the mountain, and right again into the first street. Another twenty yards brought him to the front of the tall narrow house with the Victorian verandah, the blue glass panels beside the front door, the bay windows on either side. He slowed down, but did not stop. He had no idea why he'd come. Certainly, there was no possibility of dropping in on the girl who'd once shared the house with Nina and had taken it over during the last few months. Gerda. He'd never cared much for her. And yet it *might* be comforting to have a chat over a cup of tea! Of course, Gerda would not even know about Nina's death yet. Nobody knew. Except the police; Brigadier Bester. Unless, in spite of everything, they really hadn't identified her yet.

Perhaps he could simply go up the few steps to the stoep, ring the bell; and if someone opened – but suppose it was Gerda herself? – enquire whether Such-or-such, some fictitious name, lived there? Merely for the chance of looking into that short passage again, into the Spartan, functional space of the house. But it might have changed by now. Gerda would undoubtedly have begun to clutter it up with the ballast of her own life.

On his way past, still trying to make up his mind about entering or not, he noticed a movement in a white Toyota parked some distance ahead on the opposite side of the street, its nose turned towards Thomas. A man turning the page of a newspaper. Next to the man, in the passenger seat, sat another person. Thomas felt his face grow cold. Tilting the umbrella a touch further down, he walked on, trying his best not to hasten his step. On the next corner he turned right, back to the main road, back to the bus-stop, where he sat down on the bench inside the shelter.

It took a while for his heartbeat to steady. He reproached himself. Really, he shouldn't get worked up like that. Most probably the two men in the car had only been waiting for a friend, someone who would undoubtedly emerge from one of the houses in the neighbourhood. But he knew he would have no peace of mind before he'd made sure. He got up again and started walking back in the direction of Sea Point, ordering his thoughts. Was there any point in finding out? There was. For half an hour, carefully checking his watch every few minutes, he walked up and down along the main road. Then turned back, up the hill, towards Nina's street, this time from the opposite direction, so that if the car was still there – most unlikely – the occupants would see nothing amiss in a man returning from wherever he'd gone to.

The car was still there.

He considered turning round to retrace his steps – this time, after all, he was approaching them from behind – but then they might notice him in the rear-view mirror and become suspicious. He did accelerate a pace or two. Trying to keep the umbrella in front of his face without making it look obvious. Not looking left or right. Most especially not at the house: even though it might be the last time in his life he passed before it. Straight on, head bent. The way anybody might walk on a rainy day.

Was it his imagination or was the car door opened behind him after he had passed?

If someone were to call him now, even if it were only to ask the time or borrow a light, any pretext at all, how should he react? Turn back as if nothing were the matter and go up to them? Or start running?

Ridiculous.

Imperceptibly, he hollowed his back. This, he thought, was how Nina had walked from customs control towards the escalator when they'd descended on her from behind. The swift glance over her shoulder. And then she'd begun to run. And through the glass wall he had seen it all. (The clock flicking over, monotonous and predictable, correct for one second, then wrong for fifty-nine.)

Now he was round the corner.

Was that a car starting up behind him?

For a brief moment he stopped.

No, it was all quiet.

As fast as he could without breaking into a trot, he walked on. At the first traffic lights he crossed the main road to the opposite sidewalk and headed for the next bus-stop. He rested for a few minutes. But he had a sudden feeling of uncertainty when he saw a bus approaching from Sea Point. Shouldn't he rather return on foot? It wasn't all that far. But it wasn't the distance that worried him; it was a matter of security. The bus was faster, and he had to get away from there as quickly as possible. Once back in the central city he would be safe.

Near Greenmarket Square – where he got off the bus; what route he'd followed from there, he would not be able to recall afterwards – he entered a cosy-looking café. A foreigner with a bald skull covered in brown scabs, some skin disease, came from behind the counter to take his order. Just coffee, said Thomas. The man seemed offended. Perhaps he'd been the only client all day. To hell with him anyway.

– All the nights we spent in that tall narrow house. On the balcony in summer, when at three or four o'clock, after the traffic had finally drained away, one could hear the sea sighing in the distance. On misty nights we lay listening to the foghorn at Mouille Point.

You were the only woman I've ever made love with who never closed her eyes in orgasm. You never allowed me to close mine either. 'Look at me, Thomas. Look in my eyes when you come, I want to see you.'

There was such a hard, clean quality in your love. There was compassion in it too – you *cared* about me; you cared about *people* – but nothing soft, compliant, cloying. A hardness instead, the hardness of hard wood: something live, but without the weakness of compromise. There were no ulterior motives, hidden aims: it was direct, open, sincere, searing, a flame that consumed whatever was redundant. ('Nina', remember, was the name of the Inca goddess of fire.) Some people thought you were impatient and unapproachable; rude, obstinate, even heartless. I remember how upset I was when I told you about what had happened to Ntsiki so long ago and how I'd never been able to forgive myself for it: how firmly you shook your head and said, 'There's no point in it, Thomas. I know one can't get through something like that unscathed – there's always marks, there's scars: but watch out for open wounds. If something has happened which you could have prevented, okay, then look at it, find out what went wrong, avoid it in future. But for God's sake, don't wallow in it. That doesn't help anybody. Things like torture or murder: I know it's horrible. Always, in any circumstances. But why be *sentimental* about it? What concerns us is a whole situation, a whole country, millions of people. Not somebody's private sorrow or happiness. There's no *time* for that.' –

'More coffee, sir?' asked the café owner. The light from a red lamp against the ceiling splashed like blood over his mottled cranium. On his face an expression as if Thomas had personally insulted him through his presence.

He looked at his watch. Another twenty minutes before he had to meet Rashid in front of the hotel. 'Yes, please,' he said. 'Thanks.'

A meagre glow, the merest intimation of gratitude, oozed into the man's morose expression.

As the second cup was placed before Thomas and the bad instant coffee spilled into the saucer, drenching the sugar sachet, he suddenly thought, in a wave of newly felt liberation: Something has happened; in this sad little red and white café, under the apprehensive eyes of this repulsive old man, something miraculous has happened. I have dared at last to abandon myself unconditionally to whatever I can remember of Nina; I haven't resisted or tried to avoid anything. For the first time during this whole unbearable week. I've begun to make my peace with her. The scar of her death will remain in me for ever: but a scar, no longer a bleeding wound.

4

It was in an inconspicuous suburban house in a street with a floral name that they spent the night. A narrow sandy strip of garden in front, and a front hedge of dense oleanders, cerise and white. Inside, a lounge cum dining-room with pale blue and yellow curtains, furniture with ball-and-claw legs; on the walls prints of European snowscapes, and two or three colour photographs of small children staring, toothless and precocious, at the viewer; a hi-fi system with huge loudspeakers, a TV set with video recorder. In the small bedroom assigned to Rashid and Thomas (his suitcase was already waiting on the floor when they arrived) the curtains were an unrepentant puce, with matching candlewick spreads on the two single beds.

'Remember,' Rashid had warned him on the way, shouting to make himself heard above the noise of the Volkswagen, 'for these people I am Anwar and you're Eddie. I thought you could pass for "Coloured", seeing it's night-time, okay? We're students at UWC, we've been thrown out of the hostel because we were in arrears with the board, we're waiting for money from home, and this man has offered to put us up for a while, he's a good sort and he's done it for others before.' He winked. 'He's in the Organisation, you see, but his wife doesn't know. Which is why we've got to watch out. He's at UWC, personnel or somewhere. Robbie Carstens. Got it?'

'You sure it's safe?'

'Justin arranged it personally. He knows Robbie. And he has a special reason for parking us there.'

'What's that?'

'Robbie is Judy's brother. You know, the nurse. In fact, it was through him that Justin first recruited her, long before Christine got hurt. 'Cause it's always useful, hey, someone like her in a place like Tygerberg. So she'll be coming over tonight to give us an update without anyone thinking twice about it.'

'How can she do it if Robbie's wife doesn't know?'

'Don't worry.'

'And when am I getting my car back?'

'Some time tomorrow. I'll know for sure in the morning. Oh and by the way –' He raised one buttock to slide his hand into a back pocket. 'Here's some cash to tide you over. Two hundred bucks. Don't rush it.'

Afterwards, Thomas would remember, wryly, how he'd thought, but without saying it: When will life calm down again and become more or less predictable again?

Easygoing, friendly, solid citizens in their early middle age, Thomas found the Carstens couple. Robbie was short and stout and bespectacled, with the chronic smile of a bookkeeper whose totals always tally; his wife Violet somewhat breathless, with prominent dentures and the unmistakable outline of a corset, a teacher of domestic science at Belhar High. In the course of the evening, three daughters also called 'Hi!' on their way to or from their rooms, from which, whenever a door was opened and someone went to the bathroom or kitchen, a wave of loud music broke through the house (Whitney Houston, Michael Jackson, Johnny Clegg). With a few ingenious additions of herbs Violet rounded off a stew that had obviously been simmering all afternoon, and served it with pumpkin and rice, and a sour salad; which Robbie complemented with a glass of sweet wine. The girls, it seemed, were dieting and did not join them; were 'too busy' anyway; although later in the evening, after the grownups had finished, they invaded the kitchen which resounded with bangings of fridge and freezer doors and the incessant ringing of a microwave oven bell.

After supper Thomas offered to give a hand with clearing the table, but Violet indignantly refused help – 'What kind of a man are you then?' – and did it all on her own while the men settled into easy chairs. After some time she sat down at the table with a stack of exercise books, all covered neatly in brown paper. With her so close, their conversation remained superficial, covering Western Province's chances in the Curry Cup, inflation, tensions on the campus, the rape of a schoolgirl on the rugby field the week before.

Robbie grew unexpectedly very agitated. 'Those *skollies* are still on the loose. Now if it had been a white girl, they'd have been behind bars long ago.'

'You stay out of politics, Robbie,' admonished his wife, without looking up from her books.

'I'm talking about the cops who are very quick to do their job when a person is white and who wipe their backsides on it if he isn't.'

'And I say, you poke your nose into politics and you asking for trouble.'

'If something's wrong, keeping quiet isn't going to make it right.'

'You must obey those in authority,' she said curtly. 'That's what the Book says. Right or wrong, it's not for us to question it.'

'You mean,' said Rashid, 'no matter what they do, it's okay?'

'All I'm saying is that if you try to change the world you only burn your fingers.' She put aside one book and picked up another. 'Take Moses,' she said. 'What happened when he started poking his nose into Pharaoh's business? It made life twice as bad for the Jews.'

'But in the end he let them go,' said Thomas.

At that moment, and just as well, the front door bell rang. It was a minute or two before the eight o'clock news. All three girls charged to the door, but Violet was too quick for them. It was the nurse Judy, still wearing her starched white uniform, slightly the worse for wear after what had evidently been a long day, and clinging rather tightly to her body (a generous body, Thomas thought, like bread dough that had been left overnight under a blanket beside the stove to rise right over the edge of the basin).

'Jesus!' was the first she said, gasping for breath. 'I nearly didn't make it.'

'What happened, sis Judy?' Violet looked searchingly at her. 'You seen a ghost?'

'Nearly saw my own undoing, that's what.' She turned round to look back towards the street, past Robbie; but nothing moved beyond the oleander hedge, and the solitary streetlamp stood introverted over its own pool of light.

'But tell us what happened, man,' Violet urged her.

Something of what must have been Judy's normal robust nature seemed to return to her. 'Perhaps it was just wishful thinking,' she said, giggling, 'but it seemed to me a lightie was following me from the hospital gates, just below the guard's cubicle, right down Delarey Road, all the way to your front gate.'

'I warned you long ago not to throw your body at the men the way you do. They get all kinds of ideas.'

'I never throw my body at anyone, thank you very much. I'm too particular. But every time I walked faster, he also walked faster. And if I stopped, he did the same. So you tell me.'

'What did the man look like?' asked Robbie, perturbed.

'I couldn't make out much. Grey hat, and a sort of coat, the all-weather kind, and a navy tie with polka dots. Light hair.'

'You not telling me it was a *white* man?'

'They come in all types, Violet.'

'It's from watching him like that that you put ideas into his head. And you know a man thinks with only one part of his body.'

Robbie looked offended. 'That's not a nice thing to say, Violet.'

She lashed out, 'You just shut up, hey? What do *you* know?'

'That's right,' said Judy. 'All they can think of is –' She made an eloquent sign with her right hand.

'Now don't be offensive, Judy. You haven't even greeted us yet.'

'Evening, sis Violet. Evening, Boet Robbie.' She first kissed Violet on the cheek, then her brother, before she turned, with a show of embarrassment, to face the guests. 'My goodness, I never saw you had guests.'

'This is Anwar, this is Eddie, sis Judy,' Robbie said dutifully.

She came past them to a deep armchair, and modestly pulled down her uniform across her substantial knees as she sat down.

'I'll put on some tea,' said Violet. 'Nothing beats tea when you had a fright like that.'

She had hardly gone into the kitchen before Thomas came to Judy's chair and asked in a low voice, 'Any news of Christine?'

'You got no idea.'

But Violet returned almost immediately, having obviously just switched on the kettle, eager not to miss anything.

Which was why Thomas would afterwards remember the evening as hours of endless frustration, making small-talk, mainly family talk between Judy and the Carstens couple, to which neither he nor Rashid could contribute much. The importance of the evening, and the most unsettling part of it, lay in what occurred afterwards, after Judy had risen, just before half-past nine, to announce that she was going home.

'You can't walk alone after what's happened,' Robbie said quickly. 'I'll drive you home.'

'Don't spoil her fun,' said Violet.

Thomas and Rashid offered to keep them company, and in spite of Violet's amused annoyance – 'So many bees around one open flower' – all three men went out with Judy. As Robbie reversed his car into the street to turn round, another car about thirty or forty yards away also came into motion – a grey Mazda, it seemed when it passed under a streetlamp – and started following them;

for the first block it drove without lights, but then they were turned on.

'That's no rapist,' said Robbie, his eyes on the rear-view mirror. 'This is another story altogether. Don't look round. Play it cool.'

Later, back in their virulently pink room, after they'd dropped Judy in front of her flat building in Bishop Lavis and bidden their hosts good-night, Thomas asked anxiously, 'Rashid, how much does Judy really know about us? And what does Robbie know?'

'I told you: Robbie is in the Organisation, and Judy's a helper. But all they know is what Justin told them, and you know he isn't one to say much.'

'But suppose they try to squeeze something out of Judy: what can she tell them?'

'That we're friends of Christine's. But she doesn't know our real names. In any case she won't even tell them that. Justin knows how to choose his people.'

'Stronger people than Judy have cracked up in the hands of the SB.'

'That I know as well as you do, my pal. But remember, even if they do force her to confess that we knew Christine – so what? There's absolutely nothing to link Christine with our bomb. Nobody but Christine herself can give them that information. And you heard what Judy said: things don't look so good for her. I don't like saying this, but what looks bad for her may be good for us.'

'Don't ever say a thing like that again!' Thomas was furious.

Rashid looked him in the eyes. 'Sorry, pal. But we're in a tough business and you know it.' Like so many times before, Thomas was surprised by such hardness in such a boyish face.

Thomas sat down on his narrow bed and started pulling off his shoes. Looked up again. 'You think Judy's all right?'

'Hope so.'

'That's not what I asked.'

'Then don't ask fucking unnecessary questions.'

'I've *got* to ask them.'

Without warning, Rashid, sitting opposite him on his own bed, put a hand on his knee. 'You listen to me, Thomas. Judy wasn't dragged into this under false pretences. Every one of us, and those around us, hundreds of them, bloody thousands, even if we don't know them: every single one of them has made the choice, open-eyed, to join the struggle. No matter how it turns out, it's worth while, it's what we have chosen. That's why we're in it. And if one is in it, it means going all the way. Right?'

Slowly, wearily, warily, he smiled. 'Right.' Then got up and undressed and, keeping on only his underpants, moved in under the blanket. Knowing he would, once again, not sleep a wink; but prepared to face it. All the way.

The previous afternoon, Judy had said, Christine had been moved, without prior warning, by a whole contingent of staff, from the intensive care unit to a remote wing, in total isolation. The guard in front of her door was doubled, and even nurses had to identify themselves before they could be allowed inside. When, on some pretext or other, Judy had gone there during the afternoon, she'd been summarily turned away. Only after extremely discreet enquiries had she learned that none of the usual hospital staff would be allowed to see Judy in future. A special unit had been flown in from Port Elizabeth.

'I'll try again, of course, but I don't want to attract attention by asking too many questions. All I know is that it isn't looking good.'

'How was she when you last saw her?'

'Unchanged. She won't come out of that coma soon.'

'But she wasn't worse either?'

'No, for sure.'

How should one interpret that?

And what significance should one attach to the fact that the Mazda hadn't returned to Belhar with them?

They had arranged that Robbie would telephone her at her flat early the next morning about some family matter, to make sure she was safe. But it was a long night to wait. There was much to agonise about. All that kept Thomas wide awake.

But towards morning he must have drifted off, for when he woke up – it was half-past eight already – Rashid had gone and the house was very quiet. Thomas jumped up to have a look, but the place was deserted. He went out the back door to look through the small side window of the garage; the Volkswagen was still inside. It reassured him, but he still felt annoyed at having overslept. (And yet it had been necessary. He wouldn't last long if it went on like that, night after night.)

As he emerged from the bathroom in his jeans and a checkered shirt Rashid came through the front door.

'Where the hell have you been?'

'Went to phone Justin. Robbie dropped me at the station, he took the family shopping.'

'You should have woken me up.'

'Why? You needed the sleep.'

'Did Robbie get through to Judy?'

'Yes. No problem. No further sign of last night's people. But for safety's sake someone will look her up at the hospital later today to double-check. An out-patient or a messenger or someone.'

'Perhaps it was just coincidence the Mazda followed us.'

'Don't you be so sure.' Rashid went over to the front window, but the oleander hedge was too dense to see through. 'They were waiting for us out there when we left this morning. They went after Robbie and the family after they'd dropped me at the station.'

Thomas felt a brief contraction of his heart. But he remained calm. 'It must have some connection with what Judy told us. About Christine being moved. Perhaps they're having a general check-up. But why? What are they planning to do?' he frowned. 'You think she may be regaining consciousness?'

'Then Judy would have known. She knows her job.'

Thomas stood pensive for a moment. 'What do we do now?

'You ready to go?'

'Where?'

'Into town. Can't stay here.'

'Do I have time to grab breakfast? Or are you in a hurry?'

'Not at all. Take your time.'

He cut two slices of bread, took milk from the fridge, sat down at the counter that divided the kitchen and the dining-room.

'By the way,' said Rashid, 'Justin will meet you at Mike's Kitchen in the Golden Acre. About one. But he may be late, so just wait until he shows up.'

'What's he say about the Judy business?'

'We couldn't talk on the phone. I'll be seeing him later.'

Thomas wiped his mouth with the back of his hand. 'Okay, I'm ready.'

Rashid was standing at the window again, leaning forward. After a while he shook his head. 'Can't see anything. But I don't want to take chances.' He straightened himself. 'I'm going to check the mailbox.' Without waiting, he opened the front door and went out. Through the window Thomas watched him walk to the front gate and open the flap of the mailbox, leaning over casually to look up and down the street. After a moment he came back, closing the door behind him. 'They're back.'

'So what do we do?'

'We'll just play it cool. I think you're right, it's part of a general check-up on Judy's contacts. They only saw you in the dark last night. Me they saw this morning, in the back of Robbie's car. Put on your mac and cover your head with something, then you should be okay. There's hats in the passage.'

'What about you?'

'I'll just play it straight. Even if they only had a glimpse of me, I can't change my appearance now. Let's go.'

'Won't it attract attention if I go out with my suitcase?'

Rashid reflected for a moment. 'Ja. Perhaps it's better just to pack a few things in a plastic bag, they won't look twice at that.'

While Rashid was digging in the kitchen cupboards in search of a shopping bag, Thomas selected a few bits of clothing, working quickly but meticulously through whatever he left behind to make sure it was quite anonymous. Cash slips from Pretoria and Bloemfontein, a Pretoria bus ticket, scraps of paper with cryptic notes; among them, unexpectedly, a half-page that made him frown for a moment: a name written in large lower-case letters, *lisa lombard*, a telephone number, an address in Claremont. Then he remembered: the talkative young woman on the plane. For a moment he considered burning it with his other rubbish and flushing it down the toilet, then thrust it into the back pocket of his jeans. Perhaps, he thought idly, if he had nothing better to do, he might look her up.

Five minutes later, stooping in a wide-brimmed hat and the cheap plastic coat, he opened the back gate, ducking behind the hedge to remain out of sight until Rashid had reversed the Volkswagen into the street, closed the garage door and the gate – calmly, without looking round, keeping his back to where Rashid had indicated the Mazda was parked – then got into the car through the door Rashid had opened from inside. Behind them he heard an engine starting up.

'Just tell me,' he said when they turned left at the first corner towards Modderdam Road, 'how do you plan to shake off the Mazda in this tumble-drier?'

Rashid grinned. 'It's not a matter of speed, my pal. It's skill. We don't *want* a chase. They must think it's an ordinary shopping trip into town. We've got nothing to hide, do we now?' He winked.

The Mazda remained a short distance behind them. Right on their heels to begin with, but gradually, as it seemed they were going to maintain that tortoise pace, dropping further back, allowing two, even three other cars to move in between them. The first few kilometres on Settler's Way, until they reached the cooling towers at Pinelands, the traffic whizzed past them; but as it became more dense the pace slackened. That was obviously what Rashid had been bargaining on, changing lanes several times, always at the last moment, putting more cars between them and their pursuers, but without shaking the Mazda off altogether. At the top of De Waal Drive, where Eastern Boulevard branches off, Rashid performed a daring manoeuvre: keeping in the far left lane for the upper route, he suddenly, at the very last moment, swerved right, across the yellow dividing lines, into the Eastern Boulevard traffic lanes. An orchestra of hooters blared from all sides. Thomas sat petrified in the passenger seat.

'Shook him off?' he asked after he'd caught his breath again.

Rashid was staring intently into the mirror, his knuckles showing white on the steering wheel. 'Bastard!' he suddenly exclaimed. 'He's made it. But he's far behind now.' For the first time he accelerated, weaving left and right from lane to lane, the engine roaring in protest.

'Ready to get out?' Rashid asked through his teeth as they stopped at the traffic lights beside – of all places! – the Parade. 'I'll stop as soon as we turn into Adderley. You disappear into the Golden Acre. Should be safe there. Remember to meet Justin for lunch at Mike's Kitchen.'

'Isn't that too public? Those people following us –'

'Get rid of your coat and hat. Find another bag for your clothes.'

'Right.' He was thinking fast. 'Look, if I notice anyone following me I'll put a Woolworths bag on the table where I'm waiting. Then Justin must go right past. Will you tell him?'

'Sure. Good luck.'

'When do I see you again?'

'Justin will tell you. Otherwise, phone the taxi place later in the afternoon.'

Rashid turned sharply left into Adderley Street. Twenty yards on he slammed on the brakes, nearly causing the car behind him to collide with them. Thomas had already opened his door.

'Jump!' shouted Rashid, sounding almost gleeful. Thomas hurled the door shut behind him. With a roar the Volkswagen pulled off.

As if from far away, through the traffic din, he could hear Rashid's voice: 'Now you're on your own, pal!'

5

– 'On my own', then, too. After the Special Branch has come to see me about my township photographs, my homage to Grandpa Khaya Ntshenge, there is no one to turn to. Upon receiving the message from the studio that they will not require my services any more, my first impulse is to run to Carla. But a block from her residence I turn back. No, not Carla. Am I scared that she will not understand? Do I want to spare her the anguish? I haven't thought about anything yet. All I know is: Not now, not yet. This is something I have to face on my own.

What is at stake for me is photography itself. A way of registering, of accounting for the new world I have discovered. And even 'registering', even 'accounting' is, in the long run, not enough. It is Ntsiki Yaya who guides me towards shaping the turbulent and inchoate questions which have been stirred up in my mind.

Ntsiki. He is the one I must talk to. The only one I *can* talk to.

For a whole week I stay away from the townships. Bunking most of my lectures – I, the dedicated student! – avoiding my best friends, seeing even Carla as seldom as possible, as I wander, disgruntled and desperate, through the streets of Stellenbosch and think through sleepless nights. Scared. Yes, I'm scared.

But at last I head back to Ntsiki and his world. By this time I have pondered it all. It is a conscious decision and, I hope, a responsible one. If I allow that amicable visit, that fatherly admonition, to intimidate me, I may just as well pack away my cameras and resign myself to what my parents have so diligently foreseen for me. The very fact that I've been warned makes it more important not to obey. At least it has forced me to make up my mind about what is, and what is not, important; what can be done; what I must refuse to accept.

'So, Thomas-my-bra, you're back?' Ntsiki. 'I've just decided to give you up for a bad job.' In the street scarred by ditches and potholes, where small boys play with wire-cars, a playful gust of wind churns up dust. Below the outside staircase of his building a chicken coop has been fabricated from cardboard boxes, boards and wire-mesh. From a broken sewage pipe seeps smelly brown water.

278

Some of the missing steps we follow up the staircase have been replaced by off-cuts of wood; broken railings have been repaired precariously with blue-wire and frayed rope, draped with dusters and dishcloths and mops. We sit down at one of the unwieldy tables; I've brought a couple of beers. At the zinc against the back wall a woman is doing her washing while two small children play at her feet. Through a crack in the side wall, if I move my head, I can see a segment of the outside world. Inexplicably I feel as if I have come home from a long journey.

'They told me to stay away,' I tell him.

'Who "they"?'

'*They*.'

Ntsiki gives me a sharp look. His narrow face is framed in the black halo of his Afro hair. 'You don't say?' He stretches his long legs clad in blue and white striped pants, staring for a while at the toes of his takkies. Bright red socks cling to his bony ankles. 'So why you here again?'

'I was worried about you.'

'About *me*?' He raises his legs as he bursts out laughing. 'What for? I'm a cat, my bra, I can see in the dark and I always land on my feet.'

(*Not always, Ntsiki*, I shall be forced to think later, remembering that afternoon.)

'They don't like my photos.'

'So?' Ntsiki has a way of saying 'So?' which makes one feel like a worm. 'You didn't expect them to give you a medal, did you?'

'All I wanted to do was –'

This is the question I have not yet learned to ask.

'*What* was it you wanted, my bra? Playing games? And now all of a sudden it's serious?'

'I've never played games, Ntsiki,' I protest.

Once again that devastating 'So?'

'I – all I wanted to do – to me my camera is a way of trying to see – to find out – what's going on.'

I look at him in desperation. What do I want of him? Not even approval, perhaps no more than a hint of encouragement, understanding, something. But he watches me without a word, as if he enjoys to see me flounder.

'And so what did you see of what's going on?'

'I'm not sure, Ntsiki. All I know is it must have been something that got their goat.'

279

'And now that you've seen what's going on? What next?'

'Now I want to know *why*!' I answer in precipitate eagerness: and only in saying the words do I realise what it is that has eluded me for so long.

'You sure you can live with this kind of *why*?'

'If you can do it I'm sure I can learn too.'

Uproarious laughter. For a moment, startled, the children on the floor stop playing. Through the crack in the wall I can see a combi slowly approaching in the dirt road. 'Thomas-my-bra, I was born with it. For you it's different.'

'No one's born with it. I won't believe it.'

He gets up abruptly and goes back to the door without looking round to see whether I'm following him. I am. Down that lethal staircase. Along the front of the block to the side – a wall on which huge unevenly painted white letters proclaim: *Wa funya nwabichama apha unfi leyo*: 'The one who urinates here, must die' – unzips his flies and repeats as much of the inscription with his jet as he can manage: *Wa funya nwabicha* –

'You're right,' he says laconically as he deftly bends his legs to stow away his fountain-pen. 'I wasn't born with it. I also had to learn. But earlier than you did.'

'How did you learn?'

'Picked it up.' Non-committal. 'Like burrs.' And then he launches into the story of his life: about Kwazakele outside Port Elizabeth where he grew up and had his education; his first school the rubbish dumps at the edge of the township. The eternally smoking dumps; the thick bank of fog permanently covering the township. The children playing hookey from school to go there instead. Never-ending adventures, treasure gathered from the garbage of the white suburbs. Gangs: not for the money it brings in or the feeling of bravado or power; just for kicks. Loitering around the Single Quarters: at five on a Friday morning the police raids to pick up the women and children who have spent the night with the men. With the result that, as the weather turns warm, many of the men prefer to take their women – pick-ups, whores, or their own wives who have travelled from Transkei or Ciskei for a visit – into the veld: 'That's how we learned about sex, Thomas-my-bra. We hid behind every bush and shrub to spy on them.' And then the glue sniffing. Or, for the bigger boys, meths. And soccer. On that bare red earth among the erosion ditches, an expanse of stones and rocks. 'Many of us could never play on proper soccer fields afterwards, just couldn't judge the speed of the ball. Not after that bare earth.' And then, even then, always, everywhere: *ubuntu*. If you're in trouble, if your father is picked up because he doesn't have his pass in his tattered jacket, if your mother is taken away for running a shebeen: there's always people to lend a hand, to share their food with you, offer you a bit of clothing against the winter wind or a space to sleep under a bed or on a floor or against a wall. 'But later on even *ubuntu* began to wear out. In the end it was only survival, nothing more. Life wasn't something you planned, my bra. It was just something that happened to you. From day to day. You see? That's how one learns. That's how one learns to ask: *Why? What for?*

'And your father? What did he do if you asked him?'

'My father? He was part of the problem, man. One Saturday my father takes me with him to his work. For fun. He's a garden boy in Newton Park. Good people, he tells me. And the madam brings me cooldrink in a tin mug. And when we leave, she gives my father a present, an old jacket of her husband. And he puts it under his arm and claps his hands together and says thank you: "*Nkosi*, my madam. Thank you, my madam. The Lord will bless you, my madam." And suddenly I want to run away. I don't want anyone to see me with this man who's my father. I'm ashamed of him. The way he thanked her for an old second-hand jacket. *My* father, man. You understand what I'm saying, my bra? It's not an old tramp or a beggar I'm talking about, hey, it's my *father*. But now I'm ashamed of him.' A new vehemence invades him: 'People talk about torture and violence and stuff like that, Thomas. Don't you listen to them. Let me tell you: that's not the problem. The problem is the little bit of shit you get every day of your life. That's all. The shit that goes on and on until one day you discover you're no longer a person, man, you're just a thing on a survival trip, nothing more. And that's when you start asking, "What for?"'

This is how Ntsiki nudges me towards asking the same questions.

In the beginning he still seems to look down at me – not much, but perceptibly – because of my ignorance, my whiteness; he appears both patient and amused. But about a month after my return to the townships there is a shift in our relationship. He's been away on one of his shady trips to Transkei; quite by coincidence, not having known anything about his absence, I happen to be visiting his New Flats building when he arrives back. He seems startled when he recognises me.

'What the hell are *you* doing here?'

'Looking for you, of course.'

'I'm busy.' Impatiently he brushes me aside. 'Look, man, they're waiting for me in Guguletu.'

'Can I go with you?'

'No ways. Come back tomorrow, okay? I'm telling you, man. I'm busy.'

Somewhat taken aback, I stand aside to let him go, but change my mind as I see him jump into the combi and drive off in a cloud of dust. Annoyance, curiosity, an anticipation of trouble? I don't know. But I run to my motorbike and follow in his wake.

This is how it happens that I arrive on the scene as he is stopped by police at the entrance to Guguletu. Not a serious roadblock, no sign of the automatic weapons and military vehicles one often finds at such spots; only two young constables on point duty. Just as well. Because when they stop Ntsiki and order him to open the back door of his combi for a routine check-up, and he begins to talk back, I am there to intervene. What puts the idea into my head, and what may happen if they don't take my word, I cannot tell; but I drive up to them on my bike and ask with a show of concerned good will, 'Can I help? I'm with this man.'

'How come?' asks one of the constables.

'I'm from Stellenbosch,' I reply. 'The Church Youth Society. We're distributing bibles.'

The two young men exchange a glance, then lose interest and motion to us to drive on.

I follow Ntsiki on his winding route to where he comes to a standstill at last. Whatever I may have expected, his reaction catches me unprepared as he jumps from the combi and throws his arms round my neck, collapsing with laughter. Only much later does it penetrate. After a swarm of men have appeared from nowhere to carry off, like a disciplined army, stacks of cartons and hessian bags from the combi, and Ntsiki, finally relaxing in someone's cramped lounge on a red café chair at a chrome and formica dining-table, tears open a tin of beer and hits me between the shoulder-blades with a blow that makes me gasp for breath. 'My bra, this is to you!' Still nonplussed, I ask, 'But what's going on, Ntsiki?' And as if it is the most natural thing in the world he replies, 'Grass, my bra. That's what it is. Fresh from Transkei. The best grass in the whole world. Dagga.'

It is my turn to let fly. But he laughs it away. ('Cucumber, my man. Space your *ntloko*. This is life.') And never refers to the incident again, not even when I deliberately try to bring it up. Until I have no choice but to resign myself to it, reassured at least in the knowledge that this new camaraderie between us – however dubious the grounds on which it rests – has brought Ntsiki to accept me like a blood relative.

And this is why, even if I am now in so many respects 'on my own', I am never really alone. Because Ntsiki is there; and his friends. Achmat, the 'coloured' lawyer from Athlone. Workers at the abattoir, at canning factories, at the power station, on the roads. Messengers, tea-boys, fah-fee runners, mechanics, card-sharps, swindlers, smugglers, a great brotherhood of survivors.

Out of the blue, one afternoon, Ntsiki has special news for me: 'Thomas-my-bra, my *baba* is coming home. Sunday week we're giving a *stokvel* to welcome him. You must be there. Promise! I want you to come, and bring your photo with you.' He always refers to a camera as a 'photo'.

For a while I have no idea of what he is talking about. 'Who's your *baba*? Where's he coming from? What's a *stokvel*?'

Ntsiki bursts out laughing. 'Jesus, my bra, you're too square, man.' And then launches into eager explanations: his *baba* is his father – not his real father, who stayed behind in Kwazakele after Ntsiki had been circumcised and moved to the city; but a relative, a great-uncle or something, on his mother's side, who has taken his father's place according to the custom of his people – it's Henry Bungane, who has been on Robben Island for five years, and who is to be freed next week; and on Sunday there will be a welcoming party. It's an occasion not to be missed.

'But surely you don't want strangers there, Ntsiki?'

'The whole township will be there. They're coming all the way from P.E. And anyway, my bra, you're kind of family too, aren't you?'

My face is aflame in sudden emotion.

'True?' he insists.

'True, Ntsiki.'

We seal it with the Africa handshake. And on the appointed day I meet Henry Bungane.

A small man with a shiny bald head, a perpetually smiling face – until one comes close enough to discover that his eyes never change when he laughs – expressive hands that gesticulate non-stop, unexpectedly small feet in black shoes with the shine of newness. Actually, everything about him is new: the white shirt, the striped tie, the charcoal suit; only the eyes are ancient, round, wise, like those of a tortoise. Henry Bungane. In an armchair much too big for him, late in the evening, the gaslight reflecting on his head, after the crowds have finally ebbed away into their endless matchbox houses in the loud dark. Only a few members of the family remaining – their names I cannot even remember – and Ntsiki, his lawyer friend Achmat, and I. On Henry's lap two children, a small boy of ten or eleven; a sleeping girl, born several months after her father had gone to the island. A woman with a surprisingly youthful face, on the floor at his feet, one hand raised to the armrest of his chair; gazing up at him. This is how he sits on the one photograph I shall choose later, from the many taken that day, for the exhibition abroad. *Home from the Island.* A small man in the almost empty space of the spare little lounge, back with his family, in this light which reveals him in a strange supernatural glow; a smiling, sad, inextinguishable Moses back from Sinai. What the photo cannot register is the voice: the amazing, deep, rich bass that fills all the space surrounding him, even when he is talking softly among friends. (But earlier in the day, in the afternoon of noise and sun, there was the reverberation of his words over the crowd gathered in the dusty street in front of his small house, thousands of them standing with raised fists and answering 'Ngawethu!' to his booming 'Amandla!')

'So: Thomas.'

His round eyes on my face, as if he stares at me from the whole history of his recent years, stares right through me, in search of something I cannot account for. He seems to be expecting something of me, a profound remark, a small step for a man, something like that, but I am equipped so poorly.

'You're free again,' I stammer, feeling utterly foolish.

A brief laugh, a mere rumbling of his deep voice. 'One can be free anywhere. Even in jail. Even on the Island.' A pause, lasting for so long that I accept he has finished speaking. Then he resumes, 'You see, prison, if you really think of it, sets free one's mind. It is a place where you really become, how do they put it, the master of your fate. It frees you from everything that has conditioned you outside. Especially from fear. It's a great feeling of peace that comes over one when you discover there's nothing you need to be afraid of any more. Nothing. Not the police, not their dogs, not teargas, blood, handcuffs, not what can happen to your family. Because in a way the worst has already happened. And after that, you're free. There's nothing you can do about it. You're free of everything, you're not even afraid of dying any more. All that remains is just you. Yourself. And you have all the time in the world to think.' That unnerving gaze again. 'What do *you* call "freedom", Thomas?'

How inadequate, all of a sudden, everything I can cite: Plato – Rousseau – Sartre – Camus – names, names; the second-handness of my 'Western tradition'.

He gives me a forgiving smile. 'Don't look for it too far, my young friend. If you think about it, freedom is nothing but the little bit of space surrounding you.' A pause. 'And what you do with it.'

Then he starts talking about the Island. Softly – so softly that some phrases are inaudible – a deep, reassuring drone in the room; the boy leans back against his shoulder, fighting bravely against sleep for a while, then goes limp. And Henry talks: about the journey to the Island in the belly of a boat, a long row of prisoners chained together, precariously going down the steep ladder, just as in some old slave ship (– my distant ancestor Catharijn! –); about the warders awaiting one with their crude welcome: 'This is where you're going to be broken in, right?' He talks about the hard labour: breaking stones, gardening, digging trenches, building walls. The taunts and tormenting of the guards. And the rare occasions when someone breaks down, rises to the bait, talks back; or worse, dares to defend himself. 'It once happened to a friend of mine. He couldn't take it any more. So fifteen guards took him on. The rest stood by with automatic weapons to keep us back. Not a shred of clothing left on his body afterwards. Not a tooth in his mouth. You could hardly see it was a man. Then they put him in chains. Dragged him off to solitary, for a month.'

'But how does one survive there, Henry?'

'Oh one survives.' A rumbling laugh like distant thunder. 'One survives. Because one is never alone, you see. There's no other place in the world where a man has friends like that.' (Later, much later, after he's begun to work for the UDF, once when I accompany him on a trip through the country, he confesses unexpectedly, 'You know, Thomas, some days I almost miss the Island.' I gape at him in amazement. 'It's true,' he says. 'Not the prison part. Not the warders. Not the hunger or the torture or the boredom. But the friends. The organisation. Every man knows what to do. Professionals, the whole lot of them. Now I must waste time teaching others from scratch. And there's so little time. There's so much work to do. But in that place! – we didn't waste time, man, we *worked*, all of us together, like one big beautiful machine. The best university in the world!')

And then he tells about the people. '*Those* people!' An eloquent sigh. '*Those* people!' He tells us how they used to coach the warders for their exams, Standard 8 or matric: in Afrikaans, in history, any conceivable subject. How they helped the warders with their legal problems: traffic tickets, debt, letters of demand, income tax, occasionally a divorce. '*You* should spend a few years in that place, Achmat,' he says laughingly to the lawyer, 'that'll make you the best lawyer in town.'

His eyes close for a while; he must be exhausted; it is time to leave him alone with his family. But he resumes: 'Ag yes, the Island! Hell, man, on a clear day you can *mos* see the whole coast from there, all the way from Green Point to Blouberg. No other view in the whole world like that. As that bloody old imperialist Sir Francis Drake said in his time. But he knew what he was talking about.' And to Ntsiki: 'One day we'll all go back there together, *buti*. When this place is free again. I'll go and show you. We can go out on the rocks together and look for seafood.'

'I never thought there was anything living on or around the Island,' I confess.

'Oh there's lots of life. There's game, I tell you. Hares. Guinea-fowl. Even wild peacocks. Crying at night like people dying.' This sends him off on another tangent. 'Those nights. So quiet, you could hear the sea. The saddest sound in the whole world. Or a man crying somewhere in the dark.' A long silence. 'Or a group of men beginning to sing in the dark. Very softly. So softly you can't even hear it with your ears, it's just something trembling in the walls. But growing louder all the time. Louder. Until the whole island is singing in the dark.' And then, his eyes closed again, in that great deep heavy booming voice, he begins to hum the tune: '*Nkosi sikelel' iAfrika* –' And before the end of the first line, Ntsiki joins in; and then the woman, and Achmat. And the children half-awaken from their sleep and without a moment's hesitation start humming with the others. And I too. In the background the low hiss of the gas-lamp. And outside, in the night: the inaudible hum of Africa stirring in its sleep and absorbing into itself the rhythm of the hymn and reproducing it, amplifying it, until the dark sound reverberates along its farthest shores.

*

Afterwards, Stellenbosch. For nights on end I wander through the streets until long after the traffic has drained away and the last shouts of drunken students staggering home have disappeared into their rooms and digs and caverns. Only the sound of the swift water in furrows beside the streets. Sometimes, if there is wind, the oak leaves rustling. Perhaps a single late, hasty car. Then silence again.

I remember how the place overwhelmed me when I first arrived here. The green luxuriance, the mountains, the smell of history, the stark white walls through dark green foliage. After the barren interior, the West Coast, the Transvaal, the Little Karoo, summer vacations on my grandfather's farm in Griqualand West. How elated I was to roam the shady streets in search of tokens of my individual past. Some of these buildings around me would have existed in those days; some of these thresholds might well have been crossed (humbly, cap in hand, as befitted their lowly rank) by Fransoois Lodewickus and Carel Guillaume, entering the cool Dutch interiors with their stark tiled floors and gleaming wooden beams and Delft porcelain in louring dark armoires. But now, after what has happened, I see it all in a different light: a museum town, its buildings and people petrified in obsolete history, irrelevant, pervaded by the smell of camphor, formalin, mothballs and mould. Pretension. Forbidding any space to whoever deviates or dares question the commandments, written or unwritten. Because my predicament involves everybody I can turn to for help, for the simple opportunity to talk, to unburden myself. There is no one. Among my lecturers, no one. Nor among my fellow students. Or, more precisely: there may be a few, indeed, prepared to listen, even to offer sympathy: but provided it remain between us. All are scared silly at the thought of what may happen if it is spoken out loud.

Even Carla belongs to the past.

No, I no longer belong here.

It is Henry I choose to discuss it with. His imperturbable calm, his wisdom, attracts me; in a way he has become a father to me – as he used to be for Ntsiki, earlier.

'I no longer know where to turn,' I confide in him one afternoon. 'It's not my fault that the country is in such a mess. I *want* something different. But there's nothing I can do to change it.'

'Don't underestimate what you can do, *buti*.'

But I am impatient. 'No, Henry. I don't believe it. I feel so guilty.'

'About what?'

'Everything.'

The rumbling of a brief laugh somewhere inside him. Then, gravely, 'Guilt will bring you nowhere, Thomas. We're all guilty, since Adam's time. But God didn't make us so we could spend all our time moping in sackcloth and ashes.' (Henry, I have discovered, is a believer, a lay preacher in a Baptist church; the bible is never very far away.) 'Take your guilt for what it is,' he continues in a fatherly tone. 'Then put it down behind you and move on. There's nothing God can do with your guilt. But with your responsibility He can do everything.'

It sounds so tempting. How passionately I want to believe him. But at this stage his words are no more than words to me. I even begrudge him that religious tone, because at this very time I myself am beginning to question the infallibility of the bible and everything my parents have so eagerly inculcated in me.

As a result, what happens to Ntsiki really comes too soon for me to cope with.

Out of the blue. True, Ntsiki has warned me about rumours doing the rounds in the single quarters that the police are planning large-scale raids, but there's nothing new about it. Most of the women and children who have illegally moved into the buildings have long become used to their insecure, provisional existence; they are resigned to it, take it for granted, even joke about it. But this time, as it turns out, there is solid ground for the rumours. First a couple of nocturnal spot-raids, here, there, somewhere else. Then it builds up to a week-long siege during which the townships are raffled from one end to the other. Army vehicles in a tight cordon all around the area. While inside, contingents of riot police move from one rutted street to the next, leaving purple stamps on the palms of all the inhabitants already 'processed', like grading marks on beef or mutton carcasses at the abattoirs.

I have learned long ago how to get into the townships on my motorbike – Ntsiki has shown me, especially around Nyanga, where there are holes in the hedges or the vibracrete walls: back roads through Pinelands or Athlone – and using my telephoto lens I can get photographs without running into personal danger. Time I have in abundance as I hardly attend lectures any more. After my final degree courses of the previous year, the teachers' diploma subjects are an insult to the intellect. But even if they were stimulating, it is unlikely they will ever lure me back. My interest has been dissipated: not only in the diploma, but in Stellenbosch; in all that has comprised my 'first' life.

The eventual raid on Ntsiki's building comes as a surprise because the police have already invaded the place two days earlier, carting off more than a hundred women and children and bundling them on trains, back to Transkei or wherever they came from. But the police probably realise that the people have been tipped off and that many are hiding out elsewhere at night; which is why this time they make a sudden swoop at midday, knowing that most of the 'illegals' – even though they've been living there with their husbands for eight or nine years – will be at home then, washing or ironing or keeping house while the men are at work. Of the men, only a handful of the very old and decrepit are at home, and five or six who are ill, a few who are out of work and, inevitably, Ntsiki, who is preparing for his next trip to Transkei. (I've had an angry argument with him about it: 'Ntsiki, I'm not going to help you out again. Dagga is dagga, it's a crime, dammit, there's no excuse for it.' Whereupon he laughed from his guts. 'So? There may not be an excuse for it, my bra, but there's money in it.' Suddenly very serious: 'Why are you suddenly so uptight about crime? Come on, tell me straight: if you weren't white, and you lived in this place, wouldn't you have made a grab for grass too? Or for anything else that can make life a bit more better?')

We are in one of the outside ablution blocks – shower cubicles which also serve as toilets; walls, originally dark green or blue, now stained with rust; the eternal leaking of sewage pipes; the stench of blocked toilets – when a small boy comes running in, breathless, large-eyed, stammering out a hurried message in Xhosa to Ntsiki. (I have started learning the language, but I'm not yet fluent enough to follow a fast conversation.)

'Thomas, it's the cops.' He pushes me aside. 'They'll find you here. Better get away quickly. Round that way. Keep behind the market people.'

I weave and duck my way to the first row of stalls, where I stop to make sure I have enough film in both my cameras. I am surrounded by an exodus of loudly screaming or ululating women and children swarming down the outside staircase of the building and scattering in all directions. Dogs tug at their leashes, barking hysterically, while squads of police fan out from their vans, the back doors open to receive their new consignments of human flesh.

In spite of the commotion there isn't much violence. No one

cramped cubicle, previously a publisher's storage room, four young
assistants at work behind a single board placed on trestles and
covered with brown paper; Achmat below the window at his
own small desk. Steel cabinets and cupboards, all of them wide
open, files and papers protruding from shelves and drawers. In the
passage outside, a crowd of twenty or thirty clients – 'coloured',
black, Indian – all waiting to be helped. It takes an hour before
Achmat can see me.

'Don't worry,' he says, appearing irritable about being bothered
with such a trifle: there are many cases waiting, all of them urgent.
'I'll see what I can do.'

When he telephones me the following day at my landlady's house
(I have to keep as cool as possible, knowing she always lurks round
a corner to eavesdrop), he sounds less offhand. 'Something fishy
here, pal. The cops say they don't know anything about our man.
He hasn't been arrested at all. You sure about your facts?'

'My God, Achmat, I was there, I *saw* it!'

'Can you come round to my house tonight?' He gives me the
address in Athlone.

It is easier said than done, driving there in pouring rain on my
bike. Shoved into the front of my plastic raincoat is a large envelope
bulging with the photographs I took of the raid.

A particularly beautiful woman opens the door and invites me
into the drawing-room before disappearing again, abruptly and
soundlessly. Entering after a while, still chewing, carrying a small
tray with tea and two cups, Achmat is in slippers, and wearing a
striped gown over his day suit.

'Right, spill it.'

I hand him the envelope.

For a long time, frowning with attention, he works his way
through the photographs. Twice. Three times. Then looks up and
barks at me, 'This is dynamite, man. I hope you realise it. You shown
them to anyone else?'

'No. I printed them myself in my landlady's bathroom.'

'Anybody *know* about their existence?'

'No. Except for the police who came after me. But they don't
know it was me.'

'Look, pal.' He puts the photographs on a spindly table covered
with a tiny Afghan rug. 'Tomorrow I'm going to throw the book at
them. You can bet your life on it. But you keep your mouth shut
about the whole thing. Not a word. Not to anybody. Understand?

And bring me another set of these tomorrow. Hide away the negatives where not even God Almighty will find them on the Day of Judgement. Leave the rest to me.'

I do. When the police persist with the story that Ntsiki has never been arrested, Achmat demands an interview with the station commander. With a vague promise to 'look into the matter' the officer leaves with the photographs clutched firmly under his arm. When he formally reiterates, the following day, that Ntsiki is not in detention, Achmat submits the second set of photographs to the Supreme Court and applies for an interdict. ('You just lie low, pal. If it comes to the push I'll ask you for an affidavit. But I'm trying to keep you out of this.')

Even before the interdict is granted, an unknown person telephones Achmat at home with the news that the man he is looking for has been found on Macassar beach.

What the informant neglects to mention is that the man we have been looking for is dead.

It has been evident, for quite some time now, that my first world can no longer accommodate me. Now it seems the second has also become precarious, a minefield, a Sperrgebiet. I can no longer cope with it. I lack the guts. I am too scared. I understand nothing any more. I have lost my grasp on what is happening around me. All I know is that I want to get out of here. The country I thought I knew has become alien to me.

Dad threatens to get an apoplexy. Mum cries her eyes out. Frans makes scathing remarks about the stupid little twerp. Maria says, 'I think you're making a big mistake, Boetie. But it's your decision.'

I give up my studies, pay my landlady one notice month, count my savings, and book a cheap seat on a plane to Europe. What I omit to tell anybody is that I have secretly resolved not to come back again at all. —

6

The turning-point of the day was the news in the afternoon paper. The hours preceding it, with the exception of lunch with Justin, Thomas would afterwards find difficult to reconstruct.

After Rashid had dropped him that morning, he hurried through the Sanlam entrance to the Golden Acre, ducking under Robbie's grey hat, down to the underground level where, as unobtrusively as possible, he removed the hat and took off and rolled up the raincoat. The coat he kept in a tight bundle in his arm; the hat he discarded in a bin near the escalator to St George's Street. In Garlicks he bought a canvas shoulder-bag to which he could transfer the contents of his OK plastic bag. And afterwards he sauntered aimlessly through the streets, peering into display windows, bought chocolates at Woolworths so that, if necessary, he could use the bag as a signal to Justin. For a long time he sat hunched over an orange juice and a sausage roll in a Juicy Lucy, absently watching the Saturday morning crowd.

No sign of anybody tailing him. Gradually, as he began to relax, he became more interested in the passers-by. As often in the past, relegated to the role of spectator, of observer, of photographer without a camera, he thought, almost with a twinge of regret: All those strangers coming past, children, teenagers, women, men, the young, the old: caught for a single fleeting instant in the lens of his eye – and then gone. For ever. Never to be seen again. Even if one of them were to stop briefly to address him – to ask the way to a shop, to say good morning or pass a remark about the weather – it would be no more than a brief exchange, and that would be it. Like the young man he'd given a lift on the way to Bloemfontein, Raymond. Or yesterday's blond boy, to Villiersdorp. Poor kid. Or the girl on the plane, Lisa, who'd showered him with the contents of her bag and compulsively chattered for an hour or so on the flight to Johannesburg. By now she had been reclaimed by her own existence, like the others, as if they'd never met. What difference might it have made to him if, instead, any one of those – or one of the anonymous crowd churning past him now – had *really* become involved in his life? Those individuals, each of them, like himself, the bearer of an entire and unique history. Thirteen generations, a hundred generations, all the way back to *Homo erectus* or *Homo habilis*. The odds were even: each one of them *could* have been decisive for his existence: each one passing here in front of him and disappearing among the others was an unrealised possibility, a lost opportunity.

– Those nameless ones who, a week ago, gathered on the Parade for the spectacle, when I arrived on my motorcycle to assist Nina in her stalled car. They were just as coincidental to my life, as peripheral and unreal. But then came the explosion. And six of them are now scorched into my existence and my consciousness for good, with the full blaze of their names, addresses, histories. And the same may happen to any of the multitude passing in front of me now: what a radically different person might that make of me, towards what a totally different end would that steer my life? Because nothing is fixed or determined in advance: any moment something unforeseen may occur, may implode into my life and open up a whole new range of previously unthought of possibilities. Terrifying. Yet, in a strange way, comforting too. How many other lives have already entered mine. All assimilated into myself. And I into them. Every single individual I've touched on my way, however briefly, would retain something of me. From our respective positions we illuminate each other, even without being aware of it; without all the others not one of us can ever be whole. –

Later he went up to the upper level of the concourse. It was still too early for his appointment with Justin in Mike's Kitchen, but he could spend some time in Musica, an unexpected, almost indecent luxury. Without anybody trying to disturb him, he selected records, listened to them through earphones, chose others. Chamber music, Vivaldi, Haydn, Mozart. The Rachmaninov preludes. Chopin ballades. Beethoven. The Third. Remembering a day in Lusaka, with Sipho and Noni, when they'd listened to it together, and Sipho had said, 'Did you know that Lenin refused to listen to music? Said it made him weak. I wonder whether the comrade realised what he was missing? Sometimes I think the armoured train that took him back to Petrograd shut out too much.'

At a quarter to one he went out to the restaurant. There were only a few people. He chose a table in a corner from where he could keep an eye on the entrance.

He had to wait almost an hour; to keep himself busy he ordered an apple juice which he nursed sparingly, mindful of Rashid's warning that Justin might be late. He kept a sharp lookout, but it was clear there was no one following him, the Woolworths bag he kept out of sight on his lap.

At last the familiar spare figure appeared at the entrance, stopping for a while to look about him. Thomas showed no reaction as he approached, did not even offer his hand. Justin's face looked drawn, his sad eyes weary. He shoved a key across the table.

'Your car key. Level M, number 121. Don't forget, because you won't recognise it. It's pale blue now. Bellville registration.' His eyes lit up briefly. 'You should be okay now.'

'The parking ticket?'

'In the cubbyhole. There's a credit card too. But don't use it out of town.'

'I'm not planning to leave town.'

'Just in case.'

A girl with dishevelled hair and heavily made-up eyes arrived to take their order; her nails were bitten to the quick.

'So, Freddie, what's new?' As always when they were in public, he used Justin's code name, even when there was no one near to eavesdrop.

'No problem. Waiting for news about the patient. But everything is under control.'

'And at home?'

A small flickering of pain or bitterness appeared in his eyes. 'Under control too, I suppose.'

'You think this'll be going on for a while still?'

Justin shrugged. 'You having a hard time?'

Thomas dropped his head.

After a moment he looked up again. 'I need something to do,' he said urgently.

Justin's eyes narrowed.

'I need something to keep me occupied,' Thomas insisted. 'You're all busy with this or that. You must think up something for me too. It's killing me.'

Justin leaned forward to speak in a low whisper, barely moving his lips. 'The most important thing you can do now is to keep out of sight. Until we're absolutely sure it's safe again. Then we'll give you so much to do you won't have time to shit.'

Thomas sighed. 'I was hoping there'd be something I could do while I'm lying low.'

'You can knit us all jerseys for the winter.'

'I tell you, even that would be a relief. Anything.'

'Let's get this weekend behind us first. Then we'll have it all organised. A safe place to stay, the lot.' He stared intently at Thomas, as if in search of signs – of what? Hesitation? Resistance? Cracks appearing?

Unflinching, he stared back, then nodded slowly.

Justin put his hand on Thomas's arm on the table, pressed it.

'Weather's clearing up,' he said in his usual tone of voice as he leaned back in his seat. 'Still a bit windy, but from tomorrow the Cape will be a feast again.'

Thomas looked up and smiled. There was so much he would

still have wanted to say, so many questions still to ask; but this was not the time. For the moment it was enough to just be sitting here, opposite Justin, looking in his eyes and finding in them the confirmation that he hadn't failed, that there was sense in what he'd done, even though it was as yet not possible to define that sense; that there was sense in going on. Sitting there opposite him, Justin was the guarantee of what had happened, of what still lay ahead. There he sat, his whole history enclosed in him: his great-grandfather who'd been a bricklayer, his grandfather the fisherman, his father the cabinetmaker; the house in District Six demolished by the bulldozers, and the dreary little bare-brick home on the Cape Flats where his father had yielded, unresisting, to death; the child who'd been shot by the police, and who had left a tooth behind for the tooth mouse. Convinced that the country was no longer a place for ordinary Godfearing people they left for Canada. There he came into contact with members of the Organisation. The first time he went to Lusaka from Toronto his wife thought it was for a congress; even now, after so many years, she still had no idea of his activities. She knew, of course, that he'd joined the Organisation and had remained a member even after their return from Canada, three years later, when they could no longer stand the cold; but not about the bombs. Sometimes in the school holidays, or during the long leave he took to supervise the Paarl programme, she believed he was doing 'research' in Johannesburg, while in fact he was in Zimbabwe, or Zambia, or Angola, once even in Tanzania. All of this he'd had to bear alone; of all of this Thomas was aware as he sat looking at him across the cluttered table. Since the very beginning of their programme Justin had been the one who'd warned them, like the instructors in Luanda before that, over and over: one doesn't resort to violence out of revenge or rage. To throw a bomb – how many times had he repeated it? – demands more than that. It demands reflection, calm, dedication, faith. It demands hard work. Hard, thankless, unremitting work. Without any guarantee of success. Without the presumption of expectation. There he was now, still unwavering. Lean, weary, suffering; but tough as biltong, as sinews, as uncompromising in his demands of himself as of others; more.

It brought a new sense of resolution to Thomas.

The girl returned with their plates on her upturned palms.

They ate without talking. Words, Thomas discovered, were no longer necessary. Below the surface of their silence the broad, imperturbable current of their conversation was flowing on.

When it was time to go, Thomas asked, 'Where will I be staying tonight?'

Justin took out money to pay. 'Jimmy will be waiting for you in Long Street at five. Corner of Wale. If he's late, wait. He'll come.' He stood up and briefly placed his hand on Thomas's shoulder. 'Chin up,' he said. 'You've been great so far. I'm proud of you.'

He went out first. Thomas followed a minute later.

Five o'clock, he thought. It was hours to go. And the city centre was deserted on a Saturday afternoon.

Hands in his jeans pockets, he sauntered out to the street. A few blocks away he had an idea, and changed direction, heading for a cinema. Without even glancing at the posters outside to see what was showing, he bought a ticket and followed the usherette. The film had already started.

When he came out at twenty to five he bought a newspaper from a vendor in front of the cinema.

BREAKTHROUGH IN TERROR CASE?

He drew in his breath very deeply before he started reading. The report consisted largely of speculation, suggestions, hints, rumours, tip-offs, leading up to a solitary paragraph of more solid information: the security police were urgently trying to contact the following persons who had been booked on flights to foreign destinations from Jan Smuts airport the previous Friday evening and had not taken up their seats:

Peter H. Dawson
J.L. Gerber
Dennis Johnstone
P.J. Sutton

7

– Anyway, I mean, you know, that's what he sort of said. I mean, how could I not remember it? 'You always have a choice.' Fucking easy for you to talk, I thought, hell. So who's he so likely? Okay, I mean, he was there and everything, he was, you know, like on the border, did his stint, but he said himself, I mean, it's not as if he's seen any fucking action. Just something about a fucking TV show or something, and then some fucking Swapo guys in a truck.

298

The whole fucking fortnight I, you know, sort of spent at home in fucking Villiersdorp, Jesus what a dump, anyway, all the time I was kind of *deurmekaar* in my head, thinking about what this ouk had said. Even when Janie, you know, I mean, what I'm trying to say is whenever she wasn't in school she was sort of like busy with me, Jesus, that girl's got fucking hot pants, man. Just once she, how shall I say, it's not like she wanted to talk or anything, but I suppose it just came out without her meaning to, you know, so she said, 'Oh my God, Hennie, what's going to become of me if they shoot you?' So I scheme this is my chance, hey, now we can like discuss the whole bloody thing that's been, you know, sort of eating me, but Jesus, before I could even open my mouth she was all over me, I mean, sitting down on me with that tight little bum of hers, right down on me and I mean, hell, like riding the spunk out of me, and crying and talking like mad all the while, like 'Come in me, Hennie, come in me, come in me, oh Jesus, you're driving me crazy,' you know. And all the while, I mean, shit, there I'm lying back with her on top of me and all I can think of is this fucking trip to the border that's just round the corner, and the chat I had with this ouk, and it's bugging me like hell, man, like I can't think straight any more, Jesus. 'You got a choice. You got a choice. You got a choice.' I wanted to talk to her about it, but every time I was ready to, you know, I mean, she'd just fuck it right out of me. So I mean what bloody chance did I have, come to think of it, you know, and my poor goddam mother too, in her way, just stuffing me with food and things, and every time I try to talk to her she just brings on some more, and if I just, you know, one can just *look* at her, then she starts crying all over the place. And if I say like, Ma, I've got to talk to you, she really freaks out, I mean, like bawling her fucking head off, and I mean, hell, I'm sorry for her too in a funny kind of way, so I just cool it. And then I try the old man, but every fucking time I manoeuvre him into, you know, like sitting down and sort of listening, he gets going about all this action coming up and how fucking lucky I am to have a chance of fighting for my people, all that shit, man, and how I must give those fucking terrs hell and bring back glory for the whole damn family. And then, so, I mean, when I just can't bloody well take it any more, I go to the dominee, but all he can do is bless me in the name of fucking Father and Son and Holy Ghost, and I strike another bloody blank. So there's fucking nowhere I can turn to, Jesus man, I really mean it, there's kind of not a single fucking soul to listen to me. And all the time, I mean, no matter where I go or what I'm doing, it's this ouk that keeps on talking in my head, you know, like you've always got a fucking choice, it's up to you, matter of paying the fucking price. When my fortnight was up and I now had to hitch back to fucking Oudtshoorn, long-pass expiring, I was wondering whether I shouldn't just, you know, like hitch right past, to hell and gone, but that's when I see the newspaper. Jesus, I thought I'd blow a fucking gasket, I mean, there he was spread across the whole bloody front page, his face, you know, and I thought like my God, but I've seen you before. It said his fucking name was, you know, Thomas Landman. Not the name he gave me, but so what, I've got eyes, I mean, I can see, can't I? And this was him, you know, the same fucking ouk who went on so much about you got a choice. There I was tying myself into bloody knots about going to the border or not, and this fucking turd goes about blowing up people left right and centre, just my bloody luck it wasn't Janie or someone he killed, you know, like hell, I mean, Jesus. No, I'm sorry, right, I mean I'm against violence and all that kind of jazz but, you know, I've had enough shit as it is, I'm not going to let people like him blow up the whole fucking place behind my back, know what I mean? So I decided, I mean, right there on the spot I knew I was now going to the border, I'm going to fucking shoot like every fucking terr that crosses my path. —

<h2 style="text-align:center">8</h2>

'The first moment I saw that report I had the fright of my life,' Thomas told Rashid when, at twenty past five, the young man got into the blue Golf beside him. 'But now that I've had time to go over it, I don't think we need to be too worried. No one knows I was Dennis Johnstone. As a matter of fact, I never *was* Dennis Johnstone, because I never checked in at Jan Smuts and Patrick would have destroyed the unused ticket immediately. On the flight to Johburg I was Anton Swanepoel. In the Holiday Inn I was Peter Ward. It will be impossible to trace the person who bought the ticket more than a month ago from Rennie's in Sandton; the bank account on which the cheque was drawn has been closed for weeks. And even if they do trace him, that will be a dead-end, because he himself didn't know who the ticket was for. I needn't even tell you all this, we all worked it out together with Justin.'

He could still recall the shudder that moved through his body, the sweat breaking out on his hands and face, when on his way out of the cinema he'd first read that front-page report. The feeling that all the people coming past were gaping at him as if he were naked, without any cover or defence at all.

He'd had no choice but to keep outwardly as calm as possible as he walked on, ready to react to any suspicious movement near him; relying on defence mechanisms he'd learned from Justin and, long before that, in the training camp. Ambling along nonchalantly, kneeling round a corner ostensibly to tie a shoelace, checking on the possibility of pursuit; retracing his steps; following elaborate detours to his destination – the parking garage where the Golf was waiting.

Once he'd moved in behind the wheel, the doors securely locked, he began to feel safer. The very strangeness of the car was comforting. It was not just the colour which had been changed: the car had been aged in the process, a few judicious dents and scratches – but without battering it so badly as to attract attention for other reasons. Even the upholstery had been changed, and, in addition, the front seats had been covered with sheepskins that had seen better times; from the mirror dangled a diminutive teddy bear on a red ribbon.

Here he was completely anonymous. Like an old jacket, Dennis Johnstone had been finally stripped from him. And as his apprehension abated, a new eagerness took over. He was no longer merely passive, the butt and object of events controlled by others, as he'd been for the past week. He was active again, initiative had been restored to him, the freedom to take decisions, to plan ahead, prepare.

Feeling that he'd taken control of his life again, he started the car and drove down the spiral tracks; showed his ticket at the cashier's and paid for it; turned up Long Street, and parked just after the Wale Street crossing to wait for Rashid.

'I'm okay,' Rashid replied to his routine question. 'But we've run into shit.'

'Why?'

'Christine is dead.'

'What?!'

'Well, we're not a hundred per cent sure yet. But Judy phoned Justin soon after lunch, from a tickey-box. Said she'd heard it from another nurse. Which might be the reason why they took the regular team off Christine. So it's bad news. Even if in the long run it may be better for herself. I mean, rather than lying like that for who knows how long.'

'What about David?' asked Thomas, perturbed.

'Anybody's guess. Justin was still trying to get hold of him when I left. He's going to take it badly, no two ways about that. What makes it so difficult is that one can't make enquiries, because no one outside is supposed to know. All hushed up, according to Judy.'

'When will you be seeing her again?'

'Don't know. Justin wants us all to lie low for a while, seeing each other as little as possible. Just in case they try to trace us through Judy or someone else in the hospital. That's what's worrying Justin, you see. On the one hand, Christine. On the other, this Johnstone story. As long as the two are kept apart, everything's fine. But the moment they connect there will be sparks.'

'They followed her last night and found us.'

'But they don't know who we are. And we're not going back to Robbie's place. If the cops nail them, Violet can't tell them anything because she knows nothing. And Robbie's an old hand. Our problem is tonight. This weekend. I found us a place in Athlone, but Justin thinks it's better we split up.'

'So what do we do?'

'He wants to know whether you can organise something on your own. I mean, you know the Cape inside out. As long as you stay away from old pals. Just keep out of sight, perhaps a small boarding house somewhere in the suburbs. But if you're scared, we'll cook up something —'

'I'll be all right.'

And that was how it happened that an hour later, that Saturday afternoon, the street map open on the seat next to him, Thomas found himself driving slowly along a road in Claremont until he recognised the street name he'd been looking for, and turned up into a steep, quiet, leafy lane flanked by trees and tall hedges, following it for a block or two before he parked on the sidewalk, under a spreading oak, next to a battered little beach-buggy, took his shoulder-bag, went through the white trellis gate, up three red steps to a stoep below a tall verandah.

He pressed the bell and listened to it ringing deep inside.

Once again he checked the name on the piece of paper, compared the number with that on the door, and stepped back.

The girl was wearing small round glasses, her eyes slightly hazy as if she'd been reading for a long time; her dark hair was undone. Perhaps she'd been in bed. (With whom? Suddenly startled, he realised it was a possibility he'd never considered.) She was wearing jeans, and a loose white shirt, with bright red and yellow braces crossed, back to front, on her chest. She was barefoot. She was taller than he'd remembered.

'You *are* Lisa Lombard, aren't you?'

'So?' Diffident, as if she were expecting him to offer her a tract or a brochure. (A week ago, the mouse couple in Observatory –)

'Don't you remember me? You said if ever I came down to Cape Town again –'

'Good God. You're Anton Swanepoel? I didn't recognise you, you look different. What on earth have you done to your hair?'

'Signs of the times.'

'I never thought you'd take me up on it.'

'I was unexpectedly offered a lift down. But now there are other guests at the place I was hoping to go to. Do you think I could possibly stay here for a couple of days? I'll sleep anywhere, even on the floor. I'm not fussy.'

She gazed at him for a while. Her eyes: that curious colour, like smoked agate.

– Are you prepared to take my life in your hands? Then tell me. Tell me *now*. Or forever hold your peace. –

Chapter 7

— For every kind of fish you must prepare in a particular way. Fish isn't just fish. Takes years of practice, getting used to it, learning to live with fish and the sea. First thing, you must know your boat. You must be able to stick to the right speed. Four, five knots if it's, say, yellowtail you're after. Feathers on your line. Plastic lures. A good even speed, otherwise you can forget about it. When it gets a bit deeper, seven fathoms, ten, fifteen, once you've found the right pinnacle on the seabed, it's live bait. Another story altogether. You first use your zoorie, bring in the small fry. Keep them in your bucket, or in the well. *Strepies*, hottentots, mackerel. If you can find mackerel, you're okay. Then you go for the black steenbras. Or, if you want to go even deeper, say twenty fathoms, you use chokka or pilchards. To save time, you get a five-kilo pack of pilchards, that'll do nicely. Leave it out for a day or two so they can get limp. No Cape salmon will turn that down. And snoek! To get your snoek, you bring it up to the surface with a dolly, or a *blinkhoek*. If there's a proper shoal running it's real sports. No matter where you drop that line, it's a coconut every time.

So that's why. Got to know your place. Got to read your echo-sounder. Got to know your fish. Got to know your bait. Got to know where to look, and how to look. And before anything else you got to know *what* you're looking for.

Right?

Same thing in this job. Set about this bomb story as if it was a fishing trip. Haven't been able, for God knows how long now, said it before and will say it again, to take a break. So this is where one does one's fishing. Using a net if circumstances allow it. Depends. Otherwise a line, bringing them in one by one. Tug at the right moment, give them leeway at the right moment, wind up the pulley at the right moment. For every kind there's a right way of doing it. Reason to feel satisfied. No chance yet of relaxing, of sitting back, of course. But satisfied in a way. Engine's running, nice and smooth, four knots. Sonar's working. Pinnacles showing up clearly. Bait ready. Any moment now the tug will come. And Kat Bester will be waiting right here.

Three kinds of fish on this seabed. Three depths, in a manner of speaking. Requiring different kinds of bait.

Number one: Nina Jordaan. Still trying to find this one's level, to be honest. Had the body brought down to Cape Town. Now lying in our morgue in Salt River. No one knows that she's been identified all along. Not even her parents. Couldn't risk it yet. But will have to make the move soon. So far all leads have been dead-ends. Left her job at the legal clinic last December. Moved out of her house in Green Point. The woman there, Gerda Potgieter, doesn't know anything apart from the fact that Jordaan left late last year, said she was moving in with a boyfriend in Johannesburg. Came back three or four times to collect books or clothes, then left again without a trace. Potgieter seems clean. Keeping the house under observation twenty-four hours a day, just in case. But nothing so far. Interrogated Jordaan's contacts at the clinic too. Tabs on all of them. But nothing that points to the bomb. Seems she was with that Thomas Landman until late last year. The one we picked up after the Crossroads riots, few years ago, then had to let go because her father interfered. But as far as can be established he left Cape Town late October, early November last year. Some photographic project or other, was all her colleagues could say. Probably broke off with her too. But who is the boyfriend she moved in with in Johannesburg, according to Potgieter? Something fishy there. Not happy about it yet. They've pulled out all the stops in Johannesburg – that's what *they* say, anyway – to find her tracks up there. But a blank so far. Only solution might be to have a chat to old man Jordaan. But not keen on throwing out this line unless there really is no other way. And then, literally out of the blue, my sonar picked up the other fish in the shoal.

First look at number two. The woman who's been lying in Tygerberg these last three months with the bullet in her head. Never had the slightest idea of a connection between her and the bomb. The Mabusa gang in Langa, yes. But that seemed more or less wrapped up. Then, week ago, Muller of the lab team pitched up with the first results of the car blown up in the explosion. The little Austin.

305

Not the usual kind of bomb at all, he said. More tests needed, but at this stage it looks like Semtex. First time this Czech shit makes its appearance in these parts. A real bastard. Looks like clay, brownish stuff, can be pressed into any shape, rolled out flat like dough, one can hide it in the lining of a suitcase, at the back of a picture, inside a toy, anywhere. Odourless. No dog can pick it up. Nor can X-rays. A bastard. Traces of it in the Austin's boot, says Muller. Detailed a man straight away, off to London to get all the info. Muller is in touch with the Institute for the Study of Terrorism.

And this is the link. Because there was Semtex in the house on the farm near Paarl where the woman was shot. First missed it. More interested in the AK-47s and the other arms and ammunition in the cache on the loft. Only a month later, when the team went through the place for the umpteenth time, Swanie found what he thought was a lump of clay under an armchair in the lounge. Muller identified it. But of course at that stage it still seemed like an isolated incident. Until those traces were discovered in the Austin. Which means that the woman has suddenly become vitally important to the case. Matter of life or death. Quite literally.

Christine Pienaar. Found her name a fortnight after the shooting. Another mess that could have been avoided. But after the rest had got away it was understandable the police were jittery. Somebody at CAPAB identified the body. By that time they'd been looking for her all over the place. Been such a solid, dependable worker for years. Made costumes. Wigs her speciality. Slowly everything is beginning to fit.

Thought it was a breakthrough once we had the name. But no go. Nobody at CAPAB could help us. Private kind of person, always kept to herself. The home address they had on their books, place in Parow, turned out a dud. She'd given notice there months before, moved out of the bachelor flat, no one knew where.

Later managed to locate her mother in Upington, but no luck either. Always been an obedient child, the mother's words. Later got more restless, moved on to Cape Town to find a job, but still spent all her long holidays at home. Always on her own. Never replied to questions about friends, boyfriends, that kind of thing. So in the end the old lady wasn't any use either. No one would have given it a second thought if it hadn't been for that cache at the Paarl place. Bloody jackpot up in the loft. Makaroffs, AK-47s, hand grenades, ammunition. And later the Semtex. Kept all of that secret from outsiders. Waiting to explore what we thought was the Mabusa link.

Long talks with the farmer who rented them the place. Kobus Minnaar. Difficult old man, but a decent sort, used to play hooker for Western Province way back, elder in the Church for donkey's years. Only one blind spot, and that's coloureds. Can't bear the sight of them. Constantly had problems with his labourers. Once even landed in court because one Sunday afternoon he'd shot and killed a trespasser on the farm when the man had turned up, unannounced, to visit a woman. But the old man could prove that he'd previously forbidden the hottentot to set foot on the farm again and that the deceased 'had adopted a menacing attitude'. On another occasion, funnily enough, a coloured woman had summoned him for maintenance of a child. Settled out of court. And there were rumours that he'd been paying this kind of porridge money for several offspring. In the dark all cats are grey. But it was a hard hand he ruled his workers with. Am telling this simply to fill in the background. So that one can understand the old man's indignation.

What happened was this. Oom Kobus lives on an enormous fruit farm. Solid old Cape-Dutch homestead. Another period house next to it, which he uses as a shed. And further back a smaller cottage which must have been slave quarters in the old days, now occupied by the foreman. About half a kilometre from the main farmyard is a side yard, also with a Cape-Dutch house and a restored shed. Until a year or two ago it used to be an independent farm rented out as a whole. But then the old man extended his orchards and his vineyards, so he gave notice to his tenants and began to look around for someone willing to rent only the farmstead, without the surrounding land. And Oom Kobus was only too happy when, last November or thereabouts, he was contacted by someone interested in renting the property.

Man called Jeffreys. Forty-something, Oom Kobus estimated him. Black hair, milk-white skin as if he never came into the sun. Told the old man he was English, from Durban, but for some reason Oom Kobus was convinced he was a 'foreigner'. Necessary to fill in all these particulars as the old man's impressions are all we have to go on. Jeffreys told Oom Kobus he was a writer, he and a colleague were working on a children's history book. He did the writing, the colleague the pictures. The perfect place for them, isolated and peaceful, far from the city. They needed absolute quiet to finish the project, he insisted. Which suited Oom Kobus. All he demanded, as a guarantee, was three months' rent in advance. Jeffreys paid it on the spot, in cash. And a good fortnight or so before the lease was up, he paid for the next three months. Cash, once again. Oom Kobus was more than satisfied, and the tenants looked like decent people – least as far as he could judge, for they kept so much to themselves that one hardly ever saw them. When soon after their arrival the old man's wife once took them some scones, they didn't even invite her in.

The tenants included the man Jeffreys, and his wife Maggie who they said had just found a job in the city, Jeffreys said something about secretary at the technicon, and early every morning she left in her car, coming back in the evening. She was the one we later identified as Christine Pienaar. Then his colleague, also English, name of Archie Smith, a youngish, tall chap, tanned kind of skin, long hair, old-fashioned round glasses, crescent beard, always wearing a blue beret, 'one could tell immediately he was an artist'. And another girl, allegedly Jeffreys' daughter, whom Oom Kobus only ever saw at a distance, child of about sixteen or thereabouts, perhaps eighteen, long tousled black hair she never seemed to comb. Those were the four.

But they had two coloured helpers as well, and that was where the trouble began. According to Oom Kobus one of the helpers seemed middle-aged, the other one quite young. Jeffreys told him they were decent, educated people, and he and Smith needed them for lithographs or seriographs or whatever they call the stuff. And unless they could stay there as well, Jeffreys was quite adamant about this, then sorry, they couldn't lease the place. With the result that Oom Kobus grudgingly relented. On the express condition that the two coloureds use the derelict old shed as their living quarters. The old man didn't want them near his own labourers; they'd be a bad influence, they were city folk, and that, he was convinced, was the worst kind of hottentot around.

And then his worst fears, he told me, came true. Midway through February a couple of his labourers, from spite no doubt, came to ask him whether he knew those two hottentots were spending their nights in the big house with the tenants. Oom Kobus couldn't believe his ears. He grabbed his riding crop and strode the five hundred metres to the neighbouring farmyard. Without bothering to knock, he kicked the front door open and burst in on them. Found the lot of them having tea together. On *his* farm. The old man very nearly had a fit.

'You think I don't know what's going on here?' he shouted. 'I know everything. You hear me? Everything. And today's the limit.

I've already phoned the police.' Which he just said to scare the shit out of them. Little knowing what was really going on in the place.

According to what he told me they then became threatening. He started hitting out left and right with his crop, knocking vases and ornaments off the tables and window sills. And then he stormed out to phone the police. By the time the van turned up the tenants had already cleared out, lock, stock, and barrel. That was that, as far as the constables were concerned. But Oom Kobus insisted they search the place, and when they found some papers smouldering in a bin in the backyard they became suspicious. Then came the find in the loft.

Now if that young woman hadn't tried to charge off when she arrived home in the late afternoon to find the police waiting for her, we could have had the whole lot of them right on the spot. But as it turned out, she ended up in Tygerberg hospital, bullet in the head, and nothing could bring her back again. More than two months like a bloody cabbage. First decided to wait it out patiently, thinking the most we could get out of her was more light on the Mabusa case. Was rather looking forward to the interrogation.

Then Muller came with the news about the Semtex. And suddenly the whole case looked different. Could no longer afford to mark time waiting for the lady to regain consciousness. In the beginning we were still hoping someone would turn up to enquire about her. Matter of fact, there were a few calls. Four. But all of them kosher. Since then, nothing at all. So last Thursday got all the medics together. All the specialists. Not one of them could predict how long she might remain in that coma. In fact, they thought her chances were rather worse than in the beginning. Right, so a decision had to be taken. Not something a man does lightly. But seeing that her chances of recovery were just about zero anyway, and since the team had drawn a blank in the Nina Jordaan enquiry, there was only one rational decision to be taken.

Christine Pienaar had to die. Alive, she was no use to anybody. Dead, there was at least a chance that with the right kind of publicity one of her comrades might show up, perhaps attend the funeral. We have Minnaar's description of his tenants to go by.

Look, that woman's been kept alive by machines and tubes and drips and God knows what else. Just a matter of turning them off and allow nature to run its course. As long as no one got a whiff of it. Personally gave instructions to remove all the normal nursing staff.

Each of them tailed by members of the team, just in case. Nothing so far. Anyway, we brought in our own people for security reasons. Turned off the machines. Pulled out the tubes. That was it. On Friday evening Christine Pienaar died.

Broke the news to the papers on Monday. Nothing sensational. Because not a word has so far been said about the cache. People think the poor girl was accidentally shot by police when they came to arrest a trespasser on the farm. So we arranged for a discreet report. Miss Christine Pienaar, wardrobe assistant at CAPAB, shot over two months ago by accident on the farm *La Renommée* in the Paarl district, died this weekend in Tygerberg hospital. The funeral to take place day after tomorrow, Wednesday afternoon at 3 p.m., from the Dutch Reformed Church in Parow East.

But this in itself was not enough, of course. Never underestimate a communist. They may well suspect something. Must be persuaded that we're not involved at all. Easy, really. All that was necessary was to arrange for a bomb explosion in Durban. Late last night, just in time for this morning's papers. Wimpy Bar in Smith Street. Phoned the place five minutes before the time to warn them. One doesn't want unnecessary casualties. Unfortunately there were two. A cleaner inside, who presumably didn't get the message. And a beggar outside, scrounging in a rubbish bin in search of scraps. The very bin that had the bomb in it. Not much left of the poor bastard. The cleaner died on the way to hospital. Not a pleasant story, but there's always civilians who get caught in the crossfire, and this is war. The country's safety is at stake. It's them or us.

Fed the newspapers within half an hour of the explosion. Signs found at the site point towards the same kind of explosive recently used in the attempt on the state president's life in Cape Town. Reason to believe the gang have fled the Cape and are now hiding in Durban. Public warned to be on their guard.

So, today is Wednesday. The funeral is this afternoon. And the boys have dropped their guard, think we're now looking for them in Durban. With a bit of luck they'll all be coming from their lairs now. Ought to have something on the hook, by late afternoon. 'Jeffreys'? 'Archie Smith'? The coloured helpers? With luck, the whole lot.

The third fish. This is by far the most important. The deep feeling of satisfaction when all the preparations, all the calculations about place and depth and bait and hook and line suddenly work out right. Don't believe in coincidence. Things happen the way they must.

Worked our arses off on the passenger lists of all the flights that left for overseas that Friday evening. First tracing all those who did depart. All over the bloody world. Nothing suspicious there. Then began to look at the passengers who hadn't shown up for their flights. Amazing how many people book their seats, buy their tickets, then don't arrive. Most of them telephone a day or two afterwards. Those we could trace and tick off the list. Still stuck with no fewer than twenty-three names. Even with computers and everything it took us five days to sift through them. Found nineteen. Left us with four. Had to fly up to Pretoria again for consultations. Seven hours, last Thursday evening. Worked right through until three the following morning. Back at the airport at seven to fly down for the funeral. Never miss those. Charges the batteries. Makes one realise anew what one is doing in this job. How indispensable it is. Because if it isn't done, the whole country is taken over by weeds. One acts as a kind of cleansing agent. Without it, there will be a mess.

But it all takes time. Wears a man out. All the discussions before the funeral. Have to listen to everybody, even if it's a load of shit. But they call it democracy. Until we finally came up with a decision that should have been obvious from the beginning: to throw it open to the press. Splash the four names we ended up with on the front page of every newspaper in the country, on every TV news bulletin. Give the public the impression you're taking them into your confidence. Works like a bomb. Manner of speaking.

So the bodies were barely in their graves when we hit the newspapers with the names. Alphabetic order: Peter H. Dawson. J.L. Gerber. Dennis Johnstone. P.J. Sutton. By Saturday evening everybody in the country must have known about them.

Gerber was the first to telephone, not an hour after the papers had hit the streets. Game farmer in Northern Transvaal. The hell in. What the fuck gave us the idea we could publish his name as if he were a bloody terrorist? He'll take the lot of us cunts to court, clean us out. Personal friend of this, that and the other. Had to contact Pretoria to send a top man to him. Soft-soap the turd, flatter his patriotism, promise him the world, even buy him off if necessary.

Sunday morning a sobbing woman on the phone. Mrs Sutton from Houghton. Didn't we know her husband had been in intensive care at the General Hospital since last Wednesday with a coronary? What kind of heartlessness was this? The disgrace of having everybody think he was a communist while all his life et cetera.

Two to go. Dawson. Johnstone.

Still nothing on Dawson. Keeping him on file.

As for Johnstone, a phone call on Tuesday afternoon, yesterday. Pretoria. A Dr Landman from Armscor. Could he make an appointment to see me? No, preferably not on the telephone. In connection with last Saturday's report on missing passengers. Dennis Johnstone. On condition I could guarantee absolute confidence. Nobody was ever to know about this. Not his colleagues. Not his family. If I broke trust, he would see to it that things would be made very difficult for me.

Got a shit in threats. Who the hell do such people think they are? But all right, for the sake of progress one's got to co-operate. Told him it was okay, we were prepared to guarantee confidentiality. Then gave him a gentle warning too about the risk *he* ran if he tried to conceal information from the security police.

Arrived here in my office at eleven this morning. Something about him looked familiar, but at first it was difficult to place. Until afterwards. Of course. Landman.

Dr Frans Landman. Emphasis on 'doctor'. More than once. Took an immediate dislike to the man and that was one of the reasons. Learned people who flaunt their degrees. The root of all our problems Not particularly tall, head shorter than me, well built but the waistline beginning to go. Tanned, short hair. Shifty eyes.

'Brigadier, you must appreciate it is a hard thing I'm doing today. But because I care for my country —'

Cut the crap, I thought. 'You know Dennis Johnstone?'

'What gives you that idea?'

'You said so on the phone. Mr Landman —'

'Doctor.'

'Hope you're not going to waste my time.'

'I can't promise you anything. But I decided to tell you everything I know.'

'Took you a while to decide. The report appeared last Saturday.'

'I had to clear it with my conscience, Brigadier. You must understand —'

'Afraid not. You haven't told me anything yet.'

'Johnstone is an acquaintance of my brother's.'

Stared at him in silence. In this business one learns when to pause.

'My brother is a photographer. Thomas Landman. Quite well known in his field, I think.'

'Sudden flash: My God, yes, here it comes. The tug on the line one has been waiting for all along.

But didn't bat an eyelid.

'Ten days ago Thomas unexpectedly arrived at my home to spend the weekend with us. It was the Friday evening, the day the bomb exploded here in Cape Town.'

Still didn't move. 'What's so funny about that?'

'He hasn't visited us in years. We were – well, to be honest with you, we never got along well.'

'And?'

'His suitcase. A dark green case, the lightweight type. There was a leather tag on the handle with the name Dennis Johnstone on it. I noticed it when I helped him carry his luggage from his car.' He became uneasy. Fidgeted. Sweat on his face. Refused to make it easier for him. After that first tentative nibble on the line one shouldn't scare off the fish by reacting too quickly. 'I said something about it. He said it was a colleague of his. They're working together on a project for *National Geographic*. On the gold mines, as far as I can remember.'

'When did your brother leave?'

'The Monday morning.'

'Where to?'

'He didn't say. Back to Johannesburg, I presume.'

'Address, phone number?'

'He didn't give me anything.'

'And that's all you can tell me?'

'It's all I know.' He suddenly looked me right in the eyes. 'I don't find it easy to say this, Brigadier. But I've been suspecting for a long time now that my brother is mixed up with bad elements. Perhaps this may be just the kind of thing to bring him to his senses.'

'It may already be too late for that, Mr Landman.'

'What do you mean?'

'Am not saying this is the case, but suppose he was mixed up in the blast himself?'

'But that's impossible!'

'Why would it be impossible?'

'The blast was down here in the Cape. Thomas was in Johannesburg.'

'That's what *he* said.'

'You don't mean –'

'Mr Landman, a purely hypothetical question: suppose you knew

313

your brother had really been involved: would you still have come to us?'

'Is there any point in hypothetical questions?'

'You haven't answered.'

He was silent for a long time. Stared down at his hands. At last he raised his head. 'What choice would I have had? The law must run its course. Crime is crime. Not so?'

'Thank you, Dr Landman. You may have helped us more than you think.'

The next phone call, to *National Geographic* in Washington, was a mere formality. It surprised no one to learn that Thomas Landman had not been involved in any project for the journal in more than a year. They knew nothing about an article on the mines. They had never heard the name Dennis Johnstone.

For well over a year Thomas Landman and Nina Jordaan had been together. It is possible that the affair ended towards the end of last year as our first enquiries seemed to indicate. But who says it wasn't Landman she followed up to Johannesburg when she left her house in Green Point in December? If they ever went there. Because there's the little matter of the Semtex. First at Paarl, then in the Austin blown up in the blast. On the Paarl farm there had been a man of about forty, known as Jeffreys. His wife Maggie, alias Christine Pienaar. And a 'daughter'. Nina Jordaan disguised in a black wig? And a younger colleague, one Archie Smith. Suddenly the descriptions were beginning to make sense.

Sent for Swanie. Always at hand when he's needed. 'Get me a photograph of Thomas Landman. And one of Nina Jordaan.'

Personally drove out to Paarl. Took my time. At such times there is no need to hurry. On the contrary. One has to savour the moment. Great feeling of peace descending on one. Like sitting on the boat. All the time in the world. May even start sleeping better again at night. Like before. Get rid of the nightmares.

Found Oom Kobus Minnaar in the farmyard. Just inside the whitewashed wall, cutting roses. A whole patch of those blood-red ones. Old-fashioned roses, he told me proudly, from the days of Queen Victoria. Invited me to the broad front stoep for tea. From there he shouted like the bloody last trumpet at a couple of labourers trying to take a short cut through the lower garden with their cows. His wife brought out the tea things herself. Blue and white cups on a silver tray. An old-world kind of peacefulness on the farmyard, raked and swept clean. Turtle-doves in the oak-trees, far away and close by.

Lower down, below the white wall, along a water furrow, a row of pomegranate trees in which one could see the red fruit, split open. A pomegranate has always seemed rather special to me. Sweetness from my darkest childhood years.

A black cat began to purr as it rubbed itself against my legs; then jumped on my lap. Shoved it off without attracting their attention. Can't stand cats. Started with Pa, because we did have a cat at one time. Mine. Found it in the street and brought it home. Pa said he didn't want the creature in his house, it's just hairs on everything and a caterwauling at night. So gave the animal to a friend, it was Hansie de Waal. But it kept on coming back. And funny thing, it preferred Pa to everybody else in the house. Then one Saturday afternoon Pa was lying on the sofa listening to a rugby match on the radio, bottle of beer beside him. Cat appeared from nowhere, jumped on his chest. Jesus! He suddenly went completely mad and jumped up and gave the cat a kick to the head that sent it flying against the wall. Most awful scream the animal gave. Then saw something one'd rather not see again in this world: both eyes popped out of its head, hanging from thin red threads. Pa came running after it, picked it up. For a moment thought he'd had a fright, was feeling bad about it. But what he did was this. He'd pared his toenails earlier that afternoon and the scissors were still lying on the armrest of the sofa. Pa picked up the scissors and cut off the slimy, bloody threads from which the eyes still hung. Then threw the cat out the back door. Wanted to go after it, but Pa ordered me back. 'Bring me another beer and sit here. You're not moving your arse out of this room.' Knew he was watching me, ready for action. One foot out of place and he'd fuck me up properly. From outside one could still hear the moaning sounds. Will never forget it for the rest of my days. At sunset the cat finally died on the back stoep.

Oom Kobus called his wife to take away the cat.

Finished our tea. Then took the two photographs from the large brown envelope and passed them on to the old man.

'You recognise these people? Forget about the man's beard, the girl's hair.'

With a frown of concentration he stared at them, must have been for minutes. Could see he wanted to make absolutely sure. Even though there was no doubt in my mind about the outcome.

Sure enough. Identification positive.

Thomas Landman. Nina Jordaan.

Back in my office now. Outside, the mountain, as always. Never forsakes one, never disappoints one.

This is not a single fish. It's a whole shoal. —

Chapter 8

If Thomas had had to record, afterwards, his impressions of those ten days he spent in Cape Town, in the cottage of the girl Lisa in the steep narrow shady street in Claremont, he might have begun, since chronology was of no importance, with the Wednesday. The scene in the green bathroom that morning. But even more particularly, the evening when an unexpected cold front that brought fierce showers and high winds with it, drove them from their rooms to the floor in front of the blazing fireplace in the lounge where they flung down their mattresses to spend the night, or most of it, in intimate and often intense conversation.

By that time the room had become familiar to him. Its air of reckless, lived-in abandon, its friendly confusion: a huge old sofa and two deep easy chairs in tattered upholstery, draped with extravagant multicoloured African prints; a faded moth-eaten Persian carpet; below the window two prim straightbacked bentwood chairs at a narrow table, one corner of which, since the leg was missing, was propped up on a precariously leaning pile of books and magazines, the surface littered, like some archaeological site, with an unimaginable assortment of books, files, and an ancient Remington; the floor an obstacle course of boxes, trunks and suitcases trailing and spilling clothes, newspapers, more books, records and tapes, among which might be retrieved unwashed plates, odds and ends of cutlery, and a variety of ceramic or enamel coffee mugs; on the peeling walls, art and theatre posters, a few way-out postmodernist collages, and the Bonnard print; on a small table in a far corner the two beautifully painted Balinese puppets.

The previous Saturday, soon after his arrival and while she was out to see a movie with two friends, he'd begun his exploration of the house. The bedroom assigned to him, previously occupied by her recently married friend Fransie, now bare and abandoned, containing only a wardrobe, an iron bed, and some earthenware pots that sprouted dried flowers and peacock feathers. Across the passage (watch your step, she'd warned him, there were some loose floorboards), her own room, which he'd only seen, in passing, through the open door: a double bed on a low wooden base, covered with a crocheted spread; a few stern family portraits in oval frames; a clothes dummy draped with a lacy Thirties frock, and in a corner behind an open curtain, suspended from a brass rod, a whole pawnshop of old-fashioned dresses; a chest with open Dali drawers. (My God, he thought, I need my camera for this!) Further back, another room like an embarrassing afterthought, that might at a pinch serve as a guest-room (which in fact it did when her brother Erik arrived on the Sunday and curtly dismissed Thomas's offer of changing places) although it was more useful as a storeroom for some of her more unmanageable overflow. A spacious farmhouse kitchen in which the small double hotplate appeared ludicrous, poised casually in the large open hearth; an enormous green dresser stacked with crockery of which, as far as he could make out, not a single piece matched any other. And an equally large bathroom – once, no doubt a back porch, now walled and glassed in like a greenhouse – a wilderness of potplants and creepers among which a Douanier Rousseau tiger would seem perfectly at home, surrounding an antique bathtub on curved legs, beside a copper geyser with brass pipes; and a great assortment of mirrors, some suspended from nails, others leaning against pots or chairs, one a beautiful Victorian cheval. From a large earthenware pot there burgeoned, in utter incongruity, the prolific tubers of a pumpkin plant, covering most of the floor and sporting, even at this tail-end of summer, several flowers that left their outrageous, uncompromising yellow stains on the green surrounding space. He was enchanted by the room. In the daytime, he soon discovered, it was even more extraordinary, since it had no ceiling (it must be unbearably cold in winter!) and the roof-sheets were transparent fibreglass that flooded it with light like an artist's studio, only the light was green, probably from the plants, which made it look like an aquarium in which large exotic coloured fishes might move in liquid erotic ease.

This was the light in which he saw her that morning, the Wednesday morning. On the previous days she'd gone out early to get to her Bellville school in time; by the time he came from his room in

318

the mornings, lazy and dazed with sleep, to make breakfast in the kitchen, the house would be deserted. So he was unprepared for their encounter that morning: in the spacious unworldly aquarium, its windows steamed up, bathed in unreal light, she was standing naked in front of the tall cheval mirror, arms raised, drying her long dark hair, multiplied in the many mirrors. A prize photo. Lean, almost spare, modelled in the light. The angularity of rib-cage, shoulders, hips, knees, the merest swelling of breasts, a small cloud of curly black pubic hair below the slight curve – with her buttocks, the only hint of generosity her body permitted itself – of her belly.

It was not she – the scene in front of him, its intense visuality – that made him stop, but the sudden feeling of having seen it before, exactly the same image, the same girl, standing in precisely that posture, with her hard lean tall body, as if a mental picture, long submerged in memory, had suddenly emerged from blank photographic paper, and as if he'd actually been waiting for it, expecting it to happen, like the stencil of an early recollection overlaid on what he was actually observing, the way a hunter in the bush – Frans had told him – carries the image of the animal he looks for, its outline, its shape, in his head; otherwise he would never notice it in its natural surroundings. (But where did it come from then, when and how had this image first been imprinted on his mind? Undoubtedly the original setting had been different: a wood, perhaps, dense foliage; and water, a waterfall? For the moment it eluded him; was therefore irredeemable. But the impression of something intimately known he could neither shake off nor come to terms with.)

And what reaction was *she* expecting of him? Should he duck away, embarrassed, turn back, move past, pretend he hadn't noticed? Mumble an apology? Clear his throat? Dismiss it with a joke?

She lowered the white towel slightly to peer across the edge at him, through her wet hair, and said, 'Oh Anton, won't you bring me a dry towel? This one's had it. On one of the chairs in the spare room, I think.'

He deliberately lingered in the spare room to give her time.

'Find it?' she called.

'Coming.'

He returned to the bathroom, assuming she would have put on something in the meantime; would at least have wrapped a towel around her. But she was still naked, still busy, now with her back turned to him. An array of new aspects awaited him in the many mirrors, splinter images that confronted him in Cubist simultaneity. Flickerings of shadow on her back caused by the vigorous motion of her shoulder-blades, the sinewy muscles down her spine. The peculiar gauche grace of her long narrow body and legs. Nothing rhythmic or easy, nothing supple, no sensual appeal. There was, on the contrary, an intriguing angularity about her body and its movements, something austere, a broken flow.

'Here.'

'Thanks.' Leaning forward, her hair streaming over her face, she reached back with an arm to take the towel he proffered.

'Aren't you going to work today?'

She said something which in the intricacy and energy of her motions he couldn't make out.

'But –'

'Why don't you make us some tea so long?'

Only when he was back at the hotplate in the kitchen – the immediacy of her image still imprinted on his mind – did he discover that what he really felt was anger. Sudden unreasonable rage. But why? Surely not because of her nudity as such: he was a photographer, there was for him nothing unusual about it, she hadn't stimulated him in any way. Then what? That, unclothed, she had looked at him – clothed – with such a calm unwavering stare? Yet there had been nothing provocative in her attitude; she hadn't even seemed aware of being naked. It was, evidently, a most natural state for her. Or was it precisely that which angered him? Not because he'd been embarrassed or, worse, sensually disturbed – she wasn't in the least sexy: this he repeated emphatically to himself: *She isn't in the least sexy* – but because she'd had no right, no one had the right even in the smallest, most coincidental detail, to remind him of Nina. It was an invasion of that most urgently private territory in himself dedicated to Nina; she had no right of entry into it. *He* wished no entry into it himself; least of all now.

It was time, he decided, to move out. He didn't want any further truck with her. Two days earlier already, on the Monday morning, he'd proposed to leave, not wishing to overstay his welcome, abuse her hospitality; to which she'd replied without hesitation, 'Do as you wish. But you're not in my way at all. Matter of fact, I rather enjoy having someone around.' But now it was certainly time to go. If possible, before the day was out.

However, Justin was too busy to attend to it when later that day Thomas broached the matter. There was the crisis about David. It was the day of Christine's funeral. And then, on the six o'clock news, there came the devastating report about what had happened there. Thomas tried urgently to telephone Justin again – driving to a public booth in Newlands to avoid being noticed in his own neighbourhood; no chance café owner, petrol attendant, supermarket assistant should be able to recollect and report on him afterwards; his was, had to be, an existence without traces, in parentheses - but the number remained engaged. Trepidation lodged in his stomach like a tangible lump, he returned in the falling night to Lisa's cottage behind the tall hedge; bent double against the driving rain as he ran from the gate to the front door. In the kitchen she was bustling about with buckets and baskets filled with wood and coal.

'You going out tonight, Anton?' she asked. 'I thought we might make a fire. It's the perfect weather for it. If you can get it going I'll make the food.'

'I'll give you a hand.'

'You had your turn last night. You can open the wine. And there's an *Argus* on the sofa.'

'Sounds like playing house.'

They had a rough and ready stew – she'd dumped into a black iron pot whatever she could lay her hands on – and drank more red wine than they should. Outside the rain came down in a steady wash. In his agitation about what had happened at the funeral, his concern about what might yet happen, his resentment against her subsided. (And good God, it wasn't as if she'd been to blame!) As for Lisa, she was relaxed, easy, in a generous and expansive mood. From her room she fetched a guitar, strummed for a while, then began to play, her hair falling across her face; turned inward, as if she were playing for herself only, as if she'd forgotten all about his presence. A few pop tunes, folk, then that sweet Afrikaans lullaby with the unbearably cruel words, *Siembamba* ('Siembamba, mama's little baby, Siembamba, mama's little baby, Wring his neck and throw him in the ditch, Step on his head and he'll be dead'); then, without warning, the elegiac freedom song *Senzeni na*, singing softly to the tune in her whispery gravelly voice.

'Where'd you learn that?' he asked, intrigued.

She glanced up, as if surprised to see him there. Then answered, closing up, 'I'm not illiterate, you know.'

'But it's a song from the struggle.'

'So what? I've had a taste of it too. In my own way.'

'Tell me about it?'

'It's not important.'

She tuned in to a new song. This one, too, he recognised, from so many townships across the country; so many funerals. Through narrowed eyes he watched her in the flickering dusk, but she'd withdrawn herself completely into the music. And when at the end he asked again, 'Where'd you learn that?' she declined to answer, put away the guitar – offended? embarrassed? suddenly shy? – and knelt at her music set and began to play tapes. Nana Mouskouri, Tracey Chapman, Johnny Clegg, guitar music by John Williams, a whiff of Chopin. Later they put the wine bottle and their glasses on the threadbare carpet in front of the fireplace and settled on large chunky cushions to be closer to the warmth. It was almost midnight when she casually asked, 'Why don't we bring our beds to the fire? It's so cosy here.'

And then launched into one of her easy rambling reminiscences: 'We often did it when we were small, Erik and I. My parents never approved, always scared we'd set fire to the place or get asphyxiated or whatever. And children who play with fire, we were warned, pee in their beds. But sometimes we did anyway: waited for them to go to bed and then stole out quietly. Just the two of us. It was like a story we acted out. Something dreamlike. We sucked oranges and used the peels to create blue flames in the fire. And took turns to say what fantastic things we could see in the embers. Drew pictures in the dark with smouldering twigs. Until at last we'd fall asleep in each other's arms. Then they'd find us there the next morning in front of the grey burnt-out coals. No end to the scoldings and threats and dire warnings that came down on us. Even hidings. Mother never believed in sparing the rod. But we just couldn't resist the temptation, and at the first opportunity we had we'd do it again. It was a miracle we never burnt the house down. It remains one of my best memories ever. Those nights in front of the fire, with Erik. That was happiness. It was security. It was magic.'

'You were very close, you and Erik.'

She looked at him, orange light flaming on her pale cheeks; then away again. Shrugged. 'I told you, we're twins.'

'I envy you that. My brother and I never got along. I adore my sister, but she's always been more of a mother to me, she's eight years older.'

'You don't like Erik,' she said suddenly. 'When he was here over the weekend –'

'It's he who doesn't like *me*. He made me feel an impostor.' (Thinking, as he said it, But I *am* an impostor!)

'It's just his way.' She sounded defensive, affronted, embarrassed. 'He's never approved of any of my boyfriends.'

'But I'm not –' he protested.

'I know.' She smiled. Her wide, frank mouth. 'But how was he to know? Anyway, I reassured him before he left.' She finished the last drops from her glass; the wine shone dark red in the firelight. 'Well, shall we go and get the bedding?'

He was back first with his unwieldy bundle. Hearing her rummage in the spare room, he went to the bathroom to wash, brush his teeth. When he returned to the sitting-room her things were there already. The single mattress from the spare room, covered with a duvet. He could hear her in the bedroom now. In his underpants he moved in under his blankets. After a while she came past to the bathroom. When she returned at last, carrying a new bottle of wine, she was wearing striped men's pyjamas, too big for her, the sleeves and legs rolled back. Over the jacket she wore an old frayed man's jersey, originally dark red, but mended in all imaginable colours.

'You look well protected,' he grinned. 'Against the cold, I mean.'

'Do I need other protection too?'

'I don't think so.'

She looked down at him, her strange dark eyes peering intently, almost accusingly, at his face. Then, without a word, handed him the bottle and crawled in under her duvet. He filled both their empty glasses.

'You've got nice hands,' she said suddenly.

'Exactly what the madam in my brothel used to say,' he answered. 'All that pee from the pots I cleaned. Very good for the skin.' He raised his glass. 'Here's to your arctic outfit.'

For a while their conversation returned to the level of their previous encounters: light banter, mockery, skating safely on a smooth surface. On the first evening, when he'd just arrived and she was curious to find out what had brought him to Cape Town, he'd resumed the story of his persona on the plane:

'A total disaster. My madam found out about the prostitutes' demo I was organising, so she fired me on the spot.' His imagination took flight, as often before, as in his reconstructions of his family history: 'I refused to go. She grabbed a butcher's knife. No doubt at all about her intentions. Went straight for my castration complex. What could I do? I had to kill her with her own knife. Lac'd with

323

her golden blood. *And* my girlfriend threw me out. And now the entire police force in the country is baying at my heels.'

'Then you'd better lie low here until it's safe again.'

'That's what I was hoping you'd say.'

'But seriously,' she asked, 'what really brings you back to the Cape? Coming to see your prof again? You must be stinking rich to fly to and fro like this all the time.'

'I didn't come to see my prof. And I didn't fly either. A friend of mine had to drive down and it was too good a chance to miss.'

'A CY car?' she asked, straight-faced. She had gone out with him to show him where he could pull into a narrow driveway alongside the house, under a pergola; must have noticed the Bellville registration number.

'You never miss anything, do you?'

A shrug.

'Belongs to a pal in Bellville, who's in the army. I have the use of his car whenever I'm down here.' Fortunately he'd prepared an alibi. Before she could put in another question he said, 'I usually stay with him too, but this time an uncle and an aunt of his were visiting.'

'Just as well I was around.'

'Absolutely. But I'll sing for my supper. I'm a mean hand at cooking and charring. Wash all your pots too.'

Soon afterwards the friends with whom she'd arranged to go to the cinema had turned up. He was in the bath. From the kitchen she called at him to invite him with them, but he turned it down with a clear conscience. And made sure that, by the time they came home, he was safely ensconced in his room, the light turned off; and only after her companions had left again, long after midnight, and she'd closed the front door, and hesitated, and called softly, 'Anton? Anton, are you asleep?' did he reply, 'It's okay, come in.'

'Do you have everything you need?'

'No. But who has?'

'You must be missing the noise and bustle of the brothel.'

'Oh yes, we never stopped before sunrise.'

'Shall I wake you for church in the morning?' Mischief in her sandpaper voice.

'Early Mass.'

For a moment she sounded serious. 'You're not really Catholic, are you?'

'I'm trying to keep my options open. And you?'

'I'm not really into anything either.'

'But you said your father was a dominee?'

'Still is. Godforsaken little *dorpie* in Griqualand West. But it's the surest way of breeding agnostics, don't you think? Both Erik and I are born heathens.'

'He older or younger than you?'

'Twins. He's the good-looking one.'

'And what turned you against your father's noble profession?'

'Too much of a good thing.' She came to sit down on the edge of the bed, her knees drawn up, barely visible in the faint light from the passage. 'Where did *you* turn off the straight and narrow?'

'I was all right until I was about fourteen.' He told her about his garden project: the stretch of barren soil he'd invested with mealies and pumpkins and cucumbers and beetroot and carrots and beans, and which had all been scorched to dust. 'I prayed like hell. But nothing happened. It was like the prophets of Baal, that day Elijah challenged them, remember? Not a cloud the size of a clenched fist shouting "Amandla!" And from there it's been downhill all the way.'

That was the closest they had come – in that reassuring darkness – to being serious, the closest to confession. There had been another flickering the following morning, but that hadn't lasted long, as Erik had unexpectedly arrived and interrupted the conversation. Which had been a good thing, perhaps, as she'd been on the point of keeping her promise to show him the Cape. A radiant autumn day, no reason under the sun to refuse. Yet he knew he should try to get out of it: however tempting it was, he couldn't risk too much public exposure. Moreover, that recent day of wandering about with Nina was still too quick in his mind.

'Surely you have better things to do than show an ex-brothelkeeper around?'

'You have something against being seen in public with me?' He had to step carefully: she was much too sharp for safety.

'I don't want to waste your time. And you must have' – the ice was very thin – 'there must be someone else you'd prefer to be with on a day like this?'

'Like who?'

There was no point in evasion or equivocation: 'Isn't there a man in your life?'

'–'

'I'm not aspiring to take anyone's place.'

'You've got a bloody cheek, Anton Swanepoel.'

'That's not what I meant.'

'Makes it even worse.' Going for his guts: 'But I suppose you can't really help it, can you? You *are* a male.'

He tried to keep it light: 'I just wanted to reassure you. What with killing my madam and being thrown out by my girlfriend I'm rather bruised.'

For a moment her disquieting eyes studied him. Then she turned away from the breakfast table, wandered through the large empty kitchen, stacked dishes in the sink, staring – her narrow back turned to him – at the fast-changing leaves in the pergola outside. 'Makes two of us.'

'That's bad news.'

'You see, Fransie and I shared this place for – oh ages, over a year. She with her boyfriend, I with mine. Until her *ou* went up to Pretoria, new job, and she decided she couldn't face it here alone. So I sent mine packing as well.'

'Sounds crazy to me.'

'Not more crazy than the rest of my life.' She turned round, a dishcloth in her hand. 'Or what was left of it. Because he'd taken over everything. I was his personal little colony, you see. We got along rather well to begin with, but gradually he just took over. Began to sponge on me. But that's when I said, No taxation without representation. And threw him out.'

'Bravo.'

'Help me wash up, then we can go.'

'Why are you trying to change the subject?'

'What subject?'

'The boyfriend.'

'With disarming directness she said, 'I don't know you, Anton. And I still feel embarrassed about going over the top like that on the plane. What you must have thought of me –'

At that moment the doorbell rang and it was Erik. Her mirror image. The same smoke-dark eyes, the same angular body – but his was tougher, seemed more resilient – the same pale skin, dark hair. But cut very short, army style; he was wearing his browns. Chatting, their arms round one another, they came down the passage into the kitchen. Erik stopped abruptly.

'Who's this?' More than suspicion in his voice: accusation, distance, hostility.

Now, lying in front of the fire, Thomas said, 'Tell me about your brother.' He held the glass to his eyes and peered at the fire through the wine. 'You must admit he wasn't very friendly on Sunday.'

'I told you,' she said, on the defence. Took a deep mouthful, put the glass on the floor, rolled over on her back, her head cradled in her arms, staring up at the flower pattern on the old pressed ceiling. The glow from the fire was flickering on it, and against the walls. Otherwise the room was dark. A safe dusk in which one could afford to be trusting and frank. 'I'm worried about Erik. It's the army, I think. It's come between us. I never thought it would be possible. From as far back as I can remember we've always been together, in everything; the two of us against the grownups, against the school, against the world. I don't mean it in any aggressive sense. It was just us on one side, the others over there.' She was pensive for a while. 'We shared everything. Playing, going to school, making mischief, spending our holidays, eating, sleeping, everything. We even secretly shared our baths for goodness how long. In fact, it was one of our favourite places for talking together. When my parents weren't there, of course. They'd have had heart attacks. It's something outsiders won't understand. I often thought about it, especially after my mother died, my first year at varsity. Breast cancer, without any warning, matter of weeks. Her death made me realise for the first time that parents are mortal. All of a sudden one realises that there's an end to the love between parents and children. And there's an end to the love between lovers. There's no kind of love one can really depend on. Except the love between brother and sister. Don't get me wrong. We've had spectacular fights too, Erik and I. Cat and dog. But it's different. Below all that there's something else, a kind of solid bedrock that goes on forever, that never gives way, never lets you down, something you can rely on, something that matters, for all time. There's nothing you need to prove to one another. Nothing you ever need to lie about, nothing to pretend. It simply exists. It is *there*.'

He had a curious sensation as he lay there listening to her, to that flood of words going its way, in her low rasping voice, not nervous and precipitate as the other day in the plane, but peaceful, reflective, free: here he was, he thought, with his own life continuing on its course behind and below their conversation – his anxiety about David, the questions about what had happened, what was still to happen, ultimately the acquiescence in his own death – and beside him, on her own mattress, the young woman, Lisa, her life also pursuing an invisible course of which he knew so little:

327

and then there was this flow of conversation, this tide of words through which they did make contact, by which they were touched, moved, and in which – who knows? – their separate courses were imperceptibly redrawn.

'– discovered everything together,' he heard her voice again. A chuckle. 'We were so inquisitive, and we had only each other to learn from, to share or experiment with. All the way through school and university we were inseparable. Erik took up medicine, I psychology. We always dreamed about setting up a practice together. Of course, as we grew older we started going out with other people, although it was quite traumatic to start with. Neither of us really felt any need of what we regarded as mere substitutes. At the same time one has to be realistic.' She pulled a face. 'Isn't that just a euphemism for being petty bourgeois?'

'And now it's changed?'

'I don't know.' A long silence. She rolled over on her stomach again, refilled her glass, lay propped up on her elbows to stare into the coals. 'Yes, there have been changes in Erik lately.'

'Or in you?'

'Sure, it's possible. But he – You know, he used to be so dead against going to the army. Through all the years he was studying medicine: he kept on believing something would happen so he could avoid doing military service. But when he graduated two years ago, there was no way out. And then –' She slowly turned her head and fixed her dark night-eyes on him. 'If I try to discuss it with him, he changes the subject. But I have the distinct impression that he's actually beginning to *enjoy* military life. That's what keeps me awake at night. He's become fascinated by the discipline, the order, the whole power machine. Landed with his backside in butter of course. They need medics. So he did only a few weeks of basics before he was transferred to Wineberg, the military hospital there. He can come out every weekend, sometimes even during the week. At first he couldn't wait to get his pass, spent all his free time here with me. But it's happening less and less frequently. And he snaps at me when I dare mention it. Last week he got promotion. Some or other stupid stripe on his sleeve, I don't know if you noticed. What upsets me is that he actually seems *proud* of it. It's given him a whiff of power. Things he never cared one fuck about are suddenly terribly important. It's not the Erik I used to know, I tell you. We spent almost the whole of last Sunday quarrelling.

328

You should have gone with us, you know, it might have made things easier.'

He remembered the suspicious, aggressive 'Who's this?' with which Erik had greeted him, and the uneasy pause-filled conversation that had ensued before he'd persuaded them to go on their own, assuring them he had enough to do by himself; and the long boring day until they'd returned in the early dusk. One could see at a glance that she'd been crying. She'd gone to bed early, leaving him and Erik behind in the sitting-room, warily polite with one another, exchanging a few innocuous remarks. Later Erik got up, poured wine, offered Thomas a glass.

'My sister tells me you're a rather mysterious guy.'

'I wish I were.'

'What you do for a living?'

'A friend and I are trying to run a small publishing concern. Alternative literature, mostly.'

'That's not what you told her.'

'I was having her on. You don't believe I really work in a brothel, do you?'

A pause. He could hear Erik swallowing. Outside a rare car passed in the street.

'Any money in it?'

'No.'

'Then why do you do it?'

'Faith, hope and charity.' Over his glass he looked at Erik: the narrow pale face, the smouldering dark eyes, the long thin hands holding the glass. In a way he seemed still a boy, even though he must be – how old? – twenty-five. The resemblance to Lisa continued to perturb him. 'Why are you a doctor?'

'What's that got to do with it?'

'_'

'I hear you're working on a thesis as well,' Erik went on.

'Yes. Philosophy. Just to keep the rust off. Although my job is more rewarding than Lisa's.'

'What do you know about her job?'

'What she told me.' Amused, intrigued: 'Look, do you check out all her friends like this?'

The reaction was unexpectedly apologetic: 'Sorry. I suppose I sound very possessive. But she had a rather bad deal with the last one.'

'She's twenty-five, Erik.'

'But she's incredibly innocent.' A blush Thomas had not expected. 'It's not what you're thinking. But she tends to trust people very easily and then she gets hurt.'

'Lisa seems pretty tough to me.'

'I know she is. But she's –' A sudden surge of aggressiveness. 'I don't want people to use her, see what I mean?'

'It's a deal.' He emptied his glass and put it on a stack of books on the table. He was thinking: Erik is as possessive about Lisa as David used to be about Christine.

He saw David on the Tuesday afternoon. Justin had arranged it, when they'd met briefly on Monday. By that time the newspapers had already carried the report; the news was official, no longer a mere rumour. Christine was dead, even though no particulars had been released yet. 'Please,' Justin had asked Thomas, his face haggard, 'see if you can talk him out of it. He insists on going to the funeral and I don't think it's a good idea. We can't afford him making a scene. But he's so on edge right now, I don't think it's wise to forbid him either.'

They met in the Gardens, at the birdcages, as Justin had arranged. Thomas had arrived – also according to schedule – a quarter of an hour before David. He seated himself on a bench and opened his paper. Then David arrived, and sat down next to him, with his own paper. After a few minutes he took out a small brown cheroot, searched his pockets for matches, found nothing, and turned to Thomas:

'You got a light?'

Some distance from them there were children playing, and on another bench a hobo lay snoring, his empty blue-train bottle, unconvincingly wrapped in newsprint, propping up his head. Otherwise the place was deserted.

'Yes, Abe.' David's code name. In such a public place the precaution was necessary.

He tried to hide his shock: in less than a fortnight David had aged noticeably. His hair seemed thinner on his scalp, the red blotches on his cheeks unhealthy, his nose more beaked than Thomas remembered. And the black eyes behind the thick glasses were weary.

David lit the cheroot, put the matchbox in his own pocket, then placed one hand on Thomas's knee and pressed it tightly.

'So how's it?'

'Surviving. In the circumstances that's saying a lot, isn't it?'

David took a fierce puff at the cheroot and blew out the smoke. 'True.' He still needed time to control his emotions. Then, with a conspicuous effort to keep his tone neutral, 'Lot of water into the sea since we last saw each other.'

Unable to think of something to say, he pressed David's hand on his knee.

'We were in such high spirits then, weren't we?' David glanced around him; there was no one near. 'I remember how Suzie kept all our engines on overdrive. Some girl.' (Suzie: Nina.)

'Listen, Abe,' he said quickly. 'This is not the time to crack up. The struggle goes on, right?'

'Sure. But – I know it sounds heretical – but can it really be worth all of this?'

'This isn't you talking.'

'It is me, Peter. I tell you, it's me. Me and my whole history sitting here on this goddamn bench in front of this cage full of miserable birds.' In a sudden flare of rage, 'Cathy didn't deserve to die, Peter.' Cathy, of course, was Christine.

'You think Suzie deserved it?' he asked angrily. 'You think any of the thousands of people killed by apartheid over the years deserved it? Come on, Abe. You're the last person I suspected of selfishness.'

'God.' He exhaled another cloud of blue smoke. 'You're not in a mood for pulling any punches, are you?'

'No, I'm not. Because I know you better than this.'

David flicked away his stub and immediately felt for another in his pocket.

'Cathy was the first woman in twelve years I'd dared to fall in love with,' he said after a while. 'After Abby had left me, taking the child with her and everything: I was totally cut up. So my mind was set: there would never be another woman for me. Call it stupid, or obstinate, what you wish. But that's the way I am. No half-measures. My future was cut out for me. I wanted to finish what my father had begun. You know about him, I've told you before.'

'He was a saint in his own way.'

'Bloody sure he was. Just getting out of Auschwitz alive was a miracle. A mere skeleton, a sack of bones. I've seen photographs –'

'You showed me.'

'I know you know his story.' Embarrassed: 'I'm just trying to get it off my chest.'

'Talk about whatever you feel like, Abe. I'm here to listen.'

'Well, so he and my mother came out here. Devoting his whole life to the victims. Believing he owed something to history. Even joined the SACP, although he was never a Marxist's backside. But he always said they were the only ones who cared about the victims in those days. Tried to *do* something for them. Cost him four, five spells in prison. Broke his health. Which wasn't difficult, it was already shaky when he came out of Auschwitz. A shadow of a man. But glowing with love. God, he had more love in that wispy little frame of his than twenty ordinary people. And ever since I was a child all I wanted to do was what he did, be like he was. With the result that I even neglected Abby. And she was the one person I wouldn't have wanted to do it to.'

'You never heard from her again?'

'No. Better that way, if you think about it. But it cracked me up about the child. She must be a big girl now. Fourteen. Can you imagine? Her mother's spitting image and God knows, Abby was stunning. Tiny person, the slightest wind could blow her over.' Suddenly whimsical: 'Like a little candle burning in the wind.' Then he abruptly reined in his emotion. 'But it's all over. Long ago. Sharon was only two when they left. Goodbye note on the pillow.' For a minute or so he smoked in silence. Then threw away the half-smoked cheroot and felt for the next.

'And Cathy was the first woman since then?' He knew the answer; but he wanted to keep David talking.

'Yes. After almost twelve years. Happened at the worst time imaginable too. You saw for yourself what my work was like last year. Ever since 'eighty-four, when the unrest first broke out. That was when I decided it simply wasn't enough being a doctor. All those kids. The small corpses. Some of them two or three years old. Babies shot on their mothers' backs. From behind. And the maimed. Buckshot. Birdshot. Rubber bullets. Real bullets. Batons. Sjamboks. It was no longer enough to heal the wounded, bury the dead. There was another kind of disease that had to be cured. A cancer that had to be cut out. And I knew I had to do something. I couldn't just look on while every day the country came to resemble more and more the Reich my parents had told me about. Out of the question. And then I met Freddie.' Justin. 'And our group began to work together. And suddenly there was Cathy.' He shook his head, incredulous. 'Do you remember how rude I was to her in the beginning? Vicious. I didn't want her to come near me. It was because from the very first day I realised, Oh God, this is bad news. This one I can't ward off. She's in my blood already. A malaria parasite. Sounds awful to put it like this. But that was how I felt about it.' A pause. 'But it was no use trying to fend her off or pretend she wasn't there.'

'I think I'm only beginning to understand how unbearable it must have been for you to stay away from that hospital. Now that Suzie is dead too –'

'I knew you'd understand. More than the others. Although it's hard to express what Freddie has meant to me.' He stared at the birdcages, through them, beyond them, seeing what Thomas could not see. 'Freddie was right, of course. I still hoped I could go to Tygerberg, tell them I was her GP, I had a right to see her. But he'd found out about the guards from Judy. I would have walked right into it. So there was no other option.' He looked back at Thomas and shook his head. 'But that's spilt milk. No use carrying on about it now. Cathy is dead. She's to be buried tomorrow, it was in the papers, you must have seen it.'

'Yes, I saw it. And in a way – for God's sake don't misunderstand me, Abe, but perhaps, in a way, it's better like this. At least now you can be sure they'll never get to her. If she'd regained her consciousness –'

'She's dead!'

'So is Suzie.'

'Why do you keep on saying that?'

'Because it's important you take that into account. I know it can't change anything about your pain. But we knew from the beginning' – he weighed his words very cautiously – 'it's the one thing we've had to come to terms with. I mean: that there was a price to be paid. And that we had to be prepared for it.' A pause. He insisted, 'Isn't that so?'

'I know. And I've always been ready to pay the price myself. I can take whatever comes my way. It's something I've sorted out with myself years ago. But what one isn't prepared for is the price you pay when *others* are sacrificed. The ones you love.'

'What do you think Cathy would have done – what would you have expected of her – if you were the one who got killed?'

David stared at him in silence.

'Answer me, Abe. I'm asking you this because that's what made the difference for myself. I know Suzie would never have given up, or even hesitated for one minute. Perhaps women are stronger than us. But don't you think for that very reason we owe it to them?'

David drew a deep breath, stubbed out his cheroot on the edge of the bench and flicked away the messy remains. 'Of course,' he said.

But on the question of attending the funeral he remained adamant. How could anyone expect him *not* to go? Perhaps, if he'd been able to see her again after the shooting, he might have been more 'reasonable'. But there had never been a farewell of any kind. He felt he owed it to her. It was the least he could do. To round it off. If there was any real risk involved, fine, then he'd have no choice. But what could possibly be deduced from his attending a funeral? 'In any case,' he trumped, 'didn't you see this morning's paper? That explosion in Durban last night. The SB believe we are involved, they're looking for us there. No one expects us here. It's an ordinary funeral, no special occasion. And I haven't even met her mother yet.'

And then, earlier this evening – Thomas stared past Lisa at the dying coals – there had been the news on TV: the security police have pounced on the funeral of Miss Christine Pienaar. Several people have been arrested, including a well-known Cape Town doctor, David Blumer. No further details have been released, but an important announcement can be expected at any moment. Informed sources indicate that there may be a connection with the bomb attack on the life of the state president two weeks ago.

The Bonnard print on her wall: the artist's remarkable sense of space: the scene is focused on a nude woman in front of a mirror, but in the mirror is reflected a scene from outside. Neither can exist, is conceivable, without the other.

Once he crawled from under his blankets to feed the fire with the last few vine stumps in the cardboard box he'd brought in earlier. The coals were smouldering very low by now. With a fire-iron he stirred the old embers, turning up their glowing red bellies. Bluish smoke began to whirl up into the chimney. Outside it was still raining, less violently now, a distant steady rustling in the dark.

'You asleep?' he asked after he'd wormed himself in under the bedclothes again; she'd been silent for so long.

'No,' she mumbled lazily.

'Can I ask you something?'

'What?'

'This morning –'

334

'What about this morning?' She sounded on her guard; cautious, also defiant. (Was she expecting him, he wondered, to refer to the scene in the bathroom? But there was no need at all for that any more.)

'Why didn't you go to work? When I asked you at breakfast table you didn't answer.'

'I took the day off,' she said casually. 'I needed time to think. Yesterday was pretty awful. I'm not sure what I'm still doing in that place.'

'What happened yesterday?' he asked, peering at her in the red gloom.

'Nothing out of the ordinary. I mean, if one looks at it in isolation. Problem is it builds up all the time, every bloody day there's something new.' She fell silent again; he got the impression that she was reluctant to go on. But after a few minutes she did.

A new girl in the school. Registered a fortnight before. But no one could cope with her. Obstinate as a rock. Especially towards the principal, the famous Siebert. By the time they'd handed her over to Lisa – after she'd already spent a week in solitary ('and solitary, God knows, is *solitary*, I promise you') – she was already so intractable that nothing could leave a dent on her carapace.

After Lisa had done all she could, with infinite patience, to put her at ease – playing a folk tape, offering her tea, cautiously steering their small-talk towards an interview – the girl suddenly, viciously, snarled at her, 'Ag man, fuck you!'

Unperturbed, Lisa looked her in the eyes. It wasn't her first experience of the kind.

'Fuck you too,' she said. Then sat back, crossing her legs. 'And now that we've got that off our chests, how about getting started?'

Suddenly the girl burst out laughing. It soon turned into hysterics. But it was a breakthrough. And by yesterday she was ready to talk. She'd been living with her father, but he'd remarried and begun to find her a nuisance. She took to wandering about on her own, at all hours. One evening, as on many other occasions, she ended up in a disco until two or three in the morning. Not having any transport, she set out on foot, bottle in hand. Man in a car following her for several blocks, pulling up beside her at last, offering her a lift. Better than walking four kilometres. Seemed an ordinary enough bloke, sober suit, collared and tied. But instead of taking her to Woodstock where she lived he headed for Muizenberg. Drove right on to the beach, dragged her out. At first she tried to plead with him, offered him wine, made all kinds of promises. He lost his cool, became violent. There was quite a tussle. Then another car arrived. Man got out, asked if he could help. She ran to him and grabbed hold of him, crying and laughing at the same time, said yes, yes, oh please, yes, help me, help me. Right, he said, only a pleasure. So he held her by the arms for the first man to strip off her jeans and they took turns raping her on the bonnet of his car. Then dumped her right there – spitefully taking even her jeans with them – and drove off.

Her father gave her hell when she got home the following day. There was a court case, but the men got off, said it had been with consent, actually she'd led them on. Her father and stepmother were totally confused; also at the end of their tether. Which was how she ended up in the industrial school.

'What did you do?' asked Thomas.

'Shit, man, what *could* I do? I've told you all about that place already. One tries everything, but it's like a wall right round you. There's only one magic answer Siebert and his gang have to everything, and that's discipline. An obstreperous girl like that's got to be broken in, otherwise there's no end to your problems. Time after time after time, Anton. I don't know why, but this specific girl, Loekie, really got to me. So I went back to Siebert.'

In his customary formal way the principal had let her into his office, but without inviting her to sit; she'd taken a seat unbidden.

'Trouble again, Miss Lombard?'

'I hope not, Mr Siebert. It's about Loekie Barnard.'

'Oh that little mare. Had problems with her from day one. I told you, didn't I? She needs a very firm hand.'

'Mr Siebert, all I'm asking for is one week.'

'To do what?'

'Let her go to town with me in the afternoons. Get some fresh air. She might even spend a night with me. Mr Siebert, all this child needs –'

'Miss Lombard, how many times have we had this conversation in the last months? How many more times must I tell you –'

'You haven't given me a single chance yet, Mr Siebert.'

'Because I know exactly what the result will be. Miss Lombard, you're – what? – in your early twenties –'

'I am twenty-five, sir.'

'Exactly. Wet behind the ears. I have more years of experience behind me than you've been in this world.'

She'd lost her temper. As so many times before, even though she knew she shouldn't. 'What kind of experience, Mr Siebert?' And, before he could answer: 'Destroying children's lives? Getting off on seeing them broken in your hands? Of lording it over others? It's a record anyone with a fraction of a conscience should be ashamed of.'

He rose. 'You are very close to your limit, Miss Lombard. If there's one thing I cannot stand –'

'– it's insubordination. I know. Somehow you end up saying it every time.' She got up and went to the door.

Behind her, he shouted, 'Sit!' So loudly, in such a rage, that she stopped. 'I still have a few things to say to *you*, Miss Lombard.'

She remained standing.

'The way you dress, for one. What respect do you think children can have for you if you go about like – like a – like something in a bazaar?'

She was deadly calm now. 'Mr Siebert, I don't know what's wrong with my clothes. They're clean. All my seams are properly sewn up. I'm covered from my neck to my ankles.' A demonstrative flare of the Indian kaftan. 'I'm wearing socks and shoes. I'm wearing a bra and panties. Would you like to see?'

Without any warning, she bent over and grasped the hem of her dress and scooped it up to below her chin. And remained standing like that.

'Miss Lombard!' He stuttered in rage.

'Satisfied, Mr Siebert?' She let go of the dress; it fell back. She went up to his desk, propping herself up on her hands to lean over as far as she could. 'Now let me tell *you* something about clothes.' What she was wearing at that moment, she said, was the same clothes she wore with her friends. She wasn't pretending to be what she was not. As for him and his staff, with their suits and ties and badly zipped-up flies, preparing to look God Almighty in the face without batting an eyelid, what sins were *they* hiding? 'You know what you make me think of, Mr Siebert? An old-time farm shithouse with a doily on the lid.'

Too bloody awful; well over the top. She knew it. She could bite off her tongue afterwards. Not for what she had done to him, or to herself, but to Loekie. To all the girls in her care. For it was they who would have to bear the brunt of it, no one else.

'My mother always warned me to keep a guard before my tongue, or I'd talk myself straight into hell. You know how many times she washed my mouth out with soap? And all for bloody nothing.'

All of that, Thomas thought, dismayed, had been happening to her while he was going on with the business of his life. He hadn't known anything about it at all. Suddenly it felt like a dereliction of duty, of responsibility. But how much of it was he expected to assume? Or *did* it all concern him? What right did anyone, ever, have to say: This, and this, and that I choose as my responsibility; the rest is irrelevant, I cannot, will not, cope with it?

Unnervingly, as if she knew exactly what he was thinking, she said, 'Tell me what to do, Anton. Should I stay on there? Should I get out?'

He stared into the fire, trying to think of an answer.

'There was something you said on the plane that day,' she said, 'which keeps bugging me.'

'What was that?'

'Something like: One must try to make what you *want* to do coincide with what you *ought* to do. So now I'm asking you: What do you think I "ought" to do?'

'Suppose I give you an answer, will you do it?'

A brief laugh in the dark. 'Probably not.'

'You see?'

'You think I should blow up the school?' she asked. The laugh that accompanied it was too shrill for her hoarse voice.

'Will it help?'

'No.'

'Then perhaps you shouldn't.'

'So you're one of the pacifists.'

He was being drawn into a discussion he would have preferred to avoid; and it was all the more dangerous for announcing itself in such a casual, mocking way.

'Not necessarily,' he said, trying to keep his voice neutral. 'I mean, there are situations – You don't want to blow up Loekie together with your Mr Siebert, do you?'

'Perhaps I'd be doing her a favour.' A pause. 'And you still haven't answered my question.'

'If I were in your position – if you'd asked me this the day on the plane I might have said, "Go right ahead, blow up the place. Otherwise, leave while you can still do so with some dignity." But tonight I'd say, and don't ask me why: Stay. Give it another try. Try *everything* you can. And if in the end you find there is no other way, then let them throw you out. Don't make it easy for them.'

'Mm.' She was quiet for quite a while; then shivered, and moved in under her duvet again.

'Does it make any sense?'

'Why would you have said something different on the plane?'

He must have known that she wouldn't let it pass so lightly.

'Because at that stage I still had my job,' he mocked.

'I wish you hadn't said that.'

'Why?'

'Because this isn't a game any more. Because I don't *want* it to be a game. One gets tired of playing games.' She turned her face away, to the fire. 'I've chickened out so many times before,' she said. 'Relationships. Work. The one occasion I ventured into politics. If you can even call it that. Now that was *really* a mess. Every time I chickened out. But what gets my goat is this: I mean, suppose I decide to see it through for once, isn't that just another way of being chicken? Because what will happen if I run away?'

'You need a manager,' he said playfully. 'To handle your life for you.' Realising immediately it was the stupidest thing he'd said all night.

'Thanks,' she said very quietly. And then: 'Fuck you.'

The rain, as far as he could make out, had stopped outside. But a wind was coming up. There were branches scraping on the roof.

'If I do have a problem,' she said at last, 'it's that I've always had too *many* people trying to run my life for me.'

'Sorry.'

Presumably she didn't even hear him. In a strained voice she went on, 'My dearly beloved father who tried to make me all over again. Must have been his idea of rebirth. My mother who refused to "take any nonsense". My teachers. Only one person has always accepted me the way I am and that's Erik.' Another impatient scraping of the branches in the gutter. She felt for her glass, found it, discovered it was empty and poured some more wine, held out the bottle to him. He took it from her and poured for himself. It was two-thirds empty.

'At university, my professors. Even my friends. And then the men. Especially the men. Who regarded it as their divine duty to shape me to their image. Including Martin.'

'Martin?' he dared to ask.

'The one who lived here with me.' Curtly: 'He's history anyway.'

339

A long silence; only the branches moving outside. 'Even the year I spent in Europe. I'd never felt so free before in my whole life.' Her voice was losing its angry edge, becoming an even flow of words like before, an easy stream on which he felt himself drifting as she, too, abandoned herself to it. 'Erik was supposed to have gone with me, it was what we'd always dreamt about. But he had to finish his medical studies first. I drew every cent of the money I'd inherited from Mother – she'd have turned over in her grave if she'd known what I was using it for. On the road all the time. In Arles I picked up this man. Or he me. I was on my way to Italy, so was he, and we decided to join forces. One of the best pals I've ever had. I mean, we weren't really lovers, nothing heavy anyway. From time to time it so happened that we – you know? If one of us felt a bit down, or if we'd had a particularly good bottle of wine and suddenly felt generous and sharing. For the rest it was – just good. But then –'

She drifted on; took him with her, their hands invisibly clutched. And he had the curious, unsettling impression, as he lay there listening to her and to the night rustling outside, that this was not an evening like any other, and that in remembering it later it wouldn't be either, it could never again fade away, dissolve, and be forgotten or rejected, disowned, but would remain a space which somehow, perhaps even against their own wishes, would darkly concern them; a space in which each had relinquished something to the other, had given himself, herself, hostage, had placed themselves at risk; hours which tuned them in to one another, changing them, shifting their understanding of each other and of the world, perhaps fatally, perhaps for ever. (But how?)

'Don't get me wrong,' said Lisa. 'There was no great scene, the guy was much too decent for that. I simply discovered that remaining with him was beginning to cramp my style. And one gets set on one's own independence; even if it's no more than an illusion of independence. So I broke up and went on alone. To prove I could.' Her bony shoulders moved under the duvet which slid down from them. 'But the outcome wasn't so hot either, for then I had to spend all my time fending off strangers. And Jesus, I mean, look at me, it's not as if I've got all that much to offer. But that's precisely what made me so mad. To see how practically every single male I met on my hitchhiking regarded it as perfectly natural to take a chance with me. My only choice was whether to resist or not. And if I did, they took it as an insult, which was enough reason for them to insult *me*. Because then all of a sudden I was stuck-up or a bitch or a cock-teaser or frigid or simply abnormal. Can you understand what that does to you when it is repeated day after day after day? I started missing the guy quite desperately. I wanted to be back with Erik. And that also made me angry. I mean, hell, was there nothing I could do or enjoy on my own? I couldn't make the grade *with* someone else, and I couldn't do *without* them either. I tell you, I got so sick and tired of it all that one day I just packed my rucksack and came back. Chickening out once again. Story of my life.'

2

'– and then one comes back,' said Lisa. It had grown very dark in the room now. The coals glowed a dark red through black. 'And in the beginning you think you can change the whole world. You're full of energy. You have faith. Your eyes see clearly, there are no skins on them any more, you can look right into the sun. But slowly you get used to it again. You don't get indignant any more. It all seems normal again. It's the only way you can survive. I mean, one can't live without eyelids. And so, in order to survive, you learn to compromise again. You try to persuade yourself that the establishment can be reformed from inside. That is why I've lasted so long under Siebert. Until one day one discovers that there are other reasons. The real reason is that it's simply easier not to rock the boat. Only problem is, once you realise it, how can you live with yourself any longer? How can you keep your self-respect? Because once you've lost that you've lost your freedom too.'

'I know,' he said. 'I also ran away to Europe. And came back.'

(– The tulip farm near Haarlem – harvesting grapes to the south of Aix – through Germany to Scandinavia – Amsterdam and the Hague, in search of traces of my ancestor Hendrickus Willemszoon – grey pigeons in Trafalgar Square – and nowhere do I find peace, there is no escape, everywhere I find myself pursued by what I've hoped to leave behind – and then, at last, Mum's telegram about Dad's illness –)

'I'm desperate, Anton, I tell you. One keeps on working oneself up, but it's no use just talking-talking-talking. One reaches a point where you've got to break out and *do* something. But what? I told you on the plane already, remember: sometimes I understand only too well what drives people to –' She broke off.

'Violence?' he asked, protected by the dark.

'The question is,' she said, without attempting to answer, 'how can you be sure it isn't just a subjective, egoistical reaction? What difference does it make to the world? Life gives a small hiccup, then it goes on again. If I do something I'd like it to have some meaning for others as well. To give them a bit of hope, open up some space. The difference between making love and masturbating.'

'You think violence can only be destructive?'

'Absolutely. Even if it isn't necessarily in the usual sense of the word: I mean, not simply because something or someone is wiped out. But because of what you do to yourself. I'm very confused about it all, Anton. Don't laugh at me. I'm still treading water, I'm looking for solid earth.' A pause. A small ember suddenly exploded in the fireplace, scattering a spray of sparks up into the chimney, like a shooting star. For an instant he saw her face illuminated by it, her large grave eyes. 'I think what I'm trying to say is that whenever you're forced to choose sides, to commit yourself to a programme or a cause, it diminishes something inside you because then there are so many other things you exclude, so many other doors you close to yourself.' She sat up again, spreading her open hands to the dull glow from the fireplace. 'Or do you think I'm just trying to find excuses not to get involved? But involved in what? It isn't kicks I'm looking for, Anton. I want to *do* something, I want to fit in somewhere. I don't want to go on buzzing like a fly in a bottle. Can you understand that?'

'You sure you weren't in the French Revolution in a previous life?' he asked. 'Don't you by any chance remember a man in a bath? A man with a skin disease and a turban round his head?'

'Is mocking all you can do?'

'If only you knew how serious I am, Lisa.'

'I have this feeling that for a long time, for years, I've been preparing myself for something. I'm standing at the edge of a precipice, but I'm afraid to jump because I don't know what's on the other side.'

The red glow had faded from the ceiling, but a faint glimmer still flickered from the fireplace over their mattresses. Outside, the branch was still scraping against the gutter, but it was a pleasant, reassuring sound that confirmed their snugness inside. Sleep invaded him like a slow deep tide.

'Tell me a story, Anton?' she asked suddenly, drowsily. 'When we were small Erik often put me to sleep like that. He still does, sometimes. He has a wonderful imagination.'

'I don't really know any stories.'

342

'Then make up something.'

For a while he lay sorting through thoughts and memories jumbled in his mind like so much cherished junk in boxes under a bed. Then he had an inspiration.

'Once upon a time there was a man called Hendrick Willemszoon, a very ordinary man who lived with his wife and innumerable children near Rotterdam. Nothing extraordinary ever happened in their lives. But one day he decided it couldn't go on like that. He had to break out and start a new life. So he abandoned his wife and his family and his work and his responsibilities and went off to Texel from where the ships set sail to places all over the world. He waited until there was no one near, and then crawled into a barrel of salted pork on a ship that was preparing to sail to the Cape of Good Hope. Many months later, when he arrived at the Cape, famished and half-dead from scurvy –'

Playful, relaxed, giving full reins to his imagination, he spun out his tale in the dark. When he stopped, at last, there was no sound from under the duvet on the narrow mattress next to his. He could hear her breathing deeply and peacefully. She sounded fast asleep. He could feel himself drifting off too.

But suddenly he heard her utter a small amused chuckle, so softly that he wondered whether she was talking in her sleep.

'I lied to old Siebert,' she said. 'Just as well my dress couldn't lift any higher. I wasn't wearing a bra.'

3

– The irony of it. That what is usually regarded as the most insignificant and coincidental, the least essential, the most inconsequential – the body, flesh and blood – should in the end turn out to be by far the most precious, the most indispensable, not only of what one has but of what one is. As a doctor I've always learned to respect the body. This goes without saying. But also not to overestimate it. It *is* only flesh and blood. It is mortal. Now, in the rare and unpredictable minutes I am left alone, dare to relax, I crouch in a foetal position (not easy, with the chains and foot-irons), roll myself into a ball, hug myself, inhale my own smell. There is some comfort in it. It confirms that I still exist. Here, within my private contours, my borders circumscribed, my limits fixed. I. Only when I have come to terms with this abused, repulsive, stinking thing can my thoughts soar.

Another irony. I have never been as free as I am now.

So free that I must rein myself in to control my wandering thoughts. Otherwise it leads to chaos. Father would have approved. In Auschwitz he used to say, this was how he approached life. Chose for every day a topic to explore, to structure. The Hegelian symmetries of thesis, antithesis, synthesis. The topics would vary. Sometimes he would chose a cabbage to focus on, carrot leaves, the mould on a piece of bread. On other occasions perhaps Moses on Sinai, the dating of the Pentateuch, the double narrative of Genesis. Or the nature of freedom, the limits of reason, the foundations of ethics. Never a mere wallowing in emotions, an abandonment to guilt or despair.

'Despair, my boy,' I remember him saying, 'is an insult to the future.'

How many times have I used that line to encourage Justin and the others? Because, inevitably, we had our moments of near-despair. Especially in the first days after Christine had been shot.

Christine. I am no longer afraid of thinking about her. I do not exclude any thought about her, however painful or trivial. In fact, I try to pursue these thoughts – disciplined, ordered, systematic – even while their questions break over me.

Strange that her death should have occurred at this juncture, just as I'd begun to consider the possibility of leaving the country after all. Emigrating. Haven't mentioned it to a soul, least of all to Justin. And certainly not that morning in the Gardens when Thomas was delegated to talk to me. It seemed too much like an abject admission of defeat. An acknowledgement not only that it hadn't worked out but that *I* had failed. And yet: the temptation to start again, fresh, in Israel. There is ample opportunity for me and my qualifications over there. And among my own people too. Why keep on struggling, I was beginning to think, on behalf of others, in a society not my own? That was indeed the closest I'd ever come to defeat.

Seen in this light my arrest was the best thing that could have happened to me.

The funeral. Barely a dozen people. A cold, rainy day, just like the previous Friday when the others were buried. A good omen, some believe, a blessing from above.

Her mother from Upington. Small frail woman, tubercular, quite bewildered, in a *dwaal*. I'd never met her before, but recognised her from what Christine had told me. Stood beside her, held my umbrella over her.

'And who would you be, sir?'

'David Blumer, Mrs Pienaar. A friend.'

Her brother and his wife. A young sister who'd come with the mother. A few of her colleagues from CAPAB. One or two others, strangers, who must have had some connection with her. Nothing as gloomy as a funeral among strangers. The parson, who hadn't known her, held a brief service in the ugly church, twice misread her name, expressed his sincere condolences with the family, glanced at his watch, and concluded. In the muddy graveyard, where 'dust unto dust' sounded strangely out of place as the coffin was lowered into a grave half-filled with water, the ceremony was even shorter. The half-hearted hymn was rained out. Showers, showers of blessing.

What had I really hoped to find? Illumination invariably eludes one on occasions like these. And yet there was a need to be there. A ritual cleansing. There is comfort in the very clichés: things that never change. And it was the closest I'd come to Christine since the day we had so hastily abandoned the farm.

Her mother, in a plaintive voice, 'You know, sir, they actually wanted to cremate her. Through the mercy of our Lord I was able to stop them. We're not heathens. What will happen on the Day of Judgement if there's only ashes?'

But ashes are more basic, Mrs Pienaar. Fire is a great cleanser.

At the gate, as we approached in an undignified cluster trudging through the mud, the doors of four, six, eight cars that had arrived unnoticed were opened simultaneously and men in raincoats moved in among us, in twos.

'Do you mind coming with us, sir? Security police. Just routine.'

Even her brother, I noticed, was escorted away by two men. The frail old woman raised her walking stick in defence. I could hear her thin voice screeching. They let her go.

I knew immediately. Justin had warned me. So had Thomas. But the strange thing was that instead of feeling cornered or panicky helpless I was swamped by a great feeling of serenity I had no fear This was something I could resist. Had not Father survived it? Four thousand years of survival came to my aid. I leaned back against the car seat. It is possible that I even smiled.

'You're making a big mistake,' I told them.

They thought I was referring to the arrest.

At that stage they were still very polite. 'We are sorry about the inconvenience, sir. Just doing our job.'

At the station, too, after the formal recording of name, address and other irrelevant details: 'We do apologise, Dr Blumer. There's just a few details we want to clear. If you don't mind waiting here in the office?'

They had taken precautions, of course. Bars in front of the window. Gradually, imperceptibly, the mood changed. Two armed guards at the door.

Once, an officer looked in from the passage: 'Oh it's this trouble-maker again.'

Because there had been other occasions.

Something warned me when they came to take the photograph. Not that I showed my feelings. An anonymous man in a grey suit brought me a cup of tea.

'Mind if I smoke?' I asked.

'Go ahead.' I was already beginning to suspect that it wasn't likely to happen again soon.

Three hours and twenty minutes. I registered it very precisely. Then four men came in, past the guards. One sat down at the table opposite me, an ordinary office table covered with a grey blanket; another took up position by the window; two remained just inside the door, which they had closed behind them.

'Right, Blumer. We're listening.'

There was no doubt any more: I was no longer 'Doctor' to them. I knew there was a long stretch ahead of us. Immeasurably long.

That was six days ago. No, seven. Must make sure. Once one loses one's hold on time, the erosion sets in. Trivialities are important. But it's difficult to keep track if the division between day and night gets blurred. I have only been left alone twice to sleep. There is no window in this cell. I don't know if the sun is shining or if it is night. Seven. Yes, I think it's seven.

To start with, there was only a long conversation. I was even allowed to sit. Only my watch and my glasses were removed. I find it difficult to see without them but in a way it makes it easier.

Where –?

When –?

Who –?

What –?

More and more insistent, more focused, less general and diffuse.

'Exactly what were you doing on that farm outside Paarl, Blumer?'

'Who were the others with you? Think well.'

'Why did you leave Christine Pienaar behind?'

They made a point of continually coming back to her. Insinuations gradually made way for direct taunts, more and more vicious.

346

'You got a good innings with the lady?'

'Was she a good fuck? Seems she had a whole bag of tricks. Cunt like Du Toit's Kloof tunnel.'

I manage to remain detached from it all. Concentrate on other things. Try to recall exactly what Abby looked like when I first met her in Edinburgh. Our honeymoon in Scotland. The bent little woman, tough as heather, we stayed with on the Isle of Skye.

The questions go on and on. Sharpened and honed like razors. I must think about other things. My memories of Abby are becoming precarious.

Indistinct faces swim up towards me from undefined space, are briefly focused in my myopic stare, drift away again. The voices remain constant, taking turns, working up to a crescendo.

'Listen, Blumer. Last few times you were here you were handled with gloves, right. We were playing games. This time it's serious. It's murder. Terrorism. Get that?' Another face. Broad and tanned. Stale beer on his breath. The brigadier, I remember him from previous times. 'Don't want you to have any illusions about this, Blumer. Think because you got a white skin you're safe? You'll soon find out in this place you're less than a kaffir. What happened to people like Biko or Aggett can happen to you too. Do we understand each other? We don't like communists.'

Others take over. New faces looming like poisonous mushrooms in the light. Questions, questions.

Unexpectedly – it must be some time during the night, perhaps even the early dawn – a voice sounding suspiciously sympathetic: 'Man looks tired. Perhaps we should give him a break. Take him to the showers. Then we can start fresh again.'

I was naked in the jet of cold water when the four men came in. Youngish, all of them. With lengths of rubber hose. One with a baton.

They haven't given me my clothes back yet. Just as well, perhaps, I don't think I can dress myself unaided. I believe some of my ribs are broken. Breathing is painful. Life is difficult.

The problem is that it never stops. The methods are not important. A total lack of originality, no real ingenuity, all so predictable, so crude. If one compares this to what Father told us about Auschwitz. Those were artists in their métier. Mine have been pretty basic. Too hurried. Perhaps they are pressed for results by someone higher up.

The brigadier has paid me another personal visit. Honoured indeed. Benevolent uncle. Concerned about my health. Says he.

'Blumer, what are you trying to do to yourself, man? Can you tell me why? We know everything already. Heroism is such a waste of energy.'

'If you already know everything, why do you keep coming back to me?'

'The satisfaction of a job well done.' He leans over me. His jacket smells of cigarette smoke. I'm dying for a fag. He offers me one, but snatches it back before I can light it. 'Let's first get this over and done with, Blumer.' His pronunciation lends an old-fashioned obscenity to my name. 'Then you can smoke as much as you like, hey?'

'What do you want to know?'

'Look, we already caught Nina Jordaan. Unfortunately she tried to resist, so we had to use force. I suppose you know it already?'

'_'

'And we have Thomas Landman too.'

'_'

'He's told us everything we wanted to know.'

'I don't believe you.'

'Then why don't you tell it the way *you* see it?'

'_'

'Landman blamed you for everything. You aware of that?'

I feel like grinning, but restrain the impulse. My face must be so unrecognisable as it is, heaven knows how a grimace will contort it.

'You not interested in defending yourself?'

'Bring him to me, let him say it in front of me.'

'Look, Blumer.' For the first time he is showing signs of impatience. 'Here I'm giving you a chance to tell your own story. I don't like to see you getting hurt. I want to protect you. But I'm afraid if you don't co-operate I'll have you to pass you on to Major Swanepoel. You must have heard of him.'

'I have nothing to say to you, Brigadier.'

'We've had so much trouble with you already over the years.'

'I have never looked for trouble.'

Early as 'seventy-six. You remember?'

'That child with his back full of buckshot whom I took home to look after?'

(That was when Abby and I had our first major quarrel. 'David, you cannot expose us all to danger. You have no right to.')

'It was a criminal you sheltered. A potential murderer.'

'No. A young boy who'd gone to buy bread for his mother when he was stopped by a Casspir.'

'If he really was innocent, why did you smuggle him out of the country before we could get to him? All the way to Lesotho. Where he joined the enemy?'

'I helped him to save his life. What happened to him afterwards was out of my hands.'

'And another year or so later' – he presses his finger on an indistinct green object in his other hand, presumably a folder – 'you testified in a terrorism trial where you tried to bring a district surgeon into discredit.'

'Because you'd blackmailed him. Forced him to sign a false report on an autopsy. While I'd seen the body myself. Of a man who'd been perfectly healthy at the time of his arrest.'

'You illegally entered a state morgue after the autopsy had already been done.'

'I was acting on the family's instructions.'

The brigadier gives a bored sigh. Consults his folder again. 'And on another occasion you obstructed the police in the execution of their duties.'

'I refused them permission to interrogate a young girl with a serious abdominal wound because I had to operate on her.'

'And afterwards she disappeared without a trace.'

'Don't blame me, Brigadier. I would have preferred her to go to court. It may well have been to your own advantage that she was too scared.'

'You've made quite a career out of testifying against the police ever since the troubles began in 'eighty-five.'

'I happen to be a doctor. I give medical evidence.'

'Is that enough reason to always cast suspicion on the forces of law and order?'

The split infinitive pains me, but I decide to ignore it. 'Your Terror left me no other choice.'

'Our what?'

'What you choose to call the State of Emergency.'

A warning sound from his throat. Then he turns some more pages, suddenly slams his folder shut. 'And four or five times you were arrested about illegal posters or protests.'

'_'

'Blumer, man, what I don't understand is *why*? You could have had a nice comfortable life. What's the sense of landing in trouble for the sake of others?'

'What I have done I did as much for myself as for others.'

'That is a lot of sentimental drivel.'

'I know. We Jews have a sentimental streak. As I see it, other nations sometimes experience a blessed moment of illumination when they believe in the common humanity of all people. We Jews have lived in that faith for four thousand years.'

'And where did it get you?' he patted on his folder as if to dust it. 'Where did it get *you*?'

'What I did was the least anybody with a conscience could do.'

'A communist has got no conscience, man!'

'I'm not a communist.'

'You father was a communist.'

'It's a pity you never knew my father, Brigadier. Do you know, until the day of his death, whenever he passed a crust of bread in the street, he would bend over and pick it up. A habit he could never give up after Auschwitz.'

'Don't try to move me to tears, Blumer. You denying that your father was a communist?'

'In those days the party was still legal.'

'Did he change after it got banned?'

'Brigadier, is it really necessary to talk about the dead?'

'The dead?' Suddenly he becomes very agitated. 'The dead, Blumer? Do you know how many died two weeks ago in the bomb you people exploded?'

'What do you mean by "you people"?'

An irritable gesture. 'Look man, you're not here to ask me questions. You're here to answer mine.'

I shake my head.

'Tell us about this Landman chap.'

'What makes you think I even know him?'

'You have all been identified. No use you trying to play around. Be reasonable, Blumer. Why make it difficult for all of us?'

'Brigadier, I had a relationship with Christine Pienaar. That has nothing to do with anyone else. There was nothing subversive about it.'

'Your "relationship", as you call it, leaves me cold. What we want to know about is that bomb on the Parade.' He becomes almost paternal. 'You know, Blumer, you can do yourself a favour – you can do the whole country a favour – including those underdogs you're always so interested in — if you tell us where that terrorist Thomas Landman is hiding.'

'I thought he had already told you everything?'

His large tanned face turned crimson. He turned towards the door. From there, in a theatrical move, he looked back. 'You've had your chance, Blumer. Now you'll have to explain to Major Swanepoel.'

When Swanepoel arrives he has two assistants with him.

A truly monotonous affair. All I am really concerned with is for the others to be safe. Justin, Thomas, Rashid. (How few are left!) For a moment he had me worried about Thomas. Now I am reassured again. Although it is distressing to know that they have found out about him. How, where, could they have discovered it? But no matter what happens, they will never hear it from me. This, at least, I owe to those I have so nearly failed.

I've been intrigued by Thomas. In the beginning I wondered whether he wasn't too gentle. Too soft for the job. *She* was the tough cookie. Nina. But gradually I came to respect him. During the time we spent on the farm at Paarl he was the negotiator, the strategist. He could turn the surly old man from whom we rented the place round his little finger. And his planning was meticulous; there was nothing he didn't consider. Thorough. Nothing could rush him. This was a bit irritating at times. But above all he was resourceful, original. Not that he'd try anything hazardous, but he was never content with old, hackneyed methods. It was he who persuaded Justin to use Semtex rather than the better-known explosives.

Ironical that what they found in the house was the cache of conventional weapons, ammunition, limpet mines. If it hadn't been for that, if we'd stuck to the Semtex, we could have remained on the farm to the end. Christine would still have been alive. As it happened we'd only agreed to keep the arms in the loft for a fortnight or so while they were still hot. All my fault. Thomas was dead against it, but I insisted, they were needed for another cell, of which I'd been a member before I was transferred to Justin. Something that had been arranged months before; many lives had been endangered, all along the route the consignment had followed, from Lusaka to Harare to Gaborone, across the border, to Johannesburg, then P.E., at last Cape Town. The real destination was Guguletu, but after the SB had pounced on Mabusa, we had to find a safe place. A few weeks only. Absolutely essential. And against Thomas's advice I persuaded Justin.

Right there things began to turn against us. All of it, in retrospect, quite unnecessary; avoidable. Christine's death above all. But who

351

am I to talk about 'unnecessary'? It was Thomas himself who always insisted, 'There's no such thing. If something happens, it means it had to. Otherwise it wouldn't have happened.'

An atavistic Calvinist streak in him? I often teased him about it. As he tackled me about my Jewishness. It was he, more than anyone else, who made me realise how similar Afrikaners and Jews can be. For better and for worse.

Previously, I must confess, I never had much contact with Afrikaners. Avoided them at university: the rockspiders, the hairy-backs. Thomas put me to shame.

Once, on the farm, I told him about a friend of mine who'd been active in student politics in his time, a key figure in NUSAS. Then, after he'd completed his B.Comm.-LLB., he came to me for advice. How could he use his time to the best effect? He wanted to become an activist, he explained. For two years. 'Why two years?' I asked him. He said, 'Because after that I have to take over my old man's business.' Import-export millionaire. When I told Thomas about it he gave his boyish grin. 'I suppose that's the difference,' he said. 'We Afrikaners have nowhere else to turn to one day. We have no space to experiment or play games with political attitudes. We live what we are. Which can be dangerous.'

It had taken him a long time, I discovered, to arrive where he is now. So many chains and obstacles in his laager, which the rest of us never even think about. But once he'd made his choice it was without conditions or compromises. I don't think fire and brimstone can turn him off course.

This is why I must see this through. I am ashamed for having vacillated, however briefly. In my moment of weakness, when I yielded to my private grief, I failed the Organisation. Now at least I have an opportunity to atone for that weakness.

Seven days. This is probably only the beginning, it may continue for a long time yet. But it's something. I am still here. I shall survive. And if they kill me, at least I'll have the satisfaction of knowing what it is I die for. –

4

Then that decisive day, one week later. A fine day, serene and sun-washed, autumnal, blue along the edges. At dusk, when there was as yet no hint of what was about to happen – how bourgeois

He was clearly reluctant. It took several mouthfuls before he could speak. 'Had an emergency. One of the troopies tried to blow his brains out and made a hash of it.' Another swallow. 'Can't understand it at all. He always seemed quite easygoing. Then suddenly, this afternoon, when he had to go on township duty, he packed up.'

'It isn't only on the border that people get bushed,' said Thomas, without looking at Erik.

'But one gets trained to cope,' said Erik. 'That's what the army is there for.'

'One gets trained to fight an enemy,' Thomas said cautiously. He was still looking away, into the fireplace, as if there was a fire burning. 'One gets trained to attack terrorists who want to take over your country. One goes to the army to make the country a safe place for ordinary peace-loving people.'

'So what's wrong with it?'

'All that's wrong with it is that it isn't true. No one prepares you for the discovery that the so-called terrorists are your compatriots who are also fighting to make the country a safe place for ordinary peace-loving people. No one equips you to torture a bound and defenceless prisoner and murder him in cold blood. No one thinks of warning you about driving a Buffel or a Casspir into the townships and firing on children. Not as something exceptional but as a matter of course. Because this is what it is all about. To keep the ruling power in place.'

'You know all the answers, don't you?' said Erik. But he seemed uneasy. He emptied his glass, and held it up to Lisa for more. She refilled it.

'If that was what's been bothering today's troopie,' Erik said in a sudden flush of anger, 'then why didn't he say so?'

Thomas leaned his head back against the sofa. 'How can anyone know beforehand how he's going to react in a crisis?'

'Have you ever had a bomb exploding close to you?' Erik challenged him.

'As a matter of fact, yes.'

'And what did you do?'

Thomas was ready to retort, but suddenly noticing Lisa's warning eyes on him he changed his mind.

'Washed out my pants,' he said playfully.

Erik stared hard at him for a moment, then grinned. 'Run away to fight another day?'

and domestic it all seemed later, looking back: that last time – she came from the bathroom wrapped in a large white towel, a smaller one in a turban round her wet hair, and called from the middle door (she'd returned only a half-hour before from her daily jog):

'If you feel like making your veal for us, I'll slap up a big mixed salad. I've bought us a bottle of French wine.'

'What are we celebrating?'

There were flames in her eyes. 'I've finally told Siebert to stuff his school. This time it's final.'

He stared at her for a minute.

'No,' she said, all of a sudden, as if he'd asked her a question, 'for once I'm not chickening out. I've thought about it and thought about it. Especially after the talk we had last week. It took me a hell of a long time, but now I've jumped.'

Almost confused he half rose from the armchair in which he'd been sitting, then dropped back on the armrest. 'Lisa, are you really sure?'

'I'm going out to buy the things for the salad.'

'I can go.'

'No, I will. I'm just slipping into something. There's a Greek down the road. He always saves the best for me. You can marinade your meat so long. It's in the fridge, and the Marsala is on the kitchen dresser.'

He was still sitting on the armrest, plucking with one hand at a loose thread in the colourful woven cloth that covered it, when she returned from the bathroom, in jeans and a navy and white striped jersey, carrying a basket in her hand, her hair still damp. She smelled of soap and baby powder.

'Ciao.'

She went out; the front door swung shut behind her. He remained where he was, wondering abstractedly: if, that other night, he'd told her to resign, to get the hell out of the place, would she have changed her mind and stayed on? What did he really understand about her? And why should it be important to understand?

Her life, at least, had reached a point of decision, a measure of clarity.

His?

On the morning after Christine's funeral he'd gone out to phone Justin. They'd met at noon, on a deserted beach at Blueberg. Straggling clouds were drifting away, dispersed by a fierce wind. A great cascade of cloud covered the distant mountain. The sea was a deep green. Involuntarily he looked towards Robben Island: that was the view of the Mountain Henry would have had, long ago. But in that weather, through the misty spray of the waves, the island was invisible.

Half an hour after them Rashid also approached across the sand, bent double against the wind. Their backs propped up against the skeleton of an up-ended boat on the beach, they tried to make the most of the imperfect shelter.

'So David's inside.' Justin. His eyes screwed up against the onslaught of fine sand.

'I'm worried about him,' Rashid said candidly. 'The man's shaky nowadays.'

It was Thomas who insisted, 'David won't split. He's tougher than any of us.'

'It's no use speculating.' Justin seemed tired. 'We must be prepared for anything. Rashid and I are reasonably okay. How about you, Thomas?'

'I'll keep a low profile.'

'Is it safe where you're staying?'

'Yes. No one will think of looking for me there.'

'But you don't know the girl.'

'I've come to know her better.'

Rashid shot him a quick quizzical glance. 'What does that mean?'

He grinned. 'Not what you're thinking, Rashid. I'm not interested. But we've had a long chat. She's all right.'

'Not inquisitive?'

'No. And I'm playing it close to my chest.'

Justin looked hard at him. 'You sure you're bearing up? This isn't the time to get weak in the knees.'

'I told you before. It would have been easier if I had something to keep me busy.'

'I know it's hard on you, Thomas. But this is what you've been trained for, right? When we were planning the whole thing – when the bomb exploded – when Nina got killed – when all the other things happened, Christine, David, the lot – all of that was hard enough, but that wasn't the hardest part. The hardest part is *now*. To learn to live with it. To go on. Not to let go, not even for a moment. To keep faith. You hear me?'

'I hear you, Justin.'

'And in case it's any use to you: we have faith in you.'

Thomas smiled briefly, and nodded.

The sand still came sweeping past in a steady drift, churned up around the edges of the decayed boat.

'You really don't think we should move on now that they've got David?' asked Thomas.

'No. I'm sure it's safer for you here in the Cape,' said Justin. 'As I read their thinking, they'll expect the rest of us to scatter after the funeral.' He drew his head in between his shoulders against the wind.

Suits me, Thomas thought. He wouldn't mind staying here. The girl had been good company. They were getting on well. He was making no demands on her life, she on his; it was pleasant to have someone to talk to. And she intrigued him, with her aimless rebellion, her energy, her passion. It no longer bothered him that she reminded him occasionally of Nina. She was sufficiently different, now that he'd come to know her better. She did not threaten anything in his existence.

The only possible source of trouble might be her brother.

Erik had turned up again, late the Friday evening, for the weekend. He'd seemed even paler than before, almost transparent, his dark eyes shining with an unnatural brightness.

Just inside the passage, after Lisa had unlocked the front door to let him in, he'd stopped, gesturing with his head to where Thomas was sitting reading.

'Your guest still here?'

'Yes. Anton is trying to finish a chapter of his thesis.' With innocent mockery: 'Not that I've seen him doing all that much.'

'Then he must have ulterior motives.' He made no attempt to hide his disapproval.

What had again struck Thomas was the uncanny resemblance between them. Neither, he thought, needed a mirror while the other was around. It must be an unsettling feeling, looking in the face of another to acknowledge oneself.

'What's the matter?' asked Lisa. 'You look like death warmed up. Seen a ghost?'

'In a way I have.' Erik hesitated briefly in front of the open door to Thomas's bedroom, then with a small gesture of irritation carried his bag past to the small spare room. Asking over his shoulder, 'You have something to drink?'

She'd already poured the wine – for all three of them – when Erik came back.

'Tell me about your ghost?'

'You can put it like that.' He got up and filled his glass again, remained standing with it in his hand, then announced abruptly, 'I'm off to bed. See you guys.'

The following morning Lisa and Erik had left in her brother's car. For the weekend, they'd said. Lisa had invited Thomas too, but it was obvious that she did it only out of politeness, while Erik stood scowling in the background. Faking gaiety, Thomas had said, 'No, it's time I started doing something about my poor neglected thesis.' And then had faced the dreary weekend on his own. They'd only returned on the Sunday night; and Erik wouldn't stay over. He'd just come in with her to have a bite. But his attitude to Thomas was, quite unexpectedly, more accommodating than before.

As he prepared to leave after the meal, he said with disarming candour, 'Look, Anton, if I seemed rude the other evening, it was just because I was rather fucked by what had happened —'

She must have told her brother off, he thought; he wished he could have heard what she'd said. And replied, 'That's okay. I went a bit over the top myself.'

'No, I've thought about what you said.' A pause. 'I hope we can talk about it again later.'

'Sure. See you.'

Erik paused, smiled unexpectedly, and said, 'Well, look after my sister, will you?'

To which she replied in a huff, 'That's the last I need from anyone.'

For a moment she seemed really vexed. But then she put an arm around her brother's waist and accompanied him outside to his car on the sidewalk in front of the tall myrtle hedge.

He was in the bathroom when he heard her returning from the café into the kitchen.

'Be with you in a minute!' he called, pulling up his zip, pressing the handle.

He could hear no answer.

When he came into the kitchen she was standing at the scrubbed pine table where she'd put down her shopping basket. She stared at him with her large nocturnal eyes. Her face was absolutely white.

'Hello, Thomas.' Her voice sounded unsteady.

He was so startled by the way she looked that he didn't even hear the greeting.

She was preparing, it seemed, to speak again. But then, as if her courage suddenly failed her, without a word, she just pushed the evening newspaper across the table towards him. He could see her hands trembling.

On the front page there was a blown-up photograph of his face. The caption, in white capitals on a red banner, said:

THE FACE OF A TERRORIST?

5

– Like a match suddenly flaring up in a dark room all at once you see everything at the same time this is how it was the moment I saw the picture Anton's face Thomas's face on the front page among the tomatoes and onions and green peppers and garlic and olives and feta cheese I'd brought to the counter nothing isolated or separate or chronological but all of it in one flash and most remarkable of all I didn't even realise it right then it only dawned on me afterwards was that at that moment the one overriding thought in my mind was to run home to warn him before they could find out where he was I was only vaguely conscious of what the paper said that only came later when I reread it took the first street up to the mountain sat down on a green bench under a tree to read with dumb uncomprehending eyes Thomas Landman sought by police believe he may be able to assist them in their enquiries in connection with the attack on the state president's life two weeks ago on the parade assist in their enquiries assist in that didn't mean he'd done it assist in but the caption above the photo said the face of a terrorist no oh no that isn't the face of a terrorist he's staying just up the road from here in my cottage he's quiet and helpful and sometimes very amusing all his stories about working in the whorehouse certainly not a terrorist how many people died in that explosion no I'm sorry it's quite out of the question it can't be him yet the paper says so my heart is throbbing right in my throat I'm trembling so much I cannot fold up the paper again to put it back in the basket he keeps staring at me from that page only a week ago he lay beside me in front of the fire all night and I told him everything that came to my mind absolutely everything withholding nothing I've never opened my heart so unreservedly to anyone before it wasn't just because it was dark and he couldn't see me but because of something in him that encourages one to confide in him and for the first time in God

358

knows how long I was allowed to be me just the way I am and I don't care a fuck if that means nothing to others this is *my* starting point my only landmark even if that is never enough in itself once you've started asking questions you've got to try and change the world to make it more liveable otherwise you choke this I realised in one big flash the moment I saw his photograph and knew *what* it was that made him different made him break into my life like that it was because he'd had the guts to say no to the system and to break out I'm not talking about the bomb we've spent nights and nights arguing about it an argument that may go on for the rest of our lives I'm not talking about murdering and killing and maiming I'm talking about the guts it took to do *something* right or wrong that lies beyond mere morality what matters is to have that lucidity that courage to see what is happening and then to do something about it that's what I'm trying so desperately to explain to you Erik you're the only one apart from Thomas who can understand this and it's imperative that you understand because you are like me you are me and I've been living vicariously through you for so many years until you too began to disappoint me I want to break you open too the way I was torn apart before it is too late my Erik oh God I'm so fucking worried about you if you cannot understand this it will be another failure and defeat for me this one the worst of all

I pushed the newspaper across the table towards him feeling the grain of the wood the coarse scrubbed grain of the wood under my palms but I couldn't utter a sound he must have thought I was terrified of him I just stood there trembling and after some time turned round and fled to my room I wanted to cry but I couldn't I've never been one to cry easily but this time it was quite impossible I just lay on my bed shaking uncontrollably but after a long time it went over it was dark in the house and I got up and went back to the kitchen and found him still sitting there with the paper he didn't look up when I came in and I stood behind him and then he said in a toneless voice and that was the moment time began to flow again and the flood inside me subsided and he said:

'Please don't be afraid. I'll go.'

'I'm not afraid.' I put my hands on his shoulders the shoulders that suddenly looked felt so vulnerable and without myself knowing why I said it I said, 'Is there anything I can do?'

He remained sitting like that for a long time, then with his right hand he touched my hand on his left shoulder and let go again. I went quickly round the table to the other side in a way I could not still cannot explain his touch had quite unnerved me it was I who felt completely exposed without protection as I stood there opposite him and started unpacking the vegetables from the basket and only after a long time dared to ask, a stupid question I suppose:

'How could you do it?'

He looked surprised. After a while he shrugged, and said, 'You can do anything if you must.'

'Even – a thing like that?'

He didn't answer.

But now I was lucid again, I had to talk about it. 'Surely to do a thing like that one must first kill something inside oneself?'

I never thought one's eyes could reveal so much pain.

'Don't you think I had to?' he asked.

'But you're –' it was almost impossible to find words for it. Perhaps it was myself I was subjecting to this inquisition, rather than him. I sat down opposite him. My legs were too shaky to remain standing. 'I can't see how anyone can think of violence as a solution for anything.'

'Do you think one can go on talking about justice and still exclude violence?'

'I'm not talking about principles or theories!' I was suddenly furious, I felt patronised. 'I don't want to discuss what you thought – I want to talk about what *happened*.'

'And why would you want to know?'

'Because you're here under my roof. Because you've entered, without knocking, into my life. Because it's necessary for me to know.' On what impulse did I do that? – stretched my arm across the table and took one of his hands, pulled it towards me, turned it palm up, stroked it with a finger. It looked like the hand of a pianist.

'I asked you a question, Anton.' I stopped, and said, 'Thomas. And I hope you're not going to insult me by telling me that the end justifies the means.'

'No, I won't.'

'And you're not going to tell me that because the government uses violence it demands a violent reaction. If you resort to violence doesn't it make you as bad as your enemy?'

'Would you agree,' he said, 'that there is a difference between a veld fire and the kind of controlled fire one lights oneself to prevent the other one from spreading and destroying everything?'

'The problem with metaphors, Anton, Thomas, is that they take one away from reality. Fire is fire. People are different. And whatever you may have tried to prevent with your bomb, the simple fact is that people got killed.' I could see he was ready to interrupt, but I hadn't finished yet. 'And please don't try to tell me now there are no "innocent" people. And don't try to tell me either that the bomb wasn't meant for them but for the president. *They died.*'

'And for that I am prepared to hang.'

The starkness of his words was like a bucket of cold water on my flesh.

He moved his chair back.

In a sudden panic I jumped up to stand between him and the middle door.

'What's the matter, Lisa?'

'Where are you going?'

'I can't cause you any further problems. You've already done too much for me.'

'Oh stuff all that doing-too-much up your arse!' I was beside myself with agitation. 'Don't make me out to be the SPCA or something.'

'Lisa.' He looked dismayed. 'That's the last thing I meant. But I can't endanger your life.'

'Where can you go to, at this time of the night?'

'I must make some phone calls.'

'There's a phone in the lounge.'

'I cannot phone from here. It's too much of a risk.'

'You can't go out like that either, anybody may recognise you. By this time your photo will have been on TV too.'

'But it's urgent, Lisa. Don't you understand?'

'Then give me the message. I'll phone for you.'

'Are you out of your mind?'

'Why can't I?' I became conscious of how fast he was breathing, as if he were ill.

'Security.'

'You think I'm going to phone the police?' I felt my jaws tighten.

'What do you and I really know about each other?'

I felt insulted more deeply, more viciously, than ever before in my life. Half turning away from him I snapped, 'Well, go then. Do your own phoning. Make sure you find a tickey-box right under a lamp where no one can miss you.'

I came back to the table, past him, and sat down on my chair. He remained standing for a while, then went through to his room. I sat waiting for the front door to open and close. But it was silent. Some time later I heard him coming back. I looked up. He came to the table and put a scrap of paper down before me.

'Here's the number. Whoever answers, just tell them to let Freddy know Peter is okay, he'll contact them tomorrow. Then put down the receiver immediately and get the hell out. Try to find a place some distance from here. And destroy the paper as soon as you've finished.'

It was a woman who answered the telephone. She didn't ask any questions. The moment after I'd put down the receiver I picked it up again. A reflex. To phone Erik. I believed implicitly that *he* would have an answer. But after dialling the first two figures I replaced the telephone, feeling guilty, not for my sake but for Thomas's, for having even considered such a possibility. And then drove home quickly in the buggy. When I got there – on the way back, in a rush of an adolescent sense of cheap adventure I thrust the paper with the number on it in my mouth, and chewed it, and swallowed it – he was in the kitchen preparing the meal. He glanced up. I just nodded. While he expertly went his way in front of the stove I made the salad. It was a blessing to have something to keep my hands busy, though neither of us ate much afterwards; and we both retired early.

I did not expect to sleep at all, yet at some stage I must have drifted off, because it was eight o'clock when I woke up. The house was silent. My head was bursting. I got dressed and went to the kitchen to make coffee. A very old impulse sent me back to my room: I took my *I Ching* from the bedside chest – it had travelled all over the world with me – and took it with me to the kitchen table, where I began to shake the coins in my cupped hands, eyes tightly shut, while the coffee was cooling off.

I remember it precisely. *Iü: heaven above, the lake below.* 'Treading upon the tail of the tiger. It does not bite the man. Success.'

I had a nine on the fifth line of the hexagram. 'Resolute conduct,' said the book. 'Perseverance with awareness of danger.'

Strange how the ritual, that answer, calmed me down.

I was still sitting there, the book open before me, the mug held between my palms, when Thomas came in, wrapped in a towel. He looked exhausted.

'I was hoping you'd sleep late,' I said.

He shook his head. 'It's going to be a busy day.'

Over breakfast we began to discuss the possibilities. Not that there were many. The only more or less safe option seemed to be a drastic new dyeing of his hair. He protested; it would take too long, he argued. But it was either that or tempt fate. In the end he relented.

I went all the way to Cavendish Square on foot – he'd insisted I choose either somewhere far away or a big bustling place – and told them it was for my own hair I needed the dye. A long argument with the so-called beauty consultant who tried to dissuade me from messing up what she called my lovely hair, but I told her it was either that or my boyfriend would drop me, because he only got turned on by redheads. Her snide parting shot: 'Oh my goodness me, *my* boyfriend runs a mile the moment he sees a redhead on the horizon, he always says suppose she's got red pubic hair too, you know, the mere thought gives him the heebie-jeebies.'

Even with the packet in my hands I was still reluctant to go home, although I knew how impatiently he must be waiting for me.

Stalling for time, I went into the butchery on the way. Came past the place and decided there and then to buy meat for the evening, even if there was no chance in hell that he'd still be there by nightfall. I just had to. A kind of exorcism of the unavoidable. Not just any piece of meat either. Something extravagant, something special. The best, most expensive fillet I could find.

As I stood waiting for my fillet to be trimmed, an elderly black man entered. Greying, with a small pointed beard, watery eyes, threadbare clothes, one jacket sleeve held in place at the shoulder by a safety-pin. Taking his time, painfully polite, embarrassed, he studied all the cuts, then pointed at the brawn, the cheapest he could see, and asked for a single slice. The irritable butcher cut a ratty little slice, slapped it in a piece of white paper, put it on the scales, and said:

'Twenty cents.'

The old man put his hand in his pocket and counted out change in his palm: ten cents, twelve, fifteen, seventeen. Felt through all his pockets again and brought out a single cent. Recounted it all: eighteen. Then, expressionless, resigned, he put his money away again and said:

'Sorry, boss, it's all right.'

And went out. The gauze door swung shut after him.

As I went out with my brown paper parcel neatly tied up with string, I bumped blindly into people on the sidewalk because I couldn't concentrate on my surroundings. Not because of a bleeding heart, but because, God knows, there was nothing at all I could do about the whole miserable little incident. I could have offered the old man money – and humiliated him for good. Yet not having done it was even worse. I could have declined to take my own meat. I could have berated the butcher. For what? Was it his fault? Was it mine? Suddenly the whole concept of 'guilt' was no longer adequate to contain what I felt, what had happened, what happens every day.

The helplessness – and the futility – of my entire white existence in this country had been stripped bare in an instant.

I thought: Would it be far-fetched to believe one can throw a bomb for *this*?

I went home. As I put the key in the keyhole I was gripped by sudden panic: what if he'd left already? What if he'd sent me to the shops to give him time to abscond? What if I never saw him again in my life? Because at that moment I knew: if Thomas had left, if he wasn't coming back, I would have missed an opportunity which might never be repeated.

'Thomas?' I called from the door.

'Good God, Lisa, where have you been so long?'

Normally I would have snapped back immediately; now I merely shrugged and said quietly, 'I've brought your stuff. Let's go through to the bathroom.'

It was a complicated process, as I first had to bleach his hair – the beauty consultant had given me all the tips – before we could attempt to change the colour, and the end result was yuch. But the main thing was that it made him look disconcertingly different.

'And now?' I asked after he'd put on his shirt again and began to head for the front door.

'What do you mean?'

'I want to know where you're going.'

'I've got to – talk to my people.'

'And then?'

'It depends on what they decide.'

'You think you may have to leave?'

He nodded.

364

'I'm going with you, Thomas.'

It came out so calmly, as if it was the most obvious thing in the world. All the turbulence, the uncertainty in me had subsided. It was all amazingly clear. Everything that had ever happened to me, it seemed, had pointed towards this.

'If your people have good reasons for deciding against it, I'll accept it. But at least you must come back to tell me. Will you?'

'Do you have the faintest idea of what you'll be letting yourself in for?' He was groping, it seemed to me, for arguments, reasons, excuses. 'This is not a game, Lisa. Do you understand that? It's bloody life or death.'

'It's precisely because I've had enough of playing games. Don't deny me this opportunity.'

Then he left. But I was no longer perturbed. I knew he would come back. —

6

'Do you realise the risk you're running, Thomas?'

'If she wanted to give the game away she'd have done it long ago. Last night or this morning. She'd had more than enough opportunity.'

'You hardly know the woman.'

'I trust her.'

'Do you trust her with your *life*?'

'If she's with me I have a better chance of pulling through. She said herself she could be my alibi.'

'Why? Because it gives her a kick? A bit of adventure? Or because she's got the hots for you?'

'How must I know her motives?'

Rashid: 'If you don't know her well enough to be sure about that, then you don't know her well enough to place your life in her hands.'

He was conscious of Justin's probing, worried eyes observing him.

'I told you, I trust her.'

'A bleeding-heart liberal?' Rashid.

'Maybe. But I'm prepared to take the risk. It's my life.'

'We're in it too. The whole Organisation.'

'She knows absolutely nothing about you and I won't ever tell her. For her own sake as well as for yours. The way we've always treated our helpers.'

'Does *she* know what is at stake?' Justin.

'I've asked her.'

'I'm asking *you*.'

'Does one ever know what is at stake before the crunch comes?'

'We've been trained. For months, some of us for years, we've been prepared for it.'

'Nina had no training before we went to Paarl.'

'But the Organisation spent months vetting her before the time. This one is a novice.'

'Is it her you are worried about, Justin, or me?'

'It's the struggle.'

'David's been caught,' Thomas said. 'But whether he's going to crack up or not is now in his own hands. We can only trust him. That's more or less the position I'm in too. You've got to trust me.'

'David is beyond our reach, you're not.'

'Let's look at the worst scenario,' said Thomas. 'Suppose she fucks it up. Then I get caught. At the very least I'll have the opportunity, before I'm hanged, to put my case – our case – in court. That's not much, but it's better than a total loss.'

'The hell,' said Rashid quickly. 'You'll never see the inside of a court. They'll torture you until there's nothing left of you. A messy end, nothing heroic about it. So don't kid yourself.'

Thomas walked some distance away. They were on the mountain, had come up, one by one, in the cable car, after his telephone call in the late morning. The day had a hard, polished look, blue as sapphire. Far to the south Adamastor's spinal column jutted into the cold sea. A white line of breakers indicated where two oceans met and tumultuously mingled.

– Here, irretrievably long ago, but in this same place, on a lichen-blotched rock, among the tumbled boulders of the summit, Nina said, 'Whatever happens after this, whether it's tomorrow or the day after or whenever: if ever we are tempted to have misgivings about what's happened, then try to remember, Thomas, try to remember it *was* worth while. All of it. Promise?' –

'We want you to survive,' Justin said calmly behind him, his tone concerned and fatherly. 'We've all come to terms with the possibility of failure or death, right. But it's always better to survive and continue with the struggle.'

Thomas turned back to face them. 'And that's precisely why I think we should give Lisa a chance,' he said. 'I'll be less conspicuous with her than on my own.'

'What, exactly, do you propose to do?' asked Rashid, unconvinced.

'That's what we have to plot together. That's why we're here.'

'We can slap up a letter of introduction for the two of you. Journalists on some project. How about that? *Newsweek* or *National Geographic*, we have letterheads on file.'

'Good. But let's keep it low-key. Nothing foreign. They're all suspect. What about a good solid Afrikaans magazine? *Huisgenoot*?'

'Sounds good.'

'A photographer and a journalist,' Thomas suggested with new enthusiasm. 'At last I'll be able to use a camera again.'

'Not a damn.' Justin pulled a sardonic face. 'That'll be looking for trouble, man. Two straight journalists, no photographer.'

Thomas swallowed his frustration; Justin was obviously right.

Justin turned to Rashid. 'That means two ID books. Can you arrange it?'

'No problem. Just give me names. And I'll need mugshots.' For the first time he smiled. 'Record their faces for posterity.' He looked at Justin. 'But where will they be going to? It's no use just telling them to get the hell out of the Cape. What's the destination?'

'Out of the country.' Justin stood up from the boulder on which he'd been sitting. He thrust his hands in his pockets, a characteristic posture when he was getting down to business. 'I've gone through it all last night. The airports are still too sensitive. Zimbabwe and Swaziland too far away. That leaves us with Lesotho and Botswana. The important thing is to take it slowly. At the moment everybody is jittery. Which is why I like the idea of a magazine project. Gives us time, takes off the pressure. Once it's cooled down, you slip through. But we'll have to keep contact.'

'Then we can settle on *Huisgenoot*,' said Thomas. 'No one will think twice about it. We'll be working on an article – some general topic, like the Afrikaners of the *platteland*. Gives one ample scope. Then we can head for Botswana, move up the West Coast, cut through to Griqualand West. I know those parts.'

'One thing,' warned Justin. 'Under no circumstances is the girl to know where you're heading for. She'll have to take it one day at a time as you go on. If at any stage she gets difficult, you drop her. We'll have a contingency plan ready.'

'I told you I trust her.'

'But you must be prepared to drop her if it comes to the push. Because she's just a footnote, an appendix. You're the one we're concerned about. Right? The less she knows the less dangerous it is for herself. Just in case she gets nailed along the way. You understand that, don't you?'

'Of course. All right then.'

'Got to get going,' said Rashid. 'Let's start at the beginning.'

It was almost like the old days, the Paarl days, when they'd all huddled together like this to plan the details. Except there were now fewer of them; half were missing: Nina, Christine, David. They had less time too. But they had practice in working together; there were years of preparation they could rely on. In any case there was no need, and no possibility, this time, of planning more than the outlines. The rest would have to be left to Thomas, to him and the girl, to improvise from one situation to the next, take their own decisions. The important thing would be to remain alert, read the signs, interpret them, assimilate them; and then to act from day to day. Yesterday had ceased, provisionally, to exist. Tomorrow could not be trusted in advance. There was only today.

The next morning – it was about ten; he'd waited for the early morning traffic to abate, the neighbourhood to be drained and to settle – Thomas carried out his baggage to the new car, a small white Opel, which Rashid had brought round, as arranged, the previous evening. (It was late enough to rely on darkness; early enough not to attract attention.) Lisa had obediently remained indoors, as instructed, while Thomas and Rashid had pulled the car into the narrow driveway beside the house. (Behind the Worcester registration plates, Rashid had shown him, two additional sets had been screwed into position, one from Kimberley, the other Transvaal.) Then Rashid had gone off into the night in the Golf. Lisa had asked no questions when Thomas came back. Afterwards they'd packed what they would need for the journey. She'd given him an old grey suitcase for his things. And now, the following morning, after a night in which neither had slept much, they were ready: Lisa rather pale, which made her eyes look darker than usual; but resolutely lighthearted.

In the back pocket of his jeans was his latest, carefully 'aged' ID book. They'd decided to retain the name Anton, changing only the surname to Lamprecht. Lisa had happily chosen her second name,

Karin, adding to it, not without a touch of perversity, the surname of her previous lover, Rossouw.

While Thomas was loading the grey suitcase into the car Lisa fetched her own luggage: the well-worn blue canvas bag he remembered wryly from the plane, once again bulging in an unwieldy and unusual shape; and a collection of loose articles.

He got in. She'd gone into the house one last time, returning with a red Tupperware container with food she'd prepared, as a surprise, in the early morning: a roasted chicken, some hard-boiled eggs, meatballs, sandwiches. She was still barefoot, her sandals suspended from the crook of a little finger. She got into the passenger seat, leaned back to put the red container on the back seat, then drew up one leg and began to put on the sandals.

'Well, bon voyage,' he said.

She looked up obliquely through the hair covering her narrow face. 'You haven't even told me where we're going to.'

'I'm not sure myself.'

'Perhaps I'm not allowed to know?'

'It's for your own good.'

'Of course,' she said, sarcastic.

'Lisa.' He was very serious now. 'I want you to get this absolutely clear: this is not a holiday trip. There's nothing glamorous or adventurous about it. It's going to be boring and irritating and frustrating and often difficult, perhaps even dangerous.'

'_'

'I want you to think carefully,' he insisted. 'Please. Because right now you can still get out. I won't blame you. You can forget about me and get on with your own life. You don't owe me anything and I'm not expecting anything. It may be the last chance you have.'

She shook her head and tied up the second sandal. Round her ankle the narrow strand of cheerful beads, red, yellow, blue.

'If you do come with me, God alone knows what may happen to you. I can't promise you anything. Not even protection. It may be worse than anything you can imagine at this moment. So please think again. I beg you.'

She wanted to answer. He stopped her with a gesture.

'Lisa: this may be the last time I use your real name. If you come along – and I still think it's madness to do so – then from now on you're Karin and nothing else.'

'That's what I've always wanted to be. I never liked being Lisa.'

'The difference is that from now on you won't have a choice.

"Lisa" no longer exists. Neither does "Thomas". You *are* Karin. I'm Anton. Even when we are alone together. Otherwise it's all too easy to slip up. And this isn't a game either. My life may depend on it.' He was silent for an instant. 'Perhaps yours too.'

She nodded, suddenly grave. For a minute she didn't answer. Then, in a quick, resolute movement, she shook back her long black hair.

'I'm going with you, Thomas.' With the flicker of a smile. And then: 'Anton.'

Chapter 9

1

– We're standing on a jetty staring down at a smooth sloping concrete slab that juts out from the busy sea. In the background fishing
boats are bobbing on the waves; still further back are trawlers,
where the cold Atlantic deepens from turquoise to ultramarine
and prussian blue. A crowd of labourers – men in khaki pants
and faded shirts, the sleeves rolled up, women in multicoloured
headscarves – are processing the moving mounds of newly caught
crayfish: as the wire-cages are tipped over each crayfish is measured
at a glance, the carapace clasped expertly in a knowing hand, safely
out of reach of thrashing tail and legs; with the other hand, in a
single flick of the wrist, the tail is twisted off and thrust into an ice
container. The still living torsos of the crustaceans, thrown aside on
a growing slithery heap, continue comically, desperately to scuttle
away across the bloody concrete.

'My God,' Lisa protests – pale with shock and revulsion – to the
foreman, 'how can you do this to them? They're still alive!'

The man laughs, his eyes disappearing among the wrinkles of
his weatherbeaten cheeks. 'No Merrim,' he assures her, 'nothing
to worry about, we been doing this job for years. The crayfish get
used to it.' –

2

That had been five days, six days ago, on the first day of their journey
up the coast. The memory was brought back when, looking askance
at her – on a windy, sandy stretch of beach, protected by a patch of
milkwood, they had just finished the fish and chips and the bottle
of wine they'd bought in the last village – he noticed her absently

371

sucking a knuckle of one of the fingers on her right hand. She'd shown him: there was a hint of infection in the small cut. After their brief conversation with the crayfish packers she'd squatted down for a moment to pick up, in an impulsive futile gesture, one of the maimed scuttling bodies – did she consider throwing it back into the sea, he'd wondered briefly, or taking it back to the car with her, in a senseless attempt to save its already mutilated life? – but she was clumsy, and a leg or antenna got caught under the narrow gold ring with the peace sign (a gift from Erik, she'd told him); a thorn had penetrated the skin and in her momentary fright she'd quickly dropped the crayfish.

Later, in the car, because the nick was painful, she'd moved the ring to her left hand. That was what had caused the misunderstanding on the Bassons' farm afterwards. A trivial incident. And yet –

Now they were on the road again. This strange, aimless journey. At first, after the weekend with the old couple, they'd turned inland, to the Cedarberg; and as the weather had eased into the tranquil warmth of late autumn they'd spent the first two nights in the mountains: Lisa knew the surroundings from earlier climbing expeditions with Erik, even though that had been years ago. And perhaps they should have remained there. For then they would not have known what they knew now; what was happening at this moment.

Thomas looked at his watch, a reflex motion. Yes. Ten past three. In Cape Town the service would be under way. It shouldn't take long. Then the furnace. Nina would have appreciated the irony; if she'd rejected heaven, she'd always secretly cherished the notion of hell. How long would it take for a body to be transformed into ashes?

It was difficult to keep track of it all. First the news about his father's stroke. (That was what had made him decide to head for the mountains in the first place, as far as possible from other people.) Then, last night, the TV news about today's cremation. In the bleak hotel lounge with unmatched chairs from country auctions, cheap landscape prints on the walls, a yawning waiter in black and red against the doorpost, his round tray pressed against his chest, Lisa had put out her hand and placed it on his.

'Was she really one of you?'

He'd nodded fiercely. He didn't want her to look at him.

'She was –? The two of you –?'

He'd covered his face with his hands.

372

They'd sat there without moving, for a long time. (Poor waiter.) Long after the news broadcast had finished they began to talk. It was almost like the night in front of the fire in her sitting-room. At last they went down the long passage with its worn and patchy carpet – walls dark green below, beige above, small dull lamps at long intervals – to their single rooms opposite each other. After he'd unlocked his he'd hesitated, wondering. Behind him, her back to him, she was also waiting. Then both opened their doors, said good-night, withdrew.

The room in the dingy yellow light of the 40-watt lamp beside the bed with the faded red candlewick spread. Cockroaches scuttling from cracks and peeling wallpaper; a smell of dust and old feet; on the brown carpet a large dark stain: what crime of passion by what crazed thwarted lover had been committed here in years past? Gone now, all gone; and yet not altogether, for these traces remained. A Gideon Bible on the rickety little chest beside the bed. In the drawer, when he pulled it open, a hairpin. And suddenly he felt himself invaded by worlds he didn't even know, other existences overshadowing his, questioning it, challenging it. A distant past of hotel rooms came back to him: years ago, after he'd returned to South Africa from his first trip abroad, on his many photographic journeys through the country, on his own, or with Henry, or with others. He thought about Lisa across the passage in a room identical to his. Strange how easily, checking into this hotel, they had acquiesced in their separateness again. After the weekend with the Bassons and the two nights in the mountains. A shift had occurred, undoubtedly: but they were still cautious. Especially that night. Nina, oh God, Nina. *Her bright, brave smile.* Would it never cease haunting him?

Of course not, he was thinking now, in the glare of the sun, as they drove on. The smell of ozone, of crayfish, pervaded the whole area. Nothing is ever past. It all persists.

Those two evenings in the room in the Bassons' home, Oom Dolf and Tant Nakkie, there had been a gas lamp. (On the first evening because of a power cut; the second, because they'd come to like the muted light of the lamp.) The white glare. The reassuring hiss. (A hiss from so far away in the past.)

– In Henry Bungane's house, at the close of the day in which he has come home from the Island, the children on his lap, the woman at his feet, the booming of his deep voice. What I shall always remember is the small frail bag in the heart of the light,

373

glowing white, transparent; in the morning, I know from childhood holidays on Oupa's farm, it will look like a filigree of ash. Always ashes. Unto ashes. Nina. –

(His father? That came the next morning, Monday morning, as they drove off, after Lisa had turned on the car radio for the news.)

Beside him, as they drove along (had she noticed his glance at his watch? nothing escaped her), Lisa asked, 'Is it very bad, Anton?'

'I should have been there. At the cremation.' He shook his head. 'Or with my father. I should be everywhere except where I am.'

– I *am* everywhere except where I am. –

She was again sucking, absently, the nick on her finger.

Last Saturday, on their way back from the factory, after the first half-hour of silence – neither had felt like talking – she'd suddenly said, 'Those poor crayfish, Anton. Is there nothing one can do about it?'

With a flash of bitterness he'd asked, 'A more humane death, you mean?'

She looked up quickly, then turned away to the sea again. 'They come from so deep below the sea. They look so well protected.'

'Did you know,' he said, 'that every year, sometimes even twice a year, I'm not quite sure of the facts, they get a new carapace? The old one splits open very neatly and the crayfish crawls out, drawing each leg and segment and antenna very precisely from the old one. But the new carapace is still quite soft and the crayfish has to hide for a couple of days until it hardens, otherwise its enemies will get it.'

'And in the end, in spite of everything, it still gets caught.'

'One day there won't be any left. And what will happen then, I wonder? They're scavengers, they keep the sea clean, make it a liveable place for all the other marine creatures.'

'Actually *I*'m feeling like a crayfish with a brand-new shell,' she said, her eyes lit up. 'I've left my old carapace back in the Cape.'

Now, remembering their conversation, he thought: The other night, the first night on the farm, without your carapace –

– In the spare room of the spacious old farmhouse that smells of lavender and rosemary – the sphere of light round the gas lamp, the penumbra surrounding it – as I sit on the edge of the bed, my back considerately turned to you while you're washing and brushing your teeth in the old-fashioned ewer, my wandering eyes discover a round mirror on the wall in which I can surreptitiously watch you, a photograph in deep rich colours, dark browns, and purple shadows, the creamy white of your skin; and suddenly I can no longer look away. And afterwards, when it is my turn, you covered to your chin under heavy sheets and blankets and crocheted spread, I catch a glimpse of you as you prop yourself up on an elbow to spy on *me* in the same shadowy glass. –

A gull came swooping past, describing a tall curve upward from the water that lay shimmering in the sun, suddenly turned and dived down again to skim exhilaratingly across the surface. The graph, he thought, the whole exquisite pattern of its flight, is in fact discovered only the moment after it is gone, when its imprint is retained by the retina, a photograph in the mind. Or otherwise perhaps one sees it in advance, anticipating it, calculating its inevitable sweep. The flight itself, the here and now of it, one grasps only through what is either past or yet to happen; on its own, each moment is devoid of meaning.

They were driving through plains of hard fragrant scrub. Blue upon blue the hills lay ahead and to their right, breaking into sudden rocky outcrops. To the left, visible from time to time, the shocking blue of the sea. Behind them clouds of dust were billowing up. Surfaced roads they'd left behind, a deliberate choice, long ago. Here the landscape had remained as it had been in his childhood. A vast emptiness, eroded by the wind until the bare essentials remained. The region in which the first Landmans had been shaped, had in turn shaped their minds to its image and spare contours. They came across few other travellers; it was already too far out of season. The only sign of life, at rare intervals, was a gull flung up into the sky like a folded rag; occasionally there were crows feeding on the road on the remains of a dead hare or skunk; on electricity poles, now and then, a small hawk or the tatters of a nest.

'It's a strange feeling,' he said, anxious to break the silence, 'to be on the move like this, on the road, with no fixed point of reference.'

'I think it's wonderful,' Lisa said happily. 'When I was a child this was what I loved most about holidays: just driving and driving. I never liked the arrivals. In a way they were always less than I'd expected. Papa, again, couldn't stand travelling, always drove like hell to get where he wanted to be. We used to have endless fights in the car. I kept on finding reasons to stop. For ice-cream, cool drink, a pee. Just to stretch it out, to avoid arriving anywhere too soon. It drove him up the wall. Poor man. I think life itself is an endless irritation to him. Heaven is where he wants to get to. Whereas I can't think of anything more dreary.'

Snugly, almost voluptuously – if she'd been a cat she would have purred – she shifted on her seat.

Back to the past, he thought. Here they were, nomads again. Only a few generations ago his ancestors had still lived in wagons. Driving along here like this was like immersing himself in their lives, repeating them. And were they, he and she, but a story drawing its own tentative line along this coast, still unfinished and, who knows, incapable of ending?

– And when I'm gone one day, how will others write the story of my life? How would *you* write it, Lisa Karin, if you were required to? With shock, horror, condemnation, incomprehension, forgiveness, compassion? Because, if you are honest about it, this is the only heaven or hell permitted us, our only 'hereafter': the memories of others. Not forgetting, not the void, but how those others we travel with, or who travel with us, will remember us and write our history. *Aletheia*. Sometimes I try – in this instant beside you I'm trying – to imagine how others would report on me if they were asked, what they would remember of the parentheses of my existence I have shared with them along the way. And how would I report on *them*? Anyone of them: Frans or Belinda, Maria, the black hitchhiker Raymond, or the troopie I'd given a lift, Mum and Dad, you, your brother, or Rashid, Justin, David (if he is still alive, allowed the time to think) or Nina's father, some bartender here, a newspaper vendor there, Oom Dolf and Tant Nakkie on the farm, anyone of you? *Aletheia*. My meagre truth. –

At the Ladies' Bar of the seedy little hotel in the very first village they'd visited on their journey – after the unsettling scene at the crayfish factory they needed some refreshment – the bleary-eyed bartender had been irritatingly inquisitive. Without batting an eyelid they'd told him they were freelance journalists researching material for an article on 'interesting people' along the West Coast. And this had added an unforeseen deviation to their journey.

'If you people looking for funny folk,' the old man had said, leaning heavily on his massive forearms, his left eye red and weepy over Thomas's glass, 'then there's Oom Maans Petoors, just down along this road here. Still rides on a donkey cart, keeps all his money in a trunk under his bed, trusts nobody. Then again, if it's difficult folk you looking for, there's Oom Petrus Badenhorst right there on the coast, give you more trouble than ten devils from hell. But if it's good folk you looking for, then it's Oom Dolf and Tant Nakkie Basson round the first hill, that way.'

They feigned interest – Thomas even had a green notebook ready to jot down names with a flourish of professionalism – but before they could continue, without any warning, the old man lifted the telephone from its cradle, turned the handle furiously, and asked the exchange, 'Sweetie, get me Oom Dolf on the line, ag please man.' A few minutes later, still without bothering to consult them, the appointment had been made for the late afternoon. Thomas managed, with some effort, to stop him before he could ring up the rest of the district.

Neither was in a mood to keep the appointment; but to stand the old man up might attract unwelcome attention. And that was how, a few hours later, they'd stopped in the shady yard of the big wheat farm, 'round the first hill, that way'. Lisa, especially, had no intention of staying long.

But she, too, succumbed to the hospitality of the old people. They must have been almost seventy: a dignified, straight old man wearing a watch chain on his waistcoat; a woman whose unmistakable early sturdiness had been softened and cushioned by age. They were waiting patiently for their youngest to finish his military training to come and take over the farm; he'd already earned his degree in agriculture. The older children, three of them, all married and with families of their own, had gone off in their own directions: an economist at the Reserve Bank, a professor in sociology, the daughter a doctor, an orthopaedic surgeon. The farm boasted the most modern of implements – tractors, ploughs, combine harvesters, binders, all housed in an impressive barn. Only the house was still old-fashioned. There was electricity for lights, fridge and freezer, but no sign of either a Hoover or an oven or even an electric stove. Not because of the erratic power supply – during supper the lights had gone out and candles and gas lamps, ready and waiting in strategic spots, were lit; it clearly was an everyday event – but, the old lady gave them to understand, from a kind of pride, independence, a sense of virtue.

The evening was marked, above all, by one particular misunderstanding, comic only in retrospect, not when it occurred. Upon their arrival Thomas had introduced themselves: 'I am Anton Lamprecht, this is Karin, we – and then he'd been interrupted and their relationship had remained unclarified. But towards the end of the evening meal, when the procession of servants from

377

the kitchen had cleared away the last dishes and while they were waiting for coffee, the old woman – gaslight gleaming on her glasses, illuminating wrinkles of laughter round her mouth and eyes – had smiled knowingly and said:

'All right, you may as well come out with it. This magazine business is just an excuse, isn't it?'

Thomas was momentarily unable to say a word; he didn't dare look at Lisa.

'Come on, I know people. I've seen through the two of you. You're definitely not journalists looking for a story.'

'But Tant Nakkie –' He drew a deep breath. 'I can show you the editor's letter of introduction.'

'Ag, anyone can write a letter.' A pause. 'Well, what do you say?'

Lisa scraped her chair back as if she were preparing for sudden flight.

Still with her knowing smile the old lady prodded, 'You two *are* on honeymoon, aren't you? I saw the ring. So am I right or not?'

The ring, Thomas noticed at a quick glance, had obviously been too wide for the finger to which Lisa had transferred it; and from her absent twirling of it it had turned round, the peace sign inside the hand; from above, only the narrow golden band was visible.

Oom Dolf interrupted amicably, 'Now, now, Nakkie, don't go on like that. If they don't want to tell it's their business. Remember how you lied about us when we went to Kleinmond on *our* honeymoon?'

'Oh well.' Thomas leaned back and placed his hands, palms down, on the table. 'I suppose the secret's out.' He still wasn't sure whether he should laugh or cry with relief. Looking at Lisa was now quite out of the question.

Tant Nakkie rose energetically. 'Come, child, I want you to tell me if the room is all right. The men can look after themselves for a while.'

'Tant Nakkie, really, we –'

'So when was the wedding?'

A momentary silence, then Lisa said shyly, 'Yesterday afternoon, Tante.'

'You see, Dolf, I told you.'

'Ag, Nakkie.'

By that time it would be senseless to attempt any further explanations. In a way the misunderstanding suited them. And

378

soon, after Tant Nakkie and Lisa had conferred on what was needed for the night and Oom Dolf and Thomas had gone out to sprinkle the quince hedge under the stars, their bedroom door was closed, the house grew silent around them, and they were left alone with the hiss of the gas lamp and the tall shadows on the delicate flower pattern of the walls.

'What now, Anton?'

Suddenly, clearly, she felt trapped; bashful like an old-time bride.

He sat on the edge of the big stinkwood bed, sinking into the feather mattress. 'My grandmother, my mum's mother, had a bed just like this. Once when we there on holiday I had to share it with her. I was very small. And night after night I wetted the bed. But grandma was unbelievably loyal. Every morning, with a dead-pan face, she would tell the others how hot it had been, how I'd been perspiring.'

Lisa was looking less tense now. 'I won't be loyal at all,' she promised, her shadow-eyes filled with laughter. 'If you pee on me I'll tell everybody.'

He put a finger in his mouth and held it aloft. 'So help me God.' But there was a grave undertone to what he'd meant to sound lighthearted; a tautness in his throat, a consciousness of her presence in a way that was different from what it had been before: something he hadn't wanted, something he even dreaded, yet which, now that its moment had come, he neither could nor wished to avoid. 'If you want to wash?' he said slowly. 'I'll turn my back.' His prudence matched the stern propriety of the room.

And much later, deep in the night, when neither of them could sleep, she lay in his arm and asked, 'Anton, will you tell me another story?'

And he continued — like Scheherazade, he thought! — from where he'd temporarily suspended, the previous time, the story of his ancestors. Hoping the day would never break, because he hadn't felt so peaceful and so safe in years. As if through some dark apprehension in himself he could sense how brief its span would be, how abruptly it would end: that news on the car radio when they drove off on the Monday morning, a long-winded badly constructed sentence informing the country that Mr Christiaan Landman, father of the fugitive terrorist Thomas Landman, who is hunted countrywide by the police in connection with the bomb attack on the state president's life, has been admitted to the intensive care unit of the hospital in Oudtshoorn after suffering a stroke. According to a hospital spokesman –

3

– After eight months in Europe – and still I have found no solace for the anger and despair, the questions that first drove me there; not even an escape from iniquity or racism – there is the urgent telegram from home: Pa is seriously ill. Yet when I arrive at his bedside I find him, if not hale and hearty, far from death (a mere warning signal of a duodenal ulcer which will never materialise: even in this respect he never quite 'makes' it); although he remains convinced that it must be stomach cancer, that no one has the courage to break the news to him, and that he is facing the bitter death of a martyr (the only virtue of which is that it is guaranteed to bring me to my senses, his condition being unambiguously linked to the anguish my 'irresponsibility' has caused him). On the deathbed he is so miraculously to survive, buoyed up only by relief at discovering that I have cared enough to hurry home, he breaks through many layers of inner resistance to confess to me the folly of his early life – his English girlfriend, Joan Brookshaw, the love of his life, abandoned to escape a curse from his father – without which my record of our tribal history would have been even more incomplete than it is: an act of confidence that will, I know, haunt him for the rest of his earthly life.

'But at least you've come back,' he says, resigned, at the end of it (he will persist in the fortunate belief that it is for his sake I have returned). 'Now you can take up your life again where you. I wonder whether you will ever realise how you let us down when you. Not all of us are allowed an opportunity to redress our mistakes. Let us pray.'

I do resume my life, if not in the way he would have liked or could have foreseen. Photographer with the *Cape Times*. ('But Boetie, it's only a hobby, not a career. And an *English* newspaper?') My unlikely guardian angel at the newspaper is Sean Maritz. Poor Sean. This is the way most people react when his name is mentioned. 'Poor Sean.' His appearance must have something to do with it – the dejected spaniel face, the hunched shoulders, as if from an early age, objecting against growing so tall, he's been trying to pull himself down to earth. Yet his mind is razor-sharp. If only he wouldn't expose it so defiantly to the ravages of cynicism and neat whisky.

It seems wrong to apply a word like 'gay' to Sean: he's such a morose person. I cannot tell, either, whether he has ulterior motives in taking me under his wing at the *Cape Times*, introducing me to its routine, its written and unwritten rules; even helping me to find a flat. If there is, he certainly never attempts to force his attentions on me. This may be the result of a recent devastating history with a young actor whom he literally brought in from the street, only to be swindled, for two years running, out of most of his possessions (including his records and his hi-fi), before the little shit dumped him for a more glamorous – and much richer – opera singer.

My enthusiasm about the new job elicits nothing but commiseration from Sean: 'One should never get too attached to anything, my baby. Whether it's a nation or a cause or a job or a place or another person.'

'But what's the point of doing anything if you're not prepared to get involved?'

'Involvement is for the birds.'

'I'm serious, Sean.'

'I can see that. And that's what depresses me. Let me tell you, whatever's going to happen in this country will happen without anyone asking our permission first.'

'Who are you referring to?'

'You're the one who always talks about "us Afrikaners".' A deep, dedicated swallow of neat whisky; the bottle ready in his left hand to fill up the glass whenever necessary. 'Let me tell you, it's not just Afrikaners who make my arse-hairs turn grey. It's all whites. And why, you might ask? Because we're an aberration and an abomination in this continent. We don't *belong* here. We can't even stand the sun.' (His own pale pink skin is mottled with freckles; the very edges of his eyelids are burnt red.) 'For us, merely to be human is something foreign.'

'You wouldn't say such things if you tried to get involved yourself.'

'You're boring me, baby. How many others have tried before me? "Dedicating" their lives to the struggle? Even dying for it? For what? Has that put an end to the war? Has it made a fart of difference to injustice and violence?'

'Sean, you're too young to be so cynical.'

'I feel older than God.'

'You're not even fifty.'

'I'm fifty-two, and ever since I was eighteen I've been doing my Micawber bit, waiting for something to happen, for the world to change, and now I've had enough.'

As a friend Sean is both demanding and generous. Whenever he goes away – and unlike his earlier years as a reporter he now takes every holiday he is entitled to – I am expected to look after his house in Kloofsig. I even have the use of his car to prevent the battery running down. (Sean is so helpless with mechanics that he is capable of selling the car – or even giving it away – if the battery is flat.) For the rest, his house is a useful hiding place for sensitive material. Sean never enquires about it; I doubt whether he is even remotely interested.

What *he* gets out of it, it gradually dawns on me, is the kick of living vicariously through me the experiences that have previously passed him by. Because as it happens, I am caught up in all the convulsions of the time. Those two years are, in fact, the most hectic of my life. It is the time the authorities refer to, euphemistically, as the 'Unrest' and the angry youngsters of the townships, hopefully, as *Isiqabo*, the Beginning. A period without chronology, a confusion of music, of great crowds bursting into song at demonstrations, protest marches, meetings, gatherings; at funerals, funerals. Sometimes it feels like one unending funeral that stretches through all time.

'*Senzeni na?* – What have we done?'

The melody which, years later, that night at the fireside, Lisa will strum on her guitar.

Over and over, through days and nights, even in my sleep, it penetrates my mind, far beyond the dark rim of consciousness. I shall remember it the way I hear it for the first time, at a service in Kwazakele, outside Port Elizabeth, in a small white church. A priest, hands stretched high above his head, is supplicating his audience, 'Please, please, I beg you, don't make any noise, don't even sing. The police are waiting outside. They waiting for an excuse. Let us bury our dead in dignity and silence. Let us now bow our heads in prayer.'

And then, from that hush, the sound begins to well up like a wave from the depths of the sea: so softly, to begin with, that one cannot even be sure it is there, a deep muted hum that gradually swells and increases, gaining in definition, finding words. Female voices separating themselves from the others announce new phrases, evoking a response in a deep droning bass, a liturgical harmony as ancient as humanity:

'*Senzeni na?* – What have we done?

Senzeni na sibotshwa nje? – What have we done to be caught?

La mabhulu – These whites

La mabhulu aziziny – These whites are dogs

Ayakufa ezizinya – They will die because they are dogs –'

Followed by the long list of names of the recently killed, one by one:

'*Ambulele uMahlangu* – They killed Mahlangu

Ambulele uMoloise – They killed Moloise

Ambulele uGoniwe – They killed Goniwe –'

On and on, until it reverts to that question forever unanswerable:

'*Senzeni na?*'

More and more passionately it rises in the small white building until everybody is standing and the walls reverberate with the sound, culminating inevitably in the cry:

'*Amandla!*'

And like close thunder the answer rings out: '*Ngawethu!*'

And then: '*iAfrika!*'

'*Mayibuye!*'

'*Inkululeko!*'

'*Ngoku!*'

And then the *Vivas* and the *Abaixos*. At that stage the teargas canisters come hurtling through the windows, shattering the glass, and coughing crying blinded people stampede outside to the waiting hordes of blue police. But long afterwards, much later, as the Mello-Yellos begin to drive away, I still hear voices, here, there, everywhere, ringing with sad defiance in my ears:

'*Senzeni na?*'

It is Henry who has taken me to this meeting. As to so many others. Henry Bungane, the small man from the Island, Henry with the bulging round eyes which never stop watering – at least he's acquired gold-rimmed spectacles during my absence abroad – affected as they are by the light of the Island, the naked sun reflected on white earth. ('Ten years back it was worse, *buti*, so I'm not complaining. In those days they buried the difficult prisoners up to their necks in holes. Leaving them there from sunrise to sundown. And all the warders who felt the need came to stand above them and pissed in their faces. The only moisture they were offered. Apart from that there was only the glare of the sun. Not

383

one of those who survived those times came back with undamaged eyes. So I still count myself lucky.') Henry of the thunderous voice. Small wonder that when the UDF was founded, in my absence, he became one of the top men in the Cape.

I am drawn into it without delay, the very first weekend after I've started working at the *Times*, when I look him up in the township. 'No use you trying to keep out of it, *buti*. This is war. On our own, one by one, we're helpless against the power of the government. What we need is organisation. It's no use there's one here, two there, twenty somewhere else. My people are bewildered. We don't know who we are or where we are. We're part Western, part tribal, part African. There's nothing that binds us together from inside, nothing we can hold on to, or that we can fall back on. Except for our political anger against apartheid. We need more than that. It's not just a matter of what we are against, we need to be *for* something. We must all come together now, the time is right, to attack the enemy all along the line, to mobilise ourselves. White and black, everybody. That's why I want to see you there too. You and all the others who think like you. You're not alone, you know. And today it's no longer black against white, we don't want to repeat the mistakes of the previous generations. It's democrats against racists. And good intentions and nice words are not the answer to naked power, *buti*. We also have power. It's time we started to use it.'

A great demagogue, Henry. Sometimes he addresses me as if I'm a whole audience. But not a word of what he says is mere rhetoric. He means it; it comes from the guts; he's lived through all of it. Which is why the people flock to him, a thousand, ten thousand, fifteen thousand turning up at a meeting when Henry Bungane speaks.

It is he who acts as my guide and mentor; equally important, he keeps me occupied at times when I feel tempted to yield to the depression that threatens to swamp me, especially in those first weeks after my return. (The full horror of my country after an absence of months: realities that burn into one like the sun into the eyes of a man on Robben Island buried to his neck in white sand, and not even piss to revive one.) It is he who makes me discover that I am *not* alone. And the patience with which he does it! 'Take it slowly, *buti*. There's a whole world waiting to be discovered. And I'm walking with you all the way. Don't worry.'

We certainly keep moving. Up and down the country. I take photographs while Henry addresses meetings or confers with his comrades in the UDF, grasping at the same time every opportunity to lead revival services wherever we go. Sometimes we travel in his tubercular, battered grey Ford. Often with others, in cars loaded beyond all imaginable capacity, in combis bursting at the seams, even on the backs of vegetable trucks, anything on wheels. In the daytime. Mostly at night. Through the UDF grapevine news travels at an incredible speed: this afternoon there's a march on Mitchell's Plain – tomorrow a protest meeting in Cradock or Zwelitsha – on Saturday a funeral in Guguletu – on Sunday a service in Regina Mundi. If it is at all possible, Henry's got to be there. And I'm there with him.

In the beginning my bosses at the newspaper appear hesitant; my news editor is openly suspicious that I may be malingering. It's only Sean who impulsively and implicitly believes in me and supports me in tricky moments. The others remain sceptical for much longer. But I bring back the photographs. And in the long run they cannot argue with that. When a year after my return the whole country bursts into flames – starting on the Rand, spreading to the Eastern Cape, invading the whole of the Peninsula, even the generally placid Orange Free State – I pile up on my editor's desk (usually via unimaginable detours, sometimes at the risk of my life) the photographs no other newspaper in the country can obtain.

I am contacted by the BBC. By *Newsweek. Der Spiegel.* Agence France Press. All of a sudden I have more work than I can ever handle. I resign from my post at the *Cape Times* to freelance. But this means that I am working day and night. Sometimes I catch less than ten hours' sleep a week. Many are the times when, in that untranslatable Afrikaans expression, I see my own hole. Cornered by police. Trampled by stampeding crowds. Caught in crossfire. Suffocated by teargas. On three occasions one of my cameras is demolished by boots or batons. Countless times my films are confiscated. Once in New Brighton I lose a full week's work when my camera bag gets lost in a mad flight from the police. Long days of utter exhaustion, filled with defeats and disappointments and betrayals. Often I am ready to give up. Furious, rebellious, frustrated. People I've been working with, people who have risked their lives for me, are picked up, whisked out of the world for unpredictable eternities of detention, re-emerging literally and figuratively broken. Others simply 'disappear' for good.

In the midst of all this, keeping faith in what we're doing can be more difficult than anything else. Life becomes a battered old tin drum pierced with holes: and so much seeps out, gets lost through the holes; yet through those very holes, in rare blessed moments, there is a glimpse of another world – a world that does not yet exist, but which is in the process of manifesting itself, a world as it may one day exist. And for the sake of that world I find it possible, necessary, to continue. This is what it makes it worth while. More than worth while: life is a permanent high.

Photography is no longer an aesthetic preoccupation, something that happens in a dark room, remote from the world, no longer even a way of recording events: it has become a way of fighting, an immersion in the battle, an exhilarating and often dangerous way of living with my land, of entering it in a dark and intimate way, as if it were a woman. Driven by what is at this stage still the urgent but naïve faith that once people – 'my' people – have discovered what is happening, they will change: that once I have confronted them with the evidence of my photographs that in itself will point them the way to Damascus.

In its wake it brings new enemies. My front door is daubed with slogans; the tyres of my motorcycle are slashed, the brakes 'tampered with', a cable cut through; a dead cat is deposited on my doormat. Some of my past comrades from Stellenbosch, encountered in the street, give me the cold shoulder. In my own family tensions develop. Dad becomes surly and disapproving; Frans is openly disparaging about a brother 'in cahoots with the enemy'. One day, when I run into an old girlfriend in Cape Town she gives me one look and turns away abruptly as if I do not exist. But in exchange for these rejections, what bounty! *Ubuntu*. My whole concept of history is revised. How brief, how inadequate, the three hundred years of white 'civilisation' with which I grew up, compared to the vast perspective of Africa looming behind it. (And what satisfaction to acknowledge at least a twist of it in myself, through my ancestral mother Catharijn of Guinea, and the Khoin woman Toas a century later.)

In a discussion about it, one day, with Henry, he smiles patiently. 'Don't worry, *buti*, it was only when I went to the Island that I myself discovered Africa. Perhaps we must arrange for you to spend some time there too.'

There is nothing smooth and easy about our relationship, which at times is marked by passionate quarrels, night-long arguments. Once, after yet another funeral, Henry tries to cope with his own emotions by saying, 'Well, if it must happen, then let it be so. Perhaps it is a good thing. It makes us stronger. The government is looking for victories, but the people, us: we flourish on defeat.'

'For God's sake, Henry!' I storm at him, 'we've had too much violence already.'

'Violence is the name of the world we live in, *buti*. Ever since Cain and Abel. That is the starting point. The choice we're given, the only choice, is whether we're prepared only to suffer violence or to use it against others too. And I've made my choice. As a Christian.'

'It's immoral!'

'I'm not talking about morality. Leave that to the people who have the vote. They have the luxury to opt for peace. I'm talking about us, here in the ghetto.'

'But look at what happened today!' The funeral in New Brighton. A background of shacks and shanties of wood, plastic, corrugated iron. Vibracrete walls with holes broken into them for short cuts to the buses and the station. Behind that, stretches of flat water pink with flamingoes, like a cheap postcard. And at the funeral there was a charge by the police. The bearers had to drop in the dust their three coffins, wrapped in black, green and gold. A young girl was shot in the back. Another death, designating in advance the next funeral.

'Must it all happen again next week?' I ask in helpless anger. 'It's time to start thinking about stopping the violence, not fuelling it.'

To my surprise he says, 'But that's precisely what I'm preaching, *buti*. Not retribution. Not violence for the sake of violence. But not turning the meek cheek either.'

'–'

He laughs. 'I'm an activist, *buti*, not a terrorist. What I'm doing is to encourage people to stand together and to say *no*. There's a difference, I tell you. A big difference.'

'Henry, don't try to tell me it's just saying No that landed you on the Island for five years!' It is the first time I have ever referred to it directly.

He seems amused, not offended at all. '*Buti*, I thought Ntsiki told you long ago.' Shaking his head, he takes off his glasses and wipes them with a white handkerchief; his round eyes are, as always, watery. 'What happened was very simple: I was hiding a man on the run from the SB. I knew he killed an impimpi in Guguletu who betrayed his brother to the cops. But I also knew they were going to kill him if they found him. So what else could I do?'

'And for that –'

'Sure, why not?' A bitter click of his tongue. 'The bad thing was

387

they caught him after all. Shot him dead. Then framed me in court to prove I was with him at the time he killed the impimpi. I wasn't even in the Cape when it happened. But when the Boere pull out the stops, what can you do?'

'And you didn't blame him for killing the impimpi?'

'Sin is sin. Murder is murder. Of course. But at the same time I could understand why he did it, not so? There's nothing that makes a man so blind as when he is betrayed. There's nothing, I tell you, not even murder, that drives people as mad as that.'

(I remember, again, my great-grandfather's record of the Boer War: how they – staunch Godfearing Boers all – executed traitors. Made them dig their own holes, then shot them. In my round childish handwriting I personally transcribed it, word for word, from laborious High Dutch into Afrikaans.)

This is what he says, again, on the day we both miraculously escape getting killed, in Transkei, after yet another funeral, when the crowd, believing they have discovered an informer in their midst, turn upon the man like bees swarming round a queen; and Henry flings himself down on the prostrate bleeding already half-dead body, and is set on, in his turn, by the blood-crazed mob; and as I attempt to drag him off, they turn on me as well. From nowhere tyres materialise, and bottles of paraffin, burning rags. God knows what may happen if a group of women, risking their own lives, do not whisk us off to their huts, and from there, in the dark of the night, to the next village. I shall never forget that smell of petrol and burning rubber. The blackness of that smoke. The moans of the dying young man encircled by flames. The screams and ululations of the crowd.

Gradually, through those two turbulent years, something inside me shifts, even though it is not registered in my consciousness until after the fact – like the graph of a bird in flight one sees only after it has passed; like an airport clock; like a remote star whose light reaches one long after its own extinction. What makes it finally penetrate my consciousness is the exhibition of my photographs at the Market Theatre in Johannesburg in September of the second year, sponsored by General Motors, under the aegis of the UDF.

A melodramatic title, *The Burning Land*. But it creates a stir. A week before the end of the exhibition the organisers are invited to transfer it to a church hall in Alexandra. On the day of its opening in the township it is banned. By the time I arrive at the hall to collect the photographs there is nothing left. Everything has been 'confiscated' in terms of Article something of Act something.

When, late that night, Henry and I arrive at my hotel room, I find shoved under my door a folded sheet. It is a photocopy in large print, of a quotation from Cicero (how sophisticated can they be!). At the top, like a newspaper heading:

Even a murderer is better than the traitor within

followed by the text:

A nation can survive its fools, and even the ambitious. But it cannot survive treason from within. An enemy at the gates is less formidable, for he is known and he carries his banners openly. But the traitor moves among those within the gate freely, his sly whispers rustling through all the alleys, heard in the very hall of government itself. For the traitor appears no traitor – he speaks in the accents familiar to his victims, and he wears their face and their garments, and he appeals to the baseness that lies deep in the hearts of all men. He rots the soul of a nation – he works secretly and unknown in the night to undermine the pillars of a city – he infects the body politic so that it can no longer resist. A murderer is less to be feared.

I shake my head slowly, handing the sheet to Henry. 'A traitor? Henry, I don't understand my people any more.'

All he asks is, '"Your" people, *buti*?'

All that moment – the graph of the bird's flight registered in my mind, in my conscience – I realise: No. The time for that way of thinking is past. 'My' people are not the ones who speak my language or whose colour I share (give or take a shade). From now on 'my people' include all of those I feel at home with, those who share my way of thinking, who believe in the same things as I do. Henry's people, the people of the UDF: *they* are mine.

(And yet I cannot – will not – stop thinking of myself as an Afrikaner! How many times will this come up, later, in my heated discussions with Nina? To her it will not only be irrelevant, but an annoyance, a hindrance. She will even have a revulsion, at times, against speaking Afrikaans. To her it is an embarrassment, a humiliation, a disgrace, an insult. Not to me. Afterwards, even while I work with Henry in the UDF, and much later still, in the training camp in Angola, I shall never feel the need to deny or renounce the fact that I'm an Afrikaner. The shift inside myself has not severed me from anything; has, on the contrary, extended my boundaries. That is the one thing Nina will never accept.)

As if somebody has read my thoughts there is, only days after the ban on the exhibition, an invitation from Amnesty International to reopen it in London. For two months, I work night and day to replace the lost prints. I vacate my flat in Cape Town, stow most of my belongings in Sean's house and the rest with my parents in the Little Karoo; and leave for London. This departure is unlike the first one. But not even I have an inkling of just *how* different it will turn out to be. –

4

Like the bars of an intricate piece of sheet music the power lines beside the road were inscribed with the notes of hundreds, thousands of swallows: a great soundless composition in the process of taking shape as more and more new formations arrived to amplify or disrupt the existing chords, prefiguring their fugue across the landscapes of the continent towards the possibility, the hope, the certainty of a spring beyond the seas.

'It's magic,' said Lisa. 'How do the birds know? Who tells them? And when they leave at last, how do they know where to go?' She leaned her head against the window to stare at the power lines outside. 'When I was small, whenever I was angry with somebody, usually my parents, or if I felt cornered, I tried to imagine Erik and me taking hands and going off with them. He used to make up stories about the countries we could go to. To be a swallow – Perhaps I was one in a previous life.' She turned her head towards him. 'Strange to think about it now. All those years I couldn't wait to set out with them. I never wanted to be *here*. But when I had the chance of going to Europe – I mean, it was great, but in the end I couldn't take it any more. I missed Erik too much. But above all, I missed Africa. You know those nights one sits at an open window and suddenly looks up and sees the stars enormous in the black sky, and from outside comes the smell of dust and dried grass, of raindrops after months of drought, far away there is the screeching of *kiewiets*, or a dog barking, and suddenly a huge moth flies in, a moth as big as a bird, with heavy dull wings, flapping along the walls and ceiling. That is when you know: this is Africa. And all around you there is darkness and space, space without end, and the earth below is hard and deep and mysterious, and in the darkness prowl tokoloshes and night-walkers and God knows what else, because nothing has been tamed yet, and most of the things you know are out there have not yet been named.'

'You weren't away for long, were you?' asked Thomas. As so often before he found it curiously satisfying to abandon himself, unquestioning, to the steady flow of her words.

'A year. Long enough. The best of all was coming back. Just after we'd landed at Nairobi and taken off again the plane developed engine trouble and we had to turn back. Delayed for a full day. We were taken to a hotel in town. A whole palaver to begin with, as they didn't want to allow the South Africans in, but in the end they relented. Most of the other passengers were the hell in about the delay, but I felt as if I'd suddenly been turned loose in Paradise. That joy of recognition: even though I'd never set foot in Kenya before, it was my place, my continent. I was secretly hoping the plane would never get fixed, I felt so much at home there.'

A sudden probing glance in his direction. 'What has gone wrong for us, Anton?'

'I'm afraid that after three hundred years our people have still not learned to accept Africa on its own terms. And as long as we deny the most important part of ourselves, we'll be living a lie. Or at best a schizophrenic existence. Which as a psychologist you should know all about.'

Ignoring the dig, she asked eagerly, 'Have *you* seen much of Africa?'

He merely nodded, considering for a moment to leave it at that, then changed his mind: 'I've been around. You see, at one time my best friend was able to come and go as he pleased, and he took me with him. We grew up in the same village, near Lambert's Bay, where we'll be stopping over tomorrow night. But we never knew each other as kids. I had to go all the way to London to meet him there.' He added more softly, 'Sipho. That was his name. Sipho.'

'Was?' she asked, subdued.

For a moment he closed his eyes, nodded.

Intensely, silently, she gazed at him.

– How inadequate and paltry, my knowledge of you. However well – however terrifying well! – I know you in some respects, there are whole landscapes inside you I have no knowledge of at all, landscapes you conceal from me, your secret and your mystery, to which I suppose I shall never be allowed entry. It was no sudden romantic urge that made me decide to come with you. Perhaps it was that unexpected glimpse of your world, a world so shocking and alien to me, that forced me to respond. In that instant when I first stood with the newspaper in my hands, this was what struck me: that at the very edge of my own safe existence there is this world, a world in which real events take place, in which one cannot step back, withdraw oneself, but where one lives inside the blazing furnace of the real, a world in which one is totally present, body and soul, and which is not apprehended only through hearsay or wishful thinking or fear or weird imagining. And as I'm sitting here beside you today, surrounded by the birds preparing to migrate: even though I still don't know the meaning of what is happening from day to day, or where we're going, or what is to become of us, *I am here*. And I am prepared to face the impossible. This I know now, this you have taught me: unless I am involved in everything, I am nothing. –

'All my life,' she said at last, 'my best friend has been Erik. That's why I was so upset when the army started changing him.' A wistful smile. 'When we were small we loved playing Hansel and Gretel, pretending to get lost in the bluegum forest above the town. In the late afternoon when the sun went down even the forest we used to know so well became, suddenly, a wonderfully strange place. We persuaded ourselves that we were orphans, ill-treated by adults. It was so real that I sometimes began to cry quite uncontrollably. Once we stayed out too late and really lost our way. Erik told me to wait there while he went for help. But I got scared and went ahead on my own, and so we strayed from one another in the dark. These last few months I've often had the impression that this is what is happening to us all over again. I've lost Erik.' She paused. 'But I know he'll come back.'

'How did you get home that night?'

'A whole crowd of people with torches and lanterns and dogs came looking for us. It was quite sensational, although our backsides were burning for many days from the beating we got for it. Still, I believe it was worth while in the end. You know, after I was left alone, scared to death of witches and wild animals and monsters, I suddenly came upon a cluster of glow-worms. In the cemetery of all places, at the far side of the bluegum forest. It was pure magic. The most beautiful sight I've ever seen in my life. It took all my fear away. I sat down where I found them. And that was where the rescuers finally found me. I burst into tears when they picked me up to carry me home. Everybody thought it was because of the fright I'd had, or from relief. But it was because of the glow-worms.'

'I once saw a firefly,' said Thomas. 'In the most unlikely place you can ever imagine.' He told her about the evening in the outhouse, and about the sugar water he'd continued to take out at night for heaven knows how long.

'So it was right of me to come with you,' she said, curiously satisfied. And sat up. 'What made you decide to let me come?'

'Many reasons,' he said. 'But mainly that you offered to phone for me.'

She sat staring down at her hands.

'What about you?' he prodded. 'Why, in spite of everything you'd found out, did you want to come with me?'

'Because I trust your hands,' she said. 'People may lie or cheat, but hands don't.'

She raised her hands, thumbs together, the fingers spread out, and studied them intently for a while. Slender hands with a transparency of blue veins; long fingers, the ends unexpectedly square, knuckles prominent, the unvarnished nails cut short in a no-nonsense way. She turned them round, palms up, studying the lines with critical concentration.

'I've always longed to have "sensitive" hands,' she said. 'But look at them. Nothing sensitive about them at all. And not terribly practical either. I always drop things. They're just – well, hands.'

'They play the guitar very well.'

'Anyone can play the guitar. It's not like the violin or the cello or something that really demands an effort. A guitar is a generous instrument, it sings even for a savage.'

'You're not a savage.'

'You don't know me yet.' An unexpected sigh. 'But perhaps you're right. I grew up so safe and protected.' She grew wistful. 'The nanny who looked after us. Naomi. She's getting on in years now, still looks after Papa. But in those days she was in her prime. A large woman, all soft and generous. Something Mother could never be even if she wanted to, she was always too busy being the dominee's wife. So it was really Naomi who brought us up. Carried both of us on her back when we were very small. Later she took turns with us. But she always favoured me. Even now, when I fall asleep at night, something of that early feeling of security comes back to me, the feeling of lying snugly in an *abba* blanket on the back of a large strong soft black woman. I remember the wood-fire smell of her clothes. A kind of physicality that still moves me. There was even something sexual about it, I think. I know that's how Erik remembers it, we've often talked about it.'

She remained silent for a long time, her face concentrated, a frown between her smoky eyes.

'Only much later,' she continued at last, more restrained, 'I must have been at university already, I once talked to Naomi about her own children. And realised for the first time that they'd grown up without a mother all those years she'd been bringing us up. Left in the care of a grandmother and some distant aunts. And she has so much love in her, Anton. The love her own children deserved.' She looked up in one of her quick changes of mood. 'I'd love to see her again. I always miss her when I feel lonely or mixed up or threatened.'

'I hope you're not feeling threatened now!'

'No. But I was a few days ago.'

'When?'

'That first night on the farm with the Bassons, when I went into the room and saw the double bed.'

After he undressed, he walked past the mirror in which she'd watched him wash (he her, earlier), to turn off the gas lamp beside the bed; then, blind in the dark, he felt his way to the window to open the curtains to the stingy moonlight from outside, and then came back to the bed. The feather mattress gave way deeply as he sat down on the edge. He could hear her giggling softly. Lisa lay on the near side, and he had to climb over her, feeling his way in the dark, to crawl in under the blankets on the wall side.

For a while they lay stiffly, waiting, uncertain beside each other. Trying to sound playful, he said, 'Well, Mrs Lamprecht?'

She sat bolt upright. 'Look here, Anton –' There was a hint of panic in her voice; more than a touch of warning too.

'You're not scared of me, are you?'

'Of course not.' After a while she added, 'Now you're supposed to say, "I promise I won't do anything you don't want me to –"'

'Will that convince you?'

She sniffed.

She was still sitting upright, he saw, her knees now pulled up, hugging them in her arms. The night light from behind highlighted the outline of her shoulders and her back, the texture of the frayed old shirt she wore in bed.

'What are we *doing* here?' she asked suddenly, in her voice no protest, only vulnerability, perhaps amazement.

'This is only the beginning, Karin.' He still found it strange to call her by this name.

'Aren't you scared?'

'I don't know.' He honestly had to reflect for a moment. 'I've been living this kind of life for so long. Not that one ever gets used to it, or becomes immune. But one learns to rearrange one's priorities. There's simply no *point* in being scared.'

After a long time she spoke again: 'May I ask you a very impertinent question?'

'What?'

'Do you think of yourself as a murderer?'

'No,' he said calmly.

'And yet –' She remained silent for a long time, then decided to go through with it: 'And yet you *are*.' Then, hastily, 'And that is what I cannot understand at all: why doesn't it upset *me* more? I should have pulled in my ears and ran for it and never have come back the moment I saw your photo in that paper.'

'Perhaps you cannot bring yourself to think of it as murder either.'

'No!' she said with startling vehemence. 'Because it *is*. Yet there's something that holds me back. What I read in the paper I simply cannot relate to you. It doesn't fit. Perhaps I just refuse to believe it.'

He leaned back. Waited for her to resume. Knowing how terrifyingly thin the edge was on which they lay in that darkness.

'You *must* believe it,' he said softly, almost as if he felt pity for her. 'You'll be deluding yourself if you don't.'

'I know. And yet I can't.' Another of her inscrutable pauses. 'I feel safe with you. And surely that's the last thing in the world I ought to feel. So why do I? Tell me that. Why, Anton?'

'Whatever you do, don't try to romanticise it.'

'What about you? You're also trying to deny that it was murder.'

'All I'm trying to believe is – that it was *necessary*. That we had no other choice.'

'How could you take a decision like that, and then come to terms with it and put it out of your mind?'

'That's not how it was. I have never stopped thinking about it. I don't think I ever will.'

She said nothing in reply. After a very long time she sat up. Against the gentle brush strokes of light he saw her pull the shirt over her head and throw it on the foot of the bed; she shifted down again. The simplicity of the gesture unexpectedly disturbed him. He became aware of how closely they were lying together. Of the silence surrounding them, this dark bed, the house, the farm. From time to time a floorboard creaked; outside the window a night bird screeched: sounds that merely served to define the silence, establish landmarks for it, before receding again before its imperturbable flow.

'You know what it feels like?' she asked suddenly, softly. And when he didn't answer, merely turned his head to listen tensely: 'Like Hansel and Gretel, lost in the wood. We don't know the way home. And we know the witch is waiting, only we don't know where.'

Without a word he stretched out an arm towards her. She raised her shoulders to settle in its crook, then snuggled up against him. For a long time they lay in tense silence. He listened to her breathing. He felt the blood-warmth emanating from her. Almost intuitively, certainly without consciously meaning to, he brought over his other arm and began to caress her hair which lay spread on the pillow between them. He heard the slight change in her breathing, the briefest catch before it resumed. With the tip of a finger he traced the outline of her profile: forehead, nose, lips, chin. Moved down across her throat that throbbed slightly under his touch like a bird breathing. Over her shoulders. Even more lightly, barely touching her skin, he moved his hand across the slight swelling of her breasts, hard thimbles of nipples. Becoming aware, at the same time, of a kind of desire he thought he'd already relinquished for good: an emptiness to which he'd reconciled himself, a vacuum that had to be accepted without question. Almost as of something untoward he became conscious of his erection, like the pain a patient feels, without warning, in an amputated limb.

His motion had become quizzical, almost diffident. It was a curious sensation, as if his hand were an eraser with which he tried to obliterate her, to deny her, to wish her away, like a failed drawing, a wrong word. In search of something below the inscribed surface, a different word, another name, another body, Nina.

Would she be aware of it at all? Was that why her body grew tense under his touch? How could he tell – and it was desperately important to do so – whether it was revulsion or desire, or a curious, sad, desolate acquiescence in what might seem to her inevitable? And when at last she moved her own hand to enfold his penis, was that to assure him that she was alert to his need, wished to react, felt compassion for him, wanted to comfort or reassure him, or that she wanted him, desired him, or simply wished to get it over as soon as possible? Their hands touched. Their fingers became enlaced, holding each other. For a long time they lay unmoving, tense, each waiting for the other; gradually they eased again, his erection drooped and returned to rest. In unspoken gratitude, relief, acceptance, they remained lying hand in hand, and so fell asleep.

But it was a shallow sleep, a dozing, a daze; and soon he was awake again, lying motionless in the sweltering bed beside her, until much, much later – the clock in the lounge had already struck two, and half-past, then three o'clock – she whispered:

'Are you awake too?'

'Yes.'

'Tell me a another story?'

And that was when he resumed from the point they'd reached before: the story of David Gideon Landman and the nymph in the wood: he told it the way his grandfather had done – the legend of a strange wild girl surprised in a pool below a waterfall, and eluding her captor by turning instantly into a gazelle, a small duiker or a steenbok, capering off into the wilderness; and of a young man going in search of her, a journey that lasts for months and years until he comes upon his lost gazelle in the Camdeboo; not knowing it is her, he takes aim to fire; when he begins to skin the carcass the magic girl jumps from it. But as Thomas lay telling it, he saw in his mind the story as he himself had altered it in the romantic imaginings of his boyhood: the naked girl below the cataract, the long black hair rippling down her smooth back – all the emphatic, emblematic sensuality that had inspired the first wet dreams of his adolescence – and suddenly it struck him with such violence that he had to gasp for breath, that *this* was the image Lisa had recalled that green morning when he'd discovered her among the plants of her bathroom. That was why she'd seemed so familiar: it was a scene he had anticipated long before he'd ever met her.

And now he desired her: frankly, unconditionally, yet with a troubled feeling of guilt as well, as if his desire were forbidden and incestuous; all the more so as the girl of his tribal chronicle had so disconcertingly borne the name of Thomas. He resisted the urge, tried to control his voice, pursuing the long story of David Gideon Landman, even inventing new variations and detours to prevent, at least postpone, an end; attempting perhaps to exorcise something both in himself and her. And sometime in the course of his narration Lisa fell asleep, and then he too, without ever reaching the end; as if they really were two children who had lost their way in the wood but had now temporarily found a place to rest, where they were no longer afraid, where they could abandon themselves to what in that dark night was unavoidable anyway.

— As we drive on through the silent flames of this basic landscape she is being cremated. Nina. It feels like the inevitable outcome of that night in the old couple's farmhouse, when Lisa's body briefly, under my hand, changed into hers. I know I really took my leave of her that day in Green Point when I accepted the finality of her death. But this is something different to come to terms with; and this is what happened that night. That in continuing with my life I would have to leave open the possibility of 'someone else'. I could not face it then. I cannot now.

Last night's TV news. After dinner, while I went to fetch something from the room, Lisa went to the seedy lounge. When I came back there was someone with her: a middle-aged commercial traveller with steel-rimmed glasses, chatting her up, soft-soaping her with jokes that showed the mould of innumerable retellings in similar hotel lounges where they'd sometimes worked and mostly not; stories with the stale odour of one-night stands, false bravado, prostate trouble, smelly feet, tea-stains on waistcoats.

She seemed surprisingly carefree. She was actually laughing at one of his jokes when I came in; exuding sympathy with his display of loneliness; and I discovered that she'd even accepted his offer of a drink, which was brought in by the waiter just as I arrived; red wine. 'Up yours!' shouted the stranger, his red-veined face contorted in enforced joviality, his brandy glass raised, his spectacles — dust-covered and greasy with finger-marks — reflecting the unremitting light.

She introduced us, 'Anton — Eddie.'

Could she really have been pleased — or even relieved — by making his acquaintance? I was the one who made no secret of my disapproval. (Why *should* it have upset me so?) And soon after

398

I'd settled myself on the armrest of her chair and borrowed her glass to sip from it – as crudely possessive as any dog staking out his territory with a raised hind leg – he offered an airy apology and left.

'You were insufferably rude,' said Lisa emphatically as the stranger moved off, with a stiff-legged deliberate gait, to the bar from which he'd undoubtedly appeared.

'Don't tell me you fell for his stories? It's the oldest trick in the trade.'

'The poor sod was unbearably lonely.'

'No doubt he has a wife and six kids at home.'

'Does that make it a crime to strike up a conversation?'

'He wanted to get you to his bed.'

'It was still my choice to say yes or no. It's not as if you saved me from a fate worse than death.'

'I have a shit in men like that.'

'Why? It was none of your business, was it?' Her eyes narrowed; she refilled her glass from the half-bottle on the low round drink stained table. 'It's not as if you have any claims on me, you know.'

I could feel my face burn. 'Look, you're free to carry on as you like. But we do happen to be together on this trip.'

'For as long as we both shall live?'

'I didn't say that.'

'But it must have been in the back of your mind.'

This was a new Lisa whom I hadn't seen before, and who strangely disturbed me: not only because I knew I'd deserved the reprimand, but because of the peculiar independence she asserted, which forced me to take her into account in a way different from before. This Lisa was no woman who had come along with an attitude of whither thou goest I will go, and where thou lodgest, I will lodge, thy people shall be my people, and thy God my God.

'It must be hard to be a man,' she added in stinging commiseration, her eyes on the glass she was holding in her two cupped hands.

'Are you referring to Eddie or to me?'

'I'm referring to men.'

A quiet, perilous moment from which anything might have sprung. But just then the news began and the waiter came hurrying subserviently towards us to turn on the volume. In urgent concentration, without speaking, we sat watching the screen as if it really were of the utmost importance not to miss anything.

It was the second item. With all the melodramatic embellishment the SABC is capable of. A colour photograph of Nina's face that filled the screen without warning (my God, I could swear I'd taken it myself: but where had they found it?), accompanied by the smug elocution-teacher voice of the newsreader. The female terrorist shot dead by police at Jan Smuts airport a month ago as she prepared to flee the country has been identified as Miss Nina Jordaan, a member of one of the leading Afrikaner families in the Mother City, only daughter of Mr Justice Henning Jordaan, who has presided in a number of terrorism trials. It has been established beyond all doubt that the deceased was involved in the bomb attack on the life of the state president earlier that same day, together with the fugitive terrorist Thomas Landman – at this point Nina's face was replaced by the black and white photograph of myself that had been published earlier – who, according to Brigadier Kat Bester of the security police, is believed still to be in hiding in the vicinity of Cape Town.

I didn't register anything else. Although I'd been expecting it for a long time – what was surprising was not the news itself but the fact that it had been suppressed for so long: for what reason? and what was behind the decision to release it now? and why the assurance that the fugitive Thomas Landman, condemned in advance, was hiding in Cape Town? questions, questions, questions, a whole flood of them, a building imploding – it was unsettling to hear it in that public place. I tried to shrink away from under the eyes of the tired but attentive waiter. He wasn't even conscious of me; only of the TV screen. Should we try to get out of there and back to our rooms as soon as possible? But it was obvious the man hadn't noticed anything; my disguise was effective; to make an untoward move, now, might arouse his suspicion.

That was when she put her hand on mine, and whispered:

'Was she really one of you?'

'–'

'She was –?' I could feel understanding seeping into her, like a dark liquid clouding a glass of clear water. 'The two of you –?'

I pressed my hands to my face.

At some stage, later that evening, Eddie came staggering from the bar again, stopped, aimed in our direction, waved half-heartedly:

'How's it?'

This time neither of us responded. I could hear him mumbling something – it was (fortunately?) impossible to distinguish the words – and then he moved on, evidently far gone, his steps cautious and emphatic as he sidled through the room in a peristaltic movement towards the outside stoep.

We remained sitting. The waiter, who had propped himself up against the wall, tried to stay on his feet, his face contorted sporadically by yawns like soundless screams. Once, it must have been very late by then, Lisa motioned to him and ordered two brandies. When he came back she counted money from her worn brown purse. And then told him, 'That's okay, we won't need anything else. We'll switch off the TV when we go.' He said, 'Thank you, Madam,' and disappeared for good. At last we were alone.

'How could you live with it all this time?' Incredulity broke through her voice. 'And all the while – My God, Tho-Anton!' It was the first time since we'd left Cape Town that she'd almost slipped up with my name.

'I *couldn't* say anything.'

'I know. But I wish I'd known before. Perhaps I could have been more of a help.'

'It's all right. Really.' By now I'd had time to recover; the neat brandy was taking effect too.

'Do you mind if I ask you about it? Or would you rather I shut up?'

'It depends. I can't answer everything.'

'Did you –' She seemed to check her thought. 'Were you –' And then: 'You loved her?'

'Yes.'

'Were you – together for a long time?'

'Yes.'

'Was she –' This was, clearly, more precarious territory. 'Was it difficult for her to – I mean, you know – bring herself to do a thing like that?'

'It was difficult for all of us. We would all rather live than die. But one reaches a point where you know you must go through with it.'

'Isn't it – Anton, will you please forgive me asking all these questions? – but don't you think it may be *easier*, in the long run, to turn to violence? Isn't it a short cut?'

'What makes you think it can ever be a short cut?'

'Perhaps that isn't the right word. I'm groping for something. Help

401

me!' She swallowed deeply, then resumed with more composure. 'What I mean is: one may reach a point where life begins to seem too problematic, too complicated, too confused to handle – and then, perhaps, you lose patience – you stop looking for other possibilities – and there may be something about violence that makes it seem – well, less complicated, more manageable – a way of cutting through the knots, of having done with it all?' A sudden change of mood, almost mocking: 'Or is it simply a new version of the old Boer way of shooting your way to a solution?'

When I answered it was as if Sipho's voice was talking through me: because how many times, how many hours, days, nights, had we not discussed it? In London, in Lusaka, in Dakar, in Dar-es-Salaam, Accra, up and down Africa. 'Of course that's one way of doing it. That's the way it's often done. But that's not how it was for me. Or for us. For her, for Nina. To detonate a bomb –' Instinctively I straightened up, glanced around me – no matter how softly we were whispering, I could not drop my guard – before I resumed, 'To explode a bomb one needs more than the simple energy of anger.' (In the training camp in Angola, over and over, repeated, later, by Justin, 'Get rid of the anger in you. Get rid of the hatred. Anger is the greatest threat to revolution. It makes you blind. *We* have to think through every step we take, every inch of the way.')

'But there's so much that is *denied* by it, Anton.'

'Of course there is. That's the price you have to pay. I'm not trying to shy away from anything of what happened, Karin. I don't want to cover up anything. I – and Nina – all of us – we killed people. I cannot even try to pretend that I'm innocent, that I'm anything except the thing I am.'

'And in spite of it all you could go through with it?'

'Yes. And Nina too. For her it was even harder. But at the same time she was tougher than I. Because we recognised that there are situations where doing nothing may be worse than exploding a bomb and killing people. In order to prevent even more violence.'

'The people who died are *dead*.'

'So is Nina.'

She looked into my eyes, and dropped her head.

With a disarming wavering in her voice she said, 'I'm so sorry I never knew Nina. If I had, perhaps I would have found it easier to understand.'

'What?'

'You. And about violence. Because she was a woman. Per
could have persuaded me.'

'Not I?'

'No.' A silence. The darkness of her eyes. 'I so much w
understand. It's important. But there's something in me that
to believe what you say. I cannot accept the destruction of lif
even if it is done for the sake of life. But I *want* to understan
sure it would –'

'What?' I urged her after a pause.

'It might help me to help *you*.' She unfolded from her cha
was time to go to bed. 'You must be so lonely tonight, Anton.

'One gets used to it.'

'I don't think so. Not really.'

I got up too. Down a long ill-lit passage we went to our separ
rooms opposite one another. I was wondering whether she – I was
sure I dared. Perhaps a mere gesture would have sufficed. Alread
she had understood more than I could ever have hoped for. And
was lonely. God alone knows how much. But at the same time i
was necessary, that night before Nina's cremation, for me to be, to
remain, alone. –

5

– 1. This I have not deserved. It is not that, judging from within the
rigid discipline of my profession, I demand of life, as I would of
myself, to be 'just'. But that my own child should have done this
to me, and that others – including Brigadier Bester whom I used to
regard as an ally if not a friend – should have exploited it to turn
the knife in the wound as it were, this I have not deserved.

2. What are the facts before me?

2.1. On the evening of Friday, 29 April, at about 20 minutes to 7,
my daughter Nina, having just cleared customs and passport control
at Jan Smuts airport, was walking towards the escalator leading
downstairs to the duty-free shopping area when she was accosted
by two security police officers accompanied by a detachment of
armed policemen in uniform. She started running away but was
shot dead. In her handbag were found a false passport and an air
ticket to Frankfurt, both bearing the name of Elaine Munroe.

2.2. It was established – I still have to satisfy myself of the

details of the evidence, but prima facie there would appear to be a case – that she had been involved in that morning's attempt against the state president's life in Cape Town.

2.3.   For reasons not yet satisfactorily explained all of the above information was kept secret from me and the members of my family for almost three weeks, even though Brigadier Bester and others had positively identified Nina's body within hours of her death. The body was flown to Cape Town aboard a military aircraft on the day after the event and kept in the police mortuary in Salt River.

2.4.   On Wednesday, 18 May, I received a visit from Brigadier Bester in my chambers and for the first time was informed of the fact of her death and of the events leading up to it. My first reaction was to request that the information be kept strictly confidential and that, at the very least, Nina's alleged involvement in the bombing episode be suppressed. It would serve no purpose, I pointed out, least of all the concerns of justice, to implicate a person who had already paid the price for her actions, if indeed she had been involved in the matter. On the other hand, it could cause immeasurable damage to innocent persons without bringing the guilty a step closer to what can only be regarded as their just deserts.

2.5.1.   Bester accepted my argument and indicated, as on many other occasions in the past, his willingness to co-operate with me. It was agreed that if for any reason her death had to be made public at some future stage the media would only be informed that she had died in an accident.

2.5.2.   Considering the fact that she has been suffering from acute nervous tension for some time now, I chose to inform my wife of no more than the fact of Nina's 'accidental' death, without for the time being divulging particulars about the circumstances surrounding that tragic event. One has regard for the distress of others more vulnerable than oneself.

2.6.   As he was, I thought, on the point of leaving my chambers, Bester drew a folded sheet of paper from his breast pocket, unfolded it and offered it to me. 'Would you mind having this typed by your secretary and then signing it?' he asked (or words to that effect). 'It is rather urgent. Can wait for it, if it's all right with you.' I perused the document, similar to others Bester had proffered me over the years. A brief statement, purporting to be drawn up by myself, to the effect that on such and such a date at such and such a time I had visited the detainee David Moishe Blumer in his cell in Caledon Square and found him to be in a satisfactory state of health, mentally and

physically; and that in reply to my question about his well-being he had replied that he had no complaints.

'Any problem?' I enquired of Bester. I can recall our subsequent brief conversation verbatim, since I took the precaution of writing it down immediately after his departure.

'Not really,' he replied. 'But you have no doubt seen the newspapers. All those people demanding that Blumer must be charged or released. The usual load. Only this time it seems to be more widespread. So the Pres called me in yesterday. Told me he got enquiries from the British, French and American embassies and the Scandinavians. Bloody lot of interfering shits.'

'You sure it's worth while holding on to the man?' I asked.

'He was part of the communist conspiracy that nearly blew up the Pres,' he said. 'No doubt about it. In it with your daughter. You might say he was partly responsible for her death. You wouldn't like to see a man like that getting out of it scot-free, would you?'

I did not like the look that accompanied his remark. Naturally I cannot allow myself to be influenced by anything as irrational as a 'feeling' or a 'hunch', but I wish to record for my own purposes that his manner suggested he knew more than he was prepared to divulge.

'Would there be any objection to my seeing Blumer for myself?' I asked.

I noted the way in which Bester's avuncular eyes appeared to change. Barely perceptible, admittedly, but through years on the Bench it becomes second nature to watch for such small tell-tale signs accompanying a statement. It was as if behind his customary easygoing expression a blind had been drawn. I realised of course that this was the first time I had ever offered the merest hint of querying any of his submissions; we had always found it mutually profitable to co-operate without asking questions.

'It is your prerogative to see any detainee whenever you wish,' he said calmly. 'But you are a busy man. Would hate to waste your time.' Adding with a benign smile (but without a change in his eyes), 'Matter of efficiency.'

I still hesitated, holding the sheet of notepaper in my hands. Then I shrugged, pressed a button on my intercom and summoned my secretary. Ten minutes later, during which time neither of us said another word, the statement was ready for signing; and Bester left.

2.7.   For three days I kept the matter to myself. At home Lorraine remained in bed, heavily sedated by her doctor, not even opening her eyes when I entered the room; or, at most, turning her head away. For years now she has denied me the support a man might expect of his wife – to such an extent that I have had no choice but to have recourse, from time to time, to the services of a young paid lady, Sylvia, who came to me with the personal recommendation of someone in the highest circles (whose name I am not here at liberty to divulge) and whose sympathy and understanding, more than anything else, have sustained me through difficult times.

I did my best to concentrate on the Coetzee case (a relief to be dealing with a straightforward murder case again; the recent spate of political trials has been exhausting), but my mind was perturbed. I must even confess to drawing more courage from the whisky decanter than usual. Nina's death in itself was bad enough, no need to dwell on that. But the way in which Bester had undertaken to keep the circumstances a secret and his request (request? demand) that I sign the statement on David Blumer continued to distract me. Coincidence? I do not wish to confuse my assessment of the facts with conjecture: but a brief explanation of the state of mind induced in me by those facts is indeed relevant to what ensued.

On the Saturday morning, 21 May, I had my regular game of golf with the state president and our two partners. Off the record: I loathe golf but discovered many years ago that it was indispensable for the kind of contacts I need; today, as a direct consequence, I am perhaps closer to the President than most others. It must gratify him to beat me so consistently, and the humiliation I feel is a small enough price to pay for the benefits that flow from it. But this is by the way.

After the game, when for a few minutes the two of us were alone in the VIP lounge, and after several quick White Horses, his choice, I resolved that in his own interest he should be informed about the meeting between Bester and myself. In fact, it was he who, perhaps deliberately, created the opening by thanking me for my statement on Blumer. It had, he said, and I quote, 'taken a bloody load off my shoulders'. I presented him with a brief summary of the occasion, indicating – without dwelling on it, of course – that I was concerned about possible ulterior motives in Bester's approach to the matter and reiterating that it would seem pointless to drag Nina's name into it if it could be avoided.

At that juncture our companions returned from the Gents and the subject was not pursued any further.

2.8. On Tuesday afternoon, 24 May, just as I was preparing to

406

leave my chambers, Bester entered without knocking. He looked furious, to put it mildly. My first impression was that he had had too much to drink; I could actually smell cheap brandy on his breath. Before I could say anything he barked at me, 'You went to the Pres? Would like to know why. Thought a man could bloody well count on you.'

'Look,' I said. 'Sit down. By all means let us discuss it.' I always believe in the rational approach, which I suppose is what attracted me towards jurisprudence in the first place.

'Nothing to discuss,' he said sharply. 'Just came to tell you you can have the body on Thursday afternoon.'

I felt the blood drain from my face. He did not stay to discuss the matter. By the time I opened the door he had closed abruptly after him he had already disappeared down the corridor. I admit it was past seven before I reached my home in Oranjezicht. I have no recollection of how I got there; must have poured several Dimple Haigs too many. But there were extenuating circumstances: all of a sudden I now had to confront Lorraine with the news of the cremation. My sons too, but they would be less of an obstacle than she, and I could rely on the telephone to minimise emotion. My own anguish, for it was indeed an experience of anguish, was relieved only by the expectation that Bester would keep faith and not broadcast the confidential version of the event.

2.9. However, on Wednesday night the full story of Nina Jordaan, the killed terrorist, was spilled on the eight o'clock TV news.

2.10. On Thursday morning, 26 May, only hours before the cremation, and on several occasions subsequently, when I tried to contact the state president I was informed, after being requested to hold on (once for as long as thirteen minutes), that he was unavailable. On Friday afternoon a secretary telephoned to cancel Saturday morning's golf.

3. Now what are the circumstances surrounding the facts, the background against which they are to be evaluated, the personalities and relationships involved in the situation in toto? (I resent that my own involvement, if only as Nina's father, makes it necessary to survey the nature of that relationship too. Emotions are sordid and at best unreliable; but I shall try to be as objective as possible.)

3.1 Lorraine.

3.1.1. I need not dwell too much on her, she has never been a significant factor either in my personal circumstances or in Nina's.

I believe she married me for reasons of personal ambition, although it would only be fair to mention that, seen from my perspective, her father's position as a prosperous attorney and an influential member of the Broederbond was not without advantage to myself especially when I was a struggling young advocate. I owe my induction and much of my subsequent progress within that organisation to him, and I have never hesitated to demonstrate my obligation through offering my services, often pro amico, to the friends he had in high places. Still, it was Lorraine who became the prime beneficiary of my relationship with her father, and I regret to state, not in rancour but as a fact, that she has but rarely shown much gratitude, particularly in the discharge of her obligations as a wife.

What does seem to me more ad rem is the way in which Lorraine's social life distanced her from Nina. Whereas my own primary hope within the strict context of matrimony was the procreation of a daughter, Lorraine seemed to recoil in distaste, from the very beginning, from this particular baby. She had acted commendably in bringing up our four sons, but towards Nina she was not merely neutral but actively resentful, so much so that she actually declined to breastfeed the baby.

Not wanting to interfere in what was clearly her female domain, after a few early attempts to reason with Lorraine I abandoned all idea of persuading her to be more responsive to the needs of the child or even to discuss a matter which was so obviously distasteful to her. Only once did she ever volunteer an opinion of her own, but that was in such anger and so cryptic, that it was difficult to make much sense out of it; and perhaps it is unfair even to try. 'Why should I try to bring up a girl for the kind of life *I* have?' she shouted. (It was, if I remember correctly, the last time she lost her control in such an embarrassing way; after that I cannot recall her raising her voice over anything again. That is, of course, until she learned of Nina's death, when once again it served no purpose.)

Without wishing to give the impression that I am criticising a woman who, after all, shares, and has shared, a part of my life, it is my conviction, considering all the available facts, that if Nina had enjoyed the security only a mother can offer a girl she might not have been driven towards – misled into – a course of action any reasonable person could have foreseen to be not only futile but disastrous. In which case I, too, would have been spared this Gethsemane where I now have to drain such a bitter and unnecessary cup, with only the support of the aforementioned young lady Sylvia to rely on.

408

3.2. My sons.

3.2.1. It may seem curious to introduce them anonymously like this, but this is how I have always experienced their presence. A collective inconvenience; a collective threat, perhaps. I do not mean to be anything but just towards them, but since the first of them was born I was no longer a decisive presence in Lorraine's life, except in terms of the security and status my proximity could offer her. It is by no means certain that we would have had a 'happy marriage' without them, whatever the phrase implies: Lorraine was an extremely attractive but distressingly prim girl when we got married and from the beginning she regarded the sexual side of our relationship as an embarrassment, if not an insult. (Could I, from my side, have salvaged it through being less forceful in my demands? Possibly, possibly. But we cannot dwell on possibilities.) And from the day the first son was born, she turned all her affections to him, withdrawing completely from all her other natural responsibilities. In quick succession – perhaps, ironically, as a result of my urgent attempts to 'win her back' – the second, the third, then the fourth were born.

Nina came eleven years after the last of them, by which time Lorraine had become wholly immersed in her social and public interests (fundraising for the Party, charity, women's prayer groups), which may account for the vicious edge to her resentment of the new child.

Because I was so busy with my career and the activities of the Broederbond there was practically no time to spend with the boys; I have never been much interested in puerile pursuits like kicking a ball around or hunting or fishing anyway. So I am afraid my role in their lives was limited. Yet in a curious way it was gratifying to see them fend for themselves and eventually succeed: an accountant, an architect, a lecturer in business administration, an electrical engineer.

I do not see much of them, but I am proud of them.

3.3. Nina.

3.3.1. Headstrong, recalcitrant, intransigent, difficult. We were always at loggerheads, which broke my heart (if now that she is dead I may momentarily indulge in the use of such a sentimental phrase). I had hoped to find in her, my daughter, my sole ally in the family. But she seemed to derive perverse satisfaction from deliberately disappointing, frustrating, countering or even shocking me. Yet she was the only one of my children to turn to law when it came to choosing a field of study. (Even so she insisted on doing it at UCT; which in the end, as a reasonable man and a responsible parent, I did allow, albeit reluctantly.) Ironically, she was the one least equipped for a career in law. Too emotional, unable to distance herself from issues, invariably getting involved instead of considering the facts objectively; passionate when she should have been dispassionate. Still, always inclined to give anyone the benefit of doubt, I saw her choice as an acknowledgement of the example I had tried to set; but in the end she turned it into a battlefield to attack me in ways calculated most effectively to offend me.

That she should have chosen violence as her form of action I can only interpret as the final insult. Throughout her young life I had demonstrated the efficacy of reason. An example that comes to mind concerns a contretemps I once had with our gardener. He was married – or what passes for marriage among those people – to our domestic servant and in exchange for being permitted to live with her in her quarters he was expected to tend the garden. She had been in our employ for many years before his arrival on the scene; a most faithful servant. But he turned out to be a highly unreliable character and on this particular occasion, it was a Saturday afternoon at about three, I actually caught him stealing. In flagrante delicto. When I reprimanded him he suddenly picked up a stone the size of a human skull – those were the actual words that passed through my head as I watched him: 'the size of a human skull' – and advanced towards me in a threatening manner. In the circumstances it would have been understandable, a matter of self-defence, had I responded with violence. Instead, at the risk of my own life, I chose to reason with him and succeeded in bringing him back to his senses. (Subsequently I did have him arraigned, as was only just; and much to my regret I also felt obliged to dismiss his wife from my employ. But this I mention in passing.) As it turned out, Nina had witnessed the scene. Yet not even this quite dramatic example, which surely must have remained with her throughout her life, had succeeded in dissuading her from having recourse to violence herself.

3.3.2.   One can only conclude that she had been led astray by others. The very strength of her will, it seems to me, drove her to find allies among those who rejected all forms of discipline. The Blumers and Landmans who had callously exploited her enthusiasm for a 'cause' disappeared, went underground, scattered like rats or cockroaches: leaving her to fall victim to inevitable, and just, retribution.

3.3.3. A note on this Thomas Landman. Nina did bring him home once or twice, a year or two ago. I am afraid he did not impress me. Another scruffy student, I thought. She introduced him as a photographer, which did not make much difference. Photography, like my father's painting, can be an innocuous diversion, but if it takes the place of a respectable career it can turn into a subversive force. There must be something evasive in the character of a person who shirks a decent living to rely on something as opportunistic as photography: keeping on the sidelines, always watching others, 'recording' action, avoiding personal commitment. The kind of person who would happily trick my daughter into doing the dirty work, then pick up his cameras (perhaps he actually took photographs of the explosion? of her death?) and run. I have more respect for a common murderer than for a coward of this kind who lurks in obscurity – a darkness lit only, from time to time, by the explosions of his flashbulbs – and who sacrifices others for the satisfaction of his own perverse voyeurism.

Landman must have been a supreme manipulator to drive a young woman as strong-willed as Nina to a deed of such desperation. There cannot but be a twisted and distorted personality at work, combining diabolic calculation with an utter disregard for others. I can only hope he will be brought to justice sooner or later. It is regrettable that our legal system does not permit me to dispense that justice. At least I hope I may be permitted the observation, admittedly made more by an avenging father than the judge I have with so much dedication trained myself to be, that even the death sentence would be too good for him.

3.3.4. It is ironical that, had Nina not been drawn into the deplorable affair, I would have been the presiding judge at the trial of those guilty of this act of terror. Only days after the explosion the state president had asked me to come over to Tuynhuys. He was still shaky, and drinking more than usual. 'I'll come straight to the point, Judge,' he said. 'When they round up the terrorists who tried to kill me I want you on the Bench.'

I met his probing stare. I knew exactly what he had in mind.

'I shall not disappoint you,' I said calmly.

3.3.5. I am aware that I am known as 'the hanging judge'. My reputation is built on it. I see it as a tribute to my honesty. It was because I never flinched from imposing the ultimate penalty that my minister, and the state president, realised I could be depended on, in cases of terrorism especially, to purge our society of the evil forces at work to subvert its very foundations. Through the passing interest I took in my father's painting as a child I know that every artist strives to discover that one secret which will make his work unique, instantly recognisable. Some rely on a gimmick. For the successful it becomes their true signature. In a modest way I see my own work as a form of art; and the death penalty is my signature.

Other judges, and many advocates, notably the Jews among them, censure me for it, some openly. But living, as I have always done, according to the most profound dictates of my conscience, I have made my peace with it. What I do is what in the deep core of myself I know I *must* do; what I have been chosen to do. If some of my colleagues disapprove, I know that in the Cabinet, in the State Security Council, in places where it matters, where the real power resides, there is appreciation for my peculiar artistic touch. Without being close to power, one is condemned to insignificance; I realised this from the time I first met Lorraine and her father.

Lately, specific threats to the continued exercise of my functions have forced me to decline some cases the state president has, directly or indirectly, 'requested' me to take. But my previous record makes it difficult to recuse oneself. It has become 'expected' of one to accept; then to proceed to the ineluctable end. Otherwise that power which protects one turns against one. I have come to see it as a challenge to do what many others flinch to do. In all humility I confess that I find in this the heroism each one of us, consistent with his peculiar talent, ambition or possibilities, strives after.

3.4.   In conclusion, I.

3.4.1.   It is with some reluctance that I approach this section, and I proceed only because it serves the purpose of fairness and objectivity. I must confess (I am not a church-going man by inclination although I am obliged for professional reasons to attend service most Sunday mornings; in any case I have always subscribed to Christian values like honesty and decency) that it is only with the aid of Dimple Haig that I have finally persuaded myself to do this; and the cremation, I believe, has shaken me more deeply than my public image might have led people to believe. I may, in fact, be 'under the influence' at this moment, and what I have to say may not be admissible in a court of law. But this is not a court of law, it is a private debt to be settled. And in any case I have always been able to 'take' my alcohol better than most others without showing the effects.

I cannot say that in the accepted sense of the term I had a difficult or deprived childhood, although it was not easy. We were, I should think, an average family, and happy as families go. When I was fourteen, Father died in a car accident. Returning from one of the interminable trips he undertook to sell insurance policies (more often than not a pretext to indulge his misplaced passion for painting), he must have been staring at the landscape: on a long stretch of open road the car hit a milestone and overturned. It was a shock, but it caused no disruption; he had never really been part of our lives. In a way it even turned out to be a blessing, because the policies he left behind instantly made us rich. For two years we basked in the glory of the new status our unexpected wealth had accorded us in that small Free State town. Until one day, as suddenly as it had struck us, it was gone again. Mother had handed over our whole fortune to an attorney to invest and manage. Mr Issy Goldberg, our mayor, and reputedly the richest man in the district. And then he'd gone and lost it, together with a staggering amount of other people's money, in a series of shady deals. When the police started investigating Goldberg committed suicide. No one knew us any more.

If the Goldberg scandal repulsed me, I was fascinated simultaneously by the idea that one man could have bought so much power with other people's money.

I applied for loans to go to Stellenbosch to study law. I never became a top student; but I made sure the professors knew me. By then I had learned about survival. From the moment I met Lorraine, and her father, it was never necessary to look back. I have never set much store by sentimental notions about 'my people', Afrikanerdom, divine providence et cetera; but through my father-in-law, in the ranks of the Broederbond, I discovered how useful these sentiments can be. On my own, I knew from bitter experience, I would never amount to much. But through the right connections, and working within the available structures (which were becoming enormously powerful at the very moment I was poised to make my entrance into the world, i.e. when the Party so unexpectedly won the elections of 1948), I knew there was no limit to where I might go.

4. A month ago I was on the threshold of my final achievement. After a satisfactory morning at Milnerton the state president had mentioned a vacancy expected in the Appellate Division in the near future.

Now my own daughter, used ruthlessly as a tool of destruction by this evil creature Thomas Landman and his Jewish collaborators, has sabotaged my future. I cannot forgive it. I did not deserve it.

This is a moment of deep loneliness. As a judge I know only too well the meaning of solitude. Throughout a trial one is supported and guided by the rules, the structures, by precedents and the written words of the law. But when it comes to the moment of sentence one is alone. Face to face with one's victim, in the shadow of the gallows. It is a moment of awesome responsibility. I have never flinched in the face of it. Today, facing a verdict on myself, pronounced not by a judge but by my own child, I find this solitude almost unbearable.

There is no one I can turn to in this hour of darkness. Except Sylvia, who is both attractive and sympathetic and in whom I am obliged to seek both the warmth of a wife and the understanding of a daughter. But the hard fact (and it is facts I am concerned with) is that she is a paid woman: and even if I can trust her with my life, without incurring a burden of responsibility at the same time, she can hardly, in this extremity, be expected to assuage my solitude. (I do not even know her surname!)

But I shall not succumb. It is more profitable to approach it as an ordeal not to be avoided: a challenge and a test. I have survived in the past; I know I can again. Within the context of my profession I am still comparatively young, sixty-five. I have the energy and ambition of a much younger man. I can still serve the Bench, and above all the Party. If I apply myself, I may yet succeed in obliterating the memory of this shameful moment brought upon me by forces of darkness beyond my control. –

6

And then they arrived in the small village, twenty or thirty kilometres off the Cape west coast, where Thomas had lived from his third year to his thirteenth. Even an outsider could not but have noticed the changes that took place over the years; but to Thomas, returning after such a long absence with an insider's memories, the changes were unnerving. If on the one hand there were unmistakable signs of deterioration and decay – houses and small shops standing empty, their windows broken out, doorways barricaded with corrugated iron – there was also an air of 'progress':

streets had been tarred, an ostentatious wine cellar had made its appearance, as had a furniture factory, a new filling station at the junction with the main road, a face-brick vicarage next to the gracious old church; and – this was, to him, by far, the worst, as it was built on the corner where his parents' house, *his* home, had been – a brash new supermarket; on the outskirts, a fruit co-op, a cool drink factory or two. There were more prosperous-looking 'coloured' and black people in the streets; at the same time the destitution of others, skeletal bodies draped in rags and tatters, also seemed worse than before.

What had remained unchanged (except for a hideous new projection room poised precariously on tall thin pillars) was – next to the Greek café on the tatty little square facing the sprawling low hotel – the cinema, a singular architectonic structure in what can only be described as Boer baroque. This was where, late that evening, with a handful of other people, they were disgorged, after an unexpectedly long session in which the film reel broke several times, into the night. (The majority of the inhabitants, as might be deduced from the bluish flickering visible through open windows or transparent sunfilter curtains, had remained at home to watch TV.)

'Still not bored with the film?' Thomas asked, bemused, as the other people drifted off into the dark, leaving them behind alone under the moon on the ludicrous little square with its tawdry cluster of windblown outlandish palm-trees. She'd already told him that afternoon, when they'd discussed the prospects of the *dorpie's* night life, that she'd seen it no fewer than four times before.

'Oh no, and I wouldn't mind seeing it yet again. Perhaps next time she won't die in the end.'

He laughed.

'Why should a film be the same every time you see it?' she asked lightly, her low voice persuasive in the dark. 'It's mere convention that won't allow us to expect anything but the predictable.'

'Has it ever worked for you?'

'No,' she said, unperturbed. 'But so what? I'm keeping an open mind.'

Like the premonition of an incoming tide the night wind brushed against them. With her left hand she swept the hair from her eyes. The moonlight glinted on the shiny new ring she was wearing, since that afternoon, on her left hand. (Erik's peace ring had been restored to her right hand.)

That afternoon on the beach: too upset, for the time being, to come to terms with the crude new supermarket on the corner where his parents' house had been, he'd taken her to another village, on the coast. Leaving the car on a deserted lookout terrace, he'd walked down an incline ahead of her, squatted at the edge of the beach to take off his shoes, and strode on across the fine sand. She kicked her sandals off her narrow feet and followed him, then stopped to scrutinise a weatherbeaten little café crouched below a huge Coca-Cola signboard a hundred yards away.

'Like some ice-cream?' she called at him.

Without waiting, the two brown sandals abandoned where she'd kicked them off, she jogged away barefoot across the beach — he stood looking after her, fascinated by the gawky rhythm of her running, the long gangling legs, nothing smooth or supple about the motion, her body lanky rather than lithe, no grace at all, he thought (as he'd done once before, in a green wilderness), no grace, no flow, no symmetry, and yet it had a poetry of its own, blank verse, an atonal modern poem inscribed upon the sand and time — and disappeared into the dark interior. He waited patiently, his eyes wandering over the conglomeration of astonishingly tasteless holiday homes massed against the steep incline that swept down to the sea. Years ago, when his family had often spent part of the summer holidays here, there had been a mere sprinkling of fishermen's houses, whitewashed and thatched. In the summer holidays the farmers of the district had erected their *matjies* homes beyond the high-water mark: lengths of carpet made of rushes and reeds and fastened across a framework of poles to form cosy rectangular huts which let cool breezes through on hot days or nights, and swelled from moisture on rainy days to keep out the cold and the wet. Beyond the last huts was the beach, a narrow sandy strip against a moonscape of jagged cliffs, a stretch of coast so wild and deserted one could walk for miles without encountering a living soul. Now the fishermen had sold out to the big companies and their black trawlers; the farmers had subdivided their land to sell the plots, at exorbitant prices, to city dwellers and time-share firms. Tarred roads zigzagged along the incline among the nouveau-riche dwellings where millionaires came to spend a week at Christmas. High on the hill stood a double-storeyed face-brick hotel.

After a few minutes he saw Lisa returning over the sand, walking more slowly this time, concentrating on her step, carrying in her hands two lucky-packets and two ice-cream cones piled high; and stopping on the way to collect her sandals as well, dangling from a crooked finger.

'You know,' she said as she handed him his, and with a quick flick of her tongue intercepted a dribbling of cream from the side of her cone, 'it suddenly occurred to me, when I was in the café, what strangers we still are to each other. I don't even know what kind of ice-cream you prefer. I wanted to get you an Eskimo Pie, but suddenly I wasn't sure.'

'I prefer the cones,' he said. 'Your intuition was spot-on.'

They walked on for quite a distance, turning in behind the first tall ridge of lunar rocks; there she stretched herself out on the sand, propped up on an elbow, finishing her ice-cream with great dedication, her eyes on the most remote dark blue of the ocean – beyond the litter of plastic bags and bottles, blobs of oil, even a dead gannet washed up on the beach – as if she'd forgotten all about him. Then she sat up again, licked off her fingers one by one, held the two lucky-packets behind her back and said:

'Which hand?'

'This one.'

He watched as she cautiously palpated hers to try and guess what was inside before she tore it open and picked from among the cheap pink sweets a small green plastic pistol. She pulled a face.

'Not my line. Suits you better.' Holding it by the tiny barrel she offered him the butt. 'At least we now have a weapon to protect ourselves. Just make sure no one sees it.'

Inside his there was a shiny cheap ring with a chink of blue glass mounted on it; but as he picked it out to offer it, ceremoniously, to her, the gaudy little stone fell out on the sand.

'Well, well.' He clicked his tongue. 'Now we can't even get engaged.' He studied the ring for a while, then took hold of it in one hand and meticulously bent open and broke off, one by one, the flimsy little prongs that had so ineffectively held the blue stone. Without its setting the narrow shiny ring lay naked in his palm. He looked up and held it out to her between forefinger and thumb.

'Karin Rossouw,' he said, 'do you take Anton Lamprecht, here present, as your lawful wedded husband? What do you say?'

She transferred Erik's peace ring to her right hand and offered him her finger. 'I do.'

He tried it on; it was a perfect fit.

'But we must have the whole spiel,' she said, putting her right hand on his before he could let go of her finger. 'Otherwise there's no magic.'

'What do you mean?'

'With this ring I thee wed, et cetera. You know, in sickness and in health, for richer or poorer, for as long as ye both shall live. The honour and obey part you can stuff up your arsehole. Or perhaps we can keep the honour. But fuck the obey. Okay?'

'There's a problem,' he said.

'What?'

'You realise it's a marriage of convenience, not one of undying love.'

'So much the better.' A little smile. 'Once, when we were small, Erik and I decided to get married one day. I'd just heard the phrase "marriage of convenience" and somehow it sounded good to me. But he said he'd prefer a marriage of amusement. So if it's all right with you —?'

'Sounds good to me. Well, shall we give it a go? With this ring —'

'Wait.' She pulled the flimsy ring from her finger again and put it back in his palm. 'We need to talk first.'

'About what?'

'About marriage. We can't just rush into it like this. Otherwise I'll soon be another little suburban housewife with a life in which everything is predictable: a monthly allowance, a pharmacy account, instalments on the washing machine, pink pudding on Sundays, a servant, and three orgasms per week, eventually scaled down to two, one faked. And I can't face it.'

'The orgasms or the washing machine?'

'The package deal.'

'So what do you propose?'

'Don't you think we ought to draw up a proper antenuptial contract first?'

'You're right.' He looked round in search of inspiration. 'Let's move over to where the sand is firmer.'

Hand in hand they walked closer to the doily edge of the low-tide on the beach; it wasn't easy to find an open patch of hard moist sand among the debris of oil and plasticware. She found a seagull feather and handed it to him.

'Item?' he asked.

'The first is: neither of us may ever blame the other for anything that happens.'

418

'That's a new one to me,' he said, quill in the air, looking hard at her. She'd rolled the legs of her jeans up to her knees and was standing above him, astride, her feet in the shallow water.

'It's very basic. As I see it the main reason why people get married is always to have someone handy to take the blame for whatever goes wrong. Whether it's a geyser that packs up or a letter someone's forgotten to mail or the sun scorching the flowers or stomach ache or haemorrhoids. That's what kept my mother going all her life. And even my Godfearing father. So write it down.'

Thomas etched the clause on a patch of smoothed moist sand. Then he looked up and asked again, 'Item?'

'You must never leave your toenails lying about after you've cut them.' She looked at him askance. '*Do* you cut your toenails?'

'What else?'

'Oh good,' she said, relieved. 'You see, Martin used to bite his.'

In as good a copperplate as he could manage Thomas entered the inscription on the sand and said, 'Right. And in exchange for that you're not allowed to leave your panties soaking in the basin after you've washed them.'

'And you won't expect me to wash your underpants and socks.'

'And you won't ever get rid of any of my clothes or possessions or of my sheep or mine oxen without first consulting me.'

'And you will not, when you pee, leave any traces on the floor or the rim of the toilet.'

'That's a tough one,' he said. 'My aim is not always secure. But I resign myself. So help me God. Provided you undertake not to use my razor to shave your legs or under your arms. In fact, I'd like you not to shave under your arms at all, but I leave that to you. It's only a wish.'

'And I,' she said, 'would appreciate it if you won't explode any more bombs. That, too, is only a wish.'

'Any further clauses?' he asked. 'The table of the law is almost full.'

'There's one more thing: you must solemnly promise that you will never allow them to catch you.'

'Who are "they"?' he asked. 'In a legal document you must be specific.'

'"They" are "they". Whoever they may be. Because if they catch you I'll probably have to go to jail with you and there's no sense in sacrificing such a promising young life.'

'I won't expect you to go with me.'

'I don't normally do what is "expected" of me.'

He flattened a new rectangle of sand under his palm, wrote down the clause under her watchful eye, then sat back to rub the sand from the quill.

'What made you think you'd have to go to jail with me?' he asked, looking up at her against the sun.

She shrugged. 'It's congenital. When I was still at school, Erik and I sometimes slipped out at night – through the window – to meet friends in town. Just for the excitement of running loose, the feeling of doing something forbidden. Perhaps it was the same streak in me that made me come with you.'

'That wasn't the reason you gave me yesterday.'

'I know. But ever since you first asked me I've been thinking about it. And I believe it's important to keep on finding new reasons every day, otherwise one starts believing one's own explanations just *because* you've been repeating them all the time.' A brief smile tugged at her lips. 'And for the same reason I'll go on asking you why you planted that bomb.'

He didn't reply immediately. After some time he asked soberly, 'Anything else I should write down?'

'No, I think we can sign now.'

He offered her the seagull feather. She took it, squatted beside him and signed her name: her real name.

'You.'

He added his signature to hers.

'Now give me the ring,' she said, getting back on her feet.

He also stood up.

'With this ring I thee wed,' he said, slipping it on the finger she held stiffly out to him.

'I pledge thee my troth,' she said.

'That's nice,' said Thomas. 'That's really beautiful. I pledge thee my troth. For ever and ever.'

'World without end,' she said.

A breeze smelling of sea-secrets brushed their naked faces. With a small rustling sound of innumerable minute bubbles breaking the tide began to creep across the sand, covering the blobs of oil.

'You may kiss the bride,' said Lisa.

He hesitated. Far above them a gull described a parabola against the blue of the sky, remained suspended in the high breeze, then flapped its wings and swooped down towards the sea. He took her

hands in his, leaned over and gave her a chaste kiss on the mouth. Her lips tasted salty.

'All done,' he said.

To his surprise he saw what looked like tears on her cheeks. But she turned away so quickly, against the wind, that he couldn't be sure. She began to walk away. He looked after her. The gull feather fell from his hand. He stooped, picked up her sandals and began to follow her, slowly, his shadow moving ahead of him. When he caught up with her she stopped and turned. She smiled brightly. Perhaps she hadn't been crying after all. Together, they looked back. Across the sand where they'd written their contract crept an indolent foam-covered fold of water, obliterating it, taking back with it the feather of the gull and an empty plastic bottle.

'Good,' Lisa said, content, 'now it's final.'

Driving back from the sea — more resigned, Thomas now felt prepared to face his past — they passed a small lake. A seam of tough rushes surrounding the black water, a single heron standing one-legged over its reflection.

'Stop!' Lisa exclaimed, so suddenly that, startled, he braked in a cloud of dust.

'What's the matter?'

'We have time, don't we? Can't we just sit here for a while?'

They turned down the windows. There was no sound outside. The late afternoon sun, reflected in the rear-view mirror, stood right above the ocean.

Without warning the heron lowered its leg. Glistening rings began to ripple across the surface of the black water. That was all. Yet both were strangely moved by it.

Somewhere, at this moment, somewhere in the world out there, bombs exploded, people died, violence raged, terror was sown. Yet this, this motion of a heron lowering its leg into dark water and causing circles to ripple to the edge, this was an event so momentous that all of a sudden a whole world was placed at risk; so perilous that it went beyond all understanding.

Before the houses of the white village began, separated from the townships by a bleak no-man's-land, they passed the 'coloured' area. (The black townships were even farther away, more out of sight: the townships where Sipho came from; where one distant December day Thomas had helped a black woman carry home her Christmas bags and had drunk a glass of Oros and had stared through an open door into the dazzling white glare outside towards a streaming water tap in the distance where children cavorted in the mud and the woman filled a plastic bucket which she balanced on her head.) A whole horde of children, emerging from the door of a low prefab school building, came fanning across the barren playground. A thickset middle-aged man followed in their wake, clearly worn out, weighed down by a heavy school case. Some of the children made a wide detour to avoid the car before they scattered into the township; others risked a cautious greeting; only the smallest ones smiled without reserve.

'Good afternoon,' said Thomas as the teacher came past. The man who had been walking with his eyes on the ground looked up in surprise; his greeting sounded wary.

'Lamprecht,' said Thomas, offering his hand.

The man stared at it for a moment before he took it; then Lisa's. 'Augustyn,' he said laconically. An uneasy silence separated them.

'You're working very late?' said Thomas.

The teacher shrugged. 'Where are you from?' he asked.

'We're journalists. Doing an article on the people of the coast.'

'Is it jus' about de whites?' In his strong coastal accent it sounded like an accusation.

'No, no,' Thomas said quickly, 'All the people of the West Coast.' He looked at Lisa. She stood nervously twisting her new ring on her ring finger with her right hand.

The man showed more interest. 'And if I have something to say, will it count too?'

'Of course.'

'No, what I'm thinking is so few people listen to us. So few *know* about us.'

'We're interested in anything you can tell us.' He motioned at the children streaking towards the township. 'How come the school comes out so late? The sun is almost down.'

There was a brief twinkle in the man's eyes. 'De crow makes haste to de rooky wood,' he said. Nothing could be more unexpected than hearing Shakespeare in that heavy accent. But before either of them could comment, he resumed his drooping pose. 'It's *maar* how it is,' he said. 'Double sessions. One in the morning, one in the afternoon. The building is small and there's so many children. It's a ball-crusher, if I may say so.'

'Are you the principal?' asked Lisa.

'No, no, he's still inside. Sometimes he's dere until after dark. If you'd rather speak to him?' A touch of resentment. 'I mean, what's my word compared to his?'

'We'd be very happy to talk to you,' Thomas said quickly.

'Well, thank you very much den.' A hint of eagerness flickered in the weary eyes behind the steel-rimmed glasses. 'How about tomorrow morning den? It's easier Saturdays.'

They couldn't very well decline the offer. An appointment was made for ten o'clock. In his classroom, Mr Augustyn insisted, suggesting defensively that his house was difficult to find.

As they prepared to leave, there appeared briefly a new glint in the morose teacher's eyes. Straightening his back he said, 'Good night. And flights of angels sing dee to dy rest.' The accent lay, once again, uneasily on that Elizabethan bed. Noticing their surprise Mr Augustyn explained proudly, 'Shakespeare and I come a long way, sir, madam. It's a hard thing to teach him to these chillun. But I'm doing my best. It keeps a man going. Good day!'

They drove on; in the rear-view mirror Thomas watched the man who hadn't moved yet, his shoulders drooping once again now that they had left, the sun behind him, his school case on the ground at his feet as if he couldn't bear the thought of picking it up again. Something in his attitude reminded Thomas of his father. Not the hopelessness – for his father there still were support systems to rely on; a nation and a language and a history to believe in, a conviction that in the end he would be proved right, that his views of justice and righteousness would be vindicated because God was on his side – but the solitude, the school case, the defensiveness that suggested his true value was underestimated; the unremitting weariness.

Since they'd heard the news about his father's stroke on the radio, on Monday morning, he'd felt anxious, guilty, at odds with himself, defensive towards Lisa. Then, back from the mountains, the evening in the seedy hotel, the report about Nina. It had displaced, temporarily, the anxiety about his father. It was so much more desperate. But why? Nina was dead, his father still alive. (Perhaps!) He should be at his side. Blood must mean something!

But he could not. It was out of the question. Two nights before, after he'd turned away from Lisa in the dingy passage of their hotel, after the conversation that had cut through to the very bone, and before he'd turned in, alone in his single room, he'd gone so far as to pick up the telephone. Then he'd remained sitting on the bed like that, the receiver in his hand. A few flicks of a finger, and his mother would answer. It might make all the difference in the world. But he couldn't. He had no right to. There was no doubt his parents' telephone would be tapped. And so many others beside himself were involved. He'd replaced the telephone.

In the morning – yesterday morning – they'd first driven inland from the coast again, to Clanwilliam, to ring his contact number in Cape Town. An hour's wait; when he dialled again, another number, Justin was at the other end. For obvious reasons the conversation was very brief. He enquired, in code, about developments around the cremation, his father, David. There was nothing new. All Justin could divulge, again in code, was that the Organisation's scouts had noticed increased vigilance at frontier posts. 'So make the most of your holiday, Peter. For another week or two at least there won't be any work for you. But don't worry, we'll come up with something. In the meantime, you just enjoy yourself and give my love to the auntie.'

At least his father was still alive. But the anxiety remained.

Last night, when he could no longer bear it, in the next hotel – in his memory they were becoming interchangeable – he'd written a letter. It was difficult to find the words: words were not what he needed, or could manage, now. He had to be *there*, to carry in his arms, if necessary, the father who had carried him as a boy. Change roles, care for him, assume responsibility for him, comfort him, perhaps at last get to know him. But all that was permitted him, and even that was risky, was to wring out this clumsy note. A single page. Only to tell them that he knew, that he couldn't be there – they had to understand; please, please, for God's sake, try to understand, no matter how hard it is – they must try to forgive; his father must get well again. One day – He'd struck out the *one day*. And ended with a mere *Love*. Without a name to it; they would recognise his handwriting. He'd sealed it in an envelope bearing his mother's address. Then had enclosed it in a second envelope addressed to Justin's poste restante address. At least this should be safe, even if it took longer.

He'd spent a sleepless night. At six he'd got up, taken a bath, shaved – still uncomfortable with the strange reflection in the mirror – and dressed. Then he'd picked up the letter again, stared wistfully at it, and torn it into small shreds. At the reception counter in the lobby he'd asked for matches and proceeded to burn the shreds in the dustbin in his room. It was like a final act of betrayal. Once

424

one begins, he thought, it never ends, it cannot end. And it never gets easier either. On the contrary.

At the same time it was as if, through that depressing ritual of burning, he'd taken a final leave of his father. It was more than a confirmation of death: it was an assignment to death, a condemnation, an execution.

All these memories were jerked back to life by the sight of that teacher in his rear-view mirror. And he knew: he'd made that appointment for the following morning without intending to keep it; but now he had no choice. It was an appointment with his father.

They drove back into the village. Stopped beside the square under a frayed palm, and set out on foot so that he could show Lisa what he still remembered. The café. The renovated cinema. (That was when she'd noticed the poster for the film on the front stoep and had exclaimed, 'We *must* come and see it tonight! Do you mind?') The hard-baked tennis courts of red anthill earth behind the police station. The school, his father's kingdom. It seemed decayed, dated. Many windows in the hostel next door had the blank stare of vacancy. ('Ag mister,' the hotel manager had explained later, 'that's *mos* the way it is. There's not even twenty children left in the hostel this year. They're talking about closing it down. And they've cut the teacher quota again. Everybody's leaving for the big towns, we're running dry.' Lisa had asked, 'But the "coloured" school is bursting at the seams. Can't they use some of the space in the white buildings?' Flushed with indignation the man had replied, 'But Missus, that will be asking for trouble, man. Our people won't stand that sort of thing. No, no, that is out of the question.')

And then the corner plot where the brazen supermarket had imposed itself. Why here? There was so much space in the village; and surrounding it, to all sides, stretched the open scrubland. Now a whole segment had been torn from his life, cancelled, suspended, nullified. The garage where Frans had held church services for the servants. The outhouse where one summer night he'd seen a tiny angel with shining wings for whom he'd set out sugar water in a saucer, sustained by a belief in a miracle that was never repeated and had now been ruled out for ever.

After their departure the village had become fixed in his mind like a photograph. He had never come back. In a way the integrity of the recollection had been guaranteed by that distance. And now the worst had come true: that house *had* disappeared, had been relegated to oblivion, violently torn from the grasp of his memory.

– How closely related are destruction and creation, how thin the membrane that separate our different kinds of violence. Because violence is always there; ubiquitous. It is a condition of – a prerequisite for – our existence. What can be more violent than a question? *She* spoke about questions; never stops speaking about them. Her very existence is a question mark. Her questions about violence – *any* question, *all* questions – determine our limits, define the periphery of what is admissible, of what has so far been thinkable. And it is our search for answers to those questions which prompt us to transcend limits. This is the core of the violence which defines our humanity. Physical love – love itself, the transgression of the border between 'me' and 'you' – is violence. Fertilisation, the division of cells, growth, birth, all the processes of life, are conditional upon violence, unthinkable without it. (My courageous little pumpkin plants sprouting from the hard lumps of earth, in the garden I staked out in our barren plot in that other godforsaken town.) We do not register the violence with which a tree draws its sap from subterranean watercourses and forces it to the farthest leaf and flower and pod, nor the violence with which blood courses through our veins. But it is there. It spells life. And then there are its other forms: those which threaten life, and destroy it, and cancel it. Can one always tell the difference? And who but a god or a demon can take upon himself this decision between life and death?

Here, too, someone had decided: this house is expendable, may be sacrificed to progress, to new life, a supermarket.

But *I'm* still here. *I* must survive. Because *I* remember what was here before. And now the vanished house and garden, the outhouse, the angel or firefly, all depend on me, on my ability not to forget. –

All of a sudden he was feeling very old. Centuries old. As if this futile return had made of him a wandering Jew: as if not his ancestors but he himself had lived through that whole tract of history: the marriage with a slave girl, the trek into a barren hinterland, Abraham and Isaac and Jacob, Noah, Benjamin, each of them translated into himself, restless and cursed, wandering, fugitive, seeking. Adamastor himself.

But at least, at least, he had this woman-girl with him, with her faith in lucky-packets and seagull feathers, in changeable ends, in story lines which can be displaced.

He took her hand – would she understand the nature of the

urgency in him? – and said, 'It's time we found a room in the hotel. It will be dark soon.'

Now they were on their way back, from the cinema, to the hotel. Below the high stars the fronds of the palm trees on the little square were rustling like water. They had to wait a long time for the sleepy nightwatchman behind the reception desk to wake up and – accusingly – present their key, ringed to a heavy block of wood.

In the late afternoon, after the porter had shown them to their room, this room, and had opened the heavy faded dull-green curtains and pushed a creaking window open on the stoep outside (the screw on the hinge was broken) to let out months of stale air, they had stiffly turned their backs on the two anonymous single beds against the wall, each with its own separate lamp and Gideon Bible, to unpack their few possessions. They kept on getting in each other's way, apologising every time; each considerately left for the other more hanging and packing space. Afterwards she'd gone out with a bundle of clothes to be ironed, but it turned out the iron was out of order, so she was back disquietingly soon. She'd run a bath, leaving the bathroom door ajar on purpose, to signal confidence; but he'd settled in a straight uncomfortable chair in front of the window, below a reading lamp that didn't work, to read a newspaper of the previous day – or two days before, or a week before – his back to the bathroom. Half an hour later there were gurgling sounds from the bath. She came in, wrapped in a thin dun-coloured towel. The bathroom floor, when he went in, was covered in puddles. He thought: he should have remembered to put that in the contract too, now it was too late. When he came out again, she was standing at the dressing-table mirror, wearing a rather crumpled blue dress, working on her make-up. It almost startled him, it was the first time he'd noticed her doing it. He was surprised by her striking changed looks, the stark black of her eyebrows, her high cheekbones, the firm line of her jaw, the unexpected fullness of her mouth.

Soon after that they'd gone out together, to dinner and to the cinema.

Now, as they stepped through the door into the dusty light of the room that opened apathetically in front of them, exposing the two single beds like a confession of guilt, he was again aware of her face; especially of her smoky night-eyes; and much later, when they made love, of the ingenuity of her hands, the hardness of her body, her breathing, her black hair spread – like spilt black ink – across the edge of one of the narrow beds. In him, a new sated knowledge beyond words: I shall never again take a body for granted – the feel and texture of skin, the discovery of electricity running below it, the hardness of bone in rib-cage or hips – because nothing is predictable, everything is *you*. (And *who* are you?) Her apprehension of him would be different. Thinking: Perhaps it is true that without violence one cannot know, or understand, or acknowledge, tenderness or compassion, what is happening between us here, now. They were both, still, reticent, reluctant perhaps to give away too much by being reckless or loud. But already there was this to surprise and persuade her: that it was different from the few others she had been with – not a struggle or a tussle, not a contest to see who won, a test of strength or endurance; that he made no attempt to subdue or subjugate her or to force something from her; that her enjoyment of him was without condition or calculation, that it wasn't something either she or he tried to win or achieve, and not at his or her expense: that it felt neither like genesis nor apocalypse, only satisfying and good; and that afterwards they could lie, relaxed, together and sometimes be still and sometimes talk.

In the dull yellow glow of the lamp beside the unused bed in the corner, he let his eyes wander leisurely over her, from head to toe; and she lay waiting, neither vulnerable nor provocative: bemused perhaps, and perhaps amused.

With a forefinger he traced, as on that other night, the outline of her profile: forehead, eyebrows, the straight nose with its unruly tip, the unabashed generosity of her mouth, her chin and jaw, the vulnerability of her stretched neck. 'The first time I saw you,' he said, 'I didn't think you were anything special. Now you're beautiful.'

'What can you possibly find beautiful about me?' she asked with disconcerting frankness.

'Your eyes,' he said. 'They turn pitch-black when you come. Your mouth.'

'My mother always said my mouth was too big.'

'That's why I like it.' He moved his finger further down over her as if he were drawing the tentative outline of a map, across her collarbones, the hard roundness of her shoulders, the slight rise of her breasts. 'Your breasts, he said. 'I think they're lovely.'

'They're non-existent,' she said scornfully. 'I always longed to have a cleavage for a strapless evening gown.'

'Have you ever worn an evening gown?'

'No.' She laughed. 'I'd hate to.'

'I love your nipples,' he said. 'Nothing pink and pale and virginal about them. They're so dark and self-assured.' He looked up from them. 'That morning in your bathroom, among all those mirrors, and all the potplants, I would have given anything to take a photograph of you.'

'You're the one who's beautiful,' she said. 'I love your silences.'

'Where are the silences?'

'Your eyes,' she said, leaning over to kiss them on the lids he closed. 'And this bloody stuck-up mouth.' She kissed it too, then studied his body with rapt intensity. 'I'm glad you don't have a coir mat on your chest,' she said. 'You look like a boy. You look like Erik. He's got the same tiny nipples.' She briefly took them in her mouth, first one, then the other; a slight tingling spread through his body. 'And your navel.' With the tip of her tongue she drew a snail's trail down his belly, making small fluttering movements across his penis and scrotum. Giggled as it stirred and slightly stiffened, and folded her hand over it. 'No, I want you to stay soft. Nothing is as lovely as a soft penis.' For a moment her mouth closed over the half-exposed glans. To his own amazement – if he'd been with Nina now, he thought, he would have reacted with all the aggressiveness of an erection – his penis remained limp, vulnerable, exposed to her. After a moment she shifted to move down his thighs. 'I love the colour of your skin,' she said. 'It's like an all-over tan.'

'I'm afraid it's more than a tan.'

She stroked his thighs. 'It's beautiful. Like cinnamon.'

'To some members of my family it's a source of embarrassment.'

Her hands continued their exploration. 'And your knees. They're stroppy. They won't apologise easily.' Attentively she moved past his calves and ankles to his feet. Took them in her hands. 'Can I massage them for you? Erik loves it. Nothing calms him down so easily if he's all tensed up.' She moved to cross her legs under her and took his feet on her lap, one by one, pressing the sole against the pad of her pubic hair, where with skilful hands she set to work massaging every separate muscle and sinew. 'Turn over,' she said when she had done with his feet, and began to move her fingers up along his body again, thrusting her hands in between his thighs to part them, caressing his testicles and the small closed knot of his anus, kneaded his buttocks; and then, leaning far forward, she traced with her tongue long delicate tracts

429

along his back until she lay stretched out on top of him, breathing in his neck.

'Now I know what you look like,' she whispered.

She lay so relaxed, so quiet, that he wondered whether she'd fallen asleep.

'Are you happy?' he asked. He bent one arm upward to caress her back.

'I'm frightened,' she said softly.

'How can you be frightened?'

'Not of you. Just frightened.' Another long silence. 'I never knew fear could be so peaceful. Like when one lies in the dark listening to rain that just goes on and on: you think that the foundations of the house may sink into the mud, the walls may cave in, the whole world may be washed away: yet you just lie there. There's nothing you can do about it. It's just *there*, happening. And the sound is so peaceful. Yet you are aware of death.'

– Yes, ultimately this is what it is: there's no avoiding it. Time. To love is to be drawn into time. Into a body. Whatever you touch is pervaded with mortality. So close to death I have never been. –

He could not, did not want to, say anything as obvious as, 'Don't be afraid.' Because he knew exactly what she meant. For how long had he not been living it himself?

'Can you bear it?' he asked at last, shifting his body so that she could roll off him and lie next to him. Their faces were close together, their foreheads touching, they seemed to be breathing one another in and out, their eyes gazed deep into each other.

'I can't say yes or no,' she said. 'Because I have no idea what it is I'm expected to bear. All I know is that I'm here with you.'

'It can become worse.'

'I'm not sure it can,' she said. 'Even as we're lying here now – and what can be more secure and relaxed than this? – at any moment someone can break through the window to drag you away, to break this body of yours, to kill you. So how can it get worse? But I want to be with you. Do you understand that, Thomas?' This time, unabashed, she spoke his name. 'All my life I've been looking for something that would make it worth my while to be here, a kind of magic, something I could believe implicitly, something not yet spoilt by the men with the stomachs and the waistcoats.'

'But you *don't* believe implicitly in me.'

'I don't believe in what you've done. That I reject. I abhor it.'

430

She stroked her hand over his shoulder. 'But I believe in *you*. Even though I have no idea at all why I should.'

In the dark parenthesis that enclosed them that night neither could truly know what was at stake. He would have reached out, if he had to define it, to Ntsiki many years ago, and Henry; to Sipho and Noni; to others whose lives had spilled into his along the way – Frans, Maria, his parents: his father who was left incapacitated by his stroke; to Justin, Rashid, Christine, Nina; to David who at this moment, in this night while he lay here with Lisa in his arm, might be crouching somewhere under a bare bulb, a soaked bag over his head, gasping for breath, or with his body convulsing from electric shocks: there was no end to those whose lives had become involved with his. But even that was only the surface of what was at stake: not only their separate pasts and the fraction of it they had shared, but everything that might lie ahead, all that still had to happen and of which they were, mercifully, unaware – and which already, beyond the periphery of their consciousness, was refracted, like black rays of light, on to this night, this dimly lit room, this single bed in which they lay entangled, where after some time they made love again, now in a passion that left imprints and marks and bruises, that inflicted pain and yet set free, that hurt and comforted, that made them cry and shudder in tears, or made them laugh uncontrollably at times; a passion that at last left them, cocooned in sheets and blankets, sticky with sweat and tears and his semen and the secretions of her lust, to drift into a half-sleep from which, time and again, they woke up to make love yet again – more, oh God, more, more, because we are alive, we live, we *live*, tonight we live, tomorrow we may be dead – or to resume their never-ending conversation, a conversation that had begun before them and would continue after them, and which, only fleetingly, temporarily, expressed itself in their voices, like a stream that broke out briefly above the ground before resuming its subterranean course.

7

– *Senzeni na?* says the legend in large red lettering on the banner above the entrance to the hall in the ICA building; below it, in black, the English translation: *What have we done?* Milling crowds throughout the day, especially in the evening, after work. A large contingent from the media for the opening by a leading figure in the Labour Party. Newspapers, radio, TV teams. Interviews, question-and-answer sessions, talk shows. People patting me on the shoulder or shaking my hand – especially when the cameras are pointed in our direction – as if we are bosom friends. At regular intervals a voice in the unmistakable accent of the townships at home, 'Jeez man, how's it? How are you? How are things at home?'

Dazed, exhausted, overwhelmed, as the last stragglers begin to drift off – only here and there one or two remain, like the odd shell or bit of kelp left behind on the beach by a withdrawing tide – I escape to a chair in a corner behind a screen. My head reels. The whole commotion surrounding the exhibition has been rather too much for me: the honest outrage of many viewers, their sincere indignation – the woman who broke into tears in front of a photo of a young boy attacked by three burly constables wielding sjamboks; the young black mother who brought her two wide-eyed kids with her – but also the opportunism of those who've come only to soothe their guilty consciences at a safe distance, or to squeeze some local political mileage out of it, or simply because emotion, especially that elicited by apartheid, has become cheap, a consumer article, kitsch. Some of the reactions have moved me deeply. Others – particularly the raving media extolling my virtues as a 'dissident Boer' as if, as the poet Breytenbach has protested long ago, taking a stand against apartheid were an act of heroism instead of a sign of normality – have nearly made me vomit. This isn't what I wanted. (What have I expected?) I didn't want to be used. I didn't want to be exploited. So what have I achieved? Have I really torn a scab from some collective conscience, or have I simply become part of a fashionable craze?

As I sit leaning forward on the chair, elbows on my knees, my aching head between my hands, a raucous Louis Armstrong voice – but in an anomalous Oxford accent – exclaims behind me:

'Thomas Landman! Well, I'm glad to see you have the decency to come and hide.'

In the opening beside the screen stands a large black man in a navy suit. White shirt, maroon tie. In his mouth, between his teeth, is clenched the pipe which soon, in my mind at least, is to become his signifier. Two large white crooked front teeth. I look up at him defensively, not sure whether he's mocking or attacking me.

'Aren't you ashamed of yourself?' he asks, his dark eyes not leaving mine for an instant. 'Stabbing your own people in the back like this?'

After all the interviews, the public praises, the patronising pats on the shoulder, this feels like a wave of icy Atlantic water breaking over me. Dismayed, I can only stare at him.

'Lucrative business, this anti-apartheid bandwagon, isn't it?' he continues, his words measured through the clenched teeth that hold the pipe in position.

Piqued, I come to my feet. 'Look, sir, if you think this is a joy-ride on the bandwagon –'

'Well, it must be worth a couple of quid?' he says, unruffled. 'Thirty silver pieces?'

My face is burning. 'You're the one who should be ashamed,' I lash out at him. 'If you were white I would have known where you belonged. But because you've obviously been spending your safe, pampered life here among the flesh-pots of England, you think you can sneer at what's happening over there in South Africa? And as for the money, why don't you ask Amnesty International what the exhibition is worth to them, because I'm not making a cent out of it.'

'Then you must be fucking mad. Certifiable. That's the only explanation.'

'I'm as sane as you are. Not that it seems much of a standard to go by.'

'So how's things at home?' Suddenly the accent is broad South African.

Once again I'm caught off guard. I stare at him in confusion. 'What d'you mean, at home?'

Unperturbed, he names the village where I grew up.

'How do you know that?' I ask sharply.

'I read my newspapers.'

'But what do you know about it?'

'Because it happens to be my home town too.'

'I – I'm afraid I don't understand.'

And then he bursts out laughing, so uncontrollably that he becomes convulsed, tears streaming down his face. He has to remove the pipe and hold it in his hand; it is dead anyway, I discover. At long last he takes a large white handkerchief from his pocket and wipes his eyes.

'Welcome, brother,' he says.

This is how Sipho Mdana makes his appearance in my life.

It doesn't take long before the organisers intrude on us; I've been invited to a meal after the opening. But Sipho sweeps them out of the way in a grand jovial gesture. 'Sorry, boys. Tonight he's mine. We've got too much to catch up with.'

It is obvious that he is known to them; with British resilience they stand aside to let us pass.

As we go out I notice, for the first time, the small black, green and gold badge on the lapel of his tailored suit.

'Are you –?' All of a sudden I am wary.

Another burst of laughter. 'Yes, I am a terrorist. I've got a whole arsenal hidden in my breast pocket. Two collapsible AK-47s, seven grenades, twenty rounds of ammunition and three limpet mines of Russian origin.'

'That's not what I meant.' I feel humiliated; at the same time, I must confess, I am ashamed of my own reaction. But it is the first time I've ever met a member of the banned liberation movement – the enemy; the Black Peril – and there is something traumatic about the encounter. (What have I been expecting?!)

He ambles past a few rows of photographs, considerately giving me an opportunity to compose myself. In front of *Home from the Island* he stops. I notice that he suddenly starts fiddling with his pipe. He fumbles through his pockets for matches. To my astonishment there are tears in his eyes when he turns to me to ask gruffly:

'Were you really there the day this man came out?'

'I shall never forget that day in my life.'

'Henry Bungane,' he says slowly, as if savouring the name. The pipe is burning now. 'He was like a father to me. He went to the Island just after I left the country. The man's a saint.'

I have the unnerving feeling of getting more and more entangled in the life of a man whose name I haven't even heard before tonight. Going up to him I take him by the elbow. 'Come, let's go. We do seem to have a lot to catch up with.'

We go through the entrance lobby to the broad sidewalk of Pall Mall where streetlamps hang like large glowing fruit in the foliage of the plane-trees. The air is cool. We hurry towards Trafalgar Square and catch a tube at Charing Cross. He leads the way; I am still a relative stranger to the city. In a part of London where I have never set foot before we have a meal in a Tandoori restaurant where the food draws more water from my eyes than from my mouth.

It takes a long time for the conversation to get going. After the sudden exhilaration of mutual discovery that drew us together at the exhibition, both seem now to need time to stand back and reassess the situation more cautiously. In the end it is again Henry's name that breaks the ice. I recount to Sipho the story of our first meeting; and my travels with Henry over the last two years. And he fills me in on the Henry of earlier times, before the Island. And about his own involvement in the Struggle, as a result of which, in 'seventy-six, the first year of his LlB – sponsored by Henry – after four months in detention, he left the country head over heels one night, following a tip-off that the SB was on his heels again. He tells me of the terrifying, hilarious journey to the Lesotho border, accompanied by a Catholic priest, in a combi full of nuns, Sipho himself disguised as a nun.

'Nearly died of fear, man', he laughs, blowing out through what seems to be all his bodily orifices a cloud of blue smoke. (Even while he's eating, he hardly bothers to remove the pipe from his mouth.) 'We were stopped at three roadblocks. You get that? Not one, not two, but three. And I knew damn well that if anybody were to ask me anything, *anything* at all, I'd be in shit street. Because the moment I opened my mouth they would have had me. Not just because of my voice, but these crooked teeth. They had my mugshot in every police station in the country.' No trace of the Oxford accent any more. He bellows with laughter again, exposing the give-away teeth. 'But that Father William was a master. If ever he were to land in hell one day they'll immediately second him to heaven.'

'And after you escaped?'

'Well.' He shrugs his shoulders in the immaculate blue suit. 'Never looked back once. Finished my studies, started working. And here I am.' Only much later, through the many conversations ahead, will I learn about the long road that has brought him from Cape Town to London. First there was a hazardous flight from Maseru in a small Piper Cub which developed engine trouble, forcing them to make an emergency landing in northern Transvaal; an epic escape from police and military vehicles to Bophutatswana, and from there to Botswana (even then it took all they had to evade a South African patrol which had crossed the border in hot pursuit), from Gaborone to what was then still Salisbury, with Ian Smith in power, and finally Lusaka. From there Sipho went to Angola, six months in a training base where from the outset he made an impression on the commissars; followed by another six months in Havana. After that the Organisation encouraged him to complete his studies in

435

England. A year at the LSE, two years in Oxford; another year at Harvard. In the USA he met Noni, also an expatriate, and already a professor of African literature. 'Ever since then I've been on the road. Kind of commercial traveller, you might say.' Which, translated, means: organising youth congresses – Moscow, Prague, Berlin, Addis Ababa and Dar-es-Salaam and Dakar and Accra and Godknowswhere – running parallel with a meteoric rise in the political section of the Organisation. Sipho, I soon find out, is not merely a member, one of a multitude; he's a heavyweight: though still only in his thirties, his colleagues are already speculating about membership of the National Executive. (Only Sipho himself refuses to talk about it; at times he even gets annoyed when I mention it. 'Fuck it, man, it's not a question of this or that individual; we're all in the struggle together. That's all that matters.')

What has prompted him to look *me* up? 'It's obvious,' he says airily. 'I mean, when I discovered we come from the same town. Hell, man! I never meant to go to your show. Tell you the truth, I was pretty sceptical, even suspicious. Another whitey riding on our backs, you know? But then I read about your coming from this little place up the West Coast, and suddenly all the longing inside me broke open like a fucking pomegranate. I actually resented your doing this to me, man. But I couldn't stay away.'

It is one of the most unsettling encounters of my life. All the fuss around the exhibition, my uncertainty about the response, has stirred up an ache of longing to be home inside me; and now he turns up to make it worse. As the evening grows old around us we begin to figure out – I drawing on yet another glass of ice water to douse the flames of the hot Indian food – that we must actually have roamed through the streets of that village at the same time. All right, he's six years older than I. But he was there with me. The day I helped our servant carry home her bags, I might have crossed him in one of the erosion ditches that passed for streets in the township; or in any of the streets in town. We might have stood at the counter of the same grocery shop, or waited together to buy sweets in the café (except he would have had to stand at the window, and hand over his money first, and point from a distance at what he wanted). The night I saw the firefly in the outhouse: who knows but he might have been somewhere out there in the night too, staring at the lights in the white quarters before returning to his own shack to do his homework by the light of a paraffin lamp. Sipho Mdana: a kind of invisible shadow on every step I took in my childhood. And yet

436

neither ever knew of the other's existence. Until tonight, this heavy London night.

After the meal he invites me over to his 'place': a basement flat in North London, belonging to a friend who's out of town – Cedric Scott, whom I shall meet later, and who will provide me in due course with a fake British passport to undertake journeys I do not even dream of tonight – and where Sipho regularly stays on his London visits. Never for long: most of his life is taken up by travelling, with brief hurried dashes home in between trips – 'home' meaning Lusaka, or wherever Noni may be at any given moment. (And, of course, their small son Govan, just turned two. Before the night is out Sipho shows me innumerable photographs of the child, and of his stunning mother.) It is a long way to the flat from the restaurant, two changes on the tube, followed by a brisk walk. But it is a laid-back, friendly place when at last we get there: dark in the daytime, the lights are always on; but with bright pictures on the walls (prints and posters of Chagall, Klee, Balthus; and a lithograph, an illustrated poem by Neruda) and colourful African cloths on chairs and bean-bags.

'Have a seat,' says Sipho. 'I'll put on some music. It's not often I have the chance.'

He selects a Beethoven quartet. We drink coffee – Freedom Coffee from a black and green and yellow pack – while we listen, Sipho with closed eyes; and afterwards he finds a Johnny Clegg, *Scatterlings of Africa*, of which he plays only one cut before he takes off the record: 'God, no, this makes me too sad.' And he flops down beside me on a sofa and puts an arm round my shoulders. 'Oh dear Jesus-God, isn't it wonderful to see someone from back home again.'

This is where the conversation really starts to flow: the conversation which, interrupted by so many breaks, is to last for two years: until that obscene purple day in Lusaka.

Once again it begins with the exhibition, with my misgivings about the reactions I've been subjected to.

'Do you think one can believe them, Sipho? Isn't their praise just an easy way to make them feel good about themselves? Today it's apartheid, tomorrow Nicaragua, or Iran, or Afghanistan, or nuclear weapons, or Greenpeace: tiny people, insect people, all trying to escape their own insignificance by demonstrating for noble causes?'

'So what? Whatever their private motives may be, they keep

the world aware of what's happening. They make it impossible for people to say they didn't know. And even if there's only one out of a hundred who really means it seriously, then we've gained that one. Remember what Eluard wrote: *They were but a handful: suddenly they are a multitude.*'

'It's strange to hear poetry from the mouth of a – soldier!'

'You wanted to say "terrorist", didn't you?'

'Well, you're dedicated to violence, aren't you? Otherwise you wouldn't have been here today.'

'You make it sound like a kind of religion.'

'Isn't that exactly what it is – in a way?'

Sipho gets up and chooses another record. The Chopin ballades. Then, his back to me, he says, 'No.' Comes back to his seat, crosses his legs, checks his pipe and pokes about in it for a moment. 'No, Thomas. When I talk of violence it's something very practical which I have chosen resentfully, but with a clear mind, as a means to an end, because it's the only way.'

'Now you're going to tell me that for fifty years your people tried passive resistance, which only led to more and more oppression, until you were banned and went underground. And that this forced you to respond to violence with violence. Because the only alternative was to capitulate.'

'You've listened well.'

'Because I've heard it so many times.'

'You've listened well, but you haven't *understood*.' Something in his smile irritates me. (Please don't patronise me, I think. I'm not a child.) But he goes on calmly, 'Perhaps, in our circumstances, violence, and the courage to risk it, is the only way in which one can still affirm one's humanity.' He looks hard at me. 'Thomas, if you'd been in the camp where I was, if you'd seen the hundreds of youngsters, many of them mere kids, who came in there, each of them with the scars of torture, of some kind of violence, on his body –'

'You mean: each of them had a personal grudge, a private grief to avenge? But that can't justify any principle, Sipho!'

Again that patient smile. 'No. All I'm trying to tell you is that one cannot talk about violence as if it was some "topic for discussion", a theme, a theory, a modus operandi. You can only talk about it if you know what it means, if your own body bears the scars of it. Because violence is not an abstraction.'

'It's precisely because it isn't an abstraction that no one has the

438

right to talk lightly about it. Because it has to do with *people*, Sipho. Including innocent ones.'

'Let's leave the question of "innocence" and "guilt" aside for the moment.' He presses his fingers together. 'Because then we stray into metaphysics. Let's talk about real situations. Let's talk about Camus: you will agree that his philosophy is tied to a very specific historical situation in Algeria' (If it comes as a surprise to me – yet another side to this man I'm not prepared for – I will soon discover that philosophy is his hobby. More than a hobby, a passion.) 'You ought to transplant Sisyphus to Africa, to South Africa. That's what Noel Chabani Manganyi did: you know Manganyi?' Without waiting for an answer: 'You see, Camus speaks for the West, as Manganyi clearly shows. He speaks metaphysics. Our Sisyphus is black. His task is not metaphysical but social. His task isn't suicide but murder. And why? Because you cannot fight evil with holiness or passivity: the evil *we* contend with isn't metaphysical either, it's social injustice. A matter of political and military power. To counter that with "moral superiority" is futile. It suggests that you are trying to appeal to something good or moral in the conscience of your enemy. But he has already abandoned metaphysics and morality. So all your "reply" amounts to is a small selfish attempt to save yourself from the mess. Like Pilate. It's not enough to condemn apartheid. Everybody already knows it's evil. What is necessary is to do something about it.'

'With violent means?'

'Among other strategies, yes. Your photographs, for instance, are necessary too. I respect that. But your photographs aren't exactly free of violence either.'

'I mounted this exhibition to *condemn* violence, to show how abhorrent it is.'

'Sure you did. But how can you wash your hands if people who see it are shaken so deeply that they decide to take up arms themselves to fight against that violence you showed them? Will you still say, "That's not what I meant?" You cannot be that naïve. Your exhibition is itself a form of violence.'

'My exhibition doesn't kill anybody.' I am deeply agitated. 'Sipho, I once was present at a necklacing myself. It's something I never want to see again in my life. Henry threw his own body on the young man the mob was trying to kill. And even that was no use. No one – neither you nor anybody else – can persuade me that there is *any* excuse for that kind of violence.

Even if the man were a traitor or a sellout. No matter *what* he was.'

'Not one of us has tried to defend necklacing, Thomas.'

'But you're trying to distinguish it from other forms of violence! And I tell you it's just not possible. Violence is violence. Even violence done for a "good cause", if something like that were conceivable, contains the possibility of degenerating into a necklacing. It's a difference of degree, not of essence.'

'But just now, when I tried to tell you that your exhibition was also a form of violence *you* were the one who tried to distinguish it from "other kinds"?'

Before I can answer – if an answer is possible – Sipho gets up: the first side of the record is finished; he turns it over. When he comes back he stops in front of me: 'We grew up in the same town, Thomas. But I was born at the wrong end, the shit end. I had to fight for every crumb. What you pulled up your nose for was luxury to me. But that wasn't the worst. The worst was when I went to UCT, with Henry's help, and with bursaries and loans, and working my arse off, and 'seventy-six broke over us. When I suddenly made the obvious discovery: even if I became rich one day, an advocate or a businessman, I'd still be trapped. It wasn't a matter of changing my personal circumstances. It was a matter of having to change the whole fucking society. Can you see the difference? And do you understand why I'm saying these things?'

It is growing late around us. Throughout the dark hours, to the first signs of dawn outside, Sipho continues to play music; continues to talk. As the night peters out I gradually run out of answers; he's too much for me. And yet, blindly, I keep on clinging to this one fierce conviction: I shall never, never, be persuaded that violence can be justified.

'Sipho, it's an affront to everything we think of as "human"!'

He's bending over, putting on another record (the Kreutzer Sonata). Looking over his shoulder, a sardonic grin on his face, he says, 'Music is violent too. An assault on the ears, on silence. We wouldn't even have been conscious of "humanity" if it hadn't been for the constant assaults on it.'

'Now *you*'re the one to resort to philosophical abstractions.'

'You began with abstractions, Thomas: when I warned you that one can only talk about violence from the inside.'

'Is that your official view?'

Sipho grins, exposing the large crooked teeth set in resplendent pink gums; in a curious way there is something boyishly attractive about it. And he says, 'Tonight it's just you and me talking, Thomas, and neither one represents anyone but ourselves. We're talking because we grew up in the same place. For the moment that is the only thing we share.'

Even my involvement, through Henry, with the UDF has not prepared me adequately for this encounter, for this laughing, pipe-smoking, sardonic, enigmatic shadow from my own childhood; and inside me there is an irresistible urge to learn; to know *him* better and, through him, to enter a world of which I have no experience and only the most outrageously distorted notions.

Keeping up with Sipho is no easy task. His energy, it seems, is inexhaustible; he seldom sleeps more than four or five hours a night. ('Life is too short for spending it on your back, man.' As if he already has a premonition.) And towards the end of a fortnight of continuous surprises he floors me with the casual announcement that we're leaving for Africa in two days.

'But Sipho,' I stammer, 'how can I – I've got things set – and my passport –'

'You let me have a mugshot in the morning, Cedric will do the rest.'

'But –'

And on the Friday morning we depart.

Of that first visit – four weeks of travelling across the face of the continent – I retain only a whirlwind of impressions, like an unsorted photo album.

Accra, where – because of the congress – we spend the longest time. Near our hotel (sporting a row of flagpoles, many of them sloping at haphazard angles; several of the letters of the hotel's name literally hanging by threads) sits the imposing skeleton of what seems to have been intended as a flat building before it was abandoned at the second storey, now almost completely overgrown by a rank wilderness of shrubs and creepers. In the bar a group of olive-skinned men are installed permanently, smoking cigars and consuming vast quantities of beer and speaking Spanish: mercenaries or secret agents from a Graham Greene novel, lost in time. From the hotel stretches the long main road to the city centre, past embassies and mansions from a bygone colonial era hidden behind flame-trees and syringas; one passes cavalcades of trucks converted into buses, resembling large chicken-coops on wheels;

there are goats in the street. I accompany Sipho to the State House complex for conferences preceding the congress he is arranging: a huge building with peeling paint and a defunct air-conditioning system; in the large round assembly hall – a podium resting on two wooden replicas of elephant tusks, with flags draped around a portrait of Nkrumah – several of the wood panels are warped; a number of lights are missing. From the imposing front terrace one looks out across a massive fish-pond that has clearly been empty for a long time. Beyond, the carcass of a bus. Farther into the distance, colossal buildings from the Year of Independence, depressing incarnations of Nuremberg.

From Lagos, this picture: the freelance teacher winding his way through the market-place, carrying his bench on his head and offering his services as he goes, in his hand a *First Steps in English Grammar* and Kant's *Critique of Pure Reason*; and the buses completely covered by swarms of people like mobile bees' nests swaying ruthlessly and recklessly through the noisy traffic.

Dakar: oleanders and ochre buildings, shoe-cleaners, street vendors, stalls piled high with pawpaws and mangoes and coconuts, bunches of eagerly chatting people escaping the sticky heat in pools of shade – tall beautiful people, faces like hard-wood masks, the grace of the men's flowing *boubous*. On every street corner a jovial stranger who offers me a 'present' as a talisman – a bracelet, a leather pendant, a small ornament in what looks like tarnished silver – insisting on something 'personal' in exchange, preferably a banknote, invariably destined for a new-born infant due to be baptised tomorrow. Markets. Parks with small vervet monkeys scurrying in the foliage. And Gorée. Gorée, the island of tears. The place which finally seals my bond with Sipho. The place where, with such a sense of physical shock, I rediscover my own past in the history of my most distant known ancestral mother, Catharijn. If our entire journey had involved nothing but this bitter island surrounded by mirages, it would in itself be enough to make me return a changed man. In the heavy dust of the place, among these silent peeling stone walls – the casual rustling of water at the fountain, the bleating of a goat, the murmur of melodic voices from the girls gathered in the shade to wash their smooth dark legs (my own Catharijn might have been one of such an arch group: if she had been free and not a slave) – I acknowledge irrevocably, fatally, that I belong to Africa.

How different the blue and the warmth of Dar-es-Salaam, the

voluptuous bobbing of dhows on translucent water, making luscious and fanciful love to their own reflections; flitting shadows in white robes and turbans in narrow alleys; dazzling white façades, once the palaces of sultans, with Arabic arches and columns, now transformed into government buildings; a crumbling Persian bath; Americans in loud shirts and shorts; Japanese weighed down by cameras; corner shops with multicoloured materials and earthenware and huge sensual shells. A night on the flat roof of a hotel among rows of washing, under shameless stars.

Or deep into the interior, to smaller villages, in the diesel smell of rickety dust-covered buses, rocking and swaying among smiling or sleeping people, women suckling their babies, chickens, goats, pigs, baskets, plastic buckets; small hotels with muddy backyards which proudly offer a petrol drum filled with water for whoever is desperate enough to risk a wash; windowless hardboard cubicles from which you can hear every whisper or rustling or love-moan or death-rattle from next door; blind beggars; hungry children with reddish hair and calabash bellies, protruding navels; open-air barbers; old men carrying fly-swats or ox-tails; now and then in a dusty eroded landscape a bunch of huts in the shadow of palm-trees with tattered fronds; the weird majesty of a baobab.

Harare: new skyscrapers shoulder to shoulder with low colonial buildings among masses of dark green foliage; technicolour bougainvillea in whose shade barbers and vendors find brief shelter; further away from the centre the irrepressible crowds in potholed streets crisscrossing a township of low concrete hovels, shacks of wood and corrugated iron, among pawpaw trees, bananas, jacarandas, msasas, bluegums; and directly beyond the suburbs, the mopani-dotted plains, the immeasurable expanse of my continent.

Bougainvillea and flame-trees in Lusaka too; Sipho's blue flat-building festooned with washing lines; a trip to Soweto market in the west where, among sweet-stinking piles of fermenting mangoes, we rummage through heaps of junk in search of an exhaust for his broken-down car; then a detour to the small white double-storeyed building near by, behind a wall capped with shards of glass, where in his cool office he works through piles of accumulated mail while I occupy myself with a stack of *Sechabas*.

Lusaka also means my first meeting with Noni – quite simply the most beautiful woman I have ever seen in my life – tall and lithe, graceful as a gazelle, especially in one of her long flowing West African garments; a Nefertiti profile, a tall regal head sprouting

443

innumerable perfect plaits, large smouldering mysterious eyes, strong long hands. Always in command of a situation, always smiling, as if there is no end to the surprises of life. I can only hope that her child, the lively large-eyed mischievous Govan, *knows* how privileged he is to have a mother like that. The love between her and Sipho is like a lake of lucid water in which anyone is welcome to plunge for refreshment. Sadly, she can spend only two days with us in Lusaka, as she is on her way to New York. As a cultural officer in the Organisation she is as constantly on the move as Sipho: apart from her organising duties, there are endless invitations to lecture, to spend time at this university or that as visiting fellow, to meet cultural workers all over the world. Depending on the duration of a trip, little Govan must either travel with her – even at the age of two he is a globetrotter – or be left behind with Sipho or with friends.

And then the people, wherever we go. I sometimes get the impression that Sipho knows each of Africa's countless millions personally. In every market, in every fly-ridden street, in sewing-machine stalls or lean-tos where photographs are taken and hair-oil is sold, in the lobby of every air-conditioned new building, in the public washrooms, in the backyards of country hotels or grocery stores, at bar counters, in ultramodern offices of multinational companies or the luxury of international hotels, on eroded town squares among trees sprouting obscene pods aflutter with birds – everywhere we run into people who recognise him, embracing him or pumping his hand, stopping the traffic or causing air-conditioning plants to seize up with their great shouts of glee:

'Sipho! Sipho! How are you, my friend?'

Behind all the misery and famine and exploitation and dust and flies and stench and rotting fruit and desperation and disease of Africa, every time, day after day, thanks to Sipho, this: this generosity, warmth, exuberance, this overwhelming hospitality: my brother, my brother, welcome! And it makes no difference if they discover my nationality: I'm Sipho's friend, I come from Africa: welcome, welcome, my brother!

Dear God, I think almost every night as my head hits the pillow – rarely in a luxury hotel: sometimes in a rambling ex-colonial ruin, more often in the brick homes of friends, diplomatic palaces, prefab shacks, corrugated-iron hovels, home-made shanties, semi-detacheds, flats, rooms – how is it possible that down in that distant south we think of Africa as a hostile continent, as dangerous and threatening and brooding?

444

How incredible: that thirteen generations of Landmans have laboriously, with their blood and sweat, tears, semen, shit, soaked themselves into Africa, tuned themselves in to its great sombre rhythms, adapted to its harsh and sudden seasons, become intimate with its night skies, learned from the people who have always lived here the names of tree and rock and bush and animal and mountain, forged a language from its thunderstorms and open spaces, its cliffs, the mournful challenge of the fish-eagle, the inaudible chant of stones that bear in them the curdled fire of prehistorical times – and that, after all this, in spite of all this, we are still, today, more isolated from Africa than three hundred years ago! Because we have become afraid of its people. Because we have turned away from the humanity inside ourselves which Africa has revealed to us. On this single journey – the first of several; from now on I shall compulsively return – all this is restored to me in a flood as exorbitant as that of one of the great dried-up tracts of the continent which after a thunderstorm suddenly bursts its banks and submerges everything in its flow. And whatever may have happened before, Sipho, my friend Sipho, whatever may be happening today or still awaits us in the future: *this* I owe to you; this no one can ever take from me: this gift of restoring me to my continent. *Mayibuye iAfrika!*

At the airport in Harare, as Sipho and I are checking in for the return flight to London (Noni and Govan have left several days ago), a two-hour delay is announced. In the barn-like departure hall the air-conditioning has packed up and two smiling policemen at the door do not allow anyone to step outside for a breath of air. More and more passengers are crammed into the lounge – ours is not the only flight to be delayed – and soon the bar runs out of ice; on the wall next to the toilets (fumes of antiseptic and stale urine) a grumbling queue is forming in front of the only telephone in working order. At the passenger services counter an eager attendant makes her appearance from time to time, flashes a benevolent smile at the frantic passengers and disappears again.

Sipho and I remain unperturbed; in Africa one changes into a different time gear where details are of little concern. (In Accra we also ran into a long delay and, not yet acclimatised, I entered into a desperate argument at the information counter. To my imperative 'But we *must* be in Lagos tonight!' the unflappable lady responded with an amused, 'Why?' At that moment I, too, began to wonder:

why indeed? What's the difference whether we arrive tonight, or tomorrow, or in fact next week? That was the last time it bothered me.)

But something does happen to upset us.

A departing flight is announced. Not ours, but a South African Airways flight to Johannesburg. It causes a stir among the crowd of waiting people. A jostling, sweating, unfriendly queue forms in the mass of compressed bodies. We have found a less crowded spot at the window from where we can watch them trickle across the tarmac to the waiting white and blue and orange plane. Suddenly Sipho grabs me by the arm, clutching me so fiercely that it hurts.

'Hell, my brother,' he whispers into my ear, and I can hear his voice shaking. 'That's *our* plane, man. Let's go home!'

For the first time it dawns on me just how close 'home' really is. An hour's flight perhaps? But we are on our way in the opposite direction, thousands of kilometres away. I can still turn back, should I wish to: but not Sipho. And I realise in this moving instant that there is nothing in the whole world he'd rather do than get on that plane and go home with me. The home we both come from, where we were children together – even though he did live on the dark side, I on the other. *Our* place. And here we are standing together, pressed very close together, and we are both in tears – I know it without looking at him – yet he cannot go back.

At that moment it is impossible to say anything. But later, deep in the night, in the air on the way to London, when neither of us can sleep and he orders yet another brandy (although usually he does not drink much), I say to him, softly, so that no one else will overhear:

'Sipho, I want to tell you something. I think I understand now, for the first time. What you said about violence. *I* won't ever be able to resort to it, that I know. But I understand now why you have come to think the way you do. And I won't ever jump to judgements again.'

He says nothing, but he presses his hand down on my knee. And then gets up to go the toilet.

In London news awaits me: the possibility of transferring my exhibition to New York. In order to seal the negotiations with the prospective sponsors I must catch the first available plane to the US. Sipho is on his way to Moscow. I must confess that I'm

446

more interested in going with him, but he cuts short all protest: 'You're going to New York and that's that. It's important for your future. It's important for *us* that as many people as possible see your pictures.'

At least there is the prospect of seeing Noni again in New York. And the fortnight with her turns out to be a kind of sustained high. Whenever she isn't involved in her lecturing programme at Columbia, and when I can free myself from my sponsors, she takes me on a systematic exploration of the city's art treasures. The Met, MOMA, the Guggenheim, the Frick, the libraries. It is not just her encyclopedic knowledge of art that stuns me (and art is merely her hobby; her subject, after all, is the sociology of literature), but her ability to conduct a morning tour through a museum as if it were a space odyssey. Whatever I know about art today is largely Noni's doing. And in addition, the few lectures of hers I'm privileged to attend unfold to me the literature, the cultural history of Africa in ways I have never before dreamed of. What I have experienced on my trip with Sipho is amplified with new dimensions of space and language.

I believe I am a little bit in love with her. No, more than a little bit; it's head over heels. If in my previous relationships I have been fortunate in discovering a variety of women, Noni brings home to me a discovery of *woman*. Through her beauty, yes – and in this fortnight I find her even more beautiful, more breathtaking than in Lusaka – but above all through her way of looking at art and literature and people, her way of living without compromise, to the hilt; her devotion to Sipho and her child, while at the same time she is the most liberated and independent woman I have ever encountered. She never tries to 'prove' anything: in her positive, immensely passionate presence she simply is so impressive that what I feel for her comes close to adoration. (I can imagine how uproariously she would laugh, from her very guts, if she were to learn about this: because she is, at the same time, such a spontaneous, natural, earthy person, so brimful of laughter and of dancing, so exuberant in her sometimes crude scatological humour, so derisive of all convention, that no one can be prim or composed in her presence.) I am, why not admit it openly, infatuated with the woman. Yet there is no hint of guilt in my feelings for her: because by this time I am already so devoted to my friend Sipho that my admiration of Noni is intimately part of my loyalty to her husband.

By the end of my visit we know each other well enough for her to share even her rare moments of despondency with me:

'You know, Thomas, there are days like today, when the sky is so grey – we people from the south can't survive in cloudy weather, we're sunflowers – there are days my heart turns inside out with sadness. So many of our people have been killed over these last few years. So many have been maimed in one way or another. For so many years we've gone on believing in victory, one day, soon, just round the corner, tomorrow – But it's a hard life. It takes so much just to keep going, not to give up. Every time I turn on the radio or open the newspapers there are more people arrested, wounded, killed. Children. Mere children. Then I look at my own child and my heart shrivels up like an old walnut inside me. God knows, if something were to happen to *him*. Then she sighs, raises her beautiful eyes, and the brave smile breaks through again: 'And yet he's the one who helps me to go on believing. Every morning when I wake up and see his little face, so eager and happy and uncompromising with trust and love I know once again what it is that makes me go through with it. It's for *him*. It's for the children, Thomas. It's no longer for us: we're growing old, we're mowed down, one by one. But they, those little ones who carry stones in their hands in the township streets, my God, Thomas, it's all they've *got*. And you remember what Jesus said: Cursed are those who give a stone to a child who asks for bread.'

Then she will get up and go to a window – whether we're in a museum, or a library, or in a coffee shop; or in my cockroach-infested hotel near Times Square, or the apartment of the friends in Harlem she's staying with – and look out, as if to pry, with her fierce eyes, a ray of sun from that grey sky, and say, 'If only I could go back again. Just once.'

She gets up hurriedly and rummages in her bag. 'Come on, we're wasting time. There's an incredibly beautiful Vermeer in the Frick I still want to show you.' Or something to that effect.

Two weeks only. Then she has to go back – and how eager she is at the prospect – and there is no reason why I should stay on either. The arrangements for the transfer of the exhibition have been finalised. I've been away long enough. I want to be back home, and get to work: and this time it is no ordinary journey but the overwhelming sense of going *home* that sustains me – for their sake too, Sipho's and Noni's, these two people who, in such a short time, have become the dearest friends of my life. –

– Now I see dey call 'em terrorists, dey tried to blow up de president in de Cape. Imagine. En' dey were such decent people. 'Morning, Mr Augustyn. Morning, Mr Augustyn.' Not all white people are alike, not all of dem are bed. Just like not all of us are good or bed. We're all *people*. A poor, fork'd creature.

Yes, Shakespeare and I, we come a long way togedder. We kind of sustain each other in dis dry place. But now lately he is also getting weak inne knees. Good things of day begin to droop and drowse, hey. And all our yesterdays have lighted fools de way to dusty death.

De problem is: a person lives forward, but unne'standing goes sideways or beckwards like a crayfish. Det Sat'day morning when de two of dem came here to de school, it was just ten o'clock, dead on time, I still didn't know anything. If only I had. It's only now, too late, unne'standing is catching up.

Had I kept my eyes open I would have noticed what dey talk about now, de false colour of de man's hair, but I had *mos* no reason to be suspicious. One doesn't think bedly of one's fellow man just like det. Thou cans't not den be false to any man. All I was thinking was such a nice couple, so lovey-dovey, you could see dey not married long, and very polite. Now dere's all de stories and I expect dey'll be coming beck to me to say I've been harbouring terrorists again. Like when my own son Prospero came here to hide in my place. Now de law is de law and de court is de court, but I don't want dem to come to me about dis new thing. Cornelis Augustyn can take so much but no more. Always said: Look, don't bodder with me, I'm a patient man. I'm like a landmine: I lay dere quietly for a long long time. But if you step on me den I explode. So stay away from me now because why, I'm not far from exploding.

Look at me today: my own son Prospero gone to a faraway place where he cannot even hear my voice any mo'. En' Mavis end I with a summons on our heads because why, we gave our child lodging when he was in trouble. It's a thing I fail to unne'stand.

Look, we've lived through dry times in these parts. But even in dry times dere used to be good will among de people. Now de drought has moved right into de hearts of people. Even words have dried up. Dis is how I tried to explain it to det young man en' his young woman when dey were here. En' dey listened to what I said to dem, two good people, I thought, in *your* heart dere's still some moisture fo' things to grow in. Now det's why I am confused today. It's all upside-down, and nothing is but what is not. If dose two are terrorists as dey say, what has become of de world, what has happened to de words det always used to support me?

I want to keep my faith. God knows, I want to keep my faith. En' from time to time dere's reason to believe. When we were taken to court about sheltering my son Prospero, dey wanted to lock us up until whenever dey were ready to take de case, perhaps fo' months, even a year, dey take deir time and de courts are overflowing; but den de dominee, a white man, serves on our school committee, *he* stepped in fo' us en' arranged bail en' paid it out of his own pocket. Because fair is fair, he said, en' justice is justice. De quality of mercy is not strain'd.

Dis was what we discussed onne Sat'day morning, I enne two people dey have now declared terrorists. En' it was de first time, except fo' when I spoke to de dominee, I eve' talked about de things I carry in my heart. It's part of my bail conditions, cannot discuss de case with anybody. So why did I open my mouth to dose two afte' all de months of silence? I cannot explain it. Except det dey were ready to *listen*. Dey weren't dere to judge. Just wan'ed to *listen* to me.

We were sitting right here where I'm sitting now, in my class-room, I was marking books. My little wireless exactly where it is now, on de bookshelf, playing music, I need sound when I'm working, even if it's only de beck of my head det listens. I had tea ready for dem, even though I couldn't say fo' sure they'd come, some people can be quick when it comes to promises but slow when it comes to keeping dem. But dey came anyway, dead on time too, and we were all sitting here drinking tea, de wireless playing its thin music, en' Landman – who I still took to be Lamprecht – asked me, 'Mr Augustyn, exactly what happened to your son?'

It was after I tol' him what I knew and didn't know. Because what do I unne'stand about it all? All my chillun have left me. De girls I still see from time to time, but Prospero, no, he gave me up long ago, said all I can do is talking, talking while de land is going up in flames. I asked him many times, Haven't you ever seen de fire lit by words? But Prospero stayed away, I was too old-fashioned fo' him, a fader's word counts fo' not'ing. Until det night he suddenly turned up, looking like Lazarus from de dead. Dey looking fo' him, he tells me. Who dey? *Dey*. I try to find out more. En' at last he tells me a few of his friends set fire to a policeman's house, petrol bomb, in Athlone or somewhere. De policeman and his wife inside. Prospero,

I ask him, Prospero, befo' God Almighty, tell me de truth: were you one of 'em? He looks me straight in de eyes and he says, No, Pa, I swear I wasn't. We discussed de business befo'hand and I said no, en' dey kicked me out. But now de police are looking fo' me, because why dey know I am usually in det crowd. Dey picking up everybody. And if you get picked up you don't get out alive again. Dere's dis now thing dey got in de courts, dey call it 'common purpose', and if dey pick you up you swing.

So where are you going to now? I ask him.

Only one way, he says. Out of de country. Off to Calvinia from here, den Botswana, en' gone.

En' afte' he spent de night with us he left en' we neve' saw him again. A month late' de police came to pick us up, dey tell us we were harbouring a terrorist, Mavis and I. Now we're going down from grief. Mavis, especially, she cannot take it any mo', she's had too much. En' if I don't talk to someone about it, I tell 'em, I'll just now give up and die too. So I thenk de two of dem for listening to me, udde'wise I don't think I could bear it.

En' while we were still talking like det, de police stopped outside. Dey know everything, dey hear everything, dey see everything. Dis new man, Coetzee. No patience in him, no respect for age. I'm not saying I'm so old, fifty-seven next September, but I'm in my downhill days. En' older 'n *he* is. Came in here wit' dose two men on his heels. Rocking in deir big boots, enjoying demselves.

'Well, Augustyn? You got visitors?'

'Jus' people passing through.'

Looking back now, it seems dose two young ones must have hed a terrible fright. But dey kept quite cool, said good morning, tol' de man deir names.

De officer screwed up his eyes, en' said, 'Captain Coetzee.' But didn't offer dem his hand.

'We're on our way down de coast interviewing people,' said de man who must have been Landman. 'Making notes as we go. We hope to do an article onne' people of the West Coast.'

'All de way from Worcester?' asked de captain. Must have checked de car outside. 'Dere's no newspapers in Worcester as far as I know.'

'We're freelancing,' de man said. 'It's fo' *Huisgenoot*.'

It's hard to explain today why de police didn' recognise dem, but of course Landman looked different, and dey weren't expecting a woman with him.

Anyway, de policeman seemed satisfied wit' de answer. Turned round, ready to go it seemed. But den he came beck again. 'Since when is a magazine like *Huisgenoot* interested in agitators and political activists?'

Landman says, 'We're not writing about activists. We're writing about *people*. All kinds of people in all kinds of places.'

'Why don't you talk to *me* then?'

'We *are* talking to you. Right at dis moment.' Not at a loss for words, det one.

De policeman gave him a long look, den back at me, de kind of look I didn' like one bit. Den he said, 'You aware of it det Augustyn's bail conditions forbid him to talk to de press?'

'We hed no idea de man was out on bail,' said Landman. 'Anyway, *Huisgenoot* is not a newspaper.'

'It's for us to decide.' Sounded like a declaration of war. 'Can I see your press cards?'

'Freelance journalists don't need press cards. But I can show you a letter.' Which he did.

But Coetzee gets even more obstreperous 'n before. 'It's a State of Emergency,' he says. 'We've hed a lot of trouble in dese parts. We cannot allow strangers to move in unne' any kind of pretext. Before we know where we are we're dealing with arson and stone-throwing again. Wherever Augustyn is, there's trouble.'

I kept my mouth very tightly shut. It wasn't easy. Det man is like a thorn-branch in de face.

De captain gave 'em a hard look en' he asked, 'Where you two coming from right now?'

'Upington,' said Landman. 'From dere we went to Springbok, and now we're following de coast road back to de Cape. We must be back in Worcester by tomorrow night. Before Monday in any case.'

'What's de address in Worcester?'

Landman gave him a straight answer, I can't rememme' de address. I must say de girl didn' look too happy about it. But perhaps I'm only thinking it now, looking beck.

'Where did you stay in Upington?'

'My wife's parents.'

'Dey got an address?'

'Dey do. En' I am willing to give it to you. Plus any other information you require. But may I ask what is behind dis interrogation? I'm not used to being treated like a criminal.'

What I feared would heppen, heppened. De captain blew his top and ordered dem to come to de station with him.

For a while dey stood dead still. Thinking of it now, it must have been like a death sentence.

But dis was where de girl took over. Never saw it coming. All of a sudden she started to cry, raining tears as I've never seen in my life. 'Not even married for a week,' she sobs as if her heart is going to break, 'and it's supposed to be our honeymoon en' *everything* is going wrong. De tyre det burst. En' my purse det was lost. Enne gasket det blew at Garies. Sitting beside de road all night. En' now we're trying to earn a bit of money with an article to pay for everything, now dis!'

Landman put an arm round her shoulders. She still shaking with sobs. 'All right, all right,' he went on soothing her. Den in a whisper, but so's we could hear, 'Karin,' – I rememme' de name – 'Karin, as soon's we get back Pretoria is going to hear all about it –' En' den, properly blue-white in de face, to de captain, 'All right, let's get it over.'

'What de hell's Pretoria got to do with it?' asked de captain. He suddenly seemed a worried man.

Landman was very cool. 'You'll be hearing from dem,' he said.

De policeman went to de door with his men. Dey spoke fo' a while on de steps. Den he came back en' said, 'All right den, you can go.' Adding like a fader, 'You must unne'stand, it's only routine. We got a job to do. One can't be too careful.'

He went out. I went to de bridal couple. De girl stopped crying, just as unexpectedly as she began. Through de open door we saw de two men get back into de van. De captain still stood in front of de Opel, kind of testing de number plate with his foot, den he quickly went to de passenger side of de van en' dey pulled off like all de devils in hell were on deir heels. Avaunt en' quit my sight!

Inne classroom it was so quiet one could even hear what wasn't dere. Behind me on de shelf de wireless was still talking in its crackling voice. End of a news report. Something about anudde' detainee who died in detention. Of course, now I rememme', it was de doctor from de Cape. Great big fuss afterwards. Doctor David Blumer. Hanged himself in his cell in Caledon Square, dey said. En' when I looked up again dey were gone. –

Chapter 10

— Still those nightmares. Last night Anna had to wake me, said she'd
heard me cry out for help. Bloody nonsense. Kat Bester has never
needed help from anyone in his life. Vivid memory of the dream
afterwards. On a boat in the deep sea, so far out the land was
invisible, no one else near, and then the whale suddenly surfacing
like a smooth black mountain from right below.

Know exactly where it comes from, but it's been so many years.
How can a thing like that continue to haunt one so? Off the West
Coast, St Helena Bay. Steered to the deep sea in our borrowed
ski boat. A day so quiet the sea was like a lake. Then all of a
sudden the whale. Not twenty yards away. Enormous, glossy black,
streamlined, soundless from the secret deep. A water spray like a
fountain. God alone knows how big it was. The mere thought of
being there on those depths blue-black as civil service ink, no land
in sight, the ocean stretching away to all sides, and suddenly this
creature from down there. Like something from the Old Testament,
leviathan. In a flash you realise how little you really know about the
waters below, a huge invisible world, all those smooth dark bodies
moving like submarines, a single flick of the tail and you've had
it. Never been able to find a word for that feeling. It's more than
'shock' it's far beyond 'fear'. A kind of *awe*. Yes. Because you're so
terrifyingly small in your little boat, and this thing so big. Jesus.

Nowadays it comes back more and more frequently. Dreams
surfacing like whales from the deep. Never in my life had any
trouble with my nerves. Must be pure frustration. Pressed from
all sides. Not a day without the commissioner telephoning to find
out what the hell's going on. The president himself several times.
Blue lightning on the wires. Results. They all want fucking results.
And they expect Kat Bester to come up with the answers. Everybody
eager to shit on his head. But would they ever change places? No
chance in hell.

Patience. Try to get that into their heads. Patience. But what do *they* know about fishing? What do they know about whales?

Soon's this case is over, we'll go away on holiday, off to the fish waters, gave Anna my solemn word. She needs it too.

'You've been saying that for years,' she answers. 'When are you ever going to *do* it? I no longer believe you.' Whining, moaning way she has. Needs some firm action again.

And only a couple of weeks ago it seemed the breakthrough was at hand. Any moment. All they had to do was grab the bait. But ever since it's been nothing but frustration.

Beginning with the Jew. No end to his endurance. Couldn't get a single word out of him. And the newspapers giving us hell, the commissioner, the president. The whole bloody world, it seemed. Charge or release. Good thing old Jordaan stepped in, as might be expected of him. Real brick. Except he then suddenly changed his mind. Spoke to the president behind my back. Still don't know exactly what he told him, but the president gave me bloody hell. Treated me like a snot-nosed kid. But what can one say to the president? Right off his rocker ever since that bomb exploded. Sees terrorists everywhere, behind every door and bush. Shitting in his pants. And then *we*'re expected to clean up.

But this time it was a proper crisis. No two ways about it. Had to hit back, and fast, at old Jordaan. Below the belt, just like he had done. Only way to make sure he'll keep his trap shut in future. But it makes a man uneasy. Suppose he tried to take revenge? He may be a turd but he has power. Can use it too. And now he's angry. Suppose he got it into his head to visit the Jew and see for himself? True, it won't be easy for him to explain why he signed that affidavit a week ago to confirm that David Blumer was fine, in good health, nothing wrong with him. But if the judge really decided to go for it the shit could still hit the fan. He was capable of it. Scheming against me.

So there was no other way out. The Jew had to be eliminated before old Jordaan could poke his nose into it.

'Hanging' always works best. Clean, swift, no questions. True, ever since Biko some doctors are sensitive. But in this business one soon learns who one's friends are. One hand washing the other. And two or three of them only too eager to start repaying their debts to me. So Blumer had to see his hole. Fortunately not much of a loss to us. Already too far gone. Wouldn't have spoken anyway. Dead he

455

might serve some purpose. Alive he'd become a stumbling block. Is that true or isn't it?

Strange, suddenly ran into a bit of a problem with young Swanie. Not really a problem, just a hint of unhappiness. Because he was the obvious man to wrap it up. After the neat job he did on Mabusa it was clear one needn't look any further. But this time there was a kind of edge in him.

'Hell, Oom Kat, I'm not sure about this.' Calls me 'Oom Kat' when we're alone. Shows how well we get along. In different circumstances, have said so before, might have been father and son. But anyway, this was what he asked: 'Oom Kat, you sure this is the only way?'

Became a bit irritated with him, never happened before: 'Swanie, since when is it your job to ask questions when you're given an order?'

'I'm sorry, Oom Kat, I didn't mean to object or anything. I was just wondering –'

'You sure wondering is part of your job description?' Brief silence. 'In Mabusa's case you never wondered at all.'

'But that was different, Oom Kat. This man's white. And he's locked up, he's in chains.'

'It's an execution, that's all. He's as guilty as anything and you know that. He was one of the group on the Paarl farm. Hand in glove with the Landman squad. All proven. If he swings a bit earlier rather than later, what's the difference?'

'Then why not wait for the courts?'

'Because it can be a hell of an embarrassment to every one of us if Judge Jordaan gets to see him, that's why.' My hand on his shoulder. Spoke from the bottom of my heart. 'Swanie, we people don't have an easy job. We do it because we've been chosen for it. We stand between our people and the enemy. It's war. What we're fighting is an unscrupulous lot who'll murder our women and children in their beds if we give them half a chance. Like Bloukrans and Weenen, time of the Great Trek. You know your history, man. We know we've got right on our side. God is with us. You might say it's His work we're doing, because the communists are the Antichrist. You want to tell me you can't do it?'

'No, Oom Kat, I can do it.'

Never spoke another word about it. Could see afterwards he was looking kind of pale. Only natural. This is not an easy task. But Blumer had to be eliminated and someone had to do it.

Remember my last visit to the Jew. Prostrate on the floor of his cell, just been brought back from interrogation. Looked bad. But raised his head when the door was opened. He hardly had the energy for it but he did. Looked me in the eyes. Know those eyes. Shark. Seen them many times. But what came back to me, strange, was that same day at St Helena. Shortly before the whale surfaced. Smallish shark. Was just grabbing the baton to give it the death blow when the shark jumped up. Like a vicious dog. Those eyes. Real human eyes. Criminal eyes. Strange what those eyes can do to one. Feeling of suddenly being confronted with a creature from another world, more menacing than anything from land. Suppose that's why one also reacts so much more viciously than usual. Kind of blind rage, a hatred from the guts. As if something in that darkness inside the shark calls up a darkness in oneself, something you're normally not aware of. That day in particular. But above all it was those eyes. The eyes of a terrorist. Seen them so many times in my life. That afternoon too, on the floor of that cell.

Which was why there was only one thing to do: if before that one might still have been willing to give him a chance, one last chance, it was now all over. The man had to hang. Because of those shark eyes. And he'd *had* his chances. God knows. More than anybody deserved. Even a week earlier when it seemed he was on the edge of a breakthrough, long personal chat to him, offered him pen and paper, told him to write down whatever came into his head. Then what did he do? Clutching the pen with that hand that could barely move he made a drawing on the sheet of paper. Caricature of my face. Badly drawn, but it was unmistakable. Some of the men actually burst out laughing. Made them swallow it bloody quickly. So it was clear: his days were numbered. But even then the Jew was given another chance. Decided to pay him that one last visit, offer him that one last choice. Then those shark eyes looking at me, mocking me. And suddenly there was a kind of peacefulness come over me. No more worries, no more doubts. He had to die. He'd brought it on himself.

With that, the judge was also neutralised. Least for the time being. Shrewd move. He hadn't expected it. But he'll come up with a counter-move sooner or later. Old Jordaan is not the kind of man to give up easily. Especially not when he's in a tight spot. Can be dangerous. Have to do some investigating on him. Find out where's his weak spot, every man's got one. Then go for it. Cut off his balls permanently.

If only there were progress on some of the other fronts there would have been little to complain of. But sweet blow-all. Found the right spot on the sea, right bait, right line, everything exactly the way it ought to be. But no bite.

That's when one needs to have patience. Nothing else. Patience. Time. But now it's the one thing they won't allow me. That's when a surfacing whale can catch one unawares.

Summarise the state of affairs at the time everything looked so promising. Christine Pienaar identified and eliminated. The Jew picked up at her funeral. The Paarl gang fitted one by one into the case. Thomas Landman identified by his brother, the connection between him and Nina Jordaan established. The two coloureds still somewhere in the background, but they're small fry, going after the big ones first. Roman, Cape salmon, snoek, cob, not herring or mackerel. Not *hottentot* fish!

At the time still suspected Landman to be in hiding somewhere in Johburg. Alerted the crowd up there. Then a stroke of luck when we broke the news to Landman's parents. Brought back a whole load of things belonging to him, went through it with a fine comb. Most of it turned out to be useless old stuff. Except for three unexposed rolls of film. Some bare-arsed shots of Nina Jordaan. Confirmed what we already suspected about their relationship, but it's always good to have corroborating evidence. And it may come in useful to shut up old Jordaan if push comes to shove. The other snaps didn't reveal much at first, might have been old stuff too. But personally took them up to Pretoria and phoned Landman's brother. The one who insists on being called 'Doctor'.

Always a matter of tactics. The first time he had to fly down to Cape Town. Put him at a disadvantage, strange territory, out of his element, less sure of himself. The next time the mountain goes to Mohammed. Makes him feel important, more at ease, fewer defence mechanisms. From the word go he was co-operative. Identified the snaps. The swimming-pool at his home. His wife and brats, visitors they had on the Sunday following the bomb blast. Over-eager to be of help, to rid himself of the burden of his brother. Gives one a strange feeling of nausea. People who won't hesitate to sell out their own family. Remember the way Pa and his crowd worked with traitors during the war. Lower than shark shit on the bottom of the sea. Yet where would we be without them? Our life-blood. Because *they* are prepared to be traitors we can bring in the culprits. Makes one think.

458

Doctor Frans Landman also identified a few shots he said wasn't of one of his own kids but his sister's. The other pictures were mainly landscapes, looks like Eastern Orange Free State, North-eastern Cape. Nothing important, except they confirm that from Pretoria he travelled south. Destination Cape Town, logical deduction.

Another trip, this time to Bloemfontein. Just to make sure. The sister refused to speak. Admitted the snaps were of her child, but wouldn't say when they were taken. Not necessary. Knew it already. But made a note of her. The woman can do with a firm hand and a good fright.

Interesting, the way people react. Something very basic about it. Like animals, insects. Remember my own childhood. Could play for hours with a millipede or a grasshopper or a lizard: step on it, then sit back to watch what it does; then you prod it with a twig or a nail; see how long it lasts, how it plays dead, tries to wriggle away, find ways of escape. Fascinating.

From Bloemfontein took a plane to P.E. and drove to the Little Karoo. The mother as tight as a clam. The old man incapacitated by a stroke. Fed this information to the papers. Bloody woman will still find out who it is she's dealing with. But above all the tidbit might turn out to be the kind of bait Landman would go for, one never knows. Like the Jew at Christine Pienaar's funeral.

But Landman is a pro, that's for sure. One even comes to respect him in a way: the way you respect a tuna or a marlin that tests your strength. If you're out to catch the big ones it's the struggle they put up that makes it worth your while.

Perhaps that's how he sees it too. Strange to think of it that way: to do his job he needs me. This is the antagonist that gives him reason to plant his bombs. And he is mine. If he and his kind hadn't existed there would have been no need for us. Neither can really do without the other.

That is why the bait had to be prepared with such care. To make it all worth one's while.

Yet so far he hasn't even taken a nibble. No reaction to the news of his father's illness. Even more puzzling, no reaction to the Jordaan bitch's cremation either.

At least: not immediately.

Until a fortnight later. Then came the letter to his parents. Had it confiscated immediately, of course; waiting for it all along. The old people can do without it, he's lost to them anyway. Get this into perspective: it has nothing to do with cynicism; a lot with necessity.

Many people tend to misunderstand this. It isn't pleasant constantly to be accused by others – including those who are pressing you for 'results' – about being heartless or callous or whatever. It's a job to be done. Sometimes a bloody dirty job. But what becomes of the country if it isn't done? Every shred of law and order down the drain. And it's all there is one can rely on. One is despised, condemned, even loathed by many: but who except us, who except Kat Bester, stands between them and the enemy? Would they like to see the communists take over? Lawlessness, godlessness? What one does, in the final analysis, is done to fulfil the will of God. To ensure that justice be done in the world. To ensure the triumph of the forces of good. That is what it comes down to. In humble obedience to God and His commandments. My conscience is clean.

One question, by the way: isn't 'right' and 'wrong' determined in the long run only by whether one succeeds or not?

Methods? No, not always pleasant. One learns, of course, not to be finical, to lose one's hangups. No need to be over-sensitive. A fisherman must be prepared to see his hands smeared with blood and guts. Why pull up your nose? Let's call it by its true name: 'violence'. Looking at it in isolation is not always a pleasant sight. But it's the only thing that works. Means to an end. Law and order, the reign of the good, cannot be established in our imperfect world unless evil is eradicated boots and all. Takes a *man* to do it. And it's still cheap at the price. No need to beat about the bush: hurting them is our business. Pain and fear, that's what keeps evil under control, nothing else.

Sometimes one has to cast the net wide. How many have we picked up since the bomb? Hundreds. Some got hurt in the process. 'Innocents'? Balls. Even if they might not have been involved personally they approved of it; that was what they secretly wished for. Nobody is truly innocent.

If in our search for Thomas Landman the 'wrong' people have been rounded up, just too bad. Suppose the opposite happened: suppose out of fear that something like that might happen we allowed Thomas Landman to get away, how would people have reacted *then*?! If his parents got 'hurt' in the process, that wasn't what we wanted. But to have let that letter through, for example, what risks would we have run?

Not that the letter was much use anyway. Landman evidently much too cautious to give anything away. No address, nothing. But a Cape Town postmark. The main post office. So it would seem

Landman is still there. That is, if he is to be trusted. Question is: if he really were in Cape Town, wouldn't he have arranged with his contacts to have it posted somewhere else? Johannesburg perhaps. He's a shrewd one. Matter of finding out what makes him tick. This is always the most important of all: to learn to read the thoughts of the fish you're after. One must read its mind before the fish itself knows what it's going to do next. And that's what made me suspicious. He must have known we would intercept the letter. And if he really was in Cape Town he wouldn't have posted it from there. Right? Can't put one's head on a block for it, but at least it's a possibility to reckon with.

Then the question is: *Where else?*

And that was where the frustration came in. Because there wasn't a single further sign of life from him.

Alerted every station in the country, particularly those within a radius of a hundred to two hundred kilometres from the Cape. Photograph, full description. Warning: he might be disguised, of course. Presumably on his own. Otherwise in the company of two coloured men – they're the only ones from Paarl we have still not traced – but this would be unlikely, too conspicuous. And Landman's too clever for that. Unless perhaps he's also trying to pass for coloured? His skin is on the dark side. Possibility to bear in mind.

But no luck. Not a trace.

And then the message from up the West Coast. First sent Swanie to investigate, seemed like a shot in the dark. But he came back very excited. So immediately summoned that Captain Coetzee. At first sight there seemed to be nothing untoward in his story: Saturday 28 May, two whites, one male, one female, paying a visit to a coloured schoolteacher, Augustyn, a man who'd caused previous problems harbouring terrorists. Actually awaiting trial. Suspect political inclinations. Educated man, that's what first made me suspicious. Education, especially in blacks and coloureds, never bodes good.

Should they bring the man in for interrogation? asked Coetzee. Over-zealous. Told him no: Just keep him under observation for the time being.

Description of the two visitors. White man with 'funny' hair: dark brown, reddish, doesn't look natural. Thick-rimmed spectacles. Offered Coetzee a photograph of Landman. Seemed unsure, but thought there might be a resemblance. White woman in jeans,

461

T-shirt, long black hair fastened behind her head, fringe in front; tall, thin. Ostensibly newly-weds. Got married in Upington, they said, but Coetzee established that in the last month there has been no wedding in that town involving persons matching the description. Also established that the car registration was false. As was the address in Worcester the man had supplied, and the address of the woman's parents in Upington.

Why the fuck hadn't he informed us earlier?

Coetzee was hedging. Nobody was expecting Landman in the company of a woman. If it had been Landman at all. The crux was that the man had dropped a hint about 'informing Pretoria' about the meeting with Coetzee; the captain was scared they might be working undercover for the SB, didn't want to stir up shit.

The hell in about the man's fucking ineptness. Had he been a fisherman's arse he could have gaffed them right there.

Still, everything wasn't lost yet. Far from it. Point of fact, after the long dead spell there was this sudden feeling of something actually nibbling the bait.

But where to look for them?

According to Coetzee they were on their way back to the Cape, following the coast. So we combed the whole area. Not a soul had seen two such people after 28 May. But a barman in Hopefield mentioned that two people answering the description had been in his place a week or so earlier. Same story as the one they told Coetzee in Augustyn's presence: working on an article for *Huisgenoot*. Slowly, slowly more witnesses were rounded up. A salt-of-the-earth old farmer and his wife near Piquetberg where it seemed the two had spent a weekend. Other hotel people. All of them described the same car, white Opel with a couple of bumps and dents, Worcester registration plates. All of them had been told that the two were on their way to Cape Town – but the way we tracked their course they'd been moving *up* the coast. Still the possibility of a wild goose chase, of course. But the fishy smell was becoming stronger every day. One develops a nose for it.

Only question was: Who is the woman with Thomas Landman? Nowhere in the whole story could we fit her in. If we could establish *her* identity we could count on a catch.

But where? When? The very morning Coetzee found them with Augustyn they disappeared with their car and all from the face of the earth. Or so it seemed.

Then this morning, out of the blue, the dominee from Griqualand

West came to the rescue. And suddenly, like a float dipping under the surface of the water, it was all clear. If this isn't proof that God is on our side, what is?

Contact established.

Every man knows exactly what he has to do. Up here we're waiting with the lines, down there you lurk in the depths below. The boat bobbing on a sea as flat as a mirror. Thomas Landman, Lisa Lombard: here's the hook: take it. Hope you put up a fight that makes it worth while. At the very last moment Kat Bester wants to look you full in your cold shark-eyes. –

Chapter 11

I

— When I drove into the town on Monday morning, first garage on the
main road as we arranged, Thomas wasn't there. Not a sign. But I
was early. One o'clock or later, I'd told him, and it was barely twelve.
Managed to get out of Cape Town earlier than we expected. Even so I
was a bit worried. I'm still not so sure he'll pull it off. When all's said
and done the chap is white. That's what it boils down to. I know the
Organisation is very clear on this point – colour-blind, no black, no
white, it's the cause – but when you really strip away everything
else Thomas has less reason than I to see it through, right?

I drove past, through the small town, out the other end. Spent
some time at a picnic spot beside the road, and drove back to the
garage when it was getting on to one o'clock. Asked the attendant
to top it up. Among the boxes and stuff in the back of the combi
I'd also brought along a flat tyre to make up time if necessary. 'Just
play it cool,' Justin said. As if it was necessary to tell *me* a thing
like that.

He appeared at my window so silently that I couldn't believe my
eyes. Never underestimate the guy. Anyway, he squatted beside the
combi to tie up his shoelaces. Never even looked up at me. Just
mumbled, 'Two blocks on, then up right, okay?' And walked on
without paying any further attention to me.

Filled her up, then I followed him there. Sitting under a bluegum
on the outskirts. Whistling to himself. All the time in the world. It
was the lunch-hour, no living soul in sight. Even so he was in no
hurry to get in beside me.

'Yes!' I said.

'Glad you made it.'

'How're things? Uptight?'

'Rashid.' He shook his head as if he couldn't believe himself. I still wasn't at ease with that funny hair of his, even though one gets used to that kind of thing in our line of business. No one keeps looking the same from one day to the next. There I was myself wearing a kofia and a moustache and sunglasses. 'Rashid,' he said again. 'Can't tell you how glad I am to see *your* face again.'

'Well, you survived the weekend.'

'Yes. Not very comfortable, we had to sleep in the car, didn't want to attract attention. But it was all right; one doesn't expect five-star treatment all the way.'

'The babe okay?'

'She's taking it very well.'

'She'd better.'

'I wish you could meet her. To see for yourself.'

'I wouldn't mind. But no go. The less she sees of us the better. You haven't told her where you heading for yet?'

'No. But listen, Rashid –'

'I don't want to hear it. You know the way we work.'

'I know.'

I checked him out for a while. All things considered, he was looking a bit the worse for wear. But basically nothing wrong. 'Fill me in on what happened,' I said. 'We haven't got much time, I don't want people to see us together.'

He told me the story. I didn't like it one bit.

'I want you to be clear about one thing,' he said. 'When the going really got tough it was Lisa who got us out of it. She put on an act that completely threw the policeman.'

'Least she could have done.'

'You should have seen her, Rashid. A real pro.'

'Shouldn't have happened in the first place. You had no idea beforehand of how she would react. You took a chance. She could have sunk you. And all of us with you.' I couldn't help adding with a touch of nastiness, 'Sorry Thomas, but when it comes to making war, when it comes to making decisions and taking risks, it's a man's job. Women just aren't revolutionary material. I don't trust the dames.'

He screwed up his almost-black eyes. 'You never trusted Nina or Christine either, Rashid. Did you?'

'So what?' I didn't want to start the old argument all over again.

Without warning he asked, 'Rashid, have *you* never felt anything for a woman?'

Below the belt, I thought. Made me angry. But I'd be damned if I

465

let him see it. I don't carry my heart on my sleeve. 'One day when the struggle is over,' I told him, 'perhaps I'll think about it then. At the moment it simply isn't a chance I'm prepared to take. Right?'

'Is it really so easy?'

'Sure. If the struggle means enough to you.'

So many things that's happened to me; and I prefer to keep them to myself. Only a dog returns to his own shit. But Thomas made it difficult not to remember. The time I went to Westville, all eager to get on with my studies. Bright boy and all that. Then I had to drop it all and find a job. Then the SB trying to co-opt me. I had to go underground in Johburg. Where they picked up my trail again. How? Because they picked up Faridah in Durban and hurt her. Simple as that. She couldn't take the pressure and I never blamed her. So that was where I sat down and took a look at my life. In this kind of world there's only two choices: it's either total commitment or its fuck-all. The way I saw it, a man's got a head, and a heart, and a cock. In the struggle there's room for only one of them and that's the head. The other two are liabilities. I worked out the odds and I made my choice.

So I sneaked out. Right out of the country. Apart from Justin no one else knows about this, and he's tight as a clam. Even if they break his jaws with crowbars he won't say a word. This is my own business. Six months in Angola. Target practice, pistols, rifles, automatics, grenades. Or it's survival stints. Days, weeks. Nights in the bunkers dug below the old Portuguese buildings.

Afterwards the desert in Tanzania. Flies, mosquitoes, all the fucking plagues of Egypt. And if you malinger or think of giving up you shit square bricks. Just to survive is a bloody miracle. But you've *learned*. Your body is trained. Your mind no less.

And that's only the beginning, right? Then six more months in Berlin. Guns. Ammunition. Explosives. Things they haven't even heard the names of yet in this country. And lectures. Until you can hardly keep your eyes open. But you keep listening. Learning. Finding out what makes the world tick. One thing above all: revolution isn't made by little groups who play at war, or by boys who look for kicks, or by people who try to fight other people's battles for them. It comes from a mass movement deep inside a whole nation that's been made conscious of its real needs, its rights, its freedoms. Otherwise you can forget all about it. And that's why I keep thinking: no matter how much sympathy I got for

Thomas, he can never *really* understand. It's not in his guts. He isn't black. If he talks about being oppressed it's of a different kind.

I was thinking about all this on the long road from Cape Town. Something of a luxury, that trip in the combi. In our job you don't easily get a chance like that for sorting out your thoughts.

Thought about Thomas. The kind of passion that drives him. No other word for it. So right, I respect him for it. I often get mad at him, but there's nothing wrong with his guts. My problem with him is that I cannot help being suspicious about the emotional approach. Can't help it. It's okay, trying to find moral justification for everything you do, but Jesus Christ, this is *war*. War isn't moral.

In a war, all that counts is winning. There's no fair play and no justice. It's a manner of defeating the enemy. You want to beat the system? Then you must beat it at its own game. And dirt is the name of the game. Dirt? Power. All that counts at the end of the day. All of us on the black side: we're the majority, six, seven times over. But we have to eat shit, done it for centuries. And why? Because *they* got the power. And we can only sit down to talk once it's us who got it. Position of strength. Nothing else is important.

It's not the colour of his white skin I have against Thomas. It's because, even in the midst of the struggle, he's still conditioned to try and put right what 'his people' have fucked up. Least, that's the way I see it. Because deep down I know it's not black against white, it's haves against have-nots. It's class against class. And the struggle won't be over the day 'we' get the vote. It can only be over once we are no longer the slaves of a capitalist system. And that's a struggle the whole of the Third World is still trapped in. So once this battle is behind us, fine: but that's only the beginning. The real war still lies ahead. Its battlefield is Wall Street, London, Bonn, Tokyo. *Then* we can talk again.

It's a hell of a price we paying along the way. In our little group alone: of the six that started in Paarl, there's three dead, three left. Tough. But the odds are still okay. That is why it is important that Thomas make it. But that means *making* it. Can't go on taking risks like this. Besides, it interferes with our job.

Justin and I and the three new cell members were in Bellville working on our plans for the new attack when we got the message from Thomas. It was the Saturday and a bad time to be interrupted.

467

This new attack is bloody important. We cannot let up. One needs follow-ups. Keep them jittery. They're rattled as it is. One can see that in the continuing detentions. Cape Town, Durban, Johburg, all over. They don't know where to pounce, so they pounce everywhere. To show they're still in charge. Won't take much more to make the whole situation ungovernable. Like Justin put it the other day: Not one detainee has committed a crime, not one is guilty of anything that can be defined: no matter how many of them there are, in detention each one of them exists exclusively as the possibility of some feared act that has not yet been defined. How did he put it? – Each one is a psychosis or a neurosis in the brain of some official or policeman. So this is a pretty sick society.

Anyway, so we got the message. Usual way, via the taxi place. Peter needing spare parts. He'll phone again at six, to the auntie's house. Six o'clock means a quarter past four. The auntie is the booth at the main post office we generally use. Justin went personally, then reported back. Thomas needs new wheels, the Opel is hot. He already exchanged the Worcester plates for the Kimberley ones. And if anyone started looking for him it would be in the direction of the Cape. Whereas all the while he turned inland from Vanrhynsdorp. Justin was worried about the weekend ahead, because as I said it was Saturday it all happened. But there was nothing doing, we had to get everything organised first. So he said, Let's meet on Monday, quarter to three, first garage at this end. Quarter to three is one o'clock.

Had to tune up the combi. Serviced only a few weeks ago, but Justin doesn't take chances. Rechecked everything, because we didn't know how far he'd still have to go. Right. New plates. New papers for Thomas and the babe. And Thomas wanted to drop the journalist act. Something else. We decided on a travelling salesman. Paint was my idea. But it was vetoed: too easy for shops to check up with head office. So we raided the safe houses, all the stuff Christine had collected long ago. Dresses and shoes, especially hats. Some undies as well, even a couple of boxes of make-up. And whatever else the two might need for their own disguise. That was where we really missed Christine, say so myself. For the rest, lots of empty boxes to fill up the back of the combi. Easy to explain if anybody started poking around: one could always say the stuff had been sold on the way.

The Opel I had to drive back, we'd see to it that it would be found, later, somewhere in the Cape. Take the eyes off Thomas.

Something else about Justin, no one else would think of a thing like that: on Sunday he arranged with a woman to phone the hospital in Oudtshoorn, say she's phoning on behalf of Doctor Somebody in Pretoria, wants to enquire about the Landman patient in Intensive Care. So I could give Thomas the latest update.

And it wasn't long either before Thomas brought it up. 'I'm worried about my dad, Rashid. If only there was a way of getting in touch. I don't even know if he's still alive.'

'Justin got through to them.' I told him the story. 'I can't say it's good news, but I won't say it's bad either. He's still alive. But they say he cannot speak yet. Left side paralysed. Seems his head is working okay, recognises visitors. Perhaps he'll still recover. But they can't guarantee anything.'

He nodded. He was battling, I could see that. Keep sentiment out of it, I thought. Not that I didn't feel sorry for him. But we've all made sacrifices. There'll be time for sadness or gladness later. Now we've got a war to fight. But anyway.

He took a letter from his back pocket. Rather crumpled, no address on the envelope. 'Wrote it this morning while I sat waiting,' he said. 'In a café over there. Can you have it posted to my dad, from Cape Town?'

'You think it's safe?'

'It's just to let them know I've heard the news, I'm sorry, I miss them. No address, no date, nothing. I'll give you their address, you can put it on later.'

'Okay, I'll see to it.'

Back in Cape Town I first opened the envelope to check the contents. It was like he said, straightforward, harmless stuff. No need to check it with Justin. Put it in a new envelope, printed the address on it, posted it in town. Least I could do for him.

'What now?' he asked after a while. Seemed okay again.

'Justin thinks you can stick to the plan. Up to the North-west, then on to Botswana. But take your time, the borders are still hot. Try to contact us every other day or so. Just say weather's fine. Give us about two weeks, so we can synchronise it with the next bomb. That'll bring the heat back to Cape Town and you can take the gap.'

He nodded. Then looked hard at me. 'Is the next bomb really necessary, Rashid?'

'What a thing to ask. We can't relax now, right?'

'Will people be killed again?'

'We don't intend to.'

'We never intend to. But it happens.' His eyes looked troubled. A sigh. 'I wish we could have spared the children, Rashid.'

'Those two who died wouldn't have made any difference to the thousands already killed in the townships.'

'No,' he said, 'I know. But neither will the dead of the townships bring back those two, will they?'

I was worried about him. For a long time I gave him no answer, but in the end I kind of gently asked him, 'You chicken?'

Thomas shook his head. 'No, I'm not chicken. It's just – you know? One seems to live through many years each day. Every day you grow older. And it makes one impatient. You want to grasp what's left of life *now*, before it's gone, before it gets worse. Because if you add up everything that's happened in this country, Rashid: it's too tragic for words. One cannot grasp it any more.'

'You cracking up, Thomas?' I asked him straight.

With a little smile he said, 'I told you once before, remember? – "Try me."'

He seemed thin to me as I walked away and looked back from the corner: thin against the white of the sky behind him, and the veld beyond the last houses; such a thin sliver of a person, such a big land.

Then I walked on, in my pocket the keys to the Opel he gave me, to where he told me he left the car.

It was the last time I saw him. –

2

'That Jimmy,' Thomas said when he came back into the café where Lisa was waiting at the table, a folded much-read newspaper in front of her (and the mere fact that he couldn't even refer to Rashid by name made him angrily conscious of screens, distances, chasms interposed once again between them). 'That Jimmy. Sometimes I feel like wringing his neck when he starts ranting about women. You know what he said today? "Not revolutionary material."'

'Isn't that what most of you think?'

'All he has to do is open his eyes,' he said, annoyed. 'Everywhere in the Organisation men and women are fighting alongside of each other. And many of the women are stronger than the men.'

'I guess it takes more than one generation to cure men of the habit of millennia, ever since the first Neanderthal male looked down and saw something dangling between his legs, and based his sense of power on fifteen or so centimetres of suspended flesh.'

'Simple as that?'

'It's where it begins, isn't it? What makes it dangerous is the fear in the back of their heads that goes with it. The fear that those fifteen centimetres may not be enough. They dare not admit it, not even to themselves, but it's there. I think your Jimmy is afraid of women.'

'Try to tell it to him.'

'I will. The day you trust me enough to introduce me to him.'

'Karin.' He leaned forward in urgency. 'It doesn't depend on *me*.'

'I know.' She took his hand and quickly, almost furtively, pressed it to her mouth. The mere contact brought back memories, moved him, made him think, My God, she has a kind of consciousness that has no end.

She gave a swift glance around to make sure no one could hear, then asked softly, urgently, 'Anton, was everything all right?'

'Jimmy brought us a combi.' He smiled. 'If we'd had it over the weekend we would have had more sleep.'

'I'm not complaining.'

'You never complain. That's what makes me ashamed.' He straightened up. 'I'm going to order us more tea.'

He went to the counter where a slovenly old women, her grey hair bedecked with coloured curlers, sat drooping over a photo magazine, like a wax statue that had begun to melt in the heat.

'We'd like two more cups of tea, please.'

Without looking up at him she called towards the kitchen, in the screeching voice of a caged parrot, 'Gladys, two more teas!' Then to him, but still without looking up, 'Will that be all?'

'Thank you.'

Thomas returned, making a detour round a large display cabinet that cluttered up the space between counter and tables. It was crammed with toys, paperbacks, Tupperware, even severely practical women's lingerie; on the top perched a child's tricycle on a large box; on the floor beside it, two bicycles.

'Catering for all tastes,' he said as he sat down.

'From cradle to grave.' Lisa looked at him. 'You won't believe this, but while you were away a farmer came in here, followed by five or six of his labourers, to buy a coffin. The old lady took him through to the back door, I presume there's a storeroom out there, and after a while they came back carrying the coffin on their shoulders. It was eerie. And as they went out he said quite casually, "Will you enter it, Auntie?" As if he buys one every day.'

'At least we'll know where to come to if the going really gets tough.' He reached mechanically for the paper, then pulled back his hand, as if in disgust. 'Something in it?'

'Nothing.'

'It's last Friday's.'

'I know. I asked, but it seems they only get papers on Mondays, Wednesdays and Fridays; and this morning's missed the truck.'

He lowered his voice. 'Good place to be in.'

'How are things – back in Cape Town?' she asked.

'Hard at work. As always.'

'Won't you men ever stop?'

'You make it sound like a hobby, like games.'

'That's what I'm afraid of.' She raised her eyes to meet his: a house with drawn curtains. Grey curtains. 'If there were more women present when decisions are taken I would have felt more at ease. Tell that to your Jimmy when you see him again.'

'There *are* women involved.'

'In taking the decisions?'

'Yes. And who have fewer qualms than some of the men.'

'I'd still trust them more.'

'_'

'I'm not underestimating politics, Anton,' she said suddenly, leaning forward, talking in a whisper; her black hair loose around her shoulders. 'I only have different priorities from you.' He challenged her with his eyes; an angry shake of her head, then she continued, 'You know, just after I came back from Europe, two years ago, I spent some time working in the advice office of the Black Sash in the city. Eager to do my bit. All bright-eyed enthusiasm. And they could use a psychologist. Worked sixteen hours a day. I won't bore you with the details. All the usual things: migrant workers in need of passes, people thrown out of the hostels, women following their husbands to the city and looking for a place to stay, squatters whose shacks on the Flats had been bulldozed. Then, one day, we all went out to Mitchell's Plain to take affidavits. There'd been raids the day before, horrific stories about police brutality, we wanted to find out first-hand what had happened. It was tough going, because most of the people were too intimidated to talk. But in the end we persuaded a dozen or so to give their testimonies under oath.'

A 'coloured' woman in slippers, wearing a soiled white apron over a pink housecoat, brought a round tray with their tea-things, started unloading it on the green chipped formica, spilled milk, which she wiped off with the flat of her hand, then went back to the kitchen.

'And then?' asked Thomas.

'Ag.' She seemed reluctant to continue.

'I want to know.' (– There's so much about you I still need to know. Even after the confidences of the weekend. *Especially* after the weekend. –)

'It's so insignificant really, and so awful.' She checked the tea. It was too weak. She stirred vigorously for a while, then pushed back the pot again. 'Before we were back in town the police were in the township again. Rounded up everybody we'd spoken to. They must have had informers all over the place. Kicked open doors, trampled children, terrorised everybody they could lay their hands on. We lodged a protest, but the people were detained anyway. Some remained inside for a year. One died. From "natural causes", as always. A young man of twenty-three. Same age as I was then.' Her eyes probed his. 'Do you understand what I'm trying to tell you? What we did, we did to expose injustice, to help the victims. But as it turned out we'd just made things worse for them. If we hadn't done anything it would have been immoral, reprehensible. But then at least those people would have been left in peace. That young man would not have died. Now I have his life on my conscience.'

'Why have you never told me this?'

'–'

She poured the tea. 'That was when I chickened out and decided to give the school job a go. And there my battle with the men began. The Siebert squad. Because I've come to think that *this* is the real problem. Not black and white, but men. They are the ones who have the power. It's they who keep that kind of power going.'

Dismayed, Thomas sat brooding over what she'd told him. He wanted to respond but before he could there was an interruption.

From outside came a burly bearded young man in shorts, one hand in plaster. On his hip he had a child that might have fallen straight from heaven: a little girl of maybe eighteen months or two years old, two enormous blue eyes, blonde curls, with a dummy in her rosebud mouth.

'Ever seen anything more angelic?' whispered Lisa. 'All-things-bright-and-beautiful.'

The young gorilla glanced askance at the old lady in curlers behind the counter, thrust his hand in a glass jar and took out a fistful of marshmallow fish, one for the cherub, the rest for himself; and strode past to a door in the side wall, presumably the office.

'Ma!' his voice came thundering from there a moment later. 'What the fuck have you done with the safe key?'

'What you want in the safe?'

She didn't look up from her magazine; but her shapeless body seemed to tense in resentment or anticipation.

'None of your blarry business. Where's the key?'

'You can't go on raiding the cash box, Flip. I got to live too. It's my café. Your father left it to me.'

'Old man was soft in the head. It's your fucking café as long as you keep your nose out of my life. Come on, where's the key?'

'I got it here, Flip.' With a sigh she removed the key that hung on a length of string from her scrawny neck.

The hirsute young man reappeared, this time without the fairy child, and grabbed the key with his healthy hand, giving the old woman such a ferocious yank on the arm that she nearly lost her balance on the tall stool behind the counter.

'Ag, come on, Flip, man,' she whined.

'One of these days you'll try to stick the thing up your fucking old cunt,' he shouted over his shoulder. 'You just leave me alone, you hear?'

Behind the counter the old woman lit a menthol cigarette, blowing a cloud of smoke over her magazine. She didn't seem much perturbed. It probably happened every day.

'Ten centimetres at most,' Lisa said with a straight face. Then began to snigger.

She stopped abruptly at the sound of an earsplitting noise from the room next door. A gunshot. Then another. Thomas jumped up so quickly that his chair fell clattering on the linoleum floor.

Behind the counter the old woman raised her curlered head like an unlikely artificial flower. 'It's all right, mister,' she said through a new whorl of smoke. 'It's just the flies.'

'What?' He gaped at her. With large stunned eyes Lisa stared at the door in the side wall.

'Sometimes he shoots the flies.' She sighed, brought a hand to her chicken neck where there was no longer any reassuring key to be touched, and resumed her reading.

And indeed, when Thomas rushed to the door to investigate – he *had* to check – the hirsute troglodyte was standing in the office at a smallish grey safe against the back wall, a Magnum in his hand, his bearded head turned up to look at the softboard ceiling already riddled with innumerable bullet holes.

He gave a nasty grin at Thomas. 'This time the bastard didn't get away.'

The diminutive blonde angel, bending over beside the table that served as desk, displayed between thumb and forefinger a dubious black spot retrieved from the floor. Dribbling past the dummy in her mouth she said excitedly, 'Fy, fy.' Then held it out for Thomas to inspect. A moment later she solemnly removed the teat from between her celestial lips and said in lisping innocence, 'Fucking cunt.'

How remote from the rest of the world this place was. Even on the way here, on Saturday afternoon, after Thomas had made his first telephone call to Cape Town from Vanrhynsdorp to report on their encounter with Captain Coetzee, there had been an unsettling discovery of different spaces meeting and intersecting. Driving through the scaly semi-desert landscape of the Knersvlakte, the Plains of Groaning (the intense blue of the sky above the edge of the plateau ahead), while watching in the rear-view mirror the road as it was unravelled like an intestine behind them: to see simultaneously where one will be and where one has already been; time expressed in terms of space; being here reduced to this shifting point where future and past meet, without any importance of its own. (In this godforsaken desert Fransoois Lodewickus Landman had disappeared, three centuries before, on his heavy ship.) Then, from the barren West Coast floor, up the rough brown edge sloping upward, the road carving a steep angle into the scrub: and the moment one reaches the top, everything is different – brittle grass, clumps of trees, heavy rock formations, flocks of sheep, a cooler breath of wind on one's face.

They were still, then, moving through temporarily suspended time, their only aim – for the moment secure between the new registration plates, front and back, on the Opel (the old ones removed, and buried far from the road under a layer of gravel and scaly rock) – to get away from the coast; to await instructions from the Cape. Then all could be resumed as if there had been no interruption. But the conversation with Justin had changed that hope. They had to wait until Monday. If it was urgent, Justin had said, they could send someone through in the late afternoon or early evening; but postponing it to Monday would allow them more time for the thorough preparation he preferred.

It left the weekend in parenthesis. (Afterwards, Thomas would remember thinking: Sometimes a parenthesis can be more significant than the surrounding syntax. At the very least it breaks the illusory linearity in the grammar of our experience.) They would have to spend the two nights outdoors.

The Saturday night they spent below a thin waterfall some distance from the town, in a deserted hollow surrounded by cliffs; the stars were out; an almost-full moon, patchy and unhealthy and streaked like a half-hatched egg, sat above the farthest ridge. Apart from the small moist sound of the waterfall and the hiss of their gas flame there was nothing else; prehistoric silence. And the cold was seeping insidiously into them.

She was singularly quiet; and when at last she did speak it caught him by surprise. 'I wonder,' she said, 'if Erik would understand anything of what is happening to me right now.'

'Is it so important?'

'He's jealous of me,' he said.

'Naturally. Still, I think he's working on it, he's beginning to accept it. Which he never did before, with others.'

'Will you ever be able to detach yourself from him enough to be married?'

She moved sharply against him. 'Why do you ask that?'

'You don't have to answer.'

After a long time she said quietly, 'Erik and I – there's no one I can ever explain it to. Not even you. And I'm supposed to be a psychologist, I ought to have names for everything. But this is too secret: it begins where words end. That's why people have always misunderstood about Erik and me. They try to explain us in terms of the right and wrong of a different kind of world altogether. Perhaps no one *can* enter into the world where he and I will always be Hansel and Gretel in the wood. Maybe you also think it's ridiculous, or sordid, or childish. In which case: fuck you. But honestly, sometimes I feel as if there really is no difference, no boundary, between him and me, he's an extension of myself, I of him. Not just emotionally, but even physically.'

'When I pledged thee my troth on the beach I told you it was for better or for worse – you, the whole you, and nothing except you. Whatever "you" may be.'

'Did you realise what you were letting yourself in for?'

'No. But I was prepared to risk it.'

'You're nuts.'

'Is that your clinical diagnosis or a personal opinion?'

She said quietly, 'You know, you're beautiful.'

'It's my beholder who has beautiful eyes.'

He cupped her narrow face between his hands; it was pale in the stark white flame of the gas stove that hissed energetically under their tin of soup.

– Each time you entrust something to me which I have not known of, or haven't understood before, it feels as if I am the one made more vulnerable by the knowledge. Because so much is at stake. Gambling must be like this: every time you win something, you increase your stakes; every time there is more to be lost. Yet the more you stand to lose the more important it becomes to take the risk. –

'What are you thinking when you close up like this?' she asked, taking his wrists in her hands.

'When my people – the people from the Organisation – bring us the new car on Monday, I want you to go back with them.'

'No.'

'Listen, Karin: what happened this morning when we were with Mr Augustyn: you were wonderful, I suddenly looked at you with new eyes. But I can't allow you to get trapped in another situation as dangerous as that.'

'Don't I have any say in the matter?'

'That's not it.'

'It is. It's what it's all about.'

'It's not a matter of you or me. As individuals neither of us has any importance. It's the Organisation, the movement, the cause that counts.'

'If you walk alone, you walk faster,' Lisa said absently, as if reciting a half-remembered poem, 'But if you walk with someone else you go farther.'

'Where did you learn that?' he asked, surprised.

'Why do you ask?'

'Because those are the exact words my friend Sipho always said to me.'

'I heard it from Naomi. She brought me up with it. She told me it was an old saying of her people.'

He sat staring silently into the darkness beyond the pale flame.

477

She removed the soup from the flame and left it to cool. She got up and went to the car. He heard her open a door, then the boot. After a while she returned wearing a tracksuit jacket over her other clothes; and she handed him a jersey. She also had their sleeping-bags with her, which they draped over their backs like *karosses*, huddled close to the meagre warmth emitted by the small white flame. Using plastic spoons she'd bought with the groceries from the café in town, they ladled soup from the tin.

Afterwards he turned off the flame. Immediately pitch-black darkness descended on them. It took a while before the moonlight began once again to define their surroundings: the amphitheatre of cliffs fanning out from the ghostly thin line of the waterfall, the patches and clumps of bushes, a restless horizon. The stars had grown bigger; everything was colder than before.

'We won't sleep a wink tonight,' she said. He could hear her teeth chattering.

'We'll have to keep each other warm.'

'Lie on me.'

She lay back on her sleeping-bag, and he stretched himself out to cover her, clad in several layers of clothing, the sleeping-bag on top; supported on his elbows, his cheek against her in the immemorial posture of love: except it was too cold to make love. Below him he could still feel her tremble. And only after a long time did he realise it could not be only from cold.

'Are you afraid again?' he asked in her ear.

'Terribly.' A silence, before she added, with difficulty, 'Today, while it was all happening, it was easier to bear. But now –' He could hear her trying to control her breathing. 'What makes it worse is that everything *seems* so calm. As if we're having a picnic. But it's so deceptive. I have the feeling that somewhere in this darkness a net is being drawn in around us. For all we know that policeman has started making enquiries about us. By this time they may know that the car registration was false, that we're not who we said we are. Telegraph wires buzzing, telexes, faxes, God knows what. Invisible, inaudible. All around us in the dark. And here we lie and try to keep each other warm – and there's nothing at all we can *do* about it.'

'There are other people, too, who cannot sleep,' he said. 'People waiting for a police van to stop outside, a door to be kicked in. People in a diaspora all over the continent: looking up at this moon and wanting to come home and knowing it may never happen in their lifetime. The night is full of sleepless people, Karin. And it's not separate worlds. They're all the same. That's what makes it so unbearable.'

This was the dimension in which afterwards, in retrospect – the Monday in the café, the days after that – those two nights would become indistinguishable from one another: the night below the thin waterfall, and the next, at a camping site among low outcrops of rock not far from the same town. Hours of sitting hunched up, lying foetally, then finding refuge in the car, at last driving into the night, the heater turned on fully, to warm themselves and thaw their frozen bodies; then back to the camp. Back to a very basic existence; to reflexes, relationships: with space, stars above, and a waxing cancerous moon, terrifying silence; hard earth, the outlines of koppies as ancient as God. Conversations which returned again and again to the same landmarks, the same questions, fears, worries, small comforts, desperate dreams. Somewhere in the course of the weekend her period started; she had cramps; and because she never calculated such events in advance she was surprised by it, and had to borrow several handkerchiefs from Thomas to stem her heavy flow. Which made the nights – at least one of them, possibly both – even more uncomfortable. Although at the same time it enhanced the meagre comfort of being in it together.

'It's good just to lie against you like this.'

'You must try to sleep,' he whispered.

'What about you? You lie awake so often.'

'It comes with the job.' A mocking laugh: 'Macbeth hath murder'd sleep.' She didn't answer. After a while he said, 'It's easy to kill if one has no idea of what it means to live. But to know what life is, to love it, to will it, and then to choose, coolly and clearly, to *take* a life – I don't think one can ever truly calculate what it will do to you.' With a wry chuckle: 'As Raskolnikov discovered.'

She had no answer ready; he didn't seem to expect one.

After some time he went on, almost as if surprised himself by the recollection, 'You know, when I was in Leningrad, I met a man, Sipho'd arranged it, a man whose life consisted of guiding visitors in the footsteps of Raskolnikov. He must have known the whole novel by heart. A man with the eyes of a tortured fanatic, like one of Dostoevsky's own possessed. Sergei. I've forgotten his surname. He spent a whole day guiding me through Raskolnikov's life. The cramped little cubicle in which he lived, the old woman's flat, the exact routes he followed through the city, the place where he met Marmeladov, his conversations with Sonya, the bridge across the Neva, the stone under which he buried the stolen objects, everything. What I found scary was the impression that Sergei himself had become completely possessed by Raskolnikov, he had no life of his own left. He *was* Raskolnikov, yet Raskolnikov was a fictitious character!'

'And now you've also started?'

'No!' He shook his head vehemently. 'I think what strikes me most today is how remote Dostoevsky's world is from ours. In a way it must be almost easy to have heaven and hell available as he did, to do battle with angels and demons on the bank and shoal of eternity: because it means that ultimately you're in the hands of God and Satan. Even if it drives you mad, as it almost did to Raskolnikov, at the end of it all there's Someone in whose hands you can dump it all. There's crime – and then there's punishment. In the final analysis one can cancel out the other; the balance is perfect. But once the metaphysical order has been changed into a social dispensation – this was always Sipho's final argument – what then? Then there's only oneself. The Organisation makes it a bit easier, it offers you structures to support you: but even so, beyond those structures, there's only you, all on your own, with your personal responsibility to life and death –'

'As I see it,' she said, 'the final problem is simply this: that violence solves nothing, it only postpones the true solution. And doesn't this make it worse? Stripped to the bone, it comes down to a world divided between those who have power and those who don't. The ones who have it cling to it, the others want to get it. And the struggle goes on until they change places. But what's the use? The very fact that someone gains power makes inevitable the eventual loss of that power. Perhaps I'm an anarchist by nature. Because I'm a woman? All I know is that from the day of my birth I've been living in a world in which powerful men have been telling me what to do. I don't trust *any* power, Anton. I won't trust *any* government. And what makes you think that *your* struggle is different? or that you can destroy violence with violence? or that you can stop the seesaw of the tussle for power? You *must* have thought about it, otherwise you couldn't have done this thing. You told me yourself that there was a time you believed in fireflies.'

'I think the main difference lies in this, that we're not trying to replace one group with another. We want to get rid of a small corrupt all-powerful clique so that people can decide for themselves how to run their lives.'

She sighed. 'It sounds so good, Anton. But what about reality? Don't people just want to be left alone? With the result that a new small group comes forward to make decisions on their behalf. And then it all starts again.'

'If the struggle is waged in such a way that those people are allowed to share in it, then they're no longer out in the cold. For the first time in their lives they become part of a process in which they *can* have a say in their own lives, and take responsibility for it.'

'Don't you think the lives you took would have the effect of alienating people rather than attracting them? Surely you're trying to win supporters for your cause: instead of doing that you've killed several people. And it's no use saying that wasn't the way you planned it. That's the way it *happened*: that's what you should have taken into account.'

'We have. I was absolutely sure about it all. Before the time.'

'And now?'

'Sometimes, in spite of all the precautions and fire-breaks and counter-fires, after calculating carefully the weather and the wind, one still lights a veld fire. And it still gets out of hand. Because one can never consider *everything*. Among the imponderables there is, above all, oneself.'

He seemed ready to go on, but he must have changed his mind, or perhaps she'd interpreted it wrongly, because he said nothing more. Where his thoughts were wandering she couldn't follow; neither could he pursue hers. At last she got up quietly and walked off into the night. He heard the small hiss of urine: and all of a sudden it was a sound so human, so ordinary, so undeniable, it made his heart contract. Behind all one's talk, he thought, behind the great stream of philosophy in the West, behind dreams and ideals, utopias, wishes, urges, this is what one comes back to: the individual of flesh and blood and bone; who eats and drinks and copulates, who pees and shits, who is alone and desires not to be alone, who lives and has to die.

She returned, cocooned herself once again in her sleeping-bag, sat for some time hugging her knees in her arms, pressed tightly against him, to regain her lost warmth. And at last she asked, as if returning herself from a long journey:

'Tell me about Leningrad.'

He didn't really know where to begin: in so many ways it had been a private experience, intimately coloured by Sipho's presence, and by the awareness of Dostoevsky. It was different from Moscow:

'Do you think it'll help?'

'If you really mean it. Maybe.'

'I've forgotten how to do it.'

'I'll show you.'

He closed his eyes to concentrate on a question; shook the three Chinese coins in his closed hand and started throwing them. She drew the hexagram as he progressed, from bottom to top. Broken, broken, then four unbroken lines. '*Tun*/Retreat.'

He looked up. 'Doesn't sound very promising.'

'Read what it says.'

'The power of the dark is ascending. The light retreats to security, so that the dark cannot encroach upon it. This retreat is no matter of man's will but of natural law. Therefore in this case withdrawal is proper; it is the correct way to behave in order not to exhaust one's forces.'

'Where are we going from here?' she asked in an even voice.

'I'll only know after I've seen my people on Monday.'

'Where would you *like* to go?'

'_'

'Anton, I know I have no right to ask questions. That's the condition on which you allowed me to come with. All I want to say is that *if* you're planning to go further to the north-west, my father lives near Prieska. In the vicarage we'll be safe. No one will ever look for us there. In case you think it's a good idea to lie low for a while.'

'Can you trust him unconditionally?'

'He's my father.' She seemed to weigh her words very carefully. 'I suppose I represent just about everything he finds reprehensible, beyond his understanding. And he for me. In his world God is a kind of totalitarian presence: the Great White Male. And yet I love him.' A pause. 'Does that sound like an answer?'

'Perhaps.' He smiled. 'I'll discuss it with them. It may turn out to be just what we need right now.'

From the office in the side wall of the café the young bearded savage appeared again, the small blonde girl on his hip. Without even glancing at the curlered old woman behind the counter he strode past.

'What time will you be back?' his mother asked, still immersed in her magazine.

'That's my fucking business.'

The gauze door slammed and he was gone. Moments later a
pulled off with screeching tyres.

'We should be going too,' said Thomas.

'Do you know where?'

'Yes. I decided it might not be such a bad idea to spend a few days
with your father. If you really think it will be safe?'

'Papa is a stranger to this world. He hardly even reads the
newspapers. And even if he does know about Thomas Landman
he doesn't know about *you*. You don't resemble your photograph
at all. And the mere fact that you're with me will cause him not
to give it a second thought.'

'Then it ought to be a good place to hide. Shouldn't you telephone
him first?'

'No, he's always home.' As she got up she put a hand on his arm.
'Thank you, Anton.'

With an unexpected flickering of hurt in him he thought: We're
free to go to *your* father. No one lies in wait for us there. But mine
we must avoid, even if he may be dying.

3

— Sometimes God visits a man with illness so you can. It's all His
will. The day the men of the security police arrived. Helena can
handle such things, sometimes by staying calm, with the help of the
Lord, sometimes by blowing her top, sometimes by. It happened that
day too. But in me something gave way and snapped. Like a light that
is switched off. To think that my own son, Thomas, could have.

But that was quite some time ago. The storm has died down. Let
Thy will be done. I still have difficulty moving, especially the left
hand, but. And to talk isn't easy at all. But there's nothing wrong
with my head. In the beginning it was just a confused whirling of
thoughts. Without form, and void. Now there is order again. Sea and
dry land separated. Every time, in every individual, God begins from
Genesis again. All one needs to know is. To yield, give way. There
is much I have to come to terms with. Inside myself, but also with
Helena, with God, with.

Thomas. My first reaction was that his name had to be removed
from the family Bible, it was blasphemous to let it. But how could
I undo what God Himself had ordained? One must learn to take
responsibility for what one. Thomas, I've always thought, Thomas

is like a board one shaves. Smoother and smoother, but in the end a few knots remain which, no matter how hard you try, you cannot smooth out. Not even if you. All that happens is that the blade of the plane gets chipped or broken. I've never been good with tools. It's time I acknowledged it. Helena has tried so hard, for so long, to make me give it up, whenever I went to her with bleeding hands or she found me trying to hide the expensive wood I'd. I used to go into a terrible rage when she confronted me. I've always been inclined to bottle up. I couldn't have been an easy man for her to.

Was it because of Joan Brookshaw? Her, too, I have to learn to look in the eyes. One day, the apostle says, we look face to face. If it is God's will I shall get up from this bed again. It need not be my deathbed. But whether I do get up or not, this opportunity He has given me to prepare myself. Through my child He has struck me down. Once before in my life, He intervened in this way. Then I unburdened my heart to Thomas. He is the only one I have ever told about Joan Brookshaw. Perhaps this is what I've never been able to forgive him for afterwards. That, thinking I was at death's door, I had told him all about it and that as a result. That he *knew*. Still, he has never in word or deed made use of that knowledge to. Like Shem and Japheth he walked backward so as not to make it unbearable for me.

Joan Brookshaw. In the face of the Lord I must confess that I loved her. I would have married her if Pa hadn't said. All these years I've tried to comfort myself with the assurance that a man must obey his parents that his days may be long upon the land which the Lord. But Pa was wrong. Pa hated all that was English and all that was black. I cannot take this into the grave with me. Even if it is too late for remorse, there is nothing I can do today to offset a lifetime of. And it wasn't just my own life either, it was all the Landmans in our history, all of them, all of us who. From the beginning.

My sin went far beyond renouncing Joan Brookshaw. In God's eyes it must be an even greater sin that deep in my heart I have *not* renounced her. That there are still nights in which she returns to me in dreams. In all these years she hasn't changed, hasn't grown older. Remained the way she was then. Just as young, her hair loose and long and blonde, like a sheaf of wheat; like a young foal she gallops through my. Even now. And this I must confess today, I can no longer hold back anything, that many, many times, especially in the early years, but even later, when I was with Helena in a man's way with a woman, I would close my eyes and pretend it was Joan

Brookshaw I was holding in my. Somewhere inside me there has always been a field I've kept enclosed, hedged in, to which I've never admitted Helena.

Today I know how wrong it has been. A sin. I stare at her through the many hours she spends beside my bed, often right through the night. Just sitting there, holding my hand, sometimes not even that. Just looking at me. Through everything, a long life mostly of suffering and hardship, she has been with me. Oh she often exploded, and ranted and raved, and broke plates and dishes in rage. But she has never turned against me. I don't think I have deserved her. And if there is one thing I should like to ask of God it is to give me back my speech, even if it is only for a short while, so that I could tell her, so that for once I could tell her that. Everything I've always held back. Everything I.

I should like to confide in her. The compassion that grows between two people bound in marriage. The understanding. That is what lasts the longest. I need not exclude love, or passion, or. But nothing is as important as compassion. Compassion in the acceptance, the acknowledgement, of a body growing older, facing middle age, old age, death. For a woman it must be hard to accept the signs of receding youth, like a low tide that lays bare rock-ridges, dead shells, empty hollows. But this is what I'd like to tell her, that it is this which stirs up compassion. Firmness beginning to yield, hips expanding and softening, buttocks and thighs sagging and losing their shape, upper arms receding in flaps. Because all this is evidence of what we've shared, the signs of an 'us' within the 'I'. In you I watch my own mortality, in you I learn to love mortality, in your old age I love you more than when you were young and beautiful and. I no longer miss or need Jane Brookshaw. Forgive me.

All this I see now through what Thomas has done to. No, no. I have argued too often like this in my life. What he did he didn't do 'to me'. His life is his own, it's. If I lie here today it is not Thomas's doing, but God's. He wanted to give me this opportunity of coming to rest and. All my messing around in the garage in the afternoons, all the wood and tools I broke and maimed, was just a way of escaping from what I couldn't face or. Because I.

Yes, let me say it: I have been a failure. I never truly tried to find out what was His will. Like great-great-grandpa Petrus who looked in the mirror and said it was God who had. This audacity of reading God into our own insignificant lives. I. We. The Landmans. My people. Our whole history I chronicled to force it into the mould of what I saw as God's will. Thirteen generations of Landmans created to my own image. That's not what I.

What was I called for? What have I done with my life? This is what my son Thomas demands to know of me today, and I cannot. He wants to know, he has a right to know, and I must. The more I made a mess of things the more I withdrew into our tribal history. In order to. I wanted to turn it into some kind of sanctuary. A monument. It was a lie. When I thought I was closest to the truth I was lying most. This is what I. Lied, mainly by looking the other way, hushing up, pretending it hadn't. Perhaps I've denied too much already. Lately, I have begun to think, if only God would save my life, allow me to sit up again and hold a pen in my hand, I shall rewrite my history. There are too many lacunae in it. I must fill them in, add to them, remove, reconsider rethink. It cannot stand as it is. I never wanted to admit the. The last time Thomas was here I was furious at the mere thought that. But he was right. He was right. I remember so clearly what he. 'One has to know who you are, you must learn to live with the knowledge that you're not someone else. Otherwise you live a lie.' Something like that. I remember.

Let me consider them again, one by.

– Hendrickus Willemszoon. It is his Bible that holds our whole family between its heavy brown covers like two hands God cups around us. His name in front. Yet I left him out of my chronicle. I argued that we know too little about him. I did not *want* to admit what I knew. He and his slave wife. One can't be sure of anything, but I didn't even wish to consider the mere.

– Fransoois Lodewickus. In his life I tried to demonstrate the hand of God. The man who moved into the interior, builder of the ark. But suppose his trek was an act *against* God's will, not in obedience to it? Did I ever consider the possibility that he might have been a fugitive rather than a pioneer? In his case I should like to.

– Carel Guillaume. The prototype of our indomitable race, rebel against a despotic governor. Was he really? Or did he run away because he was afraid of taking sides, neither right nor? And even if he had rebelled against his government: how can I praise him for his role in history but condemn my own son Thomas who today stands accused for doing the same? Have we really turned into a people of double standards? And what about.

– Diederik. Murderer. Savage. I refused to record that he caused the death of his own child. As a result I was also forced to omit that he protected with his own body the corpse of his son Hans against the vultures. How trivial I made him. What landscape in myself have I not obliterated through that act of.

– Jan-Jonas. I praised him as the builder of walls. Yet his own handwriting in the margins of the Bible I disowned. Blasphemously I. I said to Thomas. 'There are depths a Landman cannot sink to.' Today I have been broken open like a pomegranate. I know now there are no depths I am not capable of sinking to. Jan-Jonas's own child wrote it down, but I pretended she was not. If thy hand offend thee cut it off. By ignoring our sins I diminished my own humanity. A man without hands, feet, eyes, heart, a man without a.

– Benjamin. Him I clothed in the habit of a patriot. A hero of his people. Not even his wife I would give her due. And how lamely I handled the episode in which Benjamin and his father both landed in the same rebellion, I hushed up what I couldn't. Or his end. 'Martyr' we called him, but have I ever understood what really took place between him and the Xhosas? What do I understand about.

– David Gideon. How many times I discussed his life with. Thomas has always had this romantic streak. That story about the girl in the wood, a kind of pagan nymph, a mirage. Outrageous, undoubtedly sucked from Pa's thumb. But not knowing what to make of her I banished her completely from our. In her, I denied all the imagination of our kind. Do I not deny my own Joan Brookshaw in the process? She, too, was naked before me when we. Pa never knew about that. And David Gideon spent years of his life in search of his dream, while I. All I recorded about that girl was that she became a staunch Boer woman. But how she sent David Gideon to his grave, I did not tell. (Might that have helped me to understand my own child? But it's.)

– Frans Jacobus. In my history he hardly features at all and the document Thomas sent me, that Settler's diary, I refused to. Another mirror in which I couldn't. If only I had been prepared to understand more about Frans Jacobus, gun-runner, traitor, confidant of the enemy, then, who knows, my own child might have been more. God grant me strength.

– Petrus. The Voortrekker, the Elect. What do I really understand about the Trek? About what had driven *him*? Is it wrong to doubt his conversations with God and Gabriel? Is it wrong *not* to doubt them? How many discussions have our people conducted with a cracked mirror, afterwards interpreted as the will of God?

– Gabriel. Hero or fool? (Is there a difference?) I made no reference to the German woman he imported at the end of his life to. As in the case of David Gideon's dream girl I thought it better not to record any. But as a result I also had to suppress the palm-trees on Gabriel's bedroom wall. And that is truly a pity. What remains for the Landmans to dream about?

– Pieter Gerhardus. My heroic father. Anti-English, anti-black. Was there anything he was *for*? Can he really be understood only in terms of negatives and absences? His brother, too, I chose to ignore. Because in the Rebellion of 1914 he preferred peace to war. And because in the World War he sided with Smuts, while Pa. Yet he was family too. He was there.

– Christiaan Beyers. Behold thy servant, Lord. I thought I should leave it to Thomas to write this chapter. Perhaps it is time for me to try and. But is it worth anyone's while?

– Thomas. I have no idea of what I have passed on to you, my son, because whatever I tried to pass on seemed to cloud up inside myself. I can only judge from what you have done, from the news those men brought that day, from what I now have to read or hear about you. If I were to say, as in the beginning I was tempted to, that you have betrayed everything the name Landman has always stood for, is it not an accusation against myself? Because I am the one who. Thomas, I understand nothing at all about what you.

Is there anything I could still remedy or atone for, should I recover? Or have I waited too long? Is it too late for our people as a nation?

For three hundred years we have tried to tame Africa, instead of trying to make friends with it.

We haven't, it is true, like the Americans, the Australians, the Canadians, exterminated the indigenous populations. But we have done something even worse. We have pretended that they were not there. We have written them out of our history. In this way, one might say, we have.

An entire history, Thomas, of errors.

There is so much our people could have become. There is so little we. You always spoke about Adamastor, Thomas. I used to reproach you for the heathen image, although in a way I think I understood what you. We could have been the children of Adamastor, through thirteen generations. But instead of that we. I am not sure God has the patience to wait for. Now it's up to you to. I don't know. I. –

4

– Just as the plane begins its descent towards Jan Smuts a stranger settles in the empty seat beside me. It is tiresome, as I am sitting with my eyes closed to savour again the whole unbelievable journey I have behind me: when I left Johannesburg more than two months ago, I thought I was going to London, with the possibility of a visit to New York afterwards. Now, thanks to Sipho and the false passport supplied by Cedric – it is safely stowed in his flat in North London for future use – I have explored Africa. For the time being I have only my memories to sustain me, as Sipho was adamant that I should not bring a single photograph or other memento, not even a scribbled note, back with me; there is no sign of Africa on me. Only much later, when it seems safe, will what I need be forwarded – along devious routes, no doubt – to me.

And now the stranger beside me. An amicable, middle-aged man who has been pacing up and down the aisle to stretch his legs after the cramped night flight, evidently eager to chat to someone. Small-talk, the cost of living abroad, Mrs Thatcher (he is a supporter), films in London, how one misses home, *braavleis* on Saturdays, beer, a piece of biltong, the Highveld sun. A number of casual questions of the kind exchanged by strangers meeting by chance on planes: been away a long time? where? friends in England? glad to be home? The plane touches down, reduces speed, turns sharply into a runway leading back to the airport building; here and there passengers are already getting up to remove luggage from overhead bins.

My neighbour also gets up. Smiles down at me in innocent amicability. 'Well, Mr Landman?' I am sure I haven't told him my name. 'Lots of water into the sea since you left for London on BA 054 on 14 September, hey? And then the Hotel West-Two in Bayswater. Met Sipho Mdana and Cedric Scott. Became quite close friends? Many visits to Shirland Road. And then I believe you went on holiday? I'm sure you enjoyed it, wherever it was you went. I mean, before you left again for New York on Pan Am. When was that again? – November. Yesterday back to London on the BA flight. And here you are. Welcome back to South Africa, Mr Landman!'

That peculiar hollow feeling in the pit of the stomach which I am to experience so many times after today. In fact, a mere half-hour later, at passport control, when the surly lady suddenly, as she opens my passport, looks up at me with undisguised interest. 'Will you excuse me for a moment, Mr Landman?' And then scurries towards the door to the baggage hall where she whispers something in the ear of an armed guard who turns his head to look at me before he disappears. Of my chatty acquaintance from the plane there is, wherever I look, no sign at all. My passport is stamped; everything seems moving smoothly again. But as I carry my suitcase from the baggage control section I am suddenly surrounded by four men in checkered sports jackets. Where could they have materialised from so unobtrusively?

'My Landman, will you please come with us? Bring your luggage with you.'

In a small office containing little besides a bare brown table I am asked to make a list, on a sheet of ruled notepaper, of the contents of my suitcase, my camera case, and my briefcase, after which all my possessions, including what I have in my pockets, are unpacked on the table. Every item of clothing is inspected individually; special attention is given to the books and cameras, as if they expect something to be hidden among the pages, even inside the hard covers, the lenses, the camera bodies; afterwards two of the men systematically work through the empty cases, presumably in search of double linings. One of the others studies every page of my passport.

'If it's bombs or AK-47s you're looking for, I am sorry to disappoint you,' I say after an hour, when it seems not one of them has any intention of addressing me.

'Mr Landman, I don't find that funny at all.'

'Won't you at least give me an idea of what it is you're looking for? I'm sure I can save all of us a lot of time.'

'We have all the time in the world, Mr Landman.'

Another half-hour later, when even their ingenuity seems to touch its limits, one of the four lights a cigarette, looks at the others, shrugs, and says, 'All right, you may pack up, Mr Landman.'

By this time my anger has become very hard and cool. 'I'm sorry,' I reply, 'but you unpacked it, and I expect you to replace everything exactly as you found it.'

'*You* expect us, Mr Landman?' asks the man with the cigarette.

'Yes,' I say in my best cool voice, hoping they will not notice the size of the lump in my throat. 'I believe that is what the regulations stipulate.' I haven't the foggiest idea of which regulations I am referring to.

'You're very set on sticking to the rules, it seems?'

I look him in the eyes. To tell the truth, I can't think of any answer whatsoever. But if this is a game I can play it too.

The man with the cigarette makes a small sideways motion with his head; the three others begin to repack my possessions.

As they start on the briefcase – the suitcase doesn't look very tidy, but I decide not to overplay my hand – the smoking man asks in a casual tone, 'Was this just a vacation, Mr Landman?'

'Why do you ask? You obviously know as much about it already as I do,' I reply. 'I attended an exhibition of my photographs in London and then went to New York to make arrangements for opening there.'

'Not a very patriotic exhibition, is it now?'

'It depends on how one interprets "patriotism".'

'Doesn't it get boring always to portray blacks as the victims and the police as the baddies?'

'Not one of my photos was posed.'

'What does that mean?'

'I can only photograph what I see.'

'You're an Afrikaner, Mr Landman?'

'Of course I am.'

'And doesn't it do anything to you to stab your own people in the back like this in foreign countries?'

'Every photograph I exhibited in London had been shown inside South Africa before.'

'Rather rowdy exhibition you had in Johannesburg.'

'The spectators I saw were very well-behaved.'

'But it did provoke violent reactions, didn't it? Arson and everything.'

I am beginning to lose my temper, but I realise that this is what they are hoping for; I will not play into their hands.

'I think a court of justice should decide on that. *If* the culprits are ever caught.'

An abrupt change of front, 'Mr Landman, where were you between 9 October and 5 November?'

'In England. Where else should I have been?'

'We're asking *you*.'

Steady now. Keep your cool. Thank God Sipho has briefed me very thoroughly, just in case. He must have known what I didn't even suspect. Which is why both our departure to Africa and our subsequent return happened in such cloak-and-dagger secrecy, travelling to and from the airport separately, at the crack of dawn, and in disguise.

'I spent some time with friends in the Cotswolds.'

'Yes?'

'Mr Cedric Scott's mother. In Stow-on-the-Wold. From there I explored much of the region, as far as Malvern, and returned over Stratford.'

'Almost a month?'

'I had time.'

'What do you know about Sipho Mdana?'

'He's an expatriate South African.'

'He's an escaped terrorist.'

'Most of our discussions were about art and music. He's very knowledgeable about Beethoven.'

'Mr Landman, sooner or later we're going to find out what we want to know.'

'I hope so. I have nothing to hide.'

'We're not very happy about your attitude.'

'Frankly, I find *your* attitude offensive.'

And at long last, two and an half hours after the plane has landed, I am allowed to go through to the domestic departures lounge. My connecting flight to Cape Town has left long ago. The next one is fully booked. Only three hours later do I find a seat, and it is mid-afternoon before I can catch a cab to my flat in Gardens in Cape Town.

Where the next instalment of the serial awaits me.

It looks as if a south-easter has struck the flat. Everything inside has been turned upside-down, the contents of every cupboard and drawer strewn across the floor. My first thought, naïvely, is: Burglars. But nothing of value is missing: clothes, TV, radio, hi-fi, even my few boxes of wine are all intact. What has vanished is all the negatives in the filing cabinet in the spare room which I have equipped as a studio. Still, it could have been worse: I left in such a hurry, having worked until the last moment, that all the negatives I'd used to print the photographs for my exhibition are still at Sean's place. Which teaches me a sound lesson for future absences.

My lawyer friend Achmat is not very helpful when I approach him, not even when I tell him that my next-door neighbour – a whining, inquisitive, gossiping woman who never leaves her flat while her husband is at work – saw four men in casual clothing unlock my front door in broad daylight, emerging later with a cardboard box filled with papers.

'Of course we know who they are, Thomas. But you may just as well try to force open the gates of hell.'

Only after several days, when he discovers I have no intention of giving up, does he offer, with a sigh, to introduce me to Werner du Rand, up-and-coming young advocate, hot stuff; above all, an Afrikaner without a blot on his name. 'If anybody stands a chance, it's Werner. No use working with chaps who have civil rights records. Mind you, I'm not saying Werner will succeed. But he's your only chance. And if he says no, you better drop it. Deal?'

Deal.

To Achmat's surprise and my delight, Werner du Rand turns out to be enthusiastic about taking my case: shaky legal grounds, he readily admits, but it's the kind of challenge he doesn't like to pass up. With a combination of blustering and bluff and some insinuations about 'influence' he extracts from the head of the Special Branch the admission that the negatives are indeed in their possession ('but completely within the ambit of the law'); the next step is to obtain, on some obscure technical point, a court order for the restitution of my property.

Werner is present when two SB men arrive at my flat to return the cardboard box, request me to verify the contents and sign a certificate to confirm that everything is there; immediately afterwards to proffer a warrant which entitles them to reconfiscate forthwith all the material they have just returned. This time with watertight legality.

'Come over to my place for a drink tonight,' says Werner after they have left; he seems quite unruffled.

'There isn't much to celebrate, is there?' I say, still confused, when in the early dusk, on the top terrace of their postmodernist home in Higgovale, he pours champagne into Orrefors flutes and serves first his graceful blonde wife Hanlie, then me.

'More than you might think.' Nonchalant in his Hilton Weiner suit and striped open-neck shirt (small green crocodile on the pocket) he sits down on the bench beside Hanlie. 'Look, they didn't have a choice: they *had* to make a counter-move. To show who's the boss. But behind that façade, I can tell you, they're rattled.'

'Rather expensive rattle.'

He laughs, crossing his legs. 'That's none of your business, Thomas.'

'How can you say that?'

'I did it pro amico.'

'But Werner –'

'I've been waiting for a long time to have a go at those guys. Why is everyone so scared of taking the plunge? We're all too eager to assume that there's no limit to their power. My attitude is: test them. Test them at every bloody opportunity you get, challenge them, drive them back, don't ever allow them to take anything for granted. That's what the courts are there for. For God's sake, Thomas, we have no right to make things easy for them. More often than is good for anybody oppression is made possible by the co-operation of the oppressed.'

Charming, with a twinkle in her eyes, Hanlie adds, 'You have no idea of how happy you've made Werner today, Thomas.'

He rises to top up the glasses. 'Thomas, I hope you're staying for dinner? We've invited a few people. Nothing fancy. Friends I'd like you to meet. Who knows, some interesting deals may flow from it.'

A whole alternative world of 'new' Afrikaners is opened to me that evening. Young, smooth, streamlined, rich, detribalised, liberal – yet Afrikaans to the core. With small grape farms in Drakenstein, old restored Cape-Dutch homesteads, hunting ranches in the Transvaal, fishing holidays at St Lucia, hiking trips along the Otter Trail. Some, like Werner, are in law; others in advertising; there are company directors among them, and academics, and importers/exporters. They resemble Frans's friends, except for the conservative bedrock. What concerns Werner's crowd is 'quality survival'; negotiated settlements; the need to break out of isolation, to foster the African connection; a return to 'an old Afrikaner liberalism'. They are the ones whose ancestors did not, like the Landmans, emigrate from the Cape to find salvation in the deep interior, bible in one hand and gun in the other, succeeding occasionally and often failing; but who remained in the Colony, maintained contact with Europe, became princes of commerce, adapting with Mediterranean laissez-aller old-world 'civilised values' to the demands of a new technological age. Men with car-phones in their BMWs and their Mercs, with fax machines, with personal computers in their children's rooms, with wine quotas, access to private lodges for rugby matches at

Newlands, monthly Business Class trips to Taipeh, Tokyo, New York, Frankfurt; men who will in due course go on IDASA tours to meet the ANC in exile, and return to write books – in collaboration with Americans – on the transition phase between apartheid and a brand of democracy which will protect minority rights.

The 'deals' Werner has referred to earlier are explained over dinner (assisted by a 'coloured' cook Hanlie handles *nouvelle cuisine* with laid-back grace). One of the guests, a young and angry Stellenbosch professor, tall and athletic, with a heavy jawbone, is ready to launch, with the collaboration of a few carefully chosen colleagues, a new journal: 'up-market, incisive, hard-hitting, for the potential reading public that cannot wait to have, in Afrikaans, a publication offering a critical, meaningful alternative to apartheid. An independent journal, no strings attached. The market is wide open. We've conducted surveys from Johannesburg, we've put out feelers to Lusaka, and I can assure you they're one hundred per cent behind us. This country needs change, and we must make sure there are Afrikaners to take the initiative. Because if we lose that, we've had it.'

And they want my collaboration. Chief photographer for the journal. A portfolio of my photographs in the first issue. And more or less a free hand in deciding on picture policy.

I have reservations; at the same time there is something infectious about their enthusiasm. Their youth, their readiness to admit mistakes, their refusal to be swamped by guilt; even an endearing kind of innocence about their faith in the possibility of a new start, the acknowledgement that this start is only possible with the co-operation of the majority. And, yes, their pragmatism. ('There's no point in romantic dreams and lofty ideals. Unless we have a power base we shall soon be irrelevant.' The speaker is, of course, once again, the athletic professor, Johann Venter; his tanned square jaw bears the scar of a remote rugby match, like the sabre wound of a musketeer; and women – he evidently knows only too well – find it irresistible. 'There have been dissatisfied and dissident Afrikaners for too long: it's time to mobilise that dissatisfaction and translate it into effective political action.')

As we get to know each other better the differences between us widen into cracks: 'But Werner, but Johann! – you're still stuck in the dialectics of power, Afrikaner power. You're still thinking in terms of group action. What's wrong with ordinary democracy?'

'What will become of democracy if my group is suppressed?'

497

'Now that people are discovering that the days of white majority government are numbered you still insist on special treatment?'

'We've learned the lessons of Africa. We've seen what happens when white nationalism is replaced by black.'

'But that's bloody well *unnecessary*, Johann! It's time we got rid of the inhibitions of nationalism altogether. Nationalism is like gangs in the back streets of Chicago, irrational group loyalties, and in the end all it fosters is a new round of violence.'

'Do you expect our people willingly to relinquish power to a black majority in the certain knowledge that they're going to be swamped? Or are you trying to tell me that after centuries of oppression, the blacks aren't going to jump at the opportunity of taking revenge? Then you're totally naïve, Thomas.'

'You're arguing from your own white experience, from a Western tradition. It is my experience that Africa is more patient and forgiving, more generous than us.'

(Sipho once said, but this of course I cannot relay to Johann, 'It's a myth that our people can't wait to revenge our suffering. It's not revenge we want, Thomas, it's justice. We want to end oppression, so how can we aspire to become oppressors ourselves?')

'Your experience? Thomas, forgive me for saying this, but what the hell do *you* know about Africa?'

'My family has been in Africa for thirteen generations. Don't you think that counts for something?'

'We've all been here for centuries. And I have a rather different impression. But the whole point is that we cannot build a future on impressions. Be realistic.'

'You think it's realistic to spend so much time and energy on devising intricate systems of protecting minority rights if all those measures can be erased with a stroke of a pen? Isn't it more realistic to try and get to *know* our compatriots instead of continuing to talk about "them" and "us"? Let's stop worrying about the survival of this or that little group, and start thinking, instead, in terms of over thirty million South Africans who all share the same country.'

'Now you're being grossly unfair, Thomas.' Werner. 'We've started building bridges already. Our children go to mixed private schools. We're not trying to keep ourselves apart.'

'You're just changing the criteria of your separateness. Once it was race, now you're replacing it with money.'

Johann, patronising: 'I think you should rather stick to taking pictures. You're a damn good photographer, but what do you know about politics? You artists –'

'How many of *you* belong to the UDF?'

'That's basically an organisation for blacks, Thomas. There's no doubt about its importance in the process of conscientisation. But *we* can put our talents to better uses by –'

'It's an open organisation. *You* are ensuring that it stays black. Which creates an unnecessary polarisation. Perhaps even revolution.'

On revolution Werner's views are concise and scathing. 'This is the end of the twentieth century, Thomas. Multinational corporations, global financial strategies, common markets, world government, perestroika. The time for revolutions is past. They simply don't work any more. If they ever did. Even the French Revolution was a balls-up. Human rights, the destruction of feudalism, liberty, equality, fraternity? Come again. All the positive results of the Revolution were about to be introduced by Louis XVI. In fact, they might well have happened sooner and more effectively if that revolution hadn't fucked up everything. And the negative results turned back the clock of humanity by at least a century. Be realistic!'

'And how do you avoid revolution?'

Werner looks askance at me, an expression almost of condescension in his face: 'Thomas, who is in power in this country at the moment? Whites. Afrikaners. So: you can only have revolution if someone from outside that establishment tries to get power through violent means. If, on the other hand, the system is changed from inside, it *can* happen peacefully. That leaves the onus to Afrikaners. Not because I have any sentimental ideas about Afrikaners, but simply because they are in power. It's the only way.' With emphasis: 'Because once you start thinking in terms of violence you've had your chips. Before you know where you are it is no longer a means to an end but an end in itself. Look at the French Revolution once again. It's balls arguing that the Terror was an unfortunate side-effect of the process: I tell you it was the raîson d'être of the revolution. Of *any* revolution.'

'Is there really a choice? Look, I'm not in favour of violence, Werner. But isn't it our own pious Boer Calvinist government who first introduced violence as part of the whole system? It's easy always to expect the "opposite side" to renounce violence, while we keep on using it ourselves.'

'Bullshit. I expected more of you than a mouthful of clichés.'

'You mean the truth is a bore, so let's pretend it's different?'

Tensions, arguments, sometimes angry explosions. And yet there is something stimulating in our relationship. I am called upon to become their court photographer: their beautiful children in their beautiful pools, their smooth tanned wives and girlfriends on tennis courts, barbecues on paved terraces, often attended by a sprinkling of black or 'coloured' guests, editorial meetings, joggers, athletic bodies in well-equipped gyms and saunas. I find myself playing tennis with Johann or Werner or some of their friends; even spending a week in Werner's house waiting to move into a new flat in Vredehoek, and helping Hanlie taxi their three lovely blond children, a boy and two girls, from school to ballet to karate to choir practice. At the same time there is something deeply depressing and disturbing in the experience, and I cannot help remembering the great colonial mansions of Accra or Lusaka slowly taken over by the luxuriant green growth of Africa, waterless fish-ponds cracking up, the carcass of a bus in the gardens of State House, an exclusive white club in Harare.

Strange, disquieting flickerings of light in a country polluted with despair. Because however far apart the worlds of black and white already were between which I used to commute, in this time, after my return from Africa, the gulf that divides them is almost unbridgeable. On the one side, my new progressive friends in a safe white world where with such innocent faith plans are made for a shared future; on the other, a return, with Henry, to the burning townships of the vast land. The State of Emergency clamped like a heavy lid on the great pressure cooker of reality: a world so devastating that I find it impossible to believe, whenever I am with Werner or Johann or their friends, that they inhabit the same planet as Henry. Crossing the border from one to the other, often several times in one day, is like breaking through a credibility barrier. And what one retains of the experience, even in sleep, is that bleeding wound of knowledge Dennis Brutus once wrote about (Sipho gave me the poem to read, in a *Sechaba* in his office in Lusaka).

A dual existence, the parts of which become increasingly irreconcilable. What is a 'terrorist' in one part becomes 'hero' in the other; the 'law and order' of the one becomes the 'subversion' of the other. A bifocal view, an unsettling double vision: with one foot in a world that appears 'real' only while you are physically in it, its antithesis

500

like a hallucination in the mind: and changing places all the time, each constantly challenging the validity of the other.

A sense of compulsion invades my photographic activities. My life is more frantic than ever before; I work fourteen, sixteen, even twenty hours a day; in the Western Cape, in the Eastern Cape, where the convulsions of violence increase from day to day, in Natal where black communities are turning against each other, on the Witwatersrand, in Mamelodi, even in the previously docile Orange Free State. Rushing across the face of the country at breakneck speed; sometimes with Henry or his fellow organisers in the UDF, often on my own. 'There's work to do, *buti*, lots of work. You got to record what is happening. Otherwise people won't know about it. It's your job to tell them, to remind them, to make it impossible for them to ignore it. Here, and in Europe, and in the States, all over the world. Have camera, will travel.'

Photographs, photographs. I barely find time to sleep at night in the new flat I have moved into, on a carbuncle of the Mountain in Vredehoek; I haven't even unpacked properly. The place is cluttered with boxes as if I live in permanent transit. And whenever I am tempted to give it a break, to withdraw for a while, to disappear even if only for a week, Henry is there to urge me on: no matter how much older than I he may be, he is indefatigable; I am ashamed by his energy. 'We need those pictures, Thomas. Make sure people won't forget. People without a memory can never be free, *buti*. How do dictatorships take root? First of all by rewriting history, wiping out memory. So that nothing from the past can remain to threaten or accuse us. And this is a struggle to which there can be no end.'

'But how does one survive. Henry? Where do *you* find the energy to go on like this? How do you *last*?'

The deep rumbling of his contented laugh. 'One lasts because you're never alone. Because there are always comrades around. If there's one thing I learned on the Island, *buti*, this is it.' And then the flood of memories is released over me. 'You know, the day you are sentenced it feels as if the bottom has dropped out of your world. All you can think is: So many years, makes so many months, makes so many days, hours, minutes. Your whole mind is filled just with yourself: your suffering, your misery, your future. And the weight of all those years and hours is so great your legs start buckling way under you. But the Island saves you from yourself. No matter how bad things are for you, you discover there are always others who suffer even more. And slowly you find out that if you all share this load you do get through. Because *you* no longer matter. The struggle is bigger than all the separate lives that go into it. That's what the Island teaches you. And when you get out of there, you're prepared. Because now you know: the Island isn't a place over there, across a stretch of sea: the whole country is a jail, *buti*. It's just easier to learn things on the Island because everything is so compressed. But prison is everywhere. And even if you come from there with scorched eyes, this is what you see: that all of us are caught in that prison. Prisoners and warders, wherever you look. And whether you turn out to be the one rather than the other is a mere accident of history. Only when you've seen this can you set to work. And then you don't get tired any more.'

Photographs, photographs. Including that windy day on the Cape Flats, at Crossroads, when I try to drag the frail furious girl away from the police and we are hidden in the *kaia* of a strange Samaritan until the coast is clear at last and in the dark we are driven back to town and she spends the night with me.

Nina.

And it is only after that, when I am invited to return to London to work on a book based on an update of my previous exhibition, that I feel prepared to go abroad again (having this time made sure that all my most precious possessions are safely stowed in Sean's house) and look Sipho in the eyes.

'Thomas,' he says calmly, his pipe clenched between his strong white teeth, his eyes looking right into me, 'Thomas, the last time the two of us went on a trip, it was to see the sights, to show you where Africa was, so you could know for future reference. But this time, if we go, it's business all the way. You ready for that?'

'That is what I've come back for, Sipho.' –

5

It was the tall green roof of the vicarage they saw first, then the white walls below; the large sash windows protected by fly-screens. A curious design, with a high square dining-room right in the middle – the light falls, muted and diffident, from lanterns set high in the roof – and the other rooms arranged around it. A wide stoep of green cement below an equally green curved verandah supported on squat white columns (mothers of the congregation rather than representatives of its lither girlhood) runs right round the house like a buffer zone between interior and exterior. Behind the broekies lace of the verandah in front was, at the time of their visit, a swallow's nest; but it was empty.

To the left of the front door was the dominee's bedroom (in the walnut wardrobe, the tortured flames of which resembled monsters and demons that had always left her petrified with exquisite fear when, as a child, she'd sometimes crept into bed between her parents, still hung, eight years after her death, the clothes of the dominee's wife). To the right was the large study with dark, dangerously inclined bookshelves kept upright only by divine mercy, overflowing with bibles and concordances and commentaries and exegeses, surrounding a great heavy desk that seemed never to be tidied; in the shadowy wall-spaces between the shelves one might make out the old picture of the Broad and Narrow Ways overlooked by the disembodied Eye in the centre; a print of Rembrandt's Jewish Bride; on the floor a faded carpet, permeated through many years, possibly generations, by the depressing odour of cat's pee, as permanent as the presence of the Holy Ghost.

Lisa slept in her old room, left undisturbed through the years of her absence, at her disposal whenever she might turn up; at the opposite end of the gloomy dining-room, Thomas was lodged in Erik's room (ascetic narrow bed, a stale smell of old shoes, the walls covered with group photographs from school or university). This was the room into which, deep in the second night of their stay, when the light was still burning in the study where the Sunday sermon was being prepared, Lisa stole, barefoot, her long dark hair loose, fragrant from the bath; still wearing her day clothes.

'Move over, Thomas.'

A brief rustling as she peeled off her clothes – in the diffuse light from outside she emerged like an exotic fruit glowing in the dark – and shifted in beside him, shivering slightly as the warmth of his skin made her voluptuously aware of how cool her own body was.

'Is it safe?' he asked.

They lay whispering in the half-dark, like children in a boarding school after lights-out.

'I missed you.'

'I've been waiting for you.'

'How did you know I'd come?'

'If you hadn't I would have gone to you.'

'I always slipped into Erik's room like this. Or he into mine.'

'And no one found out?'

'Papa was always working or reading or sleeping the sleep of the just. Mother sometimes skulked around, but the creaking floorboards gave her away.'

'And you don't think your father suspects anything now either?'

'He's without sin himself. So he doesn't expect it in others.'

After supper, that evening, he'd read with slow and emphatic gravity as if, like a translator, he was listening through earphones to a text he tried to transmit simultaneously:

'He that dwelleth in the secret place of the most High shall abide under the shadow of the Almighty.

I will say of the Lord, He is my refuge and my fortress: my God, in him will I trust.

Surely he shall deliver thee from the snare of the fowler, and from the noisome pestilence.

He shall cover thee with his feathers, and under his wings shalt thou trust: his truth shall be thy shield and buckler.

Thou shalt not be afraid for the terror by night; nor for the arrow that flieth by day;

Nor for the pestilence that walketh in darkness; nor for the destruction that wasteth at noonday —'

Like deep calm water it flowed over them: a primordial stream from some collective memory more ancient than childhood or amniotic fluid, something that lingers in the mind, but only in the mind, when long afterwards one finds oneself travelling through a different landscape, desert, stone, cracked earth.

'He doesn't approve of me.'

'It's only because I never brought boyfriends home with me. He doesn't know how to handle it. He has to pray for guidance first. Then, maybe, he'll discuss it with me: but he first needs to find the words for it – perhaps that is why he's working so late tonight – you see, his life is so remote from the sinful world that he finds it difficult to communicate with ordinary mortal beings. As I see it, you're suddenly confronting him with a kind of reality he cannot cope with. Now he has to take it into account. And he feels threatened by it. He thinks it's very serious.'

'Is it?'

'It's only a little lucky-packet ring.'

He didn't answer. He was aware of how tense her body was beside him, but could not tell if it was the tautness of sexual desire, or anxiety about his reaction to the unspoken challenge in her remark.

Almost questioning, his open palms lightly, lightly whispered over her, registering the intricate responses of her body.

'Do you think he noticed the ring?' he asked.

Independent of their words their hands and bodies became engaged in another conversation. And around them the vicarage, too, pursued its monologue of creakings and mysterious sounds: history itself speaking, the house mumbling in its sleep, giving loose rein to its subconscious.

'Oh yes he did,' said Lisa in reply to his question. 'He asked me about it. He thought at first it was a wedding ring. I told him it was an engagement ring, but that the stone had fallen out. That's close enough to the truth, isn't it?'

'I wish we could have stuck to the coast,' he said. 'Something in the interior makes me feel claustrophobic.'

'Remember the gulls in the wind?' she said.

'And the heron, on our way back.'

'The tide coming in.'

'And the smell of the sea.'

'You taste like the sea.'

'Come inside me.'

While they were making love a floorboard creaked in the dining-room behind their closed door. He stopped moving, lying tensely on her, listening; her mouth urgent and open against his neck. Another board creaked, now further away, closer to the kitchen.

'He's going to make tea. He's on his way to bed.'

'Shall we wait?'

'No. Just be careful.'

In a long slow thrusting motion he glided more deeply into her; she smothered a moan.

For minutes at a time they lay almost motionless, interrupted only at long intervals by slow movements, like kelp in a quiet tide; their physical consciousness of one another so intense it was almost unbearable. (With only a wall between them and the kitchen where the Godfearing old man was bustling about clumsily, the representation of an entire dispensation of right and wrong, good and evil, of God, sin, heaven, hell: night and eternity moving against each breath and pulsation of their interlocked bodies.)

At last the muffled sounds from next door came to an end; a light was turned off with a sharp click; and the floorboards creaked again – to the threshold of their door, lingering there, pausing, then moving on. A door was closed. With a few last groans the heavy house, like an old big weary dog, settled into sleep.

He began to move more urgently on her, inside her, driven by a kind of rage; perhaps terror.

'I'm going to come,' she whispered. 'Hold me. Hold me very tight.'

Hours later, after they'd fallen asleep and woken up again, she got up softly, felt on the floor for her dress, pressed it against her and slipped out, naked – even under the sparse weight of her swift slight body the floorboards registered her progress through the sleeping house – back to the familiarity of her own room opposite. (Below her father's door she glimpsed – surprised, briefly startled – a persistent sliver of light.) Left alone in the damp bed, in the smell of their lovemaking, Thomas lay awake for a very long time listening to the night sounds of the house. (Safe? he thought, wearily. Yes, here, at last, surely, we *are* safe, perhaps for the first time we set out on our trip. But why do I feel so threatened then?) At the first signs of dawn, when the cocks began to crow, he drifted off.

Hours later Naomi, her broad dark face expressionless, rinsed in the bathroom the dark blue white-laced pair of panties she'd found beside his bed, and draped it on the back of a chair in Lisa's room; she would never make any reference to it, but she'd made sure that the diminutive garment was displayed in such a way that Lisa could not but notice it.

It was more for Naomi's sake, thought Thomas, than for her father's that Lisa had proposed the visit. A large soft woman – her body, it seemed, bolstered unevenly but effectively with pillows against hard knocks – whom they found on hands and knees, polishing the front stoep, when they arrived. She glanced up as they stopped outside the gate, examined the combi with more than a hint of suspicion, as if ready to defend her domain against outsiders; but when Lisa got out and came through the green gate, up the narrow gravel path between unconvincing flower beds, she dropped her work with an exclamation of joy and came scurrying towards them, on bare light-soled feet.

'Lisa, Lisa, Lisa!' She engulfed the girl in her arms. 'My own little *nonna!*'

'Hello, Naomi. God, but I missed you.' She pressed herself against the woman's ample bosom and kissed her; then motioned towards

Thomas.' 'And this – this is Louis.' She was still trying to get accustomed to the new name Rashid had brought him.

He put out his hand. The woman looked at it, not sure about how to react, glanced at Lisa for approval, then took it with exaggerated ceremony and started pumping it as if she expected to see water gushing from it.

'Why you not let us know, Lisa? I wanting to make you nice food, special.' With a quick look of acknowledgement at Thomas. 'For everybody.'

The dominee had appeared in the front door: also large and lumbering, but without the generosity and safety Naomi exuded: his was a body that had given up hope, as if it had become pointless to keep shoring up the wall he had instinctively relied on all his life to keep a menacing world at bay. Clothed wholly in black, with a white bib on his chest. (Lisa, later: 'I think Papa wears a bib because he's always spilling words.')

'Lisa, my darling. All on your own?'

'I've brought someone with me, Papa. Haven't you seen?'

Naomi had reluctantly stood aside to allow father and daughter to embrace.

'I mean' – apologetic, embarrassed – 'where's Erik?'

'But Papa, he's in the army, he can't come and go as he chooses. This is Louis. He's –' For a moment the silence of her uncompleted explanation hung heavily in the air between them.

Around them, separated from the street by an unkempt red-berry hedge, lay the hard-baked soil on which a patch of dried lawn had long given up the struggle against evil; only a bed of furious petunias and a few straggly faithful dahlias continued to stain the neglected yard with blotches of unpremeditated colour.

The dominee was older than Thomas had expected, his unkempt hair a silvery white, his face covered in what looked like uneven tufts of hoary moss. A sifting of dandruff on his shoulders; while on his white bib and substantial stomach one could read the menu of recent meals: egg, gravy, tomato.

(He was seventy, said Lisa when Thomas enquired, later; he'd been married before, but the first wife had died childless; subsequently he'd spent many years alone before, well over forty, he'd married the young widow organist of his church on whom he'd fathered the twins. And then this wife, after twenty years of married life, had also died an untimely death, of cancer, leaving him helpless against the demands and ravages of life. Lately his memory

507

had become unreliable. 'It's not that he's senile,' said Lisa, 'but just because life, and particularly the past, has become unmanageable; only the future is still reassuring to him. He has a road-map to eternity.')

'And what brings you here so unexpectedly?'

'I wanted you to meet Louis.'

'But my dearest child —'

'It had to happen sooner or later,' she said lightly.

'And what does Erik say about it?' the old man asked anxiously.

'Oh he approves unconditionally.'

'And you've come all the way from the Cape?'

'Actually we're on our way back to the Cape,' she said quickly; this was what they'd agreed on. 'We spent some time in Kimberley. I had an interview there for a new job, and we used the opportunity to look up Louis's parents.'

With a hint of reproach the dominee asked, 'Why didn't you come here first?'

'We had to go straight to Kimberley for the interview, Papa.' She kissed him on the cheek again. 'Come on, don't mope. Aren't you happy for me?'

'Oh well, if you move to Kimberley, at least you won't be so far away.'

'I didn't get the job. To tell you the truth, right now I'm in the ranks of the unemployed.'

'But isn't that being very irresponsible, Lisa?'

'I'll find something, Papa.'

'You can be so impulsive. I don't know where you get it from. Your mother wasn't like that.' He shook his head. 'I hope you're going to spend some time with me?'

'A few days, if you have room for us.'

'Ah.' He seemed more content. 'Naomi, will you give them a hand with the suitcases?'

'Can I park the combi somewhere out of the street?' asked Thomas with a straight face.

'It's quite safe. Nobody steals in this place.'

But Lisa, reading between the lines, interrupted: 'I think you'd better take it round to the back. I'll show you.'

The backyard was an open expanse, partly covered with gravel, lined with a row of indestructible bluegums and behind them a few outbuildings, including a garage. Naomi lived in one of the outrooms; the other buildings were derelict. No one, it seemed, ever used them. The dominee himself found it too much trouble to park his old Zephyr in the garage; more often than not it was left beside the house under a pergola; the vine that had once grown there had long given up the struggle for survival. If a man abide not in me, he is cast forth as a branch, and is withered. They drove round the entire block comprised by the vicarage yard, through the open back gate and into the empty garage where Naomi already stood waiting to take their bags.

'You really needn't help us,' Thomas told her. 'We have very little baggage.'

'Give me Lisa's.'

'I told you: *she*'s the one who brought me up, she was my real mother,' Lisa reminded him later in the afternoon, in the quietly simmering house, while the dominee was having a nap and indecent flies kept buzzing on the window-panes. 'She's always been the same. All smiles and motherliness. But God knows –'

'You told me she gets a holiday once a year to visit her children?'

'Yes, a fortnight. And she was a young woman when she started working for them. She used to be a servant in my mother's parents' house, and she moved into the vicarage after the wedding. Kind of a wedding present, you might say. And when Papa accepted the call to this place she came all the way from Bethlehem with them. I've often wondered whether she was given any choice, but that's one thing she's never wanted to discuss. She had three small children at the time. I think the eldest was only five. Left them behind with her mother, she had no husband. And then devoted her life to bringing us up, spending two weeks every year with her own. I tell you, if God ever decides to destroy this country with fire or water, *this* will be why. Not torture or murder or spectacular forms of oppression: but *this*. Ordinary people whose ordinary lives are broken up. You know, I can only remember one single occasion when Naomi rebelled and spoke openly about her kids. It was when her eldest died. It took two weeks for the news to reach us here; and when she asked Mother permission to go, Mother said she was sorry, but she had a congress coming up and it would be difficult to leave us behind with Papa: and anyway, the funeral was already over, it wasn't as if Naomi could achieve anything by going there. That was when Naomi very quietly said in that case she was giving notice, she was leaving us. She stood crying at the back door. I clung to her skirts and started weeping too. I was five or six at the time. And in the end she changed her mind and stayed on, because she didn't want to leave us in the lurch.' A long silence; the flies went on droning on the panes. 'Jesus Christ, Louis –!'

– We had long conversations on that visit, she and I. For one whole afternoon we withdrew into the cramped outroom where she lived and which she'd filled, over the years, with all the hand-downs and throw-out furniture from the vicarage. She made tea on her primus stove. In the big house Papa was having his nap, his siesta is getting longer with the years; and Thomas was reading, I told him I wanted to be alone with Naomi. It was like the old days. The only older person I could ever confide in: she always listened so patiently.

A whole world was gathered soundlessly around me, that afternoon in Naomi's outroom, a world I thought I'd already lost. Through the cups with their dainty floral pattern from which we drank our tea even Mother was temporarily restored, muted by time. But above all there were Naomi and me.

'You still all right here with Papa, Naomi?'

'Where else can I live? So many years already. I was young when I come in this place. You see me now.'

'Papa must be so lonely all by himself in that big house. Do you know how the beams and floorboards creak at night? There must be ghosts wandering about.'

'Hau, Lisa, you mustn't say things like that.'

'And he seems to be getting lonelier all the time. And you over here.' It was then the thought struck me – really 'struck' me like a tangible object, like a bullet fired at me – that Naomi was the one woman God must have intended for Papa, the one who could have made him truly happy, the one who'd been with him for so many years. I couldn't help smiling, although it must have been a pretty wistful smile, at the thought of what the good members of his congregation would say if he were to announce from the pulpit one morning that he and Naomi Mofokeng had decided to have their banns read. Yet it is the one woman he cannot have. I know the law has been changed, but it remains as unthinkable as before. Papa himself would never even think of it, neither would Naomi. A scandalous thought to both, because of black and white. And yet they know each other better than most married couples do. They could have been good for one another; they need each other. But they have no idea of it themselves, cannot even reflect on the possibility.

510

'What you got in your head, Lisa? You saying nothing.'

Hurriedly, precipitately, I started talking, about anything that came into my mind, in order not to embarrass her with what I was really thinking. The room, in which all the furniture had drawn together very tightly for a while, began once more to relax and settle in its old postures; the space inside was no longer so oppressive. I was again eight years old, or ten, or sixteen, she my mother.

Amid all the other subjects we discussed, I curled up on her high bed, she in one of the easy chairs, I suddenly asked what I wanted most to know:

'When last did you see your children, Naomi?'

'I not going any more, Lisa. Only one or two times after your mother died, it is no use, they don't want to know me any more. I heard that Zondi is in jail in Johannesburg, they did not tell me why, I am not even sure it is true. They all gone now, Lisa. You the only child I have left.' Shook her head, clicked her tongue.' And you not a child any more either, hau. Here you bringing a man home.' Adding, like a command, 'You tell me about him, I must know.'

'We're just travelling together.'

'You sleeping with him.' This was not a question but a statement, perhaps an accusation?

'You said yourself I'm not a child any more.'

'He making you a woman.' With unexpected approval in her voice.

'_'

'And you going marry this man?'

I don't know why I did it, but I showed her my little ring. What she deduced from it I don't know. But in a way it *was* an answer.

'You not having little baby in your stomach?' A quizzical, knowledgeable touch of her palm on my belly.

'Never, Naomi! What makes you think so?'

'Your eyes shining so much. I never see you like this.'

'I still bled last week.'

There was nothing I couldn't share with her. She was the one who told me what was happening when I first menstruated: I thought it must be some contagious terminal disease, divine retribution for something Erik and I must have done. For once I couldn't even tell him about it. ('So let *me* die, please God, punish me if you want to, but don't let anything happen to him.')

'And you can see for yourself I still don't have tits.'

'Tsk, tsk. But they growing in his hands, you will see.'

Only one thing I couldn't discuss with Naomi that afternoon. The most important of all. How would she have reacted if I'd told her the truth about Thomas? She could not possibly have understood. (And afterwards, afterwards!) It would have turned her irrevocably against him. She would have wanted to shield me from him with all the fury of an animal mother protecting her young.

Perhaps I *did* need protection? But then from myself, not him.

That whole visit turned out to be unsettling. I could no longer acknowledge the world I'd grown up in and by which, all of a sudden, I was surrounded. Was that why I'd fled to Thomas that night, driven by a sexual need so violent I was myself surprised by it? But what perversity is it that drives one to look for security by provoking danger? What did I want to exorcise? Whatever it was it didn't work. But that, of course, I – we – only realised afterwards. –

The journey in the combi to the village where her father lived had felt like a new beginning, a holiday excursion, a newly won freedom. The rear seats of the vehicle had been removed to make room for the boxes of merchandise; there was ample space for sleeping in, and Justin had sent two narrow floral folding mattresses for just such an eventuality. Like a tortoise in its shell they might now take their home with them, protected against the outside world, less dependent on others than before. In Calvinia Lisa had done some shopping – her hair again plaited and wound formally round her head in the new style that made her look so elegant – while he was waiting in the combi, out of sight. Food, plastic cups and paper plates, soap and washing powder, a few bits of clothing for herself. For the time being Thomas could make do with the somewhat lived-in suits Rashid had brought along, completing the image of the travelling salesman with spectacles that sported an extra set of flap-up sunglasses.

Calvinia, Williston, Carnarvon, then up towards Vanwyksvlei and Prieska, into Griqualand West. A landscape of little mercy. Jonas-rock, whitethorn bushes, three-thorn, koppies, bristly white grass, pale patches of barren earth scarred by erosion. After sunset, the dark descending swiftly, like a photograph accidentally exposed to light before it has been fixed. The unnerving brightness of the night sky. Four nights in the open. (Full moon by the time they spent the night on the endless prehistoric plains beyond Williston.) Jackals cackling and howling like the spirits of the dead, enough to make one's skin shrivel into gooseflesh, knot up one's insides. (Below his fingertips the soft dark hair on her arms bristling up; the down at the bottom of her spine.)

Even sleep felt like betrayal of the intense consciousness brought on by those nights: of space, of themselves, each other. The silent progress of the moon; later, light seeping in, introducing greys between white and black. The beginning of the solarisation process that brought on the new day. Invariably that was when they would fall asleep; then it seemed safe. And not till many hours later would they rise and light their small stove, make coffee, sometimes porridge; perform their ablutions in ice-cold water from a plastic can, and unfold the map to plan the new day's crisscross route. There was no hurry; on the contrary. (Two weeks, Rashid had said. And Thomas had telephoned daily to remain in touch: from a post office here, a graffiti-covered booth on a sidewalk there, from the bar or lobby or passage of some hotel, from a station. *Weather's fine.*) That had been the most difficult of all: suppressing the urge to speed on, resigning themselves to that slow pace while the danger was so real.

The paradox: to drive on as if the world outside did not concern them – villages, dusty roads, black children who sometimes stopped to wave; but also newspapers, radio reports emanating from a world of violence and menace, where people suffered, or rose up in resistance, or died – while, literally, their life and death was being determined from out there, in the planning of moves and counter-moves, day and night, trying to establish exactly where they were, and then to pounce.

Occasionally there had been an unexpected interruption. Once they came upon a large brown round-nosed Ford of venerable age, immobile beside the dust-road after Prieska: a scene from a Fifties black and white film. Pushed off the road; seven or eight men and women beside it, sitting or leaning back against a low bank, several of them with children. Both boot and bonnet open, all four doors ajar, a roof-rack piled high with baggage covered in striped blankets. From a distance it looked like a huge prehistoric bird, too heavy to rise, but with tail and wings spread nevertheless in a ferocious attempt to overcome the laws of gravity.

As Thomas turned off the road a few yards from the Ford and got out, followed by Lisa, a hush fell among the people. Some of them were visibly hunching up their bodies as if preparing to take flight. Even when Thomas called out, 'Molo!' there was little reaction. Partly, as he soon discovered, because they did not understand

Xhosa. They were, it turned out, Tswana people from Mmabatho, on their way home from Cape Town.

Thomas pushed himself in among the men draped like laundry over the sides of the bonnet, cast an eye over the car's engine – assembled with great ingenuity, but leaving rather a lot to chance – and asked, 'Can I help?'

There was a vague mumbling of voices, but without any clear answer. Cautiously testing the radiator with his palm he looked up in surprise. 'But it's ice-cold? How long have you been stranded here?'

'Since yesterday.'

'What's wrong?'

It was the carburettor – a portly man in striped shirt and green trousers took up a stance at once proprietorial and knowledgeable beside Thomas to explain the circumstances – which, after several earlier mishaps on the road from Cape Town, had now finally broken down.

'And no one has passed this way since yesterday?'

'They pass, but they do not stop.'

'Then we'd better do something about it.' He looked round at Lisa. 'Okay with you? We can take this gentleman and the broken carburettor back to Prieska. It's only thirty kilometres or so.'

'We'd better bring some food along too, the kids are starved.' She glanced at the boy whining in the distance. Then she returned to the combi where she ferreted for a minute, re-emerging with a plastic bag laden with bananas and apples, a half-loaf of brown bread, a slab of chocolate. 'Here, boetie.' She held it out towards a cringing child, who promptly ran for shelter behind the nearest woman, now howling with fear. Nervously Lisa thrust the bag into the hands of the burly spokesman. 'Please, will you give it to them?' He hesitated briefly, perhaps offended by the gesture, then took it with some reluctance – as if, she thought perversely, he were handling a bomb – and passed it on to the nearest woman, before abruptly turning his back on Lisa to shout orders about the dismantling of the carburettor to the other men.

Leaving the job to them, he got into the front of the combi beside Lisa. Minutes later, as they drove off, he leaned through the window, gesturing towards the load on the roof-rack of the Ford and shouted what sounded like a string of further instructions to the group of people already half-obscured by their cloud of dust.

'What's all that stuff on your roof-rack?' Thomas enquired, eager to break the uncomfortable silence.

For a while the man stared ahead of him, uncommunicative and almost surly. When he replied at last, it wasn't exactly what they had expected. 'It is my father.'

Swerving sharply to avoid a pothole Thomas almost drove off the road. 'Your father?!'

'Yes. He is dead.' He managed to make it sound like an accusation.

'But –' Thomas desperately tried to rearrange his thoughts. 'Where did he die? When?'

'He lived in a hostel in Lwandle. It is for the migrant workers at Somerset West. Then we get the telegram in Mmabatho to say he is dead. Last Thursday. So I drive to fetch him, yes.'

'You live in Mmabatho?'

'I work on the road there. My brother and I, we have a taxi too. It is his taxi standing there now.'

'And all the other people?'

'Some of them come from the Cape with us, they are my father's people. The others we pick up on the road.' Almost apologetic: 'We cannot leave them standing there, it is too bad.'

Dismayed, Lisa asked, 'But how did you get sidetracked to this place? There are other, shorter, better roads to Mmabatho from the Cape.'

'We must drive here, there, everywhere for the people we pick up. There is one must getting off in Griquatown, another one in Campbell.'

'But –' Trying to avoid the worst stones and ridges and potholes in the road, Thomas shook his head. 'But if your father died last Thursday it's already over a week.'

Their passenger shrugged. He did not seem to be in a mood for talking; when at last he replied it was almost grudgingly. 'My brother and I get to Cape Town on Sunday. It is a long road and the car is too old.'

'And now he's lying there on the roof-rack?'

'In his coffin, yes. We put the blankets around it so he can lie more better, and to keep out the dust. But he will be tired when we getting to the other side.' Grumbling, 'I hope we shall be there by Sunday for the funeral. Then he can rest, yes.'

'What is your name?' asked Thomas, unable for a moment to pursue the conversation.

The big man glanced warily in his direction, as if there was still much about Thomas to be probed before his suspicions would be allayed. 'It is Johnson,' he said at last.

'I am Louis. And this is Marina.' He hoped that his own uneasiness about the names would not be obvious.

A silence.

Thomas tried again: 'You've had a lot of bad luck on the road?'

'Yes. Not only with the car. All around Cape Town we get roadblocks. Lots of police. Soldiers too. I don't know what they looking for, but they stopping us every few kilometres.' An apprehensive glance at Thomas. 'I am not complaining. I just telling you. I do not quarrel with those people.'

'I would have complained if I were you.'

'You are white. You have a right to complain.'

'They had no right to treat you like that.'

The man didn't answer. The expression on his face became even more disgruntled than before, as if he resented being there with them.

'Did your father live in Lwandle for a long time?'

'Eleven years.'

'What work did he do?' The conversation kept stalling; every answer had to be drawn from the stranger.

'He was a bricklayer, yes. Then later he become a security guard. But it is too long, eleven years.'

'Those hostels are bad places to live in.'

Johnson looked at him but made no comment.

'I have friends living there,' said Thomas. 'Mostly in Langa and Nyanga and Guguletu. But I know Lwandle too.' The Hottentot's Holland range in the background, the south-easter sweeping across the plains, rows of washing swaying in a sand storm, small vegetable gardens desperately trying to survive; unplastered whitewashed brick walls, asbestos roofs, a corrugated-iron lean-to school fabricated along one side. In the kitchen block inside, he and Henry – or, in a more distant past, he and Ntsiki – on a visit. Women in docile postures in the background, babies in *abba* blankets. A sputtering primus stove.

'Friends?' It sounded like a challenge.

'Yes, friends.'

An incredulous snort.

'You don't believe me, Johnson?'

'What difference it making if I believe you or not?' A new

flare-up of aggression: 'Why you picking me up? Why you taking me to Prieska?'

'To fix your carburettor.'

'I did not ask you.'

'No. But how could I leave you there beside the road with the women and children? And your father.'

'The others driving past, they leave only dust behind.'

They drove into the town and Thomas slowed down. 'I hope we can find a Ford garage in this place.'

The man didn't answer. But when they stopped he suddenly enquired in a sharply accusing tone, 'You from the police?'

'What on earth makes you think so?'

'Why you asking so many questions? I got all the papers for my father and everything. I can show you.'

Thomas was flushed with anger. 'I don't want to see them, dammit. I have nothing to do with the police.' He got out. 'You wait here, I'll see if I can find a mechanic to help us.'

After Thomas had discussed the crisis with the foreman, Johnson said, a trifle more conciliatory, 'Okay, thanks. Don't wait for me.'

'How will you get back to your car?'

'There will be a lift.'

'Two days from now? Or three?'

'The lift will come as it will come.'

'What about your father?'

'That is my worries, man.' Massive, aggressive, his eyeballs an unhealthy yellow, the man stood before him, hands on his hips.

'I told you I'll wait.' Thomas had to make an effort to control himself. 'I'll wait.'

'Suit yourself.'

In an angry lope Johnson went round the building towards the backyard where the metal bangs of an iron on rubber resounded. Disheartened and frustrated, Thomas turned back to the combi, but Lisa was already halfway across the street; on her way to buy food, he presumed. From the red cool-box behind the pumps he removed three Cokes, snapped off the caps, paid the attendant, and followed Johnson. The man looked up sharply when he made his appearance, then took one of the cans. The edges were wearing off his hostility. But an hour later, when they got back into the combi and Lisa announced, 'I bought the people some food and drink,' he snarled, 'We do not need your food.'

'You still have a long way to go.'

'Charity.' He spat out the word.

'Fuck you,' said Lisa.

It was the closest Johnson's face came to a grin. But he remained silent for the rest of the road, and all Thomas's attempts at stirring up conversation drew only monosyllabic replies.

Two hours after they had left the Ford with its spread wings beside the road they were back.

Johnson jumped out, mumbling something which sounded suspiciously like thank you. Lisa pulled open the sliding door from inside and one of the waiting men approached to remove the repaired carburettor. She took out two carrier bags which she offered to the women. One or two of them smiled and said something in Tswana. The boy who had scampered off earlier peered out from behind his mother's dress, ready to make another dash for it.

Thomas went round to the front end of the Ford. 'Can I help you fit it?'

'There is enough of us,' said Johnson, scowling at him. Then added diffidently, 'But thanks anyway.' He scowled. 'Louis.'

'Well, goodbye then.' Thomas proffered his hand. After a brief hesitation Johnson took it, caught off guard by the Africa handshake Thomas gave him. He cleared his throat as if to say something, then only shrugged.

Perhaps, thought Thomas as they drove off and in the rear-view mirror he watched through the dust the people swarming around the old Ford – the blanket-wrapped coffin still perched on the roof-rack – Johnson had come close to lowering the screen of hostility that masked his true feelings. But how much more effort would it require for them to progress to mutual trust? How much suspicion and misunderstanding would have to be worked through first before they could hope to communicate? If Henry had been present it would have been different. Henry could work – had worked – near-miracles in any urban township, in the most wretched up-country 'location'. But without him, without his human pass, he and Lisa on their own, and white, what hope was there? Perhaps it was already too late to hope for understanding. What bomb could still blast the accumulated mistrust of centuries out of the way?

Depressed, in silence, they drove on. A crude landscape, gradually softened by the superimposition of unexpected memories: if they were to continue further north, towards Kuruman, they would reach the region in which his grandfather had reigned. Secretary birds in the veld, bustards, *kiewiets*. Jackals at night, occasionally the tracks of a leopard. Blackthorn, trassie-bush, honey, blue dolomite, camel-thorn, the yellow splashes of wild pomegranate in October: each rock and plant as unnerving as a metaphor or myth.

After they had travelled a long way Lisa asked, 'Do you think Johnson and his crowd will make it this time?'

'They'll probably be in Mmabatho before us.'

'Is that where we're going?' she asked without turning her head.

He felt the blood drain from his face. For a minute or more he stared ahead, conscious of his hands perspiring on the wheel.

'Thereabouts.'

'You didn't mean to tell me.'

'No.' He still didn't look at her, but placed his hand on her knee, curiously relieved by that solidity of bone. 'But I'm glad it's out. You ought to know.'

'This weekend we can take our time. Make all the plans we need to. We'll be safe in the vicarage.'

6

– 'Thomas, the last time the two of us went on a trip, it was to see the sights, to show you where Africa was, so you could know for future reference. But this time, if we go, it's business all the way. You ready for that?'

'That is what I've come back for, Sipho.'

'Well, let's see what we can do. But you'll have to duck low to keep the Boere off your tracks. Last time they grilled you. We don't want that again. The tiniest slip and you've had it. And then you won't be worth anything to us either.'

'What can I be worth to you anyway?'

'Anybody is worth something to us.'

'Even without an AK-47 or a bomb? Because that I won't do.'

'Haven't you noticed we even have priests among us, man? The armed struggle is only a small part of the scene. Sure, it's important. But it's not all, not by a long haul.'

'And I'm white.'

'We have room for the whole rainbow.'

'All right. Then I'm going with you. But there's one thing you must promise me: if you see I'm not making the grade you must tell me. I won't bear any grudges.'

And so begins our second trip. A longer one this time, intensive, exhausting. He doesn't spare me anything; refuses to make anything easy for me. But when at the end of a hard day he puts his arm around my shoulders and asks, 'How's it, Thomas?', I know in quiet confidence that this is what all the years of uncertainty, of wondering, of worrying, of trying, of frustration, of uncertainty, have led to: and that it is worth everything. And that I can rely on him, on Sipho, this man with laughter and sympathy in his eyes, with the crooked teeth, the song in his chest; my friend.

Africa once again, this time not to explore the cities or their markets or to travel in derelict buses on rutted inland roads, but to meet people, attend meetings and conferences, spend days and nights in conversation about that torn land in the south where the ghosts of Gorée still haunt the memory: about the sacrifices already made, and still to be made, and about how to minimise them, how to clothe in flesh and blood what is still only a slogan: freedom. For me, it means a revolt against my own ancestors. Yet, at the same time, who knows, an act of allegiance as well.

Luanda, Lusaka, Harare, Gaborone (how close to the bone! how distant in the mind).

The blue hills of Morogoro, two hundred kilometres inland from Dar-es-Salaam. Deep red erosion scars in the feminine contours of the hills. Thunder-clouds passing over dark green slopes. The clean cool evenings. The enclave of Mazimbu, anomalously modern with its well-built houses, furniture and clothing factories, expertly tended gardens in the midst of the colonial remains and decrepitude of Morogoro: Masai cattle grazing peacefully in the open spaces as if centuries of colonialism have simply never happened. The exuberant frescoes on the outside walls of a low Lego-block school complex, Solomon Mahlangu Freedom College. The children, almost a thousand of them, from toddlers to almost grown-up adolescents; exiles, the children of exiles, orphans. Behind the affluence and modern furbishing of the classrooms the endemic sadness of the place staining the walls like the secretions of rock-rabbits: because every one of those herded into this place yearns to be elsewhere, far to the south. Sipho takes me to a meeting with a group of Hollanders from the AAM, a delegation from UNESCO, visiting members of the Organisation. Intense discussions on exchange programmes; the feasibility of European foster parents for the smaller children during the long vacation; the introduction of European language programmes; the rotation of contract teachers; changes in curricula. And when we emerge into the twilight – the aggressive green hills now closer, like a chain drawn in more tightly around us – a solitary young boy is standing at a closed gate peering into the descending darkness, towards the south: round head, thin delicate neck, angular shoulders, still far away from manhood; but standing very erect, in that terrible straightness only a young boy can muster. I wonder about his parents, feeling in me a sudden piercing ache that cuts through muscles and nerves: left behind in a township? travelling in Eastern Europe on some mission? hard at work in Lusaka? recuperating in a hospital in Stockholm? killed in a raid by the South African armed forces? I control the urge to put an arm round his stark, narrow shoulders, knowing it will offend him. Does Sipho guess my thoughts? 'He'll go home one day, never mind,' he says. But I know he needs at least as much persuasion as I do. Because if we can no longer hold on to *this*: what then? What lies beyond this now menacing, louring enclosure of hills?

The following day we must move on. Back to Dar-es-Salaam. Maputo. Nairobi. And then Europe.

A few days in transit in London. Noni is giving a series of lectures on African literature at the LSE. In her deep red dress she glows in the dusky hall where names have been hacked into the brown benches and a janitor in navy-blue uniform sits dozing on a stool at the door: glows like a tall flame-tree from Africa, spreading her fragrance like the sun-smell of mimosa blossoms, pouring her voice over long-haired students and crumpled academics and middle-aged ladies with leather bags from Spain and sandals from Crete, pouring it like rain over a parched landscape; and afterwards, with a hoarse chuckle, Sipho asks playfully, putting on his broadest African accent, 'Hey, man, are you in love with my wife?' Which I deny much too emphatically, 'Never!' He embraces me, laughing openly, 'Hell, why shouldn't you be? Everybody is.'

A seventeenth-century hall in The Hague, wall-sized group paintings opposite the carved dark door, recessed windows with sturdy benches below, old chairs upholstered in leather that bears a stale smell of urine, the heavy folds of draped velvet curtains: around the council table we confer on trade and cultural boycotts with rosy-cheeked *wethouders* and rotund businessmen, aggressive lean cultural workers, northern hemisphere representatives of the Organisation and of Anti-Apartheid.

In Oslo, in an upper room, a formal luncheon with a charming, no-nonsense woman Cabinet minister (outside, the threadbare sunlight falls on linden trees changing colour in the Carl Johangate). Aid programmes for education, the harnessing of culture in the struggle for liberation. Sipho pulls wads of documents from his bulging briefcase: impressive, matter-of-fact, to the point – out of respect for the minister his pipe remains unlit, although it is still clenched between his teeth – as much at ease in the surroundings as any of her colleagues.

Copenhagen in the rain, the green of tarnished copper on rooftops visible through the weeping windows of the tall room in which we confer with newspaper editors, an eager junior minister in striped suit and crescent spectacles, a handful of serious young people involved with liberation movements around the globe.

A functional grey office in East Berlin where old-fashioned typewriters clatter incessantly like machine guns behind a wooden partition, on this side of which a committee meeting on education programmes continues relentlessly, item by item, around a long bare table with green blotters and cheap water carafes; from a niche in the back wall a plaster Lenin gazes frowning and disapproving at our deliberations: busy, bustling Germans in frameless spectacles, two of them elderly military men in uniform, the rest middle-aged bureaucrats; Sipho; and four or five young South Africans whose ebullience causes more than one grey Aryan brow to raise.

In an ill-lit hotel lobby in Prague off Wenceslas Square, where archly leering porters take their time inspecting, twenty times a day, our room card before allowing us through the heavy glass doors, Sipho spends a few minutes in avid conversation with some short, bulky men in drab raincoats before he escorts me outside to a taxi; we are driven through uneven cobbled streets where little allowance has yet been made for the twentieth century. On Saturday anachronistic pop music pulses from the discos in three-star hotels; in a long narrow apartment inside a green and grey gabled building with a tiny courtyard draped with white washing, an audience of twenty or thirty people, most of them young, are crowded together to listen to him, to ask questions, to discuss – large glasses of *pivo* in their hands – about what more can be done through aid programmes for expatriate South Africans. Ten or twelve of the expatriates are present too; one of them slips a Miriam Makeba tape into a transistor player on a sideboard in the far corner; several voices join in, more and more of the assembled people begin to sway their bodies to the rhythm; one girl bursts into tears. After Makeba has fallen silent the South Africans break into song, the songs I know from the townships; and after a while Sipho and I join in, and the weepy girl as well, and we all place our hands on each other's shoulders in a large circle that excludes the Czechs, as we bob and sway to the hypnotising rhythms of that distant world, the only reality that matters here: a remote, oppressed, heartbreaking land in angry seas where, cold and colossal, Adamastor still tries to stem incoming foreign tides.

And Moscow. The birches of Sheremetyevo airport in the dusk. Snowflakes fluttering, soundless, in the wide avenues. People in heavy overcoats. The floral wallpaper and sturdy serviceable furniture in my room in the Rossiya; a bathroom with bluegreen tiles, no soap provided, no plug in the bath (a sock or underpants has to do the trick), only three threadbare towels, two of them cut from table linen, and starched so stiffly as to be unusable. Meals with Sipho and acquaintances from his previous visits – large, obese, blond men with transparent blue eyes; intense lean academics straight out of *The Possessed*; severe women, their hair drawn back in buns; occasionally a breathtaking pale beauty with glowing black eyes – in one of the hotel restaurants where frowning women sloppily fling down plates of bortsch or chunks of intimidating grey meat and cabbage in front of us.

Several of our meetings take place in the brown offices of the Committee for Solidarity with Africa and Asia, in an eighteenth-century building — servants' quarters below, seigneurial salons upstairs – where we discuss the changes glasnost and perestroika must impose on relations with Africa, the front-line states, and on the liberation of the south. Some of the men are ponderous, eager to impress us with the years they have spent in Africa; questions on Afghanistan are shrugged off with answers worn smooth through many repetitions. Back at home they might have been members of the Broederbond. Some display the more healthy cynicism of Johann Venter; two or three are young, enthusiastic, dynamic, like Werner in Cape Town. The similarities leave me dazed. They might just as well have belonged to the new wave of Afrikaners.

The most memorable meeting is on the afternoon Sipho takes me to Lumumba University: he must have expected the impact it will make on me, as he has kept it for the last afternoon (in the evening we are to catch the night train to Leningrad). An endless drive down Lenin Prospect, past the tall streamlined statue of Gagarin, until the city begins to give way to woods and we reach the tall concrete buildings of the university, staring unforgivingly over their surroundings. The session with the group of South African exiles takes place in a classroom in the main building on the campus; but afterwards it spills spontaneously into the bedroom of one of the students in a residential complex.

In this cramped space: fourteen or fifteen of them, besides the two of us. Most of the exiles are men, one bouncing a laughing baby on his lap; but two are women, both appearing exotically beautiful in this cold climate, one black, one 'coloured'. Our hosts refuse to let us go: there is too much still to discuss, to ask. How are things at home? Do you know so-and-so? Have you heard from such-and-such? When will we meet again? It's so bloody far from home.

Thabo Mtuze from Mtunzini: 'One suffers in this place, Thomas. It's seven years I've been here now, I'm getting used to it. But it's tough on the new ones who come in. In the beginning it was great sports. The Russians welcomed us as guerrillas. That's just about the highest form of life around here. But they never expected guerrillas to be ordinary human beings with ordinary human needs like drinking and fucking.' ('Hey, you bloody sexist!' from one of the two women.) 'It's true, I tell you, it's true!' he protests. 'Nothing wrong with the Russian girls, hey: they actually queued up for us. I mean, it's kind of an honour to sleep with a freedom fighter, isn't it? But their families didn't feel so hot about it. And soon everybody just got pissed off.'

'Don't listen to him,' said Jamie Pieterse from the Cape Flats. 'Thabo pretends we only have one kind of worry in this place. But I tell you, it's tough, Thomas. There's problems with the language, there's problems with the people. And it's cold as bloody hell. But don't worry, we'll battle through. One day we'll be going home again. And then it will all have been worth while.'

Worth while? Everything? In so many countries, cities, distant places, scattered across the globe? That night in the train to Leningrad I lie with my head on my arms, thinking about them, about the longing in their eyes. Throughout four days in Leningrad I see their faces superimposed on my photographs of the city: the wide silent motion of the Neva, the symmetries of the skyline, the slender spire of the fortress of Peter and Paul, the baroque splendour of the Summer Palace, the turquoise and white façades of the

Hermitage, the stations of Raskolnikov's cross. There's problems with the language, there's problems with the people, and it's cold as bloody hell. But don't worry, we'll battle through. One day we'll be going home.

One last dash to Lusaka, because it's time to go home again. A day splashed with the colour of bougainvillea. A sweating man in a blue shirt reading names from a crumpled sheet of paper. Behind me, the traffic dammed up in Chachacha Road. All of this, too, worth while? –

7

– Can a thing like that be worth while? It is shit, man. Told me his name was Louis. It is a lie. He was this man Thomas Landman. It was him they looking for when they stop us at the roadblocks near Cape Town, every time. The police, the army, all the way. All the while he was there in the dust near Prieska, far away. And we on the road with my dead father, back to Mmabatho.

No, I say nothing about it. I am too much confused today.

He and the young woman, they taking me back to the garage to fix the carburettor. All the time I know there is something very wrong. If white people starting talk and act like that, trying to pretend they your friend, then you know there is big trouble coming.

I say nothing.

They make me angry. Too much. My life is hard, but I say nothing. I do not want to lose everything I got. Before you know where you are you are in deep shit. I go my way, you go your way. Black walk with black, white walk with white. I don't trust you, all right?

Why he doing such a thing? Throwing a bomb. Killing people. It is not good for nobody, it just make it more bad. For my people it bring more trouble and we got enough too much trouble. And for him? Just look at what happen to him now. No, if there is bombs to be thrown my people will do it. One day this country will belong to us. It will be our turn. We not needing whites to do this thing for us. The day we are free we shall have everything we wish for. No more breakdown cars, no more shit. Each man shall have his own house and his own car and his own everything. So I don't want to know nothing about this man.

I suspect nothing about him when he coming there by the road to me. If I did, I rather sit right there. It is a bad time for us, but we used to bad times, we can wait, another car will come some time. My father was dead already, he was in no hurry.

Now all I want to have, and this I saying to all the others too, all I want now is forget about it. Pretend it never happening. Because if we starting talk about it, then everybody coming to ask questions and then there is no end of trouble. So we don't know nothing. We not even thinking about it.

If only someone will tell me why. Why a man like this doing a thing like this. This man, this Louis, this man they now calling Thomas Landman, he was a white man. He got everything a white man need. Those people, they are white, they are the bosses, they got everything. So why?

I say nothing about it.

But this thing go on on my head, all the time, all the time. Why? –

8

– The grace of the Lord Jesus Christ, and the love of God, and the communion of the Holy Ghost. I need it all.

What have I done to my own child?

Threescore years and ten I have behind me, the appointed time for a man, unless by reason of strength he can go on, which I cannot. Now it feels as if my seventy years have become irrelevant, stripped from me like the leaves and beard of a mealie-cob.

Out of the blue they arrived here. It was Friday the 3rd. Lisa introduced the young man to me as Louis. Would it be just to say that from the first moment I did not like him? It is all too easy to make such assertions after the event. Even to affirm that I was suspicious. Certainly it would be safe to say that I was on my guard against him, even if it was, to my shame, for selfish and unworthy reasons. It was the first time Lisa had ever brought a young man home with her. I cannot share her with another.

I have always been out of touch with my children. Perhaps out of fear, dreading the responsibility for their helplessness, their innocence. Because from the outset I bore this guilt towards them. There was blood on my hands even before they were born.

Thou shalt not kill. And I did: my wife; my child.

An accident, everybody said. And in human terms, undoubtedly, it was. Who could have foreseen that a tyre would burst? But with God there is no coincidence. And I know, I have always known, that it was His way of warning me. It wasn't just that I had been careless, reckless, that I had not been as alert as a man should be; I have never been a good driver, never a practical person. But that, if God will permit my saying so, was not a sin. It was merely human negligence. The sin was this, and this I have never confided to a living soul, that I lacked faith. Not that I was small of faith, but that I had no faith at all. And God saw fit to punish me for it.

I never wanted to become a clergyman. It had been my mother's decision when, as Hannah did with young Samuel, she dedicated me to the Lord. I was never allowed any possibility of choice.

The first few years were not so difficult. But it soon became clear to me that I was not suitable for my vocation. I believed that dedication and prayer would make it work in the end, but it did not. There came a stage when I realised that my life was an abomination in the eyes of the Lord. That was when Nerina expected our first child. I decided to resign from my position. I would turn to teaching, to any other occupation available, as long as I could free myself from the service of the Lord. Because I had begun to commit the unforgivable sin against the Holy Ghost: I had begun to doubt God's very existence. And how could I devote my life to the Church if I had no belief at all in the rock it was supposed to be built on? On that holiday journey to the Cape I told Nerina about my decision. She was horrified. We had an unworthy quarrel. I started driving faster than I should, ignoring her pleas to be more careful. Near Laingsburg the tyre burst.

It must have been God's will that I should emerge from it unscathed. But my wife was taken from me.

That is common knowledge. But that she had been three months pregnant I have never divulged to anyone. Not to this day. Now I must humble myself before the Lord to speak the unspeakable. I am the murderer of my unborn child.

Every day, every day of the almost forty years I have lived since then, I have spent in hell. Even today I have no certainty and no assurance about anything. The more devout others think me, the more I am consumed by doubt. But for a long time now all other options have ceased to exist. All for the sake of the possibility, the meagre possibility, that you, God, may exist.

Towards my children, ever since at last I remarried, I have always been unworthy, unable to cope. And yet all these years Lisa has been the one who has made it possible for me to go on. Something in her, that ferocious faith she has in life, her rebelliousness, that lucidity in her, has made me believe that it might yet be worth while, in spite of everything, to persevere: for the sake of seeing, in her, what a human being can be capable of.

Provided it is put to the right use.

But she? She grew up for the devil.

Lisa, Lisa, my impossibly beloved child. That I should be the one to plunge you into hell.

It began the moment she brought the stranger into my house. Deep in my heart I feared what she might tell me. What she was undoubtedly *going* to tell me, for why else would she have come all this way without warning?

Late on Saturday night I went to the kitchen to make tea. As I passed through the dark dining-room. I thought I heard voices in Erik's room where the stranger slept. My heart contracted. I tiptoed to Lisa's room and pushed open the door, stopped on the threshold for fear the beating of my heart might wake her; but then I went inside and found she wasn't there. Like a criminal I stole back to the door opposite. That night, I think, I discovered how people can be driven to commit the basest and most despicable acts, murdering sometimes the very ones they love most.

I heard them. Do You hear me? I heard them.

I already had my hand stretched out to turn the knob. If You are there, it must be You who restrained me. Because I knew that if I went into that room my child would be lost to me forever.

(And now she is lost in any case.)

I heard them. But blindly, after I do not know how long, I walked on to make my tea. Hours later I heard the creaking of floorboards and knew she was returning to her own room. In the church tower close by the clock struck three.

They did not want to go to church with me on Sunday. Hadn't brought their clothes, she said. That's no excuse, I wanted to tell her, God sees the heart, not the outside. But I said nothing. Not then, and not that evening either. Last night: even if it seems so very distant.

But after I had come back from the evening service I could not keep it to myself any longer. I was sitting here at my desk in front of the open Bible. She brought me tea, so quietly that I did not even hear her come in. Put it down here on the desk, then stood behind my chair and kissed me on the head.

528

'Haven't you done enough for one day, Papa? God must be satisfied.'

There was inside me a sudden savage urge to say: He's never satisfied! But I restrained myself. The discipline of all those years.

She sat down on the armrest of the chair. I have so often told her not to do it, as the poor old chair is not very steady any more. Put her hand on mine. I noticed again the narrow band of the ring that had given me such a fright when I'd first seen it on the Friday.

'Where is the man?' I asked. Why? I should have preferred to ignore his very existence; just to be alone with her for a while.

That made her get up, suddenly in a hurry to leave. Which I wished to prevent; I could not bear to be without her. And as she came past the desk on her way to the door, I said:

'No, come back.'

'Papa?' Suddenly defensive.

'You didn't want to go to church tonight either.'

'We have our own way of doing things, Papa.'

'*Is* there any future in it for you?'

'I don't know.' She said it in such a curious tone of voice. Unless I am reading meanings into it, retrospectively, which were not there at the time.

'I don't want to bottle things up, Lisa. I have reservations about the man.'

'What kind of reservations?' Immediately, she was aggressive.

'I'm not sure he is the right man for you.'

'You hardly know him, Papa. You haven't even talked to him yet.'

'He doesn't give me any chance.'

'You hide away in the study all the time.'

'Are you blaming me now?'

'You started by blaming him.'

'Not once since you arrived have you even gone for a walk. Whenever I had visitors you avoided them.'

'They were your guests. We didn't want to be in the way.' A reprimand in her voice.

'How long are you staying?'

'Are we in your way?'

'I'm just asking, Lisa!'

The distance, the chasm between us. I wanted to grasp her hands – I would have gone on my knees before her – to say, For God's sake, don't forsake me. Not you too. I have nothing left. My

529

whole life has been a waste. You are the only one who can still save me.

'We are in no hurry, Papa.' And then, in a characteristic rush of passion, 'Don't you understand I *want* to be here with you?'

It made me feel guilty. At the same time I felt the need to share my deep perplexity with her. 'If only I can find some peace of mind about your choice. This man. There's something I cannot –'

'We have a reason for hiding away in your house like this,' she said without warning. 'If I tell you what it is, will you give me your word of honour to keep it between us?'

'Of course, Lisa. You make it sound like something terrible.'

'Louis is – was – in the army. He deserted, he doesn't believe in making war. Now they're looking for him.'

I did not move for some time. Shocked; yet relieved at the same time. But I said, 'What about our duty to pay God what we owe Him, and the rest to Caesar?'

'It is something he and I have discussed inside out. Now we're prepared to live with it.'

'You expect me simply to face a fait accompli?'

'I took you into my confidence.'

'I appreciate that.' It was still difficult to order my thoughts. 'But that cannot make any difference to the reservations I have about your choice.'

'That is exactly what it is, Papa: *my* choice.'

'But you're judging from the inside, you cannot view it objectively. I'm looking from the outside. I can *see*.'

'With the beam of years of prejudice in your eye?'

This was the Lisa I had always known. But this time it concerned something that touched me too, and to the quick: she herself, my child. I had to fight it with everything I had at my disposal. Even if it was dangerous. For me, especially: I had so much more to lose than she.

'Lisa,' I broached the thing that lay most heavily on me. 'Last night –' No, no, no: I didn't want to. I had no right to.

'What?'

In that instant, in that question, I lost her. So much blood on my conscience already; now hers too.

'Lisa, what is to become of us?'

She did not understand what I meant at all. She suddenly flung herself at me: 'Papa, I don't want to be preached to. What do you

530

know about me? What have you ever tried to understand? All these years, cooped up in your study, or in the church, and all around you the world is going to hell –'

'Lisa!'

'Going to hell, I tell you. As long as you can keep your hands and your conscience clean, you don't care a fuck about the rest. Injustice, violence, murder – in the name of the very God you're so eager to serve. Pious words to cover up everything. Bloody whited sepulchres. Inside there's a stink no living creature can stand. But you keep it going: you and your Church. You've fucked up your own children, Papa, and you don't even know it. I can't take it any more!'

Then she was gone. I don't even know whether she spent the night with him again. Most likely. But it no longer made any difference to me.

Deep in the night I telephoned Erik. I had to talk to someone. The only way to reach him in the barracks was to call his chaplain. I asked him please to call Erik. Told him it was an emergency.

'Papa, what's the matter?' Bewildered and befuddled with sleep.

'Erik.' All of a sudden I felt embarrassed. I should not have drawn him into it too. But I could not handle it on my own. 'I'm phoning you about Lisa.'

'What's up? Has something happened to her?' He gets upset so easily when she is concerned.

'Nothing has happened to her. Not yet.'

'What do you mean?'

'She's here. With a man. She says –'

'What?!'

'I'm worried to my very soul, Erik. And there is no one else I can talk to. She says he deserted from the army. What do you people call it?'

'AWOL?'

'Yes, I think so. Now she wants me to cover up for them. But I'm so worried, Erik. The man has an evil hold on her. I have to look after my child's own best interests.'

'Listen, Papa –'

'No, let me finish. I know you always take her side. But I'm thinking of her own good, Erik. What is to become of her? I've been thinking: in the long run it may be the best for her if I report him to the authorities. Then –'

531

'Papa, listen –'

'It's for her own sake, Erik. I have a responsibility.'

'Listen, for God's sake!'

He shouted so loudly that I stopped, quite startled.

'The man did not run away from the army, Papa.'

'What?'

'If you report him, it's the end of Lisa. It's not something we can discuss on the phone. Just believe me. All I'm asking is that you stay out of it. Please! Do you hear me?'

'But Erik –'

'Stay out of it!'

'But what must I do, Erik?'

'Nothing. Don't do anything. In the name of everything you believe in.'

That, I thought, is not very much.

All night long I remained sitting in this chair. When Naomi brought in my coffee in the early morning she must have thought I got up early. Which would not be unusual.

I wondered: Does this mean that God exists? Or does it rule out the last vestige of the possibility of His existence? Does anything mean anything any more?

I felt like Lazarus risen from the dead. It was not the return to life that mattered, but the memories of death. At breakfast table I awaited them. I did not look at either of them as they emerged from their separate rooms. (Hypocrites! Did they still believe it could be covered up? In a way, as I recall it now, it was the last straw. That casual air with which they took their seats.) All I said, my eyes on my plate, was, 'I want you to leave after breakfast. Please. It is better you don't stay here any longer.'

'Papa?'

'Don't ask me any questions, Lisa. Just finish your breakfast. And then go.' I wanted to add: And please don't tell me where. I do not want to know.

Erik had said, 'If her life means anything to you.'

That was why I could not hand them over. Not in my house. But I do have a conscience. All these years it has driven me, more than God ever has. I have an obligation to it. There is a basic kind of decency that keeps one going. No matter what happens around one – how did she put it? – violence, injustice, murder, God knows what.

They did not come to say goodbye.

Naomi appeared in the doorway, and said, 'My God, Dominee, they gone.'

'I know, Naomi. That is how it must be. Now go and do your washing.' It was Monday, after all.

After she had gone out I heard her crying in the passage; I reached out and picked up the telephone. It was like pronouncing my own death sentence. But what else could I do? Perhaps this was the ultimate, the extreme ordeal God had always planned for me. Perhaps this would bring me peace.

When the voice answered I recognised it.

I said, 'Sergeant Erasmus, can you come over to the vicarage?'

He exists, I thought. Yes, He exists all right. At long last I know it.

Because it is a fearful thing to fall into the hands of the living God.

Thy will be done. –

9

– The long road ahead. I'm not sure I'll make it in time. (In time for what?)

Papa's given his word, hasn't he? I pleaded with him. It's Lisa's life that is at stake. I'm sure his love for her is deep enough. So perhaps I'm being quite irrational. But it's a chance I cannot take.

A good thing the chaplain is on my side. And Papa personally told him it was an emergency. I didn't have to specify anything, just said it was illness. He cleared it with the brass. Agreed to contact them on Friday if I have to stay longer. By that time –

(By that time what?)

Why this unbearable anguish in me?

Lisa, my sister. God knows. (What does He know?)

This long road is killing me. I have no idea of what time I'll get there tonight. This little car is not what it used to be. Patience must be the hardest thing in the world.

However, in a way I'm grateful for these hours on the road. When last did I allow myself the time to think? Lisa openly accused me, the last weekend I was with her, of avoiding issues. Perhaps it suited me *not* to think. Afraid of what I might find there, lurking. Like when you operate on a patient for a tumour.

It can be non-malignant. Anything can still be done. Or it can be malignant, too far gone.

The day I saw the report in the paper. It was two days late, we don't always see it, especially when we're busy. And right at that time we were up to our ears. A whole consignment of bad cases flown in from Oshakati. Worked far into the nights.

I recognised his face on the front page immediately. As it happened I was thinking of them as I took up the paper. The first weekend we were in each other's hair all the time. Always happens when I find someone else with her. We're too close. What will happen if one of us is to get married one day? But the second weekend was more relaxed. I was beginning to come round to the idea that he might not be such a bad proposition for her. Quiet, strong, enthusiastic when he gets worked up about something, understanding towards her, not dominating at all. She won't get far with a dominating companion. Too independent for that.

His face. Thomas Landman. Sought country-wide by the police. Terrorism. Murder. And I knew exactly where he was. In my own sister's bed.

I telephoned her. Countless times. There was never any answer.

Some consolation in that. It meant that at least he wasn't there any longer. But where was Lisa? With him? Or had she gone to earth, dived under? Surely she would at least have contacted me first. We have our secret language.

Until I knew exactly what had happened I dared not lift a finger.

As soon as I was free to go that weekend I raced to Claremont, still almost catatonic with fear. Not knowing what to expect.

Her beach buggy was parked under the pergola beside the house. My heart jumped. But the house was deserted. It wasn't even necessary to unlock the front door. There is a special kind of silence to a house when it is empty; quite different from the silence when they are simply not making any sound inside.

Twice I went right through the house, from front door to back garden. Only the second time did I discover the letter on the mantelpiece in the lounge. Where we always leave our messages. How could I have missed it the first time round? It was lying there in wait for me like a time bomb.

dearest erik: i have gone away with him.

She had first written *anton*. I closed my eyes. For a few minutes I had tunnel vision. Around the focal point everything was vibrating, trembling, as if I stared at the room through moving water. The paper was shaking in my hand. It was a long time before I could resume my reading:

> i have gone away with him, i can't give you any reasons, i shall, one day, it's a promise. you know the mess i've been in lately. now at last i know there's something i can do. must do. all i'm asking of you, dearest, darlingest erik, is to allow me to go ahead and do it. don't try to stop me. don't try to stop him. he is not what everybody thinks he is. will you believe me? please? this last month or so something has begun to slide in between you and me. what has become of hansel and gretel in the wood? if they've got lost forever, if they have lost each other in the dark, it will be the most unbearable experience of my life. he is going to make it possible for me to find you again. i know it. allow me this one chance, will you? i know what i'm doing, even if i cannot explain it. loveyou. i.

Followed by a row of crosses.

What should I make of it?

i know what i'm doing, even if i cannot explain it.

Crazy, irresponsible, adolescent. There were many words one could use. But I know my sister, and that makes a difference. In a way, maybe, I could understand what she herself could not yet. I was watching with very jealous eyes.

Forgive me for it. Forgive me for everything, Lisa. As long as you are happy. Whatever 'happiness' means, because you've never cared much for anything conventional. For you, I presume, happiness would mean believing in what you're doing; doing what you believe in. Not to want anything but that. This is what I read in your letter. You've never had a lack of imagination. That was what we shared in our Hansel and Gretel days. Has it really begun to fade in me? Then you were right to warn me.

Will I still be in time?

I know now how much a year's exposure to the consequences of violence has changed me. I do not really see or feel anything any more: it all happens at arm's length. Even while I am working on a broken body, it happens outside myself, at a remove: it is a matter of medical skill, a professional response to this challenge or that: it does not involve *me*. All I've wanted to do was survive.

I wanted to get these two years behind me as smoothly and effectively as possible, and never be reminded of them again. Two years to be effaced from the mind, for good. But it is not so easy. As I know now: now that you have run away with a terrorist.

Terror, I know now (how obvious when one finally faces it!), need not be linked to a frontier dividing 'this side' from 'the other side', 'them' and 'us'. When I'm operating, a stomach wall, layers of fat and muscle, are the 'frontier' I must cross to what lies 'beyond': but for the patient it is the other way round, I am the intruder from outside. And once I'm inside, I have to work and judge from within: determine where the malignancy lurks, what makes it malignant, what the foreseeable consequences may be. Here: in here. There is no 'frontier' any more. And the terror I perpetrate on the diseased organs becomes an act of healing.

All those victims who have passed through my hands. And all the time I have looked at them from one side only. There must have been hundreds, possibly thousands, of dead, and wounded, and maimed on the 'other' side as well: *their* 'victims of terror': also killed by enemies from across the border. Young Cubans perhaps. Caught in battle thousands of kilometres away from home. To fight whose war? And for what? Commandeered by a government, instructed to safeguard a set of values. Civilisation, justice, good. Just as our young men have been commandeered and instructed. In the name of those same values, civilisation, justice, good.

It goes further than that. Maybe the worst consequence of becoming blunted, of getting used to things, is this: that even the victims, even helpers like myself, come to think of violence as the only way. An eye for an eye, a tooth for a tooth, a life for a life. And then there *is* only violence left. In which case I am as much to blame for what he did as he.

Is this, Lisa, why you ran off with Thomas Landman?

This is what I have to probe and sort out on this long necessary journey.

Clichés. Commonplaces. Everybody knows them. Nobody knows them. Nobody *understands* them.

All I know is that I have to start again, from scratch. My first corpse on the dissecting table. My first scalpel in my hand. Otherwise I have lost you for good. –

536

They were already ten, fifteen kilometres out of town – silent, her father's blunt anger unspoken, intractable between them – when he suddenly braked, and swerved, and brought the car to a standstill beside the road.

'What's the matter?' she asked, startled.

'Tortoise.'

He got out of the car to pick up the leisurely, resolute little animal that had just begun to cross the road and deposit it among the low scrub on the opposite side. She had been so lost in thought that she hadn't even noticed it.

'Sorry,' he apologised with a touch of embarrassment as he got in again. 'But it's so slow, somebody might have driven over it.'

This return to the present caused Lisa to think of what she might have forgotten otherwise. 'Oh Jesus, Louis, I left my *I Ching* in my room. In all this consternation about Papa's shitty mood –'

'It will be quite safe there, won't it?'

'Oh no, please. I'm quite helpless without it. And it's not all that far. We can still go back.'

He was disgruntled, after their humiliating expulsion, at the prospect of having to look her father in the eyes again. Yet he was touched by her anxiety.

They drove back to the village they had left. And as they came round the last corner and approached the red-berry hedge of the vicarage, they saw the yellow police car in front of the open green gate.

537

Chapter 12

— Served me bloody crayfish of all things. On purpose? But to be fair to him, how was he to know? Can't stand the stuff. Take one look at it. If God had meant people to eat it He would not have made it look like that. Even when it's dished up it lies in the plate staring at one with its evil little eyes as if it's still alive. Now take its habits. That one occasion, years ago, when we brought in the body at Hangklip. Peacefully catching from the rocks, then noticed this thing lying in a gully like a big bloated jellyfish, must have been in the water for over a week. No colour left in it at all, couldn't even make out whether it was white or black, let alone man or woman, and not a hair left on the body. But worst of all was the way the crayfish had disfigured it. Two of them still clinging to the one remaining leg, the other one just a stump. Bloody scavengers. Worse than hyenas or vultures on land. And then some people pretend it's a delicacy. Won't touch it.

Which turned out to be unfortunate, yesterday, when the commissioner invited me. Friendly as anything. Lunch. Thursday 10 June. At his home in Newlands. Mostly empty, only uses it when he comes down to the Cape. Lives in Pretoria of course. Flew down specially. Day before yesterday the phone call from a woman captain in his office, all honey-mouthed: Brigadier Bester, the commissioner asked me to contact you, he is going down to Cape Town and would like to invite you to lunch tomorrow afternoon. At his home, you know the address, don't you?

Not keen at all. Not with all this mess around. The Landman case. And then, my God, Anna. Hendrina too. Not to mention the thing about Swanie who used to be my bloody right hand. Taught him the ropes, everything he ever had to know. Who could have expected a thing like this from the cunt? No, in the circumstances would have preferred to steer well clear of the commissioner yesterday. Already sensed a snake in the grass, everybody knows he doesn't come to

Cape Town unless it's absobloodylutely necessary. But what choice was there?

And then he served crayfish, as if to catch me out on purpose. Out of season too, but the commissioner has his contacts, whether it's for hunting or for crayfish, he's above the law. Not complaining, my chance will come. The commissioner is on the point of retiring and the president has already dropped a hint. Unfortunately the Pres. is unreliable these days. And hand in glove with the commissioner. Realised it from the word go, when he said, breaking open the red shell of the crayfish legs with his hands to tear out the white meat, 'Bester, I was at Tuynhuys this morning and I'm afraid the president is not happy with the progress in the Landman case.'

Should have liked to tell him it makes two of us, but silence is golden. Only said, 'The case is under control, General.'

'And exactly what does that mean?' Cold eyes the man has, almost colourless but not quite. Like bluebottles.

'What it means, General, is this.' My fingertips pressed together above the plate with the red monster on it. Eyes right in his, so he could see who he was dealing with. 'What it means, General, is this. We are drawing the net in closer. Landman is on the run with a companion. A female. A dominee's daughter. Lombard. Probably took part in the assault. Working on it. Last weekend they spent with her father. Friday 3rd to Monday 6th. The dominee reported them to us himself. Co-operative man. That was Monday morning, 6th. Flew up personally to interrogate him. Back the same evening. Left my men behind to deal with the situation. Important feedback already. Expecting the final breakthrough any minute now. All indications are that they're on their way back north. Every police station from Griqualand West to Northern Transvaal has their descriptions, and Jan Smuts is on alert round the clock. Question of time. Few days at most, if you ask me.'

'That's exactly what I'm doing.' Crushed a feeler, broke it open, sucked it out. White juice on his chin. 'It's almost six weeks, Bester.'

Same thing Anna said. Never thought she'd ever be so outspoken. Always so meek and mild. Good woman, knows her place. Until day before yesterday, breakfast table. 'What I want to know from you, Kat, is when we're going to take that holiday you've been promising me for so long? I want to know *now*.'

'Already told you, Anna. Soon's this case is over.'

'That's no longer good enough, Kat.' Bloody cheek.

Never thought it would be necessary to raise my hand against her again. Never intended to. But what can a man do? There's a thing like respect for your husband in the face of the Lord. Only thing is, Hendrina should have stayed out of it. Not only did she see it, she actually tried to interfere instead of moving out of the way and showing some respect. So had to take her in hand too, whole fucking house full of crying females, even the maid in the kitchen.

So angry when it was all sorted out at last, it wouldn't have taken much to get a heart attack. Short of breath, pain in the chest. Off to work in such a hurry my briefcase was left behind. The hell with it. First poured coffee from the machine in the passage, two of those mugs, properly filled up with sugar. Always take four teaspoons, but in emergencies like this it's more. Closed the door and withdrew in here, lit my pipe to get back to normal. Ought to have been at the fishing waters to recover properly, it's the only way of really getting away from it all.

Thought by myself: Snoek. This is what one needs now. Few other catches give one such a deep feeling of contentment as snoek. In the early season, September or thereabouts, sometimes later, depending on the weather, sea streams, many things: but one day they're there, flocks of gulls on the waves, the ocean blue-black, and below the surface the waters churn. Deep, must be twenty fathoms at least, but as far as the eye can see the water is on the boil. Now they must be brought up from down there. Takes patience, takes knowing the ropes. Bait on the line, working them upward, upward all the time, let's say four fathoms, even three if you can. Then the sports begins. No need for bait at this stage, not even a barbed hook, all a matter of expertise. Bring in your fish with the snoek *dolly* until he's right next to the hook. Quick flick, it's a deft motion that takes a lot of practice, but once you've got it it's a joy, right hand under your left arm, quick jerk. Then he comes for it. Now it's lightning action. Pull in, haul out, snap the snoek's head under your arm to break its neck. If you don't get it right you get bitten so's the daylight shines right through you. Break its neck. Throw it in the box. Right for the next one. Deepest bloody satisfaction of all. Should have been in those icy waters that morning, no problem. Whole thing with Anna and Hendrina avoided too, because they'd have been there with me. The holiday she's always wanted. Poor thing, she deserved it.

But what the hell, it wasn't possible and that's that. So no choice but to have my coffee on my own. Black. Sweet. Scratched out the pipe, refilled it, pressed the tobacco in lightly, lightly, not too tight, just right, one's thumb soon gets the feel of it, lit it, pulled the smoke through, allowed the first embers to smoulder and die, topped it up, pressed it down, then lit it again, takes years to get the hang of it. Slowly, gradually, the feeling that life was getting better again. Then Swanie came barging in. Didn't even knock properly. Just back from the North-west, driven right through the night, grey with tiredness.

Wasn't expecting him at all. His orders had been to keep watch on the vicarage until something happened.

Took him up there with me on Monday. No one as trustworthy as Swanie, say it every time. Not an hour after the dominee's call came through we were in the Hercules on our way to Kimberley. Sent a squad to search the pussy's house in Claremont. Thanks to her father's information we could pounce immediately. Landman's lair. Would have liked to be in charge personally, but there's priorities. Checked everything with Swanie on the way up. Radioed instructions to the teams waiting for us. Blocked all the roads leading from the town, radius of two hundred kilometres. Taking no chances at all. Specific orders to stop every fucking combi and shake it.

Team in a BMW waiting on the tarmac when we landed. In less than five minutes we were on our way. Rather hoped the combi would have been netted by then. But no such luck. Discovered the reason only the following day of course. At the time we were all flabbergasted about how a vehicle like that could have disappeared without any trace at all, it's not as if there's so much traffic on those godforsaken bloody roads. Still the feeling that now it was only a matter of time. Line as tight as can be. Fish on the hook. Ready for the final play.

But as it turned out it wasn't going to be that easy. In this case nothing fucking well works out the way it's supposed to.

Spent three hours with the dominee in his rambling vicarage. Kind gentle man. Totally flustered though. Just kept on pleading we mustn't hurt his child. She didn't have anything to do with it, brought up in the fear of the Lord. Have heard that story before. Old Jordaan himself, and he's a judge after all. Avoiding me like the plague nowadays, as if it was my fault. Just because we were one step ahead of him, eliminating that Jew. The bloody cheek. What he'd done was nurse an adder in his bosom. But his dirty little secret was out. Had him investigated and came up with what was needed. Just waiting to play my trump. However, the dominee was a different kind of person, so tried to play the game with him. Assured him it was only Landman we're interested in. Sympathised with his child manipulated by unscrupulous communists. Assured him that one of these days she'd be home again, the murderer swinging from the gallows, his child free to come and go as she chooses. Meantime thought: This one isn't going to get away. Missed my chance with that bitch Nina Jordaan. But not this Lisa Lombard. For once nothing is going to stop Kat Bester. This one is reserved for me personally.

Exhausting business with the dominee. Poor old man quite broken down, crying and sobbing, getting all mixed up. Talking about his first wife, a car accident, the wrath of the Lord. Took a lot of patience. Decided after an hour or so to take a break, went to the kitchen to get us all some tea. No sign of the servant girl. The dominee actually had to go and call her from her room in the backyard. Took one look at her, instant dislike. Some blacks just ask for it. The way she glowered at us. But the tea helped. Got the old man back on track again.

Obvious he didn't know much. Thought Landman was a troopie on AWOL. Wouldn't have lifted a finger if the dominee man hadn't discovered his guest was fucking his daughter at night. Too much for the dominee's Christian conscience, so he threw them out and set the police on them. And that was that. After three hours we still knew nothing more.

The fish had broken free again.

But this time it wouldn't elude us for long. The nets were out.

In a foul mood as we drove back to Kimberley. Left Swanie behind. Four or five men to keep him company. Temporary quarters in the hotel to monitor the reports from the roadblocks. The rest of us back in the Hercules. Too much work waiting here in Cape Town.

Drove directly from the airport to Claremont, the pussy's cottage. Already turned upside-down by the search team. Nothing. Sweet blow-all. Worked through the night to go over everything once again, one often misses something that seems insignificant the first time round. But no bloody luck.

Then decided to bring in her twin brother. Heard from the dominee that the two of them are thick as thieves ever since they were kids. Perhaps he could lead us to something. But at Two Military Hospital it transpired he'd left. Taken his car the previous day and driven off. Said there was some 'crisis' at home and was given leave. Immediate suspicion. And early that same morning, Tuesday, the report came through that he'd arrived at his father's place. Although at first sight it didn't seem as if there was anything more to the visit.

Swanie, on the phone, wanted to know whether they should bring the boy in, give him a work-over?

Stopped him immediately. You'll be doing no such thing. If he really doesn't know anything hauling him in will just fuck it all up. And if he does know something we must find out without giving him any hint that we're on his heels. If he really is all that close to his sister it's likely that he'll know where she is. They may have set up something to stay in touch. So gave Swanie explicit instructions: Keep an eye on the vicarage and on Erik Lombard for twenty-four hours a day. But you'll have hell to pay if he notices anything. Is that very clear? And put a bug on their phone. Check out every possibility.

Seemed as if one might now sit back and wait for things to start happening.

But halfway through Tuesday the first shock when Swanie phoned to say they'd found the combi.

Where?

'Oom Kat, you're not going to believe this. Right in the garage in the backyard of the vicarage.'

Silent for a long time. Then: 'Will you say that again?'

'They never left, Oom Kat. Or otherwise they just went for a short drive and came back. We spoke to the dominee again. He swears to God he said goodbye to them at the front gate yesterday morning. Stood looking after them as they turned left to the main road. I think he's genuine, Oom Kat.'

God Almighty.

'And the brother?'

'It doesn't look as if he knows anything. His car is parked in front. He's taken a few walks in the yard, past the garage, but the door was closed all the time, he never went inside. It's possible of course that he's know all along and is keeping watch. Oom Kat, are you sure we shouldn't –'

'No, Swanie. Keep your hands off him. Stay out of sight. And leave the combi where it is. But check it over soon's you can without being seen. Inside and out. Meantime, make sure Erik Lombard doesn't wipe his arse without your knowing it.'

Could feel something coming.

Back to Military Hospital. Whole team with me. Interrogated his CO, his chaplain, every bloody soul who knew Lombard. Clean.

Never set a foot wrong throughout his military service. Even seemed enthusiastic about the army. Not one of those who just does his bit and fuck the rest. His heart was right in it. Unless it was all a pretence of course. One cannot exclude that. Hypothesis: suppose Thomas and Lisa Landman have been together all along, suppose she and Erik are in cahoots. Right? Then it is conceivable that Erik was planted in the army right from the word go. To pass inside information through to them. About the arrangements for the parade on Friday morning 29 April, for example.

A blank. Soon established that Erik Lombard had never been involved in those arrangements.

Which still doesn't rule out the possibility that he might have worked through a contact at the Castle.

Means every soldier who got close to the Castle around that time must be checked.

And every movement of Lisa Lombard over the last months.

In this respect, at last a small stroke of luck. Discovered that she left early on the afternoon of 29 April on a plane from Cape Town to Johannesburg. SA 322, left 14h05, arrived 15h55. Which might have been the same flight Landman was on, seeing he was also up north that evening. There may well be more in this than we suspected at first.

But if that is so, where would Nina Jordaan fit in? Was she really the girl with Landman on the farm outside Paarl, or was it perhaps Lisa Lombard? Oom Kobus had been adamant, but suppose he'd been mistaken?

No end to the work. And then the commissioner has the bloody cheek to tell me he and the president are not satisfied with our progress.

Still entangled in this net of enquiries and double-checking when Swanie phoned again. Wednesday morning. That was only minutes before the woman captain from the commissioner's office called to make the appointment for yesterday's lunch meeting. Right, so there was Swanie on the phone. First a report on the combi. Gone in there the previous night and took everything they could lay their hands on. Quite a haul. Disguises, wigs, clothes, you name it. But there was something even more interesting than the combi. Strange story Swanie told me. The previous evening Erik Lombard had spent a long time in the maid's room in the backyard. Over an hour.

First reaction was, 'Jesus, man, that girl is old enough to be his fucking mother. You're not trying to tell me that he —'

'No, Oom Kat, no, no. It wasn't like that at all. We were watching, it was easy enough, one of the curtains was open. They just sat talking, genuine. She on the bed, he on a chair.'

'Come on, Swanie. Since when does a young white man spend an hour in a maid's room just talking?'

'I can put my head on a block, Oom Kat.'

Began to lose my temper. 'So what the hell do you make of it?'

'She handed him something before he left, Oom Kat. Wrapped in newsprint. He took it back to his room with him. Very early this morning we observed him coming from the house, once again carrying the parcel. He buried it in a dahlia bed in the side garden.'

'And?'

'We dug it up soon afterwards, Oom Kat. Made sure no one saw us. It's a big yard.'

'Found something?'

'Hair.'

'Hair?'

'Long black hair, looks like a woman's.'

'Lisa's?'

'All we can think, Oom Kat.'

'Swanie, you've got to bring in the *meid*. It's the only way. Set up something at the police office, get them to go and pick her up in the van. Make sure it looks like an ordinary charge. You know, illegal visitors, drunkenness, problem with her reference book, anything. Easy to explain to the dominee afterwards. Administrative error. But we've got to find out what she has to say.'

'Will do, Oom Kat.'

'And Swanie.'

'Oom Kat?'

'You can go to town on that *meid*. It's bloody well time we make a breakthrough. No matter what it takes.'

And then, yesterday morning, Thursday, he showed up here. Unbidden, without permission, grey in the face. Must be from tiredness, one's first thought. But it was much worse than tiredness.

'Swanie, what's the matter?'

'We lost the woman, Oom Kat.'

'What do you mean you lost her?'

'She's dead.'

Took two swallows of coffee. Motioned him to sit, but he remained on his feet. Paced up and down. Up and down, as if he had ants in his arse.

'What happened?'

'They were too rough with her.'

'They?'

A pause. 'We.'

'What did you get out of her?'

'Nothing.'

'Don't believe it.'

Leaned forward on his arms on my desk. Something feverish in his eyes. 'Sweet blow-all. I'm telling you. And she died.'

'What about the hair?'

'Not a word.'

'Thought you knew your work, Swanie. You've never come back to me with empty hands before.'

'I'm telling you, Oom Kat, she's dead.'

'Not talking about that. Talking about you messing things up and having nothing to show for it.'

'I was wondering about something last night, Oom Kat.' Now with his back to me, looking through the window. Nothing outside to look at. Turned back. 'Suppose the other blacks in the village heard about it and got angry. Suppose they rose up. There's five times as many of them as whites.'

'So what about it? They five times as stupid too. They fighting with stones and *kieries*. We have Casspirs, machine guns, grenades.'

'That's not what I'm talking about, Oom Kat.' Back to my desk. His face flushed. Perhaps he was ill. Otherwise he wouldn't have gone on like that. 'What I'm saying is that we can't go on forever silencing and killing the ones that make things difficult for us. Sooner or later there won't be enough of us left against them.'

Rose to my feet, but stayed calm. 'Swanie, you better go home first. You're tired. Go and sleep it off, then we can talk about it again. Right now you're not thinking straight.'

'I'm thinking as fucking straight as I've ever done.'

Beginning to get irritated. But took time to refill my pipe. Gave him a chance to calm down. Which he didn't.

'I've had more than enough time to think, Brigadier.' That hit me harder than anything else. Sjambok blow through the face. Him suddenly dropping the 'Oom'. As if he was renouncing something between us. 'It's a long road to drive from there to here.'

'Swanie, what you think doesn't concern me. What matters is that you do your job and don't make fuck-ups.'

'I've kept quiet about many things, Brigadier. I kept quiet about

Mabusa. I kept quiet about David Blumer. And God knows, I should have spoken up then. But now I've got to know: how long is this going to go on? Where is it going to end? What price is it going to cost?'

'A price any man who loves his country will be willing to pay.'

'Brigadier, we've been using big words to cover up plain shit for too long. It doesn't wash with me any more. And I can't just keep it to myself. Today I've got to talk and you've got to listen.'

'You think your opinions are of any concern to me?'

'They better!' It was obvious he had no idea of what he was saying. Way over the top.

Decided to give him rope. Used to do that with my kids too when it was the only way of calming them down. Afterwards, of course, they'd get the skin ripped off their arses, once they could appreciate what was happening. 'All right then. Spill it.'

'I've been thinking hard about it, Brigadier. Look at Moçambique. Angola. Zimbabwe. Even South West Africa is heading for it. All the places where whites used to think they were in charge, today they're kicked out. We're the only ones left.'

'Good you've noticed that. Because we're going to stay here. We're not a bloody lot of English or French or Porras getting the hell out of a place once the going gets tough. We're here to stay.'

'We can't last forever, Brigadier. I've seen it coming for a long time now. But last night it really hit me. We can stay on for a while because we've got the Casspirs and the guns. But it's getting harder every day. We're moving closer and closer to the edge of the cliff. And then? They're too many for us, Brigadier. And I don't want to end up in some Nuremberg courtroom one day where I'm asked to defend what no one can defend.'

'Who said anything about a courtroom?'

'I want to make myself very clear, Brigadier. If there's going to be an inquest on that woman's death no one must expect me to cover it up. I'll tell them what I know. I've got no choice.'

'You won't dare to. You'll be cutting off your own neck. With a knife you've sharpened yourself.'

'I don't care. If they start pushing me I'll bring down the whole place with me.'

'You better think about what you're saying there, Swanie.'

'I've done all the thinking I need to. Now I'm talking. We've been blind, Brigadier. We didn't want to see what was right in front of our eyes. But it's there for all to see, clear as daylight. Our day is coming.

It's time we start preparing for it. So now I want to know: *what* is it I'm expected to go on killing for day after day?'

'To make this country a safe place for our women and children to live in. To get rid of all the weeds in our garden. To keep the place clean.'

'I'm supposed to risk my life fighting against what we call our "enemies", knowing damn well that one day those very enemies are going to rule the country. As sure's Mugabe is ruling in Zimbabwe or Whatsisname in Moçambique. Where's the sense of it?'

Felt a muscle jumping in my jaw. 'Swanie, now you're going too far.'

'Brigadier, I don't mind killing for my country. That makes sense. But this is what I've started asking myself: what have I really been killing for? It wasn't for the country or for a cause. It wasn't to see that justice was done or to eliminate enemies. So what was it for then? That woman wasn't an enemy. She was an ordinary domestic servant who lived all her life in the outroom of a vicarage. And if this is what is expected of me, I can no longer do it.'

'Exactly what does that mean?'

'It means –' Suddenly he became bewildered, as if for the first time he realised just what he'd been saying. Long silence. Then, quite overcome, 'I'm sorry, Oom Kat. I didn't mean to – I'm afraid it just got the better of me. I –'

Felt like putting my hand on his shoulder to comfort him. But remained standing opposite him, the desk between us. 'It's all right, Swanie. You're overwrought. Go home. Sleep it off.' Then more sternly: 'And you stay there until you hear from me again. Got that? It's an order.'

He closed the door behind him. All of a sudden the office was invaded by an emptiness that made it difficult to breathe. Felt like a man who'd just received the death sentence. From anyone else one could take it. But not Swanie. The best man in my squad. Trusted him with my own life.

What is going to happen if this doubt starts infiltrating our own ranks, breaking down our best men?

Considered visiting him at his home that night. Talk to him like a father. Dammit, he had to understand reason. What we're doing is something that *must* be done. *Someone* must do it. Otherwise everything our people have fought for over bloody centuries is jeopardised. Our sweat and blood are soaked into this land. The

548

English and the French and the Portuguese, the whole cowardly lot could run back to their own countries when things got too hot for them in Africa. But what about us? Where can *we* go to? Our dead have been buried here, generations upon generations. Oppression, poverty, drought, murder, we've borne it all. Because God planted us in this place. We owe it to Him. It's not as if we enjoy being harsh or cruel. But it's justified by the end. The will of God. What else? We're not bad or evil by nature. And now we're threatened with our own extinction. A lot of strangers want to take from us what is ours in the face of man and God. No, Swanie. Had to get this message through to him.

But something else took over. It was wrong to submit to fatherly concern and neglect my own duty in the process. The example of my own father. Look how hard he was. Because he hated me? No. Because it was his way of showing he cared for me. There were certain things he was justified to expect, to demand of me. Respect his memory for that. This was something that had to be considered very carefully, very clearly. Literally a matter of life or death.

Fetched two more mugs of coffee, six sugars in each. Told the corporal in the front office to keep out everybody. Closed my door.

Swanie.

It was a farewell. Sure, discussing the matter with him was a possibility. The man *was* upset, not altogether accountable. But the naked fact was that those thoughts had indeed begun to take hold of him. No matter how well he suppressed them, sooner or later they'd come back. Worse every time. Should have read the signs the day he balked at the idea of eliminating the Jew.

The Branch cannot afford to take such risks.

There really was no choice. It could only be for his own good to get this thing over and done with as quickly and as neatly as possible. In the name of all the understanding we'd built between us.

Summoned two of the men we sometimes use for outside jobs. Both converts from the enemy who know their own past is enough to hang them, so they're prepared to do anything, ask no questions. Only too glad to be alive. Gave them the address in Guguletu. Gave them the time. Eight o'clock on the dot.

Then called Swanie. Told him we'd had a tip-off. Tracked down Landman's comrades, address in Guguletu. Five to eight sharp. Asked him to come and report to me personally afterwards. In my office.

'Cheers, Swanie. Until tonight. Good luck.'

Farewell to my own right hand. A son.

God will have to reward me one day for everything He's asked of me in this life.

Barely an hour later, not five minutes before it was time to leave for that lunch, the phone rang. Judge Jordaan's clerk. Requesting an appointment. Perhaps he'd found out about the enquiries we made. Sweet little skeleton in his cupboard. Showdown looming. Bloody hell. Told the clerk there was no chance before late next week. Should give me enough time to sort things out.

To go from there, in those circumstances, to the house in Newlands for lunch with the commissioner, was one of the hardest things in this hard time. Knew my own future was at stake. And then he served me bloody crayfish of all things. Could see he was noting it against me that the thing remained untouched on my plate. Those small evil beady eyes. Bloody scavenger. But at the same time he could not help but note that Kat Bester sticks to his convictions, would not forsake them merely out of politeness. No doubt he must have respect for it. No two ways about it.

Brought him up to date with everything. Except for the Swanie business, because it was better for him not to know about that. In Swanie's own interest. As for the rest, verse and chapter. 'The girl's own brother is also involved, General. We're keeping him under surveillance day and night. He'll lead us to them. The moment he makes his move we pounce on the whole lot.' And then saw an opening to get in a hint of my own: 'General, there's only one problem. Somebody trying to interfere, making it very difficult for us to act. Blocking us every inch of the way.'

'Who would that be?'

'Judge Jordaan. All because his daughter was involved in it, you see. Now he's trying to interfere with the evidence. Am afraid, if it goes on like this we'll be up against a wall.'

Slight narrowing of the eyes. 'You absolutely sure of that, Bester?'

'Got nothing against the man personally, General. Even have sympathy with him. Can't be easy, his own daughter. But he's a security risk, General. Established that he consorts with a coloured prostitute called Sylvia. Now can you imagine what might happen if he starts sharing confidential information with such a person? Sorry to have to say this, General, but the man is cramping our style. Threatens to stir up trouble because of Blumer's death. And you will appreciate, if he ties our hands like that, we're stumped. Even more so if he starts blabbing to his little maid.'

'Mm.' Silence. Tracking down bits of food with his tongue between his teeth. 'Well, all right then. Looks like we may have a problem there. I'll have a word with the president.' Turning those pale bluebottle eyes back to me: 'On condition you fly up to Kimberley tomorrow and personally take charge of the investigation.'

'Nothing would suit me better, General.'

'And how long do you reckon it'll still be?'

Felt a lot weighing on this question. Knew my own life was now on the block. 'Give us a week, General. No more.'

'How certain are you, Bester?'

'No doubt at all.'

Just as well he couldn't see my heart jumping like a red roman on a hook. Ringing in the ears. But what else could one say?

'All right.' Nodded. Stacked the last few pieces of red shell on his plate, rinsed his fingers in the dish of lemon water, wiped his mouth with a big white serviette. 'One week. But you realise it's now or never. If you cannot show results a week from now I'll have to send down someone else from Pretoria to take over. The president can't be kept waiting any longer. After all, it was aimed at his own life.'

Bloody relieved to have the brandy afterwards. From his lounge windows one has a view of the whole city down to the cranes in the harbour. Big white ship heading for the deep sea. White specks of wind on the water. God, a day to be out there on a boat, away from it all.

Went back to the office. More than enough to catch up with. First called Jansen, the man who took over Swanie's place in Griqualand West. Any news? No, he said, all quiet. The brother still under surveillance all the time. But nothing to report.

Later phoned Anna to tell her not to expect me for supper. But no reply. Carried on working. Phoned Jansen again. Still nothing. Then got stuck in all kinds of business, waiting for the call from Guguletu. Nine o'clock, at last, the phone rang. Black mood by then. Manner of speaking.

'All done, Brigadier.'

'You didn't hurt him unnecessarily?'

'One shot, point-blank.'

'Good.'

Then just sat. One of the toughest days of my life.

Eleven before I reached home. Whole house quiet and deserted. Note from Anna on the pillow. She and Hendrina had left. Sorry, but can't go on like this, needs a life of her own. Hope you'll manage.

Hope you'll manage.

Back in the office at sparrow's fart this morning. Hadn't slept a wink. Started clearing my desk. But slowly, the way one cleans up in a house after a death. As if all my own things had become unfamiliar to me. Drank too much coffee, too sweet. Pain on the heart.

At half-past eight, Jansen on the line.

'Brigadier? I think we've got them.'

'What?'

'Just intercepted a call to the vicarage. Lisa Lombard. She spoke to her brother.'

'What did she say?'

'We're having a bit of a problem, Brigadier. Strange garbled way of talking. Must be in code. But we've got it on tape, we're working on it.'

'If it's code it means the brother is in it too.'

'Sounds like it, Brigadier.'

'Where'd she phone from?'

'Tickey-box somewhere, Brigadier.'

'Don't tell me you let her get away?'

'No, we're right on top of it, Brigadier. Ten minutes after the call Erik Lombard left the vicarage. We have two cars following him. The way I read it he'll be leading us straight to Lisa Lombard and Thomas Landman.'

'Jesus, Jansen.' Difficult to think clearly for a moment. 'The whole caboodle in one swoop?'

'Looks like it, Brigadier.'

'You sent out a warning?'

'To all the towns in the area, Brigadier.'

'Keep on Lombard's tracks, but make sure he doesn't notice anything. And don't lift a finger without me. On my way. That clear?'

'Very clear, Brigadier.'

'Want to be there personally when they're reeled in. This catch is mine.'

Erik Lombard, Lisa Lombard. Thomas Landman. You, above all. At last. For how long have we had this date? And what a price it's cost

552

so far. Lives. People. My own peace of mind, my family, Swanie. But at long last it will all be worth while.

Quick jerk of the line. Right hand drawn in sharply below the left arm. One flick up. Break its neck.

Then the next one. —

Chapter 13

Thomas would look back, much later, to that clear night on the rocky outcrop known as Massouw's Kop behind the hospital in Schweizer-Reneke, in the Western Transvaal (Lichtenburg, from where Lisa was to make that fatal telephone call to her brother in the vicarage, at this moment still lay ahead; as did all that was to flow from it!; and by that time this night might well have gained, through suffering and many-layered darkness, in clarity and definition.

Lisa, in the uncertain flickering of their fire, was consulting, for the last time on that journey, the *I Ching*. The following day the battered black book (the endpaper bearing her name torn out long ago to ensure anonymity) would be left behind, on the front seat of the young farmer's cream-coloured bakkie; discarded afterwards – he, too, had something to hide – in a rubbish bin in the next town. (Had the poor bastard but known!) But on that evening, while Thomas was grilling a few pieces of meat on a rusty old bicycle wheel they'd found beside the road, she was shaking with avid concentration the three coins in her closed hands, spilling them on a carefully flattened square of earth, and constructing the pattern of her hexagram line by line from bottom to top: broken, unbroken, broken, unbroken, unbroken, broken.

K'un / Oppression (Exhaustion)
'Shall I read it to you?'
'Will it be any help?'
Ignoring his scepticism, she skimmed a passage in silence, turned over the page, looked up, then read aloud:
'There is no water in the lake:
The image of EXHAUSTION.
Thus the superior man stakes his life
On following his will.'
He prodded the embers with a stick. 'Doesn't sound too good, does it?'

'It depends on whether you're a superior person or not.'

'*You* are.'

'You want to hear what it means?'

'Why not?' he said. 'At least I'll die with harness on my back.'

Holding the book up against the dull red light from the fading coals, she read in a schoolteacher voice:

"Times of adversity are the reverse of times of success, but they can lead to success if they befall the right man. When a strong man meets with adversity, he remains cheerful despite all danger, and this cheerfulness is the source of later successes; it is that stability which is stronger than fate. He who lets his spirit be broken by exhaustion certainly has no success. But if adversity only bends a man, it creates in him a power to react that is bound in time to manifest itself.'

'Is that it?'

'More or less. But I still have a nine in fifth place.' She turned another page and began to read with a small frown of concentration, then looked up, clearly uncertain of whether to proceed. 'You want to hear?'

'Give me the worst.'

'Nine in the fifth place means:

His nose and feet are cut off.

Oppression at the hands of the man with the purple knee bands.

Joy comes softly.

It furthers one to make offerings and libations.'

'Just watch out for that guy with the purple knee bands. As for the rest –' he poured a few drops of cheap wine from the bottle they'd bought in town just before closing time, after the truck that had been their sanctuary for the past two days had disappeared in the distance '– there's my libation. You'll have to help with the joy that comes softly.'

'You're not taking it seriously.'

'What must happen, must happen,' he said. 'So far it hasn't gone too badly.'

So far, in fact, considering the odds, it had been going amazingly well.

Immediately after that first sight of the police van in front of the vicarage, Thomas had swung round the combi – a purely instinctive action that required no intervention of thinking, feeling, deciding – and just as promptly, just as calmly, Lisa had said, 'Drive round the block. Back to the garage. Right now it's the safest place.'

Once there, back in the dusty garage — a faded smell of oil, cobwebs on the beams overhead, old paint tins on the floor, a small tin with a petrified brush in it on a window sill, a broken ladder leaned against the wall (suddenly they were hyperconscious of every detail) — they were flooded by fear.

'You think your father would have given us away?'

'I honestly don't know. I can't believe it. I don't want to believe it. Maybe the sergeant has just come round to ask him something. But whatever's happened we cannot take any chances.'

'You sure it's safe here?'

'Safer than on the open road. You saw for yourself, no one ever uses the garage any more.'

'We'd better close the doors.'

In the side wall there was another, ordinary, door, not used in years (obstructed by bags of coal, a red plastic bucket, a broken pickaxe), that gave direct access to the backyard, only a few metres from Naomi's room. And it was Naomi Lisa first went to find, even though she had to wait a long time, as the woman had to clean and tidy the whole house before she was free to retire again to her room with several thick slices of bread and apricot jam in a tin plate balanced on a mug of coffee.

She was scared out of her wits when she found Lisa sitting in her room, waiting. But with a quick shake of her head Lisa motioned to her to come in and close the door. They exchanged a few hurried words before Lisa skulked out to call Thomas from the garage. Behind the drawn blue floral curtains in front of the small window they urgently conferred.

The most immediate need was to find out what lay behind the visit of the police who, Naomi reported, had left by now. It meant returning to the big house to sound out the dominee; and that proved difficult. He was busy, he said gruffly; couldn't talk to her now, and anyway it had nothing to do with her. It was the man, the deserter, he wanted caught. Their Lisa would soon be out of his clutches; already the police were making preparations to block all the roads and waylay the combi.

So it was indeed true.

'Naomi, we need your help. You're the only one who can.'

'Yes. But this man —?' Accusing, anxious, perturbed, motherly, the large woman stared at Thomas. 'If it is as the Dominee say then this man he's no good for you.'

'He is my man, Naomi.'

'You take him by the church?'

'I took him with this ring.'

A deep sigh. She laboriously wiped her hands on her apron. 'Then it is all right.'

'Do you understand, Naomi? If they catch him, they'll take me away too. We are together now.'

'I understand. Hau.'

'Will you help us?'

'To do what?'

'We want to hide here in your room for a while.'

Clicking her tongue, like a mother hen, she went out. As if, like so many years ago, this was an act of naughtiness she had to cover up. 'But you must wait. I must first finish the house, I must cook the food.'

'We'll wait.' In a cajoling voice: 'Naomi, I left a book in my room. A black one. Do you think you can find it for me? I don't want other people to see it.'

With an amused sniff the heavy woman lumbered back to the house; only much later did they discover that she hadn't eaten her breakfast.

'What now?' asked Lisa after Naomi had closed the door behind her.

'I'll have to phone Cape Town. My people must be alerted.'

'But what can *they* do?'

'They must be told. The whole scenario has changed. I'll have to change names too.'

'Oh Jesus, not again?!'

'I'm afraid so. Your father knows about "Louis". So the next one is "Leon". Okay?' He smiled. 'You can still be Marina, because no one has heard it yet.'

Absently she tried out the name, 'Leon.' Then sighed and shook her head, a look of desolation in her eyes. 'That *he* should have done a thing like this!'

'Right now it's of little importance who did it. All that matters is that they know. Not only that we're here, but that I'm not on my own. That we're together.'

'What are we going to *do* – Leon?'

There was a weary but resolute look about his mouth. 'Listen, my love. The only way of getting out of here is for me to go it alone. You can stay here. They'll ask you a few questions and let you go. They have nothing against you. You can tell them anything. That

I abducted you. Threatened you. Cheated you. Lay it on as thick as you can. This is the time to save your own skin.'

Very pale, a tone of bitter accusation in her voice, she asked, 'Why do you think we're here together?'

'Because you let yourself in for something, but you couldn't possibly have foreseen the consequences.'

'Not at the time, perhaps,' she said. 'But now I can.' With a wry smile he might interpret as mockery, 'Because now I'm wearing this ring.'

'What's that got to do with it?'

Suddenly she was terribly serious: 'Everything, dammit!' She came to stand in front of him. 'I love you. Can you get that into your fucking head?'

'But for God's sake, don't you realise –'

'All I realise is that I won't throw you to the dogs. Don't waste time trying to tell me I'm stupid, I've got to have my head read. I know it already. But I'm still staying with you.' For the first time her voice faltered. In her strange smoky eyes a darkness within the agate. 'I'll leave you only if you tell me to. If I'm a stumbling block to you.'

He shook his head very slowly.

'I am, aren't I?' she said. 'You can move much faster without me. By tonight you can be over the border.'

'No. There are roadblocks. Naomi said so.'

'But they're expecting a couple. A man and a woman in a combi. If you disguise yourself and travel on your own you *will* be safe.'

He took a long time to reflect. 'Everything depends on what the people in Cape Town have to say.'

'I know. But all I want to hear from your own mouth is whether *you* want me with you or not. If it depended on you alone.'

'If it depended on me, yes, I want you with me. But only if *you* won't be –'

She pressed her finger against his mouth.

Perhaps she drew her determination from Naomi's room, which had become some kind of subconscious to which all the repressed objects of an earlier existence had been relegated; and back here, at home among so many persistent tokens from her own past, she was at her most intractable. And practical.

'We have work to do. Our appearances, first of all. Here, take this.' She took a pair of large scarred dressmaker's scissors from the dresser – it had once belonged to her mother's sewing box –

and knelt in front of him, her back to him. 'You can start by cutting off my hair.'

'There must be another solution. You can put on one of the wigs Jimmy brought.'

'My hair is too thick.'

'It's a crime.' That wonderful cascade of smooth black hair, the grace with which it fell beside her narrow face when she moved.

'Crime no longer scares me.'

'But your hair!'

'Now you sound just like Papa. A woman's honour and all that jazz. But my worth is no longer far above rubies. So cut. Cut short.'

He could have wept when he saw the dark mass fall from her shoulders. She was leaning forward, like a condemned woman from the remote past, an Anne Boleyn, a Charlotte Corday, he thought, awaiting the executioner's blade; and agitated, moved, he stared at the vulnerability of her now wholly exposed neck, like the thin pale stem of a drooping flower too heavy for it. The result was jagged; the blunt scissors could no longer do a proper job. Her ears seemed more prominent than before.

'Shame,' she said, pulling a face at herself in the broken mirror of the narrow wardrobe, 'I look like those wartime photos of people in the ghetto of Warsaw.'

'I should have taken a photograph of you the way you were.'

'You'll just have to learn to live with it.' Sardonic: 'You're not an oil-painting either. We'll have to work on you. That beard must go.'

While Lisa was kneeling to gather the fallen hair from the frayed carpet – momentarily held back by this close-up of the carpet's faded pattern, and the sudden recollection of children's games played on it, with Erik, years ago; of nights surreptitiously spent in front of the fire with him, all gone, irrevocable – and folding it into a sheet of newsprint, Thomas scurried back to the garage, burrowed in the half-darkness of the combi, and returned with one of the cardboard boxes into which he'd packed the few wigs, a selection of spectacles, the make-up and some of the clothes Rashid had brought from the Cape a week ago. Then he went back for more of their possessions while through the window Lisa kept an eye on the backyard.

He shaved in cold water at the small basin in the corner. Then they changed into other clothes and started experimenting. Unsettling: her narrow face with the prominent black eyebrows in a red wig

('With this thing I can make a catch on any street corner in Hillbrow, don't you think?') followed by something more demure and straight. A scarf tied over it. A pair of thick-rimmed glasses. With a shapeless housewifely dress. He was more difficult to camouflage, he'd been through so many disguises already. Still, a brown wig parted severely in the middle, new glasses, a brown suit with a thin stripe was enough to send her into stitches.

It was an hour or more before Naomi came back, with the book she'd retrieved; and with alarming news about a carload of male visitors who had just arrived at the vicarage.

No, she hadn't inspected them closely enough to give any detailed description. Only one man, the big boss, she could describe with some accuracy: large, heavily built, with a moustache and a pipe. 'He looks like a good baas.'

Thomas turned pale; Lisa noticed it immediately.

'You know him?'

'If this is the man I think it is, I've had some dealings with him before. Last time I saw him was at the funeral service in Cape Town. He looked me right in the eyes. Brigadier Bester. He's a hunter. Never loses a track.'

(Years ago, when they'd detained him, after the first night with Nina, she'd asked her father to intercede and Bester had let him go: he'd never forgotten those parting words: 'We'll meet again. Will you remember that? We two will meet again. It's a date.')

'We must get away from here immediately.'

'You can't go now,' said Naomi. 'I was listening in the passage. They looking for you everywhere.'

'But they'll be looking far away,' Thomas reminded her. 'Remember, they think we left this place hours ago.'

'You think we can take the combi? If we change the plates?'

'Not with all those roadblocks.'

'What then?'

'Hitchhike.'

'Or stay here?' she suggested, dubious.

'No. Even if we may be safe here today, if they haven't found us by tomorrow they'll come back and start from square one.' He looked at Naomi. 'They'll probably come to talk to you too. They'll ask you if you saw us.'

'I see nothing.'

'Naomi?' Lisa took one of the woman's hands in both of hers. 'We don't want to cause you trouble.'

'Come on, *tloha*,' said the woman. 'You my child. Children *are* trouble. Always they are trouble. But you my child.'

'You promise you'll be careful?'

'It's you who must be careful.'

'One day we'll pay you back.'

'*Tlohela kwana*,' she said in mock anger.

At that moment, right outside the door, the dominee's voice called, 'Naomi!'

They froze in fear.

'Naomi! Where are you?'

In an astonishingly steady voice the woman answered, 'I'm here, Baas Dominee.'

'We want some tea.'

'I'm coming, Baas Dominee.'

She turned to the door; they hid behind it. As she touched the handle Lisa caught her by the arm.

'We'll stay here until they are gone,' she whispered. 'Will you come back as soon as you can and tell us?'

Naomi went out, leaving behind the clean Sunlight soap smell of her clothes.

Minutes later, after Lisa had cautiously surveyed the yard through a chink in the blue curtains, Thomas scurried out to the back gate, and made a wide loop through back streets to the business centre of the village: first to the hotel, to make a note of the number of the call-box in the passage; then to the post office to telephone. Quite a rigmarole: mentioning the names of four towns in what, to an outsider, would sound like an innocuous conversation, but from which Rashid would deduce that they were in the third; instructing Rashid to telephone back 'any time tomorrow', meaning as soon as possible; transmitting the telephone number of the call-box in code. Then returning to the hotel; waiting. Knowing that Rashid would first have to confer with Justin before they could return the call from another phone. Now, more than ever, no precaution was too elaborate.

An hour. Then Justin's voice. As unperturbed as if he were discussing the weather, the calm only years of practice can bring. Behind the small-talk, the codes, the circumlocutions, the core of their conversation was brief. Was the girl still with him? Wasn't it wise at this stage to break up? (No, said Thomas. He'd considered it, but it was in everybody's interest that they continue together. If they caught her now her life was in danger. Not because she knew too much, but because they *thought* she did.) Well, all right then, if it must. But they should at least consider travelling by separate routes if necessary. No, not back to the Cape; at this stage it was better to move on. Here's a number in Johannesburg, in case of emergency. Try to keep in touch. Warn us before you try to cross the border, the Organisation will try to provide cover. From both sides. Otherwise all was well. Except – (Except?) Well, your father died last night.

In the heart of the conversation, hidden among the many cryptic references, there were these few questions and answers, naked and direct, words exchanged between father and son, a hand reaching out to touch his own:

'You okay?'

'Yes, I'm all right.'

'Good. You ready for action?'

'I am.'

'We're counting on you. We're proud of you.'

But his father was dead. Another grave along the way. And yet, this time, through the temporary inability of the nerves to grasp or to react, there was almost relief. Not only because in a way he'd already taken his leave, but because it seemed, in the circumstances, merciful. He felt, inexplicably, lightheaded.

But there was a question – *Who next?* – which he could not repress, even if he could not bring himself to share it with Lisa when, after following the same detour, he returned to Naomi's room to give her a summary of his conversation with Justin. Until the late afternoon – how fast the days were shrinking now; in a mere two weeks it would be the winter solstice – they remained in the room, waiting for Naomi to return and confirm that the visitors had gone. By that time they'd already packed everything they would need for the road, each taking only a plastic bag of bare necessities: a change of clothing, an additional disguise, a few packets and tins of food, Lisa's *I Ching*.

Naomi was in tears when they left. 'Look after yourself, Lisa. You will write to me?'

'I will. Stay well, Naomi.'

'Go well. I shall cry for you in the night.' In concern and admonition she turned to Thomas. 'And you look after her.'

Without attracting any attention they reached, on the fringe of the village, the road they'd followed that morning, before the tortoise had changed the course of their story. And they were remarkably fortunate: not even twenty minutes after they'd taken up position at the side of the road an enormous seven-ton truck stopped beside them. The driver, in white dust-coat and wearing a cap and sunglasses, hardly spared them a glance; it was his passenger who jovially waved at them to approach, a great, bearded, larger than life-sized man clutching a beer bottle in a hand the size of a pickled ham.

So began the strangest days they were to experience on a journey which had long ceased to be merely a trek through a landscape, a country, geographical space, even history.

Vleis Wagenaar was as solid as his name ('Vleis' in Afrikaans means 'Flesh'), well over two metres tall, they discovered at the first outspan as he unwound himself segment by segment from the cabin of the truck, and considerably wider; a figure from prehistory (*there were giants in the earth in those days*) with bulging round eyes and a formidable nose visible through wild black hair and beard that here and there, like hoar-frost, began to show up grey; like an ancestral Diederik Landman suddenly risen from the dead – and who, accompanied by his nervous, quick little wisp of a 'coloured' driver, was travelling like some feudal warlord with his court jester. He, was, they soon learned, a farmer from the West Coast, from near Doringbaai.

'So where are you on your way to?' he asked once they were all stacked on the front seat in the cabin, he with a lukewarm beer in the hand from a crate wedged between his two coffin-sized feet ensconced in boots of red kudu leather.

'Johannesburg,' said Thomas. Explaining, as he and Lisa had agreed, that he'd lost his job as an insurance salesman in Upington, which had hit them particularly hard as they'd been married for only three months; and that they were now planning to move in with his brother in Booysens until he'd found something new.

'You must be blarry hopeless to get yourself fired?' asked the big man, his voice sounding like an underground rock-fall through the earth-layers of his body.

'It's the drought, Oom. The farmers can't pay their debts, now everybody who's not indispensable gets sacked.'

'Depends on yourself, man. Take me, for example. You might say I started with bugger-all, and here I'm on my feet today, a made man.' His grandfather had been a *bywoner*, his father a labourer at the salt-works near Kleinzee. 'Hard men. Took a battle just to survive. That part of the world was like a kind of Wild West in those days.' He suddenly looked down at Lisa next to him. 'What about you, my girlie? What are *you* going to do in Johannesburg?'

If she was annoyed by the 'girlie', she kept it to herself. 'I don't know yet, Oom. I'll also try to find a job.'

'Shame.'

That had been her own reaction when she'd first looked at her severely plain reflection in Naomi's broken mirror; but coming from a stranger it was like a slap in the face. At the same time there was so much genuine sympathy in the way he looked at her that she could not help laughing.

And that clearly stole the heart of the Old Testament Nimrod. Placing an enormous paw on her shoulder, which he tentatively pressed until the bone was nearly crushed, he said, 'You'll be okay, my girlie. If a man can still laugh he'll land on his feet all right.' He let his eyes wander over her, from head to toe, skipping nothing, like a farmer who, at an auction, sees some obscure promise in a young heifer, poor thing, whom no one else is interested in. 'You should come to spend some time on my farm, man. We'll soon fatten you up.'

'And where are you heading for, Oom?' asked Thomas, partly flattered, partly offended by the massive man's appraisal of Lisa.

'I'm on a hunting trip.'

'Yes, but –'

'When I'm on a hunting trip I'm not on my way anywhere. I start at home and I end at home. In between anything may happen.'

He was, they soon discovered, in the process of describing a wide crescent through the interior – the North-west, Griqualand West, the Orange Free State – from one hunting spot he'd selected over the years to the next; from one good friend to the next. His modus operandi became clearer when, half an hour or so out of town, they turned from the main road into a dusty corrugated farm road consisting of two sandy tracks and a central ridge so tall that from time to time, as they rumbled and swayed along, it struck the bottom of the Bedford like the waves of a dangerous swell; a few kilometres on, between nothing and nowhere, he ordered his abject chauffeur to stop at a concertina gate, told Thomas to open it, and selected a place some distance on (Thomas had to jog the few hundred metres, as their host didn't bother to pick him up again), in a sheltered spot surrounded by blackthorn bushes which he evidently knew from previous visits. There his factotum, introduced to them only as Handyman – a sadly comical figure in his white dust-coat, with

564

the hint of a hump between his spindly shoulders, bandy legs, his age quite undeterminable (anything between eighteen and possibly forty), his wizened monkey-face permanently contorted in a painful grimace, always at hand for whatever might be required of him, from driving the truck to cooking food to, literally, turning somersaults at the fireside – scurried round to the back of the vast truck, opened a metal door, lowered a stepladder, and revealed to them an unexpected interior: the entire back of the truck had been transformed into a lounge, with a Chesterfield set bolted to the floor, a drinks cabinet containing an array of bottles ingeniously slotted into frames; the floor covered with an old Bokhara and a variety of animal skins; and the walls lined with large built-in deep-freezes, all of them filled to capacity, Vleis Wagenaar showed them with a proprietorial gesture, with frozen crayfish.

'From my factory,' he explained. 'The farmers here in the interior never get to see the stuff. So I bring them crayfish; and all along the way, as I visit one old friend after the other, I shoot whatever I get in my sights, and I take home springbok, blesbok, hartebeest, oryx, in exchange for crayfish. When all the deep-freezes are filled with game I turn back. Same story every year, soon's the hunt opens. So one hand washes the other. Right, what are you chaps drinking?'

'What do you have?'

'Stupid question. Say what you want, I got it.'

Playing it safe, Lisa asked for white wine, Thomas for red; Vleis Wagenaar's choice was whisky. Handyman served them on the Chesterfield suite – the hitchhikers on chairs, the farmer on the sofa which he filled from side to side – and it wasn't a glass for each as they might reasonably have expected: beside Lisa's glass, in an ice bucket, a full bottle of L'Ormarins was thrust; Thomas was given his own bottle of Nederburg, Vleis a bottle of Johnnie Walker (which had to be replaced halfway through the evening).

'It's *maar* primitive,' Vleis said after the first generous tasting as he refilled his tumbler. 'You should see the bar in my house. Big enough for a hotel.' From time to time he turned a bulging eye in their direction and asked, 'Ag no, man, why aren't you guys drinking? Come on, there's lots more where this comes from. How's it, my girlie? Don't let the worries get you down, you'll find a job all right. And if you don't, then just phone me. I'll organise something. I have buddies all over the place.'

It was to one of these hearty exhortations that she responded

565

impulsively, 'You must forgive me, Oom, but I'm not allowed to drink much in my state.'

'And what kind of shit state might that be?'

'I'm pregnant, Oom,' she said candidly.

Thomas was the one who choked in his drink. Vleis Wagenaar merely raised his two mighty eyebrows, gave her the once-over of an expert in such matters, and said, 'Why, there's no sign of a bulge yet.'

'It's too early, Oom. But the doctor told me to be careful.'

'But you're a mere child, man.' He looked at Thomas, 'And you're in too much of a hurry, I think.' His loud bellow. 'Well, cheers.' He drained the tumbler in one draught and refilled it promptly. 'Good for you. That's how I caught my wife too, years ago, when her old man didn't want to say yes. Then we left him no choice. He took me in, allowed me to run the farm for a share of the harvest. Ten years later I bought him out. Today Vleis Wagenaar is his own man.'

Whereupon he heaved his massive body from the sofa to shout at Handyman to blarry well get on with the fire and the food outside.

'I'll go and give him a hand,' offered Thomas.

'Stay where you are. You'll just be in his way.'

After an outrageous meal – grilled crayfish, pot-roasted leg of springbok – Vleis wiped some of the remains of his food from his beard and moustache with a swipe of his backhand, and said, 'Handyman, where's your music?'

'Yessuh.' More than that, during the few days they spent together, they hardly ever heard him say. From the pocket of his dust-coat he brought a mouth-organ, stuck it to his lips and plunged into music without warning or ceremony. Jolly tunes with the inevitable mournful undertone of the instrument, embroidered with virtuoso cadenzas that amazed the newcomers in his audience. But Vleis Wagenaar soon became bored. 'Ag man, stuff that thing up your arse,' he told Handyman. And in the middle of a melancholy phrase the musician stopped playing, the grimace unchanged like a mask on his puny face.

Thomas: 'But it's beautiful, Oom. The man's an artist.'

'Not if you hear it every day.' Half-irritated, half-bemused he looked at them, broke up a resounding wind, and asked, 'Well? What can *you* do to entertain me? The night's still young.' Then changed his mind and cast an anxious glance at Lisa: 'Or should you be going to bed?'

'No, I'm all right, Oom.' With a hint of provocation she said, 'Pity I didn't bring my guitar.'

'You play?'

'Yes, I do.'

'Any good?'

'I don't know.'

'I want to know if you play well or not. Because if you don't it isn't worth while.'

She gave him a candid look. 'I play well enough. But there's no guitar here.'

Without any hesitation the titan lumbered to the back door of the truck. 'Handyman! Guitar!' And then turned back to them. 'If you don't mind waiting outside here by the fire? So Handyman can go and get you one.'

Before they properly knew what was happening, all three of them, with their bottles and glasses, were transferred to the circle of light round the fire which Handyman had blown up into a spectacular conflagration; and without further ado he wriggled his spare body into the space behind the steering-wheel, and the monstrous truck rumbled off into the night. A great silence descended on the black expanse of veld where they were left behind.

'But Oom –' Lisa tried to find a comfortable position among the mound of cushions the man had had provided for her. 'At this time of the night –?'

'So what? Handyman knows all about guitars. He's been on the road with me for donkey's years.'

The vast night expanded about them, endless, in all directions.

'Good thing you're here to keep me company,' the big man said behind them, from just beyond the edge of the light where he'd positioned himself unceremoniously to urinate. 'Otherwise it gets unbearably lonesome. Like last Sunday. Hell! I gave Handyman the day off, so it was just me. I tried to phone, on Sundays I always phone my friends everywhere in the world, no matter where they are, Cape Town, Johannesburg, Windhoek, London, Tokyo, Rio, you name it. But then the blarry phone conked in. Can you believe it? After what I paid for it. Anyway, so there I was on the blarry empty plains and all one could do was drinking and longing for company. I tell you, on a day like that one starts missing people you haven't even met.' He came back into the light, still tugging at his zip. 'No, shit, a man wasn't meant to be alone.' Approving: 'You can thank your lucky stars the two of you are together.'

'You always travel on your own?' asked Lisa.

'I got Handyman. And I got friends in every town.'

'Not tonight.'

'Why the hell do you think I picked you up?'

Embarrassed, she shifted her position. 'But what about your wife and children?'

'Baby's got her tea-parties. And there's no kids.'

Thomas looked quizzically at him. 'But I thought you said when you first got married –'

Vleis Wagenaar took a gulp straight from the bottle. 'That was a long time ago.' Stared into the livid coals. Then: 'No man, he died. When he was four. Fell off a blarry horse. And after that the wife stayed dry.'

Before she could check herself Lisa asked, 'But what does a child of four do on horseback?'

From opposite the fire the ferocious eyes just glared at her. She looked down.

'You said that was long ago?' asked Thomas.

'So nowadays there's only the hunting trips,' said Vleis Wagenaar, addressing her, not him. 'Flog myself all year round. On the farms. In town. America. Japan. Taiwan. Europe. Got business everywhere.' (Seven farms between the Cedarberg and the sea, they learned in due course – wheat, fruit, tea, sheep, even wine – not to mention his own crayfish factory, racehorses, a copper mine near O'Kiep, and a vast assortment of unspecified 'business concerns' in Cape Town, Johannesburg and various cities abroad.) 'But when the hunt opens I take off my month.' Another long, pensive swallow, this time from his glass. 'Only thing is the hunting fields get smaller every year. More and more farmers going in for conservation. That kind of thing. Good in a way, I suppose. But what is left for a man like me? In the old days the world was still open, a wild place. When my father was young. My grandfather.' The suppressed rumble of a laugh. 'Knew only two languages, those two. Fist and gun. That's the way we Boers are. What you can't set right through prayer you shoot. You know, by the time my father and my grandfather died each of them had a corpse round his neck. In fact, my father had two.'

Thomas, not without provocation, 'What about you, Oom?'

Below the savage brows the two round eyes were invisible. Only a dull glow, like the coals. Curiously bashful the man mumbled in his beard. 'It's not all that difficult to kill a man.' Then cleaned his throat and added, 'But what will the two of you understand about such things? You said you sold insurance?' Proceeding without allowing Thomas a chance to respond, 'That's no work for a man. As bad as the civil service. No my boy, now's your chance. Find something where you can be your own boss. Where you know you're alive. *Do* something, I tell you. Before you know where you are your arse is the only part of your body that's known some life.'

In this manner he rambled on until, hours later, they heard the low roar of the truck approaching in the distance. Half-sceptical, Thomas and Lisa sat waiting. To their amazement Handyman did produce a guitar as he jumped from the cabin, a brand-new instrument, the price tag still on it.

Vleis Wagenaar put the guitar on his knee, tested the strings with fingers as stout as sausages, then held it out to Lisa. 'Let's have it.'

She tried a few chords, tuned the strings, improvised reflectively for a while, then moved into a folk tune. After that she played something faster, more energetic; and almost as if it was a signal he'd been waiting for their big host said:

'Handyman, dance!'

There was something unearthly about the spectacle, something grotesque: the man squatting on his haunches opposite the fire like a louring mountain, Lisa playing, her straight lifeless hair covering her cheek like the broken wing of a bird; the little man in the white dust coat dancing on his spindly legs, the grimace never leaving his face although he clearly was deadly serious, as if his life depended on it (and perhaps it did); like a stick-insect half crushed by a heel but still continuing to squirm.

The only way to set him free was to return to slower, more melancholy music; with a touch of perversity, perhaps, Lisa stroked her long fingers across the strings and hummed in hoarse accompaniment, more for herself than for them:

> 'Siembamba, mama's little baby,
> Siembamba, mama's little baby,
> Wring his neck and throw him in the ditch,
> Step on his head and he'll be dead —'

Vleis Wagenaar soon became restless, rose with a groan either of annoyance or exertion, ambled aimlessly in a wide circle around the fire, and then came to a standstill beside her. 'Ag no, man, that's too blarry sad. Give us something livelier so Handyman can dance.'

As if prepared for it, Lisa strummed a few opening bars that made

569

Thomas glance up in surprise. It was a freedom song from the Struggle. She began to hum again in her throaty sandpaper voice. And in spite of himself he joined in after the first few bars:

> 'Mandela sereletsa
> Mandela sereletsa
> Mandela sereletsa
> Sereletsa sechaba sa hesu
> Marumo o refa
> I sale retlabanela
> Tlabanela sechaba sa hesu –'

The man mountain stood listening, his head turned to one side, evidently not sure of how to react; but the most noticeable reaction came from Handyman, who perched upright like a meerkat beside the fire where he was making coffee: for the first time his blank eyes were shining, and the perfunctory grimace widened into an open-mouthed smile – except when he discovered his master's round eyes on him and quickly froze; but it lasted for a new notes only, then the laugh broke out again.

'Where did you learn this thing?' Vleis Wagenaar's thunderous voice boomed over the fire as Lisa rounded off the song with a few improvised chords.

'Just sort of picked it up.'

'It's hot stuff. You know more songs like it?'

She shrugged her angular shoulders – that gawkiness again, which Thomas had begun to find so enthralling – went through a series of modulations, then struck up a new melody:

> 'Ityala labo
> Ityala labo linzima
> Ityala labo linzima
> Bazoyitheth' inyani ngesibhamu
> Bathumeleni
> Bathumelenu ngo Mkhonto
> Bazoyitheth' inyani ngesibhamu –'

Halfway through, Handyman broke into dance again, this time unbidden, and now it was no clowning, prancing, exaggerated marionette performance as before, but a toyi-toyi; and Vleis Wagenaar himself joined in, shuffling after Handyman with his mountainous body, not very skilfully, but with an enthusiasm, an exuberance that left them speechless; and he marked the beat, as he swayed

570

and shuffled, with a clapping of hands, erupting from time to time in the kind of yodelling shout one would expect at a barn dance.

Lisa worked through her whole repertory of freedom songs – not very extensive – while Vleis Wagenaar became more and more carried away by his own dancing, until he was heaving and gasping like a bellows, his whole massive face streaming with sweat: if she didn't stop now, she decided, the man might have a heart attack.

But he begged and shouted for more: 'No, no, more, more! Hell, my girlie, you sing like a true-blue black *meid*. You got it, man! Right on, you're a house on fire!' In his enthusiasm, underestimating his strength, he struck her with a huge open hand between the shoulder-blades, a blow that sent her staggering forward, sprawling across the guitar on all fours. For a moment her head was reeling.

But Vleis Wagenaar had had an even greater fright than she. Before Thomas could react the huge farmer was already on his knees beside her. 'Oh my God, my girlie, oh my God, man, did I hurt you? Talk to me, man. Jesus, are you all right? Handyman, where's the blarry brandy?'

But it wasn't necessary. Lisa was already on her feet again, half-collapsed with hysterical laughter; and in a mixture of relief and ecstasy Vleis Wagenaar grabbed the guitar and started swinging it round his head like an Olympic hammer-thrower, and hurled it into the night, high above the rain of sparks from the fire. Invisible, immeasurably far away, it hit the rocky ground with a clanging and twanging of breaking strings and splintering wood.

A deathly silence descended.

From Handyman only a sigh of lament: 'Oh my baas –!'

'Ag sharrap!' The big man laughed. 'Tomorrow we'll buy another. Now it's time for bed.'

Vleis Wagenaar was adamant that his guests sleep inside the truck, on the sofa which folded out into a king-sized double bed. He and Handyman would bed down beside the fire – waving aside their protests with an expansive gesture of one great hand.

It was after midnight when Thomas looked out from the truck door for the last time – the farmer was lying like a speed hump on the bare earth that shuddered lightly under his snoring; close to the fire Handyman still sat up straight like a praying mantis: perhaps that was his sleeping posture – and returned to the bed where Lisa already lay hunched up under the blankets. For a while they did not speak, still somewhat dazed by the outlandish evening; but slowly it was pulled from their grip like a too-heavy blanket; and they were left alone again, feeling more naked than before.

After a while Thomas shook his head. 'You ever had a night like this before?'

'Never.' She giggled.

He also began to laugh. 'When he started dancing –'

'Without a clue of what we were singing!'

'But Handyman knew.'

Their laughter subsided.

In the silence that ensued he said, 'It was like a concert. Except it *wasn't* a concert. It's his way of life. If this were the Old Testament I'm sure God would have sent fire and brimstone from heaven to consume him from the face of the earth.'

'He's genuinely devoted to Handyman.'

'How can you say that?'

'I watched him. I thought it was disgusting, the way he treated him. And yet there was something touching about it too.'

'You have too much compassion in you. You forgive too easily.'

'Don't say that.' She sounded angry. 'I've never had *enough* compassion with others.'

'You don't know yourself very well.'

'What about you?'

He didn't answer. Softly, in sudden awe, he placed his hand, palm down, on her flat smooth stomach and asked, 'You're not really pregnant, are you?'

'No, of course not.' She giggled again, but this time it ebbed away soon. After another long silence she asked, 'Would it have made you happy?'

– Suddenly the full violence of my last night with Nina, when she cried in such desperate passion, 'I want your child. Dammit, Thomas, I want to take *something* of you with me.'

She wanted to take it abroad with her. Expecting me to join her there; but needing the reassurance of a child in case I wouldn't make it. She couldn't care less about herself. Neither of us even considered the possibility that *she* might not get through. Since how far back has it been 'my' bomb? That day in Lusaka, the sweaty man reading out the names in front of the undertaker's building opposite the market where life flowed on as if nothing unusual had happened. And then the weeks after that – all my plans changed, the whole course of my life redrawn – in the outskirts of Luanda: the rambling house hidden among trees, now the guerrilla quarters

572

for those, like myself, recruited for clandestine crash-programmes, far away from the ordinary training camps in the bush. Neither the other recruits nor, above all, the ubiquitous police infiltrators may find out about us: one glimpse, and we've had it. We: teachers, lecturers, engineers, doctors, 'ordinary citizens' whom no one will suspect. For me, with my army training, most of it is old hat, a refresher course. And God, I have such burning impatience in me, I want to get it over, I want to go back to South Africa and plant my bomb, to avenge what happened to Sipho and Noni and Govan. This is, by far, the most difficult lesson of all to learn: patience. This, and the need to rid myself of anger. Over and over, day and night, under the eyes of a young Mandela watching us from posters on the walls: No, no, no, get rid of your anger, an angry man is a bad revolutionary. Patience, patience, patience. Use your head, man, not your heart or your guts. If there's anything you owe to Sipho it's this: not to fuck up everything just because you bear a grudge in your heart. And afterwards the same drill from Justin. 'Get the anger out of your system, Thomas. Cool it, cool it. It doesn't work. In the beginning, when my own heart was still bleeding for my child I was useless. I first had to learn to be quiet inside. Calm down. Even if it takes years. Because this isn't *your* fight, Thomas. It is the people's fight. It's *our* fight. And if you throw yourself into action with an angry heart it's other people's lives you're sacrificing, not your own. There's always other people to consider, Thomas. Think, man. Think. Use your head.' 'All right then. All right. But it's still my bomb. I promise you I'll keep a cool head. As long as you let me do it.' And then it *is* someone else's life that's sacrificed. Nina's. And others' too. Those who just happen to 'get in the way'. And Christine, and David. And now, Dad. This isn't the end yet, the stream flows on: it began before me, it will continue after me, blood, blood. Always others. Think, Thomas think. And now you. Lisa. You who suddenly made my heart jump when you said, 'I'm pregnant.' –

'Thomas? Are you listening to me?'

– A child. A woman. A small suburban house. All the things that horrified Nina. Why all of a sudden this desire for everything that appears so ordinary and normal, even bourgeois? Or *is* this what it is about, after everything else has been accounted for? Not heroism, or sacrifice, not a struggle aimed at an end which justifies all means, but only what is insignificant and human and warm? What Sipho and Noni also wished for, and Ntsiki, and Grandpa Khaya Ntshenge,

573

and Henry. Justin. Even the angry Rashid. At the end of it all: just the need to live a human life. This is what everything else is subordinate to. Including my own life, if necessary. It is good to be reminded of it. One *is* never alone. —

2

— Man, I'd barely set foot in my house again when the news struck me. Full-blast. The whole front page of the paper, photos, the works. No doubt at all. Those were the two kids that spent three days in the truck with me. My first thought was, ag shame, I should *maar* have taken them through to Johburg, you know, then no one would have got them. But of course they didn't even go to Johburg after all. Just a tall story they told me. But never mind, hell, I could have taken them to the border. Damn sure I would have. Never said no to a bit of sports. And there's hunting galore in Botswana. Hell, I could have driven them all the way up to the Okavango. If only they told me. Then no one would have got hurt, man.

But I suppose they were careful. I mean, they didn't know me, did they, couldn't take chances. Fuck, it's a sad thing if you're on the run like that, no one to trust, everybody against you. Just about bloody *everybody*. Reading the newspapers one gets the idea there's never been two blarry crooks as bad as them. But you ask me, I know better. I mean, look at my own father, or my grandfather. If you want to be technical about it you can call them murderers too. (Except I'll kill the bastard who tries to say that to my face. Vleis Wagenaar doesn't take shit from nobody.) But good decent men to the bone. Their only sin was being poor. And you can't blame no one for that. Straight up to heaven I'm sure they both went.

Now it's up to me. It's a self-made man I am. With a little shove from Baby.

First time I set eyes on her, and I saw this out straight, no bones about it, I mean, she knows it too, the first time I saw her it was her old man I first thought of, not her. Because she wasn't all that much to look at, but he was rich as fucking hell. So I gave her one look and I knew this was my chance. Soon saw the only way to get past her grumpy old man was to get her up the pole. After that the road was open. Even so I was too impatient to sit it out. Worked my hands to the bone for her old man, but kept my eyes open too. And then I got a break with the diamonds, up at Port Nolloth. Bursting at the seams with the money I made there. Until I got the tip-off, just in time, I tell you. The man I worked with sank without a bubble. Got caught with a whole tobacco pouch full of stones.

Never looked back. And here I am, me and Handyman, my two hands, my eyes, my everything. He took a liking to that Landman kid. The girlie too. Saw it right away. They were always there when he had to make the fire or whatever. Hell, that first night was quite something. That singing and dancing. They kind of clicked. And those songs, hell, I liked them, man. Asked Handyman afterwards where the songs come from. He said he wasn't sure, must be from the Cape townships. Don't bullshit me, I told him, the people there don't speak those languages, Xhosa or whatever, but he just shrugged his crooked shoulders. Poor little chap, having to go through the world with a body like that. Could have become a learned man, given the chance. A great reader of books as it is. Every free hour he has his nose is buried in a book. On this trip too. Caught him several times talking to Landman about this book or the other.

Not that I knew then the man's name was Landman. Can't even remember what name he gave. The girlie called him Leon. She, I remember, was Marina. Talked quite a lot, she and I. Got rather fond of her, matter of fact. Only too pale to my liking. And much too thin. And expecting a baby too, at least that's what she said. But she's a spunky one. More than meets the eye. That I discovered the very first night. The way she played the guitar. And that voice. Kind of hoarse, unusual, makes a man sit up and notice, in spite of her orphan-girl looks. Landman must be on to something special there. Imagine the two of them taking me for a ride like that. Pretended he'd lost his job in Upington, on their way to his brother in Johburg. And all the while I thought he was just a spineless kid, a drifter. Felt like taking him by the shoulders and giving him a good shake-up, Come on, man, you only live once, get up and grab it, *do* something. While actually he had it in him to plant a bomb, blow up people, nearly a bull's-eye on the president. Look, I'm not in favour of that kind of thing. It was a shit thing to do. But I mean, hell, he had guts. For my part he could have blown up the whole government. Corrupt lot, taxing us to death. No, if it had worked out right I'd have said bravo.

But this, of course, is where the difference comes in. There are those who win and those who lose. And Vleis Wagenaar doesn't back a loser.

Question is: *Was* Thomas Landman a loser?

And she, the girlie with him, supposedly Marina, but now it seems she's a dominee's daughter, Lisa Lombard, ordinary decent people: was *she* a loser?

Makes a man think.

Not very sociable, mostly kept to themselves, thinking back now. Things always look different afterwards. Clearer, somehow.

The sports we had that first night in the veld, Balie de Wet's farm, just after Schmidtsdrift. Went on so late they both overslept the next morning. Handyman and I up and about since long before sunrise. But I didn't want to disturb them, poor kids must be tired, I thought, and anyway, if he's like me he might like a bit of one-two in the morning, what with her already swollen with love.

Stopped at Peet Coetzee's place near Warrenton that afternoon. Now that was heavy stuff. Because I already phoned him from Delportshoop to warn him I was on my way; and by the time we pulled in under the pepper-trees in the front yard the whole place was covered with Mercs and BMWs, looked like a church bazaar. Those farmers flourish on the Land Bank. Peet is pals with the minister, so he always gets his tips straight from the horse's mouth, the kind of man I like.

Hunted till sundown. Landman didn't go out with us. He sort of shyly greeted the men, and then disappeared back into the truck. I took one of my extra rifles, a blarry nice Sauer & Son, two-seventy, and said, Come on, you're coming with us, I want to see what stuff you're made of.

But he disappointed me. Gave the thing back to me, mumbling something about Marina not feeling well and he had to keep an eye on her. Quite touching, I suppose, but a man can go too far, you can't hang on to her panties all the time. Probably was exactly what the little bastard had in mind anyway, a nice leisurely fuck while the rest of us were out in the veld. But all right, I let him be. We shot the farm to blazes that afternoon, and I emptied out all the crayfish in one whole deep-freeze for Peet to make room for the venison, and by the time the sun went down the party got going. All the way to sunrise. To be honest, I quite forgot about my two guests in the truck.

The next day we pushed on to Christiana, Joos Hougaardt's farm. This time, when Landman started hedging again, trying to hide behind his wife like the day before, I told him straight, 'If she's feeling sick, Joos's wife can look after her, today you're coming with.' Once again I pressed the two-seventy into his hands and this time I didn't give him a chance to turn tail.

Tell the truth, he looked a rather worried man to me. As if he had no idea of how to handle that gun. 'Hell, man,' I asked him, 'haven't you been in the army? You scared the blarry thing'll bite you?'

Laughter all round, by that time there already was a whole crowd turned up for the hunt, the way it goes. Soon's the word gets round that Vleis Wagenaar is coming you see men turning up for the hunt who've never hunted in their lives.

Told them Landman was the son of a great pal of mine, come a long way together, kind of wanted to brag with him, you see, I often do it when I have a youngster with me, it's like he's my son. Sometimes they let one down, but never as fucking badly as this time.

Right, so there from the farmhouse we drove out into the veld, the chasers with a half hour head start to round up the game. There's a kind of ridge of hills on one side of the big plain on Joos's farm where a man can make himself comfortable waiting for the buck to come round the edge. Then it's just a matter of taking aim and pulling the trigger, almost too easy. But I must have been a bit unsteady that afternoon what with not sleeping a wink the night before, and before setting out from Joos's house we already doused the fires inside, much better, so I can tell you I wasn't feeling all that steady by the time we got into the jeep and the bakkies to drive to our positions. Anyway, so when the first few springbok came dribbling round the ridge, I selected a sturdy young ram for myself, but when I let go, can you believe it, the shot hit him low down on the shoulder, shattering the leg, and as he took off the leg kind of spun beside him like a blarry propeller. Only a hundred yards or so, then he fell. Jumped up again, the front leg whirring, fell down once more. Now I had Landman with me, thought I'd keep him company to cheer him up, give him confidence. He completely missed *his* first buck. Which might be why mine got a fright and turned sideways just as I was pulling the trigger. But I'm not trying to find excuses. It *was* a blarry shit way to shoot. But what stung me was that Landman had the cheek to say, 'What have you done now?'

Godalmighty, I felt like taking a swipe at him that would take him right through the next day and the one after. But in a way I actually felt sorry for him too, could see the thing had shaken him up. Never hunted before in his life, that was obvious. Pale as anything. But I kind of prodded him in the ribs with the butt of my rifle, perhaps a bit harder than I meant to, one can't judge so well when one's had a few too many, and I told him, 'Now you go and finish him off.'

Then he really came up with a surprise. 'It's you who made the balls-up,' he said, 'you finish your own dirty work.'

Jeeeesus, I mean, Vleis Wagenaar doesn't take shit from anybody, hey. Still, in the circumstances I stayed reasonably calm. Again for the girlie's sake, in a way. Just gave him another prod. So he could see I was serious. 'Come on, man, don't be a blarry sissy. Go and shoot him. Then you also have a trophy to take home.' Because that's for sure, it was the only way *he* would bag anything.

By this time the springbok was back on his legs again, stumbling along, the shattered leg swaying, blood spurting all over the place, then down again, then up again. Even so, he was moving further and further away. So Landman had quite a jog trying to catch up with the buck. Each time, just as he was getting close, the little ram would struggle to its feet and hobble on again. In a way it was quite funny. But I didn't feel like laughing really.

I stood looking after him for some time and then turned to move on in the direction of the next pair of hunters. We were spread out right along the ridge, two by two. And I needed company. An hour or so later I got another chance, beautiful full-grown ram, one shot in the heart, zap, the way Vleis Wagenaar usually bags them. Because I don't like a waste, man, true's God. It spoils the meat too.

Maybe we were a bit hard on Landman that afternoon. Still, I thought it would be a lesson to the chap. To be quite frank about it, I hinted to the others that it was Landman himself who'd wounded the springbok. Felt a bit ashamed to admit it was I, such a terrible shot. Anyway, so we just left him behind in the veld when the bakkies came back to pick us up again. As a result, it was already dark, way after sunset, before he arrived back at the house, the springbok on his shoulders. Neatly cut open, the intestines shaken out, one could see he wasn't such a greenhorn after all; blood all over his shirt, a good and proper hunter. That's the way I'll remember Thomas Landman. Weird, thinking about it now. Standing opposite the blazing fire in the backyard, in the red glow, the buck on his shoulders. And pale. Even in that flickering light one could see the man was as white as a sheet. Then, with a quick sudden jerk, he shook the buck from his shoulders, wiped his forehead with the back of his hand, because he was all wet with sweat, tucked in his shirt, and said:

'Here's your buck, Oom Vleis.'

And turned round and went back to the truck.

I didn't feel good about the whole thing. And as I took a swipe from my bottle again, I said, 'Look, boys, let me get this off my mind: it wasn't the boy who wounded the buck, it was me.'

That night we didn't carry on quite so late, I was feeling a bit under the weather. And the following morning there was kind of an uneasy silence in the truck as we drove along.

'Listen,' I said after the first couple of kilometres, because I'm not the sort of man who bottles things up, 'it was my fault and I'm sorry. I can see you're not a hunter's arse and I won't try to force you into it again, all right?'

He smiled, I'll say that for him. And said, 'Yes, all right. And I didn't mean to make a scene either.'

I told them what I had in mind: I wanted them to stay with me for a few more days, trip through the Free State, then I'd turn back and drop them off in Johburg afterwards. Right on his brother's doorstep in Booysens. Because I took a liking in them. Invited them to come and visit me on the farm, any time, stay as long as they wish. Just say the word. I'll send Handyman to come and fetch you.

But they were in a hurry. It was understandable, of course. The man had his pride, he wanted to get back on his feet, not lie on other people's backs. And I think that experience on the hunt must have affected him too, even though I apologised and everything. So I said right, in that case I'll take you to Schweizer-Reneke, which was already farther north than I'd planned. But what the hell. My time's my own, and Handyman goes wherever I tell him to. And when we drove into Schweizer-Reneke I first took them to the hotel for a proper meal. Handyman waited outside in the truck. I told the people at reception to have the kitchen send him a cup of coffee and a plate of food. I look after my people, man.

As we said goodbye afterwards, seeing the two of them all lost in that wide world, because it's a fucking barren stretch of land, I thought the least I could do was give them some pocket money for the road. Emptied my pockets. Not much cash on me, about five or six hundred. But at least it would tide them over. All I had to give them right there.

They refused to take it. Too proud. But I insisted, said it was for her, the girlie, Marina. When she also pulled a tight arse, I said, Ag man, keep it for the baby then, I'll be his godfather. You come and show him to me when he's ready to face the world, hey?

There was something else I noticed, in a strange way it shook me, when I suddenly looked up and saw Handyman watching us as I gave them the money. Not that I can explain exactly what I saw on that funny little monkey-face of his, he's grinning all the time, born with a blarry smile on his mug. But I suppose one can call it an expression of sadness, almost of hunger. Poor Handyman, I thought, how many times over the years have you seen me dishing it out to others, I've got this soft heart, and he's never said a word. Shame.

But it lasted only for a moment, then he ducked in behind the truck, almost as if he was ashamed of being seen. I said goodbye to the two. And then another thing: they went round the truck to shake hands with Handyman as if he was a white man. I could see he didn't really know how to handle it, no one's ever done that to him, but once he started shaking their hands he didn't want to stop. Really, two nice kids. But of course at that time I knew nothing yet.

That was the last I saw of them. Until I got back today and saw the papers. –

3

On Massouw's Kop, then, outside Schweizer-Reneke, under the stars. Cool, turning decidedly cold in the small hours; there could be no doubt now that winter was at hand. And after they'd prepared their simple supper they did not want to keep the fire going, for fear it might attract attention. In the late afternoon they'd followed the dirt road behind the hospital, carrying their plastic bags; climbed through a hole in the gate, went up the easy incline of the hill – a few cattle snorted as they passed, and moved further off; the place had a heavy smell of manure – past the hideous electrical installations and the concrete reservoir, to prepare a camping spot for the night among black and red flintstones mapped with lime-green lichen. Rolling some of the more unwieldy rocks out of the way, below an uneven ridge on the eastern slope, Thomas suddenly stooped and called out to Lisa, 'Look what I've found!' As she approached he traced with a respectful finger a faded white outline on the red surface. 'See this? Don't you think it looks like an eland? It may be a San drawing. In these parts, I've read somewhere, there are drawings twenty thousand years old.' She squatted beside him. They hunted for further signs of the little people, but found nothing. And then they just sat, staring across the plains below, a landscape from the beginning of time.

It grew dark over them.

In this place, he thought, one wouldn't be surprised to find, on the eroded surface of a rock, the imprint of a prehistoric animal. The dust on the surface had been dislodged by the fleeting passing of Khoisan peoples, of springbok, wildebeest, thousands of years ago; the koppies themselves remained like the vertebrae of dinosaurs, ready, the moment one looked away, to lumber off into the dark; or to approach. Whatever happened here was adapted to a different time scale. The crumbling of the earth crust, the extinction of stars; even the breath of the night wind carried intimations of cosmic space. How ludicrous, in this vast night, their little fire. Inadequate, in this vacancy, the small shared warmth of their bodies. Irrelevant, the beginnings and possible endings of their common journey, their separate lives.

And yet it was important; yet they were indispensable! What would be the sense of all this if they had not been there? Star and dinosaur and thorn wood and fire existed in this night because *they* were there to see and touch and smell them. And by the same token *they* were there because this night in Africa circumscribed them, acknowledged them, generously permitted their presence.

As the night grew deeper around them, everything became very hard, silent, lucid, unclouded by sentimentality, memory, hope or fear. An essence like that of stone. Transient; everlasting. The coincidence of their passing through this landscape acquired the weight of fate. The smallest gesture they made, her breath on his face, every touch of wind or rustling of dry grass, every sound that sent them into a more intimate huddle – aware, not only of the surrounding night, but of the illuminated darkness inside them: the network of nerves, ramification of veins, the miracle of bone, the secret rhythms of lungs and heart, secretions, the expanding and shrinking of skin – was memorable, profound, an involvement with the whole. (– 'Unless I am involved in everything I am nothing.' –) His constellation in the zodiac was just beginning to emerge above the horizon. It was June. (– Cancer, the crab, the crayfish. I am beginning to merge with what has been destined for me; to what is destined by me. In ten days' time I shall be twenty-nine. Does that count for something, or is it negligible? I have lived so much already: I have not lived at all. –)

Neither of them gave any thought to sleep, at least not before the predawn was beginning to stain the sky and from the town below the first cocks began to crow, and in the camel-thorns on the hill the larks began to chirp. There was too much to talk about; there was even more that could not be said. Because this was the last night on their flight in which they would be together like this, so close, available to each other, to discuss whatever still had to be discussed, to cherish for one last time the warmth of their bodies as they crouched together, their arms around one another.

'We don't have far to go now,' he said, perhaps in an effort to encourage her.

'The last stretch will be the hardest.'

'We'll get through.'

'You sound as if you're trying to convince yourself.'

'Lisa: we *will* make it.' There, in that darkness, they could afford, even if it were only fleetingly, to reject disguise and treachery and call each other by the name.

'Thomas,' she said in her candid way, head thrown back, staring up into the night sky, 'If you're honest with yourself tonight, looking back – at *everything* – do you think, do you believe, it was worth while?'

Her voice cut more sharply into him than the icy wind. (– Nina, Nina, long ago, on another, higher mountain. –)

'How does one calculate whether something is "worth while"? It's not arithmetic, something you can add or subtract. Perhaps it's not even logical.'

'All those who died. Who were hurt. Who got caught. Who are on the run. Does it all amount to something in the end? For anyone? I'm not talking about you or me, Thomas. We're expendable. But others. Because, surely, *some* time someone should be able to stop and say: Yes, it was worth while, it was necessary.'

'Would it make more sense to approach it from the other end?' he asked quietly. 'What if we had *not* done it? Wouldn't it have been worse then? At the very least we have demonstrated that it is *not* normal for evil to continue unchecked. And that it can be opposed.'

'And you believe – you really and truly believe – that one day it will be over?'

'I'm prepared to take that chance. Dammit, Lisa: it's to bring such a day closer that I did it. Otherwise it would have been impossible. Do you believe me?'

'I'm not sure. All I know is that when it comes to violence

582

there must *always* be another option. Otherwise we are forced to renounce whatever it is – and however little it is – that makes us different from the animals.'

– Even that I do not know for sure. Yesterday afternoon on the farm (was it really only yesterday? not light years ago?), yesterday afternoon as I ran through the veld in pursuit of that wounded animal, for what seemed like countless kilometres, until at last it dropped down and didn't rise again: raised its long neck, one last time, then fell back, its mouth open, gasping, breathing its last: I looked into its eyes from a single step away, right into its eyes, and then I pressed the gun against its head and pulled the trigger. It didn't even struggle. It was too exhausted, death must have come as a release. I can't tell you what I felt at that moment.

But afterwards, as I was cutting open the dead animal, shaking out the blood and guts – almost immediately there were vultures overhead, God knows how they'd discovered it so soon – I became aware of something like relief inside me. As if in that simple action I was rounding off something, performing a necessary ritual. In the death of a springbok I assumed the weight of innumerable lives. In the late sunlight, into the sunset, into the falling dusk, I walked back. It felt as if I was walking back through time, through years and centuries, through at least thirteen generations: gathering as I went on, at every step, all the accumulated blood and violence and death. It was no longer an abstraction, a thought, an idea, dream or nightmare, not an ideology, but the reality of a body that slowly became cold against my own, as it tensed into rigor mortis. This was what had always eluded me – even in Cape Town, that wretched day of the funeral – and which had now happened. At last. Almost too late. But still in time. Something of myself was restored to me in that dead weight. And for this I shall always be grateful to our savage host. –

4

When at nine o'clock on the Saturday morning she returned to the post office in Lichtenburg where she'd already been at seven, and twice the previous afternoon – all strictly as previously arranged – there was still no sign of Thomas. Early on the Friday morning, the 10th, following the instructions of 'his people' (she still did not know the names of Justin and the others), they had left Schweizer-Reneke on their separate routes – she via Delareyville and Sannieshof, Thomas via Wolmaransstad and Ottosdal. Two hundred kilometres for him, rather less for her. At most, they'd reckoned, at the utmost, they would reach Lichtenburg by the afternoon. And even with all the delays she'd run into she was there well before sunset. But not he. Now it was past nine the following morning and Thomas had still not shown up.

She urged herself to stay calm. The arrangement was explicit: if something unforeseen took place, the one who reached the post office first would return there on every uneven hour (not more often: it was necessary not to attract undue attention, all the more so as the big new police station was only yards away) until seven at night, resuming at seven the following morning.

It was enough of a blow when in the early daylight – befuddled, her head aching, her body pervaded by the smell of the night's fire – she'd reached the post office to find no sign of him. All night long this was what had kept her going, through the heavy silence of the morose nightwatchman in his trenchcoat and balaclava: this certainty that Thomas would be there in the morning. It *couldn't* be otherwise. She repressed the urge, after the wholly sleepless night, to burst into tears; tried to rekindle some spark in her with a cool drink and a cold sausage roll at a café: fortunately she still had her share of Vleis Wagenaar's handout in her jeans pocket; the rest of her possessions she'd lost. She forced herself to keep faith. Perhaps Thomas had met with unexpected delays on the road, had arrived in the early hours, had overslept: but at nine o'clock, undoubtedly, at nine he would be there.

It was now ten past.

She had difficulty repressing the feeling of panic. Suppose, she thought, Thomas had decided, in spite of everything, to cross the border on his own during the night? It was barely an hour's drive from here. The temptation must have been strong. But surely he wouldn't have left her behind, would he? He'd urged her so many times to change her mind, convinced as he was she would come out of it unscathed. Perhaps the instructions to go their separate ways from Schweizer-Reneke had never come from his nameless leader after all: perhaps it had been, from the start, Thomas's own idea to get rid of her. For her own good, no doubt. But he wouldn't. No, he wouldn't. And yet: where was he?

Unless he'd really run into bad trouble. Perhaps an accident. He might be lying beside the road trapped in the wreck of a car. Even that might be preferable to what *could* have happened, to what she'd tried to repress for so long but which was now returning to her with ever greater persistence: the thought that someone who'd picked him up might have recognised him, might have handed him over to the police; that at this moment he   And how would she ever find out?

No, no, no, she argued. It was senseless to give way to panic. This was her opportunity of testing herself, of proving that she could handle the situation, keep her cool.

Fifteen minutes past.

Was it her imagination or had the young constable with the pockmarked face on the pavement outside the post office taken an interest in her? Surely there was nothing in her appearance to attract him.

Twenty past nine.

That was when she entered one of the bright orange booths to telephone. Because now she was convinced that something had indeed gone wrong. She *had* to talk to someone. And there was only one option.

The first booth was out of order. The second she could use. Erik's number in Cape Town. It rang for minutes before someone picked it up. No, sorry, she was informed, Corporal Lombard wasn't there, he'd gone home on special leave.

She had to change a note inside at the counter before she could dial again. The young constable was right behind her as she entered the booth. She drew in her back, expecting at any moment a heavy paw with chewed-off nails to land on her shoulder. But then he ambled on, back in the direction of the police station next door. Perhaps he'd been put off by the vapour of sweat and woodsmoke that emanated from her, she thought, almost triumphantly.

Half-past.

She dialled her father's number, hoping Naomi would answer. If her father picked it up, she'd decided in advance, she would put the receiver down.

It was Erik.

For a moment she couldn't say anything, so overcome that her voice stuck in her throat.

'Hello? Hello?' he repeated.

'Erik, boetie!'

'My God, Lisa, where are you?'

And suddenly the panic subsided; suddenly she was very calm, defensive, matter-of-fact. Her head cool and clear, her hand steady on the instrument that connected her to a wire which, she blindingly knew, was humming and hissing with eavesdroppers.

'I'm just calling to tell you I'm fine, right? I hope Daddy isn't trying to eavesdrop. Remember how annoyed he used to be when we were kids and he couldn't make out what you and I were talking about?' Mother was even worse —'

'Yes, of course, but —'

From the way he abruptly checked himself she knew that he'd caught on. She was using the code they'd devised as children and which even now they often resorted to, as a game, which sounded quite normal on the surface, but which worked with opposites, switches, repetitions, riddles, cryptic spellings, key words highlighted by 'right?'.

'Remember how we spent some holidays at the sea, and some inland, right?' (He would know about those, in the Game Reserve.)

'I don't know what you're talking about.'

'On one of the sea holidays, right, we stayed over in a town, I've forgotten the name, where I was scared and came to you for help. You didn't want to come to me, right? And then Mother found out I was with you and she threatened to tear strips off me. And I pleaded with her and said it was only because I was scared of the dark, right? Because it *was* bloody dark that night. Which made her even more furious, because she never got scared, especially not of the dark, she said God and all His disciples, right, watched over you while you slept.'

'I remember how dark it was.'

She sighed with relief: he'd caught the emphatic references to 'dark', would know to translate it into its opposite, 'light', as in '*Licht*enburg', which lay on their childhood route to the Game Reserve. And the 'disciple' would convey to him that Thomas was involved.

'You say you're well?'

'Couldn't be better, right? I suppose you're much too busy to visit me some time, right?'

'Definitely not right now.'

'I sometimes wish we were kids again, Erik. Remember how we used to play Hansel and Gretel? And the night we really lost our way.

586

It was so dark! Incredibly dark. And you and I got separated. And remember where they found me afterwards, with the glow-worms, right? You came with them. It's an experience I never want to live through again.'

'Well, you can forget about it now. It won't happen again.'

'Whatever you're planning for today, I suppose, will keep you busy for a long time?' (This was terribly clumsy, but she could think of no other way to phrase it.)

'I'm not sure. I've got enough work for about five hours or so.'

'Is that all?'

'More than enough, don't you think? Come on, you're wasting my time.'

'Okay. Oh, and don't tell Naomi I phoned, right?'

A pause she hadn't expected. Then, in a smothered voice, 'I *will* tell her. She'd like to know. She's around, as always. Still not taken her holiday. A live wire, right? She – I'm sure she'd love to hear your news.'

Confusion, incredulity invaded her. It was difficult to think of something to say, to keep calm; all she said was, 'Well, get on with your work then. I won't keep you. Just thought I'd reassure you that I'm really very well, right?'

Even if she'd wanted to add something more she couldn't; the time of her coins had run out, they were cut off.

The constable was on his leisurely way back.

She turned her back to him and walked away.

She had no idea of where she was going. In her mind continued to echo his words about Naomi, punctuated by the 'right', which in their code emphasised a clue. 'A live wire.' But how could Naomi be dead? It was inconceivable. She knew that Erik sometimes took liberties with the code to confuse her; but not when it concerned life or death.

She had to get her feelings under control; now more than ever. Whatever might have happened, she'd soon know. Erik was on his way. Five hours, he'd said. But in that jalopy of his? It was now twenty minutes to ten. He couldn't possibly be here before three. He would look for her in the graveyard. ('Remember where they found me afterwards, with the glow-worms, right?') She hoped it wasn't too far out of town. In the meantime she had to return to the post office on the uneven hours. Eleven, one, three – But by that time, dear God, Thomas *must* have shown up.

The important thing was not to panic. One thing at a time. Avoid attracting attention. First of all she had to make herself more respectable. She remembered passing a fashion shop after she'd so hurriedly crossed the street from the post office. In order not to attract attention by turning back too abruptly she walked round the block. In the shop she chose a shirt and a cheap skirt, a jersey for evenings; and, on an impulse, a pair of frilly panties: the only extravagance she could permit herself, and that only because, ironically, no one would see it. (Except, she thought in a sudden onrush of desire, Thomas; except Thomas.)

She crossed the town square, past dark *karee* trees and the unwieldy statue of an old Boer general in front of the museum; and in a pharmacy opposite bought some make-up, a bar of soap, a hairbrush, deodorant, dark glasses. (Those would be identified later: oh yes, they remembered, she'd bought them there on the Saturday morning: who on earth could have expected her to be a terrorist?)

As on the previous evening she had to resist the temptation of going to a hotel to freshen up. But apart from the fear that in her dishevelled state she might be turned away humiliatingly, she had to avoid as much as possible being noticed. And so, reluctantly, she went to the public toilet building on the square. Not very tidy, and smelly, but at least it was deserted, so that she could have an all-over if furtive wash at the basin and rid herself of the worst smoke smell from the previous night beside the nightwatchman's smoky coal-can. In one of the toilet cubicles she changed into the new clothes, brushed out her wig, and put on the sunglasses.

After she'd casually dropped her old clothes in the nearest rubbish bin it was still too early to return to the post office; and she went to a café – behind the nouveau riche façade a small-town world persisted in the forms and habits of years ago – for coffee and a sandwich; she also bought, to hide behind and keep her occupied, a newspaper, a magazine, a paperback.

In the newspaper, the sudden confrontation with their two photographs published together, hers and Thomas's; already relegated to an inside page, but nonetheless, in the blatancy of their linked exposure, a shock to her. There was something indecent about the matter-of-factness of the publication: the way in which it was assumed, unquestioningly, that she'd been involved in the bomb

588

attack; the way in which it confidently inscribed her in a history of which she still knew next to nothing. The apprehension – more than apprehension: the certainty – that having inserted her into it, they would now go all the way in their pursuit of her. She was left no choice any more, no opportunity of being heard. A victim was required. Guilt and innocence were no longer even relevant. She had been written off; she, no less than Thomas, was the object and prey of their public hunt.

She felt – in the language of the popular magazine she'd bought with the newspaper – the blood drain from her face (and was aware of the phrase as much as of the sensation). She felt anger, she felt revulsion: but in an inexplicable way she also felt pride. There was a curious satisfaction in being able at least to share the shame, if not the guilt, with him.

At the same time there was something unsettling about looking at herself like that, as if gazing across a very great distance at someone vaguely familiar but impossible to acknowledge. And when, absently, she looked up and saw her reflection in a mirror on the wall opposite – that strange, stern person with the nondescript hair and the sunglasses and the cheap blouse and skirt who was supposed to be Lisa Lombard – she could understand the feeling. Because that dated university photograph (from where? supplied by her father, no doubt, where else?) belonged to another existence, a different dimension; as if she'd been sucked into a Black Hole and spat out into another time frame. This was no longer she. (Neither was that scowling female in the café mirror!) *Was* there a 'real' she left at all?)

She returned to the report. The self-assured announcement that the police were working on a number of new clues and were expecting a final breakthrough.

How many 'breakthroughs' had there been already?! Yet here she still was. (And Thomas? But Thomas? Suppose, this time, the 'new clues' really had to do with him?)

Her eyes moved so restlessly across the report that it was a while before she grasped what the caption to the picture said: *There are indications that Lisa Lombard has cut her hair very short and may be wearing a wig. The public is requested to be on the lookout.*

Indications? What 'indications'? No one in the world, apart from Thomas and Naomi, knew that she'd cut her hair.

Naomi. *A live wire.*

Could it be?

She stubbornly refused to believe it. She had to shake off the doubts. As soon as they'd settled somewhere she would write to Naomi. From across the border. It was so close now. She'd send a postcard from Gaborone. Naomi would be bemused by the strange stamp. Yes.

Those 'new clues'. Surely Naomi would not have told them anything. And her father knew nothing. Who else was there?

Vleis Wagenaar? Impossible: he knew absolutely nothing. And even if he had – she realised it was naïve to argue like this – she couldn't believe that he would have given them away. There was that curious gentleness with which, in spite of his coarseness, his smouldering feudal violence, he had treated her.

She needed, desperately, the reassurance of Thomas's presence. At the same time she dreaded it. What would he look like when – if? – he returned?

That early evening when he'd come back from the hunt to face her in the truck. She had sat up in the big bed when he entered. He stopped. She saw the blood on his shirt, on his hands. A smudge on one cheek. He said nothing.

In dead silence, for a very long time, they stared at one another. The few yards separating them seemed endless.

At last she asked, 'Thomas, you haven't really shot a buck, have you?'

He drew a deep breath, and shrugged his shoulders. Then took off his soiled shirt, ran water from the tap in a barrel in the corner, started washing himself in silence.

'Why didn't you come back with the others?'

'I just didn't.'

That night she lay wide awake beside him, tense with thought. – Tonight, for the first time, I can *believe* that you planted a bomb. I saw the blood on your naked body. I won't be able to stand it if you were to touch me now. (And yet – thank God you're asleep, you're exhausted – I desire you! What perversity is this?) It would not be difficult to find you repulsive tonight, but even in spite of the blood – *because* of the blood? – you need me; I you. Why? I don't understand it. It's as if I have suddenly, at long last, seen you in the full horror of your guilt: everything I've always *willed* myself not to see. Now I've seen you as you have been looking upon yourself. But at the same time I've seen you in your terrible vulnerability: as you can never see yourself. I love you, Thomas Landman. –

*

Involuntarily, as if that might help, she took off her dark glasses and started rummaging in her plastic shopping bag in search of something to clean them with. All she could come up with was the frilly panties she'd bought. With those, very meticulously she cleaned the lenses, wondering suddenly: Why was she taking so much trouble? Would that erase the report she'd read, the photo?

It was almost eleven; time to go. This time, she was convinced, Thomas would be there.

But he wasn't.

At least Erik was on his way. She took a listless walk through the town centre, unable to sit still again so soon. Sculptures of pelicans in front of what looked like a civic centre, bourgeois prosperity, shady avenues. At a fruit shop she asked for directions to the graveyard, and a sympathetic old man in a bulging khaki shirt and baggy trousers turned to talk to her. She explained that an aunt of hers was buried there. The old man promptly offered to drive her there in his small truck; she could not very well refuse. Once there — to her relief it wasn't all that far, a brisk walk from the centre, but manageable: on the outskirts, on the other side of the town, near the turn-off to Mmabatho, which somehow seemed like a good omen — it took all her persuasive skill to make him drive back without her; he was quite prepared to wait until she'd paid her respects to the dear departed. But in the end he left — 'Cheerio, my dear' — and she spent some time among the graves before returning, leisurely, to the centre of the town on foot.

The shops were beginning to close for the weekend. The Saturday morning traffic was draining away. She found another café to sit in, a seedier one this time, but it suited her better. Oh damn you, Thomas!

Everything — apart from the lift with the young farmer — had gone so well so far. The first wait, after she'd taken up position at the edge of Schweizer-Reneke (near the hospital, where the road made a determined curve to the right; below a huge blank billboard like an empty cinema screen, as if even the inspiration for graffiti or advertisements was lacking here), had been long, over two hours; but she was in no hurry (except that she'd approached the enterprise as a race: she was determined to reach Lichtenburg before Thomas), and there was something curiously satisfying about being left alone with her thoughts, as if a kind of independence had been restored to her. That afternoon on the farm, when Thomas had gone

591

hunting with the men, had been different; not for a moment could one exclude the consciousness of a whole house full of bustling women, spilling into the yard in desperate demonstration of their capabilities. From time to time some of them would 'look in', with tea and sympathy, disturbing her rest, keeping her on the defence. Today was different. A whole day left to herself. To take stock? Perhaps this was how she'd thought of it beforehand. But when the time came she found, somewhat to her surprise, that *that* was not important after all. There were not really any new choices, any revision of previous ones, to consider: what mattered was the solitude in itself, an affirmation of being who she was, of *wanting* to be where she was.

In the end, when a car did stop to offer her a lift, it came almost as an invasion of her new silence. An elderly farmer and his wife on their way back, via Delareyville, to their farm in the district, after they'd spent the week with their children in Niekerkshoop. They were clearly concerned about her, a young white women on her own on the road: wasn't she afraid, wasn't it dangerous? Not at all, she assured them. She was at college in Pretoria, but her mother had taken ill and she'd come down to visit her; now she was on her way back, she was writing a test on Monday. Strange, she thought, how it became easier all the time, this invention of new selves and stories. She was getting quite good at it; soon she might be lying even when the truth would do.

In Delareyville, where the village half-heartedly petered out into the veld, below a cluster of syringas and other trees planted for a show of shade in a dry land, she had to wait even longer, almost three hours, perched on an up-ended whitewashed stone, before a car drew up beside her: an old white Valiant in a cloud of smoke; eight black people inside, with their boxes and bundles of baggage, and two babies, and a live chicken whose yellow legs had been tightly tied together. But in some miraculous way they managed to make room for her too; she held one of the babies on her lap, and soon the young woman next to her, in a threadbare dress held together with safety-pins, her face drawn in the haggard look of chronic poverty, fell asleep with her head comfortably nestled on Lisa's shoulder. An energetic conversation went on around her, in Tswana, which she didn't understand. If they made no attempt to talk to her, they didn't exclude her either; her presence was simply accepted as if she belonged there with them; at some stage a white loaf was drawn from a plastic bag and passed round, to her too, and like the others she broke off a chunk and stuffed it into her mouth. She felt almost regretful when she had to get out in Sannieshof where they turned off to Bophuthatswana. On an impulse she offered the young woman who'd been sleeping against her the shopping bag with all the clothes she'd so carefully selected in Naomi's room, keeping only the *I Ching* for herself. With cries of enthusiasm all the contents of the bag were unpacked immediately, each item passed from one to the other; and then all the passengers got out so that, one by one, smiling and conspiratorial, they could shake her hand. And with a feeling of sudden emptiness and loss she was left behind, clutching her book, as they disappeared to the north in their cloud of blue smoke.

Another long wait. She settled on an oildrum at the Total garage on the far side of the village, losing herself so completely in thought that she was quite startled when, in a cloud of dust, the young farmer stopped on the shoulder of the road beside her in his cream Toyota bakkie streaked with brown and orange, tall on its wheels, obviously brand-new. And they'd hardly pulled off when he asked, 'You ever had a ride in a beauty like this? Just feel it.' And then stepped on the accelerator so that they shot forward in a roar of speed. As if it was the most natural thing in the world he put his left hand on her knee and squeezed it, a gesture of familiarity and propriety. She smiled, amused; which he evidently interpreted as willingness, for the next instant his hand was on her thigh. He turned his head to look at her, and winked, his teeth stark white against the tan of his face.

'Shouldn't you keep your eyes on the road?' she asked as sweetly as possible, trying unobtrusively to move her leg.

'I can steer this baby with no hands,' he said, removing his right hand from the wheel too; his left was now approaching the fold of her groin. He asked, 'How's it?'

She stared straight ahead as she crossed her right leg over her left knee. That seemed, for a while, to restrain him; at least his hand could make no further progress without obvious effort. For twenty, thirty kilometres he drove on without any further attempts at exploration. It was an insignificant incident that disturbed the precarious equilibrium between them. Beside the road a group of children was coming towards them, evidently on their way home from school, carrying bundles of books and waving cheerily as the bakkie approached. Lisa waved back.

At first she did not notice anything amiss. But a few hundred yards on the man asked, suddenly aggressive, 'Why did you wave like that?'

'To say hello. Why do you ask? They were so friendly.'

It wasn't necessary to wave back.'

She didn't answer.

'You one of those?' he demanded.

'Those what?'

'People who suck up to blacks.'

She felt a flush in her face but decided not to reply.

'Why don't you say anything?'

'What is there to say?'

'I was asking you a question.

'I didn't see any point in answering.'

'Because you think I'm a shit?'

She said nothing.

'Suppose you've slept with them too?'

'_'

'You women all think black pricks are the size of pick handles.'

'_'

'I mean, you're not much to look at, are you? Probably had no fucking choice.'

She snorted.

'Don't you get uppity with me, my pussy.' He braked so hard that the pick-up skidded on the gravel beside the road; for a moment she thought they were going to roll. But then the bakkie came to a stop and the dust swept over them from behind. He leaned half over her to open the door on her side. For a moment, obtusely, she didn't realise what was happening.

'Get out!'

'But —'

'Fuck off out of my car!'

He gave her a shove that sent her staggering through the open door, almost landing on all fours in the gravel. Before she could turn round he'd slammed the door shut again and pulled off. In ludicrous anger she hurled a fistful of gravel after him. Realising only much later that he'd gone off with her last remaining possession, the *I Ching*. Even so she was more relieved than upset. He could drive straight to hell for all she cared.

There was something tterribly desolate in standing beside the deserted road like that, not a soul in sight, the veld white and

594

bare, straggly, miserable. But she drew reassurance from her very loneliness in that immeasurable space below a sky almost drained of colour. Who was it who'd said, she tried to remember – a line from her student days? from her wanderings in Europe? – that God had made people the way the sea made continents: by withdrawing? In that case she was fast becoming human.

But there was anxiety in it too. More about the delay than the misadventure. She didn't want to keep Thomas waiting. If they were delayed it mustn't be her fault.

It wasn't. Not half an hour later – she'd begun to walk on, just to have something to do – another car approached from behind and stopped, a businesslike middle-aged woman behind the wheel: she wore a scarf round her head, khaki shirt and trousers, veldskoens; on the seat beside her was a bull-terrier which at first refused to budge and needed much coaxing and prodding to be transferred to the back seat. Lisa repeated the story she'd devised before, about her sick mother, and the test she would be writing on the Monday. The woman listened impassively, giving not the slightest sign that she'd heard or even cared. Just before four o'clock, still without a word, she dropped Lisa at a garage in Lichtenburg.

It was quite a walk from there to the town centre, but she was at the post office in time for the five o'clock rendezvous. No sign, however, of Thomas. And not at seven either.

That was when she'd considered checking in at a hotel; but having no luggage, she might attract unwanted attention. She enquired at a café about the town's caravan camp but it was too far away. To sort out her thoughts she bought a hamburger which she ate on the town square, beside a fountain with white sculptures. By now it was dark. She felt deserted and threatened. Worried about Thomas.

When she saw groups of people approaching across the square towards a cinema in an illuminated arcade, she decided to join them; afterwards she couldn't remember much about the film, except that it had been a thriller, with a great deal of shooting and chasing and screaming tyres. She left before the end. Back to the blackness, both comforting and menacing, of the trees on the square. It was cold; it was dark. After the cinema had come out the town subsided into terrifying silence. How much more bearable it would have been, she thought, if Erik had been with her (that distant Hansel and Gretel night in the bluegum wood;

595

in the graveyard; the owls; and then the glow-worms). But she was resolved to see it through, convinced that early the following morning Thomas would be waiting at the post office.

From time to time, when the cold began to numb her body, she walked or jogged for a few blocks – away from the daunting police station near by – and that was how, long past midnight, she discovered the garage where the sullen old nightwatchman sat beside his can of glowing coals, huddled in his trenchcoat and balaclava. She had a fright when she first saw the dark figure behind the red glow of the embers; but when she realised what it was she approached, shivering, to ask:

'Do you mind if I sit here with you?'

He did not answer.

'I won't disturb you.'

No reaction. One might think it was a scarecrow someone had propped up there for the night; but from time to time he moved: turned his head, stretched an arm, shifted a leg. And at regular intervals he got up to break thin damp sticks of wood from a bundle that had evidently been put there for this purpose, spread his hands over the flickering, heavily smoking coals, and sat down again. Sometimes he uttered a deep rumbling sigh, or turned his eyes towards her, staring at her, expressionless, for minutes on end; but never said a word.

In the first few hours she still tried, with a measure of determination, to start up a conversation, but he didn't react. And later the cold grew so severe that she didn't have the energy to put any more effort into it. Then she would get up and jog painfully round the building, lifting her knees to her chin, to get the circulation going again; or bend over the can, as close to the coals as possible without scorching herself, to absorb what warmth she could. And sometimes she dropped back her head to stare up at the stars: Thomas's stars. *He* would be reassured by them, she thought; they could show him the way, wherever he wanted to go. To her they were simply remote and irrelevant, a riddle she couldn't – and, as a matter of fact, had no desire to – solve. Her thoughts roamed freely, getting nowhere. Until the dull dawn appeared and she walked off into the slowly lightening dark: by that time, it seemed, the nightwatchman was asleep, his eyes still open and staring; and the coals had died; there was no more wood. Through the godforsaken streets she roamed, hoping desperately that she might suddenly come upon Thomas, wandering about like herself to while away the dreary hours until seven when it would be time to meet at the post office. But nothing happened; and at seven he wasn't there.

And now he'd still not shown up. But now, at least, Erik was on his way.

– My darling Erik, in this sad café I'm writing you a letter in my mind. If Thomas has been condemned to taking photographs without a camera, why should I complain about a lack of pen or paper? There's nothing I *can* claim any more, for nothing is self-evident, nothing can be taken for granted. And when you arrive here, soon, soon – for God's sake, drive carefully! – you, too, may see that I'm no longer the Lisa who grew up with you. Not because of the wig and the sunglasses and the demure little skirt, but because something in myself has changed. You and I won't be able to play Hansel and Gretel any more, you know, our magic wood has disappeared a long time ago.

I wish I could explain to you exactly what has changed, but I'm not sure I can find the right words for it. All I know is that the restlessness, the frustration that has raged in me for so long, this anger that never knew which way to go, this itch that drove me to Europe in search of a solution, then drove me back again, still in search of an answer, my never-ending feud with the men at school, with the revolting Siebert, my 'insubordination' – that all this has suddenly found what it has always sought: a course and a direction. I'm not running after anyone, Erik, this above all is what I want you to understand. What I have found is what I want to do, where I want to go. Does it sound confused? But the confusion is in the words, not in me. There is a terrifying clarity in me.

I have always been reluctant to follow others, play in their team, sing in their chorus, march in their band. I know better now, thanks to Thomas. I've always been suspicious about the way 'our' people are going against the grain of history; but I've been as suspicious of the motives of the 'other' side. Which is why I've never stopped resisting Thomas's arguments: using violence to attempt setting right what is wrong can only end in the destruction of everything, including the possibility of a new beginning. That I cannot accept. Which is why I've clung to the idea of occupying the no-man's-land between the opposing forces; I saw myself as my own only hope.

I need forgiveness, Erik. All of us who have been clinging to this

597

delusion need forgiveness. Because what can it possibly be if not delusion? These times do not permit anyone to opt out. Even a wrong choice is better than no choice at all. It is the only way of knowing who you are, of assuming your humanity.

And in order to reach that point one has no right to exclude beforehand anything, no matter what. The day I left Cape Town with Thomas I thought I knew what I was letting myself in for. Can you believe it? How profoundly have I changed since then! You may laugh at me (but I know you won't), it must sound ridiculous, but do you know when I finally knew that I had changed? It was during the weekend Thomas and I sheltered in the veld, waiting for his people to bring the combi, and all of a sudden in that wide expanse of barrenness we saw a white camel. It was so ridiculous, I thought at first it must be a mirage. Perhaps I was hallucinating. Surely it was totally impossible? As fabulous as a unicorn or a dragon. Yet it was there. We saw it. And then, just as suddenly, I accepted it, with a kind of resignation, and not without amusement. Because this was the confirmation, however absurd it might seem, that from now on there was nothing I could exclude as impossible or improbable any more. That camel had gone right through the eye of the needle of my imagination: after that everything else would be that much easier.

I hope you'll understand. Now that I've spoken to you, I can face the world again. For you. For Thomas. For – whatever.

Oh Erik, I love you. –

It was a few minutes to one. She had to go. Perhaps, this time, Thomas would be there.

He wasn't. But this time, at least, there was news of him.

5

– From Thomas's voice on the phone, the last few times he called, I could hear he was under stress. Never excited or panicky, that's not his style. But there was stress. Especially as he drew closer to the north. Which was understandable. The last time Rashid sent a message that he'd phoned again I sensed that this was now the bottleneck. Rashid's always been quick with the tongue. Especially when it was about this woman with Thomas. He could never quite bring himself to accept her presence. I tried to calm him as best I could. Rashid's worth a lot to us. Totally dedicated. But a kind of young Robespierre in his way, if one has to start looking for models. No weak spot in his armour. No women, no drink, no hobbies, nothing. He can't care less about rest or regular hours or comfort. All that matters to him is the struggle. He even dropped his own family. Singleminded. Once, before I knew him better, I asked him straight: didn't he ever feel like letting up, getting out for a bit, seeing a film, reading a book, taking out a girl, going to a disco, whatever? But that's not his line. Waste of time, he said brusquely. Culture is a dirty word.

Thomas was more difficult. From the first day. I knew about his work, of course. Everybody was talking about it. His photographs had carried the struggle all over the world. Quite something, for an Afrikaner. But he seemed too gentle to me. Still, I had very positive reports from Lusaka. One of the best recruits they'd had in years, they told me. A bit heavy on the emotions at times, but quality. They strongly recommended that I give him a chance. Also because of the anger still in him: thought it might help him get it out of his system. Or to channel it, so one could use it.

What made it easier was that he was prepared, from the beginning, to work with others. Not one of the loners. That was what Sipho Mdana taught him. There was one thing Sipho also quoted in the time I first got to know him, long before Thomas. The old saying of his people: *Ubuntu ungamntu mgabunye abantu.* A person is a person through other persons. That was what caught Thomas, what made him a useful man for us. I discovered it especially in the months we worked together on the farm at Paarl. Because this is a major part of any job, bringing the people together, getting them to know each other through and through. David was a great help. One of the best we ever had. Now he's gone too. It's turned out an expensive transaction, this one. And now this thing with Thomas and the girl and her brother added to it. Expensive. And yet, if I add it all up, we've gained from it. We hit them where it mattered. The soft underbelly. No matter that the president got out of it unscathed. They had a hell of a fright. Right now they're going overboard with the strong-arm stuff, but it's a symptom of panic. Behind it lies the discovery that brute force cannot keep them in power indefinitely. So we're one step closer to the day we can all sit down round a table and make the future happen. That is what I've been working for all these years.

If only the price hadn't been so high.

This is the hardest of all for me. I'm a Christian. I'm not by nature inclined to fight. But what else can one do when doing nothing means allowing evil to grow? My great-grandfather the bricklayer, my grandpa who was a fisherman on the boats, my father the cabinetmaker: where did their passivity bring them? The dog who crouches and wags its tail gets kicked. The one who bares his teeth is treated with respect. If there's nothing else I've learned, then it's this. And God knows it wasn't easy.

I had so much to lose: I was the first in our family to get a proper education. A decent job, a wife I love and with whom I have a good life; a good home, children. It's not an easy thing to place all this at stake, the risk is too great. But the day Frikkie was shot, I knew it was useless thinking one can stay out of it. He would have been eighteen this year, in February. The eleventh. The day he was killed he was six. And all I have of him is the tooth he left behind in his shoe for the tooth mouse that morning. That was when I went in. Not for revenge. Revenge is a cheap thing and against the will of the Lord: it never goes beyond an eye for an eye, a tooth for a tooth. No, it was more than revenge I had on my mind, more even than Frikkie himself. It was everything I learned to face the day he died. Everything I'd tried to ignore before.

And this has nothing to do with eyes and teeth, but everything with *people*. It's a vision we are struggling for. Us: not I, or this one, or that one, but *us*. It's a vision, but that doesn't mean it's pie in the sky. It's hard work. The vision is important to get you going; but what you need, what you're working for, is the power to make it come true. Always it comes down to this, when all is said and done: power. This is the bottom line, without it you needn't even try. Even if it means you have to shape that power the way God made Adam, from the dust of the earth.

I shall never forget what I read about Cambon. He was, if I remember correctly, governor general of Algeria some time in the last century. The lesson he learned too late had to do with a government that tries to rule by force. I wrote it down at the time I was in Angola, memorised it:

We did not realise that in suppressing the forces of resistance in this fashion we were also suppressing our means of action. The result is that today we are confronted with a sort of human dust on which we have no influence, and in which movements take place which are, to us, unknown.

Through Frikkie's death I realised, although the words only came afterwards, that I too now belonged to this dust. Dust unto dust. I found in it the right to hit back. It was this dust that gave us the opportunity. Because no matter what they do they can never be one with us again. And this was something we could use. Not that it was easy. It goes right against my nature. But when history itself breaks into one's life and calls one's name one has to be there to answer. Even the white national anthem says that. *At thy call we shall not falter, firm and steadfast we shall stand.*

It was at Paarl that I first learned to respect Thomas. He was the one who volunteered in January to go to Marseille and bring back the Semtex. He knew very well he would be risking his life, but he pretended it would be child's play to hide the stuff in the lining of his case, no X-ray picks it up. But I knew it takes only one inquisitive bastard at customs and you've had it. And anyway, Thomas was too valuable to us, especially right then, so I sent someone else from outside the group. But he would have done it. Passed every test.

Then came the raid on the farm. So totally unnecessary. Perhaps we panicked too soon. We should never have packed up and left in such a hurry that day. But we couldn't take chances on what the farmer knew or did not know. All he said was that he knew everything and that the police were on their way. How were we to know he was bluffing? That was the first mishap. I was all for aborting the whole plan. Or at least suspending it until the dust had settled. Especially after what had happened to Christine. But Thomas wouldn't hear of it. And for once he had Rashid in full support. And David too: he said we owed it to Christine to go through with it.

How easily a plan can get derailed. One can plan and scheme for months, preparing for every eventuality; then it takes one little cog to seize up and the whole engine goes up in smoke. It was a matter of seconds, then Thomas and Nina would have got away from that cop. The police would never have had any clue and the two of them would have been out of the country that same night. But ever since then it's been downhill. First Nina. Then Christine, killed so they could set a trap for David. And Thomas on the run for his life. We just *had* to keep him out of their way. And it was becoming harder every day.

In a way it is a game, but the stakes are life and death. Always having to read your opponent's mind before he himself knows what's in it. Over the years I've come to know the brigadier. By now I flatter myself that I can predict most of his moves. But one can't afford to relax for a moment. One miscalculation and it's tickets. Sometimes there are helpers one can rely on to make things easier. There's Judy. What she's already done for us in Tygerberg hospital cannot be calculated. There's Sylvia. High-class call-girl. Never takes on anything below Cabinet minister or supreme court judge or top brass in the army. Through her we've found out about moves long before they were ever on the books. It was through her we learned that the killing of the brigadier's right-hand man, young Swanepoel, in Guguletu was probably an inside job. And that there was trouble brewing between the brigadier and the judge, Nina's father. So it came as no surprise when the newspapers reported dead-pan that the judge had suddenly resigned. Health reasons. But Sylvia couldn't help us with anything that would make Thomas's job easier for himself or for us. Just the way the dice fall.

Two things had to be arranged to help him.

One: the next bomb had to be planted. Right here in Cape Town, under their noses. We'd been working on it since before Thomas's bomb: often a follow-up is more important than the thing itself. But the timing had to be spot-on. And that's not easy. Because first we had to get a new cell going after the SB had cornered Mabusa and his group, just before our bomb at the Castle; a bad blow for the whole Organisation. At the same time we had to adjust to Thomas's progress from day to day. It wasn't just a matter of planting a bomb, finish and *klaar*. It had to happen right inside the lion's den, otherwise it would just be one of many. The kind of job we really needed a man like Mabusa for. He was good, professional to the toes. But anyway, we did it. That's one thing about our Organisation. There's always three or four new ones to take the place of anyone who gets eliminated.

So this bomb went off exactly on target and on time, not half an hour after the brigadier left for Kimberley that Saturday morning, on his way to Lichtenburg. Right inside the Langa police station.

Semtex, once again. Because we wanted them to know the same people were involved. Knowing it would rattle them to discover we're still here on the spot; take some of the pressure off Thomas. Main thing was to get the message through: We're still alive and well and living in Cape Town.

Without our contact in the police station we wouldn't have had a chance. We'd been working on him for a long time. And when his number was called he brought his side. *A luta continua.*

Two: we had to do all we could to get Thomas across the border. When he called from Schweizer-Reneke we told him: keep it open, we may still go for Jan Smuts. But that was too much of a risk. Zeke and the others in Soweto told us no go. So Botswana was the only option. And when Thomas next phoned, from Ottosdal, on his way to Lichtenburg on the Friday afternoon, I gave him his final instructions.

From Johburg three cars would be organised that night. One up front, one on standby, one in Mmabatho. Which meant that Thomas and the young woman had to lie low for the night, stay out of sight. He never needed more than half a word. Good head on his shoulders. Our only real worry was the woman. By that time the Boere firmly believed she'd been in it from the word go, so we had to get her out too. For our sake just as much as for her own. But of course it complicated things, two are always more difficult than one. Anyway, we had to go for it.

I am still convinced it would all have gone without a hitch if the woman's brother hadn't also come into the picture. The problem was, of course, that we knew nothing about him in advance. Only when we got the tip-off from Lichtenburg. By that time there wasn't much we could still do here from the Cape, except to get a message through to Gaborone and to arrange for another car with hardware from Johburg. The first two were risky enough as it was, considering all the roadblocks and check-ups on the way, no matter how professional Zeke is with the loose panels and fake seat covers. But risk or no risk, we needed the back-up. Because it was beginning to look like there was a war coming, with the brother on his way, bringing half the SAP and three-quarters of the army on his tail.

So we had no choice, even if this is not the way I like to do things: I prefer planning carefully and meticulously, taking my time, calculating contingencies, leaving as little to chance as possible.

How different a world it could have been. But it's no use thinking like that. My own child would still have been alive if he hadn't been sitting on the pavement that day in 'seventy-six. Then I would have been an ordinary teacher today and nothing more. My head bowed patiently under the yoke like so many others.

Would that have been preferable?

It does not concern only us. There is so much more involved than our private happiness or peace. What matters is the struggle. What matters is the peace we want to leave to those who remain behind, to our children. We must go to hell in order for them to inherit a chance of going to heaven. So there are many, many people involved. All those deaths could not have been in vain. What has now happened to Thomas and to Lisa Lombard must not be in vain. It is for their sake too that we must go on. We must keep faith. If ever we lose faith we will have nothing left at all. –

6

It was just after eleven on the Saturday morning when Thomas arrived in Lichtenburg on the back of the mule-cart, still dazed from the close night; still aching and bruised from what had happened. A curious feeling, knowing that this was the last lap. Whether it was short or long, at last a target was in sight: there was, quite literally, a border to be crossed. For how long had they lived in this awareness? A knowledge as intimate as love.

He could not go straight to the post office: their next appointed hour was only one o'clock. Moreover, Justin had warned him: the discovery of their sojourn with her father, the detention and death of Naomi (nothing of which had been reported in the press; but Justin knew), meant that they had to be even more careful than before. Every town and village and hamlet in the Western Transvaal would be under surveillance. No, he could not possibly show his face at the post office. There were other ways of communication still open: there was the group sent from Johannesburg, five of them in a minibus bearing Bophuthatswana registration plates, instructed to wait at the garage closest to the turn-off to Coligny. They arranged to pick up a child in the township who would take a message to Lisa at the post office on the appointed hour; while pretending to be begging for bread he would casually drop Thomas's name – an obsequious 'Baas Leon' – and pass on the message about where to join them.

The leader, distinguished by a greasy yellow baseball cap worn back to front on his bullet head, showed Thomas, in a container inside one of the rear seats, the arsenal they had brought with them. AK-47s, Makaroffs, grenades, hand-guns. It perturbed him. Was it really necessary? They exploded with laughter. Leave it to them, they assured him. And don't worry, man. Just a couple of hours and they'd be on their way. Crossing the border would be a mere formality.

Not one of them, at that stage, knew about Erik yet.

Afterwards, the petrol pump attendant would recall seeing the combi with its load of friendly, laughing people, how they'd bought Cokes and consumed loaves of bread and chatted to him; and how the thin young white man – looking rather the worse for wear, his clothes dirty and crumpled, a bruise on his cheek – had joined them. But his testimony added little of importance to what, by then, was already surmised or known.

They made room for Thomas among them, to lie down on a bench and try to catch some sleep. For a while they joked about his lack of stamina, then, still laughing, left him in peace. He found it hard to contain his anxiety; he was worried about Lisa. What would she have been doing since the previous day? Would she still be waiting, or had she given up and gone home? (Where in the wide world was 'home' to her? She had as little to go back to as he.)

The first car, after he'd left Schweizer-Reneke the previous day (following a call to Rashid and an interminable wait for Justin to call back), had stopped very soon beside the yard filled with red farm implements where he'd taken up position; but the drive in the ancient black Chev did not go very smoothly. Behind the wheel was a thickset bearded man in a safari suit, his broad-rimmed hat – sporting a band of leopard-skin – drawn deep over his sorrowful eyes; his shapeless wife beside him; on the back seat, three children, two boys with hair cropped close to the round bird-skulls, and a diminutive girl with a shag of dark hair. Thomas shifted in beside the children. The man – Pote ('Paws') Delport, pleased to meet you, I'm a child of the Lord – first offered a rather rambling prayer for a prosperous journey (they were, he informed Thomas, on their way to his wife's relatives in Klerksdorp). Unfortunately the prayer was not answered, but that was not evident until much later. He started talking, at length, and without much coherence, about divining water, which was his work and passion in life. After a few kilometres Pote stopped for Thomas and his wife to change places. 'She feels more at home back there with the children,' Pote cut short Thomas's protests before plunging once more, without warning, into prayer, repeating all his earlier earnest entreaties, lest God had forgotten in the meantime. And then, as they pulled off, he continued in a loud voice which his wife could not but overhear (albeit without perceptible reaction), 'I'm still working on her, sir. She hasn't had much of a schooling, her father didn't believe in education for his daughters, which is why she doesn't say much in company.' He continued the exposition on his occupation: 'I am a poor man as you see me, sir. But the Lord says it's easier to get through the Gates that way. May God protect the Afrikaner from prosperity. Because you listen to me, sir, the day the Afrikaner became rich he sold his soul to the devil. Now is that true or isn't it?' Without waiting for confirmation he returned to his previous line of conversation: 'Look at the veld, sir. It's only dust, there's nothing left, not a drop of water for man or beast. While down below this dry earth runs God's streams of plenty. But do you think any of these farmers will call me in to show it to them? They're dying of thirst, sir, and under their feet is a sea of water. God will provide. But man's heart is hard. He shall humble us before His face. We must all be broken first.'

What broke was the car. Four times over the sixty-nine kilometres to Wolmaransstad. The first symptom was, invariably, the radiator boiling; but this was linked to other, more esoteric, complications. Pote Delport's reaction, without fail, was first to offer a prayer, and then to duck in under the hood of the engine where he would start plucking at the wires, at random. The moment Thomas appeared beside him he would gratefully stand back and leave it all to the ingenuity of his guest – complemented by invocations of God Almighty to witness his profound gratitude. 'You may think, sir, that I abandon myself to worries and grief when she stops like this. But I can't care less, no, sir.' Snapping his middle fingers on two amazingly broad thumbs. 'Because I know the Lord will provide, sir. It is His way of testing me. Every time we break down I feel His divine presence very close.'

The fourth time, ten kilometres outside Wolmaransstad, one of the front tyres blew out. And after Thomas had opened the boot – his host had seated himself comfortably on a bank a few yards from the road to watch – and had unpacked the mountain of baggage on the ground beside the car, he discovered that the spare wheel, worn through to the canvas, was totally useless. Which meant that Thomas had to hitchhike in to town with one of the wheels (Delport felt he shouldn't abandon his family to the mercy of the elements), have it repaired at a garage, pay for the job, and then hitch another ride back to the car. As they all got in again, at long last, Delport offered another prayer of thanks. On the very outskirts of the town the car once again broke into stutters and shuddered to a stop. There Thomas left them, much to Delport's chagrin at his guest's refusal to share in a farewell prayer.

'Perhaps, sir, if you will not wait, the Lord will at least incline your heart to offer us a small donation as a contribution to the costs of the journey?' he suggested hopefully.

Thomas thrust a few of Vleis Wagenaar's notes into the man's eager paws and strode off. It was past noon already.

In the straggling industrial area on the fringe of the town, on the road to Ottosdal, he waited for barely fifteen minutes before a talkative travelling salesman picked him up. Impassive, he allowed the man's steady string of unoriginal anecdotes to reel past him as he sat remembering, with an ache of longing, his grandfather's magic way of transforming anything and everything into story.

In Ottosdal, as arranged, he telephoned Justin again for the latest instructions.

He was hungry. In a green and white and pink café he ordered tea and a sandwich; the table was dominated by a vase of plastic flowers which didn't leave room for much else; as Thomas moved it aside a cockroach scuttled off across the chipped formica. Half an hour later he returned to the main road. This time it was a long wait. His patience was already wearing thin when a poisonous green Sierra stopped to offer him a lift. Inside were four young men, all visibly under the influence of the sorghum beer they were passing from hand to hand. The carton reached him too, and on the first round he dutifully took a sip; but afterwards he declined. Which incited them to start commenting on the whitey who obviously thought he was too good for them. Initially it sounded like innocuous banter, but gradually a more vicious tone cut through to the surface. He did his best to remain congenial, even demonstrated his good will by addressing the man beside him in Xhosa. But this had an inflammatory effect.

'What you trying to prove, Whitey? You talk to kaffirs in Xhosa?'

Sorry, he apologised, he really hadn't meant to offend them; he just wanted to prove he was okay.

'What you mean okay? You show me a whitey that's okay. You

607

haven't even got a car, you bumming lifts, you bloody poor-white, you trying to patronise us? That's shit, man. That's pure shit.'

He tried to convince them that he did own a car but that it had broken down; that he was on his way back to Johannesburg, a lecturer at Wits, nothing wrong with his credentials. But the man next to him, in the middle of the rear seat – the two in front, too engrossed in serious drinking, more or less ignored the conversation – became even more aggressive.

'Don't give me this Wits business, man. Bloody lot of white liberals. Fuck them, I say. Fuck all of you.'

Look, Thomas said at last, if he was such a nuisance to them, they could let him get off again and drive on without him. He wasn't asking any favours. Neither was he prepared to swallow insults.

'So who's insulting who?' His neighbour was really worked up by now. 'Bloody white shit getting into our car, throwing your weight around. You shit, man, you shit. I tell you.'

Afterwards he found it difficult to remember the particulars. An angry shuffling and jostling on the back seat, the car careering off the road, swaying and skidding dangerously, coming to a standstill, he thrown out. The car pulling off, stopping some distance away, then reversing towards him. Two of the men jumping out, starting to push him around, grabbing his shopping bag, tearing the money from his jeans pocket, stripping the watch from his left wrist. A knee in his stomach. Something hard striking the side of his face. Voices calling, 'Hey, cool it, man, cool it. That's enough.' And the car driving off at speed again.

In his head – through the pain and confusion – there was only one thought: he had to get away from the road. If he were found like that and people started making enquiries, taking him to a doctor or, worse, the police, he'd be in deep trouble. In a ditch beside the road he lay down for a while until he was feeling better. Then he began to walk on again, diving for cover whenever a car approached, which did not happen very often.

It must have been close to sunset when a tractor approached from behind. This seemed safe. He started waving frantically and the driver, a tall man in faded overalls, stopped. Thomas went up to him.

The man gazed at him in dismay. Thomas evidently had no idea of how bad he looked.

'The baas he's all right?'

He said something in reply. The man put out a long arm to

help him up on the tractor and managed to offer him room, half-crouched, half-standing.

'Where do you live?' he asked. The tractor shuddered and roared. His head felt like bursting.

'Is not far, is just little way ahead here. My baas's place.'

'No. If you don't mind, please –' He tried to explain without sounding too implausible: all he knew was that it was too risky to confront a farmer in this state. His saviour, on the other hand, was clearly unhappy at Thomas's entreaties not to deliver him to a higher authority. At the same time the man was too intimidated by a lifetime of obeying orders to offer much resistance. On the roaring tractor they followed the road past black dried-up sunflower fields and patches of khaki weed. At a narrow turn-off to where Thomas could discern in the distance, past a sparse bluegum plantation, a huddle of huts and shanties, the man stopped and motioned in obvious reluctance. 'Is there, my place. But is not a good place for the baas.'

Thomas shook his head in furious supplication and got down from the tractor.

The man flung his voice, like a hurtling stone, through the air to where a woman answered from the huts; the conversation continued for a while, and then the man drove on, his whole attitude translating his misgivings and his gloom, to what must be 'the baas's place'.

When he returned on foot an hour later – the twilight had already begun to turn to night – carrying a plastic bag of mealie meal and some potatoes from the homestead, Thomas was already lying prone in a hut. The people were clearly agitated, intimidated, by his presence; and as most of them could speak only Tswana, communication was inhibited. What he managed to convey – hoped he had conveyed – was that he wished to spend the night with them if they would let him; and that he had to resume as early as possible in the morning his journey to Lichtenburg.

They brought him porridge in a red plastic mug. An hour after sunset the evening meal was finished. They obviously did not want to waste paraffin or candles on lighting. Soon after, they were all asleep, Thomas in a square hut with twelve or thirteen others, large and small; the single window opening stuffed with old hessian bags, the door drawn shut. In the middle of the floor a bucket of coals stood smouldering to provide heat, spreading its bitter smoke smell over the heavy, more intimate odours of so many bodies.

609

In the hollow of the night, taking care not to make any noise, Thomas got up – outside, the dry paper rustling of mealie stalks in the breeze – and removed the bags from the window to let in some fresh air. A deep male voice mumbled something in half-hearted protest, but was soon smothered in sleep again.

He still found it impossible to sleep. Through his confused thoughts an ancient memory returned: that night in his childhood when he and his father had been driven by the flood and the storm to seek shelter with the strangers: the scorching of the hidden pages of hell-fire girls against his skin under his soaked clothes, the terrors of the yard through which he stumbled to the outhouse to get rid of them; and the dying old woman, the sour smell of death; the sound of her voice in his ear as she whispered, 'Boetie – the – kaffirs – are – coming.' Throughout his life, throughout all the generations of his tribe, this fear of the kaffirs coming. And tonight he was here in this hut with them, the only people among whom he felt safe.

His great-grandfather Gabriel Landman, it suddenly occurred to him, had also had this experience when in the Anglo-Boer War he'd stumbled back to the family farm to spend the night with the old black man and his family in the ruins of the house, sharing with them their meagre *pap* and pumpkin and *marog*. Truly, there was nothing new under the sun.

With a heavy headache he rose with the others, long before the first light, went outside, stripped to the waist, and splashed some ice-cold water from a blue plastic bucket over his face and bare body. It made him gasp for breath, but also eased the headache; and after a fistful of cold stiff porridge he left with the tractor driver, covering a few hundred yards from the parched mealie lands to a patch of dull brown thorn-trees where another cluster of huts huddled inside a windblown shelter of branches. A mule-cart was already waiting. Everything had evidently been arranged. And so he left on his last lap to the town.

– Did not Don Quixote, too, return home from one of his journeys like this? (Great-grandpa Gabriel did, on a horse-cart.) On the back of a wagon, a bundle of bruised bones. But *my* journey has been different, hasn't it? I have not gone in search of giants or Saracens, and certainly not of knighthood; my Dulcinea is an angry, rebellious, unpredictable woman, her smooth black hair hacked short below an unsightly wig, her body angular in its gauche grace, her eyes smoked agate, on her finger a lucky-packet ring. *I pledge thee my troth –*

There is something salubrious about a trip like this. Relegated to the pace of a mule, on a shaky cart with a silent man and two small boys on the front bench. Each separate thorn-tree, each tuft of white grass, each patch of blood-red earth in stripped sunflower or mealie lands I can study intimately as we pass. As slowly as a funeral procession, respectful towards the innumerable dead already returned to dust. Immeasurably ancient dust, this, the grave perhaps of the very first humanoids, the inhabitants of Taung three million years ago, followed by hunters and gatherers, herders of cattle, the first tillers of the soil, smelters of iron and copper and gold, artists who left the traces of their imaginings on rocks and stones and the walls of caves.

Circle upon circle the different layers of my existence are finally drawn in towards me, like a kaross, here, now.

The furthest circle: the children, descendants, avatars of Adam-astor. How many of them have gone into the shaping of myself: Hollander, French Huguenot, English, a wandering Jew, black African, Khoikhoin. Refugee, coward, traitor, murderer, robber, rebel or slave, believer and infidel; the meek and the savage, the forever wandering; soldier, digger, solid burgher, outcast. Each one of them, woman or man, inspired by a personal dream or hallucination, a private vision – ship in the desert, woman transformed into gazelle or mermaid, the archangel Gabriel, an outlandish camel on the wall of a small hot furnace of a room – each one in search of the impossible, each both victim and victor; each obsessed with power and survival, a personal salvation. How can I distinguish – how dare I presume to distinguish – between the good and the bad in them, the reason and the unreason, the love and the hate, the failure and the success, the divine and the demonic, between faith and heresy? Perhaps those like us require a special compassion, are in dire need of grace. What we have been, what we have become, has been our way of responding to Africa, the most bountiful, and the cruellest, mother of history: sometimes sentimental, often generous; unreasonable, enraged, gentle, violent, patient. What I myself have done: does that deserve only outright condemnation? Or dare one imagine it eliciting, somewhere, sometime, from someone, a measure at least, if not of forgiveness, perhaps of understanding? What do I know about success or failure?

How many lives have been destroyed through what we – I and my tribe – have done? (How many more –?) Have we become at last the cause of our own destruction? And yet we have loved this hard tract of earth! We have never wished to go elsewhere. This has been our glory, our misery. Our terrible, burning, misplaced, perverse love. There is a whole history with me today on the back of this rickety cart. On our way to – what? Is there still a destination awaiting us?

The second circle: private memories, photographs from my own life shoved haphazardly into the albums of my mind. A life perpetually split in two, positive and negative: the comfortable facts of home – and the explosions of story and imagination in the holidays on Oupa's farm; the reassurance of our white town – and the unpredictabilities of the townships: a black woman balancing a pail of water on her head, the death of an old man in his single quarters, a small figure with a booming voice back from the island of terror and of dreams, a friend hurled into the back of a van, desperate lives, violent deaths, burning faith, *ubuntu*; the intimate knowledge of the land in which I was born – and the discoveries abroad, the community of the exiled and the dispossessed, the violence of a purple day. And then the return to where at last I know I fatefully belong, and the shouldering of my own terrifying responsibility for this patch of earth, this garden withered by too many droughts. Our little group on the farm: Justin, Rashid, David (Christine in hospital); and Nina and I.

And already I am in the third circle, flung headlong into it by that explosion which marks forever Before and After. An old woman losing her wig – a girl collapsing in slow motion on an airport building floor – the transparency of the walls in the houses of my family: brother, sister, parents; and nowhere an outhouse with a firefly – the thwarted epiphany of a funeral – a girl in a green aquarium: I love you, Lisa Lombard – Nimrod the mighty hunter who forced me to acknowledge, at last, the blood on my hands. This violence which has been the distinguishing mark of homo sapiens, leaving its crude imprint even on the little skull from Taung, not all that far from here. I had come to believe that to put an end to the blood I had no choice but to spill some too: but whether that was confirmation or betrayal of my humanity I can no longer say for sure, because all that has happened is that I have been added to the catalogue of killers. With the loss of simple answers the questions too have become infinitely more difficult. Everything is woven into everything else, each new day has become a reflection or distortion of others.

And all of this, here on this cart which travels as slowly as fate,

I have to absorb into myself. Because no one can live without assuming the full burden of his inherited guilt: his complicity in being human, with all the good and evil that are part of it.

Perhaps I once thought that the road to a world more worthy and free than the one we have would be shorter: and in this I erred; but I cannot believe that it is wrong to devote one's life to bringing such a world closer. Because *not* to believe in it, *not* to be prepared to give one's life for it if necessary, would be the final insult to the skeleton of Taung. –

7

'Fuck that brother of hers.' The burly driver of the minibus, so relaxed and jocular when they'd first met at the garage in Lichtenburg, tore the greasy yellow baseball cap from his head and hit it several times, viciously, against the palm of his left hand as if to rid it of some invisible contamination. 'We could have been across the border and safe in Botswana by now.' He looked at the ostentatious watch, all cogs and discs and wheels, that sat on his wrist like a time-bomb. 'We said four o'clock. It's ten past. I'm going now.'

'We can't leave them behind,' insisted Thomas. His eyes were black against the unusual pallor of his face. 'We can't leave *her* behind.'

'We can. And we must. If that is what it takes to get *you* across that border. Now come on, we made a deal, you said four o'clock, right?'

'I can't.'

'Look, my brother.' The man put a big arm round his shoulders. 'I know it's tough. But you're in this business because you can take it. And because you can obey orders.'

'You can drive off at half-past. Okay?'

Thomas was aware of the four others watching closely through half-mast eyelids. The heartiness with which they had originally received him was beginning to change, slowly but perceptibly, into suspicion, disdain, open resentment. The minibus, all its doors open, was parked under a cluster of patchy bluegums, not so much for the shade – even in the open sun the warmth was wintry – as for the meagre protection it offered against prying eyes, whether from among the distant cluster of corrugated-iron diggers' homes

613

and sheds and the sad shanties of their black labourers, or from the sky above where it might not be too far-fetched to imagine a police helicopter materialising.

This was the Klipveld, the 'Rocky Earth', between Lichtenburg and the Botswana border; from above – from a helicopter? – it would be noticeable as a gravelly ridge that defines the water divide between north and south. In primeval times streams crisscrossed the territory, bringing with them the massive deposits of diamonds which early in the century drew fortune-seekers from across the globe to Lichtenburg, the 'Town of Light'; what is left of the watercourses today, after all the softer earth has been washed or blown away, is the intricate pattern of hard ridges the diggers call 'runs', the only prominent features in an otherwise level semi-desert landscape. Few diggers remain where seventy years before Thomas's grandfather tried his own brief luck; among the abandoned holes and trenches must be the scars with which he, too, marked the now impoverished earth.

But standing in the open back door of the minibus, his eyes shielded against the thin sunlight as he peered to the south-east in search of any cloud of dust that might mark the approach of Lisa and Erik in their vehicle (followed by God knows how many others?!), Thomas could not have been thinking about his grandfather. Inside the minibus he could hear the CB radio crackling; their contacts in Soweto, in Mmabatho, and across the border in Botswana, were also getting impatient. Fifteen more minutes; then they would have to continue without Lisa. And all because her brother had now become involved too. (– Fuck that man. –)

Just before one o'clock his comrades had sent a small boy from the township to the post office with a message for Lisa. And she had acted with the clearheaded professionalism he'd come to admire in her. In the brief half-hour they had been together afterwards she had told him about it (and how proud she had done him, in front of the comrades): pretending to be annoyed by the boy who had given her the message, she'd thrust a coin in his grimy hand and shooed him off; then had casually sauntered back to the café where she had been sitting, reading, before. She ordered another pot of tea. After a while, leaving her cup still half-full and her plastic bag draped over the chair as if she intended to return in a minute (what she remembered – regretted – as she spoke to him was the loss of the sexy panties!), she went to the toilet at the rear of the building. From the open backyard she made her escape. Along the way there was one moment of panic when a yellow police van approached round a corner; but keeping her cool she stopped in front of a shop window to study with ferocious interest the banal objects on display inside, almost too scared to breathe, and relaxing only after the vehicle had passed on its slow prowl.

And so Lisa had arrived at the garage where they had been so anxiously waiting. That was the first Thomas had learned about her telephone call that morning, and about Erik. (Thinking about it now, under the bedraggled bluegum-trees of the diggings, he suddenly wondered: had the police, perhaps, actually been following her every inch of the way, anticipating her movements? But that was unlikely. No one could possibly have established from where she'd telephoned her father's house that morning; and even if experts had managed to decipher some of the codes in her conversation with Erik – especially after making the necessary adjustments upon discovering that he was not heading for the coast as they'd anticipated, but north-east – the police would still have been largely dependent on Erik, and no one else, for their clues. And surely Erik would have been sufficiently on the alert soon to discover that he was being followed; at the very least he would have realised that Lisa's life depended on his caution and ingenuity. Undoubtedly the pursuers were in radio contact, as they progressed, with the stations ahead; but they could have had no way of telling in advance that Lichtenburg was to be their preliminary destination.)

She seemed more upset than he was. 'Oh Jesus, what are we going to do now? Have I made a total fuck-up?'

'*Must* we wait for him?' he blurted out without thinking. They were talking out of earshot of the others.

She gaped at him (he hardly recognised her in that outfit: the awful wig, the sunglasses). 'Of course we must. Can you think of what they'll do to him if they caught him? And if they don't find us they *will* grab him.'

'Are you absolutely sure he's on his way?'

'Of course. He said so.' She told him, briefly, haphazardly, of the coded conversation. 'He'll be looking for me in the graveyard.'

'With half the country's police force on his heels.'

She stared at him in silence. At last she said, very quietly, 'There's only one thing we can do.' From the set line of her jaw he could tell what was coming; and he dreaded it. 'I'll go and meet him. You have to go on without me.'

'Don't be bloody stupid.'

'I messed it up. I'll take the consequences.'

'Look, we're in this together. Whatever happens.' He tried to smile but it wasn't very successful. 'In sickness and in health, for richer or poorer, right?'

There were tears in her eyes, but she did not give way to them.

They returned to the others in the minibus for an impromptu conference; some of the comrades were not impressed. To put it mildly. But between the two of them they managed to placate the men, if only for the time being. The advantage they had, Thomas pointed out, was that Erik's pursuers could have as yet no idea of where the group of them were; of where *he* was. And before they actually had him in their telescopic sights they were unlikely to pounce on anyone else.

Even so there was no time to lose. Lisa would have to be dropped in the graveyard while Thomas proceeded with the others in the minibus to this more remote, and hopefully – temporarily – safe hiding place.

It was hard, almost unbearable, to leave her behind when they drove off; but there was no other way. As he looked back, after they had deposited her near the northern fringe of the town – how many times on this journey, he thought in near-despair, had he looked back at others left behind? – she appeared forlorn, and shockingly fragile. There was no certainty that he would ever see her again. It was in a curious state of suspension that he sat back against his seat in the minibus; nothing seemed quite real any more; he was unable to connect with his own emotions. At least two of the men in the group insisted again, once they had dropped Lisa off and made sure that they were not being followed, that they drive straight on to the border (and how could he blame them? it was more than temptation: the most basic common sense dictated that they should use the advantage and make a dash for freedom); but in the end, when he threatened to get out and stay behind on his own, they grudgingly agreed.

But now they were nearing the end of their tolerance.

'Twenty-five past,' said the thickset man behind the wheel as he replaced the radio microphone. He was looking at no one in particular.

And then, when even Thomas had given up hope – although he still did not know whether, when the moment came, he would leave with them or remain behind, alone, among the wretched bluegums and the depressing grey dumps of worked-out diamond runs – there was the sound of a car approaching.

They all tensed. With the deftness of a prestigiditator two of the men produced, as if from nowhere, AK-47 guns and crouched, out of sight, behind the minibus. The driver wearing the ancient yellow cap had his hand, ready, on his radio controls. The watch on his wrist caught, in a flash, the sun.

Among the gravel dumps appeared a dusty fawn-coloured vehicle. It was not Erik's car, as Lisa had described it.

They were already preparing for action when Thomas called out. It was indeed Lisa and her brother.

He ran towards them and pulled open the passenger door even before the car had come to a standstill.

'What happened? Why are you so late?'

'Lost our way in this damn maze of farm roads and dirt tracks and cattle paths after we turned off the main road like you said.' She kissed him, stifling a sob of relief.

In the background Erik gave an awkward smile. 'I thought you'd have driven off by now.'

'You sure as hell kept us waiting,' said the driver gruffly, coming up from behind. 'Anybody tailing you?'

'When Erik arrived in the graveyard he said there'd been two cars behind him most of the way.' She glanced, involuntarily, over her shoulder.

'So what'd you do?'

A quick nervous grin. 'There was an old couple putting flowers on a grave. Left their keys in the car at the side gate. So we just jumped in and drove off. No one seemed to notice.'

'Neat thinking,' said Thomas, glancing at the leader. 'What did I tell you –?'

The burly man grunted what sounded like grudging approval. Then returned to the attack: 'What happened to the Boere?'

'We took the R52 like you said. They must have thought we were heading straight for the airport, so I suppose once they picked up the trail again they all charged past the turn-off.'

'Even so, I don't think we're safe yet,' said Erik. 'They would have spread the word by now.' He seemed remarkably collected, though he was clearly nervous. In a sudden impulsive gesture he offered Thomas his hand. 'Hell, man, I'm sorry. I know it's all my fault –'

The driver interrupted angrily. 'Look, there's no time for sweet talk now. We got to get to that border.' He fired staccato instructions at them. Thomas and Erik had to swap clothes. Lisa and Thomas, armed with some of the weapons from the arsenal in the minibus, would drive on ahead in the stolen car. In Erik's uniform Thomas had a chance of eluding the enemy, while Erik could travel, under close scrutiny, in the minibus with the five comrades. There was a car waiting at a picnic spot near Rooigrond; another outside the university entrance in Mmabatho. If necessary, they could swop vehicles again and confuse whatever pursuers might materialise. Then there was the final stretch of twenty-three kilometres to the border post at Ramatlabama. On the other side several batches of armed helpers from Gaborone and Lobatsi would be on standby. With some luck –

And it really did seem as if their luck would hold.

But on that final lap to the dried bed of the Molopo that traces the frontier it changed.

The first signal was the regular, urgent, throbbing sound that seemed to come from no specific spot, yet surrounded them, intruded upon them, zooming in on them. They first thought it must be thunder, but it was too menacingly regular for that, and the sky – draining slowly of light as the sun slid downward to the grim horizon – was clear. Something wrong with the engine? But their progress was even.

It was Lisa who first cried out, catching her breath, 'My God, it's a helicopter!'

And against this all-seeing, ubiquitous pursuer, Thomas knew, there was little defence. Cars from behind might be eluded; road-blocks might be crashed, even armed vehicles in front might be circled or avoided. But this deus ex machina was relentless.

Its occupants must have realised that its presence had been discovered. In a terrifying dive it came swooping down towards them, hovering overhead, then spiralling slowly upward again, tilted, prepared for another dive. Involuntarily they ducked. It was so close they could see – if not, for the moment, recognise – faces in the glass bubble above. And perhaps their own faces, too, were discovered; or at least enough of their bodies for the men overhead to make out her blouse, his troopie uniform. Was that why the machine swerved out of the way again and swooped towards the station wagon (which had, in Mmabatho, replaced the minibus) in their wake? It was hard to keep track of it in the rear-view mirror. They were too tense too speak. Only from the tightness of her hand on his knee could Thomas guess what was happening inside her.

Suddenly – was it recklessness or bravado or calculation? – a head, then a torso, emerged from the side window of the station wagon; and an AK-47. They did not hear the shooting. They only saw the helicopter wavering, lunging, momentarily appearing to lose its balance, then streaking away out of sight.

The station wagon signalled from behind with its headlights. Thomas swerved off the road and waited for it to catch up.

'Did you hit it?' he asked, breathless.

'Don't know. But there's shit ahead, man. Just got a message on the radio. Whole fucking army massing at the border post.'

'So what do we do now?'

'Got to move up north. Another twenty or so kilometres. It's an old escape route of the stock thieves. They sending a car across the border to help us. With some luck –'

No such luck.

The car, a souped-up Sierra, did get through from the other side, its driver having cut the wires; the old river-bed was dry, no problem to cross it. But with the welcoming hills of Botswana already in sight – the sun had just set; the dark was coming down over distant outcrops huddled in the dusk like rows of small baked loaves – the helicopter was suddenly back overhead. And then, like vultures, another and another. And there was the rumbling of large vehicles in the distance, to the left; and a battery of headlights – searchlights – flaring in the dusk.

'It's a fucking trap,' said the man with the yellow baseball cap, turning towards the station wagon – they were all, briefly, huddled beside the vehicles to confer – grasping for a gun.

'Walking right into it,' said Brigadier Kat Bester in the first helicopter above, clutching and unclutching his hands as if reeling in a line.

From up there he had a clear view of the uncluttered landscape, bare as a sheet of paper, on which all movement was inscribed with the unsentimental directness of geometry: Erik – whom in the descending dark, and at that distance, they mistook for Thomas – jumping into the Sierra and speeding off on his own, obviously intent on drawing the fire, diverting the attention; the others piling helter-skelter into the station wagon and the second car; the security forces streaking across the veld like a lengthening arrow to head off the fugitive.

'This one is mine,' Bester said.

The pilot in the helicopter changed course. The second passenger, a military officer, took aim at the speeding car; on the ground other vehicles were closing in on it as it swerved, and spun, and – the helicopter now descending directly in its way – scudded to a standstill, its tyres blown out.

There was confusion, afterwards, in the various accounts of the event. But this much was clear: that Lisa, at the wheel of the second car – the others needed their hands free to handle the guns – swerved unexpectedly from the straight line she had been instructed to follow to the border, racing instead, impulsively, furiously, towards her beleaguered brother. Behind them, the station wagon also veered from its course in angry pursuit.

The big man in the passenger seat beside Lisa, reacting swiftly and viciously – Thomas, in the back seat, was unable to intervene – stunned her with a blow of his rifle butt. She let go of the wheel. The man grabbed it. But the car stalled. They were twenty or thirty yards away when Erik flung open the door of the Sierra and half-jumped, half-fell from it. But he was stopped in his tracks by the brigadier who came leaping – startlingly agile for a man of his build – from the helicopter which had just touched down. Overhead, the rotor blades were still whirring.

For a moment, peering through the deep dusk, the big man stared anxiously, disbelievingly, at Erik. And then Lisa, sprinting from the other car, was approaching, shouting hysterically. Behind them the first unwieldy machines of the security forces were also grumbling to a halt in the swirling dark dust.

Before she could reach her brother the brigadier grabbed hold of her. In his free hand he had a pistol.

'Let her go!' shouted Thomas from the distant car as its occupants spilled out, scrambling, cursing, furious, dropping on their knees, taking aim. In seconds they were joined by the men from the station wagon which had pulled up alongside, its engine still idling.

Above the scene hovered the two other helicopters.

As Thomas called out the brigadier turned his head. He could not have recognised the voice. But he knew immediately, in spite of the gloom, who it was.

At last: the two of them.

There seemed no end to that silence in which they stood staring, through the gathering night, at one another; for them, there was no one else present.

But for Lisa between them.

'Let go of her!' Thomas whispered. But this time no one could have heard him.

She tried to wrench free. Erik shouted something. Thomas bellowed. The brigadier had his gun against her head, backing away very slowly, very confidently towards the waiting helicopter.

There was, Thomas thought afterwards, over and over, nothing else he could have done. He could not let her be dragged away like that to what he knew — he knew beyond words, in his guts — would happen to her.

There was, simultaneously with his shot, a whole burst of firing, of grenades exploding, from the comrades at the station wagon and the car, from the security forces in the distance, from the helicopters above: and in that dark no-man's-land in their midst were the brigadier and Lisa; and Erik running towards them, stumbling, falling, crawling away. And Lisa, first, in the foreground, slumping, as a long time before, moments before, Nina too had fallen.

— The men, all those men, always the men. Their unbelievable racket. So much noise. And yet now I know, suddenly, at last, too late, what it is I have always feared about violence. It is not the noise of shots and explosions and screams and shouts, not the din that accompanies and surrounds it, but the silence that lurks deep inside it like the darkness in the heart of a flame. That silence which is forever beyond words. The silence of a heron dipping its foot into black water. The silence of a half-dead crayfish scuttling out of reach. The silence that is inhuman because it is beyond language. It betrays language, betrays us. Not noise, no, not noise; only silence. —

Moments later, in the crossfire, the brigadier, too, fell. Immediately one of the hovering helicopters came whirring down from above to offer help, a frantic insect; appeared to forget about the one already on the ground and suddenly became entangled in the swirling rotors. The sound of clanging, tearing metal. And then a spectacular explosion, and volcanic fire leaping into the night. The remaining helicopter dashed off to avoid the flames, made a wide detour, then returned to settle at some distance. Men burst from it in a frantic dash to collect the fallen officer. (Within the hour, it was reported afterwards, he was operated on by a medical team in One Military Hospital at Voortrekkerhoogte. Bullet in the brain. The emergency operation lasted five hours. He never regained consciousness. Still later, it was announced that a decoration for exceptional bravery was to be awarded to him posthumously; owing to a nervous condition his widow could not attend the ceremony to accept the medal on his behalf.)

While the security men were still straining to lift the brigadier into the helicopter, comrades ran, weaving and ducking, through the crossfire in what newspapers were to describe as 'the eerie glow' of the still smouldering wreckage, to drag Erik and Thomas away from Lisa. Impossible as it seemed, they reached the nearer vehicle without mishap. But as they prepared to pile into it the whole car exploded in a grenade attack. Only one of the comrades – perhaps the leader, but he had lost his cap – staggered to his feet again and scrambled into the driver's seat of the still idling station wagon; Erik, amazingly unscathed, managed to drag Thomas inside with him. The doors still open, the station wagon drove off wildly across the rutted veld, spun through the sand of a dried-up river-bed, roared and whined up a bank and into blackness.

At some stage there were headlights flashing ahead; there were voices. Shouting, talking.

Afterwards, for a very long time, there was only silence.

8

– To mark the paper, blotch the page; stain consciousness of the present with memory of the past, or conscience perhaps with history.

In this severe, functional room which was once Sipho's office (how remote the morning I sat here paging through back numbers of *Sechaba* while he was catching up on the correspondence accumulated during our trip to Moscow), in a white building on the outskirts of Lusaka, behind iron grilles and alarm systems and walls topped with broken glass, not far from Soweto market where once we rummaged in search of a spare exhaust for his car so that he could collect Noni from the airport, I must try at last, at long long last, to gather what I have so nearly lost.

They have offered me the use of a word processor. That will make it much easier. But I am keeping that for the recording of the tribal history I have worked on for so many years. (The many notes and early drafts entrusted to David in Cape Town on the eve of our attack were awaiting me here; for the rest I shall have to rely on memory and my imagination.) Not because it will serve any great purpose in itself: merely to impose again a discipline on my mind; to occupy myself; not to go to pieces.

Before I feel free to indulge myself on that pc I must grapple with pen and paper – a matter of honour, I admit, more than of necessity – coaxing a dumb if willing left hand into mastering laboriously the intricacies of writing once taken for granted by the right: a task as daunting, and for me as indispensable, as the preparations long ago for our act of terror or the journey afterwards to stay out of their reach. Five-finger exercises for left hand.

There are stacks of newspapers around me from the time – eighteen, twenty months ago (is it possible?) – but I find them, for all their assertiveness, their unbearable smugness, as unreliable and incomplete as my own recollections. How much easier to return to a remote and already partly canonised past: but that must wait till later. There is this other obstacle course to be negotiated first. In the beginning there were the months in one hospital after the other – Gaborone, Lusaka, London, Stockholm, then back here – to blame, to use as a pretext for postponement. But now, in this parenthesis between what was and what is not yet, it can no longer be postponed.

I remember the smell of the first hospital in which I came to again. I remember calling out, still groggy with anaesthetic, Lisa's name, remember groping for help, and not finding it because, as I only realised later, I had no right hand any more to grasp with.

'Lisa!'

Then there were soothing voices, and I was pushed back against the pillows, and someone said, 'Don't you know then, Lisa is dead.'

And then, yes, I remembered. I knew; as I know now. It is I who killed her. No matter what anyone says. No matter what the reason: whether it was a mistake, the bullet meant for that man; or to save her from something worse. I did it. I shall bear it to my own grave; it is the inevitable consequence of that very first decision I took, the day Sipho and Noni were killed, to take up arms myself. A fearful symmetry.

I have, they say, 'survived'. Minus the hand, minus some other bits and pieces. But such things have happened to others before; will happen; and worse, infinitely worse. I have survived, and that is, I know – I *must* believe in it – a kind of victory. Not only for us, but for the others too; for those who dreadfully accept that all who dare resist the regime must inevitably become its victim. I have crossed that border, and others.

Erik comes to see me every day. We have, at last – after groping our way through many layers of grief and anger, reproach, resentment, guilt – become friends; he has joined the Organisation. Together we try to sustain each other, each – both – drawing courage from that absence which largely determines us. All we have to show for everything that has happened is that we are here, somewhere beyond a frontier of predictability, acceptability. And the assurance that we have not succumbed; that we are still alive. It is almost in desperation that we cling to this. It is the only way to bear the burden; to honour the one we love.

Secluded here in my spare white office – waiting for the day I have sufficiently mastered my new deprivation to proceed to the pc and attempt to find, if not sense, at least coherence in my tribal past – this is what I am trying so strenuously to do in my large and urgent, unformed letters, on a growing pile of smudged pages.

How different these scribblings would have been had I written them twenty months ago. How incalculably much has changed since then: in myself; in that country in the south; in the world. Around me the unthinkable has begun to happen: the Berlin Wall has fallen, the dictatorships of Central Europe have been swept away, despotic military rule in South America has been dismantled, in the Soviet Union perestroika has begun to transform the heart of the system. Around the globe, millions of ordinary women and men have begun to say, 'No! Enough!' In South Africa, too, the people are on the march, clamouring for the freedom denied them, with so much violence, for so long. A Berlin wall of the mind, blade-wire barricades erected in the hearts of people, battalions of Casspirs and guns have begun to retreat before the onslaught of ordinary people. Robben Island has regurgitated most of its prisoners; it may well become a museum or a tourist resort in future, its walls inscribed with the legends which compel visitors to the House of Bondage in Gorée to take heed. Prisons have opened their gates. Mandela has emerged, free, from the Victor Verster prison outside Paarl, not ten kilometres from the farm where two years before we had prepared our assault.

And suddenly, from the vantage point of this new world which only months ago would have been unimaginable, I must ask the one, unavoidable, question: Have I sacrificed all this – my life, many lives, your life – in vain? Had I known then what I do now, would I have chosen a different course?

But how fair *is* such a question? Suppose that at the time, in that Dark Hole of our modern history, we – and the innumerable others like us – had not decided to put an end to what was happening, had elected instead to stay out of the fray, to renounce violence ourselves, leaving it to others to kill and be killed: suppose people like us had chosen instead to wait patiently and passively – or even to resist, but peacefully, drawing a careful line we would not permit ourselves to step over, no matter how often the forces from the opposing side overstepped it – would the changes that have happened in the world since then have been even remotely possible?

To judge today, with all the advantages of hindsight, whether what we did then was 'right', was 'necessary', was 'inevitable': would that not falsify, for the sake of the insights we have today, what was true before?

It is so easy to forget! Perhaps the whole reason for the chronicle I have been driven for so long to write and which I am now ready, at last, to embark on, is this very need to record, to thwart forgetfulness; to grasp at that truth which is not so much the opposite of the lie as of forgetting. *A-letheia.*

How tentative, perhaps deceptive, this new dawn: how far away the light still is! (Already, even in the midst of the great wave of hope sweeping the world, there are the rumblings of new wars and violence.) If we were to forget what has gone before and how we have arrived where we are: how easy it might be then to relapse into that terror and chaos and madness. Only by knowing, knowing without compromise, only by trying to understand, only by swallowing every bitter bloody morsel of the fruit from the Tree of Knowledge, can we hope to free ourselves from that madness. Without this understanding of the darkness that has preceded what now looks so much like dawn, all that turbulence would have served no purpose. To know how it *was* is the only precarious certainty we can hope to attain about knowing how it *is*: how it may yet be.

Dwelling on what no longer is: perhaps this is, inevitably, ironically, one's only way of being fully contemporary, abreast of one's time. Is this not how our very understanding of our condition functions? the awareness that the moment we grasp is already past in the grasping.

A gull in flight sweeps past in the wind, registered only when it is already gone. But without the knowledge of that line inscribed in us, what would we know about gulls?

A broken crayfish claws its way across a slithery concrete slab, not knowing it is already dead. And through that very futile action it curiously defies death.

On the wall of an airport building: a clock whose figures jump from one minute to the next, always a fraction late, invariably 'behind the times'.

And in the foreground a woman dies in her own blood. Time and time again.

This is why it had to be done. This is why it has to be remembered. And in this way, not any other.

SUPPLEMENT

THE CHRONICLE
OF THE
LANDMAN FAMILY

As Reconstructed by Thomas Landman

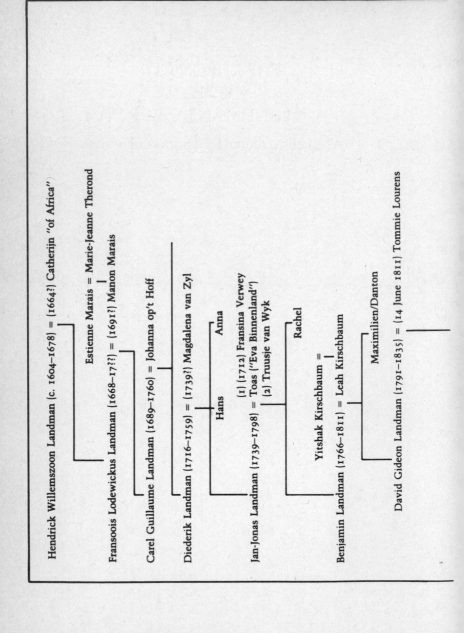

Hendrick Willemszoon Landman (c. 1604–1678) = (1664?) Catherijn "of Africa"

Estienne Marais = Marie-Jeanne Therond

Fransoois Lodewickus Landman (1668–17??) = (1691?) Manon Marais

Carel Guillaume Landman (1689–1760) = Johanna op't Hoff

Diederik Landman (1716–1759) = (1739?) Magdalena van Zyl

Hans   Anna

(1) (1712) Fransina Verwey
Jan-Jonas Landman (1739–1798) = Toas ("Eva Binnenland")
(2) Truusje van Wyk

Rachel

Yitshak Kirschbaum =

Benjamin Landman (1766–1811) = Leah Kirschbaum

Maximilien/Danton

David Gideon Landman (1791–1835) = (14 June 1811) Tommie Lourens

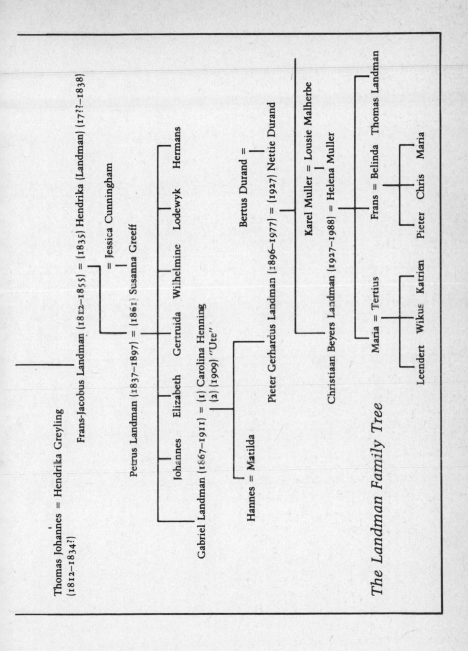

The Landman Family Tree

Contents

The past experience revived in the meaning
Is not the experience of one life only
But of many generations . . .

T.S. Eliot: 'The Dry Salvages'

Ask a Cancerian about his family tree.
He'll love to tell you.

Linda Goodman: Sun Signs

Hendrick Willemszoon Landman

(c. 1604–1678)

Ever since I first read Camoens, I have been seduced by the idea of interpreting my family history as a series of encounters with Adamastor, that dark, brooding Spirit of the Cape: how would my ancestors have shaped up, weighed in his great scales? *Mene, mene, tekel, upharsin*? But I am fascinated, too, by Nina's comment after we'd borrowed that musty little-read tome from the library: 'We're not the victims of Adamastor, Thomas, we are his children.' To see the successive generations of my family as avatars of Adamastor himself: his way of repeating, and renewing, in each new age, the challenge against intruders and violators. No, that would be presumptuous! – why should he have chosen *us*? If he really were interested in selecting a family for his successive incarnations, they could not but have been black. Surely, even if we have become a white tribe of the continent, we remain an anomaly, 'a terrible animal', in the words of the poet Breytenbach. And yet I continue to be haunted by Nina's remark. There can be no harm in playing the magic game of *if*: What *if* Adamastor had chosen the Landman family for his avatars down the centuries? – how have we fared, what have we done to him? (Oh weep for Adamastor, he is dead.) Trial and error. And error, and error. Or have there been some moments – few and far between, indeed, no more than brief and moving moments – in which perhaps we have caught, in sudden agonising or exhilarating flashes, an intimation (no more) of what it must mean to live, to express, to feel, to be, this continent, this Africa? Not moments of 'understanding', of 'evaluating', or 'judging': but of living, of being: moments as violent and haunting and brief as the double cry of the fish-eagle, the silhouette of a thorn-tree against a bleeding sky, the exclamation of a flower in Namaqualand, a smell of wood fire, the bitter taste of aloe on the

637

tongue. And perhaps, for the sake of those few, random, moments, all the rest – the waste, the suffering, the stupidity, the intransigence, the arrogance, the pathos – will yet turn out in the end to have been worth while?

In our tribe, where first Grandpa, then Dad, then I, have worked so assiduously on the reconstruction of our family tree (much to Mum's disgust: she could be very disparaging about 'all this male business about who begat whom'), there used to be consensus on regarding Fransoois Lodewickus Landman as our founder, based on the argument that he had been the first of our (male) line to be born on African soil. Whenever I asked, as I regularly did, about his father Hendrick Willemszoon (since Fransoois Lodewickus could not have arrived ready-made like Adam in Paradise), the curt reply was that almost nothing was known about the man, not even the date of his arrival at the Cape. Which is true, but only up to a point. True, in that not one of us has been able to find out from the available sources (including the Cape Archives) anything about his previous history or the circumstances of his arrival at the Cape. But then we have not yet been able to pursue our researches in the Netherlands.

My own amateur enquiries in the *Rijksargief* in The Hague, some years ago, did produce one Hendrick Willemszoon Landman, member of a carpenters' guild in Rotterdam, who appears to have abandoned his wife and a vast brood of children in 1661 or 1662 (when he was already over fifty years old). It is not at all unlikely that he should have fled to the Cape of Good Hope, at the time a useful rubbish bin for most of Europe's adventurers, failures and down-and-outs; in which case some barrel-scraping in old ships' records etc. may well bring to light more information. Unless, of course, the old rogue had been a stowaway, which was perhaps not unlikely, given the circumstances of his disappearance. But my own intention to follow up the research in Holland did not materialise, and when, much later, I tried to persuade Frans to pursue the matter on one of his periodic visits to the Max Planck Institute, his tart response was that he had more important things to do than to waste his time on a disreputable scoundrel who probably had no connection with our family anyway. It was my impression that, like Pa and Grandpa and others in our family, he'd found it convenient to close the books on our genealogy at that point.

But that unpropitious beginning was still negligible compared to the embarrassment caused to some of Hendrick Willemszoon's descendants by his life at the Cape. Because it simply isn't true that so little about him has been recorded. It requires time and patience, of course, but no more than is needed to reconstruct the biographies of his son Fransoois Lodewickus or their descendants. Land allotments, slave transactions, reports of the Council of Policy – such documents yield clues which all point to a man who, if he was enigmatic in many ways, was nevertheless a worthy root of our family tree in Africa. 'Worthy' in my eyes, that is, not in Pa's. Because through my still unfinished research it has become quite clear to me why that particular chunk of our family history – like some others, later – has been suppressed for so long. Conceived and born in lies we are. Admittedly, some rare Afrikaners of my generation have begun to count the drops of African blood in our veins, like our contemporaries in the US who are so eager to prove an indigenous 'Indian' connection: but in our family things have not yet progressed so far. Lily-white purity über alles. All the more so as a certain sallowness of complexion characterises many of the members of my family, including myself.

Of course I do not presume to know the full truth. The fistful of facts I have gleaned over the last few years I have had to interpret in my own subjective way. But this is how – to the best of my knowledge, so help me God – Hendrick Willemszoon Landman's life at the Cape appears to me:

I like to imagine him coming out as a stowaway on a ship of the Dutch East India Company, spending heaven knows how many months on a turbulent sea. I see him stealing about at night among the bales and barrels in the hold or on deck, filching the odd salted ham or draught of water or arrack in order to survive those inhuman conditions. He undoubtedly had enough time to reflect on his sins. The wife and nine or ten or God knows how many children he'd left in the lurch. Would he have felt remorse at all, or did he really believe the escape was worth so much hardship? And where was he really heading for? Did he simply want to put as many sea-miles as possible between him and his past? Perhaps he disembarked at the Cape thinking it was Batavia; perhaps he could no longer stand the rocking and swaying of the ship, the bad food; perhaps, suffering from scurvy, he'd been dumped here with all the other sick and dead of the voyage. (Except in that case, surely, his name would have featured on the sick-comforter's register, which it didn't.) Or perhaps others on board had come to regard him as a Jonah bringing disaster to his co-passengers and had hurled him ashore unceremoniously in Table Bay. (In a report on the voyage from Texel to Cabo of the *Lindschoten* in 1662, there is a harrowing account of being driven off course for four weeks near Cape Verde, of people washed overboard; of twenty slaves from the hold cast into the waves as ballast to lighten the burden; in May 1663 there was an attempted mutiny on board the *Welgemoed*, some sailors were flogged to death, others died in the hold where they'd been held in chains. And on the *Aurora*, in August that same year – The possibilities are endless. Hendrick Willemszoon Landman might have been on any of these, and paid the price. The problem is not to look for explanations but to curtail my imagination.)

Whatever the circumstances, the man was washed up on our little shore of history some time in 1662 or 1663 like so much other human debris. And if there is a God who decides the fates of men and nations, it must have been predestined that one like him should plant us in this austral soil. I salute you, arch-ancestor Hendrick.

Ten years earlier, the Dutch East India Company, in its greed to remain in charge of the fabulous riches of the East – cinnamon and coriander and pepper, coffee and sugar, silk and priceless materials, ivory, gold and diamonds, and the best slaves in the world – had decided to establish a small refreshment station for its ships at the Cape of Good Hope, known earlier, with good reason, as the Cape of Storms. Many ships had foundered along that perilous coastline where two oceans meet in a white spray, guarded by the rearing dark cliffs of Cape Point, which wise old mariners knew was the petrified shape of the titan Adamastor. But even more sailors had died of thirst and scurvy and other unspeakable illnesses caused by the months and months at sea; a victualling post in Table Bay would shorten the journey and keep up the morale of the seamen and so ensure a better service between Europe and the East. Would it be viable? A group of survivors from the shipwreck of the *Haerlem* in Table Bay in 1647 had taken home enthusiastic reports about the vegetables they'd grown and the fat-tailed sheep they'd bartered for beads and copper wire and tobacco and arrack from the slight-bodied friendly yellow-brown Khoin, whom they called Hottentots, and who had inhabited the subcontinent for countless centuries. There would be 'advantage and profit' to the Company, they submitted, in such a venture: no more than sixty or seventy men would be needed to construct a fortress, assisted by three or four gardeners to supervise 'digging and delving' by the sailors and soldiers. After cautious deliberations the Lords Seventeen, the directors of the Company, decided to risk it; and in early April 1652 three small ships sailed into Table Bay and deposited, near the mouth of the Salt River, the first Commander, one Jan van Riebeeck, and his crew.

Their task turned out more hazardous than they'd expected. Winter set in early that year. Their tents and mud dwellings were flooded, fights broke out among the men, much precious seed was lost. With the arrival of spring in September the gardens began to grow, building on the fortress started, prospects brightened; but life remained difficult. The Khoin, seeing their habitual grazing and watering-places invaded by the strangers who, as it now became evident, were not merely visitors but had come to stay, became less tractable than before. Crops failed. There were never enough labourers for all the work to be done. Quarrels became more frequent, and often more serious. To overcome the problems, remedies were applied which in the long run had devastating consequences: a first 'war' was fought against the Khoin; slaves were imported; a brave and straggly little hedge of wild almonds was planted to keep Africa out of this new small foothold of Europe.

Still, they began to prosper in a humble way. Expeditions were sent out to explore the unknown interior – inspired, among other things, by the old European dream of a fabulous empire of Monomotapa somewhere in the deep hinterland. A first group of 'Free Burghers' were released from Company service and allowed to settle on their own small plots: even if they were forbidden to engage in direct trade with the Khoin, and were obliged to sell their produce only to the Company, it represented something new. They were sprouting roots of their own in Africa; their first concern was no longer Holland. That, at least, is my (possibly romantic) conclusion.

These were the conditions under which my progenitor set foot at the Cape. I only wish I knew more about his early activities. Carpenter, hunter, cattle-barterer? He must have done a bit of everything, because his name appears in all kinds of connections in the almost illegible copperplate of yellowed documents. (The copperplate, of course, was written by others, not himself: the rare occasions on which his own signature was required yield only a cross accompanied by a scribbled note to attest that this was 'Hendr. Willemsz. Landman His Mark'.)

In due course he settled on a small plot – not inside the little Cape settlement proper, where the early Free Burghers had been allotted their land along the trickle of the Amstel River (today the

Liesbeek), but on the far side of the frontier, an action for which he and the handful of other hardheads who'd done the same were reprimanded several times, without any effect, by the Commander. Apart from this, hardly anything is known about the first Landman in Africa. Except, of course, for the central cluster of events of his life. That is, the story of the slave girl Catharijn.

From the sources I have consulted – much more remains to be done, I have only scratched the surface – it isn't clear exactly when Catharijn was imported, whether Hendrick's neighbour Jan Wijlen was indeed her first owner, or whether any other members of her family arrived with her. The latter is quite a relevant question, because she must have been very young when she was set down at the Cape: at the time of the transaction in which Hendrick was involved (and it would seem that he'd known her for quite a while by then) her age was given as 'about eleven or twelve years and not yet arrived at womanhood'. Hendrick paid Jan Wijlen no less than 50 rix-dollars (140 guilders), an exorbitant price for such a young slave girl, considering that male slaves from Guinea were usually sold for Rd 35 – which, in turn, was appreciably more than the 17 or 20 paid for slaves from Angola.

Catharijn's real name will forever remain unknown: by the time she surfaced in our history it had already been Dutchified. All that is really known about her is her place of origin, 'Upper Guinea', which on a modern map would coincide with Mauritania, Gambia or Senegal. This means that, like all the other slaves from those parts, she would have been shipped out from the island of Gorée off the coast of Dakar.

When I was in Dakar a few years ago with Sipho, soon after we had met at my exhibition in London, he took me to Gorée. I remember the cool sea-spray on that blistering day as we approached the small brown island with its formidable round fortress like the figurehead on an old-fashioned ship. The haze on the sea caused the island to drift in space like a mirage: only when we glided into the harbour, close to the first row of brightly painted houses with arches and pillars, did the fog clear up. Small boys with ancient, grave faces dived into the green water like smooth quick seals fishing out coins. What struck me as unexpected, almost eerie, was the total absence of gulls. As if even after so many centuries the birds were still shy of that island of shame.

The textures of the old walls lining narrow alleys bearing unlikely names like the Rue Saint-Germain or the Rue Saint-Denis: a palimpsest of peeling layers, white and ochre and rust and various blues, one on top of the other; the powder-dust kicked up in small clouds by one's heels. Flies. Children everywhere, most of them incredibly beautiful – 'Beautiful as the night,' Sipho called them – with the great moist eyes of gazelles, delicate hands, narrow feet, radiant white teeth, the girls small swift patches of colour in their red or yellow or blue dresses. They made no noise at all. Everything in the place was muffled, subdued, one wasn't conscious of any individual, defined sounds. Behind large arched doorways, behind dark windows framed in blue or green, one sometimes discovered sudden flashes of movement, too fast to suggest substance or solidity, without sound, like shadows. At a stone fountain in an opening among the tall buildings, in the deep shadow of a tree, a group of young girls were drinking water from cupped hands and washing themselves, first the hands and faces, then with unselfconscious grace the rest of their bodies right through their clothes, like pigeons fluttering in a puddle. Behind them lay a few white goats peacefully chewing their cuds. Immediately beyond the dense shadows of the tree everything was trembling in the glare of the sun; the air was heavy with humidity.

Sipho led me to the Slave House. Mottled yellow walls exposed to the full violence of the sun. An unimposing door in the street wall. Above it, an inscription I can no longer recall verbatim but which suggested that this slave house would be preserved to remind every African that part of himself once passed through these gates into the unknown. (Sipho: 'One day we'll have a monument like this in South Africa too, to remind people of apartheid. A resettlement camp perhaps, or a jail.') In the courtyard one finds oneself directly in front of the main building with its two wide semicircular staircases reaching down like an embrace. Upstairs, in large airy rooms, lived the dealers; below, in cubicles and cellars of solid stone, with tiny barred apertures to allow for a minimum of light and air, the slaves in their hundreds, crammed into that suffocating space like slaughter-cattle on a truck. For months and months, this crushing mass of bodies. (Even Sipho and I, able to move about freely, felt dazed from the heat.) In one wing, the weighing room. Men of less than 60 kilograms were sent to a special cell to be force-fed until they'd reached the required weight. The rest were imprisoned separately according to their categories: one room for men, another for women, one for young girls, one for small children.

Auctions were held in the main room between the two prongs of the staircase: a man's value was determined by his weight, a woman's by the size and firmness of her breasts, a child's by its teeth.

From there a final pitch-dark passage led to the door in the seaward wall through which they boarded the ships, three or four hundred at a time. (And as it was known that one of out every five would die before reaching their destination in Brazil or the North American colonies or Batavia or the Cape of Good Hope, more than the required number were herded into the ships to start with, to prevent profits from fluctuating too much.) Before embarking, they had to be branded; and on such days the whole island reeked of burning flesh. The few, the lucky ones, who managed to escape at the last moment, over the edge of the gangplank, jumping into the churning green water chains and all, were immediately torn apart by waiting sharks.

On the walls I read legends still scorched into my memory like brand marks on a slave's face:

> *Savoir n'est pas accepter*
> *Se taire n'est pas oublier*
> *La mémoire fait la force des peuples*

'Do you understand now,' Sipho said when at last we stumbled from that inner darkness into the blinding sun, 'why Africans feel about apartheid the way they do? As long as it persists, the horror of what happened in this place continues.' I couldn't answer. He looked sharply at me: 'Thomas? Are you all right?' I could still not utter a word. I just nodded. In front of my eyes the world was flickering like a TV screen that had suddenly gone blank. Somewhere, on a small square, in the hazy shade of a baobab, Sipho made me sit down until I'd recovered. How could I explain to him – even to him, my best friend – exactly how well I'd understood? It was as if, tied to a stake, I'd suddenly had my eyelids cut off so that my naked eyes could stare unblinking into my own history.

'Did you know, Sipho,' I asked him, at last, 'that the wife of the first Landman in Africa was "processed" in that house and passed through that door to board a slave ship to the Cape?'

Incredulous, he stared at me. No doubt he thought the sun had been too much for me. It was the first time I'd ever confided to anyone what I am now writing down on these pages.

Hendrick Willemszoon Landman had sometimes seen the little

slave girl Catharijn in his morose neighbour's house. He admitted as much to the Council of Policy when his case was heard; it was duly recorded by the secretary. It was not as if he'd been hatching any lewd plans – after his experiences in Holland (if that was indeed what had happened) he would have been pretty wary of women and children – but she'd made a pleasing impression on him. Her timid, gentle manner. The shyness of her smile. Her lovely eyes perhaps. She'd never spoken in his presence. He hadn't known – and never learned – a thing about her past history: if he had, he certainly never intimated anything to others. She was always reserved, withdrawn, closed: it is likely that she'd suffered too much, and too early in her life. Perhaps all he divined in her was a sad, deep longing beyond the reach of words: but I must refrain from romantic conjecture.

All I know is that Hendrick himself didn't keep any slaves; his only help was a single white – German – assistant. And two or three times, when he was ill, Catharijn's owner had sent her over to look after him. (Is this a clue? He may have been a sickly man, already advanced in years by the time he arrived at the Cape, his health permanently ruined, perhaps, by the hazardous voyage out. Which might explain why he kept to himself so much.)

In those times hardly a month went by without slaves running away from their masters. The first consignment of slaves had arrived at the Cape in April or May 1658: and as early as June that year the first few absconded. Afraid lest they find allies among the Khoin in the interior – several sources indicate that the Khoin were usually most reluctant to join in any search for runaway slaves (although there is evidence, too, of animosity between slaves and Khoin) – the Commander instructed that everything possible be done to bring them back. Tobacco and copper to the value of one ox, plus a few *sopies* of arrack, was offered as a reward to any Khoin who brought back a runaway. And those recovered were punished thoroughly to scare off others: this punishment was soon standardised as flogging and branding (on back or cheek), followed by lifelong imprisonment in chains; and in many cases an ear or two was cut off as well to ensure that the message was driven home. Behind this special cruelty one reads the deep fear of Africa in the minds of that small band of Europeans huddled behind a futile hedge of wild almonds that had to keep the whole dark continent out.

In spite of all this, the slaves continued to run away in droves – into the Table Mountain, or around it to the savage chain of the Gable Mountains (known nowadays as the Twelve Apostles), and across Cape Point to the coast of False Bay and the Hottentot's Holland range; or to the west, towards Saldanha; or blindly to the north. Neither hunger nor thirst, nor the risk of being attacked by predators or indigenous peoples, could deter them; and not even the horrendous punishments that awaited those who were caught and brought back could instil enough fear in them to prevent their absconding. Which must say something about the urge to be free.

And so the young girl Catharijn also ran off in the month of March 1664, with a dozen or so others, men, women and children. It is not known what happened to all of them. As far as I could establish, two or three disappeared forever in the interior. The others were surprised by a detachment of Company troops – famished, exhausted, and half demented with fear after a lion had caught one of the men from their midst, they were an easy prey – and driven back to Cape Town. On the way a few more succumbed. And it was but a wretched handful which was finally handed over to Fiscal Gabbema for punishment.

The ringleader was led out first. Tied to the 'horse' on the open terrain – today's Parade – in front of the claywalled fortress, he was first flogged, then branded on the right cheek; and because the authorities were by then driven to extremes by the continuing desertions, the habitual punishment was aggravated by chopping off, joint by joint, his two forefingers, followed by the tip of his nose. For their edification, the other condemned prisoners were forced to witness the whole process.

What passes through the mind of a prepubescent slip of a girl when, surrounded by a jeering crowd, she is dragged to the stake, where her clothes are torn off and her thin wrists tied up with leather thongs, and the burly officer approaches with the cat-o'-nine-tails? By that time the dust at her feet would already be sticky with the blood of those who'd gone before. (To the spectators, of course, it was a festive occasion: they would throng around in their Sunday best, carrying picnic food and drinks, well content at the prospect of the entertainment.) But I really have no desire to dwell on it.

Exactly how and why Hendrick Willemszoon had become involved in the matter, no one knows. It is logical to assume, in the light of their earlier acquaintance, however superficial, that he would have been upset when he'd first heard about Catharijn's running away; so we can assume he was relieved when she was found again – though his relief would undoubtedly have been tainted by anxiety about what was to follow. So little has been recorded of it all. One can only speculate that Hendrick may have pleaded with his neighbour, her master, to intervene with the Fiscal. But Jan Wijlen was either not prepared to get involved (arguing, perhaps, that she deserved punishment; that it might actually do her good) or else he realised that the matter was out of his hands already. It certainly would seem that Wijlen had no wish to be burdened any further by the troublesome girl, for he readily agreed to sell her to Hendrick Willemszoon – though he was greedy and calculating enough to demand a full 50 rix-dollars.

The moment the deal was closed, Hendrick hurried to the Fiscal to inform him that the girl was now his property and that he wanted to withdraw the charges against her. But this, he would soon find out, was no longer possible as the case had already been heard and the verdict pronounced. The law had to run its course. And it was this, as I like to interpret the situation, which prompted Hendrick – in an outburst of indignation? – to announce that he had decided to give her her freedom, which meant that the verdict was no longer applicable. And when even that didn't work (perhaps his intervention came at the very last moment, when the convicted prisoners had already been tied to the stake, which would explain the terrific haste with which it all happened), he told the Fiscal that he was going to marry the girl. To make it sound more credible he was prepared to declare under oath that the marriage had already been arranged, with Jan Wijlen's knowledge.

Thereupon the punishment was suspended for the matter to be investigated. Hendrick must have offered either a very convincing argument or a substantial bribe, because a month later the Council of Policy recorded in its minutes its permission for the marriage to be solemnised. And after another few months – during which time Catharijn presumably attended catechism, in order to be duly confirmed in the Dutch Reformed Church, which was a prerequisite both for manumission and for marriage – the wedding took place.

I am convinced that this was all Hendrick had been concerned about: to save a child from cruel punishment (haunted, perhaps, by the memory of those children he had once abandoned to their fate in Europe?). Having explored all avenues of intervention, he realised that this was the only possible way to ensure her safety, so he took it. There need not have been any ulterior motives. Not at that stage.

But how often have I wished I could have known more about this rough and ready old ancestor of mine. Had he really left his

647

family in the lurch to run off to the Cape of Good Hope at the very end of the known world? But if he had, then surely through that later act he must have atoned for his sins? There must have been something special about the man. It is known that in those days Free Burghers did from time to time marry slave women: it wasn't common practice, but neither was it exceptional. But the way in which he did it, the way he defied the law and all the conventions of his small, rigid society – putting his own peace of mind at stake, no doubt – makes me suspect that there was more to him than meets the jaded eye of recorded history.

His only further appearances in the archival documents concern two changes of address during the following years, placing on each occasion more distance between him and the Cape settlement, further away from neighbours and officials, deeper into the Hottentot's Holland region; and the registration of the birth of a son, Fransoois Lodewickus, born to him and the aforesaid Catharijn of Africa, anno domini 1668.

This gives rise to speculation, no doubt. Was he, when all is said and done, no more than a randy old goat? (I feel deeply enough involved with him to argue very strongly against this.) Had he merely waited patiently for Catharijn to 'reach womanhood' before he took her to his bed? Was it an 'accident'? Perhaps it happened when, like King David in his dotage, he felt weary and abandoned and cold and needed the comfort of a female body to warm his old bones? Or had the two of them, remote from any other people, condemned to solitude, grown closer to each other until the inevitable had happened?

Yet another possibility presents itself. What if Catharijn had fallen pregnant from another man – a slave, who knows?! – and Hendrick acknowledged paternity to ensure that the poor little baby had at least a name to start with?

There is absolutely no way of telling beyond doubt. It is a matter, not even of interpretation or wishful thinking, but of faith. Does it really matter so much, after more than three hundred years? What we do know is that our little tree was planted in the south of this vast continent, Europe grafted on Africa; and Fransoois Lodewickus Landman became the first Afrikaner of our line – in the sense in which the word was used originally: a person born in this country; and, more often than not, rather less than purely white. A propitious beginning: I thank history for it.

648

Fransoois Lodewickus Landman

(1668–17??)

After Hendrick's death (how did he die? old age? illness? an accident? or just like that? – over the years many people have died from the country itself, as if it were some terminal disease; they simply lacked the strength to meet its challenges) Catharijn and her son returned to the small settlement at the foot of Table Mountain where it must have been safer for her than beyond the frontier. In the Cape Archives I have managed to decipher the inventory of the estate left by Hendrick Landman: 73 sheep and 16 cattle, a plough and other implements, a small iron trunk containing 134 rix-dollars in cash; some wooden furniture, undoubtedly made by Hendrick himself – a bed and a cradle, four chests, a large dining-table (but no chairs), a small table, a dresser with enamel basin and pitcher; bedding, including two pillows; a few silver spoons and a silver bell; five iron pots, a water bucket, four barrels for fish and meat, 'one wall mirror in ornamental wooden frame' (still hanging, considerably the worse for wear and age, on Mum's passage wall), a State Bible (now on the sideboard behind Pa's seat at the head of the long dining-table; on its flyleaf the names of thirteen generations of Landmans), a brazier, two muskets; and a collection of plates and mugs, mostly of tin, but a few in porcelain, a tea-caddy, 'a doll's mug' from which the child presumably drank his milk, one large copper kettle. There is something depressing, something unsettling, in this discovery of an individual's spare possessions – with nothing truly personal among them, no real clue to the character of that mysterious distant man who had accumulated them.

With these few things Catharijn moved house, and with the money she got for the sheep and cattle (the little dwelling, I presume, had to be abandoned without compensation as it was beyond the limits of the settlement) she bought a property in the Berg Street, comprising a small house and a shop in which, as a Free Black, she was allowed to sell fish, spices, seed, needlework, and some contraband obtained from visiting ships. On a few occasions this led to difficulties with the authorities and she had to pay a fine.

The child, who was only ten when Hendrick died, helped her in the shop. An ordinary, rather poor but secure existence seemed to be taking shape for them. Nothing of it – except the few brushes with the law, of course – has been documented. (Does 'history', then, really mean, as some would have it, only 'that which has been written down'?) But by the time Fransoois turned sixteen, the pattern of their lives changed abruptly. It would seem that without any warning he sold or bartered most of their possessions, keeping only some domestic items, hired a few Khoin, and trekked inland.

It was a time when official expeditions into the interior were actively encouraged: in 1685, for example, Commander Simon van der Stel personally undertook a journey by coach, accompanied by several wagons and carriages, along the West Coast to the Copper Mountains. But official expeditions were different from the kind of journey undertaken by Fransoois Lodewickus Landman: ordinary burghers were in fact severely restricted in their movements. His venture risked stern disciplinary measures by the Council of Policy.

But whatever the risks, one day – or night – Fransoois left Cape Town, accompanied by his mother Catharijn. From the first time Grandpa told me the story (omitting, of course, all reference to her background), the move has captured my imagination. Even though I have no documentary evidence, I suspect that the whole venture had been her idea. Why? Once before, a mere child, and a slave, she'd run away. Through the timely intervention of Hendrick Landman she'd been saved from flogging and branding and chains, and turned into a free (though married) woman: but I am sure that somewhere deep inside her the urge that had first driven her must have continued to smoulder: the urge to get away from this remote Cape to which she had been forcibly transported as a young child, and to return to the land of her birth, far away up the coast of Africa.

What on earth could she have known about geography? That initial voyage by sea must have appeared an eternity to her, huddled with hundreds of others in the pitch-dark of the ship's hold. But once a week, or once a fortnight, when the slaves were brought up to the deck in long chained rows from the stench of the hold, for the dead to be thrown overboard and the living to be splashed with buckets

650

of sea-water to rid them of the worst filth and vermin, she could not but have noticed, once her eyes had adapted to the glare of the sun, the coastline far away on their left, to the east, a thin brown line beyond the white of breaking waves. And deep inside her bones, that urgent memory must have kept on burning: the knowledge that if you went far enough along that coast, you would get back to where you'd started from. And if my intuition is correct, that resolve to return home one day she would have implanted deep in the mind of her growing son.

Of course they never got there. And somewhere in the interior Catharijn died. How? When? Where? How frighteningly little one knows, especially of the things that concern one most. For Catharijn is part of me, something about myself began with her, and through her some part of myself must always grope back into the heart of my continent. And yet I don't know, I don't know anything. Always one is forced back to that first, basic, fierce act of faith to create one's own truth: Let there be light – let there be sea and earth – let there be a first man and woman – a beginning –

So: somewhere in the vast interior she died. Somewhere – close to the coast, where the cold blue waves of the Atlantic rage against the land? or deeper inland, in a barren Kalahari among flintstones and anthills and spare thorn-trees? – somewhere in the stubborn soil of Africa Fransoois would have dug a shallow grave to lay her in, rolled in a blanket inherited from his father, and built a cairn on top of it, not so much to mark the spot as to keep off scavengers. Somewhere he would have decided to turn back alone. Lost – and torn – between the remoteness his mother had come from and that other remoteness where his father had lived before he died. Back. Alone. Even the Khoin who had accompanied him on the journey had deserted him by then. And the oxen had died, or run away, or had been caught by lions. And the wagon had broken. (I don't know, I don't know.) The last hundred miles or so, from the environs of Piketberg, as far as I can make out, he covered on foot, carrying in a bundle on his back what to him must have been his most precious possessions: a plate and mug, the heavy bible, the silver bell (!), the wall mirror in its ornamental wooden frame (the handiwork, perhaps, of his late carpenter father?), the copper kettle, a few bits of clothing.

He offered his services as an indentured handyman, first to a Free Burgher in the recently established district of Stellenbosch, then to a Company official who offered better wages, and finally to one

Estienne Marais in the valley of Fransch Hoek, who as a staunch French Huguenot paid less but allowed him more freedom. On behalf of his employer he undertook numerous (illegal) expeditions to Khoin tribes he'd met along the West Coast – the distance from Cape Town made it possible to come and go without the knowledge of the authorities – and thanks to the lucrative bartering of sheep and cattle he managed to engage in with these Khoin he was soon able to go off into the interior on his own again.

This time it caused quite a rumpus, as his employer's seventeen-year-old stepdaughter Manon ran away with him. (A story of true love? Or had there been less salubrious reasons for the girl to flee from her stepfather?) They left on a small carriage stolen from Estienne Marais while he was away to Cape Town to sell provisions to the return fleet in Table Bay. This was, as far as I could establish, in April 1689. Manon's mother Marie Jeanne immediately sent a messenger on horseback after her husband, but even so the two runaways had a head start of a good three, four days. In addition, of course, Fransoois knew the region intimately, which Estienne Marais didn't.

But they were caught after all – a whole troop of men on horseback had set out with the angry Huguenot – and the escapade ended with Fransoois tied to a wheel of the stolen carriage, flogged unmercifully, and left behind for dead, while Manon was forcibly taken back by the triumphant troop. However, within days of returning to Fransch Hoek, Manon once again ran away, this time on horseback, and alone, in search of her lover. This time her family gave her up – one of the reasons being, one surmises, that it had been discovered she was pregnant, because before the end of the year, somewhere in the interior, she gave birth to her first son, Carel Guillaume. This only came to light when she and Fransoois returned from their travels two years later to have several sacraments performed at the same church service in Stellenbosch – their wedding, and the baptism of two children.

It was by no means easy to trace Manon's descent, as the official documents sometimes refer to her under her stepfather's name (Marais), sometimes under her mother's maiden name (Therond), and sometimes under Marie-Jeanne's first married name (Molines). She came from a family that had lost no fewer than seven of its members in the persecution of Protestants in France even before the revocation of the Edict of Nantes in 1685 – two of them over a century earlier, in the infamous Tour de Constance at Aigues-Mortes. The last of the seven was Marie-Jeanne's young sister Suzanne. The girl had resisted the advances of one of the four dragoons quartered in the family's home in an attempt to 'persuade' them to be converted to the Catholic faith. Marie-Jeanne, who at the time had been living with her husband Guillaume in her parents' home, was in fact pregnant with Manon when it happened. Her screaming brought Guillaume running to the stable where Suzanne had been lured. Under normal circumstances, it was attested at the inquest, Guillaume was an even-tempered and diplomatic person, but when he discovered what the dragoon was up to with Suzanne, he went into such a Gallic rage that he drew his sword and killed the soldier. Guillaume Molines and Suzanne Therond were both arrested, and nothing the family did could save them from execution. Not long afterwards, the baby Manon was born. At the time of the revocation of the Edict she was thirteen.

The covert pressure Protestants had been suffering previously now turned into open violence. Marie-Jeanne, who had for a long time been the target of a group of officials in the intendant's bureau in Nîmes (one of them a cousin of the dragoon killed by Guillaume), realised that her own safety and that of her child were at stake. But she lacked the means to emigrate, which was really the only effective – if illegal – way to elude their menacing interest.

The only solution lay in the prosperous Estienne Marais, a man twice her age, who had been courting her for years. He was a Protestant too, but it seemed it had never been a matter of deep conviction for him; and since he obviously knew how to win, or buy, the favour of important individuals, he'd been allowed openly to pursue his career as a banker. He'd even been called in on some special secret errands for government officials. For him there would be no difficulty at all to travel abroad. I have no idea of what happened between him and Marie-Jeanne: perhaps she even loved the man. (But was *he* more interested in her, or in her barely nubile daughter?) All that is directly relevant to our family history is that they were married quite suddenly and left for the Netherlands from where, in the course of 1688, they arrived at the Cape aboard the *Schelde*. (What on earth could have induced a prosperous banker to become a farmer in this distant, savage country? One can only suspect fraud or other sinister activities; but Dad used to get very annoyed if I broached the subject, even though Estienne Marais was only related to us by marriage. Slandering a Huguenot is simply not done.) At the time of their arrival at the Cape, Estienne and Marie-Jeanne Marais had no children of their own yet. Their first son was only born a year after Manon had eloped with Fransoois; which, in itself, may be revealing.

After the young couple had come back from their travels with their two children, they returned temporarily to the farm of Manon's mother and stepfather, a rather surprising move in view of the tempestuous beginning of their relationship. One can only assume that the parents' anger subsided once the marriage was a fait accompli; it is also possible, if my suspicions are true, that Manon, married, at last felt safe in her stepfather's presence.

Not that their life was by any means tranquil. There was constant friction with the Cape authorities and the *landdrost*, or magistrate and administrative supervisor, of Stellenbosch – either because Free Burghers were still allowed very little scope for initiative, or because Fransoois derived some perverse satisfaction out of defying the decrees of the Council of Policy. On at least four occasions his name appears in the official documents in connection with fines imposed for contravening regulations on bartering with the Khoin, trading with ships, or working on Sundays. Their most persistent problems, however, were with Estienne Marais. On several occasions he and Fransoois came to blows, and each time, significantly, Manon was somehow involved in it. I have nothing but suspicion to go by: everything in the official records is innuendo, possibility, suggestion. But I wonder –

All of this must have contributed to Fransoois's decision, as soon as he and Manon had again accumulated a few possessions, to load a new wagon and respond once more to the lure of the interior, with his wife and children (of whom, by now, there were three). It was quite evident that this was not, as in the case of other Free Burghers, a journey undertaken to trade or barter or explore: Fransoois travelled for the sake of travelling, because he was unable to stay put in any one place. Henceforth it became the predictable, metronomic pattern of his life, moving to and fro constantly between the graves of his parents, one in the shadow of Table Mountain, the other in a nameless spot deep in the wilderness (but still very, very far from the coast of Senegal). Clearly, he would never be free from either of them.

More than once when they briefly returned, thin and tattered, from their wanderings, there would be another baby in the family who had to be christened; on some occasions one of the older ones would be missing. In the end they had five left (but God alone knows how many others had been left behind under tiny mounds of earth and stone on the endless plains of the continent). One or two of the older boys, especially the first-born, who had never been strong, were sometimes left behind for shorter or longer periods with their grandmother and step-grandfather on the Fransch Hoek farm while the rest of the family returned into the hinterland beyond the limits.

Other travellers along the West Coast and the upper reaches of the Olifants River sometimes returned to Cape Town with reports in private diaries or published journals of the strange white family they'd encountered with some or other wandering tribe of Khoin. For long periods, it would seem, they stuck to the coast, driven to the sea by drought and thirst; there they subsisted on fish, or on mussels or kelp garnered from the rocks, or – when there really was nothing else available – on crayfish, the last resort of the poorest among the poor. When the veld improved, especially after there had been tidings of rains inland, they would move away and live off their fat-tailed sheep, or hunt small game, or gather ostrich eggs, or collect *kambro* and other roots and fruits of the veld. This held an endless fascination for the travellers who met them. Sometimes it was only after a day or two that the visitors discovered they were not aborigines: at first sight they had the appearance of Khoin, their skins – sallow to start with – tanned deeply by the sun and greasy with rancid fat and buchu as a protection against insects, clad in skin karosses, the children mostly naked. They even spoke the weird click-sounds of the Khoin language. Yet somewhere in the background, hidden among trees or rocks, there would always be the rickety little wagon that bore their meagre belongings and their good Cape clothes. And at least one of the journals made reference to the unsettling impression left on the minds of visitors when Fransoois gathered his family around him in the wilderness to read from the State Bible and say a prayer; or when Manon set down the children – her own and those of the Khoin – in a circle around a flattened patch of sand to teach them how to read and write.

In the chronicle of our tribe this scene has become transfigured (understandably, I suppose) into the image of the First Mission-ary, almost a century before the Moravian Brothers arrived at the Cape: Mother Manon, Harbinger of Light in Darkest Africa.

This, inevitably, is the interpretation Dad and Oupa have always brought to it. They've had no choice: their whole way of life has depended on it. But for me – and this may be my own distortion – Fransoois and his family represent something completely different. I do not see him as the pious believer among the heathen, but (in the terminology of one of the old journals) as the *zwijger*, 'the silent one', with the appearance of 'an old savage' (though he wasn't even forty at the time), the long dishevelled hair and beard of a man subsisting on locusts and wild honey, a man who stares right through others, as if they do not exist, seeing only the horizon, the invisible, terrifying, unspeakable truths inside the stones and earth and the hard light of Africa.

My final impression of Fransoois Lodewickus Landman comes from the journal of a little-known German traveller Oscar Petz who, in 1702, spent eight long months at the Cape, during which time he undertook an eventful journey up the West Coast. At a stage when a lingering, thirsty death seemed inevitable a number of leagues inland from what, today, is Lambert's Bay, he arrived at the place where the Landmans had temporarily settled and was saved by them. Or rather: Manon and her children nursed him back to life, as by that time, if Petz is to be believed, Fransoois was already so far withdrawn from the world that he couldn't, or wouldn't, engage in conversation any more. Apart from anything else, Petz writes, Fransoois was too busy, night and day, building a ship.

I have scrutinised this passage in the Petz journal a dozen times and more, but that is exactly what it says: at least thirty miles from the sea, in the middle of that vast desert – traversed, later, by Lisa and me – Fransoois was building a ship. His helpers he'd chosen from Khoin who occasionally passed that way; his material was wood from tongues of virgin forest in the kloofs of the Cedar Mountains. The dimensions of this task, transporting heavy timber over such a distance, in that barren part of the world, is mind-boggling. But one commodity my ancestor undoubtedly possessed in abundance was time. And, undoubtedly, dedication. Month after month, year after year, he went on building his ark, patiently, indefatigably. It was a rough and unsightly thing, as neither Fransoois nor any of his helpers had any knowledge of ships and seaworthiness; and God alone knows whether the construction would ever have survived even the shortest trip on water.

Shortly before Petz left them, the ship, unbelievably, had been completed. How the news travelled through that godforsaken landscape, no one could tell; but on the day the final touches were put to the ship, a great multitude of Khoin arrived from the ends of the earth to watch how the vessel would be set afloat in the sea which was at least a day's journey to the west. Everybody lent a hand, men, women, and children, but even when they all heaved together it proved impossible to push or drag the unwieldy thing for more than a few yards. The cedarwood was quite simply too heavy to be moved.

Only a new Flood from heaven would make it possible for our forefather to sail away from there, and there was no sign at all that God was that way inclined. Petz makes no mention of the doughty builder's reaction, except to record that when they woke up the following morning, and on every subsequent morning during the fortnight or so the traveller remained with the family, Fransoois was already perched on the stern of his massive ark, staring ferociously ahead into the blazing sun, as if he were already at sea; as if he alone knew about the perils of the mighty swells he faced. There was something unworldly about the scene, so convinced did Fransoois appear that pure will-power would set his ark moving, floating, to heaven knows where, across uncharted seas, until, perhaps, his apocalyptic eyes would recognise land ahoy, far away in the distance: the barren yellow coast of Senegal where his mother had come from: back, back, all the way back to something unknown and perhaps unknowable, something ancient and prehistoric, immemorial, Genesis itself.

And this gave rise to the final impossible kink in his story, discovered much later in a letter Manon wrote after she'd arrived back at the Cape in 1703 or 1704. She'd brought her few remaining children with her. Of Fransoois there was no sign. What had become of him? I can repeat only what I read, and that was unbelievable. After all, it comes from that dawn of our tribe where myth and history overlap. According to Manon — and surely she was a devout woman, practical and Protestant, a thoroughbred Huguenot — they woke up one morning to a silence outside as vast as the sea. It had always been a quiet place, but never as quiet as that day. Not even the cicadas shrilled. And when, with a presentiment of disaster, she walked into the great emptiness outside there was: nothing. Absolutely nothing. The ark was gone. The ark, with Fransoois Lodewickus Landman on the prow. Gone. Disappeared into the dazzling day. All that was left was a furrow in the ground, as if something had been dragged that way. It didn't point west, towards the sea, but north-east, straight inland. They followed the track, but eventually the earth grew so hard and scaly that they lost sight of it. And that is how, in the insufficient oral tradition of our tribe, Fransoois Lodewickus Landman finally vanished into the heart of Africa.

Carel Guillaume Landman

(1689–1760)

A curious symbiosis, this, between my ancestors and myself. Blindly, through fierce or furtive copulations in the dark, they invented me in return for this, their conscious if tentative re-invention by their offspring. The old joke: the patient outstretched in the dentist's chair, clutching his would-be tormentor's testicles as the man approaches with the drill: 'We're not going to hurt each other, are we?' Am I their alibi, or are they mine? But there is no easy way out, and no remittance. How can I know where I'm going unless I know where I've been? How can I imagine myself without reference to the possibilities that have preceded me? (Preceded? They are still alive inside me, irreducibly part of myself.) In these secular times one hesitates to speak of 'truth', but perhaps I'm old-fashioned enough to believe – hope – that I'm in search of it. A reminder, though. In Greek, I read it somewhere, the word for truth, *aletheia*, is not the opposite of lie as one would expect, but of *lethe*, forgetting. It is not a word, a concept, a notion in its own right, to which something else can be opposed – truth/untruth – but itself the opposite or denial of a given concept, it is *un*-forgetting. Forgetting is the starting-point, the natural state. Truth is only what has been remembered, salvaged, from that territory of oblivion. It is the bungled word that emerges at the far end of a line of whispering children. And it is in the name of this truth that I must invent those who invented me. Others consult fortune-tellers to predict their future for them: I am trying to predict my past.

In my clan Carel Guillaume Landman is remembered – this is *their* truth – as the rebel, the true patriot who defied the authority of his Governor, the despot Willem Adriaen van der Stel, and landed, if only for a few days, in the Dark Hole at the Castle for it. They would have applauded with even greater enthusiasm had he attempted, in that fateful year of 1706, to blow up the Governor in his carriage as he entered the Castle from the vast dirt-strewn potholed terrain at the front entrance (people were broken on the wheel there, or strung up on the gallows after having flesh torn from their bodies by red-hot pincers) which, tidied up into a square with palm-trees and herb sellers and parking bays, is still known as the Parade. But of course he didn't go so far. For one thing, he was too young, sixteen. For another, the circumstances did not require extreme action. In his time it was enough to withhold consent when ordered by the Governor's agents to sign a document in praise of van der Stel. To withhold consent: it is a strategy I, too, have tried, God, for how long? It is no longer adequate. We do not live under the administration of the Dutch East India Company which, corrupt and mercenary as it was, knew that trade could prosper only if malpractices were not too visible and the inhabitants of the colonies kept reasonably content. Nor do we live under the kind of British rule – cruel and autocratic yet based on assumptions of gentlemanly conduct – which made a Gandhi possible.

Not that it was easy, or even foreseeable, at the time, of course. When my ancestor, a mere boy himself, refused to sign the Governor's document he knew it might mean banishment to Mauritius or another remote island of the Indian Ocean; it might mean torture; indefinite detention in the Dark Hole; possibly death. Still, he refused. He was, remember, a contemporary, perhaps a friend, of that other impertinent (and, at the time, inebriated) youngster Bibault who told the constables of Landdrost Starrenburg in the village of Stellenbosch: 'I refuse to go, I am an Afrikaner, even if the Landdrost beats me to death, or even if he throws me in jail, I will not and shall not be silent.'

But Carel Guillaume Landman refused *twice*, not only once. And that makes all the difference. My father never told me that. Perhaps he would never admit it even to himself. To him only the version sanctioned by family tradition exists.

My own corrupt *aletheia* is different.

Here is my version:

When Manon Landman and her remaining children returned from their nomadic life among the Khoin, prematurely old, shrunken, her skin cured as ancient leather, she had little choice but to return to

660

the Fransch Hoek farm of her mother and stepfather, the Huguenot Estienne Marais. Her eldest son, that is Carel Guillaume, had spent the previous year or two on the farm as his health had been too frail to accompany the rest of the family into the wilderness; he had grown into a strapping youngster with exceptionally clever hands, especially at carpentry; and his surly old grandfather appeared to have taken a particular liking to the boy. There was even talk, it would seem, that upon his death the farm, covered in vines and orchards and already enjoying some notoriety for its heady dessert wine, might be bequeathed to young Carel rather than to Estienne Marais's own son Pierre, who'd turned into a rather useless young lout with little or no interest in farming. Manon, her bloom and good looks gone, no longer had anything to fear from her lecherous old stepfather. So it seemed reasonable for them at last to expect, after the tribulations they'd gone through, a future, if not of prosperity, at least of some comfort and peace. Unfortunately this was cut short by the unexpected death, apparently from a stroke, of Estienne Marais. True, he must have been well into his seventies by then, but so robust was his health and so impressive his constitution that it seemed he would live forever. That, at least, must have been his own conviction, as it turned out after his death that he had never made a will. Drawn by the news like a vulture to a carcass in the veld came Pierre Marais from Cape Town, where he'd been living it up, to claim the farm as his inheritance. His poor mother, Marie-Jeanne, whose health had never been good, was too frail and weary to want to get involved. And when her daughter Manon petitioned the Council of Policy on behalf of her children, especially Carel, who'd helped the old man turn the farm into a profitable venture, it only exacerbated the tensions in the family. Nowhere could I find a judgement on the petition by the authorities, from which I deduce that Manon was persuaded to drop the case before it could be heard; and it is likely that Carel himself insisted on it, as his whole life seemed to be an endless series of efforts to avoid trouble. If Pierre Marais wanted to fight for possession of the family farm, then Carel would rather opt out.

This was how he turned up as a foreman on the farm of Geert van Damme in the Stellenbosch district. No need to dwell on van Damme, except to point out that he was a good friend of Henning Husing and Adam Tas, the two wealthy ringleaders in the gathering movement among Free Burghers against the Cape authorities. His own increasing wealth threatened by Governor van der Stel's systematic campaign to extend his and his friends' farming activities (with the use of Company slaves and implements, setting an example in corruption for future governments of the country), and eager to gain control of the sale of wine and meat, the two major products of the Colony, Husing – himself a onetime beneficiary of the Governor's whimsical favours – went into action. With the assistance of a few trusted friends, including the urbane and learned windbag Tas, the excitable van Damme and others, Husing drew up a petition against the alleged malpractices of the government, and smuggled it to the Lords Seventeen in Holland aboard one of the ships of the Return Fleet which visited Cape Town on its long voyage from Batavia to Amsterdam in February 1706.

The signatures of sixty-three colonists appear on the petition. There should have been sixty-four, but when my ancestor Carel was approached by his employer, the boisterous van Damme – a man, it is reported, of over six feet tall, barrel-shaped, his small head sprouting directly from his shoulders without any hint of a neck – he declined to sign.

'Look, man, don't you see?' one can imagine the big man explaining. 'It's us against them. What are they doing on those farms of theirs? Half a million vines on the Governor's bloody farm alone. And ten thousand sheep, I've heard tell, on his farms across the Hottentot's Holland Mountains. I mean, Jesus! We poor ordinary burghers aren't even allowed to barter sheep from the Hottentots, but look at him. And he's not the only one, Carel. Even the predikant. What's his name, Kalden, the one that looks like he's been pickled in brine for three months. All he knows from Scripture is "Thou shalt not want." We've got to stop them, Carel, or there won't be a life left for any of us. What are we doing here, sucked dry by a bunch of officials who're supposed to give us a chance too? Now you just take this quill and sign for me. You can write, can't you?'

'Yes, my mother taught me.'

'So what are you waiting for? We've both got work to do, man.'

'It's got nothing to do with me, Oom Geert. I'm just a foreman. The way I see it, it's a fight between the big farmers and the Governor's men about who's going to be the richest. There's no place for ordinary little people like me in between.'

'Don't be bloody stupid, man,' the barrel boomed. 'Riches have nothing to do with it. It's a fight between the Company and the people about who has the right to live off this land. How d'you think we're going to get our sheep sold if that crooked Phijffer's got the monopoly? Spent eight years on Robben Island for fraud, did you know that? Last time the meat monopoly was auctioned he had to scrape and borrow to buy one-quarter of the lease for meat, now suddenly he's got it all. How? Because van der Stel set him up. So in future the ships won't buy a single sheep from us, only from that lot. I'll be bankrupt in a year. And what do you think's going to happen to you and your family if I go down? It's life and death for you too, my boy. One would think you should be grateful for what I've done for you lot. Turned up here on my doorstep like a bunch of trekking Hottentots. And did I send you away? Carel, like a decent Christian I took you in. Everything you've got you can thank *me* for. Is there no gratitude in you?

'I'm thankful for everything, Oom Geert. But I'm sorry. There's really nothing I can see in it for me. Husing and Tas and van der Heiden and all those big men, they're only in it for themselves. They don't care about me.'

'I'm one of them.' There would have been a dangerous edge to the big man's voice by now. 'You tell me to my face that I'm in it for myself too? After everything I've done for you?'

'You helped me because you needed a new foreman after Jan Jansen left just before the harvest, Oom Geert. I'm sorry, but you know that's the truth. I'm thankful for what you did. But you're not fighting this fight for me, it's only for yourself.'

I do not know what phrase would have been current in the Dutch of the time – already, in the mouths of slaves and others, it was turning into a more simplified and creolised language than that spoken in the Mother Country – for 'Fuck off!', but that undoubtedly was what Geert van Damme would have said in ordering Carel Guillaume Landman and his mother and their whole brood off his fertile farm on the banks of the Eerste River.

This was how my ancestor missed his first chance at immortality. And what had happened between him and Geert van Damme inevitably sheds light on what happened afterwards, when he was rounded up with all manner of burghers, sailors, slaves and riffraff from the streets of Cape Town to be entertained at a banquet in the Castle, plied with arrack from Batavia and sweet Constantia wine from the farm of the Governor's retired father, and then invited – against a backdrop of soldiers with drawn swords and cocked pistols – to sign the Governor's Counter-manifesto. Once again Carel Guillaume Landman said no. Not because, as the sacred tradition of my clan has it, he was incorruptible, or refused to bow to tyranny, but because he wouldn't be drawn into a fight of which he failed to see the relevance. If there is heroism in that, it is the innocent heroism of the little man who prefers to be captain of his own soul.

His refusal had no immediate consequence. Perhaps the Governor feared a riot in the unpredictable throng of guests at his banquet. Reprisals only came later. At that time Carel – still a mere lad of seventeen – had drifted, with his whole crowd of dependants, to Cape Town, where he joined a modest carpentry and wagon-making business set up by three Free Blacks, Malays from Djakarta. This in itself was quite remarkable. Even his decision, earlier, to offer his services as a foreman to Geert van Damme had been unusual, as very few Free Burghers at the time were willing to do what was generally regarded as slave work for other whites: even the poorest preferred to remain independent. But plying a trade in Cape Town was, for a white person, severely frowned on. Except, of course, that with a freed slave as a grandmother Carel may have had more mobility in that still fluid society. In any case, I cannot imagine that he would have wasted much time brooding on such matters. There were mouths to be fed, and he clearly loved his work.

What was even more remarkable was his conversion to Islam. A reaction against the Christian charity displayed by Geert van Damme? The expression of a mystical urge? A natural result of his daily contact with his Muslim colleagues and a whole community of underdogs turning to Islam for solace and sustenance at a time when they were allowed little access to Christianity for fear that baptised slaves might start expecting freedom? (At least one of his colleagues, Mustapha, had come to the Cape in the retinue of the rebel sheik Yussuf, banished from the East Indies for insubordination; and after the death of the sheik in 1699 Mustapha had somehow bought himself out of slavery. It is known that, apart from his skill as a craftsman, he was a particularly active missionary of the Faith among the Company slaves.) I never broached this aspect of Carel's life with my father or with Frans; they may well have been unaware of it. But I am persuaded that the evidence I have found is incontrovertible. It may not have any relevance for the 'historical role' of my ancestor; but it satisfies a deeper kind of curiosity in myself – about the man himself, the substance behind recorded history.

During the months following the dispatch of both the Petition and the Counter-manifesto to Holland, van der Stel embarked on a thorough and systematic campaign throughout the Colony to weed out every 'undesirable element' suspected of having plotted against him. It was easy to find the ringleaders once a copy of the burghers' petition had been produced from a drawer in the monumental desk of Adam Tas; but the Governor was intent on pursuing the very shadows lurking in the background. In the remote district of Stellenbosch (thirty kilometres away) Landdrost Starrenburg and a commando of armed men rode from farm to farm and house to house to round up closet malcontents; in Cape Town there were weekly raids on suspect premises.

In one such raid in mid-April 1707 several newly made cabinets in Carel's carpentry were broken by drunken soldiers on a spree. The Malays hovered in the background, their anger smouldering behind deliberately expressionless dark faces, as wooden as carved masks. But Carel tried to stop them. When he was roughly shoved out of the way, he grabbed a long smooth yellowwood plank and clobbered the officer in command over the head with it. For this he was apprehended and manhandled so severely that for a while his companions thought he might die. As it happened, the good ship *Kattendijk* sailed into Table Bay from Holland on 16 April 1707 with news of the summary dismissal of Governor van der Stel and his entourage by the Lords Seventeen, and in the confusion many detainees were released, including Carel Landman, who had been nursing both his anger and his wounds in the rat-infested clammy blackness of the Dark Hole in the Castle. This not only saved his life but, more important, at least for our official family chronicle, enshrined him forever as a hero in the struggle against tyranny. The episode represents a turning-point in my ancestor's hitherto unlucky life. He returned to his carpentry, minded his own business, became converted to Islam, then dropped out of history until some seven years later, when he married the daughter of a highly ranked Company official from Mauritius. Captivated by the beauty of the Cape and its botanical riches, this Mijnheer op't Hoff extended a projected visit of a few weeks to three years. His earlier involvement with the cultivation of the Jardin des Pamplemousses in Mauritius had paved the way for his infatuation with the Cape Gardens.

Mijnheer op't Hoff conceived an ambitious plan to proceed inland and collect samples of his own. For this he required a sturdy wagon. It would have surprised no one that he was referred to the small but highly esteemed business run by Mustapha, Baba, Said and Carel

665

Landman just off the Boereplein. Sometimes his only daughter Johanna accompanied her widower father on his visits to inspect the progress of the wagon through several months. She met Carel. They fell in love. They got married. (In the Groote Kerk, which must have cost some wrangling on behalf of the Muslim bridegroom; but op't Hoff was an important man.)

Three days before the wagon was delivered Mijnheer op't Hoff had an attack of asthma and died within the hour. Carel Guillaume Landman woke up beside his sturdy wife the next morning to find himself a rich man.

After installing his aged mother and his siblings in a new house on the Lion's Rump, he and his wife, with the driver and slaves and assistants op't Hoff had already hired, undertook the journey Carel's father-in-law had planned before his untimely death; it seemed the proper thing to do. Up the West Coast, past the upper reaches of the Olifants River and the Bokkeveld Mountains, inland through the splendid desolation of the Hantam and Namaqualand. (It was September, after the first spring rains, and the whole desert had broken out, miraculously, in such a gaudy sea of flowers, purple and orange and yellow and white and blood-red, it seemed like the Promised Land.) There are indications that they may even have reached the broad muddy river the Khoin called the Gariep, much later renamed the Orange. After the flowers came the dry season and the heat, lucent and white, like the oven of Nebuchadnezzar. When they came back from their honeymoon, almost a year later, Johanna's pale Dutch skin was blotched and blistered, red as a crayfish, and she seemed to be continually gasping for breath. She was five months pregnant.

One would think that this should have cured them of the urge to wander. On the contrary. The return to regions Carel had lived in intermittently as a small child with his parents and the Khoin (even though he'd experienced less of it than his siblings) seemed – in more senses than one – to pave the way for what happened later. Or am I indulging in the biographic fallacy? – the urge to impose patterns and sense on random events, to shape a life into a chain of cause and effect? It is so much easier, at such a distance. The urge to whittle away everything that cannot be explained or 'fitted in', to pick all the untidy bits of meat and gristle from the bones and leave the skeleton clear, unambiguous. How comprehensible and neat those lives appear, stripped of coincidence and anomaly. (What will remain of my own life, one day, should someone decide to clear

666

it of what, to them, appears obscure, contradictory, or redundant? Look, they will say, he was destined from the beginning to become a terrorist, everything in his whole life and in his ancestry points to it, it should have been evident to all around him.) To shape our world in the image of a story. To reduce a life to a symmetry of bones, the *dolosse* from which a witchdoctor can conjure up past or future. Yet a skeleton is what it is precisely because all vestiges and signs of life have been torn from it.

For a couple of years Carel and his wife remained in Cape Town. But there are indications that he was growing increasingly restless: though his wife and children stayed on in the house he had bought immediately behind the Company Gardens, Carel bought a farm at Klapmuts, then sold it to buy another at Drakenstein, then sold it to buy yet another in the Land of Waveren. For the sheep and cattle he had acquired he obtained grazing rights in the Swartland. He spent more and more of his time away from home, although in the fashion of a patriarchal society he amply made up for his absences whenever he returned, judged by the steady increase of his family: in the end they had fifteen children, nine sons and six daughters. Soon after the birth of the sixth child (and the death of Carel's mother Manon) he sold the house in Cape Town and made the move that, I suppose, had been predictable all along. They settled, provisionally, on the farm in the Land of Waveren, but after the ninth child had been born they moved to a remote stretch along the coast near the present Eland's Bay. At least two of his brothers were already living in the region, towards Piketberg, but as far as I can make out they were not farmers in the accepted sense of the word: they simply squatted among the Khoin their parents had once adopted as their clan, subsisting on fish and crayfish when they found themselves near the sea, or trekking far into the interior when their sheep needed grazing. And what became of this branch of the family I simply do not know.

Of course, Carel had a different life-style altogether. In the subsistence economy on those far fringes of the colony he was something of a gentleman farmer. I suspect, in fact, that his whole slow but deliberate move away from Cape Town had much to do with his newly acquired status as a rich burgher, after having grown up in poverty. It was, perhaps, not so much the wealth that embarrassed him as the change in the attitudes of the high and mighty in that small society. Previously he'd been frowned on as a labourer; he was acceptable only in terms of the services he could render. The only invitation he'd ever received into the glittering world of officialdom had been to the Governor's banquet where he'd been expected to sign the Counter-manifesto. Now, with Johanna op't Hoff at his side, buxom as a Rembrandt Bathsheba and loaded with her father's money, all kinds of doors were suddenly opened to him. The Fiscal, officials from the Council of Policy, the surgeon, the predikant, officers off visiting ships, eventually even the Governor himself, began to invite them to banquets and balls and rare sporting events. Johanna, used to a social life, would have been in her element – if she declined invitations it was because of her perennial pregnancies – but Carel became increasingly resentful. Once, it is recorded, he caused something of a stir by insisting on taking his three carpenter friends to a ball with him (for he'd refused to break his connections with the workshop); but eventually even this kind of behaviour was accepted, indulgently. What finally drove him from the fashionable Cape society of his time, I believe, was the same refusal to be drawn into the world of the powerful which had first caused him to clash with those above him.

The rest of his long life has left little precipitate in recorded history. It was marked mainly by domestic events surrounding one curious exploit which I must confess I find rather endearing. One of his carpenter companions, Said, had accompanied him up the West Coast. (The others had been comfortably installed by Carel in new premises, built of solid stone, the thatched roof supported on stinkwood beams, the dung-floor smooth and cool.) Once settled, the two of them temporarily left the running of the farm to Johanna and her formidable brood while they spent their time on the meticulous construction of an exquisite, very small mosque at the back of the house, where he would retreat to meditate whenever the commotion of his vast family or the activities on the farm became too much for him. An object of much curiosity to passing travellers for many years (several of them commented on the exceptionally tall and graceful minaret), the little mosque fell into disrepair after Carel's death; today not even a whitewashed wall remains. Soon after the completion of the outlandish little building Said married one of Carel's daughters and in due course the couple – as well as several of the other children – drifted back to Cape Town. But Carel Guillaume Landman remained, assisted and supported by his staunch wife whose skin never got used to the sun she'd come to

668

love, so that her face and arms were always covered in blisters and running sores.

As he withdrew more and more into prayer and meditation in his outlandish mosque, the running of the farm was really left to Johanna. From the few cryptic comments left by others on his long life I get the impression that his numerous children were something of a problem to him. Certainly, the stone house (in spite of constant additions that, over the years, turned it into a kind of rambling family nest) remained too small comfortably to accommodate so many of them, which in itself may have contributed to Carel's increasing withdrawal symptoms.

One rather charming detail recorded by a visitor concerns a habit he developed to control his children at times when he really felt in need of peace and quiet: at some distance from the house, it seems, there grew an enormous milkwood tree, something quite unusual in those arid parts; its huge, wide-spread branches were festooned with sturdy ropes, at the end of each of which was tied a coarsely woven hessian bag. And on Sunday afternoons, or at other times when Carel couldn't stand the rumpus of his brood, he would stuff a child into each bag, tie up the open end below the child's arms, and hoist the bags up into the tree. They were positioned in such a way that the children were out of reach of each other; and there they remained suspended until Carel – or, more likely, his wife – remembered to set them free again. From a distance, the curious visitor records, it was a fascinating sight: that great green tree with children dangling from its branches like exotic, outsized fruit, a veritable Tree of Life.

But even meditation, in the end, was not enough to keep Carel interested in a life that simply went on for too long. A few years after settling on the farm, he made the annual journey to Cape Town with a wagon loaded with accumulated produce, there joined an expedition along the south-east coast of the land to the forests of Tsitsikama where he personally selected and felled the biggest stinkwood tree he could find; and upon his return set about the long and loving task of fashioning coffins for himself and his entire family from that hard, beautiful, fragrant wood. Johanna did not approve, but he ignored her bickering and persevered. The pile of coffins was stored in the loft of the stone house, except for his own, which he kept, immaculately oiled and daily dusted, in his mosque, where he began to spend most afternoons lying in a posture

669

of peaceful death. Convinced, after several years, that he was now fully prepared to meet his Maker, he boiled several large copper cans and kettles of water, meticulously washed himself, rubbed his body with oriental oils he'd bought on his previous trip to Cape Town, donned a shroud, said goodbye to his stunned and disapproving family, and lay down in his coffin to die.

After three days, when he was still very much alive, Johanna marched into the mosque, hauled him out of the coffin, ordered several of her sons to lug the objectionable box up the stone staircase to the loft and lock it up with the others, and more or less force-fed Carel a meal of many courses. He survived for more than twenty years after that, but having already taken his leave of life, there seemed nothing left for him to do; and all those years he simply vegetated in the twilight of his little mosque while his wife's skin grew ever more cancerous from toiling in the sun and his swarming, robust brood flourished and yelled and cavorted around the Tree of Life.

His actual death is not recorded. It wasn't necessary. He had, by then, been dead for so long. But at least its physical occurrence, when it came, finally restored him to the earth that had eluded him for so many years.

Diederik Landman

(1716–1759)

The Savage. This is the term with which Dad, when he had no choice but to mention the man, chose to designate a link in our chain he would have preferred to ignore. I must confess, perversely, to a fascination with Diederik Landman.

More and more, as I go on, it seems to me that the life of each of my predecessors as I invent or reinvent them can be seen – among other things, of course: no life can be reduced to any simple formula – as the expression of a relationship with some form of power. Sometimes this power appears to be lodged in government, or in society, or the family itself: in parents and ancestors, or in the unborn generations of the future; it may reside in nature, or in religion, or in sex, in custom and tradition, in love or money, or even in death; but invariably, behind whatever power the many members of my family have had to contend with, there is the ordeal of Africa itself.

And inevitably the reactions to such manifestations of power have differed widely, from flight to several degrees of aggression, whether reactionary or prophylactic; from passive resistance to refusal to confrontation; from reluctant co-option to active collaboration (sometimes for survival, sometimes with a view to establishing a power base for themselves) and to revolt. Often, neither the specific nature of the power involved nor the reaction to it can be defined very clearly; more often than not a whole variety of responses is involved in the actions of a single generation. But in the case of Diederik Landman, the Savage, there does not seem to be any problem at all. He lived, and died, in terms of brute, physical violence. That, at least, has been the traditional view in my family. But I have my doubts, precisely because it appears too glib.

What if Diederik Landman was really an artist at heart, a man with enormous creative energies, who simply lacked the means of expressing it in his environment? How else could he vent all that pent-up exuberance, that appetite and passion for life, within the social parameters available to him? There is, wrote Sir Richard Burton in a line Sipho loved to quote, 'all Africa and her prodigies in us'. The expression is all.

It is recorded (by his granddaughter Rachel) that he was the only one among Carel's great brood to revolt against his father's practice of stringing up the children in the milkwood tree when he was in need of spiritual peace. The second or third in the long row of siblings, Diederik ignored the threats and dire warnings of his older brothers and hid a knife in the hessian bag reserved for him. With this, one Sunday afternoon, he managed to cut down the rope that held him suspended from one of the massive branches and promptly tumbled to the ground in a cloud of dust, not having taken any precautions to prevent such a consequence. Their father, secluded in his coffin in the mosque, ignored the rumpus until several hours later, by which time Diederik was quite weak from the loss of blood. He'd broken an arm, a hip and an ankle, resulting in a limp for the rest of his life, although it affected neither his prodigious growth nor his physical strength and prowess. There used to be in Oupa's farmhouse in Kuruman a pair of rawhide trousers said to have belonged to Diederik: two grown men could fit into the garment with ease, one in each leg, with enough slack at the waist to allow for a third. And it is rumoured that he was over seven feet tall before he was twenty.

By the time he was a robust youngster of fifteen or sixteen, he announced his decision to go to Cape Town to make an independent life. His father, upset at already having seen three or four of his offspring leave the home (if their presence oppressed him, somehow their absence was unbearable), tried to restrain him. But Diederik, short-tempered since birth, threw such a tantrum that the other sons were called in to hold him down for a thrashing. He took it without even a grunt; then, released, aimed at his father's face a blow that broke his jaw, which may have hastened the old man's decision, recorded above, to give up on life and will his own death.

Not long after that, in a dispute with his oldest brother over who should run the farm and how it should be done, Diederik once again lost his temper and the brother was never heard of again. Perhaps he left the farm. It is possible that he was killed.

A third incident of the same kind marked a turning-point in Diederik's tempestuous life. He must have been about nineteen or twenty when, on his way home with two of his brothers from a hunting expedition into the upper reaches of Namaqualand, they spent a night on a remote farm belonging to a widow van Zyl who had three daughters. Diederik's eye fell on the youngest, Magdalena, who was barely nubile. Never a man to hide his feelings, he promptly proposed. The widow, considering the advantages of a male presence – and such a one – on the farm, first tried to palm off her older daughters, one of whom had a harelip and the other an unfortunate squint (which would explain why, in that hard male country with its dearth of women, they were still unmarried); but when Diederik began to show signs of impatience she accepted. Only, she pointed out, he should consider that Magdalena had just turned twelve; if, following a Biblical precedent (the only mythological framework available to my tribe), he was willing to work on the farm for three years they could get married on her fifteenth birthday.

Diederik went home with his brothers to collect what he regarded as a fair share of the family's possessions, and ignoring his father's melancholy silence and his mother's righteous Dutch anger he returned to the widow's place to commence his duties. The farm began to prosper, owing not only to Diederik's rage for work but to three years of quite exceptional rains.

A month before Magdalena's fifteenth birthday Diederik took the widow's biggest wagon to Cape Town to sell their accumulated produce – cured hides, biltong, ostrich eggs and feathers, candles, soap, lard, whips and sjamboks, herbs, and ivory – and buy some special things for the wedding. On the way home he stopped at his parent's place to pick up some bits and pieces he thought his bride might like, including the wall mirror in its hand-carved wooden frame and, curiously enough, the family Bible. Upon his return Magdalena was missing. Gone to Stellenbosch to marry a widower of fifty to whom, it only now turned out, her mother had promised her five years before.

Once again Diederik was offered his pick of the older sisters. Instead, he smashed most of the furniture in the house and set out for Stellenbosch, two hundred miles away, where he discovered the whereabouts of the newly married couple, rode his horse right into their home and claimed his bride. When the bridegroom tried to intervene, Diederik killed him.

Back on the van Zyls' farm he turned the lady and her daughters out of the house, though he was magnanimous enough to offer them the shed to live in, while he took over the family home with his petrified young stolen bride. (Did she love him or was it sheer terror that kept her to his side? Did he love her, or was she merely part of his earthly possessions, less valuable perhaps than his wall mirror? Once again, the terrible frustration of not knowing. Yet there are flickering signs teasing one into drawing conclusions: the beautiful, incredibly soft jackal-skin kaross he made for her with his two rough hands; the innumerable pairs of handmade shoes and slippers she was reported to have left behind: I think he loved this frail girl to distraction. Only, he had no way of articulating it – apart from curing skins and making her shoes and useless garments.)

In due course a handful of militiamen turned up to arrest Diederik for the murder in Stellenbosch, but he put up such a fight that they soon scurried back to Cape Town. A few months later another, larger, commando arrived, but he'd had Khoin scouts posted along the way to warn him well in time, and with the (no doubt reluctant) help of his farm-hands and the women, all armed to the teeth and formidable shots, once again drove off the representatives of the Company.

Annoyed at the prospect of being plagued in this manner for perhaps years to come, he loaded all his earthly possessions – a bed, some chairs and a dining-table, implements, pitchers and kegs and barrels, his heirloom mirror and Bible, a coop of chickens, another with geese, three indentured servants, two slaves, and his wife – on the widow van Zyl's wagon, selected a fair number of fat-tailed sheep and cattle from his mother-in-law's stock, and set off on a trek of many months which finally took him to the Little Karoo. But here is the kind of touch which makes me suspect that there was more to the man than our history tends to give him credit for: knowing beforehand that the journey would be arduous, and hard on the hoofs of his animals, he first enlisted the womenfolk to make little sheepskin boots for all the sheep and cattle.

In a very ancient sense it was a tragic journey. Not because of any mishap, but because of the deep misunderstanding at the heart of it. To Diederik Landman, at least as his granddaughter later recorded it, it was a trek through virgin territory, never before occupied, or even visited, by man, woman or child: plains and open stretches, hills and the rocky outcrops of koppies like the vertebrae of the earth showing up through the stretch-marked skin, mountain ranges and prairies and plateaux that sometimes carried the dust-clouds of migrating springbok or wildebeest; and the only signs of life visible to his raging eyes were rock-rabbits or meerkats, lizards, tortoises, the occasional snake, buck and antelope, ostriches, once or twice a pride of lions, a small herd of elephant perhaps, and many birds. From time to time they would come past a mound of stones left there by trekking Khoin in honour of the great god-hunter Heitsi-Eibib; under overhanging rocks they would discover the red and yellow ochre painting smudges or etchings of the San. But these he discounted. They were like the tracks of animals in the veld. He was the discoverer of a vast new land unrolling before his imperious veldskoen-shod feet. Like a dog staking out its territory with its urine, Diederik mapped the lines and limits of his land with the remains of the animals he shot, the ashes and charred stumps of his fireplaces, the blood and sweat of tribulation, and two small mounds of earth marking the miscarriages Magdalena, still a mere child, suffered on the way. His: all his.

How could he know that in reality he was travelling through a landscape already inhabited by myths and legends? There was no koppie or dry river-bed, no tree, no rock that had not already been named, no table-topped hill or breast-shaped knoll that had not yet been celebrated in poetry or song. The shy imprint of the feet of Khoisan peoples who had wandered there for thousands of years proclaimed the land their mother; their stories had sung it into being, their moon-dances had moulded its contours. But Diederik didn't know. He thought it was nameless. He thought it was his.

There was no fixed destination to their journey. Several times they made a halt, where the grazing was good or the water abundant, or when the sheep and cattle had to be reshod. In any of these places they could have settled; and every time the frail, exhausted Magdalena's heart would contract with joy at the thought that they had finally arrived, that the unbearable, bone-numbing jolting of the wagon had come to an end. But every time they had to reload their possessions and move on again, either because familiarity with a spot revealed its defects, or because one day a smudge of smoke from another trekker's camp-fire would suddenly stain the distant sky; and Diederik could not stomach the knowledge of a neighbour in the vicinity, not even on the open plains where the horizon was days away.

He was friendly enough to strangers they met on the way; and once they had staked out the farm that was, finally, to be theirs, in the harsh but fertile valley beyond the Tradouw, Diederik's hospitality to visitors became legendary. (This, he used to joke, was because one never knew when God or his angels might decide to visit one in human guise, the way they'd done with Abraham; and in this heart of the country the light was so blinding, that any visitor appeared transparent.) He would make sure that Magdalena supervised the preparation of mammoth meals – thick soups, joints of mutton, roast venison, chicken pies, pumpkin, rice or wheat: all richly flavoured with cinnamon, or saffron, or cumin, coriander, tamarind, and rounded off with liberal draughts of neat brandy – and they would be given the best bed, and invited to take part in the daily family prayers, and be accompanied for miles when they left, to make sure they headed in the right direction. But this robust hospitality was prompted by the advance knowledge that in due course – even if it might take days, or weeks – the visitors would depart and leave one in peace again. Neighbours were something else: rivals for grazing or water, potential poachers, a perpetual nuisance.

It must have been a good season beyond the Tradouw when, after more than a year of wandering, Diederik announced that this was where he would stake out their farm: abundant water, tall grass for the cattle and succulent green scrub for the sheep, the veld covered in small yellow, white and purple flowers. And there they stayed, even when the droughts came and the place became a moonscape of shale and red and grey rock, withered and contorted trees, anthills, and the bleached white bones of many dead animals.

They would trek away in winter, to the east, where Diederik had staked out other grazing farms in the limitless land for his sheep and cattle; and in those places they would live on the wagon or put up a temporary shelter of wattle-and-daub; but they always returned to the farm Diederik had called *Rust-mijn-ziel*, or Rest-my-soul. The only other times he left the place were the long annual trips to Cape Town. (By that time the authorities had either forgotten about the giant's early misdeeds or had decided, wisely, to ignore him.) It is likely that he would have preferred to cut all bonds that tied him to that remote outside world, but retaining them was a matter of simple necessity: he needed those products from that unlikely, far-off place called Europe, and which could only be had through Cape Town – tobacco, spices, salt and sugar, coffee, items of clothing, and above all, ammunition. He resented those month-long treks which impinged on his independence, and only became tractable again when he was back at *Rust-mijn-ziel*.

Over the years, other trekboers moved into the region too, but at the first sight of an intruder's smoke Diederik would ride out to warn them against coming too close. The few who did settle, out of sight, were scared enough of the wild man to keep their distance; and at least it was useful to have womenfolk in the vicinity, even if they were several hours on horseback away, in case Magdalena fell ill, which often happened, she was so fragile. In due course they had two sons; then, after a few more miscarriages, a daughter. Magdalena died within the week and Diederik and his sons – and, a slave woman, Nenna – had to look after the puny new-born creature, as thin as a dragonfly but without the wings, with an inappropriate shock of black hair above its wizened face. At birth there was no sign of life in the baby. Resigned to the fact of another failure, Diederik rolled it in an old frayed dress of Magdalena's – no sense in making a coffin for what looked like a stillborn kitten – took it outside to the bottom of the garden where Magdalena's miscarriages had been buried, and dug a shallow hole to rid himself of it. As he picked up the bundle to bury it his hands sensed a faint wriggling motion and he heard what sounded like a whimper. The baby was alive after all. He called her Anna, and promptly christened her himself at the fountain behind the stone homestead, nearly drowning her in his enthusiasm.

Diederik became a legend of terror in his own lifetime. The scourge of his valley, as he saw it, was the San, the 'Bushmen', who had lived there since time immemorial, and who regarded cattle and sheep as fair game, especially when these wandered about in what had always been *their* territory. To Diederik they were subhuman predators, to be shot on sight. In fact, he offered his Khoin labourers a reward for each pair of 'Bushmen' ears they brought him; round his enormous waist he wore a leather thong strung with ears. Visitors who met him for the first time, like the traveller Larsson, initially mistook them for sun-dried peaches. Not all of those ears, it was rumoured, were San in origin; a few, in fact, were – or had been – white. Whoever crossed him, whether stranger or servant or son, encountered at close quarters the power of his tree-trunk arms, the range of his fury, the singeing fire of his hippo-hide whip, or the explosive force of his gun. Yet it was touching to witness the gentleness and patience with which this savage man handled his daughter.

It is said (my source once again the notebook of his granddaughter which Dad persistently refused to acknowledge) that after he had buried Magdalena in a grave he had dug with his own hands, he howled for days like a mad dog at the moon, tore at his beard, smashed whatever came in his sight. Then he disappeared into the mountains and only returned days later, lugging a dark red boulder so huge and heavy that no one could subsequently believe that a single man had carried it; and this he planted on Magdalena's grave, and chiselled her name, misspelt, on it. Only then did he come back into the stone house, solemn and silent, but at peace with himself. He boiled water in a copper basin, washed himself from head to toe, and took over the care of his daughter. When she was ill — she was as frail as her mother had been — he would sit rocking the weightless little body in his arms all night; when she was well, he carried her on his broad shoulders wherever he went. Nothing could separate him from the waif; even at night he would get up several times and tiptoe to her bed where he would bend over, an anxious ear against the pale smudge of her little face in the dark, to make sure she was still breathing.

Thus was prepared the parchment for the terrible poetry of the main event for which he is remembered.

He had always had problems with Hans, his younger son. His first-born, Jan-Jonas, took after his father. He wasn't quite so big, nor quite so impetuous, but he was a strong and robust boy who even as a twelve-year-old could carry a full-grown sheep on his shoulders; and before he was fifteen he could outdo any slave or Khoin labourer on the farm in hunting, riding, ploughing, harvesting, and — especially — building stone walls. But his father did not like him. Perhaps he saw in Jan-Jonas, from an early age, a possible rival and eventual threat to his authority. But if Diederik was hard on his first-born, he was inhuman in his treatment of Hans, who was slight and introverted, his mother's child. In different circumstances he might have become a musician. Even as a small boy he would slip out on full-moon nights to join the Khoin labourers in their dances; in the beginning they allowed him to shake a calabash filled with pebbles to the rhythm of their music, but later they taught him to play the *ghura*, a curious bow-shaped stringed instrument. The

678

first time he was old enough to accompany his father on the annual trip to Cape Town he was enraptured by a musical performance on the Parade in front of the Castle; and back home he spent months fabricating a fiddle. This was soon broken by his father in a fit of rage when he caught Hans making music while he was supposed to help the reapers bring in the wheat. But it was characteristic of the boy that he simply made a new instrument. And through the years the relationship between father and son was marked by the furious smashing of fiddles and the patient fashioning of new ones. Worse than the breakings were the beatings inflicted on the boy for the most trivial misdemeanour; and in spite of his physical frailty, or because of it, Diederik persisted in demanding more of him than of Jan-Jonas. That the boy survived at all for so long is a miracle. At times even Jan-Jonas fled from the house or the outbuildings when he could no longer bear the sound of those floggings that stripped the skin from a back like bark off a tree.

To Anna, too, her father's abuse of Hans caused much distress, because she loved her gentle, inventive brother. And there were occasions when she did succeed in averting punishment; but usually Diederik simply brushed her aside or, when she persisted, even hammering at her father with her fists to make him stop, he would lock her up in a room until he had done. Perhaps the very special tenderness between Hans and Anna contributed to the father's harshness with the boy: Anna was his, he would not share his daughter with anyone.

This was made very clear when, shortly before Anna's sixteenth birthday, an itinerant preacher arrived on *Rust-mijn-ziel* with his family. They had been there for just over a week when the man's oldest son politely asked for Anna's hand in marriage. Never before had Diederik flown into a rage of such proportions. He nearly killed the preacher and his whole family, who fled on foot, limping and broken; after they had disappeared, urged on even faster by a salvo of shots, Diederik broke to bits all the possessions they had been forced to leave behind, and finally set fire to their wagon. He was on the point of shooting their oxen when Anna intervened, hysterical. Her father struck her a blow that sent her reeling against the newly whitewashed front wall of the house. It was the first time he'd ever raised a hand against her. Aghast, he stared at her as she stood there, one hand raised to her cheek, too shocked even to cry. He began to tremble. He was ready to fall on his knees before her. What a difference it would have made had he done so. But unfortunately Hans had witnessed the scene and, beside himself, stormed at Diederik with his ineffectual fists. This time he was flogged to within an inch of his life.

For weeks, Anna refused to speak to her father and spent her days and nights tending to Hans, emerging from his outroom only to ask for other herbs and ointments and remedies from old Nenna; a Khoin herbalist was even brought into the house. Smouldering, Diederik avoided them, his sorrow subsumed by rage against a world over which he seemed to have lost control. There was a great thunderstorm brewing within the stone walls of their house, alone in that bleak wilderness, and it was only a matter of time before it would be unleashed.

Hans seemed intent on provoking it. He would lie in his bed playing the new fiddle he'd made from wood which Anna had carefully chosen for him; at night he would keep the candle burning to read the bible, knowing it angered his father who was overly possessive of the book. (It had been Magdalena's last wish that all her children should be taught to read and write; resentfully, but unable to go against the will of the dead, Diederik had hired, for two years, a Dutch ex-soldier who'd offered his services as a teacher. Jan-Jonas was satisfied with the basics, but Hans and Anna were taken with a passion for reading, and the only book in the house was that bible Hendrick Willemszoon had initially brought with him from Rotterdam.) Hans was barely back on his feet again, when he committed an act of such enormity that he must have known he was putting his life at stake. Diederik came home one night announcing that he'd caught red-handed a group of Khoin just as they were driving a number of sheep through a breach in the kraal wall. No one dared to challenge him, although they knew that only a few weeks earlier he himself had forcibly taken the sheep in question from a passing band of Khoin who'd refused to accept the paltry price he'd offered. Now he'd locked up the alleged thieves in the shed for the night; at first light, he announced, he was going to shoot the lot and add to his collection of ears. But when he arrived at the shed the next morning the door was unlocked and the prisoners were gone.

Diederik stared in disbelief. In pure frustration he fired a shot into the empty heavens. As he turned round, Hans was there, standing calmly in the first colourless light, arms folded on his wiry chest.

It is easy to imagine what was said between them.

'What the hell has happened here?' stormed the father.

'I let them go,' said Hans.

'What?'

'It was their own sheep they came for,' said Hans. 'You can't kill them for that.'

'*Rust-mijn-ziel* is my farm, Hans. No one is going to tell me what I can or cannot do on it.'

'Those people lived in these parts long before we came here.'

'Are you talking back at me? Only the other day you raised your hand against your own father. You realise you can burn in hell for that?'

'If I must burn for what is right, I'll burn.'

'I've had enough of this. I'm going to saddle my horse and run those bastards down. And when I bring them back you'll help me shoot them.'

'I'm sorry, Pa. But I won't.'

Diederik spat in disgust. 'Have you forgotten that last thrashing I gave you?'

'You can't just go on killing people, Pa.'

'People?' The big man's voice boomed with scornful laughter. 'A bunch of bloody Hottentots?'

'They're made in the image of God, like us. Isn't that what you yourself read in the Bible?'

Diederik was livid. 'How dare you blaspheme in my face like that? You think God looks like a bloody Hottentot?'

'You think God looks like *you*?'

Diederik raised his reloaded gun. I have little doubt but that he would have shot his son point-blank. But then Anna appeared. She always seemed to be around, wherever Hans went. Without a word she came to stand in front of Hans.

'You'll have to shoot me first, Pa,' she said.

Diederik lowered the gun and stared at her. She didn't move. It should have been very easy to shove her aside, but he didn't. For a long time he stared at her in frustrated, uncomprehending rage. Then he turned round and strode towards the stable. A minute later he came out again, riding bareback on his big black horse. But he didn't go in pursuit of the Khoin. As far as they could make out, he just rode and rode all day, and then came back. The following day the horse was lame.

The next confrontation did not end so peacefully. Diederik had ridden out, with Jan-Jonas, in pursuit of a clan of San who'd attacked his shepherds in the veld the day before; having trapped them in a mountain cave whose walls were covered in primitive paintings (Hans had seen the place before and had marvelled at the delicate figures of eland and wildebeest and little stick-men with bows and arrows and erect penises), they'd shot the grownups and brought two young boys home with them. In due course they would be taught to tend the sheep and cattle, even though Diederik knew from previous experience that it would take many months, and countless beatings, to break them in. Occasionally in the past, from a safe distance, Hans had raised some cautious objection against the practice. This time there was nothing hesitant about his resistance: when they arrived at the stable he took out his pocket knife to cut the thongs with which the children had been dragged behind Diederik's horse.

'Don't do that, Hans,' warned his father, his voice a deep rumble in his throat.

'They're only children, Pa.' He cut the first thong; the small yellow-brown boy scampered away like a frightened hare, with Jan-Jonas in pursuit.

'Children? I know them. They're vermin. They're worse than baboons.'

Hans took hold of the second thong. His father lashed out at him with his famous hippo-hide sjambok, leaving a bright red gash across his cheek. Hans gasped with pain, blinded for a moment, then proceeded to cut the second boy loose. He saw the next blow coming, and ducked, and grabbed the sjambok.

'God is my witness, today I'm going to kill you!' said Diederik, jerking the sjambok back so sharply that Hans lost his balance. The second blow cut right through his moleskin jacket. He fell. When he scrambled to his feet again he was staggering under the weight of a sneezewood lintel they'd cut the previous day for a doorway in the new shed Jan-Jonas was building.

'For Heaven's sake, stop it!' shouted Anna who came running from the kitchen door.

Diederik hissed something through clenched teeth. He aimed another blow, missed, stumbled slightly on his bad leg; then his son felled him with the beam. Hans was frail, but sinewy, and at that moment he had the strength of someone possessed. For a minute Diederik lay unmoving where he'd fallen.

'Hans!' Anna called out.

But Hans hadn't waited to see the result of his blow. He stooped to grab Diederik's fallen gun, and was gone.

Anna kneeled beside her father's prostrate body. A lesser man might well have been killed by that blow, but Diederik was only dazed. He shook his head, and mumbled, and sat up.

'Where's the bastard?' he growled. It was the sound of an old lion driven from the pride by a younger male.

'He's gone, Pa. Let him be. Come, I'll take you home.'

He shook himself loose. 'Anna, where is he?'

She took hold of his arm again.

'He tried to kill his own father,' said Diederik. He briefly pressed a hand against his head, then lowered it again, staring at the blood on his blunt fingers.

'He was scared, Pa. He didn't mean to.'

'Let go of me!' He brushed her off again. 'His own father. God will curse him into hell for this.'

'Please, Pa. Didn't you tell us how you once struck down *your* father?'

Diederik chose not to answer.

At that moment, behind the half-built new shed a shot rang out.

'Good,' said Diederik. 'Must be Jan-Jonas who got one of the little monkeys.'

But it wasn't. Hans had shot himself.

This was the beginning of that stark poem they wrote together.

Helped by old Nenna, Anna brought the broken body into the stone house, to her narrow room. They undressed him, and boiled water on the kitchen hearth, and washed him very meticulously, and clothed him in a shift which was too big for him. Anna spent the night kneeling on the dung floor beside the body. Jan-Jonas was somewhere outside; from time to time one could hear his footsteps as he wandered about in the night under the huge stars. The Milky Way, Orion, the Plough, Scorpius ascending. In the *voorhuis*, under the heavy yellowwood beams of the roof, Diederik, a large hulk, sat hunched over the open bible. It was impossible to tell whether he was reading, but his eyes were open; and even after the candle had flickered out, he remained sitting there in the darkness that bore the heavy smell of wax, staring out in front of him as if the words were smouldering in the dark, still visible to his savage eyes.

When Jan-Jonas found him there in the morning he looked up at his son, squinting slightly as if he had difficulty recognising him.

'We'll have to put him away,' he said.

'I'll make the coffin. The slaves can dig a grave,' said Jan-Jonas.

'There'll be nothing of the sort,' said Diederik. 'A man who tries to kill his own father does not deserve burial. We must put the body out in the veld and leave it there.'

'You can't do that, Pa,' Anna whispered, horrified. 'What about the jackals, and the vultures?'

'What about them?'

'They'll –' She stared at him. 'Pa, *please*! You can't do that. For God's sake. They'll devour him.'

'Then let them. It is the will of God.'

Nothing more was said. Diederik ordered his slaves and labourers and all their families from their hovels, and when all were assembled in the farmyard (only Anna had refused to come out) he and Jan-Jonas carried the body, stripped of its shroud, out of the house, through the small throng of solemn spectators, past the stable and the sheds, past the kraals and the wheat fields, past the little stonewalled graveyard where the massive boulder sat so heavily on its solitary grave, across the scorched brown veld under a sky drained of colour – it was January, at the height of summer – growing smaller and smaller as they went, until they disappeared into the shimmering distance.

Anna spent the whole day in the graveyard, perched on the boulder on her mother's grave, oblivious of the sun, staring.

In the late afternoon the first specks of vultures became visible in the distance, high up in the sky, circling very slowly.

When Diederik went out to call her in for supper after dark, she just shook her head.

'You'll come to sit with us even if you don't eat,' he said.

'How can you eat with Hans out there?'

'Anna.' He went up to her. He spoke very slowly. 'Hans is gone from us. No one on this farm will ever speak his name again. You understand?'

'How can you do such a thing?' she asked.

'I have to do what is right,' he said. 'Otherwise it will be an abomination in the sight of God.'

'*You* talk of abomination?!'

He put a hand on her shoulder, felt her flinch.

'Don't turn against me,' he said in the dark. 'Years ago I had your mother. Then she died. Now you are all I have.'

'If you deny Hans, I'm not your child either any more.'

'Anna, you don't know what you're saying.'

She didn't answer.

'Anna, speak to me.'

'I'll speak to you if bury Hans.'

'I cannot go back on my word.'

He felt the shrug of her thin shoulders.

He could crunch her bones in his huge hands, she was so fragile, a small bird. But suddenly he turned away, and walked back to the dark house where yellow candle-light shone through the small *voorhuis* window. He and Jan-Jonas were already eating – mutton, and bread dipped in milk – when she appeared in the doorway and came to sit with them; folded into a small white bundle on her lap was the shroud Diederik had torn from the body of her brother.

After supper Jan-Jonas brought Diederik the bible and he read for a long time, laboriously stalking with his blunt forefinger each word on the page as if they were insects to be crushed. I have no idea of the chapter he read, or of the book it came from – Job, Ecclesiastes, Jeremiah, Ezekiel? For all it mattered it might as well have been a mere catalogue of names, one of those endless genealogies.

Afterwards the men knelt at their chairs – Anna remained motionless on her chair, her hands folded on the cloth in her lap – and the father intoned a rambling prayer.

Before sunrise the next morning the house was awakened by Diederik, who came storming in from outside, bellowing like a wounded bull.

'What's the matter, Pa?' asked Jan-Jonas.

'I've been out in the veld. Someone has buried the body. Covered it with a heap of stones.'

'But who on earth –?'

'Took me an hour to take them all down again.'

All that lived and moved on the farm was summoned to the kitchen door where Diederik, sjambok in hand, swore in the name of God that he would personally kill any man, woman or child who went near the body again.

The following morning a new mound of stones had been piled up to hide the body from sight.

Once again everyone from the house and the huts was rounded up. Diederik started striking out at random with his sjambok, but no one could – or would – offer an explanation.

'Perhaps some Hottentots came by,' Jan-Jonas suggested at last. 'You know they build these cairns all over the place.'

'No Hottentot did this.'

'But how can you be sure, Pa?'

'I know what I know.' He stared hard at Jan-Jonas, at Anna, at

685

each labourer in turn. They shuffled and flinched, some women and children whimpered in fear, but they all met his stare and there was no reply.

He fetched his gun and strode down to the graveyard, clambered on Magdalena's tombstone and fired a shot into the clear sky. This he repeated at intervals all through the day. His people were quaking. Only the vultures in the distance were unperturbed.

After they had all gone to bed that night he crept out of the house again. The moon was out, half full. Black against the darkness of the night his large shadow strode limping across the endless expanse of the veld to where the body had been exposed. There was not much of it left. The stench was terrible. But he sat down under a gnarled wagon-tree and waited. It wasn't long before he saw the girl approach, running furtively in the dark, stopping from time to time to look back.

Near the scattered bones she scooped up her long white nightdress and began to gather stones in it. He waited until she began to stack them before he got up. The sound of a twig crunched under one of his heavy feet made her look up. Her face was very white in the moonlight, her hair streaming over her narrow shoulders like black water.

'Anna.'

She was breathing heavily. 'I had to do it, Pa.'

'I knew it could only be you.'

He could see her trembling lightly, but she didn't move.

'I warned you, didn't I?' he insisted.

'He was my brother,' she said. 'He was your son.'

'I said I would kill anyone who came near this place again.'

'Then kill me, Pa,' she said quietly.

'For God's sake!' He was silent for a long time. Then – dare I imagine him uttering such a thing? – he asked rudely, 'How can I kill you? I love you.'

'Then I'd rather you hated me, for I cannot bear your love.'

He struck out at her with his whip: it was, after all, the only language he knew.

'Yes, kill me,' I imagine her saying, grabbing him by the arms. 'For I hate you. I hate you! I've never hated anything in my life so much.'

It made him blind. He struck at her again, and again, thrashing wildly about him as she jumped and fought and howled, until suddenly she was gone from his grasp, free, running into the night.

686

She was screaming like a madwoman. But the screams grew fainter. The pale blotch of her nightdress in the dark, too, grew fainter. Until she was gone. And then there was only the veld around him, the hulking outlines of mountains far away, the moon and stars, and nothing else, not even a cricket chirping in the brittle grass.

The next day they went out in search of her: Diederik, and Jan-Jonas, and all the farm workers. But they found nothing. The earth was so hard, and she so light, that her small feet had left no imprint.

From time to time, through the years, there were reports that she'd been seen with a band of wandering Khoin deep in the hinterland. Some said she was like one of them, others that she was their slave. No one could tell for certain that it was Anna at all. She may simply have disappeared, like her great-grandfather, like so many others.

That night, after their fruitless search, Diederik and Jan-Jonas sat down for supper alone. Like every evening of their lives the father read a chapter from the Bible, said a prayer, and then they went to bed. The next morning *Rust-mijn-ziel* was deadly quiet. All the workers had fled in the night, taking their families with them. Only old Nenna was left. There was a curse on the place, she said quietly when Diederik spoke to her; that was why they'd gone. And if he tried to bring them back, they would just go off again. She would have gone too, only she didn't know what he would do then, a man alone was such a helpless creature. He walked off into the veld, carrying his gun, past the boulder that marked the grave of his long-dead wife. Was he shocked to find the bones of his son once again covered by the funeral mound? Truth is, his first reaction was one of almost boundless joy: she was back! It was the only explanation.

That was what he called out when he saw Jan-Jonas coming towards him: 'She's back! Jan-Jonas, Anna's back. Look, she's covered him up again.'

With something of his old exuberance he clambered on the heap and started tossing stones away in all directions. Pausing once to rest his back, he called out, 'Aren't you going to help me?'

'No, Pa.'

'Come on,' he said, too eager to be angry. 'Let's get this done, then we can go and find her. She'll be hungry. Thirsty. She must be exhausted.'

'It wasn't Anna, Pa.'

He narrowed his eyes. A terrible premonition settled in his

stomach like nausea. 'What d'you mean, man? Can't you see she's covered him up again?'

'I tell you it wasn't Anna, Pa. It was me.'

'I don't believe you.'

'I came here last night to bury what was left of him, Pa. It can't go on like this.'

'You did it to defy me? Just like that?'

'Pa, you're destroying everything we've ever had.' There was a sob in his voice. 'Please!'

'You realise what you've done, Jan-Jonas? You realise what you're forcing me to do?' Diederik stooped to pick up his gun. 'I gave my word to God!'

'Don't, Pa.'

Something broke inside Diederik. Grabbing the long gun by the barrel he aimed a ferocious blow at Jan-Jonas. But his son jumped out of the way, and picked up a rock and hurled it at his father. Then another. Realising he wouldn't be able to get near Jan-Jonas, Diederik pressed the butt of his gun against his shoulder and aimed to fire. Another stone struck him. He staggered just as he pulled the trigger, and missed. The next stone struck him on the forehead. He fell to his hands and knees. Then Jan-Jonas was on top of him. Rolling, wrestling, kicking, hitting, biting, they fought like dogs.

Our family tradition, which favours the epic approach, has it that the battle lasted all day and deep into the night, until it was too dark to see and each thought he'd killed the other. When Diederik came to again, he was lying on his back, staring into the sun through dried crusts of blood. In his ears, one can imagine, was the shrilling of cicadas; around him stretched the emptiness of the veld. There was no sign of Jan-Jonas. High, very high above, the vultures were describing their slow terrible circles in the sky. They were spiralling down, taking their time, their great wings outstretched and motionless, drifting on invisible currents of hot air. He tried to move, but couldn't. It felt as if every bone in his enormous body had been broken.

Still they swooped downward in their wide slow loops, until he could see the bald heads and necks, the beaks thrust forward, the vicious yellow eyes.

This is how I imagine it (for how else can one explain the only remaining evidence of his end?):

They've done enough damage, he must have thought. *The time has come to bury Hans. I was wrong. I should have listened to her. Now I have lost them all. Everything. Only emptiness is left on* Rust-mijn-ziel, *this place where my soul had sought to come to rest.*

This, I am sure, is what he thought. *All I have left is this: the bones of my son. I'll cover him up against their talons and their greedy beaks.*

I can see him struggling again to move. Pain shoots through his limbs, into his eyes. But he persists. Dragging his broken body after him, he moves along on his arms. Picks up stones to cover what remains of the bones. But the vultures are coming nearer; there will not be time enough to stack the mound again. Yet he must do something. It was his son. He crawls this way and that, gathering what bones he can find – God, there are so few of them, such a sad little bundle – and finally lies down on top of them, like a giant bird settling on its nest, protecting, with his body, with his life, whatever memories remain of happier, greater, simpler times.

Jan-Jonas Landman

(1739–1798)

I remember the trip on my motorcycle, with Nina, that early summer, to the hamlet of New Bethesda in the Camdebo. After we'd spent a few uneasy days with my parents in the Little Karoo (it was the first time – the only time – I'd taken her home) we proceeded to the coast, into Transkei; and on the way back we made a wide loop towards Graaff-Reinet. Not the most comfortable of journeys, I suppose, what with the two of us, a rucksack, and my camera bag all on a 500cc bike; but it was exhilarating, especially coming only a few months after we'd first met, a kind of pre-marital honeymoon on which I introduced her to childhood memories and places, and to some of the friends I had met over the last years, on my travels from town to town, from township to township, with Henry Bungane. And Nina loved slumming it.

Gradually, as we approached the Camdebo from the east, from King William's Town and Grahamstown, Bedford, Cookhouse, the landscape became more restless, turbulent with mountains and kloofs. This was Bruintjieshoogte, where from the middle of the eighteenth century an early race of pioneers had clung to the heights like rock-rabbits or baboons, scanning the rolling plains below, watching warily from afar the approach of any stranger. Now it seemed peaceful, almost desolate. The turbulence subsided; across a vast open prairie we drove to the placid little town set in its semi-circle of hills, far behind it the Sneeuberge, the Mountains-of-Snow. That was where we were heading for, following the main road that leads to Middelburg. Not a soul in sight, except once a cyclist with a guitar strung over his shoulder, and once a donkey-cart with a bunch of 'coloured' people huddled together in their Sunday best. We turned left on the dust track to New Bethesda, down a sudden decline, past a tall red cliff – and then the valley opened up below us. An archetypal village with wide dusty streets, pepper-trees, bare backyards with chicken runs and outdoor toilets (how well I knew them from my youth: the wooden seat, the smell of Jeyes' Fluid, the newspaper squares on a long nail behind the door, the box filled with mealie cobs). Windmills with broken blades. A store dating from 1863. An ostentatious Dutch Reformed church. It was this ordinariness, this predictable and wholly unimaginative pattern, which made our discovery of the Owl House so extraordinary. We'd recently seen Athol Fugard's play inspired by the place, *The Road to Mecca*: that was Nina's reason for coming; my own was more arcane.

A morose old lady with her grey hair in a stark bun behind her head, her glasses reflecting the afternoon sun, took us – with obvious disapproval, for it was Sunday – to the house where Helen Elizabeth Martin had lived. Not even the many images and statues of owls on the front stoep prepared us for what awaited us inside, and in the yard. All the walls and ceilings covered with coloured glass ground in a coffee-mill, shimmering in many colours in the light of lamps and candles. Red window-panes which turned the views of the outside world into pure fantasy. Mirrors cut in crescents and crosses. An Aladdin's cave, a phantasmagoric recess of the mind, a dream unexpectedly recaptured in daylight. And outside, the 'Camel Garden' densely inhabited by imaginary creatures in cement. Monsters and outlandish fairytale chapels and pyramids. I thought of Carel Landman in his mosque, of Fransoois on his dreamboat in the desert: would they have recognised a kindred spirit in Helen Elizabeth Martin? To her contemporaries in this stark village she must have appeared mad: how could they hope to understand the passions and imaginings which drove her to such weird shapes and fantasies?

The sun above, the pepper-trees and painted rooftops, the windmills in the backyards around us seemed anomalous: this was a completely different kind of world, as if we'd taken a wrong turning into another time-frame.

Disapproving of our holding hands as we wandered through that house and garden, the old lady who accompanied us was reluctant to part with even the most mundane information. We had to drag the few basic facts from her: Helen had married twice; had gone away; had come back after her parents' death to lead a life of total seclusion; her only helper and confidant a 'coloured' man. At seventy-eight, Helen had been taken with a terror of going

691

blind – all her life she'd lived for light and glitter, bright colours, extravagant hues – so one Friday, at noon, she'd swallowed caustic soda, and on the Sunday night she'd died.

'People say all kinds of things,' said our stern guide, staring accusingly at us. 'But I tell you there was nothing wrong with Helen. Nothing at all. They just didn't understand her, that's all.'

'Of course,' said Nina, just as severely. 'How *could* they understand?'

'She had a vision, you see,' said the old lady, relenting a little. 'Not many of us have that.'

We returned to the bike, parked under a pepper-tree a block or so away. We waved goodbye to our guide, but she turned her head away stiffly and walked on. We were back in the drab little village in its lost valley under the hills. But somehow it looked different now. Its subconscious had been revealed to us, a few of its angels and demons had briefly, like the shadows of clouds, flitted across the landscape of our minds. But it was not Helen Elizabeth Martin I was thinking of: it was those ancestors of mine who'd also fought against the confines of their crude or unintelligible world, each in his own way. Hendrick Willemszoon, who'd married a slave girl because it had seemed the only way he could save her from the stake. Fransoois Lodewickus, who'd turned his back on the 'civilised' world to sail off into the desert in search of his mother's birthplace. Carel Guillaume, who'd willed himself dead in a coffin in his private mosque, from which he returned, like Lazarus, into a world in which he had become a stranger. Diederik, whose demons finally got the better of him. Jan-Jonas, who'd tried to reconcile his passions with the demands of the 'real' world: Jan-Jonas, the builder of walls to contain the wilderness. This was his territory. He might have lived in the very valley where New Bethesda now nestled. Helen Elizabeth Martin might have been one of his descendants, like me: he had many, few of them legitimate. Perhaps, somewhere quite near, a stone's throw from the Owl House, might be the remains of some crumbling wall built by his hands. What had he built them for? A pointless question. Why did Helen Elizabeth sculpt mushroom humanoids with camel heads?

There is much uncertainty about Jan-Jonas's movements immediately after his father's death. It is known, from his daughter Rachel's little notebook, that he must have remained in the vicinity for some time because she records that he buried the old man's body where

692

it lay, still shielding the bones of his son. But after that he must have gone away, living in the mountains or off the veld for God knows how long, perhaps too scared to return to that ill-omened farm alone. Perhaps it was starvation that finally drove him back.

The place was deserted. One can imagine the trepidation with which he approached the homestead. The front door was closed. He stopped in the doorway, called out, every muscle in his body taut as he stood listening. But there was no sound at all. As he moved from the *voorhuis* to the small room where Anna had slept, and from there to the kitchen, the only sign of life was a family of swallows nesting under the rafters. They must have flown in through one of the small windows (none of them had glass, of course). They had left their droppings all over the place. Everything was covered with a film of grey dust. Nenna had obviously gone off too. And it was clear that there had been no visitors in his absence. It surprised him. He'd expected to find the place ransacked. But the runaway workers must have spread the word about the farm being cursed.

Outside, the vegetable garden lay parched in the sun. Only a few white pumpkins had survived among blotched and scorched leaves. There was a smell of death in the stable; the horse had died. But at least some of the cattle and sheep, which had been driven from the kraals to graze before sunrise on that fatal morning, should still be somewhere in the veld. A few scrawny chickens were scratching behind the shed.

Jan-Jonas surveyed the desolation of the place. All this was his now. He could start again. But he had no stomach for it. There was indeed a curse resting on the farm and if a new start was to be made it had to be somewhere else, as far as possible from this place of death. He spent a week or so rounding up a handful of cattle scattered here and there over miles of veld, repaired the wagon and loaded everything he needed from the house into it. When everything was ready, he clambered up the back of the oven in the kitchen wall and put a torch to the thatch. He waited only to see the flames leap up. Then, without looking back once, he drove off slowly, driving his little herd on ahead of the lumbering wagon. Which way to go? North and east lay the emptiness of still mainly 'undiscovered' land; south and west was sparsely populated territory, other people, companionship, contact with a rudely civilised world. Jan-Jonas headed north-east.

Two days from home he encountered a small band of travelling Khoin and after much argument two of the younger men were persuaded to join him in exchange for an ox and five sheep, a roll of tobacco and a keg of bad brandy. From then on his trek was more manageable. On a modern map one can trace his route through the years that followed – Prince Albert, Willowmore, Aberdeen, Graaff-Reinet, New Bethesda, Cradock, Somerset East. Every time he found a place to stay he would set up home and begin to stack stone walls, miles and miles of them zigzagging across the plains, to make sure, and doubly sure, that his territory was demarcated and contained, the arid wilderness excluded. For two years, or three, or four or five, he would settle in a spot and claim it as his own; then, as if all those magnificently stacked walls counted for nothing, he would load his wagon and move on again, driven by some unexplained urge in his mind. The more solid his walls, the more uncontrollable the urge to move beyond them.

Loneliness was part of it, I think. The need of companionship; the need of sex. (This is all too evident from the scalding lines he scrawled, obviously in moments of guilt-ridden despair, on the endpapers or in the margins of the family bible: I'm sure my father would have torn those pages out to destroy the evidence were such an act not sacrilegious.) Yet the paradox was that the greater his need of companionship, the further away he moved from other people. A desire for purgation, perhaps? Escape from temptation? Or mortification of the flesh?

And then, suddenly, he met – and married within a week – his first wife, Fransina Verwey, in Swellendam where he'd gone to take communion in the winter of 1762. Like most of the other frontiersmen, Jan-Jonas never missed *nagmaal* if he could help it. Much more than holy communion was involved on these occasions, even though one did attend three or four church services over the weekend and a couple of prayer meetings as well: the farmers, some of whom might have been on the road for two or three weeks to arrive in time, came to sell or auction or barter their produce, to have children baptised or marriages regularised, to fill each other in on whatever had happened in the meantime; above all, it was an occasion for merrymaking, and sport, and communal eating, and dancing, and drinking. Potent honey-beer, which the Khoin had taught them to brew, was much in evidence. Those few who had stills on their farms brought along the fire-water they had extracted with rough skill from whatever veld fruit or bulbs or berries they could lay their hands on (prickly pears, imported from abroad, had already taken root here and there, and yielded a particularly fierce distillate), and the consequences were invariably devastating. What brought Jan-Jonas to *nagmaal* was, most likely, the growing urge to find a wife. Which explains his unseemly haste the moment Fransina Verwey indicated her interest, one evening after several rounds of dancing, when he'd taken her for a walk behind the outspanned wagons to show her, among other things, the stars in the deep black winter sky.

There was nothing particularly attractive about her. She was, from all accounts, grossly overweight, sickly, and pious to a fault; but she was willing, and it seemed her prosperous parents were only too eager to be rid of her, for she was packed off with a dowry quite considerable for those days, chests and chests of hand-embroidered linen, and copper kettles and pots and pans, two mattresses stuffed with feathers, a span of oxen and fifty sheep.

Jan-Jonas would probably have taken her without any dowry at all. Previously, apart from coming to *nagmaal* at least twice a year, he'd undertaken a laborious annual trip all the way to Cape Town: not just to trade his wares, to buy another a slave or two, or look up those descendants of his father's innumerable brothers and sisters who'd drifted back to town from the West Coast, but mainly to spend as much time as possible in the Slave Lodge which served as the town's brothel. (These are the escapades his passionate guilt-ridden lines in the bible refer to, mostly.)

It is my guess that Fransina was seen, the poor woman, as the remedy to his urges, his loneliness, and his previous lascivious outbreaks. If so, she turned out to be more of an affliction than a solution. For one thing, she was barren: certainly her childlessness could not be ascribed to lack of trying on Jan-Jonas's part. In that stark patriarchal world his manliness was at stake. He was obsessed with the need to produce offspring: not only, I surmise, because he must have been painfully conscious of being the sole surviving male of his line, but because children were in those days a material asset. The more sons one had the more overseers there were to keep an eye on slaves and 'unreliable' Khoin. That was the time, as far as I can make out, when he was living in the New Bethesda region. In the still practically uncolonised interior there was no obstacle to staking out a farm; the only formality required would be to register it, at some stage, in Cape Town and pay an annual quit-rent; but in practice even that hardly ever happened. The Company simply lacked the means to control such a vast hinterland. The new farm Jan-Jonas had occupied was larger than the previous ones; the walls surrounding it more formidable than anything he had built before. But skill and hands were needed. His father had been one of fifteen children; Jan-Jonas as yet had none.

This undoubtedly weighed heavily in his decision, about three years after his marriage, to bring a young Khoin woman into the house as his second wife. It could not have happened without great domestic upheaval: in fact, as soon as they got word of the disgrace, his in-laws travelled all the way from Swellendam to have it out with him. But Jan-Jonas had the better of them. Certainly his arguments (which can still be reconstructed from marginal notes in the bible) made sense: When Sarai realised she could bear Abraham no children, she said unto her husband: I pray thee, go in unto my maid; it may be that I may obtain children by her. And when Jacob's beloved wife Rachel bore him no children, she gave him Bilhah her handmaid unto wife: and Jacob went in unto her. And Bilhah conceived, and bare Jacob a son. And then there was King David. And what about Solomon, the wisest man of all? So how could any man or woman reproach Jan-Jonas in the face of the Lord if he went in unto his wife's handmaiden Toas whom he had duly christened Eva?

The Verweys returned to Swellendam, presumably chastened by the justness of their son-in-law's cause, and turning down all poor Fransina's tearful entreaties to take her with them.

Did they regret their decision when only days after their departure Fransina hanged herself twice from a beam in the stable (at the first attempt the beam broke and half the roof fell in on her)? I could find no record of their reaction. Perhaps the fact that they decided against another journey to attend the funeral is eloquent in itself – although the summer heat may have been reason enough. Neither did they visit Jan-Jonas after his handmaid had given birth to his daughter Rachel, or, not quite a year later, to his son Benjamin.

There is less ground for condoning Jan-Jonas's subsequent actions which resulted in the birth of a considerable number of offspring to all the other Khoin women on the farm; but maybe he began to have some reservations of his own about the religious justification of all this, because in 1776, on the occasion of his annual trip to Cape Town, he unexpectedly took to wife Truusje van Wijk, the daughter of a surgeon from one of the Company's ships en route from Amsterdam to Batavia. She was clearly a woman who would stand no nonsense, and within a month of her arrival on the farm the Khoin woman Toas (Eva) and her son (then about ten years old) were turned out of the house and sent to live with the other labourers. (Little Rachel, it seems, was never regarded as a menace, being of the female sex; in fact, there is evidence that Truusje became curiously fond of the little girl. The other bastard children on the farm did not seem to pose any threats either, as they and their mothers, unlike Toas and Benjamin, had no delusions about their status.)

For a few months an uneasy calm reigned in the farmhouse surrounded by its many rough concentric circles of brown stone walls. Then Truusje fell pregnant; and before the birth of her first daughter (there were four more to come) she instructed Jan-Jonas to order Toas and her child Benjamin off the farm.

Was it in retaliation, or in a sudden panic, that within days of Toas's departure with his son – he would remember, I am sure, for the rest of his life that last view of them as they rode off on the ox-cart he'd given them, with two small bundles and a yellowwood *wakis* containing the few possessions they were allowed to take with them – Jan-Jonas announced that the wagons had to be loaded, as they were vacating the farm? Truusje ranted and raved, threatening to throw everything off the wagons again, or alternatively to stay behind all by herself, but Jan-Jonas was a man as stubborn as his father had been. So her baby, a girl, was born in the main wagon, in the open veld, between the farm they'd abandoned and another they'd not yet found; and Truusje swore she would never forgive him for it. But he did the same just before their next daughter was born, and again when Truusje was pregnant with the following three (which may be one reason they discontinued having children after that). Every time he built a new house and surrounded it with walls; and then abandoned it all – though it is said that in later years, on the annual trip to Cape Town to do his business with the corrupt Company, he would visit all his earlier abodes again, and check the walls, and rebuild what had decayed or caved in, until the journeys became so long and complicated that he would barely be back home before it was time to set out again on the next. Which may be another reason for the abrupt end to the expansion of their family. One thing that must be said, is that Jan-Jonas never touched another woman: at least our family tradition has denied him that. It may be that Truusje finally cured him, after all. She certainly was a formidable consort.

Formidable, but lonely. In Jan-Jonas's long absences she had to run whichever farm they were living on at that time, supervise the slaves and the Khoin labourers, keep an eye on the vegetable garden and the kraals and the daily cleaning of the house where chickens roosted in the *voorhuis* and a hand-reared lamb or two slept under the kitchen table. She'd known nothing about farming life when she had married Jan-Jonas, but she was determined to learn: from her husband, her neighbours (few and far between as they were), from the labourers she was expected to oversee. They taught her about the seasons and the skies, how to read the spoor of a duiker or the mood of a cloud; they showed her which roots in the veld were edible, which bitter berries to avoid. And the Khoin and slave women in the house initiated her in the use of herbs and remedies: the urine of a young hare for kidney stones, fennel on brandy for palpitations, buchu for the bladder, wild honey and pulped 'hottentot' figs for bronchitis, cow dung and vinegar to stop gangrene; wild wormwood, aloe juice, dog-piss shrubs and kambro, pollen from yellow thorn-tree blossoms, dried heather from the mountains, ground porcupine quills, the secretions of rock-rabbits, lichen, snake-skin powder — how could she ever have survived without such knowledge?

Her main occupation was the rearing of her children. When they were small she had a Khoin wet-nurse to help her, but it was a passion with her that her daughters should be 'educated', and having had a pretty thorough schooling herself in Amsterdam, she spent hours every day teaching them not only reading and writing but a fair amount of history and geography as well. Rachel, the little half-caste child left behind by Toas when she rode off into the wilderness with her small son Benjamin, sat in on the lessons. In fact, it was soon evident that she was rather more prone to learning than Truusje's own daughters; and it says much for the lady's character that she not only accepted this, but spent more and more time on extra lessons for the enthusiastic girl-child with the bright brown eyes and the innumerable little plaits in her frizzy hair. Thanks to her efforts, Rachel became the one who later, in a formal little book in a dark blue binding now in the Cape Archives, wrote down what she had learned of her father's history; and this has been an invaluable source book in my own research.

(Once again, just as when I was confronted with Hendrick Willemszoon's slave wife, I am frustrated by a whole line leading from Toas back into Africa, irretrievable even to the imagination. In addition to anecdotes from her father's chronicle, Rachel mentioned stories Toas had told about her own ancestry, reaching back to a half-mythical hero T'kama who had allegedly taken to wife a woman from an early Portuguese ship on its way to the East:

but whether that was even possible I cannot tell. And beyond this T'kama the line, it seems, goes back all the way to the legendary hunter Heitsi-Eibib. But the trail is lost; even Rachel did not elaborate.)

One sad note must be inserted here. None of this has survived in the official history of my family. *Aletheia*. In their versions, Jan-Jonas had never associated with Khoin women; Toas had been no more than a domestic servant. And Benjamin had been the son of poor fat Fransina, who had brought the roof down on herself in a fit of nerves because she couldn't cope with the child. All those copious notes in the Bible were no more than the blasphemous ramblings of a mind probably disturbed by alcohol. And Benjamin had not been expelled from the farm either: enterprising youngster that he was, he'd run away, tended by that poor loyal servant Toas, also known as Eva.

There is little more to record of Jan-Jonas until his death, in his sleep, in 1798, only months after Truusje had been killed by the bite of a puff-adder (all her remedies had sadly proved to no avail). His real history is written in the walls he built, even if their language is not always intelligible to others, or to me: they formed all kinds of geometric patterns in the veld, barricades against – what? Sometimes they just seemed to run on and on into the distance, without any apparent function or purpose whatsoever, containing nothing, enclosing nothing, defending nothing, pointless linear assaults on space. Surely there must have been more to them than the mere statement: *Jan-Jonas Landman was here*?

Those walls have cost me many nights' sleep. In a way they encapsulate the problem I have with Jan-Jonas's whole life: sometimes it seems self-contained and focused, at other times it takes off blindly without arriving anywhere – without, above all, really linking him to history. I know we all, to some degree at least, tend to think of history as a mere footnote to our own lives: what matters to us is our own presence. But when it comes to others, it is reassuring to be able to 'place' them within some kind of context, to evaluate their 'significance' in terms of their position in a larger historical framework. But perhaps that is the point of Jan-Jonas's life: that in his time our tribe *did* opt out of history, ignoring all the large currents of events sweeping through that much-vaunted Age of Reason. Their non-history *was* our history. *Not* conforming, *not* fitting in, *not* arriving anywhere, *not* making sense: perhaps that was the true call Jan-Jonas responded to. It wasn't the Dutch East India Company, or the depressing succession of governors at the Cape – each more extravagant, more corrupt than his predecessors – or the great events of that age (the Seven Years' War, the American War of Independence, the reign of Louis XV) that constituted *our* history. Ours was written in the heart of the country, not in gunpowder or in flourishes of the pen, but in stone walls and furrows and small ploughed fields, in drinking and merrymaking at *nagmaal* times, in making children, in teaching a little brown girl to read, in disowning and sending away the woman one has loved and who is no longer acceptable or useful, the woman and her small fierce son, straight-backed as a meerkat, flesh of one's flesh, a single insignificant link in a human fuse running through the ages, seemingly without aim or purpose: until it explodes one day in a bomb blast on the Parade in Cape Town.

Benjamin Landman

(1766–1811)

Like a subterranean mineral vein emerging in brief outcrops at unpredictable intervals before disappearing underground again, our family chronicle makes its appearance, several times, in the daylight of recorded history during the lifetime of Benjamin Landman. What befell him and his mother, the Khoin woman Toas, christened Eva, in the months immediately following their departure from the farm at what is now New Bethesda, is not known. Even if, as seems likely, they were joined on the way by a few of Toas's people who would have lent a hand with the trek – the small cart with its few bundles and odds and ends (including the last-minute gifts Jan-Jonas had pressed on them behind Truusje's forbidding back: the hand-carved heirloom mirror which Toas had found irresistible from the very first day she'd glimpsed herself in it; and the bible that bore so many revealing marks of Jan-Jonas's lifelong struggle with the flesh; two spare oxen; a cow; eight sheep) – it must have been no mean feat for them to travel all the way to Cape Town, where the woman was employed as a housemaid by one Barend Retief in August 1777.

They had both been there before, the first time when Jan-Jonas had taken his son, then a child of two or three, to be baptised by the Dutch Reformed predikant in the Groote Kerk (the mother was vaguely – and disingenuously – designated as 'Eva Binnenland', a surname meaning 'Inland'). This event, and the document recording it (which first the mother and later her child preserved close to their bodies from the day Jan-Jonas had driven them away), was the determining factor in Benjamin Landman's life. To have been baptised, to be acknowledged in an official document as a Christian (even though this was qualified by the designation 'Bastard'), opened doors which otherwise would have remained very tightly sealed.

Already Cape society was becoming less fluid than before; already race was becoming a factor – if not yet the decisive factor – in defining one's social horizon. If liaisons between white trekboers and slave or Khoin women were frequent in the distant frontier territory, the children born from such unions were doomed to a twilight world with little hope of advancement: unless they were baptised. And from all contemporary reports Benjamin had the additional advantages of being both handsome and intelligent. He had his mother's beautiful eyes and sómething of her grace (we know from many accounts, especially from Le Vaillant's, that Khoin women, though more often than not distasteful in appearance to prejudiced European eyes, could sometimes be quite stunningly attractive), his father's height and bearing, and the shrewdness of both. So although he was officially not the equal of a European, he was more than a slave or a Khoin or a 'tame Hottentot' or a simple bastard; and there was some scope for personal endeavour to earn him the possibility of a future.

After that initial baptismal visit mother and child had, jointly and severally, returned to Cape Town with Jan-Jonas on some of his annual trips, usually in the first months of the year when one could count on the maximum number of passing ships in the harbour. For the father these visits had been fraught with problems: there was a simple choice between clandestine meetings with officers or sailors from the ships to strike illegal deals (sometimes unscrupulously using Toas as a decoy), running the constant risk of getting caught and sentenced to a heavy fine or worse; and an interminable wrangling with Company officials, the only ones legally allowed to conduct trade, trying to persuade them to raise the ridiculous prices offered to inland farmers so that they could personally pocket most of the vast profits. But to Toas and Benjamin these visits had been a source of unmitigated enchantment. (Even the occasional forced encounter with a ship's officer in order to secure a deal for Jan-Jonas's sheep or ostrich eggs or ivory Toas seemed to take in her stride.)

How remote, how unreal, became the harsh monotony of the farm in this town where every day seemed to throb with magic. Smells: curry, and dried fish, and overripe fruit, and fermenting grapes, and nutmeg, and cinnamon; buchu and acrid woodsmoke from the Mountain; *kukumakranka* and beeswax in the homes. Sights and sounds: a formal band playing in the Church Square or under the trees of the Company Gardens; improvised dances or the whine of oriental music on the Boerenplein; merrymakers spilling from the taverns into the streets, laughing, drinking, or brawling; Malay slaves in brightly coloured shifts scuffling past, soundless on their bare feet, straining under the weight of long carrying-poles with buckets of water or baskets of produce suspended from them; doughty burghers strutting along the potholed streets with long-stemmed pipes or silver-topped canes in hand, accompanied by their overdressed wives with tall coiffures and Parisian décolletées, dexterously shaded from the sun by slaves carrying umbrellas or palm fronds; artisans squatting in their small open-front shops making furniture, cobbling shoes, weaving mats and baskets and rattan window-blinds, cutting and sewing clothes, repairing copper kettles, stuffing coir mattresses, cooking spicy meats and saffron rice with raisins; on the beach below the Castle, groups of people piling up great mounds of shells and covering these with billet and brushwood to burn them to lime. It was even possible, if it was really spectacular entertainment one craved, to attend an execution or the flogging or branding or maiming of some convicted criminal. (The gallows for white offenders stood on the lower slope of the mountain known as the Lion's Rump; slaves and Khoin were taken to the shore, near the mouth of the Salt River. For special occasions a huge gallows was erected in front of the Castle, where Carel Guillaume had been imprisoned; on the spot to which, two centuries later, with a sense of real occasion, Nina and I returned.)

No wonder Benjamin and his mother were lured back to this small town below its tall cloud-capped mountain, exposed to the south-east wind and the spray from Table Bay, its whitewashed or Dutch-green houses set among oaks already a hundred years old, with in one's ears the miraculous sound of water running in stone furrows along the main streets, carried down from the mountain in long wooden pipes.

It was different from before, of course. Then they had been visitors, and Jan-Jonas had been with them; this time they had to fend for themselves and eke out a living on the meagre wages earned by Eva (the only name by which she was known henceforth). But she had in her an indomitable will to survive. Her whole life was directed towards her child: he was both her answer to the world and her revenge on it. She sent him to the school where the children of the Company's slaves and officials were taught. (Once a fire broke out in the building; Benjamin ran back into the flames: not, as the others thought, admiring his bravery, to save the single small screaming child who'd got caught inside – although I'm relieved to say that Benjamin did manage to drag him out as well – but to salvage the coat which had his baptismal certificate sewn inside its lining. Without it, he knew, he might as well have been incinerated himself.) When he was not at school he was supposed to help Eva with the housework, which invariably went on until long after nightfall; but when she wasn't looking he often slipped out to run down to the harbour and watch the ships, and the vendors, and the soldiers and sailors, and the prostitutes, the coming and going of people in outlandish clothes, and speaking outlandish tongues. He had a flair for languages: he spoke the inland vernacular of his father, and the Khoin language his mother had taught him; and soon picked up the creolised Malay-Portuguese of slaves and sailors, the High Dutch of visitors from the mother country, and even a smattering of English and of French. (In those days, when the Cape was known as Little Paris, there was quite a traffic of French ships anchoring in Table Bay.) And it is likely that, with the odd doubloon or ducat or shilling or guilder he earned through fetching and carrying for the free-spending visitors, he also brought home confused notions about liberty, equality and fraternity transported through the turbulent Atlantic from pre-revolutionary France.

In 1783, when Benjamin had just turned seventeen, there came a major change in their lives: the daughter of Barend Bothma, Eva's employer, was married to a sergeant from the Castle garrison, Ludwig Jansen, who by undertaking to pay the Company four rix-dollars a month, promptly became a *pasganger* or passman with the right to ply whatever trade he wished. Having been trained as a teacher in the Netherlands, it had been Jansen's ambition for some time to travel into the interior as a freelance schoolmaster. In spite of some misgivings on the part of the Bothma family, the newly married couple left for the distant Eastern Frontier, taking Eva and Benjamin with them. During the six years or so they had lived in Cape Town, Eva had been Liesbet Bothma's personal maid; in some respects they were closer than mother and daughter. So it was natural for young Liesbet to insist on Eva's company on that long journey into the unknown.

Were they reluctant to leave the town in which they'd managed to escape from the unhappy past – or was there some secret eagerness in them to return to the region where they'd both been born? I wish I knew. What I do know is that all his life, deep inside himself, Benjamin nursed, like a sickness of the blood, a resentment – no, more: a slow-burning rage – against the father who had disowned him and whom he'd desperately loved. I doubt that he cherished any plans of active revenge. But it would seem, at least at this great distance, that much of what happened later was determined by that rage.

To be sentimental about it would be unfair to the man. Yet it is necessary, if one wants to understand anything at all about him, never to forget that during the first ten years of his life Benjamin and his father had been inseparable. However profligate Jan-Jonas may have been in his affairs with women, however uncaring about most of his children, this first-born son had been to him, as one of his melodramatic but revealing notes in the margin of his Bible attests, what Rachel's sons had been to Jacob. The birth of Benjamin vindicated, in the father's eyes, all the sins he'd committed in the eyes of others; it offered an issue to the dead-end his own father had landed him in. This was the child who, in some obscure way, made sense – in his eyes at least, for no one else could understand it – of all those walls he felt himself driven to build. And Benjamin had thrived in his father's love. A spoilt child, no doubt. But such a beautiful boy, with such endearing manners, that most people were willing to forgive him anything. Except Truusje: she firmly believed he was being raised for an ignoble end. In the beginning Jan-Jonas simply laughed it off, and continued to take Benjamin with him wherever he went, to share with him whatever he knew. But Truusje persisted (and who can blame her?). So one can imagine the child's shock when, out of the blue, his whole familiar world was torn from him. It might still have been possible for Jan-Jonas to give his son some plausible explanation when Toas and the boy were instructed to move from the *opstal* to the labourers' hovels; but how does one persuade a ten-year-old who has been one's favourite child that he is suddenly no longer wanted, that he must get on an ox-cart with his mother and be driven into the wilderness, never to return?

He never looked back once, that morning when the swaying, lumbering cart bore them from the valley that had defined his early life: straight-backed, dry-eyed, he sat on the *wakis* beside his mother, the heavy leather-bound Bible his father had given him on his bare knees. Through the years that followed he never went to bed at night without that unwieldy volume which he used as a pillow, his face pressed hard against the leather, breathing in as deeply as he could the elusive smell of the past – tobacco, sweat, sheepskin, flint, tallow, grease, dust, earth, everything that spelled 'father', the most hated, most beloved name he knew in the world.

It is likely that the hard edge of his pain had been blunted during the years in Cape Town. But now they were on their way back, which could not but whet the knife again.

In the region of Bruintjieshoogte, not all that far from Graaff-Reinet, Ludwig Jansen found his first appointment as schoolmaster to a bunch of unruly children raised on a cluster of farms belonging to the Prinsloo clan. But the pay was bad, the Prinsloos an aggressive lot, and Liesbet, heavily pregnant, couldn't stand the tension; soon they moved on. And so began their itinerant life, which eventually took them to the Zuurveld, the lush green country stretching for a hundred or so kilometres along the coast between the Sunday's River in the west and the Great Fish River in the east.

They could not have chosen a more difficult time for such a move. The Zuurveld with its billowing grassy hills (blazing red in winter when the aloes were in flower) and its thickets of euphorbia and *kiepersol* and blue plumbago, had become a precarious frontier region where, during the preceding decade, the trekboer pioneers moving inexorably eastward in search of new grazing had begun to run into the vanguard of an even more massive westward movement of the Xhosa peoples. It had been easy, until then, to deal with the small bands of Khoin scattered through the vast inland regions: there were relatively few of them, especially after several great smallpox epidemics had decimated their numbers; and their nomadic life had made it possible for them to stay out of harm's way by moving on when conflict threatened to become serious. But the Xhosa were different: a strong and stably organised society of people peaceful by nature but ready to fight when threatened, and already firmly established in the region by the time the white farmers arrived.

These Xhosa in the Zuurveld were linked to the massive main body of their nation beyond the Great Fish River (proclaimed in 1780 by the Cape government – with more wishful thinking than practical sense – as the eastern frontier of the Colony) through an intricate network of kinship and client-and-patron relations; and in their many internecine squabbles and scuffles, some of the groups would enlist the support of white farmers against others; while some would seek allies among the Khoin also scattered through the region, or lured from the service of trekboers they

706

appeared to stretch out endlessly in all directions, was closing up. And from the rear the once remote Cape government began to move inexorably closer: first, in 1743, the district of Swellendam had been proclaimed, with its own *drostdy* or legal and administrative headquarters, its inspectors and soldiers and officious officials; now, in 1786, in Graaff-Reinet as well. Previously, if you were pestered to pay the 24 rix-dollars 'recognition fee' required annually for a loan farm, you could simply move on, further away, and claim a new stretch of land as your own; now escape was no longer easy, and if you didn't heed the warnings to pay up, soldiers – some of them, to add insult to injury, recruited from the Khoin – might turn up to evict you and install a stranger in your place.

It didn't take much for the simmering tensions to flare up in violence. Benjamin experienced this at close quarters within months of his arrival, with schoolmaster Ludwig Jansen and his young wife, on the farm of Peet Bonthuys near the mouth of the Bushman's River in the very heart of the Zuurveld. They'd lived there very peacefully: Jansen tried his best to teach the four Bonthuys children and a handful of others from neighbouring farms; his wife Liesbet devoted all her time to her new-born son; Benjamin gave Jansen a hand with the younger children under the great wild-fig tree at the front door, while his mother worked in the Bonthuys kitchen. But one morning there was a sudden commotion. A handful of Xhosa warriors arrived at the house and demanded to see Peet Bonthuys. He came out with his gun. There was an altercation. A shot rang out. When they left, Peet Bonthuys lay on the kitchen floor with seven or eight assegais in his chest and stomach; Jansen, reverting to the soldier he'd once been, ran to his wagon to fetch his own gun, shouting to Benjamin to come to his help. Fortunately for them, Jansen was restrained by his hysterical wife, while Toas came running to stop Benjamin. Together with the womenfolk and the screaming children they watched the group of Xhosas opening the kraals and driving off all the cattle and sheep. Among them Mrs Bonthuys had recognised two men, Xaba and usi, who'd worked on the farm for the past year.

That held the key to the whole shocking episode. After their ar's work, when the two men had approached Bonthuys for ir wages (two sheep and an ox each, as well as some beads trinkets, a few bags of flour and a roll of tobacco), the farmer bluntly refused: they hadn't worked properly, he'd said, and eover, they'd borrowed food in the course of the year which had accompanied as labourers, whether free or indentured. Many of the Xhosa welcomed their new white neighbours as potential powerful allies against some of their personal enemies across the border; from the farmers it was possible to obtain not only the copper and beads but some of the guns and ammunition previously supplied only sporadically, and at great cost, by *tochtgangers* or travelling merchants, as well as the seeds of mealies, pumpkins, sorghum, beans and other vegetables they'd begun to grow among their pastures; young men in need of cattle to pay their *lobola* for a bride could hire their labour to white farmers and earn solid, regular wages. So there was much to gain from a close and friendly association. In return, the farmers were only too happy with their new access to a constant supply of cattle and ivory (even though the government in the Cape had officially prohibited all such transactions), and with what they regarded as a more dependable and robust labour force than that supplied previously by the Khoin with their frail physique, 'mischievous' habits and wandering nature. The proximity of whites offered the Xhosa a new kind of security, and access to new kinds of luxury; the Xhosa, in turn, made it easier for whites to survive: from them they learned how to read the skies and the wind of the region; they learned to burn the veld in winter to ensure better grazing on th hills in the summer months. Each improved the other's chances prosperity.

But in the very heart of the potential for friendly relations lay the seeds of strife. Both groups needed grazing for huge he both felt a fierce attachment to the soil. (Only the nature of attachment differed: the trekboers were greedy to obtain as of it as possible – even if they never thought twice about aband it once it had been trampled and grazed into an eroded was the Xhosa believed the earth was inalienable, provided by all to use, for no one to possess.) Neither could turn ba where they'd come: from across the Great Fish River the Xhosa nation continued to push westward to escape pres the expanding amaZulu; while the trekboers discovered had appeared to be 'empty' land behind them had slow as newcomers had begun to stake out their farms in the of land among those occupied earlier. It was impossib course, as the farmers in the northernmost Sneeuberg r into more solid resistance from the San than ever befor else. All of a sudden the vast land, which for over

708

had to be offset against their wages; but if they worked for another year, and borrowed less, perhaps there would be something for them then. This had been a widespread practice between farmers and their Khoin servants in the past, resulting invariably in a kind of forced labour. But with the Xhosa it didn't work. The two men had absconded to report the matter to their chief, whose people were settled not far away beside the Kowie River; and this was the result.

Nor was it the end of the unhappy matter. Within days, as soon as the news had spread through the neighbourhood, a commando of farmers was assembled and – although such action was expressly forbidden by the Cape government – they led an attack on the kraal Xaba and Vusi had come from. The place was destroyed and the huts burnt down, a great number of cattle was taken in retribution and driven back to the Bushman's River, and ten or twenty small children were taken prisoner to be indentured with the members of the commando.

The refugees from the Kowie River crossed the Great Fish River to lay their case before one of the more important chiefs, and a substantial force of warriors was sent back into the colony to recover the lost children and cattle, burning several farmhouses on their way. And then the white farmers rode to Graaff-Reinet to demand that an even bigger commando be called up to avenge the depredations they had suffered. And then the Xhosa chiefs in their turn –

Ludwig Jansen moved on to other farms. Eva remained with him, mainly because Liesbet, changed from a carefree young town girl into a nervous, whining, fretting wife and mother, could not cope without her; but Benjamin joined a team of woodcutters hacking yellowwood and stinkwood from one of the great virgin forests in the region, which they hauled to Graaff-Reinet and sometimes even as far as Swellendam, where good timber was in great demand for all the new buildings going up. Their profits were small, but it was a start, a first step towards realising the secret dream he'd been cherishing in his heart: one day to own a place of his own and be as free and proud as his father.

However, it soon became obvious to him – especially when he discovered that the foremen of the team had been cheating them out of most of their earnings – that woodcutting was a dead-end. He returned to the farm where the Jansens and his mother were living at the time. Then Eva died. I have never been able to establish, beyond all doubt, the reason for this sudden death; but there are indications that it was the result of a thrashing from the farmer, who'd suspected her of selling some of his cattle off to the Xhosa. Certainly, there was a fight between Benjamin and the farmer immediately after her death; and then he moved on to a farm further inland where he became a foreman, or *bywoner*. This entitled him to a few sheep and cattle every year, and half of the income from whatever cereals and vegetables he produced.

He changed employers a few more times, usually because some of his wages had been withheld for abstruse reasons or because he'd been suspected, rightly or wrongly, for common cause with Xhosas or for inciting Khoin labourers or slaves in the employ of his baas to abscond. It is known that an increasing number of such fugitives had begun to settle among the Xhosa; in many cases they'd run away with some of their employers' guns and ammunition. Every day the situation was becoming more explosive. It also became more complicated, in that relations among the different groups were no longer unambiguous: not all whites were ipso facto masters, and those not white were not all servants.

1787, known among the farmers as the *stormjaar*, the 'storm year', was one of almost continuous upheaval – worse even than the period immediately before Benjamin had arrived in the Zuurveld, when the boer commandant Adriaan van Jaarsveld had given a decisive turn to relations with the Xhosa through an act of treachery the black people of the region recall with anger to this day: having summoned a number of Xhosa leaders allegedly to negotiate peace, van Jaarsveld suddenly instructed his companions to scatter an amount of carved tobacco on the ground. While the black negotiators scrambled about in undignified eagerness to pick up the tobacco, van Jaarsveld and his men opened fire, killing most of the 'enemy' and winning for themselves, among the white population, a long-lasting fame as heroes of the people. But 1787 was worse, following a devastating year of drought which exacerbated, for both boers and blacks, the need for grazing. At the same time a new wave of Xhosas moved into the Zuurveld, following the death of the paramount chief Rharhabe and a fierce succession struggle beyond the Great Fish River.

In these circumstances work as a *bywoner* became too insecure. The turning-point came when the handful of cattle and sheep Benjamin had accumulated were lost in a Xhosa raid on the farm where he was working at the time; as this seemed a direct consequence of a raid the farmer and some of his neighbours had conducted on a

Xhosa settlement a month or two earlier (allegedly to punish them for having incited their few remaining Khoin labourers to abscond: unfortunately, however, the boers had attacked the wrong kraal), Benjamin asked his employer for compensation. The farmer, an irascible old man called Lemmer, who had lost both his sons in the war of 1779, refused outright. Why should Benjamin be compensated if everybody else had suffered the same loss? Because, reasoned Benjamin, he'd had nothing to do with it: the quarrel had been between Lemmer and his friends on the one hand and the Xhosa on the other. In fact, if anyone was at fault, it was old man Lemmer himself for having attacked the wrong people, which had been, practically, an open invitation to retaliate. (At the time of the incident Benjamin had been in the newly established village of Graaff-Reinet to buy ammunition for his boss.) What the hell, exclaimed the old man. You think I care a damn about a *bywoner*'s few scabby sheep and cattle? But I worked hard for them, Oom, he pleaded. And how d'you think I got mine? retorted old Lemmer: it's blood and sweat and shit they cost me, I've already paid with the lives of my two sons to be on this farm, so don't come to me with this kind of talk. Benjamin was beginning to lose his temper too. When I came to work here, he said, you offered me protection, among other things. And it's through your rashness that I lost my herd. Lemmer: I won't let a *baster* insult me to my face, you hear? He raised his stick to attack Benjamin, who wrenched it from the furious old man's hands and hurled it away. He loaded his meagre possessions on the small wagon he'd bought the previous year – how many times had he gone through that performance already; how many more times would it still have to be repeated? – inspanned a few of Lemmer's remaining oxen and drove off.

And so he trekked to the village of Graaff-Reinet.

The Graaff-Reinet Nina and I visited on our way to New Bethesda was a placid little town, with white Cape-Dutch gables flashing through green foliage, and verandahs covering the shady stoeps; an old-world peace had settled, heavy as dust, on the residential streets surrounding the few main thoroughfares around the hub of the solid Dutch Reformed church. But at the time Benjamin had arrived there, even 'village' would have been too proud a word for the small rectangle of streets, each wide enough for a full team of oxen to turn in it; the sprinkling of clay houses perched in spacious gardens; the modest little church; the barracks housing a mere handful of militiamen. But it *was* the seat of a *landdrost* – the well-meaning but ineffectual alcoholic Mijnheer Woeke – and it did represent, with whatever ludicrous ineffectiveness, the once remote and almost mythical power of the Cape.

I remember how Nina and I drove along the winding dirt road into the mountains behind the town, where we left the motorbike to follow the footpath to the edge of the precipice: the sudden breathtaking view of the Valley of Desolation below, its outlines blurred in early morning mist. 'Listen!' Nina exclaimed, catching her breath. Through jagged cliffs came echoing the organ-tones of winds and nesting pigeons, a continuous, deep, mournful sound as if the landscape itself was lamenting the burden of its history. Any wagon trekking along the vast *vlakte* of the Camdebo below our feet would be minimised by space; whole families, whole tribes might disappear down there without leaving a trace. Millions of years ago that had been a vast inland sea: the hills still bore its prehistoric water marks; incrusted in the layers of rock were the fossils of long-extinct sea creatures – fishes, snails, the ancestors of crayfish. And then God said, Let the waters under the heaven be gathered together unto one place, and let dry land appear: and it was so. And God called the dry land Earth: and God saw that it was good. And the earth brought forth grass, the herb yielding seed, and the fruit tree yielding fruit after its kind. And the prairies were covered with scrub. And the Khoisan came, hunters and gatherers and later shepherds and cattleherds, and for thousands of years they roamed the great plains. Then came the members of my tribe: this was the region where they spent their hundred years of solitude, their seeming endless aimless wandering through a wilderness more ancient than the bible.

And to this small town far below our vantage point – its rectilinear streets and minuscule white buildings superimposed so bravely, so ineffectually, on the contours of that ancient landscape – came my ancestor Benjamin in search of God knows what. Admittedly, his years as a handyman in a variety of trades in Cape Town and on the border stood him in good stead, as he soon found work with a builder whom he'd met a few years earlier when he'd delivered timber to the man. He lived in his own wagon, pulled under a tree in his employer's ample backyard; and he was allowed to graze his oxen on the village common. Still, he was really only marking time; and the excursions he continued to undertake into the frontier region – north to the Sneeuberge, east to the Great Fish River – seem to indicate that he had not yet come to rest.

But at least he found a wife in Graaff-Reinet. She was called Leah; and she was the daughter of a Jewish *smous*, or itinerant trader, who for several years past had been making the long trip from Cape Town to the outlying districts of the colony at least once every four or five months, peddling his wares which ranged from dress materials and needles and safety-pins to sugar and coffee and tea and gunpowder and lead for bullets. Benjamin first met Yitshak Kirschbaum when, on his way back from a trip to the Zuurveld, he came across the trader's heavy wagon stuck in a treacherous river-crossing. Leah as well as two young brothers and an older sister were with Kirschbaum (since his wife's death a couple of years earlier he'd always taken his children with him), and it did not take long for Benjamin to fall in love with the dark-eyed girl.

Initially there was some resistance from the father who, although he'd never been an overly religious man himself, was reluctant to see his daughter marry a goy. But the affinity between them was greater than whatever scruples Kirschbaum might have felt; and Benjamin's name undoubtedly counted very much in his favour. As did his history. Yitshak Kirschbaum could empathise with anyone who'd ever been rejected, insulted, or persecuted because of his race, and many were the nights the old man spent – right through until daybreak – regaling Benjamin with stories of the accumulated sufferings of his tribe through the centuries, starting in Egypt and Babylon and imperial Rome, through medieval Italy, Germany, France and Spain, to the most recent history of countries the young man didn't even know existed. His eagerness to learn new things was amply and fantastically rewarded by Yitshak Kirschbaum (who'd drifted down to the Cape from the Baltic, via Germany and the Low Countries): what the old man didn't know he invented, and the more outrageous his inventions, the more vehemently he defended them. He had personally visited the Kublai Khan in Mongolia, where he'd been shown the broken Tables of the Law Moses had brought down from Mount Sinai; he'd been entertained by the Emperor of China, who had subsequently thrown him into prison because he'd refused to renounce his faith – but he'd managed to escape in a small rowing boat to America where he'd joined the war of the thirteen colonies against the Eskimos; he had founded a synagogue among the Red Indians, wondrous men who sprouted feathers instead of hair, and he would have married the princess Scheherazade of Baghdad, had she not refused at the last moment to be converted to the true faith; he had fought against the Saracens on the highland of Golan where the great skull of Goliath could still be seen, petrified, like a big black boulder; and he'd ridden on the back of a unicorn through the frozen steppes of Russia to convert the tsar to Judaism (in which he had succeeded, only the tsar was then murdered by the Philistines).

If it seems I dwell on this too much (but there is so much more I could tell!), it is because from Yitshak Kirschbaum my tribe must have inherited a love of stories and of telling them (the Talmud, he explained, averred that God had created men and women so that they might tell Him stories), and through him and Leah a certain melancholy strain was reinforced in us: the assurance of being the elected race of the Almighty, yet at the same time inviting persecution from all mankind. If we are misunderstood, praise God, it is a sure sign of having right on our side. If we are vilified, hosannah, it vindicates the justice of our cause.

They all travelled to Cape Town for the wedding, because Leah first had to be catechised and christened in the Dutch Reformed Church – which nearly broke old Yitshak's heart and inspired him to many nights of stories about the persecution of the faithful and the vanity of the world; and then they all went back again, and Yitshak engaged Benjamin's employer to build a house at Graaff-Reinet, and the whole family moved into it to live happily ever after.

Far away, in the Zuurveld, the situation was growing worse every day, and by 1793 most of the inhabitants, black and white, lived in fear of one another; appeals from the farmers to the government, via the *landdrost* of Graaff-Reinet, elicited the regular response that the Xhosa should be appeased, not provoked – until a sizeable band of farmers, led by one Barend Lindeque, decided to take the law in their own hands. Knowing that paramount chief Ndlambe, who lived beyond the Great Fish River, was eager to impose his rule on the tribes inside the Zuurveld, they mounted a joint force with Ndlambe and launched an attack on the Xhosa settlements inside the Colony, capturing some two thousand head of cattle. But then something went wrong, Ndlambe withdrew from the alliance in anger, and the Zuurveld Xhosa turned on the white farmers. Almost none of the hundred and fifty or so boer families in the region remained on their farms. Now it was open war, and the *landdrosts* of Graaff-Reinet and Swellendam led a considerable burgher force into battle, rounding up eight thousand cattle and driving most of the Zuurveld blacks across the Great Fish River, into Ndlambe's hands. However, instead of pursuing the war, which was what the boers wanted, the recently appointed *landdrost* of Graaff-Reinet, Honoratus Christiaan David Maynier, a man imbued with Rousseau's philosophies, insisted on restricting violence to a minimum and proceeded to negotiate a peace settlement with the Xhosa. This earned him the vicious resentment of practically all the farmers in his vast district, and of most of their descendants.

The Kirschbaum-Landman family in Graaff-Reinet experienced little of all this. In fact, the most notable event in the relatively even tenor of their lives in those days was the birth of a son, David Gideon, in 1791; though in retrospect there was considerable significance in two trading trips Benjamin and his father-in-law made to the frontier in 1792 and 1794, when they met a group of young Germans who had settled there a year or two earlier, all of them tremendously knowledgeable and excited about recent events in France. I have no doubt that their tales of the Revolution, and their ebullient espousal of the cause of liberty, equality and fraternity found fallow ground in Benjamin. (His next two sons, twins born in 1794, were actually christened Maximilien and Danton; and I suspect that, had not the rest of his children been girls, all the luminaries of the Revolution would have been represented in our family tree.) But outwardly those were tranquil years for my ancestor.

Until 1795, that is, when one morning in early February a group of self-styled armed 'Patriots' rode into the peaceful little village, led by the popular commander Adriaan van Jaarsveld – a young John Wayne, I like to imagine him – and some others (including the hot-headed Prinsloos from Agter-Bruintjieshoogte), and sent Landdrost Maynier packing. His officers, who had helped enforce his policy of peaceful negotiations with the Xhosa, were summarily deposed. This was the beginning of high drama, at times interspersed with low comedy. The Cape government sent a commission of enquiry, which was promptly expelled by a large group of armed rebels; during the following months all the simmering resentment of so many years came to the boil as a spirit of rebellion swept through the whole district. Staunch burghers and their ample wives strode through the dusty streets of the now bustling little village, addressing each other as *citoyen* and *citoyenne*, attending boisterous meetings to celebrate the *volkstem* or 'voice of the people', waving the French tricolour, and refusing to acknowledge any longer the authority of the rulers at the Cape.

The mouse that roared. Still, it was just possible that the Dutch East India Company might have lost – or even relinquished – control of the defiant little 'republic' (which soon found an ally in a similar 'republic' of Swellendam). But unfortunately it happened at a most inopportune moment. In September of that year, Britain provisionally took control of the Cape to counter the recent French invasion of the Netherlands; and even though the occupation was temporary and the British had no wish to alienate the population, they were certainly not going to tolerate any resistance from a bunch of unruly frontiersmen.

They confirmed the ammunition boycott the Company had already placed on the frontier districts, dispatched a new *landdrost* to Graaff-Reinet and demanded that all inhabitants take an oath of loyalty to the King. A boisterous crowd, many of them sporting tricolour cockades and shouting, 'Down with the aristocrats!', awaited the emissary, although it is to be doubted that they really understood what the banners and slogans were all about: they simply saw a good opportunity of ridding themselves of the nuisance of a more and more restrictive government, and the French example seemed as useful as any. Led by one of the wild Prinsloos, Marthinus, who'd styled himself 'Protector of the Volkstem', they presented the terrified man with a petition and drove him back to Cape Town. Benjamin Landman, my father was always proud to point out, was among them – but so of course was practically everybody except the crippled, the senile or the insane. Still, I like to believe that there was a touch of pure revolutionary fervour in my ancestor. He'd had, perhaps, more exposure to those French ideas than many of the others: what concerned him was not just the heavy hand of a distant and uncaring Company, but the notion of unreasonable power as such, and the experience of rejection, denial, suppression. One can imagine Yitshak Kirschbaum haranguing his son-in-law for nights on end on the long history of the Just and the need for never-ending resistance.

Whatever the real motives of the uprising, many of the rebels, faced by increasing pressure from the Xhosa in the Zuurveld and San in the Sneeuberge and finding their ammunition still cut off (even a counter-embargo on meat for Cape Town had had no effect),

716

began to waver. Benjamin Landman was among a group of young men commandeered by the Prinsloos and van Jaarsveld to ride from farm to farm and encourage the boers to stand firm. It was the most hectic time of his life. Leaving Rachel behind with her father to look after his first-born David Gideon and the now two-year-old twins Maximilien and Danton, Benjamin rode his horse like a madman. It was as if his personal honour was at stake, and the urgency of his mission unleashed in him an eloquence he himself had never suspected. Now was the time to stand together and throw off the yoke of oppression. All men are born free, yet here we are in chains. I know we're suffering, exposed, without the means to defend ourselves, to all our enemies. But there's one thing no one can take from us and that is our patriotic sense of honour. Et cetera. If he had a copy of the Declaration of the Rights of Man and of the Citizen in his possession, and I love to think he had, he would have read aloud to his bemused audiences those resounding articles, all the more impressive since none of his listeners could understand the language:

'The aim of society is the happiness of all. The government is instituted in order to guarantee man the enjoyment of his natural and imprescriptible rights.

'These rights are equality, liberty, security and property.

'All men are equal by nature and before the law.

'The law is the free and solemn expression of the general will —'

Ending with this, the grandest of all:

'When the government violates the rights of the people, insurrection is for the people, and for each part of the people, the most sacred of rights and the most indispensable of duties.'

Oh yes, I'm sure Benjamin had a copy, and used it, until the paper became crumpled and sweaty from those long frantic dashes from Graaff-Reinet to Bruintjieshoogte, to the Baviaans River, to the Sneeuberg range, the thickets and billowing hills of the Zuurveld, galloping, galloping, his heart burning in his chest with a joy he could hardly contain. Something was at hand, something immense was about to happen, he was ready to break into history.

The culmination of his activities during those mad, exhilarating months was a ride into the territory beyond the Great Fish River, one of a group of impetuous young men who saw in their plan a solution to all the turmoil in their region. It was a rash venture by anyone's calculations, hatched late one night in Yitshak Kirschbaum's house,

when they were bold and lucid from a new consignment of brandy;
afraid of being put down, and eager to get involved in a bold,
spectacular initiative of their own, they kept the whole idea secret
from the leaders of the revolt. In the dark of the night they rode
out from the little sleeping village, continuing for several days and
nights almost without unsaddling, until they reached the place of
the paramount chief Ndlambe. They were kept waiting for two
days before the chief granted them audience, and by then they
were so nervous that all were speaking at the same time. Let us
all act together in this thing, they said. Help us to drive that evil
foreign government out of this land forever: then we can settle the
differences between us, and equitably divide the land between us,
and be done with strife and violence for all time. Unfortunately
the petition was in vain – either because Ndlambe had his hands
full with some of his own unruly subjects, or, more likely, because
he couldn't trust the negotiators or take them seriously. He was
gentle enough with them, not giving them a straight no at first but
intimating that he would reflect on the matter and contact them in
due course.

'But there isn't time to wait!' protested Benjamin. 'We need an
answer *now*.'

Then Ndlambe said, 'Look. Suppose some of my young men came
to your leaders with a proposal like this. How would they react?
Would they not say: What proof have we that your chiefs are with
you in this matter? Do you understand? And if I discovered that my
young men had done such a thing without consulting with me first,
what would I do? Would I not give them a proper thrashing and tell
them to keep out of the business of war and peace in which many
people may get killed?'

It was a dejected group that rode back all that weary way to
Graaff-Reinet. But as they approached the little settlement of mud
houses in the great semicircle of mountains, their enthusiasm
returned: they were young. True, their impulsive mission had
failed. But the revolution was going on. Great things were still
waiting to burst upon them.

The rest is indeed history.

Great numbers of Xhosa still came pouring into the Zuurveld,
in spite of which the new British government at the Cape ordered
all the boers who'd fled from their farms to return immediately,
otherwise their property would be confiscated. The rebels decided
to mount a new assault. When van Jaarsveld was arrested in January

718

1799 on what his friends interpreted as a trumped-up charge of fraud, a band of rebels, headed by Marthinus Prinsloo, and once again counting Benjamin Landman in their midst, galloped after the small detachment of soldiers who were taking the accused man to Cape Town for trial, surprised them, and freed their companion.

Both sides were now preparing for the final clash. But when three months later a sizeable military force arrived from Cape Town, the end of the rebellion was a mere formality. Several of the ringleaders were imprisoned; van Jaarsveld and Prinsloo received death sentences, which were later commuted. Van Jaarsveld died in prison, but when the Cape was restored to Dutch rule in 1803 Prinsloo and the others were given a general amnesty.

By that time Benjamin had disappeared from the scene of visible activity. We know that he'd been a member of the rebel group that freed van Jaarsveld from his captors in January 1799: and he was among the hundred and fifty rebels who prepared to face the British troops that April. Yet before the confrontation materialised he'd disappeared from their ranks. Both Oupa and my father have puzzled for a long time to find a reasonable explanation. Fear? Benjamin had been too committed, for too long, to drop out when everything he'd been expecting so eagerly was on the point of happening. Despondency? Surely he wouldn't have waited for the last moment. Pragmatism? He was not the type of person to forsake his ideals at the first real opportunity of testing them. Et cetera.

I, too, have pondered the question for a long time. And perhaps the answer is not all that difficult after all. We know, from a reference in his sister Rachel's notebook, that her father had seen his son on only one occasion since the day he'd sent Benjamin and Toas off into the wilderness, and that was many years later. She did not elaborate, apart from mentioning that this had happened on commando, 'during the uprising'. So this is the scenario as I imagine it: in that final mustering of rebel troops to confront the British in the mountains of Bruintjieshoogte, Benjamin recognises his father. Jan-Jonas, white as death, stares at his long-lost son, then makes a move in his direction. The son looks at him, pale through the olive complexion of his skin, and turns away, and leaves the revolution. Not just because he cannot, will not, face the man he's loved and hated all his life; but because suddenly everything that has been so clear has turned into confusion. His rebellion against a government he's never even seen has been, all along, the expression of his rebellion against his father. Now, unexpectedly, he finds his father a member of that same revolt, fighting on the same side; yet they are adversaries. How can anyone expect him to handle this?

He settled, later, in the Zuurveld. That was after old Yitshak Kirschbaum had died, carried away by a violent bout of coughing, one winter's evening, in the middle of a story about the French Revolution being in fact a mistake of history, as Louis XVI had never really been beheaded, only circumcised.

Benjamin's own death, praised by my family as martyrdom, may have been something of a mistake. His neighbour had severely flogged a young Khoin who upon the completion of his period of indenture had left his master's service against the farmer's wishes, and then had come back to claim the few head of cattle he'd earned. After the beating he returned to the Xhosa settlement where he'd left his black wife, and when the people heard his tale and saw his wounds they sent a raiding party to the farm. The farmer managed to escape on horseback (leaving his wife and two small children behind) and called on Benjamin for help. The latter was in no mood for another punitive expedition, but offered to try and intercede with the Xhosa who'd driven off every hoof of cattle on the neighbour's farm.

At the Xhosa 'kraal' there was an angry shouting match to start with – possibly some of the men had mistaken Benjamin for the culprit farmer – but then the visitor was invited to sit down with them and smoke a pipe of peace. While they were puffing away in silence the men suddenly rushed at Benjamin and stabbed him to death with their assegais. Perhaps some among them had remembered the way Adriaan van Jaarsveld had scattered tobacco on the ground, many years ago, to betray and kill the men who'd come to discuss a peaceful settlement.

David Gideon Landman

(1791–1835)

I remember a discussion I had with Mum about this chronicle one summer vacation at home in the furnace of the Little Karoo: it was, in fact, the last long holiday I spent there, that disastrous Christmas when Frans and I had the stand-up fight. Most of the time, to avoid the quarrels that always broke out when he and I were together, and to escape from the festive spirit and the horde of children (Frans's, Maria's), I was holed up in Dad's study on the back stoep working on the notes which have now, after so many years, debouched in this writing (done as much for the sake of therapy as for the record).

Mum came into the room while I was sorting through the bits and pieces of paper on which I'd accumulated my notes. Asked me what I was doing. I told her. 'But Dad's already put everything together he could find,' she said, more disapprovingly than I would have expected. 'It's all done and finished. Don't you think you're just wasting your time?'

'It's a wonderful way of concentrating the mind,' I said.

'I can think of more useful things to do.'

'One keeps on making new discoveries. Dad had his point of view, I have mine, everything depends on the angle.'

'You mean you just look at it the way it suits you?'

'Not quite as simple as that,' I protested. 'It's a matter of interpretation.'

She persisted. 'But then it isn't history any more, is it?'

'I think that's what *makes* it history.'

She glanced at the page I'd just started on; if I remember correctly, it was the very section I am working on now. 'David Gideon Landman,' she read, then sniggered. 'All those Landman men again.'

'But it's the family tree, Mum.'

'It must be because men are closer to baboons that they're the only ones who get put into family trees.'

'I mention all the wives.'

'I should hope so. But what do you end up with? Thirteen generations, including yourself. Thirteen men with thirteen little pricks.' (She wasn't always so outspoken.) 'Adam begat Seth and Seth begat So-and-so and So-and-so begat Whatchemecallit and all the rest. I can tell you stories about some of the women among my ancestors who probably did a lot more about turning you out the way you are than most of those men.'

I smiled indulgently. But after she'd gone out again – leaving a glass of cold ginger beer at my elbow – I began to do some basic arithmetic of the kind organisers of tennis tournaments get involved in. To produce me (the champ!) two parents were required. They were the offspring of four other progenitors. Then eight, then sixteen. Thirteen generations ago, I discovered, four thousand and ninety-six people must have had intercourse to result, just over three hundred years later, in me, Thomas Landman. A whole subcontinent and much of Europe was involved in the making of me. And then I have the temerity to single out twelve individuals and say, Look, that's the line that ends in me, lucky Number Thirteen.

Even if I had not remembered that conversation with Mum I would have been tempted to start this section on David Gideon with the story of his wife. Not that he was unremarkable in his own right, but because the woman Tommie was such an extraordinary person. From what history prompts me to conjure up of her I find it easy to understand why the youngster became infatuated with her; I believe I am a bit in love with her myself. She has certainly helped me to understand more deeply and more disturbingly my love for Lisa. Her very name haunts me. She was actually christened *Thomas*. Not Thomasina or any other feminine derivation of the name, but Thomas: just like that. Her father, a hard angry man, had expected a son – it had never even occurred to him that he might spawn females – so when she was born he simply gave her the name he'd already chosen. It had been his father's, it was his own.

(After that first disappointment, his wife did give birth to a son, who was duly christened Thomas too; but he died before he was a year old, so the next son was again called Thomas; unbelievable as it may sound, this Thomas also died young, and after that the father gave up, convinced that there must be a curse on the name. The next eleven children were all given other names, and all survived; then, with the last son, a *laatlammetjie*, the father thought the curse had been lifted and reverted to the family name. Within three months this baby, too, was buried.)

It happened in David Gideon's nineteenth year, one day when he was working in a clearing in the forest among the hills near his father's Zuurveld farm. He'd come out on foot early that morning with the twins, Max and Danie, and three or four Xhosa labourers to fell some trees for a new kraal: a lion had recently made its appearance in the neighbourhood and the sheep and cattle needed more sturdy protection. It was September, and there was quite a number of calves and lambs on the farm. David had soon selected the blackwood tree he wanted to cut down just inside the fringe of the forest, but the others insisted on going further. And so he was alone (that is how I have always imagined it, from the hints Oupa gave when he first told the story) when he heard the wildly galloping hoofs approach – but it stopped abruptly just before the horse could come in sight, beyond a thicket of *fynbos*. David Gideon sat up, listening. Nothing. Only the sounds of birds among the trees. Surely it couldn't have been his imagination? Perhaps the rider, whoever it was, had stopped for a drink of water. There was a spring of fresh water there, David knew, welling up through reeds and coarse ferns and spilling musically into a pool so deep it was almost black, set among dark green boulders, and fringed with prehistoric cycads; at its far end it broke into a stream down the easy green slope of the hill, finally to run into the Kasouga.

As he came round the outcrop of boulders he saw the horse, foaming at the mouth, its flanks white with saltpetre. But there was no sign of a rider, and the horse bore no saddle either. David Gideon was mystified. He began to advance very cautiously, feeling himself on the brink of a mystery. The horse, still breathing heavily, looked up at him and snorted through wide nostrils.

David Gideon made soothing sounds to calm the animal down.

He crept closer. And then he saw the naked girl.

In the fairytale Oupa turned it into, the girl was a fey creature with long green hair and violet eyes; it became a story of magic and miraculous metamorphoses. But what haunted me, above all else, was that first meeting, the immemorial male fantasy scene. And from here I deviated from Oupa's version. Long after I had discarded the more fantastic bits, the image of the girl, of that primal encounter, continued to obsess my adolescence. Like David Gideon, I'd never seen a naked girl. Not in the flesh: my sole experience of the kind was that disturbing day when Dad and I were caught in the flood and forced to spend the night in the house with the dying old woman; the stolen lurid girlie magazine burning my guilty skin under my drenched clothes. So this girl – who had actually been christened with my own name, Thomas – was drawn into all the fantasies, and most of the wet dreams, of my youth. I spent afternoons, long evenings, writing out the story, dwelling in the rage of my awakening masculinity on every anatomical detail – her arms ('supple'), her hair ('streaming'), her legs ('lithe'), her buttocks ('round and hard'), her breasts ('firm'), her nipples ('taut'). But it was more than libido. Even in writing my poor purple phrases I knew I was really straining after something else I could not define, let alone find. It left an image deposited on my mind like silver nitrate on bromide paper. When I became articulate in photography, that was the first image I tried to recapture. ('Sylph-like' girlfriends posing 'long-limbed' among 'verdant' trees in Jonkershoek –)

Over and over I invented the scene, my urgent sexuality a stepping-stone to bridge the gap between Oupa's fairytale and 'real history': the boy crouching among the ferns, the girl diving into the pool and swimming towards him ('her hair streaking after her like a green stain on the green water': later changed, for the sake of greater credibility, to 'black on black', and her eyes turned blue; but her nipples remained as taut as before to feed my incipient sexism), emerging a few yards from him, stepping out, shaking the water from her, swooping her hair back from her face with her hands, suddenly looking at him through her fingers.

('I have never seen a girl's breasts,' he thinks. 'There can't be anything in the world more beautiful than this.')

She came past him, moving so lightly it seemed she didn't touch the ground, 'a smooth flowing motion like water or the wind'.

'Who are you?' he croaked.

Looking back from her tall black horse, she made a movement with her head which might signify anything.

'What are you doing here? Where do you come from? Where are you going?'

'Does it matter?'

'Please,' he said urgently. 'Just tell me –'

'I've got to go.'

'Where?' he insisted.

She shrugged, looked around vaguely, made a tentative sweeping gesture with her right arm. 'The Lourens farm,' she said. (This was my way of writing her back into history.)

'There's no Lourenses around here that I know of.' He looked hard at her.

She jumped back on the horse, kicked her heels into the horse's flanks, and rode off, still naked. (Only much later did it occur to me how uncomfortable, how damn painful, that must be.)

When the others returned, he was still in a *dwaal*. He hadn't touched his blackwood tree again. They seemed incredulous when he told them about his encounter. 'I know what happened,' said Max knowingly. 'You fell asleep and had a dream. One of *those* dreams. Now you're trying to find excuses for not doing your work.'

That was the way his parents reacted too. (If only his grandfather Yitshak Kirschbaum had been alive, he thought. *He* would have believed every word of it. And more.) No one had ever heard of a Lourens family in the neighbourhood, and his father knew the region like the palm of his hand. David Gideon became sloppy in his work. He'd always been the most solid and dependable of Benjamin's sons, but now he seemed to wander about in a perpetual daze. Whenever he could – and even sometimes when there was urgent work to do – he saddled his horse and rode off ('in ever widening circles') in search of that mysterious girl. But no one had ever heard of such a one in the Zuurveld. Some of the neighbours began to suggest quite openly to Benjamin that his son must be suffering from some kind of sickness. Sunstroke, perhaps. Or worse. People began to watch him warily for signs of a more dangerous disturbance. After a full year had passed David Gideon himself must have started wondering whether it hadn't just been a dream: incredibly vivid, but still a dream.

For the purposes of writing history I must regretfully discard most of this. (For once, Pa would approve.) The naked girl in the wood is not entirely impossible, of course. But it is more likely that David Gideon just found her sitting there, perhaps even dressed in men's clothes – a faded, once dark red shirt, sheepskin trousers too big for her? – so that he first mistook her for a boy. But then he would have noticed the hair. The full mouth. (And, of course, the breasts.) The rest might have happened in much the same way.

*

It is not – merely – from fondness that I dwelt on the episode, but to illustrate the kind of problem I have in trying to reconstruct my chronicle. So much of what I know about the girl Tommie has been passed on orally from generation to generation; and from the word that emerges at my end of the line I can but guess what was said to begin with.

She had been – again according to the stereotypes favoured by our patriarchy – a wild thing since her birth. The old Malay slave woman who had accompanied the Lourens family from Cape Town to the Long Kloof years before, when Tommie's father Thomas had still been a child, had warned them from the moment she removed the caul with which the girl had been born that they should take special care with her: she was a demon in human shape, said the wise old woman, and it depended entirely on them whether she would use her supernatural powers in a good way or a bad. Thwart her or cross her, and she would become a witch; treat her with respect and she would bring them happiness and prosperity. Thomas Lourens forbade the woman even to talk about such heathen things again, but his wife remembered and was always wary of the fey creature.

The first sign Tommie gave of being 'different' was her propensity for wandering off into the veld on her own. She was only four or five when it happened for the first time. 'Don't go after her,' warned the old Malay woman. 'Creatures such as her must go back to the spirit world from time to time. She'll come back.' It was indeed enough to make one feel eerie: no matter how and where they looked – Lourens would not be put off by the old slave's nonsense – she was nowhere to be found; and although it had rained the day before and the ground was soft, she'd left no track. Yet two days later she was back as if nothing had happened; and not even a whipping from her father could draw anything from her.

It happened again after that, many times. Sometimes her father found her, and beat her, and brought her back; on other occasions she simply disappeared, like the first time, without any trace. The most the old slave woman – her only confidante – ever managed to coax from her was a vague smile and the remark: 'I was all right, Aia. I went to see my friends.' Her friends, as far as anyone could make out, were creatures of the veld: meerkats, tortoises, quick little lizards, rock-rabbits, birds. But she also brought back stories of encounters with snakes, jackals, a leopard, hyenas, a lion. 'You'll burn in hell for all your lies!' warned her father. She only shrugged, as if it were too much trouble to explain.

Birds were her favourites. She would sit with knees drawn-up beside the spring to watch them drink and frolic in the water right at her feet; they would perch on her hands for crumbs. And in the corner of her parents' room where she slept, she had a whole collection of tiny bird skulls in a camphorwood chest: with these she would conduct endless conversations as if they were live creatures; and she firmly believed that when she died she would become a bird herself.

Once, when she was eight or nine, her father was a week from home on the annual trek to Cape Town when she suddenly appeared beside the camp-fire one evening, smiling in her secret absent way, staring into the flames. She'd pleaded to accompany him on the trip; he'd refused, it was too exhausting a journey for a little slip of a girl. But here she was. More from a sense of duty than real anger he gave her the beating she deserved; as always, she didn't make a sound or shed a tear. He had to conclude that she must have hidden on the wagon all along. But when they came home again, her mother swore she'd been on the farm for a week after he'd gone.

On another occasion, after a particularly bad beating, she disappeared for several weeks. The mother, confined to bed with another baby, nearly died with despair. Only old Aia was unperturbed: 'I tell you, she'll come back.' And she did. With a group of Xhosa warriors who said they'd found her on the other side of the Great Fish River. She was, of course, unharmed.

Stories, all stories, I know: but this is how our oral tradition has canonised her.

As she grew up she spent more and more of her time on horseback. No one in those parts had ever seen a rider like that. The wildest horse became meek as she approached. And when she got on his back it didn't seem like an animal and a girl: they were one creature, a centaur, sweeping across the veld like fire, like the wind. It was said (once more that improbable vision) that she often rode naked. No one saw her, only old Aia knew about it. But once her father caught a fleeting glimpse of her, as she swept across the landscape in the distance, very far away: but he had the eyes of an eagle, he couldn't miss the hair flying about her bare shoulders, the long straight bare back. He was beside himself. What if the labourers saw her? She was provoking the wrath of God himself. Unspeakable things would happen to her. But nothing did.

In terrifying innocence she continued to go her dangerous ways and always returned unscathed.

'You must get married,' her father said when she was sixteen. 'It's the only way to tame you.'

'I'll never get married,' she said.

'I have a man in mind for you,' he said.

'I tell you I won't marry anyone.'

'You'll do what I tell you.'

'I'll run away. Then you'll never see me again.'

David Gideon Landman had grown up a sensitive child, religiously inclined. This was perhaps inevitable, seeing that before he was one year old – and that was just the beginning – he'd been both baptised and circumcised. (The latter ritual was carried out, unauthorised, by his enterprising grandfather Yitshak Kirschbaum, whose enthusiastic wielding of a pair of shears very nearly maimed the boy for life and put an end to my branch of the family tree.)

When David was about nine, the first missionaries – what a strange bunch they were: the little hunchback van der Lingen; the tall, gaunt van der Kemp, strutting stiff-legged like a secretary-bird, trailing his frayed coat tails; the ruddy-faced Englishman Read – arrived in Graaff-Reinet. By that time almost a thousand Khoin refugees from the recent disturbances in the district had congregated on the outskirts of the village. This had an immediate effect on the Landmans' family life as first David, then the twins, were enrolled in the school run by the eager young Reverend Read. David also became an avid church-goer, enthralled as he was by the unworldly appearance and almost incomprehensible High Dutch spoken by the missionary van der Kemp, with his enormous domed forehead shining like the face of Moses coming down from Mount Sinai.

It was this feature which endeared the missionary to old Yitshak Kirschbaum as well. I'm afraid he must have taken up more of van der Kemp's time than was polite; and when he got home he would regale the family for hours with his impressions of that extraordinary man, medical doctor, philosopher, natural scientist, ex-soldier, fluent in eighteen languages: 'And you know why he gave up all that to come and work among the Gentiles in this remotest corner of the globe? I'll tell you. In his youth this man was a reprobate, a drinker, a fornicator, a trouble-seeker; there was no sin in this world he didn't commit. Then he fell in love with a girl he'd picked up in the street, and he married her, although he

728

already had a daughter with another woman. And then they all went for a boat trip on a river in Rotterdam – I think it was the Volga – and the boat sank and his wife and his daughter got drowned. See how God works in mysterious ways? And so van der Kemp took an oath that he would devote the rest of his life doing penance by serving God. Now the most remarkable part of all this is that I don't think he even really believes in God. Anyway, not the way other people do. I couldn't follow everything he said, the man is too learned for a simple soul like me, I'll ask him again next time, but from what I could make out he isn't even sure there *is* a God. But just on the off-chance he's prepared to sacrifice his whole life to make up for what he'd done wrong when he was young. I can tell you this in confidence: I think he's totally mad. But what a man!'

Especially in those early days van der Kemp often confided in Yitshak Kirschbaum about his difficulties in settling into his work. In the beginning the boers of Graaff-Reinet welcomed him among them and even invited him to become their official minister; but as he'd come out to the Cape to be a missionary he was eager to move on into what was then known as 'Caffreland', beyond the Great Fish River. On the other hand the great concentration of refugee Khoin in the village was a great challenge to him. And this was where the trouble started. The boers were offended when van der Kemp invited his Khoin followers into their church.

Soon the whole district was up in arms. 'You know what's happened now?' Yitshak reported one evening, still out of breath from running all the way from the *landdrost*'s house where he'd heard the news. 'Hundreds of farmers have drawn a laager at Zwagershoek and they're threatening to march on Graaff-Reinet unless van der Kemp is thrown out.' He took his gun from its rack on the wall, spat on the barrel and started polishing it with his shirt-tail. 'This is going to be war. I won't stand for it.'

'Calm down, father,' pleaded Leah. 'How can you get involved in a thing like this?'

'I'm on God's side,' retorted the old man. 'And van der Kemp is my friend. Together we shall conquer. Thou shalt tread upon the lion and adder: the young lion and the dragon shalt thou trample under feet.'

Violence seemed unavoidable. The rebels rode down to Graaff-Reinet where Landdrost Maynier awaited them with all the troops he could muster. At the last moment van der Kemp intervened personally. After talking to Maynier and his officers, he rode out,

729

unarmed, to meet the angry farmers. Offering himself as a hostage, he persuaded them to take part in peaceful discussions first. In the end sense prevailed. But one of the consequences was that the Khoin were expelled from the church. In protest, the Landmans never again set foot in the little white building either, attending instead the special services the missionary offered in his own house, and which were open to all. As a demonstration of his sentiments, and convinced that van der Kemp's word carried a special weight in heaven, Yitshak Kirschbaum asked his friend to baptise his grandson yet again.

Not long after that, the missionary left Graaff-Reinet for the Zwartkops River where he'd been invited by the Khoin chief Klaas Stuurman to come and minister to his people (in itself an amazing occurrence, since Stuurman was known – in van der Kemp's own description – as 'the terror of the country, who has committed, perhaps, more murders than any man upon earth'). His departure left little David Gideon Landman sick with grief – he is on record as affirming, many years later, that 'no matter what anyone says about Johannes Theodorus van der Kemp, and no matter what sins he committed, and no matter even if he himself believed in God or not, I know God will have a special place for him in heaven' – and the only comfort he found when, in 1803 or thereabouts, his father decided to move to the Zuurveld, was that they would find a farm 'close to van der Kemp'.

As it turned out, it was years before he saw the man again. That was after the death of his father. By that time he'd lost his appetite and all his interest in life, and the only consolation in his father's shocking death was that he now felt free to leave the farm and devote the rest of his life to the pursuit of the dream girl he'd met, or imagined he'd met, more than a year before, that miraculous morning in the wood. It says something about the young man that his first destination was the mission at Bethelsdorp, where van der Kemp had established a sanctuary for all the dispossessed Khoin of the Colony.

He must have felt some trepidation, though. There had been so much gossip about the place doing the rounds among the Zuurveld boers for years: the collection of wretched, vermin-infested huts on a waterless plain stripped of trees and vegetation to fulfil the constant need for firewood, the squalor in which the missionaries themselves lived, wallowing in filth like pigs, their flock of vagabonds and vagrants, runaways from the law or from honest work.

The village he found was rather different from the stories he had heard: filthy and overrun by refugees indeed, yet thriving and buoyant in its way. He saw a familar figure approaching from behind the church, and suddenly he felt reassured. The rake-thin body seemed more stooped than he'd remembered – the old man was well into his sixties by now – and much more frail, but he'd lost none of his aloof dignity, and his huge bald head, hatless even in the blistering sun, was as proud as ever. He was dressed in a threadbare black coat, frayed waistcoat, and breeches, without shirt, neckcloth or stockings, his feet in leather sandals like those worn by the Khoin.

The old man stopped and peered at him, a quizzical, almost accusing look in the small eyes below the bushy eyebrows. (It was then that David realised, with a shock, that van der Kemp was going blind.)

'Oom Johannes!' said David. 'Don't you remember me? I used to come to your church in Graaff-Reinet with my grandfather. He was Yitshak Kirschbaum.'

'My God!' exclaimed the old man, as if he was literally calling God to witness. 'David? You were a little boy then. Come in.'

There was a young girl in the dusky *voorhuis* of the missionary's decrepit little house – a slave or servant, David assumed at first, but it was van der Kemp himself who made tea (bush-tea from the mountains) and served both David and the girl. She withdrew with her bowl of tea, and they were left alone. For a while, David sat looking around him in silence, suddenly tongue-tied, as if embarrassed by the meagre furniture: two narrow beds consisting simply of oxhides drawn over a wooden framework; a single rickety table; two benches. That was all.

Did van der Kemp notice, even with those faltering eyes, the furtive glances? 'One doesn't need much,' he said. It didn't sound like an apology, more like absolution. 'What matters is not visible anyway.'

'I envy you,' David blurted out, surprised by the sudden need to confess. 'You seem so – content.'

'Aren't you?'

For the first time in years the young man could pour out everything that had been fermenting inside him: his frustrations, his uncertainty, his urge to do something with his life; above all, that magical meeting with the girl in the wood and the fruitless search he'd been engaged in. 'And now,' he said, 'all I want to do is to get away from the world. I want to join you here. Let me work with you.'

'Religion is not an escape from the world, David,' said the old missionary, the dull light filtering through the reed-mats in front of the windows reflecting from his great bulbous head. 'On the contrary, it means taking up the full burden of the world.' He sighed and fell silent for a moment. 'I'm weary, David,' he suddenly confessed. 'I feel worn out to the bones with struggling and fighting and campaigning for others. But if we – the few of us in this place, a handful of others scattered through this vast land – if we withdraw from the task, what happens then? All these poor people who depend on us. *They* are concerned about their safety, about food, about clothing. What matters to me is the salvation of their souls. But their souls will be lost unless I can protect them against the people who call themselves their masters. And so the struggle must go on.'

'But I would *like* to help you.'

'What about that girl you're pining for? She won't stop burning in your chest.'

'I'll try to forget her.' He avoided van der Kemp's eyes.

'No,' said the old man. 'It doesn't work that way. We cannot deny the flesh. If we try to, we damage the soul as well. I know.' He must have noticed David's questioning gaze. For a moment a rare little smile flickered on his his lips. 'You don't believe me? Yet you met Sara just now, didn't you?'

'Sara? You mean the young girl who – Isn't she a slave?'

'She *was* a slave. I bought her to set her free. It soon became clear that her freedom wouldn't amount to much unless I married her.' (Did something in David's subconscious tribal memory respond – his ancestor, over a century before – or was he too confused?) The old man gave a brief, perhaps embarrassed, cough. 'Also, she made me conscious again of the needs of the flesh which I thought I'd given up so long ago.'

'But what can I *do* then? How will I ever find her?'

'We can start by making enquiries.'

'But I've been riding up and down the Zuurveld for months and months already!'

'She may not be from the Zuurveld. And there are people here at Bethelsdorp from every part of the Colony. I can't promise you anything. But at least we can try. Unless you really think of giving up?'

And that was how, three weeks later, David learned about a family in the Long Kloof, Lourens people, whose daughter was said to be wild and unmanageable, perhaps a witch, an incredible rider who sometimes disappeared for days on end, a girl reputed to be endowed with supernatural powers: she could make herself invisible, she could change her horse into the wind, she could tame a lion by looking him in the eyes.

'So much superstition. You see how much work I still have to do in this place?' the old man asked with an old fire flickering in his fading eyes.

The girl called Tommie was skinning the carcass of a springbok in the backyard when he came riding up to the farm in a side valley of the Long Kloof. The sun was in her eyes when she looked up as his shadow fell on her. But the next moment she recognised him. Her tanned face went pale, or that was how he told it afterwards. She stood up slowly, wiping the bloodied knife on her sheepskin trousers. Her long black hair hung down her back in a thick plait. Her bare feet were dirty; there was a smudge on her cheek. But she was beautiful.

'What are you doing here?' she asked at last.

'I've been looking for you ever since that day you –'

'Why?'

'I want to marry you.'

She stooped down quickly to pick up the gun that was lying on the ground next to the half-skinned carcass. 'Go away,' she said calmly. 'Or I'll shoot you.'

'Then go ahead,' said. 'For I'm not going back without you.'

She hesitated. Her father came round the house and stopped when he saw the stranger.

'Who are you?' His voice was impatient, even threatening.

'Oom, I'm David Landman from the Kasouga River in the Zuurveld. I want to marry Tommie.'

The burly man burst out laughing. 'You've come a long way for nothing,' he said. 'This one's a wild thing. I've already tried to marry her off many times, but she runs away every time.'

The girl glowered at them for a moment, then dropped the gun. Without saying another word she swiftly ran towards a long low outbuilding on the far side of the farmyard.

'She's going to get her horse,' said Thomas Lourens. 'You'd better hurry if you want to catch her.'

'If it's all right with Oom,' he said, 'I'd rather wait here.'

'You don't know her,' warned her father. 'She may stay away for days.'

'I'll wait for her.'

He'd waited for so long already. Even after he'd discovered where she lived there had been a long delay: the old Khoin man who had accompanied him from Bethelsdorp had fallen ill on the way; a trip they should have made in three or four days had taken three weeks. It was April already. But now he had found her: he would wait, even if it took the rest of his life.

When she came back four days later, not haggard and hungry at all as he'd expected – it was only later that he discovered how easily she lived off the veld – she stopped in her tracks on the threshhold of the *voorhuis* when she saw him sitting at the dining-table with her family.

'What are you still doing here?'

'Waiting for you.'

She looked round like a duiker sensing a snare.

'Please don't run away again,' he said.

She didn't answer, but her body was tense, as if at the slightest move he made she meant to dart away.

'You should have a wash, Tommie,' her mother sighed. 'You look terrible.'

'You shouldn't say that, Tante,' David said sternly. 'She's very beautiful.' Some of the brothers and sisters sniggered.

Tommie's nostrils flared. Suddenly she narrowed her eyes. 'See if you can catch me,' she said. 'I don't want a husband who's too *vrot* to run me down.'

'And I don't want a wife who keeps on running away,' he said quietly.

She stared at him, dark eyes blazing.

'I haven't come all this way to play games with you,' he said. 'I want to marry you.'

'For heaven's sake marry the man,' her father said. 'I want you off my hands.'

'All right,' she said.

After the wedding at Graaff-Reinet he took her to Bethelsdorp to have their union blessed by his old friend. He'd originally proposed that van der Kemp marry them, but that had nearly wrecked the whole thing.

'That *kafferboetie*?' shouted Thomas Lourens. 'That child of Satan? Ever since that man came to this Colony the place has become a hell to live in. Luring away our hottentots, telling them there's no need for them to work, preaching freedom to our slaves, stoking up trouble among the blacks: how are we supposed to do our farming with no one around to do the work?'

'But Oom –'

'You bring that Beelzebub into it and the wedding is off. I'll rather see Tommie dead than have her defiled by that man's hand on her forehead.'

David raised no further objection, but it was characteristic of him that he should have decided there and then to have a second, secret, wedding as well, without even warning Tommie about it.

But disappointment awaited them at Bethelsdorp. It turned out that barely a fortnight after David's departure van der Kemp had been summoned to Cape Town to elaborate on representations he'd made to the Governor about the way many of his Khoin congregation had been treated by their masters.

They remained at the mission for a few weeks, hoping to have news from the Cape, but it became clear that van der Kemp would not return soon. David attended services conducted by some of the other missionaries, Tommie took some interest in the weaving shop; but there really was no reason to prolong their stay. The bride, in fact, was relieved to go.

'I don't like the place,' she told her husband. 'Too many lazy louts just lying about. And the place is filthy. That van der Kemp doesn't seem to care very much about doing things properly.'

'*You're* a one to talk!' chuckled David. 'Running about wild, wearing men's trousers, with face and feet unwashed –'

'I'm wearing a dress now,' she said calmly. 'Haven't you noticed?'

I can imagine David feeling disconsolate as they rode away, as if missing his old friend's blessing on their marriage had deprived them of something important for their future. Perhaps he already had an intimation that he would not see the man again? (If so, he was right; van der Kemp died in Cape Town seven months later, without ever having returned to Bethelsdorp.) Undoubtedly, as their wagon lumbered along, David would have drawn to him – like a beggar wrapping himself in his tatters against the cold – all his last images of that unworldly old man, gaunt and proud in his long frayed coat, with his high bald head and his dirty feet in sandals, sitting on his rickety bench at night to read by candle-light from books in many languages, or standing in his little church to preach freedom and salvation to the oppressed and the illiterate. Turning his back on that overcrowded, smelly, squalid, yet strangely blissful little village (was Lambaréné like that, so many years later, I wonder?) must have been, for David, like the closing of something inside himself, possibilities denied, a candle snuffed. On the other hand, here he was taking home – wherever that might be, they hadn't found a place of their own yet – the wild girl of the wood who had been transformed, so incredibly, into his wife.

'Wife': a strange word indeed to associate with a girl like Tommie. Yet Tommie seemed to be adapting extraordinarily well to the taming processes of wifehood, motherhood. As if all those wild energies that had previously erupted in fugues and rebellion and acts of deliberate provocation had suddenly found a focus.

Certainly I cannot accept Dad's patronising, chauvinistic view that in the functions of wife and mother she had at last found her 'natural expression'. I can imagine that in the twentieth century, with other choices available, she might have become a Miriam Makeba, perhaps even an Ulrike Meinhoff. (A Nina Jordaan? A Lisa Lombard?) But what choices were available to her at the beginning of the nineteenth century on the eastern frontier of the Cape Colony? What is important is not *what* channel Tommie found for the expression of her passions, but the simple fact that she did discover it. Hurling herself into it was like diving naked into a deep black pool in the wood.

Their first child, Thomas Johannes, was born a mere seven months after their marriage. So they must have started sleeping together almost from the day Tommie came back from the veld to find David still waiting.

Their second child, Frans Jacobus, was born eleven months after the first. There were twelve more in the next thirteen years.

The Zuurveld was once more a troubled region when they returned to it, devastated by the mounting strife between boers and Xhosa; and before the end of that year it erupted in the worst violence ever, when the British moved in their own troops with the boer commandos to drive all the black inhabitants over the Great Fish River; by that time most of the whites had already moved out too, dispossessed and apprehensive about any possibility of a secure future. Yet David, in his quiet adamant way, was resolved to remain there; and after a few months with his family he left with Tommie

736

to settle on one of the many abandoned farms not far from where the military post of Graham's Town had just been established.

From the very first, Tommie ruled her household with gusto, and with an iron hand. With her children she was not only strict but tyrannical, beating them into submission at the least sign of disobedience: how strange (or is it only to be expected?) that one so unruly in her youth should be so unforgiving with her own offspring. David was the one who would try to make allowances, give them another chance – but Tommie brooked no interference when it came to disciplining the children, or running her home.

What I find most difficult to accommodate in our accepted version of her (illuminating once again, distressingly, the shaky ground one ventures on in any attempt to reconstruct another's life), is that the wild girl who once made friends with all manner of wild animals, and spoke to birds, now in her new role as frontier woman slaughtered the cattle and sheep and poultry for their domestic use, or shot buck or wild fowl when they needed venison. (On two occasions she is reported to have shot lions, but that was only because they'd been stalking the same prey.) When their cattle were raided, which began to happen again with alarming frequency after a few years of relative quiet, she thought nothing of riding out with the men to retrieve them – except when she was forced to stay behind with another lying-in. She could fell trees, and dig irrigation channels, and build walls, and thatch the roof, or smear the floors with mud and dung. But she never acted 'improperly' again: swimming naked, or wearing men's clothing, or running off into the wild.

Above all, she became famous as a herbalist and healer; and after the birth of her sixth child she was much sought after as a midwife, sometimes travelling for two days on horseback, all on her own, to assist with a difficult confinement. She seemed to thrive on 'complications' and it was generally believed that not even God himself would dare to take a child away once Tommie Landman had taken charge.

Having lost, quite early, the litheness of her girlhood (which may have existed only in the gaudy imagination of my adolescence anyway; perhaps she had been a stocky peasant girl from the start), Tommie became, first, in our canon, a sturdy woman, then a formidable and massive matron. Seeing her approach, it was said, horses winced and trembled like young foals; one stallion reportedly sat down on its haunches every time she prepared to mount. At sixty

– for she outlived David by many years – she was known, when it was necessary to replace a wagon wheel, to lift the wagon from the ground with one massive shoulder.

And then there was her strange fascination with death. Whenever there was trouble in the neighbourhood, and God knows there was enough, one would be sure to find her in the graveyard on the farm (where only strangers lay buried, ancestors of the previous owners; as none of her own family had dared to die while she was around), having long conversations with the dead, to inform them of whatever events she believed they ought to know about. Also, when they visited, at long intervals, the Lourens farm in the Lang Kloof or the Landman farm beside the Kasouga River, she would first go to the graveyard to pay her respects to the departed, talking to them in a loud voice (they had soil in their ears, she explained) to bring them up to date and enquire about their peace of mind: only then would she come up to the house to acknowledge the living.

Beside her, it would be easy to imagine David dwindling into insignificance. He certainly could never match her aggressive, exuberant extroversion. But in his own quiet way he earned his due of respect from other inhabitants in the region; not least of all from Tommie herself. He'd relinquished something of a dream when he'd chosen married life above religion; on the other hand, to have found Tommie was in itself the realisation of a dream. (Only, as he discovered, a dream come true is, somehow, no longer a dream.) Essentially, I see him as a man content with himself and his world. What he needed for a peaceful life he had inside him, and within his home. So forays into the world outside had no appeal to him.

This did not mean, however, that the world outside was content to let *him* be. And the main theme of the rest of his life became the tussle with the new British rulers of the Cape who kept on, at least as he saw it, assailing the small enclave of his domestic happiness and integrity.

Within months of the Battle of Trafalgar, in her worldwide drive against France and her allies, Britain had conquered the Cape of Good Hope and entrenched herself in that strategic position on the route to the East. In contrast to 1795, when Britain had merely occupied the Cape in a caretaker capacity, this occupation was serious and permanent, and the effects began to reverberate throughout the Colony. Administrative officials, backed up by garrisons, were posted in centres all over the country; and if that made life easier

Then he was arrested and taken to court – which, thank God, sat in Graham's Town by this time. He would ask for postponements. There would be more delays caused by his refusal to speak English, which by now had become the official language. In the end a large detachment of soldiers in red jackets came to evict him and his family from the farm.

Tommie was furious: Oupa used to tell with great enthusiasm how she took her gun and prepared to shoot the lot of them off the farm. But once again David stopped her – this time, it is said, by interposing himself between her and the soldiers. Violence was not the way to do it, he said; there was another way. Tommie, one can imagine, snorted in disgust and disbelief. But he showed her: the day after they had been dumped in Graham's Town, with all their earthly possessions loaded on two wagons, David simply returned. They were removed again. They went back again.

The third time the magistrate ensured that another family, Dodsons, British settlers who'd had a dispute with their leader, was installed on the farm as soon as the Landmans had been driven away by their armed escorts. But once again David went back, outspanned his wagons in front of what had been his house, and gave the new occupants twenty-four hours to move out. They refused. David collected a handful of neighbours, they drew a laager of wagons round the house and announced a siege. Thirst rapidly led to surrender. And as soon as the English family, poor things, had left – on a wagon David himself had generously offered them – the Landmans took occupation of their house again.

There was an unexpectedly happy end to all this. A year or so after the confrontation with the Dodsons, a pale and breathless young Englishman from the town turned up on their doorstep one evening to ask for help. His little sister had taken seriously ill, they'd tried to find the doctor, but he was out somewhere in the district and the child was dying of convulsions. Someone had mentioned Tommie's reputation as a healer, so in despair the young man had been sent to fetch her. In spite of being, as always, heavily pregnant, she went to lend a hand, the child was pulled through, and the Landmans became staunch friends of the English family. Through them, they met the young firebrand journalist Godlonton: when in due course another summons was delivered on the farm, David took it to Godlonton. No one knows exactly what took place, but it was the end of a tug-o'-war that had lasted for the better part of fifteen years.

*

few head of cattle, and went to Graaff-Rei[net]
to pay the fine – a wagon journey which [...] she asked.
only she did it in nine days. When Dav[id]
what had happened, he went to the ma[...] *apbroek!'*
the money, and returned to prison. A ma[...] and Bezuiden[...]ers,' he said,
laconically; and anyway, he needed the m[...] involved in so[...] good.'

Tommie found lodgings for her family in[...] [...] now, those [...]ing to squash
to be released.

Back on the farm they found that, des[...] [...]ust asking fo[...]
neighbours, most of their cattle had bee[...] [...], I'll go.'
all his friends and they followed the track[...] Your time is [...]. You're going
where they were stopped by soldiers at[...] [...]ing to be he[...]
constructed frontier forts. It was illegal to[...]
told. David and his group turned back, dis[...] [...]ake time to t[...] it you'll stop
they reached, waited for nightfall, and th[...] to the smith[...]ckyard where
At the settlement where the tracks stop[...] [...]od.
men at gunpoint, selected only the cattl[...]
and went back. [...]might have [...]ad her cramps

A government official turned up soon a[...] [...]rought on b[...]stic upheaval
the matter. David asked him to leave. [...]et out on ho[...] was their firs

Then it all started again: the messen[...] [...]ter when a m[...]rom Grahan[...]
monses. This time he spent six months[...] [...]ead to reque[...]ars' payme[...]

The third time he was told that he wou[...] [...]e money,' sai[...]And anyw[...]
in the Castle at the Cape; but fortunat[...] [...]thing. It was[...]rm. Jan G[...]
particularly bad year for the frontier dist[...] packed up a[...]en the X[...]
was attacked by a Xhosa force of some[...] [...]er lying he[...]k it. No[...]
government sent all its available troops,[...] [...]ly explained[...]lexities [...]
up every farmer within reach, which yie[...] [...]ly patiently[...]to budg[...]
and invaded Xhosa territory, laying was[...] [...] with anger[...] left. A[...]
the cattle they could find, and driving [...] [...]ummons. D[...]it up. [...]
child between the Great Fish River and[...] warning tha[...]ould b[...]
end all wars, it was said. [...] up at the c[...]raaff-[...]

Because of his services on comman[...] [...]d, and igno[...]warni[...]
David were dropped. But the following[...] [...]lers came t[...]him[...]
once again declined to pay his annua[...] [...]n, but he res[...]her.
started again. This time there were mor[...] [...]tersnek?' he [...]e p[...]
had to cope with the needs of four th[...] his wife and [...], [...]
who'd been shipped to Algoa Bay and[...] [...]te allowed h[...]n[...]
form a densely populated buffer zone b[...] time he was j[...] [...]
and the Colony. But even though it took[...] [...]g up their ne[...]
finally catch up with David again. Sum[...] the children[...]

The end is not fully documented, and most of it has survived only in the oral tradition of my family. But in a way, I suppose, David may be described as a casualty of the terrible war that began in December 1834 when fifteen thousand Xhosa, driven to despair by the loss of more and more of their traditional grazing in the Zuurveld, incessant 'punitive expeditions' into their territory, and recent attempts by the colonial government to open their homeland between the Fish and the Keiskamma Rivers to white settlers, poured into the Colony. It was the beginning of the Sixth Frontier War.

David's whole family and several of his neighbours had assembled in his house to discuss the news; it was just before Christmas. Even his two oldest sons, the first already married, and both of them recently installed on a farm much closer to the border, were there.

'I suppose we'll all be called up now,' said young Thomas.

'I don't think we should wait for that,' one of the others replied. 'Let's mount a commando right away and try to stop them before they can do any more harm.'

'There are *thousands* of them!' said another.

'But they don't expect us to retaliate so soon. If we can surprise them, it'll give us the advantage.'

Et cetera. Then, in the midst of all the excited discussion, David announced calmly that he refused to go to war. There was a sudden, total silence. Tommie, especially, was aghast. She stormed at him: 'All these years I've stood by you in everything, even when I didn't agree. But this is madness!'

'How many times have I gone on commando?' he asked her. 'I've never shirked what people told me was my duty. But I no longer believe it is my duty to continue this killing. Someone's got to put an end to it by saying no.'

'This is war, Thomas,' she said. 'How can you stay out of it? If you don't fight we'll all be killed. *You* will be killed.'

'I don't think so,' he said. 'But if they want to, let them. Then it's their responsibility. *I* won't take part in any more killing.' He looked around him. 'And I would prefer my sons to stay out of it too.'

'Your sons aren't cowards,' she shouted at him. 'They'll go to war and be ashamed of you forever.'

It was a terrible moment for the family.

Soon after, when the British soldier Sir Harry Smith rode from Cape Town to Graham's Town – almost nine hundred kilometres – in six days to take command of the frontier troops, David Landman's three oldest sons (twenty-three, twenty-two and twenty-one years old) joined the armed forces. The father stayed behind with his wife, his daughters, and four youngest sons. Only the second son, Frans Jacobus, returned. Both the others, Thomas Johannes and Petrus Lodewyk, had died in a Xhosa ambush in the thickets of the Riet River. The eldest left a widow of nineteen, Hendrina, five months pregnant with their first child, whom she lost a few weeks later.

After Frans had come home with the news, Tommie spent two days and two nights down in the small cemetery among the unfamiliar dead – her sons would never lie there; had been buried in a trench somewhere – to make her peace with God and the world. When she came back, our legend has it, her beautiful black hair had turned white. David stood waiting for her, but she paid no attention to him at all, as if he wasn't there. She went to their bedroom and took out from a yellowwood chest the black mourning dress she'd always kept ready; brushing aside the family gathered on the threshold, she marched out again, took a spade and a pick from the shed, and returned to the little graveyard where she began to dig a new grave in the ground as hard as rock.

The children kept a safe distance. David followed her after a while to ask her what she was doing, but he might as well not have been there. Throughout the whole blistering day she toiled, heaving spadefuls of earth from the steadily deepening trench. When it was done, in the first cool of the evening, she strode right past David, to prepare the evening meal. But she set no place for her husband. And when at last one of the smallest children anxiously dared to ask her what was going on, she informed them in a flat voice that their father had died, and she had dug his grave.

She never spoke a single word to him again. As far as she was concerned, he really *was* dead. It would have been no use arguing that he hadn't wanted his sons to go to war in the first place; as Tommie saw it – if I dare presume, once again, to read her mind – he somehow bore responsibility for their deaths by refusing to take up arms himself.

The truly eerie thing about it all was that in less than a month, David did die in his sleep. She had, quite simply, willed him into the grave she had dug for him.

Frans Jacobus Landman

(1812–1855)

Very little trace of Frans Jacobus Landman has survived in our family chronicle. On the basis of a few references to his wife and child it has been assumed, even by my father after diligent research, that he must have joined the Great Trek with his family in 1837. It was only by accident that I discovered it was untrue. (Dad still refused categorically to accept my evidence without corroboration from other sources and perhaps in doing so he was a more dependable historian than I?) Certainly, even the little that has been handed down about him is suspect, and it has become customary to treat him simply as a link between his father David and his son Petrus.

What has been recorded officially is that in 1832 or 1833 he left the family farm to join his elder brother, Thomas Johannes, on another, smaller farm near the mouth of the Riet River, which he used as a base to ply a trade between all the outlying farms and Graham's Town; that after the frontier war of 1834–1835 he married his brother's young widow Hendrina soon after she'd given birth to a premature child; that following a brief failed venture as an auctioneer in Graham's Town he clashed with the British authorities and moved as far away as possible, deep into Xhosa territory, where he seems to have made a living as a trader.

Not much to construct a whole life from. Even the more arcane material I later found in unpublished papers by some British settlers does not add a lot to it. Yet the most revealing of all this, the record of a conversation Frans – by then a broken, prematurely aged man, riddled with fever and alcohol – had had shortly before his death in 1855 with the diarist Bernard Cunningham, affords an almost terrifying glimpse of a frustrated life.

This Cunningham, at the time a tanner in Graham's Town,

narrates how he had gone to Frans Landman's remote trading post in 'Caffreland' with the intention of 'giving him Hell', the reason being that Frans had allegedly 'stolen' the Englishman's daughter from him and was now living in sin with her. Instead of their having it out, however, Cunningham was so moved by the dying man's plight that he stayed on for a month, assisted by his prodigal and now pregnant daughter, to nurse Frans to the end. Although he records that Frans seemed irredeemable – 'a poor Sinner so set in his ways & so bitter against God & man that one can but pray for Mercy on a sole [sic] that refuses to pray for himself'.

In the last night of his life ('a Storm raged outside the little wattle & daub hut the likes of which I had not Experienced not even in this part of the wilderness where we are used to the violent elements, as if Hell itself in all its Fury rag'd against us') Frans told his would-be father-in-law about an incident during that frontier war, twenty years earlier, in which he'd lost two brothers. The commando had come upon a group of Xhosa driving along, through the dense bush, a herd of cattle presumed stolen. They'd opened fire. Abandoning the cattle, the group of suspected thieves ran towards a thicket of euphorbia, the commando in hot pursuit. It turned out to be an ambush. Suddenly they were surrounded from all sides. Seven of the boers and one of their British officers had died before they succeeded in driving off the Xhosa. The survivors inspected the battlefield and collected their dead. Among the fallen Xhosa was one young man, still alive, but rolling about in agony with a stomach wound from which his intestines protruded. Frans and some of the others knelt down beside him to determine the extent of his injuries. Gasping, he pleaded with them to shoot him and end his agony. But the oldest man in the group stopped them. The 'Caffre' was going to die anyway, he said; why waste a good bullet?

They rode on for some distance, carrying away their dead to a clearing in the bushes where it was safe to dig a trench and bury them. But the memory of that young dying man kept haunting Frans: all the more so, it seems, as the death of his own two brothers lay heavily on his mind. (In what I regard as a strangely significant phrase in that deathbed confession to Cunningham, he admitted that 'I could have saved my brother Thomas, it was all my fault.') He could not expel that image of the young man writhing on the ground, clutching his entrails in his hands. Towards nightfall he slipped away from the commando, unseen, and rode back to the scene of the ambush.

The young man was gone. The trees surrounding the place were black with vultures, but there was no sign of the bodies that had littered the place in the morning. As he stood there an assegai came whizzing from the fringe of bushes opposite, missing him by inches. He realised that the Xhosa had come back for their own dead. It was only instinct that sent him scampering back to his horse; and he got away unscathed.

'I felt a numbness within myself,' he haltingly told Cunningham those many years later. 'But the one thing that burned like a flame through everything else in my mind, was this: that young black man was fighting, just like me and my brothers, for the same piece of land. And his death, to his people, was no different from the death of Thomas and Petrus to me. So why were we enemies?'

It was the turning-point of his life. And the anxiety it had instilled in him became part of the profound uncertainty that marked the rest of his life. 'How is it possible,' he asked Cunningham in the lucidity that precedes death, 'that boers and blacks are fighting each other for the land of their birth while the English rule over all of us?' ('I tried to explain to him,' comments the diarist, 'that there was a Difference between the British settler people and their government too & that although matters have now improved, in those days we were as much Oppressed as he, but I am not sure he understood as the fever again got the better of him & he beged [sic] me for more Brandy to ease the Pain, which I gave to him, praying to God to forgive both his sins & mine, & soon thereafter he passed away, to meet his Maker with Alcohol on his breath.')

What frustrated Frans, even in the most ordinary activities of his life, was, as I see it, the lack of choice. The social fabric of the colony was such that, apart from farming, there were practically no other options open to him, lacking even the rudimentary education required for teaching. In and around Cape Town Free Burghers, many of them affluent and well established, could turn to trading or smuggling; there was, at least, a limited range of services they could provide to visitors: inns, taverns, travelling facilities and the like. Or they could join the Company as soldiers, clerks, inspectors, or whatever. But the further inland one went the more restricted became one's choices to make a living. Slaves and Khoin labourers did the menial work; no white would touch it – so even working for a farmer as a foreman or a *bywoner* had a stigma attached to it; woodcutting brought in very little money, and trading could be a hazardous business in what was practically a war zone. Administrative posts were more or less out of bounds for all but a handful of people who were fluent in English and had had at least a modicum of education. Frans Landman hated farming. But what else was there for him to do in that narrow intermediate zone between 'European' overseers and slave or Khoin labourers?

(What would he have done had be been born a century later? Teacher – businessman – politician – even a musician like one of his failed ancestors? Perhaps, faced with a whole array of options, he might actually have *chosen* to become a farmer. But then it would have been his choice, not his fate.)

Caught in a similar snare, our savage ancestor Diederik had reacted with mindless violence. But Frans was not that kind of person; especially after his experience in the Sixth War. In the end, of course, he succumbed to alcohol. Perhaps it was the only alternative to madness, or violence. Unlike his father, his grandfather, and the whole line before them, he could not come to terms with his horizon, he would not make his peace with it. That is what moves me about the man, what makes him tragic, rather than merely pathetic.

I read that first move of his – leaving his father's home with his eldest brother Thomas to settle on the new farm on the Riet River – as the first sign he gave of the urge to do something different, to break away. (Unless it was quite simply a matter of expediency: his parents' home might have become too small for all the dependents.) It was no real solution, of course. For a time the effort of getting a new farm going – building a house and outbuildings and kraals, clearing some land for ploughing – would no doubt have calmed something of the itch in him, dulled the ache of restlessness. But that could not have been enough. Yet he stayed on even after his brother had married Hendrina Greyling, which couldn't have made things easier either for the young couple or for himself.

Unless Frans also had an interest in her: this is a crucial consideration for my whole reading of his life. 'At last I married Hendrina,' were his words to Bernard Cunningham on his deathbed. A mere turn of phrase? But in my continuing attempt to foretell the past I prefer to read more into it: *at last –*

The brothers met her at *nagmaal* in Graham's Town. Hendrina Greyling is yet another female ancestor I should give much to have known myself. We know she was a waif from the Sneeuberge, orphaned when her father was killed by the poisoned arrows of the San who regarded him as an intruder in their traditional hunting territory. (Her mother, it seems, had died at her birth.) A brother not much older than herself – she was about seventeen at the time – took her to an uncle and an aunt living hundreds of kilometres away in the Great Karoo, a journey lasting months, and meriting a book in its own right: several times they nearly died of hunger or of thirst; once they were attacked by a pack of wild dogs, on another occasion by an old male lion, himself nearly dead with hunger.

However, not long after her brother had at last delivered her into the care of their relatives, the aunt died, and the girl absconded. An itinerant trader, a morose old German ex-sailor, picked her up and left her in the care of the *landdrost* of Swellendam, who placed her with the family of one of his *heemraden* as a domestic help. Once again she ran away, joining this time a group of trekking Khoin. After a few months she was spotted in their company by some hunters who, believing that she'd been taken captive, shot dead several of her benefactors and 'freed' her. At Graaff-Reinet, where she was next taken, she met the family of a travelling schoolmaster cum doctor with whom she journeyed to Graham's Town. There she was at last taken in by the wife of the farmer Piet Retief (a proud moment in our tribal history, for this was the same Piet Retief who was to become one of the heroes and martyrs of Afrikanerdom). For a while she commuted with the family between the town and a number of Retief's farms. It seems likely that there may have been a distant family connection here, as Retief's wife had previously been married to a Greyling.

Through Piet Retief's numerous activities – among other things he was a builder, sawyer, miller, baker, butcher, wine merchant, property speculator, general dealer and field-cornet: there were times when his many irons got entangled in the fire, and when Hendrina arrived on his wife's doorstep he was actually serving a prison sentence – she met a colourful assortment of people, and it was when she was attending her second or third *nagmaal* with the Retief family that she was introduced to the two Landman brothers.

My impression of the older brother, Thomas Johannes (but I have little to base it on), is of a rough-and-ready, matter-of-fact person who did what was expected of him without wasting much time asking questions about anything; whereas Frans, I like to think, was far from practical, more romantically inclined, something of a

749

brooder. Which may account for the fact that Thomas was the first to ask her: there was a farm that required a woman's hand, a future to be attended to, the girl was available, so why not marry her? To Frans, if my surmise is true, this would have been a stab in the heart. (But why didn't he protest, while there was still time? And why did she accept Thomas in the first place if she also, as I suspect, preferred the younger brother? I admit my interpretation is tenuous. But everything hinges on what one reads into those words: *at last* –) Whatever the reason, the wedding took place without undue delay, the boys' mother took charge of everything, and soon the couple – and the stricken brother (if that was indeed what he was) – returned to the farm on the Riet River.

Then came the war. Thomas was killed, true to the fate of everyone with that name in his mother's family. This is where Frans's role becomes decisive: I do not suggest for a moment that he had been actively guilty of it; yet how should one read his deathbed words to Bernard Cunningham – 'I could have saved my brother Thomas, it was all my fault' – if not as a confession of having at least *willed* it? And for what other reason could this have happened except something involving Hendrina?

As we know, Hendrina went into labour when she heard the news of her husband's death, and gave birth to a premature child (sadly, and perhaps perversely, also named Thomas); and in spite of protests from other members of the family she returned to the farm with Frans. Before the customary time of mourning had run out – surely this, too, is significant? – the two were married. It was August 1835. Not one of Frans's family attended the wedding. Which again suggests that there may have been something untoward about it.

(There is yet another piece of evidence. In his deathbed confession to Bernard Cunningham almost twenty years later, Frans told the Englishman the bitter tale of how, in January 1837, less than two years after their marriage, Hendrina had left on the Great Trek in spite of all his attempts to make her stay. 'I told her,' Cunningham noted down his words, '"How can you go away from the place where our child lies buried?" But she went.'

Admittedly, it is a tricky bit of exegesis. Perhaps it was a slip of the pen, writing 'our' instead of 'your'? Or perhaps it refers to another, unrecorded child, born after their marriage? And what could he have meant by 'the place' he referred to? – by the time she left, they had already settled in 'Caffreland' and were no longer living on the farm where the child had been buried. Such are the ambiguities on which I must rest my case.)

They did not stay on the farm for long. Perhaps feelings of guilt became too much for them; it is also possible that the memories of Thomas Johannes still attached to the place made it difficult for them to begin a new life of their own. My own guess is that, with all the reasons removed which had initially driven Frans to the farm with his brother, he *had* to give it up to explore other possibilities.

They left for Graham's Town, where Hendrina may have counted on her connection with the Retief family to secure a job for her husband; unfortunately, as it turned out, Retief had by then moved away to a farm on the Koonap, below the Winterberg, and although he still from time to time dashed in to the town on business (he continued to have innumerable irons in the fire), he was so hounded by creditors and litigants that he was in no position to help. For a few months Frans joined a tannery set up by one of the British settlers, but there was friction with his fellow workers and the pay was too meagre to support a wife. The position of auctioneer fell vacant and Frans was appointed: but it must have been a mistake from the beginning, as he could speak no English. He clearly did not take his abrupt dismissal lying down, and ended up with a week in prison for 'assaulting an officer in His Majesty's service'.

That was the first time he equipped a rented wagon with whatever odds and ends of merchandise he could afford and, ignoring all advice and warning, drove right across the border, through the recently proclaimed no-man's-land to the Keiskamma River, where he acquired from the Xhosa a small plot for a trading post. There he settled with Hendrina. He'd had enough of British rule. But I find no suggestion of escape in this: on the contrary, it seems to me a calculated act of defiance to His Majesty's government. Because as it turned out, the bulk of his trade was in guns and ammunition.

There is evidence enough that the authorities were furious, and tried on several occasions to send expeditions for his retrieval; but it is significant that his Xhosa neighbours protected Frans with such diligence that no one from the colony could lay a hand on him. He had to make regular trips back to Graham's Town or Algoa Bay to replenish his stock, and it is amazing that he was never apprehended. He certainly became a much sought-after character, and at one stage there was a price of five hundred cattle on his head. This made him even more daring in his exploits: no longer content simply with gun-running, he actually trained a band of Xhosa to help him ambush and attack the detachments of British militia regularly sent to patrol the region beyond the Fish River; in this way he and his bandits amassed even more arms and ammunition. The British authorities made counter-moves. Sometimes it was by the very skin of his teeth that Frans Landman avoided being caught: the traps set for him, the elaborate preparations made time and time again to apprehend him, became the talk of the frontier district.

That, at least, is what Cunningham reports: unfortunately he assumes that his reader must be familiar with the details and consequently supplies none himself: fallow earth for the novelist, not for the historian I am trying to be. According to the diarist, one officer was known to have taken an oath that he would not cut his hair or beard until the outlaw was arrested: when he died, miserably, many years later, he was such a tangle of grey growth that he seemed like some wild creature from the woods. No matter how hard the authorities tried, Frans continued to elude both the military and their many ingenious hirelings. Which explains his dubious status in our family history: celebrated as a hero for his exploits against the British, he is nevertheless regarded with some uneasiness because it also implied common cause with the blacks. No wonder there has been little inclination among our family chroniclers to pursue his life too closely.

Much of his reputation was only acquired later; but he was already firmly established as gun-runner, freebooter and traitor by the time Hendrina deserted him, leaving on a wagon Piet Retief had sent from Graham's Town to pick her up.

Ever since 1834 frontier Boers had begun to trek from the colony in search of a less troublesome place where they could order their lives the way they wished. After the war it became a stampede, and although present-day historians suggest that the exodus was not nearly as vast as Afrikaner mythology has portrayed it, it would seem that at least one out of every five people in the frontier districts joined the Great Trek. In the course of 1834 several expeditions – or 'commissions' – were sent in different directions to explore the lie of the land; in February 1837 Piet Retief followed, with yet others in his wake.

Hendrina insisted on joining the Retief trek. She must have had enough – but of what? Was it the uncertainty of their existence, so remote from the colony, which had become too much for her? Or had the guilty relationship with Frans finally turned sour?

With hindsight, one may even be tempted to wonder whether her decision was not prompted, at least partly, by the discovery that she was pregnant, which must inevitably have rekindled too many memories. This, the most vital moment, perhaps, in their life together, remains a mystery. All I know is that they parted.

A particularly vexing question raised by her departure is why Frans did not accompany her. True, from that final confession, when he was, for all one knows, already hallucinating or demented, it transpires that at the time she left Frans did not know she was expecting their child. (Had she deliberately not told him? – But then why, for God's sake, why? – Or was it so early that she herself had not known about it yet?) Mere stubbornness seems an unlikely explanation for giving up the woman he'd sinfully loved even while she'd still been married to his brother. Unless he regarded losing her as the price he had to pay for that sin? Deliberately seeking out punishment, and revelling in suffering, are experiences not unfamiliar to my tribe.

In any case, it seems reasonable to presume that this was the time Frans first turned to the bottle. I have only Cunningham's word for it that his drinking became legendary in the border region. He seemed to be driven from one excess to another, not only in his drinking, but in his defiance of the colonial authorities. He had to do *something* to alleviate his loneliness during the almost twenty years of unremitting solitude he remained in that wilderness. It was only towards the very end that he 'stole' Jessica Cunningham from her father – but whether they'd fallen in love and eloped, or whether he had abducted her, there is no means of telling. The girl was with child when her father found them, and four months or so after Frans's death she gave birth to a daughter who has subsequently disappeared into other genealogies. (I am tempted to trace her sometime: there must be an extended network of my relations spread across all regions of this land by now; through all layers of its society. There is a multitude clamouring in my voice.)

Of Frans Hendrik Landman himself no more is known, apart from the few fragments of the last delirious confession which Cunningham thought fit to commit to paper, undoubtedly after considerable editing. (And even what he left is, in part, illegible.) He died. His unmarked grave must still be somewhere among the shrubs and bushes of 'Caffreland', now Transkei. In real, 'historical' terms, his life – his heroism, or revolt, or treason, by whatever name one chooses to call it – was insignificant; a waste. Did he even understand what was happening to him, what he was trying to do?

Do *I* understand?

I am not sure. At least, in sparing him the indignity of being forgotten, of *letheia*, I am trying through my own choices, and my own life, I hope, to complete something he was forced to abandon uncompleted.

9

Petrus Landman

(1837–1897)

There is an expression in Afrikaans, 'to see your own hole', meaning that you have made a complete fuck-up; that you are forced to face your ruin. It was first used in the Anglo-Boer War with reference to traitors who had been forced to dig their own graves before being shot. In due course its origins became obscured and in its modern usage the phrase is taken to refer to one's arsehole. And whenever my great-great-grandfather Petrus Landman is referred to as 'the Seer' of our family, this is the irreverent – if anachronistic – phrase that occurs to me. The image it inevitably conjures up is the one in J.M. Coetzee's wonderful story 'The Narrative of Jacobus Coetzee', where the pioneer is surprised by a group of Khoin youngsters as he contorts himself into weird postures trying to discover a boil on his backside. (As a result, he leads an expedition into the interior to annihilate the tribe that has thus insulted the dignity of a white man: 'No more than any other man do I enjoy killing; but I have taken it upon myself to be the one to pull the trigger, performing this sacrifice for myself and my countrymen, who exist, and committing upon the dark folk the murders we have all wished.')

From the beginning everything was against him; it is a marvel that he survived at all.

He was born on an ox-wagon somewhere in the Eastern Free State (in those days still – if only in white settler history – a nameless, unmapped tract of rolling grassland between the Orange River and the Drakensberg, or Dragon Mountains), late on a stormy day in July 1837. Such a quarrel was raging among the Trekkers – I imagine men shouting and cursing, some with fists flailing, women tearing at each other's hair and clothes, children clawing and rolling about – that even the midwives had forgotten about poor Hendrina Landman's protracted agonies; and by the time someone did remember and went to investigate, both mother and child were so feeble with exhaustion, pain and cold that they were almost given up for dead. In fact, the wretched, cross-eyed old clergyman, Erasmus Smit, was hurriedly summoned to say one of his interminable lachrymose prayers (subsequently recorded verbatim in his diary) to escort them safely, if desperately, to the waiting arms of Father, Son and Holy Ghost; whether it was repugnance at his halitosis, or sheer guts that pulled them through, is anybody's guess, but they survived.

The reason for that particular squabble was not recorded; there were few days without arguments – often erupting into fights – among the different clans: about grazing or water, lost sheep, firewood, minor accidents, servants (the Trekkers barely outnumbered the host of servants they had taken with them); gossip; broken implements; or about religion (could the unordained Smit be permitted to preach? to administer the sacraments? was it acceptable for an Englishman, the Rev. Lindley, to look after their spiritual welfare? should they try to restore their ties with the Dutch Reformed Church at the Cape which had virtually anathematised them, or found their own?); or about leadership (whom should they follow and obey; Potgieter? Maritz? Uys? Retief?); or even about where they were supposed to be going (to Natal, to the sea, said Retief; north, said Potgieter, to the Transvaal, to be sure they would be free: 'for wherever you find the sea, you find an Englishman') –

I wonder sometimes whether Hendrina did not regret her decision to leave her husband and join the trek of Piet Retief. Did she, in moments of darkness, with futile tears, take out the few heirlooms Frans had pressed upon her when she'd left – the ancient mirror; the great leather-bound bible – to indulge her miserable memories or rekindle a dream burnt out? If she had left in search of adventure and excitement, the dreary reality and hardships of the trek must soon have stifled all eager expectations; even the pregnancy was a difficult one, and she was sick most of the time.

For Retief, it had started with the grand gesture of his Manifesto, drawn up no doubt with the help of a few journalist friends in Graham's Town not entirely unfamiliar with Jefferson:

Numerous reports having been circulated throughout the colony, evidently with the intention of exciting in the minds of our countrymen a feeling of prejudice against those who have resolved to emigrate from a colony where they have experienced for so many years past a series of the most vexatious and severe losses; and as we desire to stand high in the estimation of our brethren, and are anxious that they and the world at large should believe us incapable of severing that sacred tie which binds a Christian to his native soil, without the most sufficient reasons, we are induced to record the following summary of our motives for taking so important a step . . .

1. We despair of saving the colony from those evils which threaten it by the turbulent and dishonest conduct of vagrants, who are allowed to infest the country in every part; nor do we see prospect of peace and happiness for our children in a country thus distracted by internal commotion.

2. We complain of the severe losses which we have been forced to sustain by the emancipation of our slaves, and the vexatious laws which have been enacted respecting them.

3. We complain of the continual system of plunder which we have ever endured from the Kafirs and other coloured classes, and particularly by the last invasion of the colony, which has desolated the frontier districts, and ruined most of the inhabitants.

4. We complain of the unjustifiable odium which has been cast upon us by interested and dishonest persons, under the cloak of religion, whose testimony is believed in England to the exclusion of all evidence in our favour; and we can foresee as the result of this prejudice, nothing but the total ruin of the country.

5. We are resolved, wherever we go, that we will uphold the just principles of liberty; but whilst we will take care that no one shall be held in a state of slavery, it is our determination to maintain such regulations as many suppress crime and preserve the proper relations between master and servant.

6. We solemnly declare that we quit this colony with a desire to lead a more quiet life than we have heretofore done. We will not molest any people, nor deprive them of the smallest property; but if attacked, we shall consider ourselves fully justified in defending our persons and effects, to the utmost of our ability, against every enemy.

7. We make known, that when we shall have framed a code of laws for our future guidance, copies shall be forwarded to the colony for general information; but we take this opportunity of stating, that it is our firm resolve to make provision for the summary punishment of any traitors who may be found amongst us.

8.   We purpose, in the course of our journey, and on arriving at the country in which we shall permanently reside, to make known to the native tribes our intentions, and our desire to live in peace and friendly intercourse with them.

9.   We quit this colony under the full assurance that the English government has nothing more to require of us, and will allow us to govern ourselves without its interference in future.

10.   We are now quitting the fruitful land of our birth, in which we have suffered enormous losses and continual vexation, and are entering a wild and dangerous territory; but we go with a firm reliance on an all-seeing, just, and merciful Being, whom it will be our endeavour to fear and humbly to obey.

Without wishing to insult a national hero, I must confess that it strikes me as much the kind of document – the same arch phraseology, the same holier-than-thou morality, the same naïve pretence at 'diplomacy' – the South African government has so often submitted to the UN in defence of a new raid into a neighbouring country or a new set of repressive measures.

It is unlikely that a young woman like Hendrina, weighed down by anxiety about what she'd undertaken, and bearing alone the burden of her pregnancy, would have discussed the terms of the document with Retief: though he was known as an amiable and sympathetic man, she would have been in awe of him; even had she ventured to voice misgivings or a simple question, he would no doubt have replied, as he so often did to others, 'Don't worry, child. Leave it to me. God is on our side.'

Perhaps he needed that reassurance as much as she or anyone else on the Trek: it was a journey hazardous enough to tax the faith of a saint. If, as he often insisted, they had left Pharaoh's house of bondage behind, the Promised Land continued to elude them. Beyond the Orange River a vast expanse of territory had already been occupied by the half-blood Griqua people who regarded the Trekkers with mistrust and not without disdain. So the newcomers had to move on into a strangely desolate land littered with the bones of cattle and people. Here and there were scattered black tribes; the devastation in between did not mean that the land was uninhabited, only that the threshing wind of the *mfecane*, the great black diaspora, had passed through it, caused mainly by the belligerent convulsions of the great Zulu empire on the east coast of Natal, through which communities that had been settled inland for centuries were uprooted. On the hilltops, on the distant mountains, as the string of wagons and the vast herds of cattle moved slowly into the interior, there were fire signals by night; patrols on horseback would glimpse by day small groups of black herdsmen or scouts in the distance, but on approaching they would be gone. Always the uneasy awareness of being watched, unremittingly, by an invisible, hostile adversary: as if the land itself was shrinking back from the intruders. For what to them was an excursion, must have appeared a dangerous incursion to those already there. And however sincere their intentions may have been, there was menace in their mere presence, as they trekked, unwittingly, through a landscape already shaped in song and myth – like that other, earlier, one through which a century before the savage Diederik Landman had lumbered towards his destiny.

Feeling threatened, no doubt, by everything that might follow in the wake of this incursion, blacks living near the confluence of the Limpopo and the Olifants River massacred the vanguard of the Trek, led by Hans van Rensburg, in July 1837; to avoid a similar fate, the second group, Tregardt's, swerved eastward, towards Delagoa Bay where, decimated by malaria and yellow fever, the last few remnants arrived a year later. By that time Potgieter had already called a halt in northern 'Transorangia', near the Vet River, on a stretch of land bought from the Bataung, an arrangement that angered the Ndebele in the north and resulted in an attack on the Trekker laager at Vegkop. The outcome was a military victory for the Boers, but in the process they lost a number of lives (duly recorded separately as '20 Christian' and '26 coloured'), as well as a hundred horses, almost five thousand cattle and a staggering fifty thousand sheep and goats. Fortunately for them, the Maritz trek from Graaff-Reinet arrived soon afterwards and a punitive expedition of Boer, Barolong and Griqua soldiers was mounted against the Ndebele in the north, bringing back one and a half times as many cattle as had been driven away.

Having temporarily subdued the threat from outside, the Trekkers promptly turned on each other in what became an endless petty drama of internal squabbles: these were the circumstances in which Retief arrived among them in April 1837. In electing him as 'Governor and Commander-in-chief' they managed temporarily to suspend the internal strife, but all too soon it flared up again, aggravated by the arrival of yet another clan, that of Piet Uys and his son Jacobus. From that moment onwards there would be brief moments of respite – as in the particularly beautiful spring month of October, when for obscure and ominous reasons yet another military expedition, this time wholly unprovoked, was mounted against the distant Ndebele, driving them far beyond the Limpopo – but these were the exception, not the rule.

The baby Petrus Landman lost his mother when he was barely seven months old.

Piet Retief had firmly set his mind on the territory of Natal as the Canaan to which, as the elect man of God, he was destined to lead his people. Resolved to do so peacefully, he persuaded King Dingane of the Zulu nation – 'clothed in a splendid robe of various colours, black, red, and white, in broad stripes, from the top to the bottom', wrote the missionary Owen who was involved in the negotiations – to promise him a tract of land in Natal (as it happened, this was land already ceded to British immigrants in Port Natal), on the condition that Retief first retrieve some cattle allegedly stolen from Dingane by a petty chief called Sikonyela. So certain was Retief of the outcome that he'd given his followers permission to descend into Natal from the Drakensberg, and by the time he left for Sikonyela's seat in November 1937 well over a thousand wagons had already moved into the Zulu pastures. This must have caused Dingane some alarm, all the more so as he'd already received a 'tactful' reminder from Retief about what had happened to the Ndebele who had incurred the Trekkers' wrath ('From God's great Book we learn that kings, who do such things are severely punished and not suffered to live and reign').

The cattle were brought back, but Sikonyela was allowed to go free after he'd been manacled for a while to humiliate him properly – another source of annoyance to Dingane, who'd wanted to deal with the alleged thief himself. Retief had planned to return to the Great Place of the Zulu king with a great show of force for the final signing of the treaty, but misgivings among most of the Boers about the wisdom of such a demonstration resulted in a mere hundred men ('servants' included, as always) accompanying him to Ngungundhlovu. In the midst of an impressive show of war dances arranged to celebrate the occasion, Dingane suddenly shouted that fateful command that still reverberates through the Afrikaner consciousness – *'Bulalani abatagati!* Kill the wizards!' – and all the visitors were massacred on the knoll of Hlomo Amabutho, habitually referred to by my father as 'the Golgotha of our nation'.

Within hours, impis counting thousands of men erupted from Ngungundhlovu and began to spread like lava across the green hills of Zululand towards the whole wide land already dotted by the white-hooded wagons of the Trekkers, some arranged in circular laagers, others encamped peacefully at Bloukrans and other outspans beside the many streams of the Tugela. Hendrina Landman was among the hundreds of white and 'coloured' men, women and children massacred in their sleep during the night of 16/17 February 1838. Her baby escaped quite miraculously, shielded it seemed by the massive State Bible with which the mother tried to fend off an assegai: deflected, it entered just below the child's left clavicle, missing the heart; he must have lost consciousness, leading their assailant to believe that both mother and child were dead. The lower right-hand corner of our family bible's solid binding still bears the dark stain of their blood. It was, as it were, the little creature's second death: there were several more to come.

In a sorry state, and not really expected to survive, he was adopted by a Greyling woman – presumably another distant relation of Hendrina's – who had lost her own baby in the massacre; in the midst of so much suffering it must have come as some relief to her aching swollen breasts to suckle the poor little mite.

It was a year of blood and battles, some lost, some won; culminating on Sunday, 16 December 1838. On the previous Sunday, their fifty-seven wagons lashed together in a laager on the Wasbank – the stream where the washing was done – a commando of Trekkers had held a service where a vow was taken that if God granted them victory over the Zulus, 'we should note the day of the victory in a book, to make it known even to our latest posterity, so that it might be celebrated to the Honour of God'.

Exactly one week later, on the bank of the Ncome River – soon to be renamed Blood River – four hundred and sixty-eight Boers, with their servants and some sixty black allies, repelled a Zulu force estimated at ten thousand, of which three thousand were killed; within the laager there were no casualties, only three lightly wounded. I can still recite by heart the purple passages in which our history books at school recounted the event. And how well I remember the solemnity with which my father would intone a prayer every year on the Day of the Covenant, praising the Lord that He had truly intervened on the side of the Afrikaner on that miraculous day: what he did not mention, possibly because he was unaware of it, was that the great majority of Trekkers who had made the vow had themselves quietly forgotten about it for the next quarter of a century – until it was deliberately revived to bolster a new sense of nationalism in the Transvaal.

By then young Petrus Landman had also arrived in the Transvaal, after a long detour through the Transorangia territory. He was of course too young to have been personally involved in the events of the time, but his daily contact with a particularly pious group of people who reacted very emotionally to every new convulsion of history must have left on his mind a scar as indelible as the mark of the Zulu assegai which had caused a permanent droop of the left shoulder. These people were the Greylings, the Enslins, the Gouses and others, who were among the first Trekkers to leave Natal when, soon after settling their scores with the Zulus, they found themselves once more confronted by their old enemies, the British. Even before the territory was formally annexed by the Cape governor in 1843, these clans had begun to trek back across the Drakensberg into the grasslands of southern Transorangia which had seemed like El Dorado long before Retief had persuaded them to move on.

As it turned out, it was a mere interval, no final destination. For the Griqua farmers in the territory, apprehensive about the threat of Boers encroaching on their grazing, appealed to the Cape Colony for help; and after a humiliating defeat in battle the Boers were forced to acquiesce, once more, in British rule in what was now the Orange River Sovereignty. Once again the wagons were loaded and the Trekkers moved north. But this time, at least in the group where Petrus Landman found himself, it was different. These people were no longer on the move merely to remain out of reach of the British: they had begun, quite literally, to set their sights on Jerusalem as their true destination.

A halt was called in the Northern Transvaal, in the district of Marico: but they all knew it would be only temporary, a period of rest, a recovery from fatigue, a mustering of forces, before they would set out again on the remaining stretch through Africa to the Promised Land. With deadly, almost terrifying seriousness, Petrus would record many years later the impression made on his youthful mind by the pictures of Jerusalem the 'prophetess' of the group, the redoubtable Tant Mieta Gous, showed him in her extraordinary Picture Bible. What they were after, he notes with disarming simplicity, was not the New Jerusalem, the city of God, the true destination of all devout Christians, but the real city, situated in that land flowing with milk and honey from which Joshuah and Caleb had brought back those enormous bunches of grapes, truly a Lotos land, 'without English, without taxes, and with very little work'. (He'd copied most of those pictures from the old lady's Bible on to paper; and where there were no originals, he imagined them: even as a small child he'd shown unusual talent as a draughtsman.) He recalled a surveyor, a Mr de Kok, who had visited the area and who had tried to explain to the 'Jerusalem Trekkers', as they called themselves, how impossible such a journey would be – seven or eight or ten times as much as the distance from Cape Town to Marico, through territories infested with malaria and tsetse flies, cold and heat, impenetrable marshes, rivers, deserts, the Red Sea itself – and even if they did manage to reach Palestine, he pointed out, they might be massacred by Arabs.

Petrus records that no one was put off by these dire warnings. The inhabitants of Marico were convinced that Mr de Kok must have been mistaken about the distance; not even Africa could be so big. Anyway, they were in no hurry: it had taken Moses forty years to reach the land of Canaan, why should they expect to do it in less? If there were flooded rivers on their way, they would find a ford, or wait six months or more for the waters to subside; in the desert God would provide, as He had for the Israelites; on the coast of the Red Sea there would undoubtedly be skiffs or boats on which to row across. And if Arabs and other (undoubtedly black) Canaanites awaited them on the other side, so let it be: surely they could not shoot as well as the Jerusalem Trekkers. As for tsetse flies, Tant Mieta Gous said haughtily, they were the least of their worries: she had personally concocted a brew of cramp-drops and rue which spelled death to any insect, crawling or flying.

On her farm Tant Mieta Gous began to assemble wagons, oxen and provisions, patiently preparing for the exodus. Ironically, just about that time, in 1852, after considerable wrangling, Britain did acknowledge the independence of the Transvaal (followed soon afterwards by that of the Orange Free State): but in the Marico district no one trusted the word of an Englishman. Tant Mieta Gous swept up the emotions of her fanatic band, their leader Jan Adam Enslin inspired them with accounts of visions of divers angels and other heavenly emissaries, and at last the trek to Jerusalem began. Within days they made a momentous discovery: to them the Magalakwena, a tributary of the Limpopo, was none

763

other than the River Nile itself. Truly wonderful are the ways of the Lord: they need but follow its course and they would arrive in the Promised Land. It happened even sooner than they had expected, for to the north-east of the spot where the village of Nylstroom was later founded, they witnessed from afar a steep conical hill like the base of a ziggurat, and knew immediately that it was a pyramid.

In his memoirs, Petrus is – understandably – reticent about the sequel. Within weeks, if not days, the trek was stopped in its tracks by the ravages of malaria. (Curious that such fanatically devout people should not have seen the hand of God in this.) Jan Enslin and eighteen of his relatives died on the spot, with more than a hundred others, including both Petrus Landman's foster-parents. (Petrus himself was found, in a state of delirium, among five dead bodies. According to his own report, so much later, his grave had already been dug by the time he made an incredible recovery. His third death.) It was a rout. In a laconic observation a contemporary issue of *The Graham's Town Journal* reported that if there had indeed been a trek, it was 'trekking from fear of the plague'.

There were some diehards who tried again, later: this time, wisely, no longer in search of Jerusalem, but on a devastating westward journey through the thirstland into the upper regions of today's Namibia, and even into Angola. But Petrus Landman – only fifteen at the time of his third death – was spared that bleak adventure. I have been unable to establish how or why, or even exactly when, it happened, but Petrus was removed, presumably by caring relatives or friends of the Greylings, to Lydenburg in the eastern Transvaal; and some years later, again without explanation, he found himself in Potchefstroom, adrift and penniless and alone, his only recorded possessions – his only links with his long past – that excessively ornate mirror we know so well by now, and the bible stained with his own blood.

In many respects the desperate situation in which Petrus found himself was but a reflection of the general misery and chaos in the Transvaal: dirt-poor, unorganised, largely lawless, with no sense of unity or direction. True, the Trekkers had established a *Volksraad* or National Assembly which had even adopted something resembling a constitution, known as the Forty-three Articles: but it was a peripatetic body more often ignored and even defied than acknowledged; the infighting characteristic of the whole Trek persisted, and in the large new territory claimed by the emigrants small concentrations of Boers in different regions clustered round their old leaders, with great tracts of almost unpopulated land separating them. If this imposed a geographic limitation on the possibilities of friction it also strengthened suspicions and animosities (on more than one occasion commandos from different clans actually engaged in battle), while exposing each isolated group to raids and attacks from black communities who felt themselves more and more threatened by these invaders.

During the period of the Great Trek proper, in the spirit of Retief's Manifesto, attempts had at least been made to find *some* allies among the indigenous peoples; to obtain land through treaty or barter; not to subject blacks to slavery. But in the Transvaal a different attitude became prevalent (although I'm writing this as a 'Capey', with an innate diffidence towards my compatriots from the more northern provinces, I really am trying to be fair!): unprovoked attacks, the forceful evacuation of land one coveted for oneself, and a system of forced labour, involving especially black children captured on raids, became prevalent in many areas. Such practices were exacerbated by the dire poverty in which so many of the people subsisted, causing them to feel threatened on the most basic level of their existence, and driving them back to the tooth-and-nail laws of the jungle, or the eye-for-an-eye law of the Old Testament. It must have seemed, many times, like a society subsiding slowly into a morass of pettiness, suspicion, viciousness, indolence and despair. Perhaps a century of deprivation and isolation in the deep heart of the country had been too much: they had become a race of angry and indigent individuals incapable of living within the give-and-take framework of organised society.

In such circumstances only exceptional factors might change the whole direction of such a community and act upon it as a unifying force: two such factors would be a great common threat from outside, and the appearance of a charismatic and forceful leader. In the case of the Transvaal both occurred. But only after years of confusion.

By the time Petrus Landman turned up in Potchefstroom, which temporarily seemed to have gained the edge over Soutpansberg, Rustenburg, the Magaliesberg region around Pretoria, and Lydenburg/ Ohrigstad as a centre of influence, the general situation, like his own, was still both fluid and depressing. He appears to have made a precarious living out of his pictures: illuminated texts, or scenes meticulously drawn or painted from his memories of Tant Mieta's Picture Bible, or from his dreams; invariably they were of a religious nature, although occasionally he did paint a remembered or imagined incident from the Great Trek. He was haunted by Blood River; even in scenes of Canaan his rivers would always be a lurid red. Only five or six of his pictures, as far as I know, have survived: they have a naïve, even primitive, charm; in their cloying sentimentality they are embarrassing, yet – especially if one looks at them with the prejudiced mind of a descendant – there is a certain visionary quality, a Blakean streak, in the best of them which I find quite disturbing. It is a quality that became evident only later in his life, but with hindsight it is not difficult to recognise signs of it much earlier: in his obsession with dreams; his fondness – even in his youth – for 'explaining' the bible, especially the Book of Revelation; in his gift as a diviner: of water, of bones, or of minerals. (It was even rumoured in later years that he'd 'seen' the gold of the Witwatersrand long before it was mined; but that no one had paid attention.)

Once, when a small child had disappeared on a farm, Petrus heard about it at *nagmaal*, where it was the main topic of conversation. He listened to the avid discussion in some perplexity, and at last ventured to ask, 'But why has no one looked in the *donga* behind Oom Wynand's sheep kraal?'

'What would he be doing there?' asked the father, annoyed.

'He fell in when he went after the little jackal cub that ran away,' said Petrus.

'How do you know?' the father sneered.

'I saw him there.'

'This is no time for jokes,' someone grumbled angrily.

After they'd hauled the child from the ditch, Petrus was questioned more closely. But all he could offer in explanation was that he'd 'seen it in the mirror'. What mirror? The one in his room, he said. (At the time, he was lodging with a pious widow who accepted pictures in lieu of money; her walls were covered with them.)

From that day, he was treated with some respect; and whenever a farmer in the district lost some sheep or cattle, Petrus would be consulted. Provided he was in the 'mood', for he was known as a whimsical young fellow, he would divulge what, if anything, he'd seen in his mirror. He was never wrong. And it was the widow who insisted that he be given a reward every time he'd found something; soon he had the beginnings of a flock of his own.

It went beyond that. One Sunday morning he suddenly ran out of his room, saddled his horse, and rode out to a farm two hours'

766

distance away from town: he hardly knew the people, and they were surprised to see him at all, let alone in such a hurry. He seemed somewhat embarrassed himself as he tried to explain that he'd just come to say goodbye to the farmer's oldest son, Dries, a burly young man in his early twenties.

'But why should you want to say goodbye to me?' asked Dries with a touch of aggression. 'I'm not going anywhere.'

'Yes, you are,' said Petrus. 'Only you don't know about it yet.'

'Get off this farm!' shouted the young man. 'You're just wanting to stir up trouble. It must be old Koot Vermaak who sent you.'

'No one sent me. I saw your face in the mirror this morning when I got up.'

Dries went into the house to fetch his gun; his father restrained him, but Petrus was forced to get on his horse and ride back to Potchefstroom. The following day news came that Dries Vorster had died from the bite of a mamba.

Some people began to accuse him of being an agent of the Devil. Fortunately these rumours were scotched when he married Susanna, the daughter of a predikant. There was something weird about this too. One morning he just turned up at Dominee Greeff's house and asked to see Susanna, whom he'd never met before; and when she appeared, visibly on the defensive (Petrus was not a particularly handsome man), he said without further ado, 'Look, Susanna, we're going to get married, so can't we just arrange it and have done with it?'

'What?' she gasped. 'You must be mad.' She flashed a ring. 'Anyway, I'm already engaged to Freek Britz.'

'I know,' he said impatiently. 'But you're not going to marry him. So why not save yourself a lot of tears and trouble and say yes to me?'

He was not allowed to wait for an answer. Family tradition has it that several copper and iron cooking utensils Susanna had been hoarding for her marriage were hurled after him as he ran off in a cloud of dust. If any member of the Greeff household, mindful of Petrus Landman's reputation, had felt reservations about her impending wedding to Freek Britz, these were dispelled as the preparations progressed, the banns were read, and the reception planned. On the eve of the wedding the bridegroom's parents and a host of merrymaking relatives arrived from Rustenburg; they caroused until daybreak, and then returned to their wagons to put on their Sunday clothes for the service which was to begin at nine.

A prancing procession on horseback escorted the bridegroom to the church. Along the way, a few geese, scared by a barking dog, swooped across the street with fluttering wings and necks outstretched, cackling like mad. The bridegroom's horse reared up, the young man was thrown, landing with his head against a stone, and died three days later without having regained consciousness.

It would have been fascinating to follow the progress of Petrus's wooing of the grief-stricken bride, but unfortunately nothing more has been recorded. All that is known is that they did get married less than a year later, in 1865, and that their oldest son, Gabriel (the name is significant), was born in 1867, the first of seven children. As Petrus galloped off into the night to fetch the midwife – the child was a fortnight early – his horse trod in an aardvark hole and fell heavily, landing on top of his master.

The animal returned home riderless, but Petrus was not found until next morning, after Susanna had already given birth unassisted. She seemed none the worse for wear, but Petrus only came round seventy-six hours later: exactly the time that had elapsed, several people pointed out, between her first bridegroom's accident and his death. ('God doesn't sleep,' some remarked; and would have crossed themselves had they not been such devout Calvinists.) In fact, some of the eager laymen who attended to Petrus swore afterwards that his heart had stopped beating for some time. If so – and who am I to doubt their word? – it would have been the fourth death of Petrus Landman. As if in corroboration, he produced quite a body of paintings in the following months depicting scenes from the hereafter he said he'd witnessed with his own eyes – though there were some who averred that most of them bore a striking resemblance to images from the Picture Bible (except for the addition of Blood River, and the Transvaal *vierkleur*, which featured so prominently in his work).

It was in 1877 that a new phase in the life of my strange ancestor began. First, Susanna died. (They were living in Rustenburg at the time, but she was away from home on a visit to her ageing parents in Potchefstroom, taking with her the three youngest children; when he looked into his ancestral mirror on New Year's morning to comb his beard – he had no more hair – Petrus saw, not his own face, but Susanna's; and promptly collected the older children, put them on a horse-cart, and drove to Potchefstroom in time for the funeral.) It was a heavy blow, for in spite of its inauspicious beginning theirs had been a good marriage; but he'd always made provision for death, so the damage was not irreparable. Much more portentous was the vision he saw, in the same mirror, barely a fortnight later, when the archangel Gabriel appeared to him draped in the British flag.

One might think that it did not require an archangel to predict an imminent British annexation of the Transvaal. (In any case, both family and strangers demanded to know, how had he recognised Gabriel? Because he'd met him before, he answered very simply. It is enough to make the imagination run riot. Suppose it had been the archangel who'd initially announced the birth of their first child, duly named after him? But I prefer not to pursue such blasphemous possibilities.) The imperialist threat to the shaky little republic had been building up for some time. The proud BaPedi nation of Chief Sekhukhune in the north, often victorious in previous skirmishes with the Boers, had recently come under increasing military pressure and had appealed to Britain for help. In Natal, the Zulus had been urging the British for some time to aid them against the Swazis, their traditional enemy and an ally of the Transvaal (in fact, Swaziland had been annexed by the Transvaal to move a step closer to the sea). From London, via Cape Town, attempts had been mounted to move towards a federation of all the states in Southern Africa under British rule. Above all, alluvial gold had been discovered in the Eastern Transvaal in the Seventies; and if the Empire could afford to ignore a strife-ridden Boer republic while it was poor, the possibility of untold riches kindled the good old mercenary spirit that underlies so many noble and philanthropic endeavours. (Britain had by then already brazenly recovered the south-western territory of the Orange Free State after the discovery of diamonds.)

Transvaal really was ripe for the plucking, all the more so as its president – the remarkable, liberal-minded, erudite Thomas Francois Burgers, who was desperately trying to drag his recalcitrant people into a modern age – had lost the support of almost all the Boers. (Significantly, even the charismatic and ferociously pious military leader, Commandant Paul Kruger, had resigned his position as he refused to serve under an 'unbelieving' president.)

So it should have surprised no one when on 22 January 1877 Sir Theophilus Shepstone from Natal, on behalf of Great Britain, marched into the Transvaal with a force of exactly thirty-three men (twenty-five police and eight civil servants) and, after tedious discussions that lasted until April, hoisted the Union Jack in Pretoria, which had become the capital some years earlier.

Yet it would seem that very few inside the Transvaal had really expected the move. Not that it prompted any immediate or widespread reaction: such was the level of the continuing internecine strife that it took almost four years for the Republic to mount a response. But it was four decisive years in which much of the future character of the Afrikaner people was determined; and for Petrus Landman it was the busiest and undoubtedly the most 'successful' period of his life. Previously his wife Susanna had had a calming and restraining influence on him; and he himself had not shown much ambition. But now Susanna was dead. (Her parents assumed responsibility for the rearing of the children; and because they were too old to take an active interest in education, this was largely left to some of the new Dutch teachers imported by the liberal President Burgers. Thus the ground was prepared for a future angry clash between Petrus and his eldest son.) Petrus was free to move about and spread the news of his visions. Certainly, reports of that famous apparition of the archangel Gabriel ensured him a notoriety he had never experienced before. In the past, few people had paid much attention to his obsession with Blood River and the Trek; now, all of a sudden, he found fallow ground for his ideas, confused and hesitant as they may have been.

Of course, his voice was but one – and not by any stretch of the imagination the most noticeable – among many. Ever since 1865 the Transvaal government had celebrated 16 December as a public holiday; but it was only after the annexation of 1877 that the Covenant was suddenly resurrected and incorporated in the solemn commemoration of that victory. According to the historian D. W. Kruger, this was first done at Paardekraal in December 1881, at a ceremony attended by some fifteen thousand people, 'by piling a cairn of stones, symbolising both past and future: the past because the covenant had freed them from black domination, and the future because they saw it as a sign that they would continue fighting until they regained their independence from the British imperialists.'

At the same time, the disorganised and haphazard episode of the Great Trek was reviewed, to be reshaped into the divinely inspired tale of a people elected by God, a new Israel led from their house of bondage to their own new Canaan. Petrus, of course, had grown up with these views; but the Jerusalem Trekkers had been frowned on as an extremist sect by most other Boers, and it was only after the shock of annexation that those others discovered its mythic relevance.

Petrus thrived. Never in his life had he painted so much; there were more orders than he could handle in a lifetime. His visions were in great demand as well, to underpin the new gospel preached from pulpits and at political gatherings. One day none less than Freek Bezuidenhout appeared to him in his mirror to demand vengeance from beyond the bloody graves of Slagtersnek. His much more cynical son Gabriel later noted it as his conviction that his father had never even heard of Slagtersnek before: it had become submerged as a minor accident of history until, in that interregnum of fear and anger following annexation, its potential as anti-British propaganda was rediscovered. In 1868 a play about the episode was performed in Cape Town; news about it spread first to the Orange Free State, then further north. And in the fateful year of 1877 the Rev. S. J. du Toit of Paarl, in the first history book published in the infantile Afrikaans language, exploited the full potential of the episode. So it was already 'in the air' by the time Petrus was inspired to interview Bezuidenhout in his mirror.

I have no wish to discredit my enterprising ancestor by casting doubt on the originality – or the effects – of his thinking. I am only trying to place him in the context of his confused time: after years of obscurity and not a little bit of ridicule, suddenly history afforded him the resonance previously denied him. A greater, or more unscrupulous, man would undoubtedly have profited spectacularly from the opportunity, would have became truly famous as a prophet. That even in these ideal circumstances Petrus Landman achieved no more than a relative notoriety points, sadly, to his overall insignificance. Which stands in contrast to the revered position this Seer has always occupied in the private history of my family.

Slowly, but very surely, a defiant new sense of national unity forged all the disparate and turbulent factions in the Transvaal together; and with an impressive new leader in their midst, Paul Kruger, the ebullient little republic dared to challenge the full power of Great Britain in war. For at least a year, after all attempts to negotiate a peaceful settlement had failed, everybody had seen it coming. But inevitably Petrus announced it in his own way. In his mirror, he informed the people, he had seen the archangel Michael in full military dress, bandolier over the shoulder, Mauser in hand, brandishing the Transvaal four-colour flag, announcing his decision to do battle against the Forces of Evil. That was on 'Dingaan's Day',

1880. And it did have an inspiring effect on those close to him, if not so much on others.

The First War of Independence did not last very long. Within a month or two the British garrisons stationed in the larger Transvaal towns had been subdued; and troops massing in Natal for a march on the rebellious territory were humiliated at Laing's Nek and Ingogo; on 27 February 1881 the combined British forces led by General Sir George Colley suffered the final crushing defeat on the hill of Majuba. Ninety-two British soldiers, including Colley himself, died; among the Boers there were, officially, two dead and four wounded. But to their number should be added Petrus Landman, who in his own way also died at Majuba.

He was not hit by a bullet, but died of pneumonia, contracted during an unexpectedly cold, wet spell in early February; he had been advised to stay home, but angrily persisted that the archangel Michael had personally summoned him to the battle. Presumably it was the intercession of Michael, too, which restored him to life after the *veldpredikant*, Vosloo, had already said a last prayer over the wasted body.

Content that he had done his bit for freedom, the resurrected Petrus retired to the Rustenburg farm which, after many years as a *bywoner*, he had finally acquired as his own (with the generous help of his older children, it should be added). The only noteworthy event from the following fifteen or sixteen years of his life, before he finally went out with a curious combination of bang and whimper, was the unfortunate quarrel with his son Gabriel who had returned to Rustenburg in the late Eighties as a teacher. (In those times it was not unusual for youngsters with a mere smattering of education to be appointed teachers.)

Inspired by the new ideas introduced by the Dutch teachers, Gabriel caused quite a sensation in his small community when it became known that he was trying to persuade his pupils that the earth was spherical and turned round the sun. Humiliated that his son could expose his stupidity so publicly – surely anyone could see with his own eyes that it was the sun that turned, not the earth – Petrus first tried to reason privately with his eldest. When that had no effect, the mirror was called to witness. The archangel after whom Gabriel himself had been named intervened personally to confirm the motion of this 'little remote and forever wandering star'. Young Gabriel paid no heed. Old Petrus himself

772

laid the matter before the church council. Gabriel was suspended, pending a full enquiry and consultations with neighbouring church councils. In the end, consensus was reached, and the decision of the elders can still be consulted – written in an elegant and flourishing hand, in High Dutch, and signed by all twelve members and the predikant:

'*Vanaf heeden zult de aarde niet meer draaijen* – From this day forth the earth shall turn no more.'

Gabriel resigned his post and left the district. He never saw his father again. And Petrus, vindicated but deeply saddened, all but disappeared from public sight.

It was becoming clear that it was only a matter of time before Britain would move to repossess the Transvaal, a territory thrown open to fortune-seekers from all over the world after the discovery of the fabulously rich gold reef of the Witwatersrand. These *uitlanders*, denied citizenship by the increasingly intransigent President Kruger who saw in their demands the prelude to the loss of his republic, became more and more influential in their representations to the British government; while Cecil John Rhodes, dreaming his imperial dreams, more and more saw in the Transvaal the major obstacle on a British route from Cape to Cairo. Even to non-seers the signs were ominous. To Petrus those last few years of his life were spent in increasing distress, aggravated by the fact that his health had deteriorated to the point where he was almost permanently bedridden. That was when he saw his final vision: a vision so resplendent, and so awe-inspiring, that it left him half-blind and nearly cost him his life. When two of his daughters finally brought him round after they'd found him slumped to the floor in front of the prophetic mirror, he told them in a whisper that God Himself had appeared to him. At least, that was what he deduced from the brilliance of the light that had suddenly appeared in the glass. It was, he said, as if he'd stared into a deep well of absolute light, a hole of dazzling brightness that had opened up in the mirror and sucked him into its vortex: so unbearably intense had it been that the very mirror had been cracked by it.

His son Gabriel noted afterwards that his enquiries had brought to light that the crack had been caused by a servant who'd dusted the mirror so vigorously that it had fallen from its nail; fearing the consequences, she hadn't told a soul but had simply hung the broken thing back on the wall. But we must remember that Gabriel had reason to slander his poor father; and how could he have persuaded the woman to confide in him what she'd been too scared to breathe to anybody else?

Disregarding the warnings of his daughters, Petrus rose from his bed, ordered his one-horse carriage to be inspanned, and rode to town to mount a commando. He needed thirty-three men, he said, the exact number that had accompanied Shepstone on that ignominious day almost twenty years earlier, to ride forth and annex the whole of Southern Africa for the Transvaal: that was the only way to rid the subcontinent of the Antichrist.

He had considerable trouble persuading the people of Rustenburg of the authority of his message; but once he'd collected five or six young adventurers they were sent out to other parts of the country, and after about six months Petrus had his little commando equipped to ride out towards Armaggedon. They met no resistance on their way. Sorry to say, most people regarded them as a joke. Still, they pressed on, southward, Cape Town their destination.

Not far from Bloemfontein, with perhaps half of their apocalyptic journey behind them, Petrus Landman one night died quietly in his sleep: his poor old body simply could not bear it any longer. This time nothing could revive him. And the members of his commando, possibly more relieved than perturbed, buried him under a thorn-tree, marked the grave with a cairn of stones, and rode back to where they'd come from.

Petrus Landman had finally seen his own hole.

Gabriel Landman

(1867–1911)

If many of my ancestors did little to enhance the reputation of our rude guardian angel in Africa, Gabriel's life does seem to me to recapture something of Adamastor's essential quest: to rid the land of those who merely come to rob or rule; to preserve an angry freedom which is not defined in any manifesto of human rights but which is as ancient and inalienable as the cry of a hadeda or the arc described by the horns of an oryx defending its calf against a predator.

Perhaps this impression is the simple result of the fact that Gabriel left behind a more extensive and more personal record of his life – or at least of one vital period from it, the Anglo-Boer War – than any of my other ancestors. Jan-Jonas had left behind, apart from his broken, pitifully defiant walls in the wilderness, those few cryptic, agonising comments in the margins of our family Bible; his daughter scribbled random memories in a small notebook; Petrus marked the binding of our Bible with his blood, and there is, of course, that eloquent crack in the mirror. But what – apart from some traces in the records of others, a granddaughter, a cousin, a neighbour, a British settler – have the rest of them left behind? Their names and dates inscribed laboriously on the open pages following Revelation in the Bible; here and there the name of a farm – *Rust-mijn-ziel* ('Rest-my-soul'), *Wag-'n-bietjie* ('Wait-a-while'), *Verlatefontein* ('Desolate Fountain'), *Drogeputs* ('Dry Well') – but that is all. But Gabriel handed down to posterity a whole book, an old-fashioned, foolscap-size *Minute Book* bound in faded, marbled black, with a frayed red leather spine, 193 ruled pages filled with his meticulous handwriting, and dedicated on the front endpaper 'To My Children Hannes and Pieter'. It is dated August 1903, but it is clear that this must have been a 'clean' manuscript based on a journal kept throughout the war. (There are several references to his comrades teasing him about making his copious notes while everyone else was waiting for the enemy to attack; and once, after being forced to evacuate a camp near Belfast, he rode back under heavy fire to retrieve his journal and, incidentally, to save a wounded friend.) And I must confess that, no matter how decisively I myself have broken out of the Afrikaner laager, and how cynical I am about the notions of volk and fatherland, when I read my great-grandfather's account of the war I feel an atavistic resentment of the English rekindled in my guts. I am not proud of it. But I am forced to reacknowledge how difficult it is to rid oneself of the frightful conditionings of one's youth.

(At the same time the feeling is complicated by the discovery that those attitudes and actions of the English that provoked the deepest resentment among Boers are identical to the attitudes and actions of 'my own' people, today's Afrikaners, which have prompted the revolt of my black compatriots, and which have turned *me* into an activist.)

After his mother's death in 1877, Gabriel had seen his father only sporadically, as he and his six siblings were brought up by their maternal grandparents. In due course one of his brothers, Johannes, got married and took charge of the Rustenburg farm while the old man spent his time hallucinating; his twin sisters, Gertruida and Wilhelmina, also moved in with their father to take care of him when his health deteriorated (which must have been the main reason neither of them ever got married); the oldest sister, Elisabet, married a young Dutch lawyer and moved to Bloemfontein; and the two youngest brothers, Lodewyk and Hermaans, were employed by the post office in Pretoria. Gabriel, as we know, returned to Rustenburg as a teacher, but left in disgust after the clash with his father about the Copernican behaviour of the planet earth; and after failing to secure another teaching post (even the cantankerous old President of the Republic believed in a flat earth, so redress was ruled out), he took a position as clerk in a Boksburg mine. After a few years, just after he'd married Carolina Henning, on the day of her eighteenth birthday, he was promoted to paymaster.

His relationship with Carolina must rate as one of the true love-stories of our family history. She had been a mere child when he became her teacher in the little school in Rustenburg; in fact, she'd just turned fourteen when he was forced by the church council to resign. It is said that she came to him in tears while he was packing his books at the end of his last day in school, begging him to stay on, even if it meant changing his mind about the earth and the sun. He was moved by the lovely child's emotional outburst, but explained that it was quite out of the question to retract.

'But I love you!' she burst out, clinging to him, sobbing.

He tried his best to calm her down: he must have realised that things really would look bad for him if the two of them were caught like that, embracing in the classroom. But nothing could restrain Carolina. 'I love you, I love you, I love you, I want to marry you,' she insisted.

'Look,' he said in the end, gently pulling up her head by the two long blonde pigtails, 'you're only fourteen. I'm ten years older than you. By the time you're ready to marry you'll be the most beautiful girl in the country, you'll be able to pick and choose, you won't even give me another look.'

'I'll wait for you,' she promised.

He tried another approach: 'Your father will kill you. He'll kill both of us. He's on the church council. He's the richest farmer in the district. When the time comes he'll want you to marry someone more suitable than an out-of-work teacher.'

'He'll never force me to marry against my will, he loves me.' One can picture the defiance in her dark blue eyes, still bright with tears. 'And if he says no, I'll stay unmarried to the day I die, even if I live to be a hundred and twenty-three. I'm yours. I'm going to marry you. So there.'

'All right,' he smiled in the end, still believing he was dealing with an over-emotional child. 'Let's talk about it again when you're sixteen.'

He never expected her to remember. But the day after her sixteenth birthday she arrived in Boksburg. She'd ridden her horse to Johannesburg, she told him; there she'd left the animal with a cousin of her mother's, to take the train to Boksburg. He was shocked. But more than anything else, he was struck dumb by her beauty. At sixteen, Carolina Henning was undoubtedly the most beautiful girl he'd ever seen.

However, first of all he had to take her back to her parents. This was even more hazardous than he'd expected. Her father very nearly shot him. His feelings in turmoil, Gabriel returned to his rented room in Boksburg, resigning himself to the inevitable. But a month or so later there was a terse letter from her father, inviting him to the farm. It transpired that Carolina had gone on a hunger strike, threatening to fast to death unless she was allowed to marry the man of her choice.

There was much heated discussion during the weekend Gabriel spent on the Hennings' farm. In the end a compromise was reached: they would be allowed to get married, but only when she turned eighteen. Her parents were hoping, no doubt, that she would change her mind before then. They certainly tried their best to expose her to as many eligible young men as they could round up. Some came from as far away as Winburg, and Bloemfontein, and even Port Elizabeth. Most of the time she refused even to meet them and kept herself locked up in her room; when she did deign to come out, she would be either downright rude to the hopeless suitors, or treat them with a cold civility which soon got rid of even the most ardent. And on the day of her eighteenth birthday the wedding was celebrated on the farm *Blyvooruitzicht* ('Happy Prospect'), some ten kilometres out of town. His brothers and sisters (but not his father) all came for the wedding: Elisabet with her family from Bloemfontein; Johannes with his wife and four children from the family farm in the district; the twins Gertruida and Wilhelmina came from the *tuishuis* in town, where they'd moved after their father's death because they no longer felt welcome in Johannes's house; and the two younger brothers, Lodewyk and Hermaans, from Pretoria.

Gabriel and Carolina had their first son within a year, late in 1895, and another the year after; the third child, a little girl, died in infancy, and Carolina herself remained bedridden for almost a year. Her health remained frail after that, which was a constant source of anxiety to Gabriel. But by September 1899 they discovered that she was pregnant again, which restored to them the happiness of newly-weds.

Then came the war.

Lodewyk and Hermaans, who worked on telegrams in the post office, were among the first to know that Britain had rejected President Paul Kruger's ultimatum in the bright spring of early October 1899. In a way everybody had been expecting it; on the other hand, it seems that each side had, until the very last, counted on calling what was firmly believed to be the bluff of the other. The two youngest Landmans left their jobs without even bothering to resign: Lodewyk borrowed a horse so that he could personally break the news to Johannes and their twin sisters at Rustenburg (as it turned out, it took considerable wrangling to persuade Johannes to join the war); and Hermaans took the train to Boksburg to warn

Gabriel. There followed one of those curious moments of old-world gentlemanly behaviour which, especially in those early stages of the war, characterised relations between Boers and Brits: Gabriel's boss on the mine, an Englishman called Maxwell, distressed at losing his paymaster, requested – and obtained – permission from Gabriel's field-cornet to keep Gabriel in his post for a few more days. Only after all the black workers had been paid off, was the mine closed, and Maxwell and Gabriel left, after a hearty farewell, to join opposing sides in the war.

All *uitlanders* and British sympathisers were graciously allowed eight days to leave the country; which meant that by the time the Boksburg commando was supposed to depart for the Natal border, all the trains were crammed with 'Kaffirs, Jews and Englishmen, trampling one another for a place to sit or stand', as Gabriel described it. But at least this gave him time to transport the pregnant Carolina and their two small sons, Hannes (4) and Pieter (3), to her parents' farm. Her father and two brothers had already left *Blyvooruitzicht* on commando by the time they arrived, but her mother and her ailing old grandfather assured Gabriel that she would be safe with them. He was sick with worry about her – she'd been ill all the way on the horse-cart from Johannesburg – but she was the one who insisted that he go.

'With a heavy heart' – his words – he returned to Boksburg. Was this depression due only to his wife's condition, or were there more personal reasons too? A single short paragraph in his war journal offers a glimpse of his state of mind:

'At 8 o'clock that Monday morning we left Boksburg station. I suppose we were all happy that at last we were going into action. Except, in such things one knows so little. I could not talk about it with the others, of course, not even with my brother Lodewyk. What was it we were really going to war for? The gold mines? Freedom? I am still not sure what that means. Here I was going to fight for people who refused to believe the earth is round, people who threw me out of the work I loved. Yet there I was, and I had no choice. In such moments one cannot give way to doubts. There was an enemy waiting for us. Yet my heart was broken when I thought of Carolina.'

And off he went on the crammed troop train, 'equipped with my volunteer's uniform, gun, bandolier, and a few bags of provisions'. Johannes had already gone off with the Magaliesberg Commando, while Lodewyk, recently engaged to a Winburg girl,

779

had dashed to the Free State to serve under his future father-in-law.

From Volksrust the Boer troops were transported on open flat wagons to a camp in Charlestown in Natal – a huge 'tent town' where they had abundant food and no shortage of black servants to pamper them. A motley crowd they were: old men with grey beards and gnarled hands, a new breed of pale young town-dwellers, young boys of fourteen or fifteen with the eagerness of untrained puppies; there was much joking and storytelling around the camp fires at night, interspersed with moments of solemnity when all would join in the slow and ponderous singing of hymns. 'It was,' wrote Gabriel, 'like a great gathering preparing for a hunt.'

But soon it became serious. As they pressed on towards Ladysmith, their food ran out; the rains came down and for days on end they had not a shred of dry clothing or blankets; when the sun did come out again, it was sweltering and clouds of flies descended on them. They had other problems too: their field-cornet, Dercksen, was an unloved character, 'especially with the more enlightened burghers' (whatever that might mean): Gabriel hints darkly at 'dirty acts committed only a little time before' – and soon a large number of the burghers serving under the man requested to be transferred to another section of the Boksburg Commando. A year later their dislike turned out to have been well founded, as Dercksen deserted and joined the British forces as a National Scout. One fortunate result of the move, for Gabriel, was that he now landed in the section of Christiaan Beyers, then an assistant field-cornet, who became his friend for many years.

If life on commando was difficult, there still was an inspiring sense of purpose during those early months when nothing could go wrong for the Boers and even their clumsiest and most half-hearted initiatives turned out successful: Ladysmith and Kimberley and Mafeking were under siege, at Stormberg, Magersfontein and Colenso the British were defeated. Gabriel was involved in the battle of Colenso (he reports with glee how the British sent two batteries of cannon too far ahead to cover the river, with the result that they overshot the Boer positions and lost three successive teams of men and horses sent in to recover the cannons): 'at two o'clock in the afternoon they finally had to give up, withdrawing in great confusion. How great was our relief when everything was quiet again, many of us were almost dead with thirst as the day had been so hot, and we hadn't had a bite to eat since the previous evening.'

Then followed Platrand and Spioen Kop (unfortunately, having lost his horse, Gabriel could not take part in the latter); and soon they were so accustomed to war that on hot days they would go swimming in the river under a hailstorm of British bullets.

But the turning point was close. By the time Spioen Kop was taken with such resounding success, Lord Roberts, assisted by Kitchener, had already arrived in South Africa; within weeks Kimberley had been relieved, and at Paardeberg a broken old General Cronjé had surrendered, with four thousand men, to Roberts. The news had a devastating effect on the Natal commandos at Petershill where Gabriel found himself at the time. 'It was as if an evil spirit had taken possession of our men,' he wrote. 'They started a stampede, leaving behind tents and food and everything, as if there were ten devils on our heels.' Apart from the general depression, there was for him a very personal distress as well: his young brother Lodewyk was among the prisoners of war taken at Paardeberg. Most of them were transported to the already overflowing camps at Green Point and Bellevue in Cape Town. Some time later came the news that several batches of prisoners, Lodewyk among them, had been sent overseas to Diyatalawa and other places in Ceylon.

Even so, the immediate aftermath of the news was unexpected. For a brief, strangely idyllic interval which lasted until May, the Boksburg Commando withdrew into the Drakensberg – 'Here the tall mountain peaks were overgrown with trees, bushes and ferns, here were bright cool streams running below rocks and trees, here we lived as if there was no danger and no future' – and like many other burghers, Gabriel and his brother Hermaans were granted a few weeks' home leave. Hermaans went to the family farm, where he found Johannes already home: but assuming he was on leave like the others, Hermaans saw nothing untoward in his brother's presence. It was only much later that they discovered the truth. Gabriel, of course, made a bee-line for *Blyvooruitzicht*, and much to his joy found Carolina recovered from her illness. She was still frail, but bubbling with energy and plans for the future, firmly convinced that the war would be over within months. Greatly relieved, he returned to the mountains where the Boers were still whiling away the time with cricket, football, and quoits.

But soon afterwards the withdrawal began, back from the Natal border, slowly at first, but with growing signs of panic as they were driven back ever more deeply into the Transvaal, pressed hard from all sides by the British forces moving relentlessly upon Pretoria. Bloemfontein had already fallen. On 28 May 1900 Johannesburg was taken by the enemy; a week later, without firing a shot, the capital surrendered.

The British assumed that they had won the war; hundreds of dispirited Boers, equally convinced that all was over, laid down their weapons and returned to their farms (only four of the eight men in Gabriel's tent stayed on). But as it turned out, the fall of Pretoria was only a beginning, a 'first sifting', a prelude to the most serious phase of the war, and those Boers who remained, Gabriel grimly noted, 'were determined to fight to the bitter end, even if we did not yet know how bitter that end would be.' From now on there would be few head-on clashes and conventional battles, as the Boers resorted to what Gabriel in all good faith termed 'gorilla tactics'.

Their commandos immediately began to push eastward along the railway line to Delagoa Bay, to where the Transvaal 'government-on-wheels' had called a halt at Machadodorp. Past Donkerpoort, Balmoral and Bethal they trekked, carrying out swift hit-and-run attacks on whatever British bases or forts they happened to pass on their way, holding up trains carrying ammunition or food (how disappointed they were one night after capturing a train loaded with provisions, when what they'd taken for flour turned out to be lime!), and raiding the farms of the hated 'Bush lancers' ('they were those Boers one never saw in battle: too cowardly to fight, yet at the same time too scared to give themselves up to the English').

But suddenly they were halted in their tracks by a message from Kitchener: all the women whose husbands were still in the field were to be rounded up and dispatched to the Boer commandos. 'Some kind of armistice was arranged so that we could proceed to Belfast Station to take charge of them. Altogether some 3000 women and children were sent to us in this way, and imagine my anguish as I stood there as one train after the other arrived. I could not bear the thought that my dearest wife and my sons might be among them. But they never came. We learned later that the Khakis had rounded up all the most destitute women and children from the poorest classes. It was almost unbearable to see them in the condition they were in when they arrived. Yet, may the Lord in His infinite mercy forgive me, my first reaction as each train was emptied on the platform, was, Thank God, oh thank God, Carolina is still safe. I could not wait to see her again.'

*

He never did. If only Carolina and her children *had* been among those dispatched to the front. Instead, there appeared on *Blyvooruitzicht*, late one afternoon, a detachment of British soldiers accompanied by an even larger group of armed blacks. The officer in charge called Carolina's mother to the front door (the old grandfather was in bed in a bad state) and ordered her to vacate the house before sundown. The proud woman refused and moved to close the door, but on a sign from the officer the black soldiers ran forward and kicked it right off its hinges. The noise brought Carolina out of the house, her two small sons clinging anxiously to her dress which clearly showed the advanced state of her pregnancy.

'If you don't vacate the place voluntarily,' said the officer, 'we shall burn it down over your heads.'

'I thought the English were civilised people,' said Carolina. (The dialogue is recorded in one of the statements collected by Emily Hobhouse.) 'Now I see they are worse than animals.'

Whereupon the black soldiers were instructed to drag the women out by force and keep them outside while the British searched the house. Two of them carried out the gaunt old man in his striped nightgown and laid him on the ground. Several others climbed a ladder to the roof to set fire to the thatch. After the first furious struggle the women put up no further resistance. In utter silence, their backs straight, their heads erect, they looked on as the whole place was burnt down. In the meantime the soldiers had spread in little groups all over the farm to round up the animals. The horses were kept out, and enough oxen to pull a single wagon. The other cattle, the sheep, the goats, and pigs, were driven into the kraals and slaughtered with bayonets. Following that, in the rapidly descending dusk, the soldiers had great sport running down the dogs and even the poultry, to see who could kill the most in the shortest time.

The women were allowed to sleep on the wagon that had been saved. Early the following morning they set out for the concentration camp in Johannesburg; even before they arrived there the old man had died. After a month in the camp Carolina and her mother complained to the commander about the food (women with husbands in the field were restricted to a few hard rusks known as *klinkers* a day, and a mug of coffee), the overcrowding, the vermin, the lack of proper clothing. As a result, the family was transferred to the camp at Standerton, which turned out to be incomparably worse.

Carolina's baby died, mercifully, at birth. She herself died a week later. Her mother lasted for eight more months before she, too, was buried. Both Hannes and Pieter contracted, first, measles, and then whooping cough: some of the other women hid them in their tent to prevent their being taken away to hospital, as 'we all knew that no child came back alive from that place'. No one expected the two little boys to survive. But, miraculously, they did. They were like two little mosquitoes by the time the war ended, their eyes sunken deep into the sockets, their hands and feet disproportionately large. But they were alive.

When the Boksburg Commando reached Lydenburg, Gabriel's friend, assistant field-cornet Christiaan Beyers, who had recently distinguished himself in several daring raids on British forts, was suddenly promoted to general of Zoutpansberg and Waterberg — 'truly a difficult position,' wrote Gabriel, 'as most burghers from those commandos had already gone back to their homes, while the remainder were quarrelling so much among themselves that their commandos were no good.' With a number of other Boers Gabriel petitioned General Louis Botha to be transferred with Beyers; and as soon as the request was granted they commandeered all the provisions they could find in the shop at Kruger's Post, and set off for the Bushveld. However, the direct route to Zoutpansberg was cut off by two hostile black chiefs among the BaPedi, so they had to make a wide detour through the hot, humid Low Veld. Along the way, Gabriel noted with disapproval, they occasionally passed small trading posts tucked away among palm trees and banana groves, where 'white men, who had first gone there in search of gold, now lived with their Kaffir wives among their new black brothers.'

At last they reached Pietersburg and, moving crisscross through the region that once was home to the Jerusalem Trekkers, began to round up Boers who had run away from the war. So inspiring was Beyers that a sizeable Boer force was soon assembled at the Warm Baths, from where they descended into the kloofs of the Magaliesberg to prepare for one of the rare conventional encounters of the period, the battle of Nooitgedacht, in early December. At one stage Beyers attacked an English post with only a sjambok in his hand. This provided a great boost to their morale and a massive celebration was organised for 'Dingaan's Day': several thousand Boers assembled for prayers, followed by a procession up a steep hill on which they planted the Republican four-colour. ('The standard-bearer,' wrote Gabriel, 'was an Englishman who could speak no word of Dutch, but no matter, he was a true Afrikaner.')

In the lull that followed, Gabriel obtained permission to go home for two weeks: he had not yet received news of his family's internment. It was a hazardous journey, which took him through territory of blacks who had sided with Britain: 'Linchwe's Kaffirs had already murdered several of our burghers in those parts, so I had to keep away from the road.' No wonder he got lost, fighting his way through the dense bush; and after three days his food and water ran out. He was in a sorry state when two blacks on foot came upon him. 'I was sure my last hour had arrived. But imagine my surprise when they helped me up and took me to their place about a mile away, where they gave me porridge and a calabash of sour milk. After I had rested, I gave them my horse in exchange for a bag of flour, and then one of them went with me to show me the way.'

When at last he saw the familiar ridge of koppies marking the farm in the distance, he began to run, oblivious of the *wag-'n-bietjie* thorns that tore his clothes to shreds. 'Carolina!' he shouted. 'Carolina! Carolina! Carolina! I'm home!' It took a while to grasp what the charred veld meant. The burnt-out mealie lands. Then the blackened skeleton of the house. He found a few pumpkins behind the broken kraal. But that was all.

As he stood there, an old black man with a grizzly beard came from the gaping front door of the ruined house. Behind him hovered other members of his family.

'Kleinbaas?' the old man said, hesitantly. 'Is that you, Kleinbaas Gabriel?'

He recognised the old man, who'd lived on the farm since Carolina's father had been a child. 'What are you doing here, Outa?'

'Ai, Kleinbaas. The *nooi* she send me back to my home in Sekhukhune's land. They send a message that my brother is sick, so I go. But on the way there someone come from behind to tell me what happen here. That the bad peoples come to burn the place and take away the *nooi* and the *kleinnooi* and everybody. So I come back to look after the place.'

'There's nothing you can do here now, Outa.'

'No,' the old man said stubbornly. 'One day they will all come back. Then I must be here for them.'

Gabriel stayed with them in the ruin; they shared their scant food with him – a handful of porridge, pumpkin, *marog* leaves boiled up in water. But before sunrise the next morning he left for the next farm, to be met by the same scene. And again on the third. And so it went on until, more dead than alive, he was picked up by a black family on a one-horse cart. Two days later he arrived on what had been his father's farm to find it prospering and green, a fat and smiling Johannes on the front stoep.

Only then did he discover that Johannes had given himself up soon after Cronjé's surrender and was now left in peace by the English. There were angry words between them. 'Had I not been so weak from my experiences I think I would have throttled him with my bare hands,' confessed Gabriel.

But Johannes argued with great eloquence: 'Think of it, Gabriel. The English are pouring more and more troops into the country. There's no way we can win this war, so I decided to get out.'

'What makes you think *anybody* can stay out of a war like this? It's us or them.' Was he aware of the irony that *he* should be speaking like this? – the same man who, not a year before, had not known what he was fighting for? Now, here he was, ready to wage a hopeless war to the end, even though, as he himself had confessed before, 'we did not yet know how bitter that end would be.'

Johannes was still arguing; possibly because, in the meantime, his wife had come out on the stoep and was listening to them. 'I *love* my land, Gabriel. That's why I'm doing what I'm doing. I can't bear to see it devastated. And think of all those women and children, your own among them. Don't you want to put an end to all this suffering? We can't win. I tell you. We don't have a hope in hell. If we really care for the land we must stop the war. I did it for the best of reasons –'

Gabriel stared at him in silence for a long time, then spat out the single word: '*Hensopper*!' And turned on his heel, and walked away. Johannes sent a carriage after him, but he refused to accept any help from his brother. He walked all the way in to town – he had no shoes left on his feet when he got there, and he looked like a scarecrow. But there, at last, his two sisters took him in, gave him food, forced him to rest. From an old shopkeeper who'd been a friend of his father's and who was now too old and weak to fight, they obtained new clothes; he even found a horse for Gabriel – which, God knows, was well-nigh impossible in those times. ('It's the least I can do,' said old Oom Karel. 'I'm too old to fight. So you better go and fight for both of us.')

*

After their defeat at Nooitgedacht, the enemy went all out to capture Beyers, which meant that his commandos were kept on the move all the time, trekking crisscross across the High Veld for the next eighteen months. There was little plan in their movements: it was simply a matter of eluding the enemy, striking at outposts whenever the opportunity arose, sabotaging the railway lines and capturing ammunition or provision trains, breaking to and fro through the enemy lines with the sole purpose of demoralising them. Only once or twice did they risk larger offensives: most of the time this was not possible, as the British often kept women hostages with them in their camps to discourage attacks. And when they did score a victory, it was impossible to take prisoners as there was nothing they could do with them: so the caught Khakis were simply 'shaken out' – stripped of all their arms and clothes and dumped naked in the veld. Boer prisoners, on the other hand, were herded off in their hundreds in cattle trucks to Durban or Cape Town, to be dispatched to camps in India, Ceylon, St Helena and Bermuda.

There were brief intervals when they could let their horses rest a while; but when they were on the go, they might be in the saddle for three days and nights at a time. There were days when, as they rode, men would tumble from their horses as they fell asleep from exhaustion. Often they went hungry: for months on end the haphazard nature of their movements made it impossible to arrange a regular supply of provisions, so they were forced to rely on raids on British camps or trains, or on the farms of *hensoppers* which they felt they had a moral right to plunder. But as the British forces resorted increasingly to scorched-earth tactics, it was becoming ever more difficult to find food for men and horses. Their clothes and blankets were infested by lice, of which they tried to rid themselves by boiling everything – but opportunities for this were few and far between. In the winter of 1901 Gabriel had to share a single blanket with his brother; they took turns wearing an overcoat. Neither had a jacket. Gabriel went barefoot. Once, after his horse had been shot dead under him (he would undoubtedly have been taken prisoner had not Beyers personally charged back right into the enemy fire to pull him up on his own horse), he had to wander about on foot until he was able to surprise a couple of enemy scouts and capture one of their horses while they were drinking water.

One night on the High Veld, not far from Heidelberg – it was in the early spring – they found themselves cornered in a triangle between the railway line running from Elandsfontein to Delagoa Bay and the line from Elandsfontein to Natal. A force of thousands was closing in upon them. The only way out was to break across the Delagoa line: but at that stage the blockhouses guarding it were barely a hundred metres apart. It was a reckless thing to do, but the only alternatives were death or capture and banishment. So in the clear moonlight night they launched a sham attack on one chosen point to draw the enemy fire while as many Boers as possible broke through in twos and threes further along the line. In the circumstances it was surprisingly successful: but there were many casualties. And among the dead was Hannes Landman.

This was, perhaps, the moment Gabriel came closest to giving up. 'My wife and sons herded together in a concentration camp like cattle before an auction,' he wrote bitterly. (At that stage, mercifully, he had not yet heard about Carolina's death.) 'One of my brothers a prisoner in Ceylon, another dead, a third living shamefully as a *hensopper*. What was it that kept me going? Perhaps Hannes was really the luckiest one of us all.'

He repeated this sentiment – only in a tone of even deeper despair – when, not a month later, news came that Johannes had left his farm to join the enemy as a National Scout. Gabriel refused to believe it; but it was General Beyers himself who confirmed it. Two *rapportryers* or messengers from the commando, sent to Rustenburg and the Magaliesberg to plead with the returned farmers for new provisions, had actually visited the Landman farm where Johannes's wife had personally told them the news. ('They told us that she didn't look them in the eyes when she spoke to them. If that was so, I prayed God to reward her for it one day. But even of that I was no longer sure. How can there be a God of love if He allows such things to happen?')

This, more than anything else, haunted Gabriel through the final months of the war. That a man could actually forsake his own people and join the enemy. (Oh my poor ancestor: what would he have thought of *me*? Or would he have understood that, today, our 'own people' themselves have become the enemy?) There are several references to that anguish that kept him awake at night, even when his body was so exhausted that he could barely move. One concerns a 'Kaffir spy' caught in the veld after a particularly disastrous encounter with the enemy: they had carefully prepared a surprise attack on a large camp near Standerton – but as they moved in, under cover of darkness, they found themselves surrounded in an ambush. More than half of their group were killed or taken prisoner. It was obvious that they had been betrayed. And when they came across the young black man who had deserted from their commando just before the attack (he had been an *agterryer* to one of the field-cornets) it was logical to jump to conclusions.

The man was flogged to within an inch of death, then 'forced to swallow a Mauser pill to finish him off', Gabriel records, and it was all their commandant could do to prevent the men literally tearing the body apart like a pack of wild dogs. (If there had been tyres in those days, would they have 'necklaced' the man?) The victim kept on pleading that he'd only run away because he was hungry, because he could no longer stand life on commando, because he was worried about his family whom the British had taken away to a camp in Johannesburg: but how could they believe him? 'It is the devil himself that gets into a man when he thinks he has been betrayed,' confesses Gabriel. 'Is there anything worse in this world, any man more justly hated, than a traitor? And my own brother was one too! I do not feel proud about what we did that day. We no longer thought clearly. We were like the Gadarene swine, driven forward by that madness stoked up in us by the knowledge that we had been betrayed. But what knowledge was it? We had no real proof. We were simply unable to think as individuals. The mob took over. Legion drove us over the edge, into the abyss. May God have mercy on us.'

Another entry concerns six National Scouts caught after a skirmish on a deserted, burnt-out farmyard. One, seriously wounded, was 'shaken out' and left to his own devices; the five others, including a boy of sixteen, were taken away by the commando and kept tied up and under close guard for three or four days until a court martial could be arranged. One of the five was found to have come from the Cape Colony, which meant that he was not, strictly speaking, a burgher; he was allowed to go, but the remaining four were sentenced to death. However, a petition by the burghers to spare the boy's life was accepted. At sunset the others were taken outside the camp to a low koppie to be shot. Lots had been drawn to select the members of the firing squad. 'As luck would have it, I drew a blank,' wrote Gabriel. 'Still, from where I was working on the food wagon cooking the evening meal, I could see everything. It is easy to talk about shooting the enemy when he can fight back, and one often heard burghers saying that if only they could lay their hands on such and such a Scout they would do this or that to him. But it is different when you face the man in cold blood and see the fear of death in his eyes. So I thanked God I was not one of the squad. I thought: Suppose it had been Johannes. Would my hands have shaken? Yet I hated him so much —'

The war whimpered to an end. During those last months the scene was like a landscape from hell. They were on the run all the time: it was impossible to stay in one place for more than a single night. Every day more of the men deserted to surrender to the enemy and return to their destroyed homes. They seemed to be moving through moonscapes: the veld burnt, the homes broken down, not a living creature in sight. All the black inhabitants of the Eastern Transvaal had been driven away from their razed huts to the camps in Heidelberg, Standerton, Nigel, Potchefstroom, Middelburg or Nelspruit. This is, sadly, a dimension of the war of which one catches very few glimpses in Gabriel's journal: the devastation it caused to the black people of the country. True, in many respects it was a white man's war; but the innumerable blacks who just happened to be crushed in between, and dispossessed, and killed, were treated — by both sides — with nauseating callousness. Gabriel notes calmly: 'At least we no longer lived in fear of Kaffir spies, and we managed to survive for months on the supplies of mealies and kaffir corn we found buried underneath the mud or dung floors of the burnt huts. Often the grain was quite sour, but once we'd washed it and spread it open in the sun to dry for a few hours, it got its natural taste back. I wondered many times about the surprise waiting for the Kaffirs when they came back from the camps after the war —'

When even those supplies dried up, their situation became desperate. 'My clothes consisted of trousers made of a horse-blanket, a shirt I had cut out and sewn from a half-burnt mattress found in a home destroyed by the Khakis, and a jacket someone had thrown away. On my bare feet I had soles cut from an uncured oxhide, tied round the ankles with *riempies*, no doubt like the sandals worn by the Israelites in the desert.'

Tidings of the humiliating peace concluded at Vereeniging at the end of May 1902 came while the tattered remnants of Gabriel's group (the Boksburg Commando itself had disintegrated months before) were gathered round the graves of their commandant van Niekerk and one of his men, killed in one of the very last skirmishes of the war. 'And I wondered in my heart how God, if He really cared about us, could allow such men to be killed while cowards and traitors like my brother Johannes lived on —'

Immediately after handing over his gun and ammunition, Gabriel rode to Standerton to enquire about his wife. After a week of frantic toing and froing he was shown the graves of his mother-in-law, Carolina, and the baby. With his two tiny, stick-like sons on the back of a wagon he set out on the long journey to Rustenburg. Afterwards, there was nothing at all he could recall of that week.

He returned to the farm. The old black man and his family were still there; they'd even managed to restore the roof over one of the rooms of the house. The baas, they said, had not yet come back from the war. Gabriel wasn't even touched when he heard it; nor did he react when confirmation came a week or so later that Carolina's father had indeed died. The only other member of Gabriel's family left, apart from the traitor Johannes, was his younger brother Lodewyk who had been exiled to Ceylon. It was several months before a warship deposited him in Cape Town; but he was so ill he had to be taken immediately to hospital, where he died within a few days.

Gabriel despaired of nursing his two half-dead children back to life. Still moving about and reacting like a man walking in his sleep, he took them in to town where his sisters could look after them. For days he did not speak at all, remaining in an upright chair by the window, staring out: but not as if he was waiting for something, someone: he just sat.

One day he unexpectedly left the house and, without saying anything to his sisters, set out on foot for the farm where Johannes lived. He was greeted apprehensively on the front stoep when he arrived, Johannes keeping an eye on the front door in case he had to make a dash for it. But Gabriel spoke very calmly. They had twenty-four hours, he said, to vacate the place. He was not going to allow joiners to live on the farm their father had left to him as the oldest son.

Johannes was flabbergasted. 'But — but you refused to take it when Pa died,' he croaked.

'That was because I was angry with him. But I have made my peace with Pa. There are others in the family I hate more now.'

He went to the stables, chose the best horse, and rode back towards Rustenburg. But before he reached town, he suddenly pulled in the reins. Now I am just as bad as the English, he thought. And promptly returned to the farm.

'You can stay,' he told Johannes without getting off the horse. 'For the sake of your wife and children. As long as you never make contact with me again, for you are no longer my brother. Tomorrow I shall send a wagon to collect everything in the house that belonged to Pa, for you are not fit to have it.'

Among the things transported to Rustenburg were the cracked mirror in which Petrus had seen his visions; and the family Bible. Gabriel did not want anything for himself, but he left it all with his sisters, while he returned to *Blyvooruitzicht* to start again.

But it was no use. Even after his sons had recovered – still unsteady on their thin legs, but no longer with that stare of death in their sunken eyes – he could not find any enthusiasm in himself to begin his life afresh. There was too much hate in him, he explained to Wilhelmina and Gertruida. As long as there were Englishmen around – and now they were everywhere – he could never believe in life again. They tried their best to help him. Why not write down all his war experiences, they suggested: copy out all those hurriedly scribbled notes from his field journal? Perhaps that would rid him of the weight on his chest. He did, but it was no use. He still could not sleep. A few hours of fitful dreaming every night, which left him more exhausted than before; thin as he already was, he was still losing weight.

'I must go away,' he said. 'Otherwise I'll die here. And there have been too many dead already.'

There were others who felt like him: for many among them it was the start of yet another trek. Some actually emigrated to the Argentine, in an attempt to put as wide an ocean as possible between them and the British. Gabriel was tempted, briefly, to join them, but he was afraid that his sons might not survive such a long journey by sea. So he bought a wagon with money his sisters had advanced from their savings, and set out on a trek without any firm destination in mind. An illogical but irresistible urge drove him back to the regions inhabited long ago by past generations of his family: the Eastern Cape, the Little Karoo, Cape Town, the West Coast. But nowhere did he find the rest he sought; everywhere were English.

After two full years on the move he ended up in German South West Africa, with his two small listless sons. At least there were no English around. He found work as a bookkeeper at a mine in the far north. The routine concentrated his mind; after a few months, for

exploits, irreverent and fantastic inventions; stories of transport riders, hunters, fighters, wars, ghost stories, animal stories, stories of the exploits of our family through heroic ages. It was in him that, for the first time, I heard our tribal past explode into language: he did not merely convey the past to me, he embodied it. Those others, those shadows lurking behind him, had left behind them only traces: a few bits of furniture, the massive family bible, the cracked magic mirror, a handful of faded sepia photographs (Great-great-grandpa Petrus, over-exposed and badly developed, two fierce eyes burning with visionary intensity in an ectoplastic expanse of face and beard; Great-grandpa Gabriel, erect in cocked hat, bandolier over the shoulder like a presidential sash, Mauser in hand; or, in the pictures from later years, sorrowful and lean). But Oupa was there in the flesh, in all his furious exuberance, a link with the whole mythology of our past, affirmation of their own reality.

Was it something borne in our family genes since the time of Yitshak Kirschbaum? Oupa would turn in his grave at the thought of owing anything to a Jew, but to me it makes sense. After all, Yitshak Kirschbaum had been the first of our tribe wholly to invent himself by turning history into story. Knowingly or unknowingly, Oupa merely followed his example.

I presume he exaggerated and fantasised and invented for our benefit – in his more responsible 'research', passed on to Pa as an uncompleted project, he was much more meticulous, though I believe his 'facts' were often informed by wishful thinking – but the impact was unforgettable. It was Oupa who hooked me, irremediably, on the story of our past. Even as a ten-year-old I could practically recite by heart the lives he had reassembled or invented for my ancestors, plucked at random from history and the Bible.

– Fransoois Lodewickus Landman, who married the heroic Huguenot girl Manon (with a gleeful disregard for dates, she had survived, with Joan of Arc, the massacre of St Bartholomew night, plunged a dagger in the heart of an emissary from Richelieu, and sailed all the way to the Cape in a dinghy) and ran off into the wilderness with her; there, finding themselves surrounded by hostile Hottentots, they had prayed God for deliverance; Manon managed to steal through the enemy lines with her children (disguised as loaves of bread), but Fransoois, under cover of darkness, built an ark of gopher wood, whereupon a great flood of waters came upon the earth and transported him to safety.

– Carel Guillaume Landman, who led the revolt against the evil

Governor van der Stel, for which he was thrown into the Dark Hole among the lions for forty days and forty nights, whereupon he escaped and trekked into the desert of the West Coast, where God gave him a great number of children, all growing from the Tree of the Knowledge of Good and Evil.

– Diederik Landman, an incarnation of Nimrod, Moses and Samson: he led his tribe through the wilderness for forty years, preserved the lives of his herds by making leather sandals for their feet, and the lives of his family by fighting off the Philistines (killing several hundred with the jawbone of an ass), until they arrived in the Little Karoo, where, as a very old man, he sacrificed his life by protecting with his own body the slain corpse of his beloved son.

– Jan-Jonas Landman, who tamed the wild interior by building walls that nearly reached to heaven – only, at the last moment, God interfered, causing the Kaffirs and Hottentots and slaves working for him to start speaking in different tongues, so that they could no longer do as he told him; in disgust, he married the fattest woman in the land, who pulled down the roof of the house upon all of them, so that only her small son escaped, tended by a devoted Hottentot women called Toas (herself a descendant from the man with the largest prick in history).

– Benjamin Landman, who led the frontier farmers in revolt against the English, married the beautiful daughter of the Wandering Jew, and went forth into Darkest Africa to spread the Gospel among the heathen, becoming a martyr to the cause when he was treacherously killed by at least ten thousand Kaffirs, against whom he stood all alone, armed with only a sling and a stone.

– David Gideon Landman, who fell in love with a sprite in the wood. This was my favourite story, and Oupa knew it, and wickedly embroidered it. In his version, the girl young David Gideon saw bathing in the magic pool below the waterfall – that unworldly nymph with the green hair and violet eyes – was transformed into a gazelle the moment she became aware of him. David Gideon mounted her horse – the fairy girl must have ridden bareback, as there was no sign of saddle or stirrups or reins – and galloped off on a journey that took, not days, or weeks, or months, but years. One day, close to death from hunger in the desert, he saw a duiker in the distance and took aim at it. The little buck fell down. He raced to the spot and took out his long hunting knife; but as he knelt down and began to skin the carcass, it changed, right in front of his eyes, into the long-lost girl. They rode away on the horse, and lived happily together until history caught up with them again, which was another story.

– Frans Jacobus Landman, who single-handed killed innumerable English and then escaped from them by trekking across the border where he lived among Xhosas and Amalekites, until he finally disappeared, probably boiled alive in a pot by cannibals.

– Petrus Landman, who embodied all the sufferings of the Afrikaner people: born in a wagon surrounded by yelling impis, surviving the massacres unleashed by the Zulus on sleeping women and children at Weenen and Bloukrans ('Look, this is his own blood'), sleeping under the cannon on which the Trekker leaders proclaimed the Covenant, living through the Battle of Blood River, and ending his days as a prophet called by the Lord to warn His people against the Forces of Evil ('And this, this, this is the mirror in which the archangel Gabriel appeared to him').

– Gabriel Landman, hero of the Anglo-Boer War, who fought side by side with General Beyers at Colenso, at Spioen Kop, at Nooitgedacht, sometimes shooting so many Khakis on one day that the corpses lay five deep on a battlefield of ten miles by twelve; Gabriel, whose wife and child – 'my mother, my sister' – were murdered in a concentration camp when the English put ground glass in their porridge.

– And Oupa himself, Pieter Landman, the man who never took orders from anyone, rebel and soldier, saboteur, prisoner of war and great escape artist, digger and farmer and self-made businessman, pioneer in a world running out of frontiers.

'But Oupa, why did our people suffer so? Why didn't God make it easier for them?'

'Because when God really loves you, He gives you hell to put you to the test.' His eyes glowed with the burning of his faith; his great voice rumbled through the shadowy house. 'Because it's only when you suffer that you know you're right. That's the greatest lesson God has taught us.'

But a picture of Oupa is always a double portrait: he was what he was because he and his elder brother, Great-uncle Hannes, could only define themselves in terms of their opposition to each other. Never have I known two people who differed so much, who argued so violently and interminably, who fought so spectacularly (about everything – politics, the future, the past, the present, the behaviour of children, the attitude or the beauty of women, the forecasting of

799

weather, the merits of different kinds of food, cattle, manure, shoes, the English, the government, the condition of blacks, the advantages or disadvantages of travel, the meaning of texts and prophecies in the bible, the veracity of newspapers, the taste of different brands of pipe-tobacco, the origin of Eskimos, the geography of Russia or Mauritania, the choice of checks or stripes on shirts, the dangers of Communism, of the Pope, or of the British queen, *everything*), and who were at the same time so unashamedly attached to each other. They should have been twins, most people said. ('Twins?' snorted Ouma, never one to mince her words either, 'they're birth and afterbirth, only I don't always know which is which.') When Great-uncle Hannes died in 1975, it was as if a light in Oupa himself had gone out: the last two years of his life he was morose and moody, hardly ever raised his voice above a grumble, and the blame he heaped on God was such that one shuddered at the thought of what would happen – either to him, or God, or both – when he finally got his own summons to the Throne.

While Oupa lived, we spent at least two weeks of our summer holidays every year on his farm in the heart of Griqualand West, close to the Botswana frontier. Other people went to the sea for Christmas; not us. We had to drive to the most arid region in the land, shimmering colourless in the heat of hell, where even the thorn-trees seemed to shrivel up in summer and the rust-brown Jonas stone eroded in flakes like sloughing snakes. The children put up a fight every year (Frans, especially, could sulk for weeks), but Dad and Mum merely shrugged (we knew she was, deep down, on our side); they had as little choice as we. And every other year Great-uncle Hannes would also be there: having first hosted his own offspring over Christmas, he would come to see in the New Year with Oupa. In the in-between years, we would be packed off two days after Christmas so that Oupa could take his turn celebrating New Year with his brother in the Eastern Transvaal.

Oupa ruled over his vast territory like a heathen warlord; he literally wielded his whip and his *kierie* to keep the host of abject black labourers on the farm 'in their place'. Yet he could be amazing in his generosity towards them. If a child was ill, he would get up in the middle of the night to drive it into town where he would terrorise the doctor into performing near-miracles. He had endless patience with his grandchildren, among whom I was his unabashed favourite. For whole days at a time he would take me out to 'show me the veld'. The mysterious 'Eye' on the outskirts of the town, which according to Oupa was the place where Moses had struck the rock with his staff. ('Actually this was the Garden of Eden,' he regularly told me. 'This is where the first people lived.' He may not have been far wrong, of course: Taung, where the first skull of Australopithecus – three million years old – was found, is not so far away.) Or the dry bed of the Gamagara which, he said, had once been the River Jordan. Or Gamohaan – once Mount Ararat, he told me in confidence – a hulking flintstone outcrop, its boulders marked with ochre and siena-coloured San paintings, where we would sit for hours as he made up stories or showed me the landmarks of his world. ('This is where God Himself used to sit in the Beginning, to watch over his creation,' he would say. 'There is nothing He could not see from here. Look: down there is Mamorata, the Place of Love. And over there, Maroping, the Place of Mysteries. And right there on the horizon –')

But when my great-uncle was visiting, all else had to wait. In spite of their interminable arguments (or because of them?) they were inseparable.

Great-uncle Hannes was neither frail nor small, but next to Oupa's robust, massive frame he looked both. He was bald and bony, with a benign, almost shy smile and gentle eyes; Oupa was boisterous and hairy: an unkempt silver-grey mane, a walrus moustache, full beard, bristles on every inch of his body not covered by clothes, bushy eyebrows, aggressive tufts sprouting from ears and nose. In one respect they were alike: the tenacity of their will. Soft-spoken and placid as he was, Great-uncle Hannes never gave in once he'd set his mind on something. True, it took him longer to come to a decision than Oupa, for he would first try to gather all the facts and weigh the evidence, but when his mind was made up, neither fire nor water could erode his will. Both drew on vast reservoirs of humour, but Oupa's was explosive and massive ('like a piss-pot falling from a roof', he would phrase it), while Great-uncle Hannes had a wry and understated way of probing the secret inanity in the heart of things. Perhaps this was at the very bottom of the difference between them: to Oupa life was really a terribly serious business, to be lived and explored to the hilt because it was so short and vulnerable (and humour was one way of masking that vulnerability), whereas Great-uncle Hannes had seen through the absurdity of the world at a very early stage and had learned to smile forgivingly at folly.

*

For several years after the Anglo-Boer War both boys remained sickly; the slightest cold would rapidly develop into something serious and carry them to the edge of death. But by the time they reached puberty they seemed, quite strikingly, to emerge from the shadows of their early years and catch up with other boys their age. Times were still difficult, especially at school, where Lord Milner's callous drive to stamp out the Afrikaans language made life a misery to a whole generation of children who not only were almost totally unversed in English, but who actively hated it as the language of the oppressor. Innumerable were the times when the Landman boys were forced to wear round their scrawny necks the humiliating board proclaiming I AM A DONKEY, because they'd been discovered speaking 'Dutch'. Whoever wore it at the end of the day had to bend over for an unmerciful beating. After Hannes had twice fainted under the blows, Pieter discovered a remedy: if Hannes was still wearing the board five minutes before the final bell, he would deliberately address one of his mates in Afrikaans, so that he would get the beating instead of his older – but so much frailer – brother.

In due course they developed different strategies to cope with the situation. Hannes rapidly learned to speak English fluently. ('Even the teachers can't speak it properly, man,' he explained. 'So I'm going to show them I'm better than them. That'll make *them* look like donkeys.') Pieter, enraged at such signs of a 'joiner' spirit, simply shut up altogether in school and refused to say anything. When the teachers tried to bully him into speaking, he started playing hookey. Let them beat him if they wished – and they certainly did – he would only go to school on his own terms. Inevitably, his education suffered, and after Standard 6 he dropped out altogether while Hannes went on to Matric.

After the four provinces in the country were united in 1910, largely independent of Britain though still part of the Empire, these pressures diminished. But by then Pieter had already set his mind firmly against school and everything that smacked of 'government', which to him represented the enemy. What he hadn't been taught at school, he picked up in other ways – from Hannes, from his devoted aunts, from whomever he could persuade to share something with him. Like Hannes, he had a mind as sharp as a whetted sickle, especially for figures (even when I was sixteen he could readily outwit me with ingenious mathematical games he'd invented for the pure joy of it); and I was often saddened by the waste in his life.

802

Given the chances of a modern education, he might have ended up governor of the Reserve Bank or something, instead of honing his mind on games or cheating the Receiver of Revenue.

The first real test of their mettle came in 1914, when the South African government, headed by Louis Botha and Jan Smuts, decided to go into the Great War on the side of Britain: that two of their great generals were prepared, a mere dozen years after four thousand men and twenty-six thousand women and children had been killed by the British, to become allies to the arch-enemy, devastated thousands of Boers still smarting with humiliation. When shocked and furious pleas to the government were turned down and Botha used a minor skirmish as a pretext to attack German South West Africa, the situation exploded. General Christiaan Beyers, commandant-general of the Defence Force, resigned his position and went to Potchefstroom with his old friend General de la Rey to address a meeting; as they drove through a roadblock at Langlaagte railway station, police, lying in wait for a notorious gang of criminals, shot and killed de la Rey. Open rebellion broke out. In German South West, General Maritz and his united commando of 500 men defected to the German side; in the Free State, thousands of badly armed but enthusiastic Boers poured into the field under General de Wet.

'I never even thought twice about it,' Oupa said every time he told the story. 'I immediately signed up with Major Jacques Pienaar. I was eighteen years old. For years I'd been dreaming of fighting the English for what they'd done to my mother and everybody, I wasn't going to let this chance slip by. But Hannes!' His face would go red with rage. 'When I told him to pack up so we could go, he said no. Just like that. No. If we go on fighting each other all the time, he said, there'll never be an end to war in this country. Started preaching to me about Jesus and turning the other cheek and forgiving people and loving your enemies. Jesus had only the Pharisees and things to worry about, I told him, in those times there weren't any English around. Anyway, if you read Revelation properly, it's as clear as daylight the English are the Antichrist. We've got to fight Satan, I told him. But the old *papbroek* –'

If Great-uncle Hannes was present, he would join in, patiently and peacefully, but with great conviction: 'Sometimes it takes more guts to stay out of a fight than to rush in like a bull and make a fool of yourself. The way you all did in the Rebellion. Three months, four months, and it was all over. And all you had achieved was to turn Boer against Boer.'

'You think one only goes into a fight when you know you're going to win? That's not fighting, that's bullying.'

'I'll fight when I know something is worth fighting for. Not if it goes against everything the Bible says. Children think they can sort out everything with their fists. Grownups know there are better ways.'

Then there would be an argument lasting for the rest of the day, and sometimes for several days.

There was a poignant sideline to their story: their uncle Johannes, who had defected to the British in the Boer War, saw in the Rebellion a chance to rid himself of the guilt that had been weighing him down. He came to see the boys, announcing his intention to join Beyers. Pieter curtly told him to stay out of his sight: once a traitor, always a miscreant. And Hannes tried to talk him out of it altogether. White-faced and sad, the old man returned to his farm where he shot himself the following day.

Hannes stayed on as a clerk in the Department of Agriculture in Pretoria, resisting severe pressure, even harassment, from colleagues and superiors to join the government forces, led by General Botha himself. 'I won't fight for the rebels,' he said, his words echoing those of his ancestor Carel Guillaume two centuries earlier, 'and I won't fight for the government either. This is not our war at all.' Pieter joined Beyers. After the sad incident in which the general, hard pressed by government troops, drowned while trying to escape by swimming across the Vaal River, Pieter pushed on to German South West Africa to join Maritz and Kemp in their last stand; and after the unsuccessful attack on Upington he was taken prisoner with the rest. Most of them were freed within six months. Hannes waited for him at the prison door in Johannesburg when he came out. They embraced, had a long and violent quarrel, and went home together. In a way each seemed proud of the other, although neither would ever admit it. Certainly, the warmth of their love for each other glowed on even more resolutely than before.

Twenty-five years after the Rebellion (which soon became known, with considerable justification, as the War of Weeping because of the way in which it had divided families and turned blood relatives into foes) there came another moment of historical choice when the two brothers joined opposite sides: the outbreak of the Second World War. This time it was so serious, and their positions so dramatically, even spectacularly different, that the rift might well have been permanent. Hannes signed up in the army; Pieter joined the resistance movement of the Ossewa-Brandwag and became an underground activist and saboteur.

There was, of course, a whole complicated history leading up to that moment.

Pieter returned from the 1914 Rebellion a ruined man. Although the rebels had received an amnesty, they were held responsible for repaying the damages caused by the insurrection. A popular organisation, *Helpmekaar* ('Help-each-other'), sprung up spontaneously all over the country and collected hundreds of thousands of pounds to pay off these debts, but Pieter was among those who refused help. 'How could I keep my head up if I had to take money from other people like a beggar?' Two years before the Rebellion his aunts had died within months of each other, and the brothers inherited their property in Rustenburg. Hannes knew his brother well enough to realise that there was only one way out to salvage his pride; so the house was sold and the money divided equally between them, and with his share Pieter paid off his war debt. Hannes urged him to take a job in the civil service, but Pieter refused to have anything to do with 'a government that turned against its own people'. He also refused an invitation to share with his cousins the old family farm left behind by Oom Johannes: he would not touch a property defiled by the memory of a traitor.

He joined the many thousands of destitute drifters left homeless by the war and the rebellion, and defiantly entered the darkest period of his life. For a while he subsisted in Johannesburg doing a variety of odd jobs, but he resented having to take orders from anyone, so he never lasted long in any position; that was also the reason why he wouldn't consider going into the mines like most others in his situation. But he needed financial security, and that drove him out of the city; after a year of restless, often desperate wandering he landed on the diamond diggings in the Lichtenburg Klipveld, having swallowed, for once, his pride in accepting a loan from his brother to get started.

A few small finds in the first year kept him going, but it was like living in one of the lower circles of hell: sharing a small corrugated-iron shanty with several others – a blazing furnace in summer, a leaking, draughty, wretched cold-box in winter – surrounded by a teeming, noisy, writhing mass of down-and-out people: squealing, coughing, brawling, thieving children; haggard, grey-faced, vicious wives and grimly gaudy, fat prostitutes; aggressive or browbeaten men begging for cigarettes, cowering before their superiors, beating up their black labourers. Day and night the sounds of quarrels and fights, women whimpering or screaming, children shrieking, men bellowing.

'Still, I kept on for six years,' Oupa said, 'always believing the very next sifting would bring the big one. I wasn't hooked on it like some of the others: the reason I didn't stop was that it was the only hope I had of getting back on my feet. But in the end I had to give it up. I did what I'd sworn I would never do in my life: I went to the mines. I was there in the early Twenties, you know, when we tried to fight the big bosses, when Jan Smuts sent in his troops to break the resistance of desperate men fighting with picks and shovels. That was a weird time, I tell you. You know, our own leader, General Hertzog, urged us to become Bolshevists. I remember what he said: "Bolshevism, I tell you, means the will of a nation to be free, to govern itself, and not to be subject to a foreign oppressor." We picketed, we stayed away on strikes, we fought open battles. You know what we adopted as our slogan? – *Workers of the world, unite for a white South Africa*! But it was no damn use. In the end they won. They had everything on their side. They had money. But I tell you one thing, my boy: the people I met there, the friendships we had, the ways we learned to work and stand together – no one could ever take that away from us. Those meetings we held – big formal affairs, or small secret get-togethers in someone's house, with the blinds drawn, lasting till daybreak – they're some of the best things that ever happened to me. All right, the bosses won: but it was only the beginning. We were laying the foundation for much more important victories in the future. We *knew* that. And that helped us to survive.

'After 'twenty-four it got a bit better. At least we now had a Nationalist government in power, even though they needed the support of Labour and *uitlanders* to stay there. But we couldn't complain. I mean, those days we Afrikaners *were* the labourers. We were disinherited and oppressed in our own land, the country of our birth. But I tell you, we were already on the way back.'

The friendships were solid and good, but he was still in financial straits. Hannes was already married – Pieter never got on very well with Mathilda, but he was honest enough to admit that he would regard *any* woman in his brother's life with suspicion – but Pieter could not even think of it. So once again he packed up what little there was to pack, and took to the road. He went as far as South West Africa, even spent some time at the mine where his father had worked, then moved on again. At night, alone in his tent or beside his fire under the open sky, he would read and read to improve his scant education; he would play chess against himself ('I won every time!'); he would devise new tricks and games with figures; he taught himself to write a beautiful copperplate.

With these skills, he was employed as a salesman and bookkeeper in a small shop in the North-West Cape. Weekends he would load a wagon and visit remote farms to offer them a special delivery service; the profits were split fifty-fifty with the old man who ran the shop. At the same time Pieter made friends with an auctioneer, and once a month he would take leave to give a hand with auctions in the district. Through his jovial manner he made friends with many farmers who would insist that he, and no one else, conduct the auctions where their cattle were put up for sale; and he received a percentage.

One day a farmer, Bertus Durand, approached him with a special offer: his oldest son had just died in a freak accident, gored by a bull; his two other sons had no interest in farming: would Pieter consider becoming his foreman? Pieter knew the farm well, a vast stretch of land in Griqualand West; he had also met Bertus Durand's daughter Nettie. He made some calculations which were not purely mathematical, and accepted the offer. They were married in 1925. A year later Bertus Durand died. Another year later, soon after the birth of their first child, Pieter took a calculated plunge, borrowed ever penny he could, and bought out Nettie's two brothers. He nearly worked himself to death – eighteen, twenty hours a day – but slowly he began to move towards independence and security. There were terrible years ahead. In the Great Drought of 'thirty-three he had to leave the farm in Nettie's hands (she had by then four small children to cope with as well) and went to work on the railways for three years. Even so, their debts were staggering when he came back.

'I didn't have a nail to scratch my arse.' Grandpa would sound almost satisfied when he spoke about those days. 'But these two hands have never been scared of work. Look at them. Every callus and scar on them can tell a story. And once again, with the help of God, I pulled through. Mind you, even God had a hard time with the Afrikaners those days. Thousands of us just didn't make it. The Thirties were our crucible, Thomas. You young people have got it easy these days. You should have seen us *then*. We were a nation of poor-whites. What the Boer War couldn't do to us, poverty very nearly did. We were on our knees. But there were a few things I learned the hard way. One is that the only way we could beat the English — for right through Union, and the thing they called "dominion status" and so on, the English still kept the reins, make no mistake: *they* had the power, *they* had the money — so I say, the only way to beat them was to get a proper education. Not war. Not weapons. Education. We had to beat them at their own game. That was why I decided: even if Nettie and I had to work ourselves to death, each and every one of our children would go and get educated. No matter what it cost. It was the only way to get our land back.

'And another thing was this: you can't do anything on your own. What you need is an organisation. You've got to get people together. The whole nation. In the Twenties, on the mines, we tried Bolshevism. But it didn't work for us. Now we had to try something else. But it was hell, I tell you. In those days we were scattered worse than the children of Israel. Not in a real desert, but in a wilderness of the mind. Broken by poverty, by misery, by being *bywoners* in our own land, by going this way and that without really knowing where we wanted to get to. Now, all those years, whether I was on the farm or on the railways, I kept in touch with the people I'd worked with in the mines. I kept on going back there. Sometimes Nettie was so angry with me for leaving her like that, she threatened to take the children and go away. I was sorry for her, deep down, I tell you it was a hard life for a woman, but I knew in the end she would understand, and she did. So I kept on meeting people. There were several of them, later in the Thirties, who came back from Germany. They'd studied there, you see. And all of them spoke about the same thing. The Germans had been broken by the Great War just like us Boers before them. Broken. Beaten right down into the ground. But they were rising out of the ashes again. They were beginning to be a proud nation again. There was a lot we could learn from them.'

'But Oupa!' I would protest. 'What about all those things Hitler did —?'

'Don't you try to teach me about things I lived through myself!' he would snap at me. The mere sound of his booming voice would shut me up. 'I'm talking about the Thirties, about the Third Reich, in which a destroyed nation learned to lift up its head again. And dammit, man, I tell you we were just the same.' A sigh. 'Only, there were so few of us who realised it. The rest were so damn repressed, they couldn't care less. They thought politics was a luxury. They didn't realise it was bread and meat to us, it was the only way we could survive.'

'So how did you get the people to stand together?' I knew the answer in advance, of course; I'd heard it so many times. But it was a joy — a feeling of warmth and pride spreading through my guts — just to listen to that great deep voice.

'Ah! That came in 'thirty-eight. When we celebrated the Great Trek, you see. Ox-wagons trekking from all the points of the compass, through the whole land, converging on Pretoria. It started as a small thing. To some it seemed an idea that would interest only a handful of people. But my God —!' Grandpa hardly ever took the name of the Lord in vain; when he did, it was no swear word, it was really God himself he was calling to witness: 'My God, man, it turned into the greatest event our people have ever lived through. In the towns, in the *dorpies*, in the most remote little hamlets, thousands and thousands of people came together to join the wagons. All of us in Voortrekker clothes, the men with beards, the women in *kappies*. You remember what I told you about our forefathers wanting to trek to Jerusalem? Well, this was just like it. Only, this was no dream, this was real. Suddenly, a whole nation came to life and discovered what it meant to stand together. After that, there was no stopping us. Even if there were still bitter years ahead.'

During the past few years the conciliatory movement in politics had gained momentum; even the two Boer war leaders who had been opponents for so long, Smuts and Hertzog, had joined in a new coalition government since 1934, in an attempt at long last to transcend the old animosities dividing the whites in the country. This new surge of Afrikaner patriotism brought a new factor into play, and the whole situation was precariously poised when war broke out in September 1939. Smuts decided to join the Allies against Germany; Hertzog refused. Parliament was divided. The whole country split.

Thirty years later, during summer holidays on that farm in Griqualand West, the argument still raged on.

'Nothing, you hear me?, *nothing* can give a man reason enough to support the nation who first killed thousands of your people and then tried to thrust a foreign language down your throat.'

'In 'thirty-nine,' argued Great-uncle Hannes, 'Germany was a greater threat than England had ever been. It threatened the whole of the civilised world.'

'It didn't threaten us. It would never have touched us. But if we had supported Germany and defeated England, we could have won our own independence back.'

'We were already independent, Pieter,' said Great-uncle Hannes.

'What independent country flies the Union Jack from all its public buildings? Every stamp one put on an envelope meant licking the arse of the King of England. Which is why I never stamped one of my letters. Only in a Republic would we ever be free again.'

'You've always had more emotions than common sense in you. Don't tell me you didn't *know* what Germany stood for in 'thirty-nine.'

'It was a nation that had won its self-respect back. I salute her for it. But how often must I tell you? – I wasn't fighting *with* Germany, I was fighting *against* England.'

'So if you were wronged by somebody and you met a murderer and a thief plotting against that man, you would join a bunch of criminals just to get back at him? Don't you have any principles of your own?'

'If a man threatens my life I'll take help from anyone who can help me get rid of him.' He would lean forward, or even raise his *kierie* at Great-uncle Hannes at this stage. 'But don't you try to draw all kinds of little pictures to suit yourself! What were *you* doing, hey? You joined a country that had once been your enemy, to attack another who hadn't done you any harm, a country you didn't even know.'

'We knew Germany very well, Pieter. And we knew it wasn't going to stop once it had overrun Europe. It was going to establish the empire of the Antichrist over the whole world.'

'That's shit, and you know it. You're just trying to deny that when you were asked to choose between England and your own people, you chose England.'

'It was *not* a choice between England and my own people. Jan Smuts was as good an Afrikaner – and probably better – than any one of us. The difference is, you only looked at one small country while he was looking at the whole world.'

'A man who keeps looking at the moon and stars easily trips over the first heap of dung in his way.'

'And a man who only looks at the dung before his feet will never even know there are stars in heaven.'

810

And so on, for hours, for days on end, through months and years.

Great-uncle Hannes joined the troops and was shipped off to the 'North', and fought at El Alamein, and was taken prisoner, and landed in a camp in Italy, and came back in 'forty-five – a hero to some, a traitor to others. While Oupa, already a member of the OB, joined its most active and militant wing of 'Storm Troops', the *Stormjaers*, and blew up trains and bridges and post offices (more and more of them in every retelling, until it seemed he'd singlehandedly reduced most of our main cities to rubble), and was caught, together with a whole bunch of his comrades, one night in November 1941 as they were waiting for an ammunition train near Colesberg, and interned at Koffiefontein.

(My wonderful old Oupa, how often have I wondered: if you were still alive today, would you have understood the choices I have made? If in so many ways I personify what you abhorred and fought against all your life, still there is not so much to choose between us. You took up arms against your government as I chose to do against mine. Even our causes are essentially the same: the freedom of an oppressed people. It is only in the definition of the 'people' we represent that we differ.)

All that time Ouma remained on the farm, bringing up seven children who ranged in age from ten years to eighteen months when the war broke out. 'Weren't you mad at him?' Mum would sometimes ask her when the women were present at our conversations, which wasn't often. Ouma would smile: 'Of course. I didn't see any sense in it at all. But that's what men are like, they can't help it, playing with toy guns all their lives. And I was his wife, wasn't I? Even if I didn't agree with what he was doing, he was my responsibility. I'd taken it on myself the day I'd said Yes in church. And no one was going to point a finger at me. When he came home, the farm and the children had to be prospering. It was my pride.'

His homecoming happened rather sooner than they'd anticipated. Within months of landing in the concentration camp at Koffiefontein, Oupa started planning his escape. He could regale us for hours on the wild plots hatched and – thank God – abandoned before he hit on a plan so obvious and simple it was strange no one had thought of it before. There was a large delivery truck that brought vegetables from Bloemfontein into the camp at six in the morning, three times a week – Mondays, Wednesdays, Fridays. And after cautiously keeping watch on the security measures which, as it turned out, were surprisingly lax, Oupa contrived a kind of harness from some straps and wires with which he attached himself to the underside of the truck while the vegetables were being unloaded one morning, having arranged several weeks before to be made a member of the food squad. A week later he arrived on the farm, on foot, covered in dust and grime, famished, but none the worse for wear.

'But that was where the trouble started,' Oupa would say, his eyes narrowing with glee. 'I was like a prisoner on my own farm. In the daytime I had to hide in the house. When there were visitors – and there were even a few callers who thought they could start paying their respects to Ouma in my absence, she was still a beautiful woman after seven children – I had to crawl up into the loft and lie there until they left again. Only at night could I go out into the veld. Not even the black labourers could see me, one never knew when their tongues might start wagging. To make it worse, all my best friends in the district were gone – either in the camp, or in hiding, or planning new attacks on government property. So it was hell in the long run. Except your Ouma couldn't really do without me –'

'He was a damn nuisance,' Ouma would chip in. 'You know he's not the kind of man you can keep in the house for long. And he can never keep still, he's got red ants up his backside. So there I was, glad to see him home, but almost wishing he'd rather stayed in the camp and left it to me to get on with the farming.'

Oupa would chuckle with contentment. 'Right, so what did I do? I decided to go back. But of course I couldn't just walk up to the camp gates and ask them to let me in. There would be too much explaining to do and anyway, it wouldn't be much fun. So one night your Ouma drove me to Kimberley – which was quite a feat, for she never got her licence – and from there I took a train to Bloemfontein, where I tied myself to the vegetable lorry like the previous time, and six o'clock the following morning I was back with my mates.' A malicious wink. 'You should have seen the faces of the guards at the next roll-call when they discovered they had one prisoner too many!'

In the farmhouse lounge, near the corner where the bulky old brown Atwater Kent radio used to sit on its table, there was a big hole in the floor which Oupa refused to have repaired. It was, we all knew, his 'election hole'. Ouma had been complaining for years about termites, but he'd always had more urgent or interesting things to do. Then came that historic night at the end of May 1948, when the crackling space-ship voice of the announcer brought the news that General Smuts had lost the seat of Standerton in the election of the previous day. And Oupa jumped right through the floor.

With the slimmest majority imaginable the National Party had won the election. For the first time ever Afrikaners had come to power without the aid of others. Within days, when it became known that the new prime minister, Dr Daniel Malan, would be travelling from Cape Town to Pretoria by rail, Oupa was ready. He drove the almost two hundred-odd kilometres from Kuruman to Kimberley in a horse-cart, Ouma seated beside him. They were wearing the Voortrekker clothes they'd kept in mothballs since the oxwagon trek ten years earlier. They could of course have taken Oupa's battered but still proud green 1937 Ford, if not the *bakkie* which bore so many signs of Ouma's enthusiastic but undisciplined driving, but he believed the horse-cart was more suitable to the occasion. Had there been time for such a journey, I suspect he would have gone by oxwagon. Even with the precautions he'd taken for changes of horses along the way (everybody in those parts knew Oupa, none would dare to refuse) it took them several days to Kimberley. As on every other station platform along that epic train journey, a moving mass of people had turned up – in cars and carriages, in donkey-carts, on horseback, some even on foot – to pay homage to the thickset, myopic man in black who'd suddenly become the incarnation of a people's fiercest hopes. They waited there in the sun for hours to catch no more than a glimpse of the man of God. The train stopped for three minutes, Doctor Malan appeared on a bridge, intoned a few clichés which were received as if they were the Tables of the Law straight from Mount Sinai, and disappeared. Oupa and Ouma returned to their cart and drove the many miles back. 'But it was worth it,' said Oupa. 'I tell you, I felt like old Simeon who said: "Lord, now lettest thou thy servant depart in peace, according to thy word: for mine eyes have seen thy salvation."'

There is something devastating about it: that long struggle, all that suffering, all those hopes and expectations. On one of the many photographs I took of Oupa before his death – he was strangely

813

vain, he loved to be photographed, even if he invariably took an hour to prepare for it: everything had to be 'just so' – he is seated in an armchair in the corner of the lounge by the radio, at the edge of his 'election hole', the Dutch family bible on his knees. His huge hands clutch the ends of the arm rests in an attitude both threatening and defensive. 'This is my corner,' he seems to say, his eyes staring straight at the camera like live coals under the bushy eyebrows. 'Don't come any nearer.' Behind him is a window, but the bright light from outside has washed out all detail. There is something disturbingly contradictory about the photograph: this man of the great outdoors, cornered between walls, with that glaring emptiness outside, as if there's nothing there. But to me this is my grandfather. His whole existence represented such a narrow corner: the whole wide country surrounding him, with all its space and light and its millions of people, was obliterated in his mind, like that blind window. When he spoke so genuinely, so movingly, of the 'freedom' of his people, of his country, he was thinking only of two million or so Afrikaners; the rest did not figure, did not even exist.

Christiaan Beyers Landman

(1927–1988)

It is the basis of perspective that objects grow smaller as they recede in space; but in writing history, inevitably, people grow smaller as they approach in time. It is difficult to think of Adamastor when confronted by my father. On the other hand, if Ivan Karamazov could visualise the Devil as a little man in a bowler hat, it may not be too far-fetched to imagine Adamastor, in the second half of the twentieth century, as a decent, inconspicuous bourgeois, a teacher in grey or brown, thin moustache, balding head, steel-rimmed spectacles, briefcase in hand (discreet engraving on small silver plaque: *From the Matric Class of 1960*). Perhaps it is the last of his desperate avatars. If you can't lick 'em, join 'em.

Behind the severely ordinary appearance, it is true, lurked unsuspected passions and rages that expressed themselves in curious ways. He drove, not like a maniac, but like a calculating killer, screeching to a stop inches before running down pedestrians, chickens, dogs or other cars: because he was so ferociously law-abiding, he went into a frenzy whenever someone else broke the law – and whenever he saw a pedestrian jaywalking, or a car ignoring a stop sign or neglecting to give a signal before turning, he would not rest before he had 'taught the fool a lesson', invariably leaving near-destruction in his wake. If there were water restrictions in town and he discovered someone illegally hosing a garden, he would not hesitate to call the municipality, the police, and the fire brigade. He was also an inveterate writer of vitriolic letters about civic issues (most of them obscure) to newspapers, averaging about three a week over the span of his adult life. The rawest nerve in his body was touched by the misuse or neglect (suspected or real) of the Afrikaans language. I remember cringing with embarrassment in my youth when we went into shops or banks or cafés in Cape Town and he insisted on being served in Afrikaans; if the assistant happened to be unilingual, he would demand in peremptory tones to speak to the manager and explain at the top of his voice to all and sundry, while waiting, that Afrikaners had been suppressed long enough in their own country and that it was a shame in this day and age still to encounter people so inadequately educated and/or mentally deprived and/or downright vindictive that they could not, or would not, serve a customer in his mother tongue. He would terminate the discussion with a few extremely convoluted sentences in English to drive home his point that 'if I found it possible to acquire fluency in the medium of a language invariably associated with the traditional enemies of my people, it should not be unreasonable to expect of others to reciprocate', or words to that effect. (Ironically, English was one of the subjects he taught at school, but with the exception of situations where he could use it to put someone down he refused in principle to speak it outside the classroom. Which caused some problems at home when I was a child and my mother, who came from the more tolerant Eastern Cape and associates English with culture, introduced one compulsory English day a week – with a one-rand prize for the child with fewest 'black marks' every month – to make sure we could speak it fluently.)

Weighed down, no doubt, by the illustrious name he was blessed or cursed with at birth, he suffered all his life from grandiose but unspecified ambitions that had something to do with waiting to be called upon 'to serve my people' – but apart from three or four unsuccessful attempts to be elected to the municipality, nothing ever materialised to suggest the true nature of his 'vocation'. He compensated, I'm afraid, by elevating mediocrity into a major virtue: never to be conspicuous (except in situations like the ones mentioned above), never to step out of line, never to draw attention to oneself (the worst, the most utterly damning admonition he could think of was: 'What will people say?'), never to do anything unexpected, always to conform: to be the greyest among the grey, the equallest among equals. In spite of bitter complaints to my mother that 'people just don't seem to recognise my true worth', it suited him perfectly to be vice-principal of the school, not principal; committee member of the local Party branch, not chairman; church councillor, not chief elder; member of the church choir, not soloist; seconder of motions at meetings, not proposer.

Most people drop their defences when they are working on a hobby, but Dad always kept me wondering. He spent most of his spare time in the garage doing carpentry; the place was always cluttered up with his tools, and no month went by without expensive and lethal and totally unusable new items being added to his collection. But this doesn't mean he loved carpentry. In fact, he loathed it. And he was no good at it. Every evening there were new cuts and bruises to be nursed with Mum's infinite patience; and every day new messed-up lengths of boards and beams, bent nails, stripped screws, broken bits, chipped chisels and hacked blades were surreptitiously dumped beside the black rubbish bins near the back gate. Yet he never gave up, persisting with solemn determination – not in the hope of ever getting it right, but because 'discipline is good for the mind'. He did it *because* he hated it. Grimly, silently, almost triumphantly, as he sawed away at his wrists and hammered his thumbs into a pulp and chipped chunks off his fingers, he was earning, in sweat and blood, his predestined place in heaven among all the other martyrs of the true Calvinist faith.

In my parents' generation, I have always found my mother's family much more interesting than the seven dour offspring of my wonderful paternal oupa. Mum was the *laatlammetjie*, the 'afterthought' of eleven children (not counting the thirteen her father had had in his first marriage). I never knew her father, Oupa Karel Muller, who had died when she was only twelve or thirteen, but he came from an old East Cape family who had never budged from the frontier. ('We worked out our problems right here,' he used to say, Mum enjoyed repeating to us, 'we didn't run away like those stupid Voortrekkers.') He was an estate agent in Cradock; but he also ran the old family farm in the district.

Her mother, a Malherbe by birth, belonged to a staunch Huguenot family that had lived on their farm at Paarl for three centuries – affluent and cultured people who had nurtured their ties with Europe and had produced advocates and judges, doctors, political leaders, several scholars, two robbers and one murderer over the years; a family as well matured as a bottle of very old Constantia. This whole new dimension was introduced into our tribal memory by the spirited young Louise Malherbe.

Specifically, her father had been active in the movement, late in the nineteenth century, to promote the Afrikaans language as a vehicle of political aspirations. An extraordinary episode, really: a vernacular spoken by peasants, and shaped largely by 'non-white' speakers – the early slaves, Khoin, and their mixed descendants –

was taken over by an aggressive and increasingly influential group of white nationalists, appropriated as 'the only white-man's language created on the continent of Africa', and promoted in opposition, not only to English, but to High-Dutch as well. Louise Malherbe's father was not a firebrand like some of the others; but the 'language struggle' lay close to his heart. As he saw it, Afrikaners in the two Boer republics to the north were being drawn together by a surge of chauvinism provoked by the threat of annexation by Britain; those already living under British rule in the Cape Province needed a another source of strength: and the language could provide it. He personally translated a few chapters from St Matthew, and Solomon's Proverbs, into the fledgling language, and published a few rousing poems – under a pseudonym – in *Die Patriot*, the first Afrikaans-language journal.

Karel Muller first met the lively young Louise Malherbe when after the death of his first wife he went to Cape Town to deliver a petition from a group of Eastern Cape farmers to the minister of agriculture. No one remembers what the petition was about, but the minister, it seems, was much impressed by the energetic farmer. They had several meetings; and Karel Muller was invited to the minister's farm in the Paarl valley for the weekend. There he met Louise, the daughter of an affluent neighbour. She was twenty years younger than he; but before the weekend was out, Muller had asked her father for her hand (in Dutch) and had been refused outright (in Afrikaans) on account of the age difference between the two. They eloped and were married by special licence on the Monday morning (in English). They lived happily almost ever after.

Among the eleven children they raised – my aunts and uncles – were all kinds of unusual people. One of them became what was fashionably known as a 'speculant', although I suspect he really was a confidence trickster. (Once every three or four years in my childhood, suddenly one morning when one woke up, this weird man would be in the bathroom trimming his beard and moustache, his pockets stuffed with sweets and foreign coins.) Another was an acrobat in a circus, but he'd fallen to his death before we ever met him. One girl became a doctor and emigrated to America, another a journalist, a third an actress. One son became a politician: he never actually made it into Parliament, but in each new election he would represent a new party, each one more way-out than the previous. One was a big-game hunter in East Africa, another a game warden in the Kruger National Park. One became a director of companies. The most humdrum among them all must have been Oom Boet, the gentle police sergeant. We seldom saw any of them. But whenever one of them arrived on the doorstep (Dad would *always* complain about their lack of manners, because no one ever gave prior warning of his or her arrival) the house would be turned into an electrical field in a state of constant vibration. Things would just start happening and only stop when the visitor left as suddenly as he or she had appeared, leaving us all – except Dad – half-dazed and high.

Our visits to Ouma Louise in Cradock – not nearly as regular as the annual pilgrimages to Kuruman – were always memorable, if morbid. For by the time we were big enough to take note, Ouma was already 'funny'. She'd become that way, Mum said, after Oupa Karel's death. Whereas previously she'd been inexhaustible in her pursuit of excitement, her energies were now tuned in to death. She would attend each and every funeral in town or in the district, whether she'd known the deceased or not; and if there was an auction she would buy up all the photographs of the dead. Every wall in her long narrow house was covered with oval or round or octagonal frames hemming in the stark daguerreotypes or sepia photographs of long-dead strangers. When the moon was full she would place a tall ladder against the kitchen wall of her house and climb on the roof to spend many hours in contemplation, hunched like an owl. She didn't actually howl or hoot at the moon, at least not audibly, but no one doubted that she was holding communion with the spirits of the dead. In the graveyard, right next to her husband's grave, the hole for her own resting-place had already been dug, covered with a sheet of corrugated iron. And every Sunday, when we were there, the whole family was expected to accompany the proud old lady, perennially clothed in black, on a silent excursion to the graveyard to contemplate 'Ouma's hole'. Her whole life became a celebration of death. And it seemed fitting, if horrifying, that in the end she should die of cancer: a long-drawn-out suffering lasting for two years, that slowly laid waste her tall bony body as it gnawed away at the soft flesh until only the skeleton remained, the flimsy skin stretched taut over it like papyrus from an Egyptian tomb. Every day for two years she almost lovingly prepared herself for death, undoing meticulously the network of strings that threaded her to life, the way a very fine piece of lacework is detached from its frame; singing hymns to herself in a small thin voice like an insect on a summer's day, and all the time wasting away, wasting away, until all that was left was the exquisite and transparent desire to be reunited with the man she'd loved.

Ouma Louise never approved of her youngest daughter's choice of a marriage partner. 'What's he doing with a name like Christiaan Beyers Landman?' she often sneered, deliberately within earshot of my poor father. 'That's just asking for trouble. I wonder how many times poor General Beyers has already turned in his grave.' (Even so, I suppose there was much to be thankful for: Oupa had initially considered christening him *General Christiaan Beyers Landman*.) And any objective observer might concur: in so many respects they seemed ill-matched. Yet from the inside I know theirs was a marriage that worked – on the one hand, judged cynically, because both had compromised and sacrificed and relinquished so much; on the other, in a more generous judgement, because their love was a broad, peaceful current that swept or wore away whatever was redundant or obstructive, covering up inadequacies and smoothing the rough edges of rocks and banks, leaving a green and fertile tract as it moved on. Whatever differences and fights they might have had in early years, before I was born perhaps, each grew so much into the other, each *needed* the other so much, that neither could be complete without the other. What angered him amused her; where she is volatile and emotional, his even calm was soothing and reassuring; his lack of imagination was complemented by her enthusiasm, her moments of inspired madness; his secret undefined dreams were kept in check by her sure sense of the possible.

She brought to their union her memories of a cherished, even spoilt youth as the youngest, by more than ten years, of a great brood of loving eccentrics: if she was used to having her way, she was also used to sharing; she brimmed with eagerness to explore and experience, but she also knew how never to lose sight of the feasible. From both her parents she got her love of life; from her mother's later years she learned to keep an eye on death.

My father dragged with him the weight, not only of his splendid name and the expectations of *his* father, but of the difficult years of his childhood. He almost seemed to take pleasure, more and more as time went on, in recalling the Thirties, especially those years his father had been away to earn money on the railways, when he had to walk five miles to school every morning and five back in the afternoon, barefoot most of the time: memories of dirty feet cracked and blue with cold in the hard crisp frost of winter mornings, daubed with dubbin at night in futile attempts to smooth what seemed like tortoise scales. After school he and the other children had to help their mother, each according to his or her age and abilities, to run the farm: bring in the sheep, milk the cows, collect the eggs, water the garden, chop firewood, repair fences. Later, during the war years, when their father was in the camp, there was the additional responsibility of running the hardware store Oupa had bought in town. At school they had to contend with children whose fathers were in the army and had become lieutenants or captains or majors, while theirs was an internee; there were teachers who rubbed in the ignominy of illegal, underground action against one's legally elected government. There was, always, the fierce resolve to 'show them' – whatever 'show' meant, and whoever 'they' were.

After he'd finished school – neither spectacularly nor poorly – he had to wait another year before they could scrape together the money (most of it borrowed anyway) to send him to a teachers' training college. University was out of the question (he had dreamed about becoming an architect: thank God he didn't) and the teaching profession was as much as his father could afford right then. The next children in line were more fortunate, for that was after 1948 and Oupa had become a wealthy man: if the two girls also became teachers – it was either that or nursing if you were female – the boys had a wider range of choice: one became a lawyer, one a predikant, the third went to agricultural college and came back to take charge of the farm, the last one took a degree in commerce and went into banking.

It was during the year Dad spent at home before going to college that he met the girl who remained the secret love of his life, I doubt whether Mum ever found out about it. Only once did he confide in me, and that was just after I had come back from Europe the first time, when he'd fallen ill and thought he might die; and I wasn't even very sympathetic. It seemed to me a small thing blown up out of all proportion through years of brooding and wishful thinking (but who can really tell, who can imagine, the secret of another's experience?). Cut down to size, it involved a young teacher, Joan Brookshaw, whom he'd met while running Oupa's shop in town. They saw a lot of each other, they fell in love, and after a month or two he eagerly invited her home to his family one weekend.

A deep, oppressive silence lay over the farm from the moment Joan Brookshaw was introduced to Oupa and Ouma and Dad's brothers and sisters until the Sunday afternoon when Oupa drove them back to town. Instead of dropping Dad off at the *tuishuis* where he was living during the week, Oupa got out of the car with him and accompanied him inside to the front room. 'Christiaan,' he said, 'what are your plans with this girl?' It was the first words the old man had spoken since the Friday evening.

'What do you mean, Pa?'

'You know what I mean. Are you going to marry her?'

'We don't know yet, Pa. She's – she's very nice.'

'An English girl.'

'I think I'm in love with her.'

'An English girl.'

'But Pa –'

'After everything our family has been through. After a century of injustice.'

'We are Christian people, Pa. The Bible teaches us to forget and forgive.'

'Are you trying to tell *me* how to read my Bible?'

'Pa, what has Joan got to do with anything that's happened to our people in history?'

'I didn't come in here to argue with you tonight, Christiaan. If you want to bring shame on the man whose name I gave you, it is a matter for you and your conscience. All I'm telling you is that it's up to you to choose between your family and this girl. If you choose her, I shall draw a line through your name in our family Bible and no one among us will ever speak your name again. Good-night, Christiaan.'

The matter never came up for discussion again. At the end of that school term Joan Brookshaw left the town. 'I think something inside me shrivelled up and died that night.' Dad melodramatically told me on the bleak winter's day, years later, when he confided in me during his illness. 'But what else could I have done? I couldn't turn against my own father. It would have been like turning against God.'

At the beginning of the following year he was sent to college at Graaff-Reinet. He met Mum within a fortnight. She loved telling the story:

'We'd just written our first English test, you see. I'd noticed this very worried young man battling his way through every question, ruffling his hair, crumpling his tie, staining his hands and face with ink. When we got outside, he came up to me with a look of despair on his face – I think I fell in love with him right there – and asked me, in English, mind you, "Excuse, Miss, but was it very bad for

822

you too?" He spoke English like a goat chewing cabbage leaves. So I just burst out laughing and told him I was Afrikaans. He was so relieved, he invited me for a cold drink on the spot.' It must have been, I've often thought, the last time Dad ever voluntarily addressed a stranger in English.

At the end of their three years at college Dad took up a post in a small town on the West Coast: they were all for getting married straight away, but Oupa put his foot down and insisted on a year's separation 'to test their feelings'. So the wedding only took place in December of the following year, by which time Dad had rented a small house near the school. A decent fifteen months later Maria was born, another year later, Frans. There was a second son two years after Frans, but he died within months; which probably explains why it took so long before Mum would risk her life again having me.

Among other things, they shared the resolve to offer their children what they called 'a start in life'. To Oupa this had meant providing his offspring with an education. In my parents' generation, this was already taken for granted. The 'start' they had in mind was often expressed laboriously by Dad: 'A person needs to live both vertically and horizontally.' The vertical axis meant history (even if that was generally narrowed down to the chronicle of the tribe); the horizontal was geography. And our childhood holidays – those not taken up by obligatory family visits – were spent travelling in a carefully planned grid across the length and width of the country, sometimes by train, mostly by car. Occasionally, when Mum had her way, we simply went off blindly 'to see where we get to'. More often, Dad took over, spending weeks and months on meticulous preparation (even so he invariably took the wrong turn somewhere and got us hopelessly lost; and Mum derived a special kind of glee from not telling him about it before it was too late).

But apart from these voyages of discovery into the known, Dad did not like moving about. He needed the security of a fixed abode. Only once, when I was about twelve, did he decide we had to move from the West Coast where the earliest Landmans had taken root: it would do us good, he announced, to return to the Transvaal which had also been home to the Landmans for so long. (Mum once hinted, long afterwards, that the real reason had been an argument with his school principal; but one could always count on Dad to subsume private experience in what he termed 'matters of principle'. Hence her laconic comment: 'Your father doesn't always know how to spell "principle".') But that did not last long, and barely a year later we returned to the Cape; this time the Little Karoo, the ancient stamping ground of Diederik and Jan-Jonas Landman. Our 'geography' remained, in the final analysis, a small circle strictly defined by family experience.

Dad; Mum. What turbulent times they lived through. History came past them like a river in flood, all swirls and eddies and whirlpools, carrying with it uprooted trees and torn-off branches and bits and pieces of destroyed houses, dead and bloated cattle: but in its midst, unperturbed and content, they pursued their small private lives, raising their children in the fear of the Lord and inculcating in them the values of their people, building a home, following a career, voting in elections, going to church, attending rugby matches or school fêtes, paying their bills and taxes on time. The Fifties resounded with the great marches of hundreds of thousands of blacks protesting peacefully at the increasing burden of oppression the new apartheid policies of the Nationalist Government heaved on to their shoulders. It was the time when through infamous measures coloured voters were removed from the common electoral rolls, mixed marriages were prohibited, and communities separated on the basis of their colour; a time when the race group of babies was established by looking at their nails and the texture of their hair to determine, for the rest of their natural lives, the limits of their mobility and their freedom. In the Sixties, heralded by the massacre of unarmed protesters by the police at Sharpeville, a whole new chapter in history began. Driven to despair by the violence with which their peaceful protests were suppressed, and by the banning of the organisations which for decades had clamoured for their rights, blacks embarked on programmes of controlled sabotage and violent struggle: it was the decade of Rivonia, when Nelson Mandela and Walter Sisulu and Govan Mbeki and their comrades were sent to the Island and innumerable others forced into exile; when the mass uprooting of settled communities began in order to remove 'black spots' from areas declared white; when the 'coloured' quarter of District Six in Cape Town was laid waste by the bulldozers; when the first small groups of idealistic young whites began to turn to underground action; when the great Afrikaner resistance leader Bram Fischer, scion of one of the foremost Boer families from the Orange Free State, was sentenced to life imprisonment and

Beyers Naudé was driven from the Church; the decade in which a poor mad messenger, representing (without even being aware of it himself) the great despairing majority of South Africans, plunged a knife into the heart of the smiling, avuncular apostle of apartheid, Verwoerd. Then came the Seventies, the eruption of Soweto which sent its seismic ripples throughout the country, the boycott of the Afrikaans language in black schools, the large-scale labour unrest, the collusion of the apartheid regime with Britain, the US, West Germany. And the Eighties, when the country seemed to explode into chaos, eventually controlled only by total oppression and assassinations perpetrated openly by the Security Forces under the protection of a State of Emergency –

And through all this, through all this, Dad and Mum continued their calm, secluded lives, she looking after the household and winning silver cups with her canned fruit, crocheted tablecloths, brown bread, iced cakes and lemon meringue pies at competitions organised by the WAA; he inculcating in generations of schoolchildren the white values of Afrikanerdom, and spending his afternoons in the garage wrecking costly tools on unshapely pieces of wood. Of course they were duly shocked by the murder of Verwoerd and attended a memorial service in his honour; they prayed for new prime ministers and state presidents as they were sworn in or departed under clouds of corruption; they shook their heads about the mindless violence of blacks who do not appreciate what whites are doing for them. But these events made no *difference* to their lives. Nothing induced them to stop even for a moment, to reflect perhaps; not for an instant did they consider changing course. Below the dirty foam that sometimes disturbed the surface of their lives, the bedrock was sure and dependable, predictable, unchanged.

When I survey Dad's history – his own accounts of his life and times – there is again that unnerving emptiness surrounding him: a landscape with no sign of a black figure anywhere in it. As if they didn't exist, had never existed. While I know that the whole direction and texture of his life, as of all our lives, the deepest sense of it, was *determined* by those invisible black multitudes. Their presence has shaped us and defined us. He didn't know. I do. And that has made all the difference.

Glossary

*of words and phrases not clarified
in the text*

AAM: Anti-apartheid Movement (international)
abba (Afrikaans, from Malay):   to carry a child on one's back in a
  cloth (*abbadoek*) draped round the body
ag (Afrikaans):   oh, oh well
agterryer (Afrikaans):   batman
aia (Afrikaans, from Malay):   previously a respectful form of
  address for a black woman; now pejorative
amakweta (Xhosa):   youngsters undergoing initiation
'Amandla ngawethu!' (Xhosa):   'Power to the people!'
Armscor: South African government corporation for the
  development and production of arms

baas (Afrikaans):   boss, master
baba (Xhosa):   father
bakkie (Afrikaans):   small van; on the West Coast, a fishing boat
baster (Afrikaans):   halfblood, bastard
bergie (Afrikaans):   vagrant who lives on the slopes of Table
  Mountain
biltong (Afrikaans):   strips of meat, salted and dried
Black Sash: pioneering women's organisation for human rights
blinkhoek (Afrikaans):   fishing hook without any bait
boer (Afrikaans):   farmer
Boere (Afrikaans):   (usually) the police; specifically the security
  police; it may also be used as a term for Afrikaners in general
boetie (Afrikaans):   little brother; used as fond term of address
  for any young boy, or for a (younger) son in the family
boubou (West African):   long flowing garment worn by men
bra (township slang):   brother
braai(vleis) (Afrikaans):   barbecue

828